DEVIN, DEVON

DEVIN, DEVON

Devin Murfin

ATHENA PRESS
LONDON

DEVIN, DEVON
Copyright © Devin Murfin 2008

ISBN 1 84401 980 2
ISBN 978 1 84401 980 9

First Published 2008 by
ATHENA PRESS
Queen's House, 2 Holly Road
Twickenham TW1 4EG
United Kingdom

Printed for Athena Press

The events detailed in this account are based on Devin L. Murfin's life and travels, and are true and actual to the point of his recollection and perceptions at the time they occurred. However the names of the characters have been changed, and some details have been altered to protect the innocent who may otherwise suffer harm.

Buffalo Son
From Van Morrison's song "Have I Told You Lately."

Have I told you lately –
        That I love you;
        That my wings open wide
        At the sight of you?
Have I told you –
        That your crooked river smile
        Rafts my father right through you;
        Clicks me complete –
                Into memory
                        Of talking tigers
                And bullet black eyes
                        In a cradle of
                Baby Boy love?
That hearing you hum to Morrison
Rolls us once more
Into an undertow of laughter
Across our little
Living room floor:
        Me, an innocent seventeen,
        You, a ten pound wonder,
        Smiling even before
        I got you home from the hospital?
Have I told you of
The smell of your perfect
        Curl-clad head;
        Of those first bone teeth
        That gave you reason not to eat even then
                What you didn't need;
        Of those tiny tadpole hands
        That always wanted to be fins;
        Of those ten-year-old dreams
        Of being the Catfish King who
        Belly-down scored truth onto
        The nether soft floor of the
                Mississippi;

Of your bank of stones,
            Feathers,
            Sticks
            (rubrics of the dead)
That you collected to make
            Ceremonial staffs
                        To honor Geronimo, Black
                        Hawk and Red Cloud
Calling down like an initiate (even then)
The Great Buffalo Spirits that shroud
            You still
            As you hang O-Kee-Pa
            In the silent breeze
            Of these Holy Warriors
Have I told you?
            Will telling you heal
            The pain of unacknowledgment?
            Can it cleanse away
            The war paint
            From your scarred face?
            Stay the hate that collects
            In streams on your sheets?
            The sorrow of rituals, rites,
            And a father –
                        Lost?
            Will it calm your prairie rage
                        That blazes for the right
                        To be
                        A man
                        That hangs?
What happens to a hero
Whose own people cannot see him?
Does he just freeze-frame
Like Ghost Dancers buried
In the snows of Wounded Knee?
            Or does he ascend to record his own history:
            On his arms, his chest, his thighs – his body
                        A codesi
                        For a Warrior Son
                        Who dives deep
                        And swings alone –

Hallowed –
His body a chant
In the
Great Chiefs'
Trees.

By Dorothy Payne
(Author's mother)

"Bye... Goodbye. Okay, bye."

This was one of those very uncomfortable goodbyes—you know the kind—where both parties just wanna get the hell off the phone, yet aren't quite sure how to gracefully go about it. Pushing the big white button, having blue stripe, I return the NOKIA cell phone back to designated spot on my small corner writing desk. The desk was meant for a computer, but damned if I could ever get the hang of the whole computer thing. So, layin' the little phone down beside my cheap and obsolete typewriter, I do what is always done when sittin' here at this desk deep in thought and/or confusion. I stare, trance-like, over the top of typewriter, right into the gorgeous, bright blue eyes of an exquisitely beautiful, innocent looking eighteen-year-old young woman going down on my wife's smooth shaven pussy. A photo this is—and what a photo! My wife and I had many such printed for a short-lived but very profitable business. Though the business is no longer in operation, this photo—an eight by ten glossy promo—stands proudly framed behind typewriter, kept for keepsake, and for admiring. The image is indeed real boner material, to be sure. The photographer, bein' yours truly, had used an elegant (expensive) and ornate fabric for both femme fatales to lay upon together, in frolicking poses of succulent form, with lighting a-glow.

My wife is extremely attractive... having a long, lean, tan body, narrow hips, a firm, little, round bottom (and yes, unlike some of you other prima-donna cunts, she can, and does, take it up the ass!). Add breast implants of almost double-D proportions to complement her exceptionally large, proud nipples, broad shoulders, elongated face, sexy mouth, high cheek bones, big brown eyes and thick, long, flowing black hair and you've got yourself one hell of a class act piece of ass! Also, my wife, bein' the exotic she is (of course), keeps her entire genitalia shaved—not a pubic hair is to be found. Her pussy is one of the prettiest ever seen—having a baby soft, puffy appearance with a pouting, protracting clitoris hood that only manages to cover the peeking pink clit halfway—resulting in visual delights of salivating deliciousness.

Since, not all that long ago, I used to be a professional tattoo artist and body piercer, owning several studios all under the name *Tattoo Blue*, I just couldn't resist tattooing long pointy antler-like designs (black tribal) on her—two of them, both bein' identical. Narrow and graceful, they are—each springing forth from opposites sides of the clitoris base—flowing up across tight abdomen, flaring out over both small jutting hip bones. Exotic? You bet! I have the same (though much more) black tribal work on myself. Mine starts at the base of shaved cock and balls, runnin' up abdomen, spreading out and about, branching for wrappin' around left side of rib cage, over chest, forking with sharp points and endin' on collar bone, right and left. Hurt? Oh Skippy!

My wife has also another intriguing tattoo: a large bird of paradise riding high on the right side of her entire hip and upper thigh. She used to have a labia piercing as well—a good-sized gold bead ring (ten gauge, for those that know). The ring went right through pretty pussy lip of labia majora. Sexy? Oh, you better believe! However, the piercing just wouldn't take and therefore had to be (reluctantly) removed. Bummer! Not only was the ring visually stunning, and great fun for mouth play, but it also matched mine. Well, sorta; my own is a much larger—the size for bein' custom-made—solid gold bead ring of quarter-inch thickness. (Four or two gauge? Hhmm, I forget.) The inside diameter is one and a half inches, having a bead the size of a small gold marble, and weighin' so much to require two separate piercings (flaps of skin) for holding. The ring is carried high up on through the left side of my scrotum. I love it; have had it for years and plan on dyin' with the damn thing.

Anyway, back to my wife: her name is Nancy, and she somehow managed birthing us two perfectly beautiful, smart, healthy sons. The youngest upon exiting the vagina weighed a whoppin' ten pounds, and from this not even a hint of stretch mark! The breast feeding did deflate her firm natural breasts right down though. They looked like something resembling voluptuous skins having been drained empty. Hence the boob job—breast implants. Nancy loves the implants, as do I and everyone else viewing and/or fondling them. There are many that have done both. You see, we have been married (as of date) thirteen years. We've always had multiple sex partners, both male and female. Monogamy is not a realistic practice for people as us. However, we do insist on honesty. So, for reasons obvious, my wife gets way more action than I do (lucky bitch). Besides her striking beauty she is extremely multi-orgasmic, cumming with ease—over and over—sucking dick for literally hours and, like myself, believing that when it comes to sex, the more, the merrier! Especially when the cocks are big, and the woman sultry hot! She loves bein' the center of sexual attention, radiating from herself a strong natural aura for seducing that comes out on film like you wouldn't believe. Yes, my wife is indeed an exotic.

The enchanting barely legal, that modeled with my wife in this particular photograph, was and is also big-time photogenic. Oh the face! Man, what a sweet, sublime, luscious, innocent-looking face. Childlike it is, having a flawless complexion and big crystal blue eyes that a flash from camera exaggerated, making them appear sur-fucking-real! This woman-child is so angelic in features, that my wife and I refer to her as Angel Face.

The shot was taken with Nancy sprawled out flat on her back, having legs open and arms stretched overhead, thus pulling glorious firm breasts upwards. Angel Face, with her pearly fair complexion contrasting ever so nicely against Nancy's golden tan, is laying between my wife's open legs, having her delectable mouth planted over pussy, while staring with those lustful, bright blue eyes up and over, directly into my camera's lens. The young nymph's flushed flesh-pink cheeks are ever so enticingly drawn inwards for suckling, resulting in black exotic tattoo work spillin' forth from sensual, ruby-red lips, glistening. (Again, a very cool contrast.) Beyond Angel Face's own flowing hair is the hint of her petite, white, round, arched bottom, fading into infinity of surrounding black space, containing within itself, in the upper right-hand corner, lettering explaining the purpose of such eye catching imagery:

Blue Fetish International

We do what the others won't.

Local nude figure models available for private photo and
video shoots.
Have a favorite fetish?
Capture it on film.
Your camera or ours.
Become the director or the leading man.
Group rates available.

E-mail: bluefetishinternational☐hotmail.com

Uh, obviously, this was more of a call girl service than anything else. Living in a smallish Illinois university town, having Tattoo Blue, our tattoo and body-piercing studio, enabled us access to most of the local, and non-local, young, hot chicks who were adventurous enough for that kind of work.

A shiver shoots up spine, as beads of sweat trickles down the back, feeling much like insects crawling, pulls my attention away from pretty photograph. Fuck, my whole body is perspiring profusely, with bare ass, balls, and thighs sticking in a slippery sort of way (if that makes any sense) to this cheap, vinyl covered swivel chair. Lifting weight, obeyin' urge, hands go through motions for lighting a cigarette (Camel non-filter), inhaling deeply, while settling back into butt clinging chair, tossin' white Bic lighter to land beside the little cell phone. Cell phones: Jesus, what a marvel these things are. Who'd a thought, aged forty, this idiot would be usin' such a gadget, quite similar to that of Captain James T. Kirk on the Star Trek Enterprise?

Glancing back up, eyes again meet constant stare of Angel Face with mouth full of pussy. Geez, what a weird life I lead, and man, what a depressing phone call that had been.

Nancy had purchased the small telephone upon starting *Blue Fetish International*. The business was my idea, formed after returning home from Central America. Central America. Goddamn, what a living hell that had been. The type of nightmarish hell that one doesn't expect to survive. Yet, I did. Yepper, sure did, but doin' it required all our money. Plus we had to max out the credit cards. Well, Nancy's anyway. Mine had already been maxed out by police, goons, whatever the fuck you wanna call 'em, down in the good ol' town of Livingston, Rio Dulce region, Guatemala.

We were broke and needed money fast! So, with apprentices workin' *Tattoo Blue*, Nancy and I began selling sex and drugs. The sex was—you know, the Blue Fetish thing—basically safe and harmless; other girls did most of the dates. Nancy really only went out on the girl/girl gigs, and a select few where she personally knew the client—thus was pretty confident of discretion. It is a smallish town after all, and we do have young children. Hhmm, and the drugs? Well, they were, for the most part, only psilocybe (magic) mushrooms, which I grew and was very good at. Something that had simply started as a challenging hobby resulted in exceeding success, creating one mean strain of spores. Hell, I never met anyone that could even grow the damn things (knew many to try). My mushrooms became the strongest hallucinogenic drug out there (way stronger than any LSD available). And after Central America, the unique hobby rapidly became a work of labor that was soon producing a pound or more of kick-ass dehydrated 'shrooms a week, having a demanding price of $3,000 per pound, and still buyers came the distance from Chicago and St. Louis for purchasing.

Needless to say, sound financial footing was quickly regained, though not without cost. Methods for the rebound had played major havoc with our physical and mental psyches. Fortunately, both of us are past the age for personally enjoyin' hallucinogens. Still, the risk factor in growing and selling is... Well, if caught, there are very crushing consequences. Yes—retarded as it may be—mushrooms, like marijuana and other organics of the sort, are, in the eyes of the law, illegal narcotics. A town of such size, and the weight bein' cultivated, not to mention the amount of cash exchanged... Well, you get the picture. And adding I was literally *jumpin'* off the Goddamn walls with post-traumatic stress syndrome (just gettin' back from Central America and all).

That hadn't even been two years ago. Tonight is July 31, 2002. It's your typical muggy hot summer night in Illinois. I'm sitting at the small corner writing desk, nude, sweatin' my balls off, not from the heat so much, no, it's from the damn phone call. Typical night this is; typical phone call, that was not. The phone conversation had left me feeling hollow, sad, very sad, and honestly, a bit afraid. It had gone on for over two hours, and brought forth—made fresh again—memories and visions of horrors endured, experienced, whatever in Honduras, Guatemala, and Cuba.

   Having been forewarned, I was expecting this dreaded phone call tonight. The better part of the day was spent free diving for mussels in the Mississippi river to use as bait on trot lines (also for calming nerves, and clearing head). You see, I now live alone in a cabin here on the river. Alone, except for two cockatiel birds, somehow acquired from, ahem, young sons. There is also a stray pregnant calico cat, living out on my waterfront deck. Since I do feed her, well, some would consider the cat mine. I want a dog, a Great Dane, but haven't gotten around to locating one. My loving wife and our two gorgeous sons live some forty miles away, in our small, simple, unique house in town. The little old house is unique for the remodeling I have done, mostly the installation of a commercially equipped, industrial type kitchen. Yes, I do have a passion toward cooking (much more so than actually eating). However, this kitchen was built out of necessity required for the psilocybe substrate mixing and sterilizing before inoculation. A procedure (obviously) no longer practiced, since, after all, I now live here, on my beloved river.

   Simple cabin this is. Cheap, it was not. The place was bought last fall, from the money made selling explicit nude photos of an old girlfriend of mine. She had recently married a very rich Italian guy. She is very beautiful, and he is your typical insecure macho jerk that just couldn't stand the thought of another havin' such photos of his new wife. Some would say I had blackmailed him. Fuck 'em. He was the one who tracked me down via telephone, and for some reason, thought I should be a nice guy and just give him the photos. He was very persistent. Why? Beats the fuck outta Sparky! Man, I owed this guy nothin'. The photos were damn good—and mine. He succeeded in thoroughly pissin' me off. I told the chump he could have my photos of his new wife, for the low low price of $50,000. And if he didn't pay, they would be shared out over the internet. Mr. Dumb Ass paid, and fast! Hee-hee! Shit, to this day, I wish the amount demanded had been a $100,000 instead of $50,000. Funny thing is, I still have all the negatives! Aaah! Oh boy, naw, can't do that; a deal's a deal. Anyway, the fifty was just enough for buying this river cabin.

So here on the river is where I live and work. I am licenced for both commercial fishing and mussel diving. Though really, the diving, these days, is freestyle only (without supplied air), and this is for mussels to use as bait. The good old days of spendin' hours on end belly crawlin' twenty feet under surface, along pitch-black river bottom, in search for thick, pearly white, hard shelled mussels—while suckin' foul air blastin' down from homemade, rigged contraption having 200-foot hose, empty beer keg, and converted lawnmower engine—are long over. Hhmm, also, unfortunately, the days of commercial fishing on the great river are pretty much over as well. Man, how I do miss 'em. See, the booming fish farming industry saw to this. Still, a little money can be made fishing the river; but only by selling catches to restaurants buying illegally, and, of course, organizations that throw fish fries.

I fish hundred-hook trot lines and sixteen-foot-long hoop nets. And these are for the wondrously cool catfish only. There is still a small loyal following of folks that believe (correctly so) that the wild catfish caught from the river tastes way better than the farm-raised ones.

Fishing, however is not the only reason for purchasing and living in this cabin. No, the place was bought simply because I love the river; I always have, and always will. It's mud is in the blood, having tranquil healing with peace and purpose. Here, my being is grounded and anchored; sorta like belonging.

After Central America, a place such as this was, and is, greatly needed. Not only for myself, but for my wife as well. You see, I can be a real handful to live with, even at the best of times… and so can she. From the very beginning, we have always had this serious love/hate, yet need-each-other kinda thing. Man, thank the whatevers for the power of sexual attraction, because fuck me, if there hasn't been a whole lotta times when just that has been the only thing for holdin' us together. Well, that and of course, now, our young sons. Real hard heads we are. Consequently, almost everything between us becomes a Goddamn power struggle. Strangely though, somehow we both, more often than not, in turn attain control for achieving pressed wills, however exhausting. Yes, we have had marital problems for sure, fitting the old saying: "Can't live with 'em, and can't live without 'em." Solution? She has her house and I have mine. An arrangement highly recommended for couples having the means, and wanting the kids kept from the daily bullshit Mom and Dad throw at each other.

Every weekend, Nancy and the boys are here, on the river. Plus, I go to town at least once a week for spending an evening with them. Thus, quality family time of positive accord is maintained. Yes, even when apart, cell phone contact is always open. Added benefit? Enables us to do most of our arguing via phone. Yepper, phone fighting is indeed good... avoids fighting before the boys. And if things hotly escalate as is common, just hang the fuck up on the bitch!

Really though, nowadays we don't even have that much for even fighting over. Nancy has her space and I have mine. I no longer grow illegal mushrooms or sell narcotics of any kind. That all stopped when the imbeciles workin' *Tattoo Blue*, started getting busted for sellin' drugs (including shrooms) from the business itself! Dumb-asses. I told them, never ever do that! One is, right now, doin' a seven-year prison sentence. Poor stupid idiot! And he was a real nice guy, wouldn't hurt a soul. Aughg, fuck these fascistic drug laws! Anyway, I had to shut everything down, and fast. We even sold *Tattoo Blue* (got a damn good price for it too).

Nancy is now getting paid quite well—under the table—by a very wealthy local business man. They are good friends, and really, he created this job so she can work from home. She does menial computer work. Uh, sometimes. Actually, it's a make-believe job. The guy is old-fashioned and pays her, mostly out of opposition towards the Blue Fetish gig. Somethin', obviously, he feels a beautiful mother of two should not be doing. And me? Come on—the guy hates my guts. But, so what? I live here on the river, fishing, tending to my property, and acting as self-appointed groundskeeper for all adjoining properties. Also I write, write about a crazy weird life—bein' mine. It's my entire life story, from beginning to death. The writings are a no holds barred account of personal experiences, thoughts, opinions, and general *attitude*! This will be left for my sons. When I am gone—dead— they will read and know more about me than I do. Both boys will, of course, know me through their eyes. After reading the writings, they will then know me through my eyes. Sure wish I had such self-inscribed memoirs from my father and grandfather. Man, how I'd love knowing (in their own words) just what they truly felt and thought the first time gettin' hands on pussy, or winnin' their first fight, or first gazin' upon their own newborn sons. Whew, that stuff would be priceless—worth way more than all the money they did not have for leavin' behind.

Anyway, writing is *hard*! Hair pullin', head beating hard, especially when you are writing about yourself and a past you've spent most of your life tryin' to forget. Sorta like opening a deep dark closet, letting out all the dwelling ghosts, while tellin' the whole world you banged your sister! Weird, weird, weird! But hey, if you're gonna do it, then you gotta go all the way, right? *Right?* Aw, fuck you! Writing is Goddamn hard, putting one in a very very strange place, in the head that is. And if the person (yours truly) is already in a strange place upstairs, well, it does make for somethin' even stranger than strange. Hhmm, what a weird word "strange" is.

So, I'm living life on the river, doin' the whole fishin', writing, never-ending grounds keepin' thing; and there is healing, healing from that post-traumatic stress crap. And honestly, I feel like it's all comin' along quite nicely. There is no drinkin', and no abusing prescribed Valium or Darvocet. My habitual chronic smokin' of Camel non-filters is, uh, regrettable. The nightmares have, for the most part, stopped their nightly torments. And physically, the body is a strong, lean, mean machine. All in all, this simpleton feels pretty good, considering. Then my mother arrives for a visit.

Ma, had just come in from Israel, after completing a two-year teaching gig. Her stay with us here on the river is brief, as she must leave for a new job, teaching in Indonesia. Before goin' though, Ma hands over a newspaper article. I give her a quizzical look. She explains that this article is about the death of an American journalist in Guatemala City. "Devin, I think it was the same journalist that was murdered the night before we got you out of there." (Ugh. An all too familiar chill worms up spine.) "Devin, the family is having a difficult time getting answers or cooperation concerning the murder. I didn't know if you would want to read the article or not, but I brought it just in case."

Thanking her, I put the article down behind my typewriter, right beside the—now turned around facin' wall—framed glossy of Angel Face eating Nancy. Can't have Ma seein' that now, can we? Though it would hardly surprise her. Man, there was no rush for readin' this article. Nope, no-sirree-bob!

Ma leaves and a week later Nancy's visiting parents arrive from their home in Westport, Connecticut. They stay two whole days on the river, before the bugs and heat get to 'em, whereupon it is decided things would be more comfortable for them back at the house in town. So to town they, Nancy and the boys go, leaving me (gratefully) behind, alone, here on the river. There is a ton of mowing (grass cutting) to be done, plus the fish are runnin'! Over the weekend there was a drowning, actually a couple; however, one body hadn't yet been found.

The day is perfect. Bright blue sky, hot 'n' humid with not even a breeze for wigglin' a leaf. The big river is glassy smooth and shining ever so pretty. My old beater, fourteen hp Noma riding mower, is ardently chuggin' along, doin' its best to imitate the Little Engine That Could; and I'm just plain feelin' good. Yepper, despite bein' completely covered with sweat, dirt, dust, itchy grass clippings, and having one persistent hard-biting fly on my tail. (Ouch, this ain't a typical dung eatin' son-o-bitch fly. No it is not. Normally, my speed, once the bastards land, is superior. Thus squashed, the annoying buzz-heads do become. *Smack!* Shit, missed him again.) Yes, I am feelin' good. The ground presently bein' mowed along river's edge, is dry. (This is not always the case, since it is mostly low marsh/swamp ground, underwater half the time). Lester, the Great Blue Heron, being only some twenty odd yards out, is, as usual, standin' on his favorite half submerged log, midst a long patch of lily pads he claims as his territory. He's fishin' of course, though will eat most anything (of size) that swims, slithers, or crawls among his lilies. Lester, is a big, magnificent bird and is by nature (as with all his kind, this time of year) a loner and very territorial.

Ught! Looky, he's turned his back on you know who, actin' all cool, ignoring and pretendin' my presence on this loud obnoxious machine is not a major nerve racking assault of all senses contained. Silly bird. The rigid long neck, having head ever so slightly cocked betrays him: instead of fishin', he's keepin' look-out on my progressing advance. Those big wings aren't tucked tight either, and his awesome legs are stiff like a soldier's standing at attention. Every impulse in the bird is screamin' lean forward, open those glorious wings with a flap, and fly, baby, fly! But he don't; no, not good ol' Lester. He's gonna hold his post until instincts seize full control.

Normally, these big long legged birds won't let a human get any-where near this close... and that's on foot... No way could such be expected while sittin' on top a riding mower—forget it. However, Lester has, over time, become somewhat permissive with me; still, he will only tolerate just so much.

Taking eyes off the great bird, I turn the mower, makin' another bumpy swipe with grass a flyin'! In doing so, a glance is shot up river for a quick look-see. Well well, whatta ya know; there's Ranger Rick, the prick-river patrol and it appears he's got a boater stopped. They are about a half a mile up river floatin' steadily down.

Here where I live, the river bends greatly, bein' over a mile wide from bank to bank (the other side is the state of Iowa). One of the things that makes our river bend so unique is that its main channel is broad, deep, and all open water. The barge captains love this part of the river. They take advantage of the channel's width and curvature for holding positions and/or passin' one another. Usually this takes place right smack dab in front of my place. I've seen up to three tugs, pushin' maximum number of laden barges, pass each other at the same time—right there! Just out from Lester's lily field, where muddy shallows abruptly meet with steep drop-off for main channel. All very cool! The downside, of course, is that most everything that floats down river (because of directional turn in the bend) will more than likely, beach itself here, on our banks. Spring flooding is a real trip. Yes Sirree!

Ranger Rick (or whatever the fuck his name might be), for reasons obvious, does try blending in, attempting to appear much like any other pleasure craft boater. His boat, despite havin' adhered lettering "River Patrol" in purposely small print and thus rendering legibility from a distance impossible, is an inconspicuous, tan, twenty-foot V-hull runabout. Or rather would be. See, this Ranger Rick is always alone, indeed a rarity among such pleasure craft boaters. Boats like these are (while on the river) usually full of loud, beer guzzling, fat people. Man, here in the Midwest, fat is where it's at! Also, Ranger Rick always wears the standard issue, red coastguard approved life vest. And Skippy, his boat might look like a typical runabout, but be damned if she is. Havin' a tricked-out, souped-up IO (inboard/outboard), the bitch does run hot! The distinctive roar of that engine can be heard easily from over a mile away and this is over the sound of your own outboard runnin' lickety-split! Also, the patrol boat has a very tall bright white antenna mounted on the foreword-most front of the bow. The thing can be spotted from a long long ways. Thus, here on the river, Ranger Rick and boat do stand out pretty much how the unmarked cop car does in town. You gotta be surely darn preoccupied to not know he's in the area (or be a dumb-ass weekend boater).

Personally, I do not know this Ranger Rick, but I do know I don't like him, and visa versa. When not fishin', a fun time is had runnin' the river with my wife and kids, playing, you know, like pullin' our boys behind the boat via an old car inner tube. Man, tie one of those on to a hundred-foot rope, throttling the outboard all she got, and look out, 'cause little boys will be havin' a blast! Yepper, and in doin', there ain't much that attracts attention more than we do on this ol' river. My boat is a twenty-foot Jon boat, completely open (no fixed seats) and of appearance for bein' an evident work boat. The outboard is a fairly new fifty hp Mercury, having tiller throttle (no steering wheel). Like all men that work the river, I operate the boat from the stern, in standing position. Our tattoos and long hair are the boat's flyin' colors and flag. My hair is blond, with white (natural) sun streaks. I wear it in a two-foot long, tight pony tail. (Hhmm, pony tails; you don't see many men wearin' them much these days. Nope, even the rock 'n' rollers have all cut their hair—and, like, *short*! Fuck 'em! Sparky has always been, uh, different. And after Central America this hair will never ever ever be cut... not without bloodshed it won't.) None of us wear any clothes when we are in the water. Why do people wear swimsuits and stuff when goin' into warm water? It's actually sorta goofy, unless, that is, you are washin' the things bein' worn. So we got a large working Jon boat, tattoos like not seen in these parts, long hair, naked little boys shrieking with joy while getting bounced all over the place, clingin' to that inner tube; and then there's Nancy, the real main attraction. I place her up on the bow's small flat deck, where she lies topless in a tiny black or red thong, complementing everything, including tattoos flaming. Yes indeed, Nancy is the boat's marvelous hood ornament! Don't matter if she is layin' on her back, stomach, or side; with her up there I've got the coolest and by far sexiest boat on the river. Even the big several hundred thousand dollar cruisers can't match my boat when Nancy is aboard. Why? Because their women are all usually fat pigs! It's not like we flaunt ourselves either; no, we do try stayin' clear away from everybody. Still, be damned if other boaters keep distance from us. Ranger Rick, for example; every time he spots us, here he comes, haulin' ass, stoppin' short... just close enough for gettin' a good look-see. We all give big smiles and happy waves! Nancy, sitting upright, will join in on the courteous greeting. Her one forearm is used for attempts at somewhat (barely) covering strong large nipples, always seeming to want to make salute themselves. Ranger Rick—clearly agitated upon seein'—is gawkin' and glarin', however, doin' so while revealing an uncertainty for next move. Should he approach, come alongside, pull standard safety check, or not? Haa haw! Wouldn't the uniformed idiot feel stupid doin' this, what with Nancy glistening, exposed as she is. The guy would probably get a boner or somethin'. Therefore, always (as of yet) the conclusion has been to send a disgusted scowl, conveying disapproval, drop the throttle lever and vaROOM! Bye bye. And away he will go, for continuin' his oh so important job of river patrollin'. Geez, a young man the guy is, meaning he wasn't around back in the old days, when I seriously worked the river. Yeah, well, at least this Ranger Rick keeps clear during my fishin'. Commercial fishermen (what's left of us) really aren't his jurisdiction; not that he couldn't, or wouldn't raise hell with us, if there was want, or calling cause. See, fishermen are more of the Game Warden's charge. And Skippy, the Game Warden is a whole 'nother story. We do know each other from the old days.

The old NOMA riding mower starts coughin'—much like a giant cat, hackin' up a hair ball. Acknowledging, right foot eases off the accelerator, enabling the beast ability to chuck out congested accumulation of wetland lily foliage now bein' mowed. Ranger Rick's boat and the other have presently drifted down and in, close enough. Hey, the other boat ain't a pleasure craft boat. No, it is not. She's a runabout, bein' used for official patrol. Hhmm, yes, though wonder from what department? And, ught-o, there's somethin' in the water, floatin' ahead of the two boats. Oh shit-fuck... it's a body, a dead human body!

Years ago, during the period of teaching myself tattooing and body piercing, before such things became so mainstream, like even when the simple naval piercing was considered an exotic act and, for most, taboo (uh-huh, way back then), I was, at the same time, battling alcoholism, maintaining an agonizing sobriety, while also going to school for a degree in mortuary science, a degree havin' title sounding much more impressive than rightfully deserving. Yet, still, the thing is earned, especially considerin'.

My past history with schooling—from kindergarten on—has been... well, a... hhmm, let's just say that as a child, during the sixties, this fool was subjected to the then very popular IQ testing and, in doin', somehow scored higher than expected (go figure). Unfortunately, in those days, the education system placed much emphasis on these tests. (Personally, I prefer ol' Forrest Gump's motto, "Stupid is as stupid does.") Thus, the dreadful teachers believed a student having an IQ level such as mine, should, with proper motivation and direction, excel in the academics. And so, in the beginning, determined, they set out to prove (enforce) this rationale, using every means deemed necessary and consequently igniting a challenge, a challenge (crediting my apparent natural aptitude for rebelling) they lost. I won, becoming an academic retard.

Most of grade school was spent sitting alone, out in the hall. There, the time peacefully passed with reading and drawing. Sixth and ninth grades were skipped altogether—without even so much bothering to enroll—and, of course, I became a high school drop-out.

Before enlisting into the army infantry, the GED (General Education Degree) was required, and passed, with surprising score. (Good guessin', huh?)

College? Yeah Skippy, that was very difficult, and like really weird. I was twenty-eight years old when first enrolling, and it certainly wasn't from any desire of mine. No, it was not. The blame must be placed on Nancy. See, we met in San Francisco, where I worked the winter months doin' construction. Early spring comes around, so it is time for headin' on back to the river, for the seasonal commercial fishing and mussel diving thing. Well, Nancy follows—moving into my trailer on the river—and immediately becomes all bossy—even tryin' to chase off my best beer drinkin' and fishin' buddies.

The time had indeed come; I demanded she either marry me, or hit the road. A bossy wife, there might be potential for working with. A bossy live-in girlfriend, forget it! And you can kiss my ass, if you think marriage is merely a signed piece of paper. Marriage is the ultimate contract, not to be taken (so commonly) lightly, where one bails at the first indication of trouble. Nancy ardently agreed; and so we got married. Yep, courthouse marriage, by same judge that had, the previous year, revoked my driver's license, for driving under the influence (sucker took five long years, before reinstating).

The following spring of marriage, Nancy, bails! No more did she want an uneducated, alcoholic river rat for a husband. Yeah well, fuck her (or so I thought). Much inner turmoil resulted, followed by a month-long drinkin' binge, while still diving the river (which was, by the way, at rushin' flood level). Add a hospital stay, with painful perforated stomach ulcers, lung infection, makin' me hack up strange orange mucus phlegm of toxins, resulting from underwater pressures and breathing in over-pumped air, contaminated with exhaust fumes from the now poorly-maintained lawnmower engine that powered the supply of air (such as it was). Combine this with a very annoying ear infection in both ears, a bad case of ring worm, festering lower extremities, and a bruised right testicle! Conclusion was my wife must be won back at all costs.

Her terms? Move off the river, enroll in college, and—for real this time—stop drinkin'. (Whoa, AA here I come!)

Okey-dokey. Havin' head hung low and tail between the legs, this dog limps off the river, for St. Louis and does make good on the demands—admittedly, surprising even myself. Nancy worked, supporting us by bein' a class act bartender, and I, in turn, stayed true to sobriety, kept a 3.5 grade-point average, tattooed and body pierced mostly gays, head-bangers, industrial rockers, and anybody else that was into such things, before all the (goody-goody) cool wannabes got into it. Also—get this—I applied for, and received an FFL (Federal Firearms License). Yeah! Sparky couldn't drive a car, but, I sure could deal in firearms, both nationally and internationally. You gotta laugh over that one! And so, some guns got bought and sold, with most transactions, ahem, bein' legal.

Mortuary science was chosen, mostly because the major was just morbid enough for (at the time) holdin' my interest. Also, the mortuary field of study impressed the hell outta the steadily growing tattoo/piercing clientele. Man, come on, how many people could say they were an embalmer, tattoo artist, body piercer, gun dealer, and, oh yeah—because of active sexual appetite with very willing, hot wife participant—swinger. God, how we both do hate that silly, ridiculous phrase.

My practicum was served at an all-black funeral home, located in the heart of north St. Louis. Nobody else wanted the position, so of course I got slotted for it. Despite bein' the only "whitey" in the place, everything worked out cool. There, I sold a few cheap handguns, and the house turned over an average of twelve bodies a day! Can you even believe? Twelve new stiffs a day; most were autopsy cases, having been cut wide open, from collar bone to pubic. Top of skulls would be sawed off, with brains removed and tossed haphazardly (along with the rest of the misarranged organs) amongst the entrails (viscera) that now the cavities could not fully accommodate. The job required removing all viscera, bagging it into red bio-hazard bags full o' guts within, followed by an overstuffed baseball stitch. And for the stuff that simply did not fit? Well hello bio-trash bin. Geez, not like these people were gonna give two shits! Lordy, they'd already had their poor dead bodies mutilated enough. And that's before we pumped 'em full of formaldehyde, stuffed skulls with newspaper, stapled jaws shut, and super-glued eyes (and everything else possible). Also, mustn't forget the trusty ol' mallet, for persuading that stubborn elbow or knee.

At first, despite the grisly sights and constant foul, rancid odor (which really, because of personal past history, was no problem), I found it all fascinating, and at those embalming tables, Sparky did excel! So much that the house quickly had me instructing and demonstrating procedure to fellow students that were now coming to the all-black north St. Louis funeral home.

From the very beginning, I wanted nothing to do with the funeral director part of this business. Really, sellin' overpriced caskets and services to sad, grieving people was not my idea of a worthy job. Plus, there is the whole suit and tie thing. (Yuck!) Embalming though was different; or so I thought, before actually doin' and becoming proficient. Soon, true clarity is revealed (at least in my view).

Instead of bein' the "ultimate form of preservation" as we students were taught, embalming is one of the most decadent bizarre forms of degrading and mutilating a corpse that I can think of. It's not like the dead person is surrounded by caring loved ones, gently, respectfully tending, washing, and preparing the body for burial or cremation. No, embalming is not like that at all! Hell, family members can't even be present for ensuring the corpse is not being disrespected, which of course it is, just by the act of embalming itself. Forget the autopsy crap, superglue, mallets, and all that. Forget the joking and comments made by the bored embalmers; and if there are new students present, well, forget all their stupid conduct, and yes, you can guess what goes on, and it does... Forget all that; just remember, a pointed steel tube of approximately the same diameter as a standard garden hose gets stabbed into the lower abdomen, where it is violently shoved back and forth, up and down, all around, and oh be sure to hit the heart, liver, and those nasty bowels! The tool is called a "trocar"; purpose bein' for sucking fluids (and such) from upper and lower cavities of non-autopsy cases. In doing, the insides are turned into minced meat; and still, the procedure fails to get all putrid fluids out, hence making complete preservation of the corpse impossible. Don't matter what the spiffy funeral director tells you. After aspiration, it's time for raising an artery (or two) and pumping in the known carcinogen formaldehyde, not too much though—don't want the corpse lookin' like a bloated pig—only enough for keepin' the body from stinking and/or purging (leaking), during open casket ceremony, etc. Then comes the make-up/cosmetics that is used for attempts at making that dead person appear as if he/she were in deep blissful sleep. Face and hands, ha! Having personally embalmed over one hundred bodies, becoming quite good with makeup, injections, and putty applications, there was still no way for creating the desired illusion and I knew of no embalmer that could. Human taxidermy? There's no foolin' the living. So why the fuck even bother? The attempt is a degradation, especially for the men that would have never been caught dead wearin' make-up when alive. Hhmm... and why are these self-revealing opinionated memories surfacing now?

Sittin' on the old mower, she's chompin' at the bit for a goin' (the little mower does have spirit). Still, I keep 'er right there not movin'. The two boats and floating body keep drifting in closer and closer. And in doin' has brought... Aughg, fuck me! Honduras/Guatemala, Honduras/Guatemala... visions, smells, fear. My upper lip is quivering with struggle from inner anxiety. Sparky is getting' *spooked*, and nerves are red-alert jumpin' for. What-where-who's there? Sneakin' up behind. Shit, no one. Whew, Christ. Man, breathe. Fuckin' breathe. Nice and easy, shake the crap off. It's only a mild case of pestering heebie-jeebies. Out there is just some poor drowned bastard. Ain't no big deal. (Uh, okay, sure, you bet.)

Turning key, shutting down mower, the old girl (like always) grumbles, then sounds off a loud poppin' BANG! (Gaseous bitch, huh?) Leaning forward, standing on mower deck, I see the other boat is from the Des Moines Sheriff's department. Wow, he sure is a long ways from home. Ranger Rick and the Sheriff are clutchin' hold of each other's boats, just chattin' away as they stay course, drifting a few yards up from bloated dead man. Gee, is he ever floatin' good. Many corpses I have seen, but never one floating. No wonder they're called "floaters." He's face down, having clinging black stringy hair. Eugh! Creepy spook shiver goes through again. Cuba. Fuck Cuba! That Cuban guy had it comin'. Oooh, I gotta get off this mower. The river's a mile wide and this corpse must come driftin' right here—right there—out from the end of my dock. Why, why, why?

With a leap, I begin pacing nervous, tight circles around the mower, but quickly realize the ridiculousness of such behavior, and so stop. Lester decides he's had enough! I'm acting weird, plus those boats are comin' in way too close. With a loud *squawk*, he takes flight, tipping his large right wing toward both boats (as if givin' the finger) before swinging a turn, soarin' on down the river toward a dense stretch of timber. There's a sun-bleached giant of a tree down there, that Lester uses for roosting.

Even though not really wantin' to. I jump up on my dock, and march out toward the very end. Why do I march? Who knows. It's just somethin' done, when pumped with spooked adrenalin. Why march out to the end of my 250-foot dock, while tense with nervous Jimmies? Well because it ain't everyday ones sees a dead human being float past their dock. I've seen a lot of things come down this river—even a cabin once, during spring flooding—but never ever a dead human floater!

Standin' there, out on the end of my dock, I become a dumb ass *gawker* (despicable behavior, gawking is). Ranger Rick and the Des

Moines Sheriff are watchin' me watch them. Both are pompously smirking, and not because of my gawking. No, it's because Ranger Rick the prick is sharing sarcastic opinions concerning this tattooed long-haired river rat, wife, and sons. (Sound travels over calm waters, like most would not believe.) Both men are actually chuckling. Fuck 'em!

On a spin, I march for the cabin, grab a Nikon camera with zoom lens, and return to end of dock. "Click, click, snappity snap." Say cheese, you redneck pukes! Instantly, they drop their smirking' grins, straighten backs, attempt lookin' all serious, while directing' oh so official attention to floating corpse.

I hold point of aim zoomed, even after annoyed subjects have drifted on past, sending' nasty glares, which are received with accomplished amusement. Hee-hee, hee! This is a lot funner than bein' spooked. However, it don't last long. No, just can't shake that Goddamn feelin' of sneaky bastards creepin' up. Aughg! Turning, I head on back for the cabin: some serious grounding is needed, and Nancy's voice is it. With cell phone to ear, standin' out on the deck, eyes spot Ike Teal, the Game Warden, approaching from up river, for pullin' alongside other two boats.

Ike Teal I do know from the old days. He is very intelligent, having much experience on the river, and takes his job extremely serious, but (unlike others) ain't a prick. Ike drives a custom made all-weld Jon boat, having center console steering, pushed by a seventy-five hp Merc.

Since not everything done on the river is legal, keepin' look-out for Ike's boat (obviously) is much more difficult than watchin' for Rick the prick and others of authority. At the moment though, Ike has two men sittin' in the front of his boat. Both are appearing' very much as if they have just come from behind a desk of an air conditioned office. Their bright red life vests contrast greatly with that of Ike's olive green. (All official personnel, when on the river, must wear life vests.) Ike's guests are guessed: one bein' the coroner, and the other a detective.

Man, if they don't make quick and get that corpse into a boat, like soon, it's gonna be beached up on shallow mud flats, right in front of Lester's big tree. Ught, there goes Lester! Ranger Rick and the Sheriff have started revving their V-hauls, backing them out from the shallows. Ike Teal, and two passengers, in the flat bottom Jon boat, now have a hold of the dead body and are tryin' to roll it in plastic sheathing. Actually, Ike is doin' all the work (no surprise there). "Devin, are you all right? Devin? DEVIN!"

(What? Oh crap!) "Yes Nancy, I'm fine. They're rollin' up the body now."

"Devin, when are you coming home?" I assure her, it will be after the mowing. "Devin, just hurry and come home, soon as possible. Okay? Devin? DEVIN!"

"Huh? What? Yeah right. I'll be home later today. I love you, bye bye."

"Wait! Devin, are you sure you're all right?"

"Yes babe, I'm fine. Love you, bye."

"Devin, you don't sound fine. God, how I hate this. Okay do what you must, and please hurry home. I love you too. Bye."

Pushing the big white button, having blue stripe, I regret calling her. She will now worry. I step in from the deck, through sliding screen door, returning cell phone back to spot beside my typewriter. In doin', the hand, on own accord, reaches behind the photo of Angel Face eating Nancy, for the folded (tucked away) newspaper article my mother had brought, and left, regarding the American journalist murdered in Guatemala City. The thing has not been touched or looked at since bein' tossed there. Out of sight, out of mind. Hhmm, until today—until right now. Why? Why now, when the nerves are a jumpin' crazy? Aw, who the hell knows! Guessin' though, Sparky would have to blame it on that blasted bloated corpse, floatin' past my dock. The article is slowly unfolded. Oh damn, fuck me...

Post-traumatic Stress, they call it. However, in my case? Post-traumatic "Red Alert", might better describe. And whoa, the first few months of arriving home from Guatemala were the worst. I couldn't even compre-hend still bein' alive, much less safely home. How could this be? A simple airplane ride, and I'm safe? Safe from the bad guys? Bullshit! Couldn't buy it. No sir. That's just what those deranged psychopaths down there want me to think. Then, when least expecting, they will hit. Hit hard and fast! This time bein' in the United States. The attack will be on my home, wife, and young sons. Yeah well, they ain't gonna catch me with guard down! Let 'em try. Mother fuckers!

At the time, my gun collection was very extensive. You know—more than I need, but not as many as I want, that sort of thing. It was indeed a fine collection, and a large one at that. First order of business, when arriving home from Guatemala, was to place strategically about the house (out of reach of the children of course) an assortment of rapid firing handguns, tactical shotguns, and assault/multi-purpose rifles. Also, I began purchasing quantities of large capacity magazines for my AKs, AR-15s and Ruger Mini 14s. Twenty and thirty-round mags they were, though experience had taught preference for the twenties. Thirtyrounders are just too long, protrusive, hindering, and more susceptible to feeding problems, thus, not always making them worth the extra ten rounds provided. Twenty-round mags, on the other hand, are just right. Still, more often than not, the thirties cost less(for whatever reasons). So, what the hell. Along with the high cap mags, came ammunition, ammo, by the bulk case load (thousands of rounds). Some would consider this stockpiling, and yes, it is. No bein' caught this time, without *firepower*! No sirree-bob! Oh let 'em come… Let 'em come!

Hhmm, obviously, half of me wanted, craved, needed an attack. How sweet it would be! Live or die, this time, there would be some payback! The other side of me, however, wasn't so gung-ho. Terrified I was, for my wife and young sons. Hadn't there been enough blood, guts, shit, horror, terror, and killing!

Man, I was spooked! Spooked like big time, full of fear, anger, hatred, guilt, and grief. I cried often, ate little, and slept even less. From Guatemala, 200 ten-milligram tablets of Valium were brought back home. At first, there was major reluctance in using any Valium for the desperately needed relief from wall-bouncing anxieties bein' severely suffered. Valium, though calming, would not only dull hard-earned, honed, sharp edge, but would also provoke sleep, deep sleep! Sleep was an enemy. Sleep made you vulnerable, and brought those Goddamn dreams! Sleep was for people that had no bad guys after them. Whew, how long had it been since last sleepin', really sleeping? Seems like for ever. Gotta stay busy—*balls to the wall*—finish remodeling our house and work the mushroom cultivating. And tattooing? Uh, forget it. These days my hand is steady for a gun, but not a tattoo gun. No, best leave the business to the apprentices, with Nancy acting as overseer. Yeah, they'd been doing just fine thus far. The quality of artwork (tattoos) coming out of the place sucked, but what the fuck! People kept comin' for business anyway. So, there my being was not needed.

However, it was at home. My family needed me to be a Dad and husband again. My wife and sons feared me; they tried not to show it. Still, how could this strange behavior not be scaring them? My body was present, 'cept the head was still down in Central America. At my insistence, Nancy and I slept nightly on bedding in the middle of the living room floor. Our house is small, and so from the arranged location, both doors, front and back, can be watched. The boys sleep in their bunk beds, the next room over. There is no door separating us; every sound can be heard. Night after night, the same. Hours would slowly pass, and though exhausted, my mind races around complexities of abstract thoughts, visions, and memories, to focus on mission at hand. Mission?

Mission impossible. Pull guard duty suspecting hostile attack while flat on back, resting mind, body, and whatever remaining of doubtful soul. Laying there listening—always listening—left hand resting on loaded go-everywhere carry gun—.40 Smith and Wesson. (Yes, I am left handed.) Carefully placed near hip is the gun's sister mag. Beside this is my carry knife—a COLD STEEL folding lock-back, having thick five-inch-long blade, clip point, and shaving sharp edge. On my right, is my wife. Placed between us, is the steel twenty-inch-long black MAGLITE flashlight/baton. Paranoid much? Or just bein' prepared? Both knife and flashlight (or rather same models of each) had been used and proven, down in the land of horrors.

Needless to say, my jumpiness with all the weapons at hand, was making Nancy a bit of a wreck herself. She wasn't getting much sleep, and I was only getting' light drifts (if even that). Every time, with the start of the drifting, a dog would bark, car drive past, house creak, refrigerator kick on, old lady neighbor fart, etc. Man, everything and anything would have my ass bolted upright! Sweat covered, adrenaline pumpin', gun at ready!

A fuckin' mess, I was: seriously suffering from paranoia and insomnia. My constant stomach ulcers are on fire, with bowels all screwed up—when not constipated, they're shittin' a storm. My right ear is infected, having perforated ear drum, constantly seeping fluid smellin' like gangrene. This ear has always been overly sensitive, becoming problematic during times most inconvenient. Since returning from Central America, I can hold my nose and blow air out from inner ear, literally making it whistle (weird). To add, there is the perpetual headaches, stress headaches, they are. While in college, the damn annoying things got really bad. Doctors kept prescribing the always "new and improved" antidepressants. None of them ever worked; plus (for me) the side effects were, well, downright strange and worse than the headaches themselves. Finally, a doctor prescribed Darvocet. He wrote that script out like it physically pained him. Why is this? How come getting painkillers from doctors is like pullin' teeth, yet they are always ever so eager to throw you on "new and improved" antidepressants? Oh well, the Darvocet worked and without side effects. My required dose is four tabs a day, every single day. It has been this way for almost ten years now. Some (most) would say there is an addiction here (no argument). So fuckin' what! The pills work and you know what? There has often been periods when the ol' four-a-day dose has been doubled, and even tripled. Again, so what!

Despite the very real fear of sleep, I know it is needed. The hours of laying in wait every night tryin' to control the alert state of drift resting, is not working. A time-out is desperately needed, and unfortunately, that means sleep, real sleep; not this shady drift stuff. Like it or not, sleep is gonna have to be risked. Yeah okay, use the Valium, but man, only for a night, or possibly two. The rest of the week, nights must be spent awake, alert, and on guard! Upon resolution, that night, at bedtime, all lights (except for insisted five night lights) are out—sleepy time! Jesus, let's hope to hell no attacks. Swallowing two ten-milligram tablets of Valium and layin' tired old body down between warm wife and cold weapons, I wait almost excitedly for the coming anticipated flush of relaxation, followed by deep sleep. Goddamn, how long has it been since feeling truly relaxed? Hhmm, okay. Where is it? Where is my Valium induced euphoric state of relaxation? Guess two tabs ain't enough. Jumpin' up, I swallow two more... Still waiting, still nothin'... What the fuck? Down goes two more! Sparky has now consumed a total of sixty milligrams of Valium... Then it comes, oh damn straight. This is sweet heaven! All muscles are simultaneously fusing. I'm melting into the floor, then lights out. Out, that is, until four hours later, when eyes pop open (wide awake) with disgusting revelation of having just shat myself! Aaaughg, fuck me! Now this ain't embarrassing or humiliating, huh? Oh, my ass! Geez, perhaps sixty milligrams was a bit much. After cleaning up the stinkin' mess, sleep would not come, but a most welcomed relaxed calmness did... Yes, and without jeopardizing ability for alert speed.

Therefore, within one month's time, 200 ten-milligram tablets of Valium were consumed. And yet, though less jumpy, I was still on guard, very afraid. Couldn't even take a shower unless Nancy was home, with bathroom door open and my carry gun resting on vanity sink. Yepper, I still went everywhere locked and loaded! Oh, and when the Valium did run out? My doctor, after hearing only a few brief parts of some horrors endured while in Central America (and after givin' the required antidepressant spiel), basically writes out a lifelong, as needed script for Darvocet and Valium. Hey thank you Doc! To this day, two ten-milligram Valiums are needed nightly, for dream haunting sleep.

April before last, of buying my river cabin, we, the family, get an invite from one of Nancy's sisters living in New York City, to a free stay with her and family at an exclusive, pricey hotel on Florida's South Beach strip. Her husband holds an impressive position with this particular upscale hotel chain; so they often get trips like these. The offer is indeed generous, and Nancy is greatly excited, but not me—no, not me. South Beach? Man, fuck South Beach! Bogus playground for the flaunting super-rich and vulture like wannabes. My tolerance for such is nil. Plus, these days, I am wanting no travel. After Central America, there is a personal, big-time phobia of all hotels and motels. Also, there's my writing: a commitment, averaging eight-hour work days, six days a week. It ain't easy.

See, a project for Sparky becomes an obsession to crawl inside, absorbing my mentality until the challenge wears off, seeding boredom, whereupon I simply crawl out, give the project a kick, and move on for another. Uh, this is probably why I'm no good at keepin' a "real job." Unfortunately, this has yet to happen with the writing. A miserable curse it is! So, to write, since I write of my past and present, I must crawl deep inside for the core, prying open inner doors. Within, all must be relived through viewing, like a film reel bein' played backwards (if that makes any sense). Sometimes it's hard to shut the damn thing off and crawl back out. Sometimes I can only do so halfway. And that's when things become real interesting…

I'm deep into the writing—struggling fiercely with internal demons—when Nancy receives invite for free trip (fuckin' South Beach). The writings, at this point, are of my old army days, when alcoholism was rampant, and despite the many bad times, man, there were some really good times! From the writings, booze is smelled, tasted, and salivatingly craved! Thus, triggering typical alcoholic mind-fuck for justification. Yes, after more than ten years of sobriety, I can now drink. Yepper, this time (it's always "this time") my drinking will be different. Sparky has children, serious obligations; he is older, wiser, and will certainly know his limits for stopping. Yeah! A responsible drinker, just how it has always been dreamt. Besides, after the horrors endured in Central America, wouldn't such a simple pleasure be deserved? (Hhmm…)

There is some heated arguing between Nancy and myself concerning this offered family trip (fuckin' South Beach); I simply cannot do the travel hotel thing. Nancy, of course, knows full well the state of my present being. She, however, will not be deterred: feigns ignorance, retaliating that my fears are a paranoid selfish excuse for depriving her and the boys of a wonderfully good time. Goddamn hard headed bitch! I'm on the verge here of a glass-eating, nervous *breakdown* and still the dumb cunt is goin' anyway. Bummer.

Nancy and the boys catch the 7 A.M. train for Chicago, where they are to board their flight for Miami/South Beach. After sadly dropping them off, and seriously wondering if we will ever be together again, I head 'er straight for the liquor store, and buy two cases of old Milwaukee. Yes, this was an awfully early hour in the day for drinkin' (especially now bein' a responsible drinker and all), but so what; it would help chase away the blues. Plus, this was gonna be a gorgeous spring day. A bright, warm spring day for drinkin' beer and writing (or so thought). The beer didn't taste quite as good as remembered. Still, the stuff did flow with gusto, and… Oh Skippy, there is that so missed feeling of warming glow. Spank my ass 'cause the beer is a-goin' down! And the writing? Well, that wasn't flowin'. Spring is in the air, bringin' about too many distractions. (Uh, like drinkin' beer.) Then, out of the blue a brilliant idea comes through! Why not get the boat ready? Charge batteries, hook up depth finders, and install those new rope cleats. Yeah, gear up the boat, and hit the river. I'll just camp out on the river islands for the whole week Nancy and the boys are gone! Damn, why wasn't this thought of before? The river for me, is a safe zone. No one can touch me out on the river; man, just let 'em try!

Now, one of the many problems befalling my drinking, is the natural ability for attracting bored loser-type people. It's always been this way; these characters just sorta come out from, uh, wherever, like night bugs fluttering around a light. Why? Well, it's been said, that drinkin' puts a spark in my eyes, that is eerie, unpredictable, and very wild. A "loose wire", hence the ill-favored calling. These strange people think I'm gonna bring about some excitement! Shake things up, raise a little hell! You know, that sorta thing. However, the problem is they are usually right. So much that, more often than not, I end up scarin' the piss right out of them!

That night, instead of goin' to the river and peacefully passing out on an island as planned, I end up spending the night in jail, having been charged with three (yes, three) counts of aggravated assault. Gee, how did this come to be? Especially now, that I had become a responsible drinker and all? Okay. It started outside. I was minding my own business, enjoying the day, readying my boat, drinkin' beer to deep-rooted harmonies of George Jones and Tammy Wynette (I've always had a thing for old, classic country music. Hate the new stuff, but sure do love the oldies, especially the sad ones.) When from around the corner of my garage alleyway, comes this unknown, good-sized, young man with beer in hand. A university student he is, living in a rental unit several houses over. Politely, yet, in that very annoying MTV hip hop sorta way, the young man informs me that he and fellow roomies are throwing themselves a barbeque party, whereupon they've run out of charcoal. And for some reason, instead of simply goin' to the store and buyin' more, they thought I might have charcoal for them. Why? Well because for me, this is just how things go. The young man gets no charcoal;

however, he does succeed in learning that I am indeed the founder of *Tattoo Blue* and *Blue Fetish International*.

In a flash, he is gone and back, havin' with him several buddies. They are all standin' between trailered boat and open garage, drinkin' beer and excitedly askin' a hundred questions concerning genitalia piercings, erotic private placement of tattoos on women, and (surprise, surprise) they want information concerning the girls that work for us.

Some of these guys had seen Nancy and the girls in the studio (all had heard of them). The dress code for the girls was simple: "less is best." Sheer, see-through tops without bras is the norm, same with thin camisole slip-dresses, having visible thongs (or not). Such divine scenery made for good business (both businesses). Most of our girls had at least one nipple pierced; all had tattoos and great asses, and, of course, Nancy has those truly wonderful breast implants.

We are all drinkin', with myself bein' in a way more chatty mood than usual; still, I had long ago grown tired of answering the same old questions regarding tattooing and piercing. And those of our girls? Forget it! That information is never shared (not even when drunk and in a chatty mood). Instead, I want to shoot the shit about fishin', the river, and my boat here. But all attempts at changing the subject towards such, got rudely ignored. These idiots were only interested in pursuing topics concerning pussy, which consequently resulted in persistent requests for the presence of our girls themselves. Now, this was becoming ridiculous, hence the inner mood change within. (Must get rid of these oversized slack-jawed pansies, and finish the work on my boat.) Abruptly, one from the group, who had 'til then remained silent and in the background, speaks, announcing he heard that I had just been in Central America and got into some serious trouble down there. The guy introduces himself—bein' Chuck—and by mannerism of stance, combined with how the others are lookin' to him, it is more than apparent that ol' Chuck here is top dog among this group of clowns. Upon hearing this, they are now asking for Central America stories. (Sure, you bet.) Don't fuckin' think so! (Oh Christ!) Then one spots my .50 caliber BMG (Browning machine gun).

The weapon is indeed a real brute of a heavy machine gun, and yes, due to the original (unaltered) right side receiver plate, completely illegal for me to own. Still, I had plans of someday restoring it. The .50 caliber is only missing some easily available, yet expensive, parts and some of the internal bolt assembly is frozen with rust. The big boy gun had been bought cheaply off some old farmer, having brought the thing back (somehow) from WW2. The farmer thought it could never be made to fire. He was wrong.

All (except for this Chuck) have hurried over to my .50 caliber resting so proudly, there on its tripod mount, in the corner of the garage. These assholes begin treating the dignified old war weapon as if it were nothing more than a piece of playground equipment. Like kids playin' army, they are shouting "Bang, bang, bang!", while pushin' and shovin' each other aside for a turn to rotate and rock the big gun, pulling back heavy cocking handle and thumbing butterfly triggers between wooden spade grips. One jackass actually straddles the weapon, as another spins him, with mount tripod pintle creakin' in protest.

The whole scene is pissin' me off. Inner loose wires are a-snappin', with eyes glarin'. Of this, the clowns (fortunately) take notice. Using quick, lame excuses they split, though not this Chuck guy. No, he stays, grinnin', coolly commenting, "Those guys are all fools. I only hang with them for a place to stay. Plus, they get all their drugs from me. They have the money, and I have the contacts."

This Chuck wants to chat; I'm wanting my good mood back. Steppin' over, flippin' cassette of George and Tammy. While shakin' out a Camel and reachin' for my lighter, Chucky, grinnin', quickly flicks his own Bic, offering the light while commenting, "Dude, I hear you grow mushrooms by the pound, and they are the best!" His sly grin broadens.

Opening a fresh beer, "Chuck, you seem to hear a lot of things." Taking my comment as a compliment, he shrugs his shoulders in mannerism matching that dung-eatin' grin. (Cocky fuck, this one is.) Damn, the sun is beginning to go down… Too late now for goin' to the river. I will wait and take off in the morning. Man, those clowns had really pulled my loose wire, makin' me feel all rowdy with no direction.

Goin' against better judgment (common among drinkers, when drunk), I invite this Chuck character into my house. The drinkin' was far from bein' over, and really, some company might be nice. Who knows, maybe Chuck here will turn out bein' somewhat cool, someone for shootin' the shit with, possibly even sharing parts of my Central American story? After all, some of the best talkin' takes place over a table full of empty beer cans, right? Right? (Sure, you bet.)

Ol' Chucky turns out not bein' such a good drinkin' pal. He wanted juicy gossip on our girls. He got none. He wanted information and advice on cultivating mushrooms. He got none. Chuck then wanted fifty bucks for splitting a gram of coke. He got that. Only thing (of course), Chucky didn't have the coke on him. He would have to take my fifty and go get the gram "from a real reliable dude" who has the best stuff around. (Blah, blah, blah. Same old stupid line of crap. Over the years, you hear 'em all a million times plus.)

Twenty minutes later, Chuck returns, empty-handed, no gram no money. He does however put on quite the animated show at assuring the coke is soon coming. "Anytime now dude and this blow is the best! After a taste dude, you are gonna want quantity, guaranteed!"

Yeah right, whatever. If he rips off my fifty, then man, I'll just have to kick his "dude" ass! Hell, fifty bucks will be worth the excuse for that privilege. It will be fun. Go ahead, rip me off, mother fucker! (Wow, there goes that loose wire thing... The bitch is really startin' to spark!) With topic now bein' cocaine, inevitably the conversation turns towards Central America and the cocaine down there, you know, the abundance, quality, and low-low price, stuff like that. Of this, there is no problems in discussing, but then ol' Chuck starts diggin' deeper and deeper. He's tryin' to pick my brain for details regarding rumored stories about the "deep shit" I had experienced while "down there." Memories begin floodin', with visions flashing, in not knowing order of sporadic sequences. Chuck is sensing this, and still, with that annoying persistent grin, keeps right on prodding, provoking. (Fucker thinks he's Mr. Tricky.) I would change the subject, and Goddamn, if Chuck wouldn't bring it right back up again.

Finally, in hopes for ending all talk concerning Central America, I tell him (using voice flat and hollow), "Look Chuck, once somebody goes down there and gets sucked into the region's underworld, that's it. That's all she wrote. You become victim to, literally, an insane hell. They force you to witness and partake in unimaginable atrocities. They use you and then kill you. And if you're lucky, your death will be somewhat quick, instead of bein' tied to a bed, slowly tortured and dismembered before a video camera, as deranged crack head cannibals orgy in blood. They are really, really big on making these sick torture snuff films; understand? Man, nobody gets out of that shit alive."

"Dude, you got out alive."

"Yes Chuck, but only due to sheer luck of events. I don't like talkin' about it; so let's not, okay?"

Chuck's smirking grin and eyes have a mischievous arrogance; and, from within', they are exposing a true nature of evil. Not pure evil, though certainly the starting seed for such. Chuck, slowly pushes himself from the kitchen table, leaning back in his chair, while crossin' his arms in deliberate self-conceit. "Dude, if you can go down there and come back alive, then I definitely could. Plus dude, with all that top grade cocaine around... ha ha! I would have made the trip worth my while."

Geez, this asshole is indeed pissin' on the wrong tree... and that grin of his is really getting' on my nerves. (Loose wires are whippin' inside the head, with sparks a flyin'!) Knowing I'm bein' baited, yet not willing to resist, I ask "And Chuck, how would you have done this?"

"Dude, by outsmarting them; that's how. Obviously, intelligence doesn't run too high among these people. Ha ha! Right? How hard could it be to outsmart—"

Wrong answer! Then again (considering circumstances), there was no right one. Of its own accord, my body just reacted, blink of an eye mid-sentence interruption, beer cans a flyin'! I am over the top of that table, having pulled .40 caliber Smith and Wesson. Racking the slide back for ejecting a live round, and releasing it to slam forward into the chamber a following round! Make no mistake, the toying son-o-bitch now knew a for-real loaded cocked pistol was bein' held against quivering temple of his head!

"Outsmart them! OUTSMART THEM? How the hell do you outsmart this, mother fucker?" Needless to say, ol' Chucky drops his smile, and like fast! Damn, this is the first time I've seen him without the wretched thing. His lips are trembling tight, face is all scrunched up, with eyes clamped shut, and arms up in the air, doin' little spazzy bye-bye waves! "Dude, you're crazy! You're fucking crazy, dude! That thing is loaded. It's really loaded! Look, dude, I get the point! Okay? Devin, dude, I get your point. Please just lower the gun... Please dude!"

Now, ain't this the predicament? Chucky here is about ready for peeing himself. I'm holdin' a loaded gun to his head, and really—other than just for kicks, from having the wrong buttons pushed and me bein' drunk and agitated—I've got no real justification for such action as this. Uh, well hhmm, excepting of course, it really feelin' good, this time being on the other end of the gun. Jesus, Sparky must think up somethin' for smoothing this over, and quick. "Chuck, Chuck! Open your eyes man." Trembling, he does, starin' down at the .40 bullet that had been ejected and now lay before him on the table. "Chuck, if you're gonna talk the talk, then man, you gotta walk the walk!" (God, I need somethin' better than that. Hhmm... Oh yeah!) "Uh, Chuck, Chuck! Where the fuck is my fifty bucks? We both know there ain't no coke comin'."

Ole Chucky, now no longer the pompous cocky prick, is urgently rambling, in hopes of convincing coke will soon be here. "Dude," he is so sorry for "dissin' " me, while talkin' "shit" about my experience in Central America. Chuck promises not to bring any of that up again! (Central America, right.) Lowering the gun, laughin' while playin' this all off as just bein' a silly, big joke, I succeed in getting' Chuck to giggle along, even callin' me "One crazy ass dude." Good buddy like, Sparky smacks him on the shoulder, opens fresh beers, and hands him over the Smith and Wesson, demonstrating how it operates etc. Obviously, this was the first time Chuck had ever handled a pistol. (Real fuckin' tough guy here.) Seeing his delight, and, uh, really needing to secure this smooth over job, I reach into the nearby cabinet and pull out my bushmaster AR-15, having short barrel and collapsible stock.

Removing twenty-round mag and ejecting out chambered cartridge, the now unloaded weapon is handed over to Chuck for playin' with. He is big time enjoying himself, askin' questions, throwin' in mention how he had heard of my large gun collection. The noted comment sends red alert light blinkin'. Okey-dokey, time to lock and load both weapons, and put them back where they came. We are now seemingly getting along just fine. Chuck has become humble, and there is no more talk concerning Central America. Instead, we are drinkin', tellin' jokes, and laughin' the way drunks do. Still, there's somethin' really bothersome about this Chuck guy. (Forget the previous challenging behavior, no coke, and mention of my large gun collection.) Chuck is now suspiciously overworkin' the good buddy thing, like repeatedly goin' to the fridge for fetchin' fresh beers, even before need be. A fast drinker I am, though not this fast and neither is Chuck. Man, what's this guy up to?

Hhmm, could it be ol' Chucky is wantin' Devin drunk? So drunk for passin' out? (Uh, this ain't gonna happen. The same had been tried with drugs in Guatemala. That trick didn't work there, and it won't work here. But damn, I am getting' drunk.) Let's think about this. With me passed out in drunken state of comatose, Chuck and his pals can come in here, stealing what they please, including my gun collection!

Pondering probability of such... Slap my balls! Who should be loudly gathered at my back door, wantin' to come inside? Why it's Chuck's oversized pals! And by the sound, they are as drunk as we. "Chuck, don't let them in unless they have coke." They, of course, don't have the coke; and, of course, Chuck lets them in. Also, he's resumed his haughty prick demeanor that the loaded gun to head had so quickly subdued earlier.

Now, these guys are all pretty good size (college wrestlers my lawyer was to later inform). They are obnoxiously rambunctious, and keep splitting up for goin' into the next room where my safe is kept (among other things of value). My head is beginnin' to swarm, and those loose wires are startin' their sparky spark dance! I ask the guys to leave. They merely laugh. I tell them to leave—an order mockingly ignored. Fuck this! Opting for full shock effect, out comes the bushmaster AR-15, live round is ejected, and another is slammed forth! (like Hollywood has learned for effect in movie making, the sound of chambering rounds into such weapons is, in itself, a real attention getter. And Skippy, you had better believe it is!) As intended, the snappy slide rackin' does indeed get their attentions, with sight from origin, claiming imposed shock! Chuck knew what was comin', and just sits there laughing. His pals though ain't laughin' now; nope, no-sirree-bob. Two instantly freeze, while the others fly out the backdoor!

With gun pointed towards those frozen in place. I unleash a fury of verbal assault, plus order 'em "Drop, and give me forty!" (Push-ups.) The pussies can only barely manage pumpin' out twenty, and that's with the muzzle of my weapon to their heads! Geez, what sissy whimps. After the lame push-ups, they too are sent out the back door. Chuck stays seated, laughin' hysterically! Yeah, real fuckin' funny, haw, haw. The drinkin' continues for two more hours, before Chuck's company grows tiresome. Remembering my fifty bucks, knowin' it to be gone—not gonna ever be seen (by me) again—and hopin' the same of Chucky here. I insist he go and get it. Chuck leaves, gleefully assuring return of that promised. (Yeah right, and Cindy Crawford is droppin' by later to play pony girl.) Goddamn Nancy is gone for not even one whole night, and I've been suckered out of fifty bucks, had strangers in the house, put loaded guns to their heads, and oh yeah, I'm drunk as a skunk!

Much to my surprise, Chuck does return, showing up at our back door, having with him only that intolerable grin, for informing "Dude, the cops are coming for you! Ha ha ha!" A ridiculous wave and he is gone. Well, fuck me! Grabbing a beer, lighting a Camel, I go and sit out on my front porch in wait for the arrival of nice policemen. They arrive alright, speedy and in numbers. Twelve squad cars! Christ, bored cops much? Obviously they were expectin' some action; they got none. To jail my ass does go.

The next day, I'm charged with three counts of aggravated assault. In the police report, even ol' Chuck had signed off on how he feared for his life. "That crazy dude was going to blow my brains out. And he's got a machine gun."

Before the Judge, bail is made, with agreement: my entire firearm collection be relinquished over to the police department for holding, pending outcome of future trial.

Upon arrival back home, there are, parked out in front, six squad cars and two unmarkeds. Inside our small cozy house is shoulder to shoulder cops; all here for court-ordered seizing of my firearm collection. Why so many cops? Well, golly! Guess these ol' boys thought they just might luck out, and find themselves somethin' a bit more exciting than a personal gun collection. Umm, like perhaps a grow room down in the basement? Nope, nope, nope, the cops found nothin' of the sort. (Sure glad to have shut that operation down.) So, the guns only they were obliged for seizing. The pricks actually looked disappointed.

With stupid cops on my heels, I went about unlocking wall lockers used for storing guns and showed them various other places where guns were placed. The dumb-ass detective in charge didn't even know how to operate half of my guns, for inspecting if loaded or not. He admitted (pathetically) to having limited knowledge concerning firearms. And the other cops? No kiddin' here, they were of the same ignorance! Yep, you should have seen 'em; and of course, they wouldn't allow me to demonstrate procedure for pullin' standard safety checks on any of the weapons. It became a Goddamn cluster fuck of retard cops milling over this gun/and or that, tryin' to figure out bolts, latches, safetys, magazines, etc. One young cop even got his thumb split wide open when the bolt from a French MAS-49 slammed closed on lingering digit. (Un-Fuckin'-believable!) His blood went all over the gun; he had to leave for the station house and receive treatment. God, this just couldn't be happening, yet you could bet the farm it was! The cops finally left, promising to take real good care of my firearm collection. (Yeah okay, and Cindy Crawford is still comin' over, right?)

Alone, leaning against the wall, crouching a squat to the floor, tears surface for dropping on crossed forearms, as chest heaves, while, like a million billion trillion times before, the brain beats the crap outta nothin' 'cept itself. (Man, what a foolish alcoholic loser… surviving Central America; and for what? To come back home for purpose of bein' a paranoid drunk? Fuck, can't believe I actually fell for the ol' "I can now be a responsible drinker" ploy. And this living in constant fear? Must stop! Post-traumatic Stress? My ass! Real men aren't supposed to suffer from such… and if by chance they do? Well, they suck it up and move on. March or die! Right? *Right!*) Aaaughg, Sparky is falling apart here. The shame is overwhelming. Still, like always, inevitably the tears stop, with body back on feet for doin' that needing done: shit, shower and shave, a few Darvocets swallowed, and the small comfort knowin' at least they didn't get seven high quality, expensive handguns hid where no one would find. (Rule number one: when possible, never surrender all guns.)

House cleaning time, clearing our trashed-out kitchen table of the many beer cans. All of Chuck's are for the most part full! That punk bastard had indeed been setting me up. I'm gonna kill him! Hhmm, after the court date, that is.

Nancy calls, and gets to hear all about drunken night of stupidity, and (like with all my fuck-ups) the pricey consequence. We both cry in frustrated agreement, concluding my head ain't screwed on right and serious changes are in order. Despite all, regardless, Nancy does want those guns back. Some, she knows are very valuable and cannot be replaced; plus, she actually owns a few (several were deliberately registered in her name). Also, Nancy doesn't want me doing any jail time. She gives the number of a lawyer acquaintance. We are gonna fight these charges!

Well, spank my ass and call me Judy! A lawyer? Wow, I was just gonna take whatever the o-mighty judge decided to dish out. But hey, if Nancy wanted to fight this, cool! However, I did feel deserving of a firing squad, if for no other reason than breaking *sobriety*. Yeah well, it won't be broken again. Mr. Alcohol has played his last dirty trick on Sparky. Yep, I might overdose on heroin, but damn, if booze ever again gets touched. (Uh, just kiddin' about the heroin thing. Really! Still, snortin' good heroin is pure heaven; save fortunately this is not a drug easily had in these parts. So therefore, the odds of personally overdosin' on such are about the equivalent as, uh, let's say Devin drownin' in the river. Ha! Ain't gonna happen.)

Having just ended phone conversation with Nancy, when ught, if the doorbell don't ring. Why it's Mr. Detective, alone, explaining (almost apologetically) how he must search my garage. They'd forgotten to do so earlier (an oversight not missed by yours truly). The detective shares how, in the report, there is mention of a "huge machine gun" on the premises, in the garage. He's gotta check it out.

Laughing, I lead the way outside, around trailered boat, to the garage. Entering, steppin' over tools and the sort, "There the ol' gal is! Ain't she a beaut?"

A look of confused astonishment comes over the detectives face, as he asks "Okay… But what is it, exactly, and can it fire?' (Dumb cop. I hate cops, always have and always will.)

Looking at him as if he were the idiot he is, "Uhm, detective, you weren't ever in the military, huh?" His head slowly shakes no, with unintended facial expression indicating that this just might be a topic of discomfort. (Despite feeling like a stepped on donkey dick, I am enjoying this.) "Hhmm, well okay, to answer your question, sir, no, she can't fire. This baby is a genuine World War 2 Browning .50 caliber machine gun! A war relic, completely de-milled, similar to how you see the big artillery pieces displayed in public parks and such. Trust me, the gun cannot be made to fire. She has been de-milled, grandfathered, and

BATF approved (not) as relic incapable of fire. Trust me, if this wasn't so, you could bet those BATF boys would be down on my ass quicker than flies on… uh, anyway, detective, you got any more questions? Or need to look around some more?" He doesn't and so leaves.

That was little over a year ago. Now I'm sitting here at my desk, having just talked to Nancy via cell phone, tellin' her of the dead human body, floating past my dock, for beachin' before Lester's tree. In my hands, is this newspaper article, staring out from which is a somber photo of a man. This man, like the one in the river, is dead. Yet, unlike the man in the river, this man had been an American journalist living in Guatemala City, where he was brutally murdered. His name is Terry Scott. The name rang no bells, but, whoa, that face sure does! I was in Guatemala City at the time of his death. (Yeah, and so were about three million other people). Hhmm, why does this man look so Goddamn familiar? We have crossed paths, he and I. Still… where, and how? Oh Jesus! It would have had to of been in the paramedic van, and later in that stinkin' emergency room (or whatever one would dare call such a place). God, was Sparky ever fucked up, having just survived goin' down in a fire and sufferin' big time from carbon monoxide poisoning (among other things). Yes, I'm sure of it. This had to be the same man, a journalist. He was American and gay.

Terry Scott, Terry Scott, you poor poor man. The article claims you were gay and had been stabbed numerous times before finally gettin' throat cut, spattering blood throughout the room! Yeah well, ain't that just how those deranged psychopaths down there like doin' these sort of things. Oooh, Terry, I know who tortured and killed you. Hhmm, I know who's responsible anyways. See, those responsible had said they were gonna "Kill the fag American journalist."

Why? Well Terry, mostly because you were gay, gay and American. They (the phychos) had been tryin' to kill me for quite some time (while down there) and failing, losing face miserably. For a few, the pursuit of my torture and death became an in-fucking-sane obsession.

At the time, I was a thirty-eight-year-old American, they thought to be gay (actually bisexual, but no matter, this to them is the same as bein' gay). You Terry, a forty-one-year-old gay American, became the next best thing. Plus, they knew your death would weigh heavy upon remaining battered remnants of my soul. Christ, how many people (and those oh so poor beautiful children, tortured and murdered) had died down there because of my being?

Hhmm, Terry, this newspaper article also states your murderous death took place on December 28, 1999. Uh, this is indeed a falsity (typical of how things are in that region). Sparky knows for a fact that they killed you on the night of the 30th, myself having been escorted out of the city and country December 31, 1999, New Year's Eve. Your death (as intended) was my send off, farewell, goodbye.

Reading further into the article, it's learnt (among other things) that since Terry's murder, there have been seven other unsolved American killings reported in Guatemala. (Lord knows how many were unreported.) Aw, I felt like cryin', not so much for havin' such great love for my fellow Americans—I don't. Goddamn though, if they should be killed, tortured, or maimed while traveling or living abroad in other countries.

According to the article, this Terry Scott's family seems to be havin' a hell of a time getting any cooperation from anyone in Guatemala (including our poor excuse for an American embassy down there) concerning Terry's murder. The family was/is, of course, seeking closure to Terry's death, yet, for them, they can't have this, without the results of a serious investigation. Man, such things don't exist in places like Guatemala. Personally, I felt that the Scott family should consider themselves lucky in that at least Terry's body was found; at least they had a body. Yes, this might sound cold, still, it is better closure than what many receive in Guatemala. For most that are tortured and killed there, they just simply disappear and are dumped in some remote spot, body's never seen again, leaving live family members always wondering, not knowing. When I was down in that horrid country, this had been one of my biggest fears—havin' my body up and disappearing. Nancy and the boys would never know what had happened. Without a body, or confirmation of death, they would never know; and this would be the worst—not knowing!

After months of frustration, the Scott family has hired a private investigator and is asking for the FBI to be brought in. Damn, the family's persistence is indeed admirable; however, the problem is that no matter what, no fuckin' way will those responsible for Terry's murder ever ever become accountable. No, instead, some poor bastard having absolutely nothin' to do with Terry's death will be targeted, thus blamed. Havin' rap pinned on him—*him* of course—bein' in all likelihood some inculpable homosexual. Hence, trumped-up charge: crime of passion…, hmm…, or somethin' similar. And uh, the FBI? Ha! Forget it. They wouldn't/couldn't (even if wanted) induce a conviction on those deserving. Not in a country such as Guatemala. No sirree-bob. If anything, the FBI snooping will only get more innocent people killed.

The blasted article also briefly informs, how the screwed-up country (Guatemala) had been under ruthless military rule for like ever and how, in 1954, the American CIA did what it does best (besides drug running, which ain't mentioned). Those boys started a forty-two-year-long bloody civil war! Finally, in 1996, the UN came in for settling things down with attempts of instilling a democracy. The author's name is Michael Garcia. Fuck me... another shiver brings forth sweaty goose bumps. Garcia. Popular Latin name much? The name was certainly heard often enough while down in the land of horrors... Aughg!

Gosh, now regret having even read the depressing thing. Yeah, but man, at least this Scott family is tryin', tryin' to find answers and understand. Hhmm, the article should have mentioned that fifty percent of all reported Central American cases involving human disappearances occur in Guatemala. That's fifty-fuckin'-percent, out of all Central America! People just up and disappearin'—dead—never found again. No body, no nothin', just gone.

Well now, ain't this the cheery day. Time to finish mowing. Outside, despite the weather bein' perfect hot, humid, and summer bright, my head and inner self is a shadow fog of gloom, fusing with nerves and reflexes over-alert-jumpy.

Glancing up and down the river, the patrol boats, Ike Teal, and dead body are gone. Also, no signs of Lester. Damn, with this *eerie,* spooked feeling now within'; it sure would be nice havin' ol' Lester back in his spot (amongst lilies), standin' guard (fishin'). The riding mower's loudness is difficult to hear above. Also, this terrain is rough ground, requiring most of my visual concentrations. Not bein' able to shake that somebody sneakin' up sensation... Yes, it sure would be nice havin' ol' Lester back in his spot. He could warn if anyone were approaching our area. He would alarm my attention by flappin' his butt outta there! But with him now gone, instead of given quick darting glances towards Lester, I gotta do the whole paranoid, every other second, look up, look down, look all around thing! Geez, post-traumatic stress, much? Is this (under present circumstances) fuckin' normal? Whew, I honestly don't know.

Lordy, it seems like I've been sorta this way for most of my entire life. Actually, the on-guard thing got really bad (or good) back when I was sixteen years old, after cutting a guy's abdomen open (and Sparky does mean wide open). The cut was a deep gutting one, goin' side to side on sliced horizontal curve, spillin' out the man's intestines, slopping forth to the floor... and still, he stayed a foot for bulldozin' us both through a glass shower stall! A hard stab to the man's thick sinewy neck finally dropped him, there, on the tiling, amongst shattered glass and everywhere blood. Blood, covering us both, and seemingly the entire bathroom. The son-a-bitch deliriously begged for me to stop, "No more cutting; call an ambulance" and, oh yeah, he was sorry, "real fuckin' sorry." The whimperin' pile of shit was a big, black, seasoned ex-con. He thought raping my white ass would be a great sport. Fucker picked on the wrong white boy! At the time, I barely weighed 125 pounds. Such experience, goin' from victim to victor makes one a bit giddy, thus presenting wicked pleasure to verbally torment and taunt the pleading, beggin', dying predator of a rapist, while watchin' him piss all over his own sloshed-out bloody guts. Mother fucker! Hhmm, and the point of this reminiscence? Uh, can't remember... Oh-right, the red alert mode. Wow, after that incident, I was on guard twenty-four seven for a long-long time.

Yep, yep, yep. Anyway, due to last year's charges of three counts of aggravated assault... You know? Where the cops came and took away (most) of my firearm collection? Well, my final court date is comin' up soon for determining if any jail time is required, and, if not, possibly reclaiming possession of beloved gun collection. My fat lawyer wants Sparky to go in for a psych evaluation beforehand. Mr. Fatty is hopin' that a shrink will write up that, yes, at the date of arrest, I was a little nuts. However, with time passed, I've regained solid stability—thus, becoming normal as apple pie. Geez, in the past, this sort of thing would have been no problem. Shrinks, for me, have always been easy to snowball, but, these days? These days tears come so easy... Who knows how it will turn out.

One of the things about mowing is that you think while doin' it. Mowing don't do a Goddamn thing for getting' your mind off nothin'. Still though, not wanting thoughts of that obvious, there is somethin' within capturing intrigue (if intrigue is even the right word) and this would have to be the mention (in article) of Terry Scott's family hiring a private investigator.

While down in Central America, I had gotten myself into some very deep shit, which, more or less, revolved around this horrific, satanic cult worshipping, drug running organized crime ring. And Skippy, flip my lid they did!

Third World corruption, organized crime, and drug running is pretty much expected (accepted?) and would surprise nobody. But man, that cult religious thing that those deranged psychopaths practiced really threw my entire being for a loop! Uh, that, and those torture/snuff videos they make. Oh, how they love getting it all on film. And just like with their sadistic religious cult ceremonies, the more shockingly grotesque the torture (combined with lots of sex, cocaine—crack—smoking and can't forget the for-real cannibalism), the better!

What kind of people would do such things? Hhmm, good question. One thing's for sure—they are not the run-of-the-mill, God fearin', Christian, Catholic whatevers. No sir, they are not! Although, that ain't sayin' nothin', huh? Especially with myself bein' a full-blown stout, stomp-down atheist. Always have been; even as a child, just couldn't swallow the whole God/Creator thing. Nope, never could. I did, however, believe in Santa Claus there for a spell. So, God-fearin' I am not. But those sadistic cult people? Whoa, I sure as all mother of God, Jesus fuckin' Christ, fear them! Most are Garifunas. And what are Garifunas? Well, they are English-speaking, black Caribs that mostly inhabit coastal regions of Guatemala, Honduras, Belize, and, word is that many have and are migrating to the United States. (Oh goody-goody!)

The Garifuna people's history is an interesting one. Let's just say that in 1665, two Spanish ships carrying Nigerian slaves sank off the coast of the Caribbean island of St. Vincent. Surviving slaves swam to shore and co-existed with the Carib Indians. The two people intermixed, and fused into a single culture, calling themselves Galibi. The Spaniards, however, thought dubbing them "cannibal" more fitting. This is the origin of the English word "cannibal." Why? Uh, because the fierce warlike fuckers *ate people,* that's why! Hhmm, anyway… Eventually, they became known as the Garinagu people. Yet, most everyone (including themselves) just call 'em Garifunas.

Now, obviously most Garifunas don't eat people, or even practice this insanely cruel, bizarre cult-religion (at least I hope most don't). However, the ones after me sure did, and surely my experience was no isolated case. So even if most Garifunas don't practice this sort of shit, a hell of a lot must. Plus, many of their participating followers (personally witnessed) were young people, meaning that popularity is growin' strong. And what is this decadent murderous religion? Well, that's the big question, huh? The religion is some kind of Santeria voodoo-type cult. And it sure wasn't no chickens that those people tortured and beheaded. No, it was not! The victims were men, women, children, and infants! To this day, I can't stand hearing the sound of a baby or little girl cry. Those sick bastards really messed my head up good.

Of course, there is a name for that religion; and within regions subjected for practice, secret it is not. Whew, upon bein', shall we say, personally introduced? There is great regret in not havin' ability for sharing correct verbal term for such psychotic denomination.

Police, detectives, FBI, CIA, American embassies ain't gonna openly cough up nothin' concerning the terrorizing cult religion; however, a private investigator just might. Also, there sorta is/was this video circulating down there, involving an umm, hhmm... certain person (me) committing, uh, incriminating acts of desperation?

"El Zorro" the video was at the time titled (or so I was told). Jesus. Having done such things, with added effect in memory of that wretched camera light always beaming non-stop, producing wretched video of madness ghosting. My God! There is no God!

A private investigator snooping around down in the land of horrors, investigating a murdered American, just might come across such video involving another American (ahem). Obviously, this would not be good. Still, look at the time frame. *El Zorro* was hot and in local (underground) circulation at the time of Terry Scott's violent death. The thing (video) could be quite easily stumbled across.

El Zorro is only one of literally thousands of such home-made porno/torture/snuff films that are first circulated throughout the region from which they are savagely produced and then routed onwards for Europe and the United States, where they are sold via ultra discretion to high paying individuals that are sick in the head for such things. Man, do not let anybody tell you these types of films/videos don't exist, because they sure as hell *do*! And if guessin' correctly, (which you can bet the farm I am) the now low-low priced, ever available VCR, video camera, and computer are allowing such inhumane horrific things to be produced and distributed at an alarming rate never before known to mankind. Of course, most of the victims (not all, but most) are women and children. The horror of dying in such a way is literally indescribable.

To be forcibly sexually violated, tortured, and mutilated, for sake of video that others will profit from and "Get off" on, is so barbarous that those responsible are no longer human beings. No, they are hideous monsters! And if there was any sort of God out there that allows for such things—well, that mother fucker can kiss my Goddamn atheist ass! Honestly, I don't mean to offend good people believing in God and religion, practicing an intelligent, respectful, non-cruel way of co-existing with fellow humans, animals, and mother earth. No, it is not my intentions to offend those having kind beliefs. It's just that somethin' must be done for stopping the atrocious acts. I can still hear them. Ught, hearin 'em right now: the cryin', shrieking, wailin' of little girls... Oh, until the fright, pain, shock becomes so intense that even this, they cannot do. Only moan, gasp breath, and wish for death.

There is nothing like the sounds of someone bein' tortured, and I do mean nothin'! Just ask anybody that's heard the appalling suffering... Unforgettable it is—forever haunting. (Oh not again! I'm cryin'.) The tears are wetting all the layered dirt and dust around my eyes, into like mud, which is only making the eyes water even more. Aughg fuck! I hate cryin'.

Blowing snot from nose and wipin' muddy eyes with dirty hands, I turn the mower for another cutting swipe. Hey, there you are! Ol' Lester's come back, and is now standin' out on his half submerged log. Geez, even though sentiment is far from bein' mutual, I do love Lester. He is one cool bird and a darn good fisherman! The other day, he caught himself a flathead catfish. It was a small one, but not for Lester. The fish was like threefold the size of Lester's head. At the time, my thoughts were, *man, ain't no way that bird is gonna be able to swallow Mr. Catfish* (right). With some well coordinated manipulations of gripping beak— *gulp*. Wow! How does he do that—swallow those things without 'em shreddin' his inner throat? Catfish have extremely sharp, pointed, spear-like dorsals, you know? I am still babying my right index finger from where, not long ago, a catfish dorsal went completely through. Yep, went right on through the whole finger. This happens easily when handling lots of catfish. Over the years, their dorsals have on several occasions, gone through my thumb and fingers, once through left hand, and twice through my right foot. And yes, I am talkin' about goin' clear through— in one side, out the other! So, maybe now you can understand my sense of awe with Lester's ability in swallowin' those puppies down whole like he does? Whatta bird!

Whatcha think, Lester? Is that Goddamn incriminating video still circulating down there? Lester could really give two flyin' fucks... Hhmm, yeah well, I hope the ghastly thing isn't; however, if it is, so be it. At least, instead of them from the land of horrors spilling my blood, it was me that spilt theirs... even killing... (Shush man, must proceed cautiously here. You are opening doors that have been purposely closed, locked, and fearfully guarded. Well duh. No-shit-Sherlock!) One was a girl, uh, not really a girl-girl, no, more like a young skinny crack whore of a woman! Honestly, she was a woman, okay teenager. Still, she weren't no girl, or kid. No she was not! I damn near cut her fucking head off! They were workin' at tying me down to the bed, while shoving a (large) flashlight up my ass; the young bitch had a knife and was gonna do the cutting... Aw fuck! How I hate remembering this shit, 'cept it just don't go away. The visions and memories are always here, even when they're not. Just gotta stay busy and avoid goin' too deep into the head (Uh, okay, Roger Dodger that. Hhmm, wonder how much this

Scott family really knows of the goin's on, down in the land of horrors?)

The Scott family obviously doesn't fully understand/realize that Terry's real killers will never be brought to legal justice. Also, if they (the Scott family) don't already know… they need to know about the torture/snuff videos bein' made and distributed. I just bet Terry's murder was filmed. Christ, does the Scott family need this knowledge? Whew, that's a hard one for anybody… knowing (or even thinking) your loved one's torturous death is on film and in the hands of perverted monsters; whoa, that's a mind fuck in itself! Still though, the Scott family must have some good contacts with journalists, for getting such coverage concerning Terry's death what with Terry himself also having been a journalist and all. As hard as it might be on this poor grieving family, they need knowing.

Perhaps, just maybe, through Terry's death and known journalist contacts, the Scott family can expose, draw some international attention to, these Goddamn in-fucking-sane torture/snuff videos; thus, more can be done for stopping production of such things. Yeah but, sharing this with the Scott family would require surfacing and, at very least, disclosing some of the horrors personally experienced down there; and man, that means also admitting unintentional responsibility for Terry's murder. Lordy-Lordy, what a difficult step. Still, this must be done. The body floating down river, the newspaper article adding mention that besides Terry Scott, seven other Americans have been murdered since (of course, all unsolved.) Yes, it is time. Glancing up toward Lester, while making a last swiping turn with riding mower, I find he's staring right at me (somethin' he rarely does). Hell, even ol' Lester is conveyin' it is time. Fuck, fuck, fuck, this really sucks!

Parking the hard rode NOMA mower, smellin' strong of gasoline, fresh cut grass and such, I feed both cockatiel birds and young pregnant calico cat, grab the newspaper article, jump into old Ford truck, and head for the house in town, some forty miles away.

Arriving home, entering the house via back door, Nancy is there, greeting with a warm loving embrace (she does have her moments). My jumpy mood is evident, and noticed (time to pop a Valium). With sugary Valium quickly dissolving in back of throat, I'm ambushed by two little boys (my sons). Rushing for givin' great big, excited, strong hugs! The Valium is kickin' in, and here at the house in town, everyone appears bein' in very good spirits, the in-laws especially. Here there is more room, ceiling fans, no bugs, and there is cable TV! (The in-laws are educated people having an addiction for world nightly news.) Of course, they are wanting details concerning the floating human corpse. After giving brief answers, pullin' Nancy aside, handing her the newspaper article, which, upon fast reading, I suggest possibly she might try finding the journalist Michael Garcia's email address for contacting. Nancy's expression becomes perplexed, asking, "Devin, are you sure?"

"Uh, no baby, I'm not. But this Scott family needs to know some of what I know. They should be informed about the torture/snuff videos."

Nancy gives encouraging squeeze, asking "Does this mean you are going to begin writing about it—your story?" She is very much aware that most of my story is untold, even to herself. Nancy also has some understanding how difficult an undertaking writing such a thing would be.

Hearing my sigh of uncertainty, she is answered, "Yes dear, I'm gonna try." However, fuck only knows if the courage and strength is there for goin' so deep into self—as will be required.

Nancy lays the article down beside her computer. Her folk's are wanting to take us all out for dinner; they will be leaving early morning, on the first train out.

7:30 A.M., with sleep still in eyes, there are groggy embraces of good-byes, have a safe trip, come back soon, etc. The in-laws are then taken to the train station—bye, bye! With that over, it's haul ass around town time, pickin' up necessary supplies for the river. The fish are runnin' (biting) and so I must get back there as soon as possible. Today is gonna be a long one. Trot lines will be dropped tonight; but first, clams (mussels) need to be had, opened, cut, and baited on each and all of the 1,000 hooks.

Arriving home, with newly bought supplies for the river, Nancy excitedly informs she had found Garcia's e-mail address, sent him a simple message, and (get this) he has already responded back! "Thanks for writing. Have forwarded your note to Elaine Porter, Terry's sister. She would also like to speak with you, so if you can, please call me at [such and such a number]."

Oh Jesus Christ! How the holy hell did Nancy find Garcia's email address so fast? And who woulda thought he'd be responding back so quickly? And now this guy Garcia wants me to call him? Fuck that! My thoughts concerning this crap ain't even straight. It's all too fast, way too fast! Sparky needs time—time for thinkin' some of this dark, new step through. Uh, like what to say, what not. How to tell that needin' to be told and that that don't. Oh fuck me, I'm not ready for this.

Despite Nancy's persistence, that call to Garcia just ain't gonna happen; not today, it ain't! On the hurry, tossin' more supplies into back of rusty Ford truck, which I love and owe my life to (another adventure not told), the phone rings. My eyes meet Nancy's. We both instantly know it's Michael Garcia callin'. Her e-mail sent had included our home number. Shit, shit, shit! "Nancy I'm not here! Gone, left, on the road, can't be reached!" She goes inside for answering the phone.

Sure enough, it's Michael Garcia;ught-o, this guy wasn't wastin' any time. The little red warning light inside my head is doin' a blinkity-blink-blink thing. Why, oh why is this Garcia bein' so quick to personally follow up on some out of the blue email sent from an unknown woman (my wife), stating her husband (me) had been in Guatemala City at the time of Terry Scott's death, and might possibly have information concerning Terry's murder, a murder that had occurred quite some time ago? Hardly a hot news flash. The article covering Terry's death had come from a hugely prominent American newspaper, having worldwide circulation. So, obviously, this Garcia is a very distinguished journalist, right? Hey, the man is no small time reporter. No he is not. Why then is he personally callin' up my house? For all this guy knows, Nancy is just some nutcase wantin' attention or the sorts. (Enough of them kinds out there, yes?) Wouldn't a big time journalist such as Michael Garcia have an intern, or the likes, for following up on these possible leads, you know, for legitimacy? Seems like such would be routine. But nooo! This Garcia reporter has to call my house personally, and like right now! Maybe the man ain't even American; maybe he's also one of those voodoo, Santeria, cult-worshipping whatever the fuck they ares! Hell, during the big satanic *hoedown,* those evil sick bastards threw in Guatemala City, a week or so before Christmas, while I was there, they had followers comin' in as far as England! Yeah, so much for your good ol' proper English blokes, huh?

So you see? This fucked-up, evil, cruel cult religion thing has some very long arms! Very long indeed; yes it does. Damn, and Michael Garcia? Who's sayin' this guy ain't one of these cult-following sick deranged psychopaths? Maybe he's snoopin',\ for learnin' the extent of my intent? Jesus, am I bein' a bit paranoid, or what? Hhmm, yeah, probably, 'cept man, there was a young doctor down there (land of horrors), in that stinkin' emergency room. Puerto Rican he was (doing his practicum/internship) while bein' an active follower of this bloody gruesome cult, which he openly admitted, even to his objecting colleague. The young doctor supported, defended and justified the barbarous religion, by braggin' it bein' older than Christianity. Uh, go figure. Anyways, this young philosophical genius of a doctor took great pleasures in tormenting, and forcing me to watch acts committed by those revealed as bein' no longer human. Aughg, fuckin' Puerto Rican prick! Also, there was in the same emergency room, an old doctor in charge, having strong authority, and he too was/is, very much involved, working closely with the Santeria, voodoo, older than Christianity, cult religion. Thus, obviously, a trivial sect of torturing maniacs this is not. Michael Garcia... Hhmm, is he with 'em?

Gosh, before goin' down to Central America, I didn't know squat about voodoo or Santeriaism (and still don't); pretty much just thought both were basically African origin, bein' big time popular in Haiti; and that they (practicing followers) insisted on torturing and sacrificing poor animals for the strange ceremonies. There had been some controversy back in the early nineties, disputing whether or not these people could legally practice this animal cruelty here in the United States. At the time, I couldn't imagine it bein' all too popular on US soil; probably just an obscure group or two that had migrated over from Haiti, possibly some curious satanic wannabes, and/or your back-to-Africa-roots sorta people. Hell, who knows? Never even gave it much thought. I did know that animal torture was *wrong*, and that nobody should ever be givin' the right for doin' such things—*ever*—religion or no religion. And plus, if you gotta torture and kill some poor critter to please your God, then, well, your God is a demented asshole!

Anyways, my ignorance on this subject is obvious. After Central America, I really have no stomach (or nerve) for even researching the bizarre topic. Whew—can't even deal with religious convictions of any sort, including my wife's Judaism. Now clearly, she is non-practicing, still, Jewish the woman is. And since she is, well, so are my sons, which is cool, but do, leave me out of the ritual ceremony crap! Same goes for my ol' granny's religious reverence; she's some sort of weird ass Baptist, or somethin'. Uhgh—it all gives Sparky the heebie-jeebies. And yet, even in keeping within self-contained bubble of ignorance for such things, knowledge still comes—both Santeriaism and voodoo are way more popular than what most know. Man, that shit is not only spread thick throughout the entire Caribbean, Central America and Mexico, but is also now filtering big time into the United States!

The phone conversation between Nancy and this Michael Garcia appears, uh, awkward, to say the least. Nancy keeps givin' nervous looks, as if asking, "Devin, what the hell am I supposed to say here?" Fuck only knows. She's on her own; I can't deal with this *heavy* right now. Gotta get to my river, work the trot lines, and think.

Shrugging shoulders, wavin' goodbye, I head on out for my old Ford truck. Opening the rusty door with required push, jerk, pull, the door obliges, though not without protest of crunchin', corroded steel, grinding itself. Goddamn, if Nancy ain't right on tail, saying, "Here! Here, talk to Devin!"

(O-Fuck me!) She hands over the phone, while pleading silently with those big beautiful brown eyes. (Cordless phones… Gee, how'd we ever get along without 'em? Right? Damn). Wishin' now very much for a Valium (or two or three). "Uh, hello."

"Devin? Hi, this is Michael Garcia." Following the introduction, Michael Garcia quickly informs that he works the Caribbean and Central America as an investigative reporter. He also shares under-standing, from speaking with my wife, that I have not spoken much to anyone concerning my own Central American experiences; and that it is very difficult for me to do so. (Golly Wally, that's an under-fuckin'-statement!) Garcia claims sympathy toward what little Nancy has told him. He then wants confirmation that I had indeed been in Guatemala City at the time of Terry Scott's death.

Clearing my throat, finding voice, Garcia is briefly told how I had been escorted out of the city, December 31, 1999, by Ambassador Todd Boil, my mother, and baby sister (baby sister, in that at the time she was twenty-one years old). With scrutinizing hesitation, Garcia cautiously questions, "But you claim to have left the day after Terry Scott's death? Devin, Terry Scott was murdered on the 28th."

"No, no sir, he was not. Terry Scott was murdered on the 30th." (My voice is shaky with agitation settin' in. Garcia's slight Spanish accent is comin' through amplified, bringin' forth ugly flashes of visions. Aughg, at least he got my name right, and ain't callin' me Devon.)

"Devin, why do you think Terry Scott was murdered on the 30th, and not the 28th?"

Letting out a long sigh, while kickin' the bumper of my truck, "Well, because it was on the news or so I was told. And uh, Ambassador Todd Boil had confirmed it, not only to me, but also my mother and baby sister. Were there any other American journalists killed on the 28th or 30th?"

Garcia answers no. Then there's a spell where we both are silent. Quite uncomfortable you bet. Finally, I break the annoying silence, asking in tone reluctant, "How exactly was Terry murdered?"

Garcia pretty much goes into a repeat of what he had written in his article.

I ask him if Terry's hands had been tied to the bed? "No!" Garcia's tone is almost defensively sharp. (Red warning light in my head is blasting!) I don't believe him, and think he's hiding something. "Uh, and the private investigator the Scott family hired, what did he find?"

Answering, Garcia tells that the Scott family had actually ended up hiring three private investigators. All they did, was take the Scott's money, finding nothing.

Clearing my throat again, "Um-uh, and the other Americans murdered since Terry?"

Garcia gives a dry rundown (summary) on their deaths: they were all shot or stabbed numerous times. One was a nun. No convictions of course. He then asks for my story and how it might pertain to Terry Scott's death, etc.

Garcia receives the brief of my tell-tale. Upon hearing I had first been in Honduras before Guatemala, he is (for whatever reason) particularly interested. "Devin, you were in Honduras prior to Guatemala?"

"Uh, yes, and Cuba too, but I'm not gonna talk about that."

"Okay. Will you tell me about Honduras?"

Biting my lower lip, I tell him a little (very little) of my left out part version, and really, due to him having played ignorance to all knowledge regarding ever popular torture/snuff films from the region, Garcia doesn't even get much of the left out part version. He does, however, learn some of the first hotel room attack. Mostly (without detail), it just endin' up being a gruesome blood bath, the whole while bein' filmed by a white man, *gringo*. The escape from there, consequently became my run from chase—across Honduras, and into Guatemala. Also, Garcia hears how at the airport in Honduras, they had tried forcing me to mule (transport on flight, traffic) a large duffle bag full of crack-like cocaine; and how this was an attempted coercion by the PRISA International Airlines themselves. They were wearing their uniforms and everything! Surprisingly (much to my suspicion), Garcia has no interest in the airport tidbit, and ignores it, not responding. (Hhmm, wonder why?)

Fumbling into left front vest pocket for Camel to light, "Uh, sir, you are aware that this goes on regularly, aren't you?"

He answers (meekly, just like how was done when asked about the torture/snuff videos), "Yes." Garcia had heard of such things occurring, though hadn't personally witnessed anything proving. And, as for the forced mulling? Again, "Yes." Still, he had never heard anything indicating the airlines themselves being directly involved.

(Oh bullshit! Man, there is somethin' about the undertones within this guy's answers.) I don't believe him. Lighting the much needed Camel, inhaling deeply, while glancin' to Nancy, who is now all ears, with hand over mouth. I ignore the speck of tobacco left on the tongue tip from non-filtered cigarette, to exhale for a hopeful calming tone. "Well sir, forced mulling does go on down there, and like big time. And PRISA Airlines is all up into it." (My voice is doin' a wimpy jiggle number.) "You do know that the people made to mule are murdered after so-called services rendered. Right? Never to be seen again. This needs to stop! Same with the torture/snuff films; God, it all needs to stop." (Jesus, don't break down and start cryin', not now.)

Garcia says nothing. (Oh great, another awkward silent moment.) "Uh, sir, you are then, at least aware of the full extent of the *coca* (cocaine) abundance down there, and how everyone and their mangy dog wants in on the *coca* trade market, and how there is now so fucking much of the stuff down there bein' produced, that no way in hell can they ever get that much cocaine up into *gringo* land... so they have now taken to consuming it themselves? You know about the strange crack cocaine they manufacture and smoke? They pour gasoline, or preferably ether, on large piles of cocaine and then apply heat and pressure. Depending on the amount they are working with, they can make solid crack rocks the size of duffle bags! They call it crack, but also *basco*? *Basuco*? Whatever! It's their version of crack cocaine; and this is what they smoke, makin 'em fuckin' insane!" (Whoa, gotta calm down. Can't fall apart here.)

"Yes." Garcia is aware of this. (Geez, at least the guy is admitting knowin' straight up about this.) He then wants more information (details) concerning my travel route while down there: where I stayed, towns, motels, and for how long, etc. My answers are slight and juggled. Sparky really don't trust this Garcia. But damn, the door has been opened, right? Fuck, this conversation is indeed strange. Garcia wants to know what I know, and I want to know what he knows, and neither one is all too inclined for revealing much of anything. Terry Scott's violent murder? Murderers seem no longer even the issue.

Reaching up under baggy shorts legging, I pull on right testicle to relieve tension; it at times stresses. I ask Garcia if he is familiar with the Garifuna people? Oh Skippy, yes he is! Even corrects my pronunciation. (Yeah, whatever.) Everyone thinks the Garifunas are cool, including myself, uh, that is, before they wanted to rape, burn, scalp, skin, and *eat* me! Okay-okay, they all aren't like this. Whew, a few even stuck necks out for helpin'. So obviously, they all are not into this bizarre satanic voodoo shit.

Garcia is very quick for answering a sharp "No!" when asked if he knows anything regarding the black Carib Garifuna religion that practices savage ceremonies (cautiously described, without goin' into much gruesome detail).

Oh, okay. How can this be? How can it be that a big-shot newspaper journalist, covering Central America and the Caribbean, does not know of the vicious older-than-Christianity religion and its bloodthirsty, inhumane, sick atrocities exercised with relentless fanaticism? Hhmm, everybody else I ran into while down in those countries knew all about the "Satanico" religion freely using mostly indigent women and children for ritual torturing sacrifices. Yes, it was/is very well known by the locals. So, how come this Garcia knows nothin' of it? Suspicious much? Fuck, he's lying.

After another seemingly long uncomfortable pause of silence, I (not bein' able to resist) ask Garcia if he is an American citizen? "Yes," he is, having home in Miami. Golly, this hardly eases my mind. Time for gettin' off this phone!

Pacing nervously around tailgate of old truck, "Look, as strange as this may sound, the man responsible for Terry Scott's death is named Captain Matrix. His name is not spelled anyway like it is pronounced, but it is pronounced *matrix*. He is the head honcho to this bizarre black Carib Garifuna cult. His title within the cult is Orc, short for Oracle. Matrix commands a small unit of heavily armed soldiers, thugs, whatever you wanta call 'em, and he always has a large street gang of young Garifunas—both male and female—that do everything he orders, and I do mean everything! This gang is also very much a part of his religious cult following. Matrix is feared by everyone, and does whatever he damn well pleases. The man wears all black military BDUs and drives a black Chevy Blazer. Matrix is a murdering monster, having his hands into everything evil and terrifying, including, very much, the torture/snuff films and big time drug running, which, obviously, helps in financing his personal army and exploits. He has close ties with the corrupt police, and he might even be a police captain, but man, this guy is also, for sure, military. Find the source of Matrix's snuff film business... There is a white man, a blond *gringo*, having a southern California accent; he works for Matrix—and others—doin' the camera, video filming. Ask around for him. You probably won't live long, but if by chance you do, he will be easy enough to find. From him you'll find the torture/snuff films, and from them, well, they will lead you to the deranged religion of butchering bizarre. Believe me, Matrix won't be hard to find from there; and then you got him—the man responsible for Terry Scott's murder. But, of course, we both know there ain't no way in holy hell that such a man as Matrix will ever be brought to justice. Not unless someone just ups and slams a bullet into his sick brain! The CIA won't do it; ha, they use the man for guard doggin' their drug routes, and I'm guessin' they use him for other little jobs, like terrorizing poor indigent people of the region, which you can imagine, he's very good at!"

My emotions are surfacing. Voice is crackin' and shaky. And Garcia is sensing the stress. There is another long moment of silence. Bic flicking, another Camel, exhaling, "You know all that crap about there bein' a war on drugs?"

Garcia, softly answers, "Yes."

"Well sir, it's all bullshit! Those military road blocks and check points down there, don't do squat. All any savvy drug runner's gotta do, is punch in the correct numbers on a cell phone, give ID, and they won't even have to slow down for the damn things—they get waved right on around and through, like fast! They can traffic smuggle like this, all the way up through even Mexico. And as for gettin' the dope across our border? Well hell, that's nothin'; just unload it onto an American vehicle of an informed American driver, and have him drive it across through customs, say, in darkness of early morning hours of around 3 or 4 A.M. US customs? What little will even be there, at that time of night? Man, they won't even search. Christ, they won't even have snoop dogs there workin', not durin' those hours, they won't. I know 'cause I've done it, crossing from Matamoros into Brownsville. And, *and*, the CIA and BATF know all about this established practice, and they not only allow it, but support it! Man, they're the ones that set the routes for trafficking!"

"Devin, as you know, in Guatemala, nothing is as it seems."

Oh Skippy, you got that right! Feeling like some serious exposure has been brought down upon me, by myself, this little chat can probably be added to the long—very long—list of things regrettable. Garcia knows the conversation is over. We close politely, with him informing that he is gonna share our talk with Terry Scott's sister, Elaine Porter. Garcia then thanks me and asks if it would be alright to call again, in the future, if there are any more questions?

"Uh, yeah sure." My tone is anything but enthusiastic. I pretty much knew Garcia wasn't gonna ever dig up nothin'.

Eugh, more got spilt than what was intended, that's for sure. And Elaine Porter? Geez, what is she gonna think after speakin' with Garcia, poor woman? Oh well, at least I surfaced, told a bit of my story, and shared some knowledge of the man responsible for Terry Scott's murder, and probably many other now dead Americans. What else can be done? Nothin' 'cept haul ass for my river. Trot lines must be dropped tonight!

On the drive to the river, alone, deep in thought, non-filtered Camel hangin' from lips, as warm air rushes in from window, firin' cigarette, blowin' ashes about without care, the small cell phone rings. Pushing the big white button, having blue stripe, "Uh, hello."

The caller is Nancy; she is informing that Elaine Porter had just called her, wanting to speak with me. (My mouth drops; cherry lit Camel flies across cab of truck, for doin' a little sparkle dance, before getting' tossed out).

"Devin, she sounds very sweet. Elaine hasn't spoken yet with Michael Garcia, but she has received his forwarded e-mail. Devin, she seems to be a little nervous, and excited."

"Nancy no! Oh fuck. Why is she excited? Why the hell is she fuckin' excited? I didn't know her brother! I wasn't in his apartment when he was murdered! I got no solid proof, or anything, and God, even if I did, it would all be pointless. Man, I was goin' through my own hell at the time it was heard they were gonna be killin' her brother; besides, just because his picture looks familiar, that don't mean nothin', it could of…"

"Devin, Devin! Hush, just calm down. I explained all of that to her. I shared with her what little I do know; and I told her how we got you out of the country with help from Ambassador Todd Boil, and that two weeks later he called your mother to inform her just how lucky we were for even getting you out alive. I've also explained to Elaine how you have had a difficult time dealing with what did happen down there, and that you are far from being comfortable in talking about it. Devin, she understands; she understands that your experience might have nothing to do with her brother's death. Elaine expects nothing from you. She just wants to hear whatever you are comfortable with sharing. Devin, Elaine seems to be a very sensitive woman, and yes, she is a little excited. She and her family have been trying very hard to get closure to Terry's death. They have many questions, but no one is cooperating. What little information they have been able to dig up has all been contradictory. A perfect example is how they were told Terry was murdered on the 28th, but now, you have informed them that he was killed on the 30th. Elaine said the whole case has been like this—a botched investigation from the very start—and still, they have learned that there are live leads, but no one is willing to pursue, or investigate."

"Nancy, of course there are live leads! Fuck, nothin' is secret down there. There's no reason for secrecy when you have an entire population whose survival depends on see nothing, say nothing. And for investigating live leads? Ha! Man, baby, no one would be stupid enough to go poking around in that! I was a fool for even thinkin' it possible a private investigator could have worked the case, and live to tell. Jesus I'm amazed Todd Boil and his assistant, Laura Simms, are even still alive!"

"Well Devin, this is what you need to tell Elaine. I honestly believe that she and her family haven't a clue as to how things really are down there. You need to share with them at least some of your knowledge, if for no other reason than to hopefully convince them to stop wasting their time, money and hopes on attaining information that is unattainable. Also Devin, Elaine has another brother; he's been down to Guatemala twice since Terry's death, in attempts of acquiring answers."

Oooh… That one struck home, just as Nancy knew it would. Whoa, this family had to stop goin' down there. They will end up dead!

"Also, Devin, Ambassador Todd Boil and Laura Simms are no longer stationed in Guatemala. Todd is now in Bosnia, and Elaine didn't know where Laura is."

(Bosnia? Damn, ol' Toddy Boil's specialty must be embassy work of post civil war countries. Hhmm, still, who knows what his real work might be in such countries. The guy is, in himself, a mind fuck.)

"Devin, I explained to Elaine that you are a commercial fisherman, and you now mostly live alone in a cabin on the Mississippi River. I told her you write there as well, and that it would be okay for her to call you this evening at eight o'clock. Devin, she understands you will be tired having just gotten off the river; and Devin, I warned her you will be a little overly nervous as well."

Oh shit, shit, shit… Tonight? A chat with Terry Scott's sister Elaine? God, poor woman; and now, poor me, for havin' to tell her that needin' told. Aughg, what was I thinkin' to open such doors?

The old truck bouncin' down gravel river road, stops, to be thrown into reverse for backing onto cabin's narrow dirt/rock driveway. Jumping out, it's a quick unloading of supplies, grabbing my nylon mesh clammin' (mussel) sack from spot hangin' amongst much other related gear and equipment of the sort (all bein' around an outside weathered refrigerator, and wooden work benches loaded with disarray). Overhead corrugated tin, jutting from side of cabin, serves as roofing to protect the small perimeter of organized disorder from rain and snow (somewhat).

With clammin' sack in hand, I march 'er on down to the dock, for my boat. Whole time, thoughts are whirlin'. Shit, shit, shit… Seein' Lester standin' proud, out on his log, a yell erupts, "It's all your fault! Dumb ass bird!" Lester rolls his eyes, leans forward, takes flight, does his half circle thing and with a loud "SQUAWK" lets drop a long stream of loose feces, and in no time, he's down river to his big tree. Yeah well, guess he showed this idiot, huh?

Sequential order is put to motion; unscrew an air intake valve to one of the two gas tanks I run, disengage the transom lock up, push power trim button for lowering outboard's lower end (only halfway), while at the same time (with other hand) squeezing rubber gas line bulb to where it feels solid-full of gas. Depress the ignition, containing on/off key, a few times for priming (choking), turn the key—va-ROOM! Glossy black Merc fires right up, and in no time, is chompin' at the bit. One thing about Mercury outboards, they sure like to getty-up go! Untie the tie-downs, walk back for growlin', smokin' outboard, drop side mounted gear lever, put anxious gleaming motor into forward drive. A twist of tiller throttle handle gives her some gas, and away we go, slowly at first 'cause boat is in very shallow water. Glancin' down at the stainless steel prop spinnin' just an inch or two below surface, the water is a dark brown with globs of mud bein' obliterated from semi solid to pure liquid (always resembling chocolate milkshakes bein' made in a blender). A quick glance confirms the pee-hole on right side of outboard is indeed spewing forth a strong narrow steady stream of water. Good. As long as she is peein' hard and constant, I know nothin' is clogging her cooling system. Turning on both depth finders, while at same time pushing power trim button, gradually lowers outboard's lower-end all the way down. The ol' girl gets throttled wide open and up on plane she goes, for always exuberant ride! Yes, even in calm waters, a boat goin' up on plane, is always a hard-on for me. I just fuckin' love it: standin' up straight, in back of boat, hand on throttle of happy outboard. (A good outboard bein' run wide open, is much like a dog chasin' a rabbit—it's in pure heaven!). The rolling of the boat cutting through water, with wind in face blowin' wondrous smells of gasoline, oil, outboard exhaust, and the earthy musk scent of the river itself—Goddamn—the combination is almost intoxicating!

The boat cruises, crossing river for favorite clammin' spot (actually, there are no clams in the river, only mussels, but everyone just calls 'em clams). My clammin' spot is in Iowa state waters, meaning that it is on the other side of the river's main channel, across from Illinois. Therefore the water is legally considered Iowa's. Yeah, it never made any damn sense to me either. Christ, the river is the river. Yes? Who gives a flyin' fuck what side of the main channel anything is on. It's still all the Mississippi River, right? So my thinkin' is, and has always been, that as long as my ass is in/on water, and not ground, well… you get the picture. See, Iowa has different state laws than Illinois, like, for example, size and catch limits on both fish and clams. Aw, fuck 'em! I've always pretty much done as pleased on this here river; just gotta keep good look-out for Game Warden Ike Teal and that moron, Ranger Rick the prick.

The spot was discovered years ago, while clammin' during peak demand. Wow, in those days, how we did haul out boat loads from this spot. The bottom is both sand and mud, having continuous, long, gradual sloping incline for strong, deep main channel.

Here, along the river's edge, there are formable embankments—jagged with imposing, large, mystic looking log jams and eerie (skeletal) duck blinds—each in its own varying stage of dilapidated ruin.

Slowing the boat, gliding into quite calm shallows, a Great Blue Heron (similar to Lester) flaps up and away from perch atop one of the taller (barely still standin') stilted wrecks, built and long abandoned (derelict) by infant souled men, havin' desire to kill ducks, for sport shooting only.

With the Blue Heron taking flight, so do about a hundred pelicans, joined by seagulls numbering twice that. Seagulls… Hhmm. Though loud and undignified, you gotta love 'em for their sleek beauty and animated, high-spirited persistence.

In three feet of water, the front anchors get tossed and tied off, with boat spinning, bow pointin' up river. Thus, a true hold is had, only a few yards east of big, knurly log jam. This is a pretty stumpy area—curbing old huge broken trees, limbs, roots and logs, pushed here by current for settling until spring flooding.

Shutting the outboard down, and raising lower end, my binoculars are used, carefully scanning both sides of the river, up and down, for as far as the glass will allow. Gotta make sure Ranger Rick the Prick, and Game Warden Ike Teal ain't within' spying range. All clear. Time for goin' to work! Droppin' khaki shorts—nude, except for old, faded red Converse high-top tennis shoes, and mesh clam sack in hand—I slowly lower myself over the side, entering cool, soft, muddy brown water, with feet sinking through thick suction layer of heavily silted squishy muck, before settling on to firmer, sandy, clay like loom mud beneath.

The contrast between cool river water and warm skin from hot sun above, strikes shiver, goose bumping. Submitting temperate acclimation, body submerges for emulating buoyant bullfrog havin' only head above surface. Uh? Anyways, a clammin' I do go! Feet and left hand begin bottom combing for any and all clams that might be within reach, busy doin' what they do.

Clams, though outrageously slow, are way more active than what most people know. However, despite existing in a world environment providing cover of zero visibility, they are still easy prey for those of us having motivation to enter and hunt by method, blind feel.

Accordingly, oftentimes, all that can be felt of 'em at first, is only a small bit protruding; then you gotta go under, diggin' down, pryin' them up and out, from sucking mud. Needless to say, all this crawlin' around, stirring things about, pullin' clams, in doin'—turns over throngs of empty shells from those long dead, now housing craw daddies, leeches, and many other little whatevers. The activity attracts much attention from certain (larger) neighboring water critters, such as turtles and snakes inhabiting nearby log jams. They like to follow me around for catchin' and eating all the small darting goodies that my clammin' stirs. Yes, the turtles are usually snapping turtles (some quite large), and the snakes? Well, they are mostly the big ol' dark water snakes, appearin' much like the southern water Moccasin (and just as ill-tempered), save, these are non-venomous. I have never been bitten by either snake or turtle while in the water, but have been bit by both while out of the water; and despite common belief, neither hurts all too bad. The water snakes (even the big grouchy ones) barely break the skin, drawing blood only slightly. And the snappers? Golly, their bites do smart; though it's not like they snap off fingers, or anything. You see, I should know; back in my younger and dumber years, I did, for a brief spell, trap snappers for butcher and sale. In the state of Illinois, using traps and/or nets to catch turtles is illegal; and it didn't take long for understanding why. Jesus, it's just too damn easy! The poor ol' snappers don't stand a chance. In a short time, my traps were harvesting snappin' turtles by the ton, with many individually in the forty—and fifty—pound class. After learning that such magnificent snappers of that size could possibly be a hundred-plus years old, well, it sure didn't take long to loose all heart in killin 'em.

I began viewing them as the river's dignified elders; and really, that's just what they are. Man, a turtle bein' a hundred fuckin' years old—that ol' boy has seen his share, for sure! Hell, in commercial river traffic alone, he would have seen the big boats go from paddle wheel, to coal/steam, to diesel. And geez, just imagine all the changes he's seen in pleasure craft development.

So, becoming thoroughly disgusted with myself, all traps got pulled and tossed down a ravine, never to be used again. Nowadays, I'd have to be in a pretty hungry way for killin' a snapping turtle; also, the meat on those boys ain't what it's all cracked up. Gosh, a nice fat catfish tastes much better any day.

I like to belly-crawl the muddy shallows first, gettin' enough clams into my sack for actin' as a drag-along-weight. The heavier the sack, the easier it is to work deeper water. These clammin' sacks are approximately four feet long, and can hold a lot, thus becoming very heavy. After acquiring the sufficient amount of clams for weight needed, my sack then gets dragged out towards deeper water—nearly comin' level with nose tilted up. Out here, clammin' is best; and if it were possible to become "one" with the river, this would be the way of doin' it.

After goin' under, and comin' up for usually much needed air—eyes and nose just barely clearing waterline—the vast surfaced world must be viewed similarly to that of Mr. Snake's or Mr. Turtle's. Just because our eyeballs are larger than theirs, don't mean we see any bigger, or smaller. The river is still the mighty Mississippi, and as all creatures emerging from, we do so under sky infinite.

Opening eyes, it is often quite common (and humorous) finding yourself confronted, practically butting noses, with certain curious water critters, mostly snakes and turtles, swimming seemingly effortlessly against the forever current, observing, and intently scrutinizing as to whether you are a goofy nut-case, or what? There are many humans that have wondered the same. Most people cringe at the mere thought of clammin' the way I do, mostly for my preference in area's personally chosen. "What, around all those awful log jams, full of snappin' turtles and *snakes*! And, *and*, he's completely *nude*!"

Aaa-haw, ha! This stupid shit is always a crack-up. Boy-oh-boy, if the retards only knew of my big, shiny, gold scrotum ring; golly, wouldn't that flip their square lids. They'd think for sure, some snappin' turtle or Billy Garfish would certainly come along, and bite the thing right off! Hhmm, to be honest, the thought of this happening has crossed my mind—though only while swimmin' nude in ocean waters where barracuda and other similar toothy fish are known for striking such bright shiny things.

My clammin' in the nude is for reasons of practicality, and I'm slightly a nudist by nature. However, with life bein' as it is, clothing of some sorts is more often than not required, even during warm summer months. For moi, this means red Converse high-top tennis shoes and shorts. The shorts are French military surplus, khaki-tan, and of solid construction, having very baggy (airy) cut. For some reason, the only size I can obtain these unique shorts is in waist size forty and greater. I'm a thirty-two waist (if even that). Baggy these shorts were meant to be, but on my ass, they are really baggy, which is fine. I just cinch belt tight, and roll those shorts up short! The leg openings are so wide that they become almost like wearin' a miniskirt, and because I haven't worn underwear since age twelve, air-a-plenty gets down there—just how it should be.

If shorts are worn while clammin', well, they just fill up with grit, mud, and tiny squirmy critters; plus, the shorts create a drag, enabling the river's ever present current to pull all the more. And when getting out of the water? Uh, Sparky is then stuck wearin' heavy, muck-filled, squirmin' shorts—always a itchin'. So, the hell with shorts for clammin' (or swimmin'). Also, another neat thing about clammin' nude, is often curious boaters will take notice, start nosin' over, actually comin' in, up on close, for gawkin' what ain't their business. When they do this, I like to make my way back into the shallows, thus baring nudity. "Aw-yuck, it's a naked man! Let's get on out of here! Yeah, okay, but first, let's see if he's got himself a naked woman with 'im. Nope, no naked woman, we're gone!" Bye bye, you gawkin' sheepheads!

Now normally, for myself, getting clams is a very special relaxing chore... but today wasn't a normal clammin' day. No sir, it was not! Although, clammin' was helping with anxieties bein' felt; you know, the whole Garcia conversation, and now tonight at eight o'clock, the expected phone call from Terry Scott's sister, Elaine Porter. And, just what was I supposed to tell her? That her brother was brutally murdered because of me; and there wasn't a Goddamn thing she could do about it? That she should just be grateful for even having gotten his dead body back? Man, fuck, fuck, fuck! This sucks! Elaine, of course, like everybody else, would want to know why I had gone down there (Central America) in the first place? Whew, how answering this question has indeed become tiresome. Yet, required it is, and often because people thought/think the trip was mostly for the purpose of smuggling drugs. They are wrong! Ironically the person most needed reminding of the real reasons for my travels to Central America, is my wife! The bitch has a very short memory, especially when in an ugly argumentative mood, wanting to push buttons. (Eh, screw her.)

My explanation is that I had simply went down there to volunteer help in rebuilding a jungle orphanage that had been devastated by a hurricane months prior, and while en route, sorta got (big time) sidetracked. Yes, this is the truth, but like with most things, there was more to it.

With my clam sack gettin' heavier and heavier, the vast, bright blue sky acts as highway to roving, shape shifting, stark white clouds that occasionally pass above, filtering, ever softly, the hot rays of sun beamin' down upon head. Spitting muddy water from mouth, having lapped in with rolling, brownish wake, my bein' is bobbin' up and down, in this big awesome river. Wow, I always feel so small out here! Just another critter catchin' other critters in the river. Geez, despite all anxieties, bein' in the river is just way cool. Still, for the millionth time, the re-hatching of all reasons for leaving my family to travel Central America comes to swirl for order.

Honestly, boredom had a lot to do with it. I've had the problem my entire life. I'm always searching, hungry for somethin', but never knowin' for what; never feeling content, no matter how good life is; always havin' to be challenging myself with new skills, yet, never reaching a level of complete mastery. Well, except for sharpening knives and eating pussy. Uh, that last is meant as a funny, save really it's just plain stupid, right? Okay, and what makes it all the more stupider (and pathetic), is the truism. Yepper, if someone was to ask what I'd mastered completely in my years of life, right off the top of my head, I would have to say, knife sharpening and pussy eating. Yeah, whatever. But what would your answer be? Comin' right off the top of head and all.

Man, don't you ever feel like there must be more to life? I sure do; and it's not the whole "Grass is greener on the other side" thing. No, more like the other side is just the other side, always callin' out personal invite—an invitation, for better or worse—granting appearance. Now, don't get this wrong. I love life, and surely do think it's a real trip of a ride. But damn, when the ride starts slowin' down, sometimes you just gotta kick it in the ass for gettin' things up and goin'! And, of course, like with most things that get kicked around (sooner or later), they will (in their own way) kick back!

My first big kick came in June 1995, when my father, unexpectedly, suddenly up and died from a heart attack (or so determined the coroner). He died alone, in his own cabin, here on the river. My father had been a good-lookin', hard working, hard playing, hard drinkin' man. He was (on his own turf) aggressive like an alpha guard dog. Yet (when not drinkin' heavy) he was quick witted, funny, and sensitive. A man very likable, beholdin' the respect of many. However, there were sides to him that I personally hated, though, despite these, I loved him very much and was greatly bonded, of course not knowing full extent, until death took him away. My father, bein' only sixteen years older than myself, taught his only son much and was truly my best friend. I miss him horribly. His death was indeed a kick in the gut shock, that sorta jump-started thinking thoughts towards my own death, which, in itself, is not feared, but rather… Fuck, life is short, right? And can be taken away at any time, and, what with my knack for attracting trouble, Goddamn, I shoulda already been dead a hundred times over!

So, grieving the loss of my father, and believing myself to be in a race with time for achievin' all that is desired before stumbling a fall, there is still a whole lotta life needing livin' first.

Always the project fiend, man, I now became a hoppin' project maniac, bouncin' from one thing to the next, like a fruit-loop retard! Just for the hell of it, I did a few more O-Kee-Pa hangings. At one time, a man alias Fakir Mustafar and myself were the only documented so-called "modern men" to have done this ancient Native American ritual. You hang completely off the ground, suspended by two hooks pierced through the flesh. It's a heavy ride, to be assured.

Having already an acquired knack for electric-vibrating needles, following course of designated lines, I took up sewing, focusing on erotic wear. Yep, with motivation on high speed roll, Sparky even went and opened another *Tattoo Blue* studio in San Francisco, but that didn't last long, so back I came to relocate and build a bigger, better studio, while at the same time tearing out my basement under pretense of remodeling, though really, the accomplished project was only to create a sterile grow room for the mushroom cultivating. This was enjoyed so much, that I went and rented a small apartment across from the city police station (cheap rent). There, I set up another grow room, this one, for growin' kick ass weed. In no time, the hydroponics system had hundreds of little plants budding. Problem was, the little gals really produced a very strong distinctive odor! The ozone regulators had to be goin' all the damn time, plus, wow, the required high pressure sodium lights really suck the juice (electricity) like not believed.

Despite my attempts at bein' discreet, neighbors became nosey. Also, it didn't help bein' spotted humpin' an eighty-pound CO_2 cylinder up the stairs, in the middle of the night. No, that definitely did not help. Ironically, I don't even like smokin' the stuff. Sure did as a kid, but not anymore. And the money made? It wasn't all that great. Not when compared to the profit yields growin' 'shrooms, which required exceptionally low overhead expense. Therefore question arises: why grow weed? Conclusion: hhmm, besides the sheer enjoyment of growin' an illegal substance (my stupid way of rebelling against organic "drug" laws), it also became a strange method for dealing with inner anger and grief. The fear factor of possibly gettin' caught was just enough for stayin' on edge, thus, forcing mind and body to be sharp and focused. The adrenalin outweighed the depression. Fortunately, upon revelation, decision was had: shut down the weed growing operation (and like fast!). No easy feat, since it required making disappear 125 fully mature female plants.

During this period, my second son was born. People say, "Births are a miracle." Well, I don't know about that; but do know for me, to witness the birthing of both my sons, is, and always will be, the most awesome complexity of all that is humanly good. My wife and I, no matter what, ever, and I do mean ever, we did *good*! And you know what? Any man that does not shed tears at the sight or news of his newly born baby, is a loser prick, needin' to be taken out back and *shot!*

I then built an attic to my garage for storage and hoisting boats. The boats were small run-abouts, which I bought, restored, and sold. However, after a few, Mr. Boredom comes a-knockin'... thus, time for sky diving. I went to Florida, and took a "one of a kind" accelerated free fall course. There, all the basic fall maneuvers are quickly learnt—aerial rolls, spins, team jumping for star formations and, of course, pneumatic ball playin'. Still, despite my highest jump bein' made at 15,500 feet (500 feet above legal limit without oxygen) and constant reprimands of tossing out (opening chute) way below the legal height of 2,000 feet, there was very little thrill. Personally, a much bigger rush could be had from a good blow job. A skilled blow job will make your knees knock with toes a curlin' as if getting' rocketed right up, through and out a blasting cannon! *Boom, boom, boom!* Sky diving, even when speed droppin', can't match such a surging, exhilarating charge.

For quite some time, I had toyed with the idea of moving my family to Mexico, Central America, or the Caribbean. My mother being an international teacher, had years ago given me the opportunity to spend some time in Jamaica. The island became enchanting—glorious tropical climate, with lush blue mountains, towering plateaus of landscape, bein' varied as the surreal beaches and waterfronts confronting pristine hues from reef ridden oceans surrounding. The cost of living was cheap, having lifestyles simple. Plus, there were many opportunities for clever Americans that could come and go. The lack of petty rules I really liked, and the people? Well, "Everyting's cool, mon." For the most part, they were alright, practicing a pretty laid back attitude. Uh, that is, until you got 'em pissed off! Though really, it took quite a bit to stir 'em. However, that was a long time ago. Times have changed, the word is Jamaica has become a very angry, violent people. "Cool runnin's" ain't so cool no more. Still, there must be somewhere similar to how Jamaica once was.

How about Costa Rica? Okay! And because I think it's really clever, and have like a million other things goin' on, bright idea comes—hey, why not send down my wife and sister (not the baby sister, the other one)? Yeah sure, two hot chicks will be able to cover more ground, making contacts, thus acquiring information in the shortest amount of time. They will get a free trip and I will get photos, a video, and "intel report" informing whether it's worth personally goin' down there for further scouting. Darn clever, huh? Wrong.

They just went down there and partied. Right away, they meet up with an American film crew working on a new movie for a very famous action hero. The star's body double/stunt man had some time off, so he and Nancy hook up and start fucking. They, with boozing sister in tow, take to the roads exploring the little country (hardly). They did it as Goddamn tourists, not as scouts lookin' to find a cool place for living and operating a business. They bring me back nothin', nothin' uh, well, Nancy does bring home a mean ass yeast infection! Aughg! I wanted to strangle them both. Fuckin' bimbos! After that, realization comes—I would have to go and do these scouting trips on my own. Determined, I decide to drive my old Ford truck from Illinois down to Belize. Now, that trip was a trip. Oh Skippy, it was! You see, Sparky don't speak anything remotely resembling "fluent" Spanish. Still, myself and that truck bounced all the way down there, following the region's worst flooding in like fifty years, and this was during the so-called "Chiapas Revolt." I did succeed in reaching Belize's border, before turning to roly-bounce all the way back up through Mexico and home again. During that trip, I did find a cool little town south of Cancun, in the Yucatan region. The town is Playa del Carmen. (Yeah, I know, maybe a couple of decades ago, it would have been perfect, but not now the small town is bein' built up, and like fast!). My wants were for somethin' similar, 'cept not yet in that tourist growth mode, while still attracting young backpackers on a budget.

The goal was to find an exotic, rustic location (preferably on the water) that could still be bought cheap. There, I would build a place for young backpacking travelers. You know, a sorta place providing the simplest of basics, such as large communal open-air hammock shelters for sleeping, having nearby latrine/shower house. And, of course, a café would be on the compound, serving (inexpensive) delicious strong coffees and simple, staple, local foods, such as large bowls of beans and rice, fruit, tasty soups, etc., anything fulfilling and costing little. I knew from personal experience that there was/is a demand/need, for such places, and always wondered why there weren't more available. Really, while traveling, all young backpackers (of class targeted) are needing a super inexpensive place to shit, shower, shave, hang their hats for sleeping, and get a bellyful; and if you could provide a cool non-restrictive atmosphere, safely encouraging freedom to openly intermingle, fuck, party, whatever, without draining their very limited funds, so much the better! And why not have a tattoo/body piercing studio handy as well? And psilocybe mushrooms? Oh Skippy Joe! Man, you know those puppies would go over good in such a place! Hhmm, well, that was my goal, and really, why couldn't it be easily achieved?

The goal wasn't making big bucks. No, rather, goal was a simple means of creating an interesting lifestyle, while providing humble income for the family to live modestly in an exotic location, diverse with culture and whatnot. Also, I honestly thought it would help my marriage. Nancy and I have always had our ups and downs. You know, the whole love/hate thing? Geez, we were now havin' way more downs than ups. The reasons for this are complex. Hhmm, maybe not. Christ, my father's death had thrown my world for a loop, thus making things a little more nuttier than usual. And Nancy? Eh, she's always been a bit of a wild card herself; however, after the birth of our second son, *whoa*, she turned into one of the most illogical people I've ever known (the emphatic directive bein' "one of"). Understand, Sparky has known many illogical people. And yes, most are women. Whew, Nancy becomes the stupid bitch from hell. Nevertheless, my love for her stayed true, and we still fucked like rabbits, but honestly, Mr. Boredom had turned against us. Something had to be done; and (of course) thinkin' myself the strongest, I sought the solution, 'cept to succeed would require goin' further south than Mexico. So, I began researching Central America, via travel guide books, having titles like *Paradise in Belize*, *Exciting Honduras*, *Charming Guatemala*, etc.

My life then receives a second big kick! June 1998, three years following my father's death, my beloved grandfather dies. He was my father's father, having a goodness, pure and simple, a rarity among human kind. Since birth, I not only loved my grandfather madly, but adored him like no other. His name was Murf, and he was my Murf. Upon exiting life— laying there, in that hospital bed, with all those degrading tubes and machines—the doctor came in and pronounced my Murf dead. The nurses followed, shutting down all the attached contrivances. My Murf had lost his exhausting, long endured battle with emphysema. I just stood there, holdin' on to his thumb like so often done as a little boy. I held on to his thumb, and just kept hangin' on (squeezing), and sorta crawled up inside myself, as if hiding. Finally, a voice came—it was time to let go. I had to leave with Grandma, and help make funeral arrangements. Goddamn funerals.

Coming up for much needed air, opening eyes, while workin' at clearing right ear, shakin' water out. The ear is constantly infected, and clammin' really does a number on it. Yep, this puppy will be poppin' and drainin' tonight!

From corner of eye, Mr. Snake is detected bein' just off to my left. He's a few feet away, checkin' me out, and by how he's holdin' his head so high, Jake the Snake is indeed scrutinizing with contempt. He's a big boy, tryin' to act tough and all. This snake would like nothin' better than to scare my ass outta here, so 's he can skim water's surface in graceful slithering form, back to the large log jam, and proudly show off, and brag before his buddies, (surely) watching. However, since I'm easily a hundred times bigger, his little brain is processing uncertainty. Still though, Mr. Snake is holdin' his ground (water).

We begin eyeballin' each other; the whole while, I'm slowly bobbin' my way up river, using feet for feelin' clams down in river's underworld. Jake the Snake stays the course, never getting any further, or closer. Ught, there's one (a clam), and big it does feel. Time to dive, 'cept, first let's get rid of this dang ol' persistent snake… "Shoo! Get!" Stickin' out my tongue, a loud *raspberry* sputters! Still, Jake the Snake stays. Uh-hmm, this is unusual. Normally, they dart underwater for retreatin' at least a few yards, but not this ol' boy. Damn! For some reason, Sparky always hates goin' under when these guys are intent on stayin' so close; however, if I don't dive, like now, the current is gonna push my foot from this big clam, thus losing position. Rats! You better not be here when I resurface, blasted snake! Of course, he is.

Putting the big "washboard" (nickname given for the species' large size and textured resemblance) clam into the sack, I lurch out with a *splash* toward Mr. Smarty Pants Snake! Haw-hee, hee, hee! That did it! Sent him right under! Soon his little head pops up, surfacing, with tail zigzaggin' to beat all, back toward the log jam.

After my grandfather's death, I had mind set to explore Central America, finding the right spot to create my backpacker's compound/retreat. While pondering the trip, time is spent completely tearing out my old kitchen and rebuilding a new one. Then, I just sorta kept a-goin', right on into the living room, and then bathroom.

Nights are spent studying Spanish for retards, and reading travel guide books. In one, I find a very brief mention of a jungle orphanage. The orphanage is in the Rio Dulce region of Guatemala. It is called Casa del Corazone, and they were in need of volunteers for performing any number of tasks from childcare to carpentry. All volunteers must sign on for a minimal one month commitment. The work would be demanding, and living arrangements simple—basic and rustic. The orphanage did have a gasoline generator for providing some electricity, during set hours of the day. In return for the volunteering, one would get three meals a day, shared sleeping quarters, and the satisfaction of knowing they are helping children. Plus, this orphanage, Casa del Corazone, is right smack dab on the banks of a big jungle river! Things there are still pretty much considered the frontier (frontera) with many indigenous Indian peoples living life (more or less) as has been done for like ever.

Now, this all sounds pretty fuckin' cool. I'm a-goin' to Guatemala! And how about Honduras as well? Oh you bet! The luring "final frontier: the Mosquito Coast," having Central America's largest remaining virgin rainforest. Man, that just couldn't be passed up. Damn straight, gotta go check this out, before they cut it all down, right? I also read there is a little island off the coast, called Utila. This island is very small and unique. Unique, in that it has yet been built up for major tourism; and the island is (somewhat) known for offering the cheapest scuba diving, and dive courses within the Caribbean. Supposedly you can get PADI open water certified for under 200 bucks! This, combined with cheap lodging and such, makes Utila a hot spot for drawing large numbers of young backpackers, mostly European. Hey, was this right up my alley, or what? Oh Skippy, yeah!

Hhmm, even though Sparky had been a mussel diver (black water diver), I had never been PADI certified. Now would be my chance, and off one of the world's largest reefs! Also, the island is reputed as still havin' builders of the traditional, long dugout canoe type boats, "Cayucos." Geez, since early childhood, I've always wanted to build a dugout canoe. On Utila, it shouldn't be very difficult finding someone from that region to teach the craft, and they build really big ones. Wow, gotta get my ass down there! Yes sir, I'll document the whole process of Cayuco construction, from start to finish, with detailed notes and photographs. What a cool project. This will be an adventure of positive accomplishment.

Nancy and I will get our deserving break from each other; there will be exploring of the Mosquito Coast, PADI certification, good scuba diving, traditional dugout boat craft will be documented and learnt, plus, there's the scouting of location for my desired backpackers retreat/compound, and I have the volunteer work at the remote jungle orphanage on that big tropical river.

Man, the fishin' has gotta be really somethin' there. Hhmm, let's see, anything else? Uh, oh yeah, and because countries down there are so poor, my mission can be accomplished costing fairly little. Anything else? Hhmm, probably, 'cept damn if any come to mind. Overall, it's a pretty good plan, huh? Well, I certainly thought so, and after a while, so did Nancy. Uh, that's not completely true. She did like the volunteer orphanage part, but the rest? Hey,she wasn't keen on that. It's because of my natural ability for attracting trouble; Nancy is very much knowing, and deeply worried about my traveling alone in countries like Guatemala and Honduras. Funny, huh? Even though we hate each other, we are still best friends, deeply in love, and bonded like you wouldn't believe (weird). In attempts at setting her mind at ease, I confide that, sure, while both countries had a recent history of much turmoil and violence, neither is like this anymore. The governments of both countries are now quite stable and the people as a whole, even though impoverished, are warm and friendly to tourists and visitors. Hell, why wouldn't they be? They need the Goddamn money! All the travel books say so (sorta).

Deep down, Nancy wasn't buyin' it, and honestly, deep down, neither was I, but, what the fuck. No risk, no gain, right? Nancy searches the internet to see if the jungle orphanage Casa del Corazone has a web page, site, whatever. Oh Skippy, they had one! It gave the whole synopsis of the project, including photographs, and even a monthly newsletter. What's this? Most recent events—hurricane had just hit the region, practically devastating the little orphanage. They desperately needed money and volunteers!

Calling several listed numbers, talkin' to some people based stateside, part of an international network for sponsoring Casa del Corazone (most had adopted a child or two, from the orphanage), all confirm the urgent need (now more than ever). And no, none had ever themselves personally experienced any troubles with crime or violence while traveling in the region. "All of the guns in Guatemala have now been put away" as one man put it during a phone conversation.

Thus, excitement grew big time towards the undertaking of my new adventure! Still, there was a strange little somethin' from within, blinking a silent, tiny red light for cautious warning; though subtle, it could not be ignored, resulting in boosting my already wall-bouncin' state. See, my daily Darvocet intake had increased with the death of my father, and yes, it really increased with the death of my grandfather. I was now doin' ten a day. A person would think swallowing ten Darvocet tabs a day, every single day, would settle one down a bit, Right? Jesus, such don't apply for Sparky. Nope, nope, nope, and so, I set about mapping my route.

The plan: get most of the exploration traveling done first, then, when funds start runnin' low, head 'er for the orphanage Casa del Corazone.

I began packing, repacking, and re-packing! Not such an easy task, since there was need for travelin' light; but damn, due to the trip bein' a solo expedition into the Mosquito Coast and all, a lot of stuff was needed. Well, stuff (equipment/kit/gear) I did have, and plenty at that. Always the outdoors man, and self-proclaimed amateur military history buff, particularly French military history and especially all that even remotely concerns the most elite (and unique) fighting force ever to be assembled: the French Foreign Legion! My biggest regret in life has always been not ever gettin' my act together for goin' to France and signing on with those true warriors of discipline and hardship. Yepper, in thick black lettering, I even have one of their mottos tattooed on my right upper arm: *Marche ou Crève* (March or Die). The motto is a worthy one, and living up to such is challenging, you bet.

For this journey, I chose a French military backpack for hauling most of my stuff. The backpack (like much French gear) is clever. It's sort of a configured water-resistant backpack/duffle bag combination, lacking protrusive side pouches and aluminum frame. You can somewhat comfortably haul a ton of kit in such a pack, yet still toss 'er about like a duffel bag. In this pack went most everything, including small light tarp, fifty foot of rope, short machete, and a twenty-inch heavy steel black MAGLITE flashlight. (This model can be used as both fighting club and flashlight. I should know; as a rascal of a teenager, Sparky was once knocked out cold with one, by a cop.) Loaded, the backpack ended up weighing over eighty pounds. Camera's and the sort went into my old favorite shoulder bag, and little miscellaneous stuff filled my very well made multi-pocket, khaki fishin' vest. Shit man, I am ready to *go*! Just kick back, spend some quality time with the boys (my sons), and wait for Nancy to find the best deal on airfare outta here.

I have always been the type of father for wantin' in on everything concerning my sons. Hell, I was jealous with envy because Nancy got to be the one for feelin' them grow internally, and have honored privilege of giving birth. And breastfeeding? Hey, do we men get ripped off on this deal, or what? Finally, enough was enough. After letting Nancy breastfeed for seven months, it's decided best she should go see a doctor for getting on ever popular antidepressants. (The second birth really had her out there!) She did, and thus had to stop nursing. Yee-haw! Now I get to feed the baby! And Skippy, there ain't nothin' like it, laying down with your warm, teeny tiny baby tucked between the crook of your arm, as the little tyke sucks away. (Even though this is bottle feeding and not breast, it's still cool as all get up!) And when baby is full, driftin' off into sleep... aw gosh, what a sight. And that petite, rhythmic, soft baby breath's wafting, combined with intoxicating aroma of perfect, lopsided infant head, the best, man, the very best!

Yes, it is heart wringing to leave the boys for any lengthy period. Then why do it, especially now that (no longer subtle) little red light inside head giving warning, has grown a flashin' brilliance, demanding acknowledgement? This journey will involve danger! Why leave family for risks unknown? Uh-duh, good fuckin' question? Hhmm, must just be my nature. An idea comes to mind, wheels go into motion, and damn, things just sorta fall into place, or rather, advance with myself in lead, or tow, but rarely havin' ability for applying brakes. Hard to explain, though like with this trip, if Sparky backs out now, there will be lifelong regret.

Nancy, in her search for my flight out, learns it's cheaper to fly into Cancun Mexico, and from there purchase tickets for flyin' further south. She suggests an idea: involving the whole family. We all fly together to Cancun, have ourselves a nice vacation, just outside the cool little town Playa del Carmen, after which, I could go on my merry way from there. Okay, sounds like a plan. Maybe the goodbyes will be easier. Through further searching, Nancy discovers that since my travels coincide with the "off season," many big resorts are now offering super cut-rate package deals. A ten day stay at some of these all-inclusive, four-star resorts is now quite the bargain, bein' less expensive than any other way we could go (who'd 'a guessed?). Geez, Nancy and I had both done our share of traveling (especially her); however, the resort thing would indeed be a new experience. Hell, we'd always scoffed at the mere thought, but that had been before. Now though, what, with the kids—golly, this just might be really cool! Besides, the boys will have a blast!

My sack is now very heavy with clams; I drag 'er to the boat, whole time scannin' the river, on look-out for you-know-who. The sack-o-clams, mud water, and little squirmies is a hundred-plus pounds, and a real chore gettin' up, over side of boat. Plopping into the big blue barrel tub, pulling my feet out from the sucking mud, I follow suit. Once in the boat, time to haul! Stepping into khaki shorts, anchor up, lower-end down, va-RRROOM! Away we go! Throttle wide-open, while keepin' constant look-out. If any boats are spotted approaching, the clams (illegally taken from Iowa waters) will have to be hurriedly heaved overboard! And since they are still in meshed sack, they will all die, wasted for nothin' (nothin' 'cept to keep my ass from bein' arrested); a bitch of a deal, this is for sure. It's one thing to kill the poor critters for use as bait, but fuck, if you gotta waste 'em just 'cause the Game Warden or Rick the Prick is barrelin' down on you! What a shame. And yes, unfortunately, I have had to do this, both with fish and clams. Sickening the act is, and though justification (sorta) can be made, it is nevertheless wrong; and always comes with haunting guilt. So, very good I have become in preventing such wastes of precious gifts given by the river.

Pushing the kill button, while at the same time raising the lower end, my boat swiftly glides for docking: *thud!* Damn, always hate hitting the ol' dock hard, however, comin' in at such speed, sometimes, it's difficult avoiding. Shutting everything down, and pullin' on center dock rope, spinnin' boat around, so her bow is pointin' outwards as she gets tied down. Weighty blue tub of clams is heaved up onto the dock, and dragged laboriously down entire length. These blue tubs are actually just hundred gallon plastic drums (barrels), sawed in half, with cutouts on both sides for handles. Man, they are indestructible, and last for ever. I can remember the days before plastic barrels: they were steel, sharp edged, heavy, and got rusted. These plastic ones—along with a reliable outboard motor, sharp knife and handy-rag—are a fisherman's best friend. No time for spare! It's balls to the walls! All clams must be opened, meats pulled and trimmed, and then diced into chunks for baiting hooks.

From my dock, blue tub-o-clams get dragged with much exertion up to skinning work bench, just a few feet from my back deck, under a large beauty of a maple tree. Catchin' breath, it's a quick jump onto the deck, for bringing out a CD player havin' Van Morrison live in San Francisco. Crankin' loud! Van is the man, and he's my favorite musical artist. Hhmm, Van would like my river. Yeah, whatever. Gotta fly, if I'm gonna get these clams cut, hooks baited, and lines dropped, all before dark.

The last jug spins to stay afloat from weighted trot line bein' dropped for river's bottom. The jugs are empty antifreeze containers, used as markers, indicating location of each and every dropped trotline. Well, that's it—ten lines and a thousand hooks, every one baited with fresh clam. The sky is clear, dusk is setting in, air is calm, and Old Man River smells like that bein' similar to warm, clean pussy. Tomorrow morning, the catch will be good.

Breathin' deeply, feelin' exhausted, yet having a sense of gratifying achievement, I turn the boat and head 'er on back up river to my dock. I won't eat tonight, but will shower, and then wait, wait for that damn cell phone to ring. O-yippee…

Pacing the floor with dreaded anxiety, amongst shadows cast against glowing soft light from oil lamp upon tabletop, I'm nude, having just showered, and there's no need for clothes. Outside, it's darker than usual, and the crickets seem louder than should be; however, on this night, so do all the other nocturnal sounds. Time to cover the cockatiels, and in doing whisper "Night, night". They both tilt their heads in unison, looking absolutely adorable. The male hops up, clinging to the bars—he wants to play nibble-finger. Gently brushing my fingertip against his little beak, "Not tonight, my friend." Letting the sheet fall, the tiny guy sweetly chirps out a "Night, night."

Turning to reach for my pack of Camels, "MEOW!" Ught-o, forgot about feedin' puss, the cat. Through big screen double doors leading out onto the deck, there she is... making presence known. Puss is a good cat—or rather kitten, having only been born herself this spring. Christ, and here she is already swellin' with kits of her own. Whew, babies havin' babies. Hope it don't kill her; this happens, you know? Puss is also very beautiful (despite bein' clearly blind in one eye). Calico she is, sportin' a sleek shiny, black, orange, and white fur. And like with most calico cats, she has a really cool playful streak. Some people consider 'em (calicos) to be more ill-tempered (ornerier) than other types of cats, only this ain't true. They just express themselves differently, that's all. For example, most calicos play with claws out, and when they've had enough, well Skippy, they have had enough! I like her way more than what anybody is aware, 'cept her; she knows. Sliding open the big screen door to pour food into her bowl, puss swats at my hand, and, purring, rubs herself against my leg in show of affection.

Steppin' back inside, sliding behind screen door closed, again my Camel cigarettes are sought, but before reachin' them, guess what? The little cell phone rings. Oh fuck! God, here goes nothin'. Pushin' the big white button, having blue stripe:

"Uh, hello."

"Devin?"

"Uh-mm, yes."

"Hello Devin, this is Elaine Porter. I spoke to your wife earlier today; she said it would be alright to call you, and that you would be willing to talk to me concerning some of your own experiences in Guatemala. She said you had gone to Guatemala to do volunteer work for an orphanage, and in doing, you ran into a group of people that are part of a bizarre cult? And they had tried killing you? And you think these same people might have something to do with the death of my brother?"

The woman's voice is quite soft and gentle, having a lot of grieving sorrow within. Obviously she is a very sensitive person, and this phone call cannot be easy for her. Jesus, the inner pain the poor woman must be in, and still, the determined strength she possesses to personally make this phone call. Whoa, I must walk lightly here. Turning my writing desk light on, while sitting down into the chair (glancing for much wanting cigarettes), my nudity is immediately felt, stickin' to cheap vinyl chair. Clearin' my throat, in attempts for bringing forth voice equal to gentle sensitivity as she.

"Yes, you see, it all started…" I begin tellin' my tale; well, at least the left-out-parts version of my tale. It was however, the truth; just not complete. As I talked, the words began to come easier and easier. Elaine, for the most part, just let me ramble on—politely interrupting only for asking a question or two. Obviously, she is taking notes. After a spell, I ask her about the private investigators she and her family had hired. She explains how they (the family) had hired three (PIs) in all, and nothing came of it. One, however, did return their money, claiming he could not pursue the case: as for reason why? He would not reveal.

"Uh, and the US embassy, Elaine, have they been any help?"

In sullen tone, Elaine shares: though sympathetic, the US embassy claims their "hands are tied." They have done everything officially dictated, including requesting the FBI be allowed to enter and conduct its own investigation—not only for the murder of Terry, but also the other Americans murdered since. Problem is, Guatemala must grant permission; and as yet, this, Guatemala will not do.

"Geez, that sounds like Guatemala alright. Elaine, did Ambassador Todd Boil ever mention bein' good friends with Terry?"

After a moment's silence, she answers, "No, he never mentioned anything of the sort. Actually, Todd Boil commented the contrary, saying he had not personally known Terry, but wished he had, for Terry sounded to have been a very kind, special man. Devin, why do you ask? Do you think they were friends?"

"Uh, yes, well, that's what Todd told me anyways, the morning after Terry's, uh, death. He said the journalist murdered had been a very close friend. And, uh, since there were no other journalists murdered on that night, well, he would have to be referring to Terry. Also, Elaine, I truly believe it was Terry with Todd, checkin' up on me, after my fire… Uh, hhmm… look, it doesn't surprise me that Todd Boil denies knowin' your brother; man, Elaine, gettin' straight answers from that guy is like, well, like impossible. Ambassador Todd Boil is either very good at his job, or very bad at it. The only sure thing about the man, is that he is very intelligent, which makes dealing with him all the more frustrating because you never know if he's screwin' with you, or bein' on the up and up, ever! Elaine, two different times I made it to the American Embassy seeking help, after runnin' for my life, escaping atrocities you wouldn't believe, and all Ambassador Todd Boil would talk about was his soon to be divorce."

Elaine gives a short, soft, sad laugh. "It's funny you should say that, Devin, because my other brother has complained of the same thing, commenting that on both trips down there, all Todd Boil would talk about was his wife leaving and divorcing him."

"Well, Elaine, I personally don't know whether to hate the guy, or love him. Gosh, without him I would not have survived, but damn, because of him, I sure went through more hell, and caused more death than ever should of. Elaine, do you know how in the movies, they always portray American embassies as these grand huge elaborate buildings protected by tall iron fences and snappy squared-away American marines? And uh-uh, how in the movies, once a person makes it to the embassy, they are then safe, on American soil, and under American protection? Yes? Well, not in Guatemala! For some reason, our embassy there looks like a run-down DMV [Department of Motor Vehicles] office. It's attached to other offices that aren't even a part of the American Embassy. There is no tall iron gate or fence. And the marines? Ha! They are all brown-skinned UN troops; every one of 'em! And, everybody has to be out of the building by eight o'clock! No protection, no nothin'!"

"Yes, Devin, my brother also mentioned something of this. He was not expecting the embassy to be as it was."

"Well it sure is, and who the fu—, uh, heck knows why. But like what your reporter guy Garcia said to me earlier today, "In Guatemala, nothing is as it seems." Oh, he's got that right. By the way Elaine, how well do you personally know this guy Garcia?" She seems to understand the real meaning of this question, and tries assuring me that Michael Garcia is indeed on the "up and up." They have already communicated twice today, via e-mail and phone. Elaine will talk with him again tonight, after our conversation.

"Devin, Michael is leaving for Guatemala and Honduras, in two days. He was especially interested, learning that you had been in Honduras as well. Another American has recently been murdered there. Also Devin, Michael is very curious about your experiences with the Garifuna people."

(Yeah, I just bet he is.) "Uh, Elaine, do you know about the Garifuna people?"

"No, Devin, not really, only what you and Michael have told me. Devin, my family and I know very little about that part of the world. Actually, we know nothing, except for that it seems to be very dangerous, and corrupt; and we can't get any cooperation in catching the man that murdered my... brother."

Feelin' her silent, unseen tears, but bein' unable to afford the inevitable pause, for fear of tears of my own. "Uh-huh, mm, hhmm, Elaine, Garcia is an American citizen and lives in Miami, right? But where is he from? Really from?"

"Devin, he's Puerto Rican; and a catholic. Michael is not a Santeria, or whatever you might believe this cult thing to be. Trust me Devin, this I do know."

(Uh, sorry lady, but Sparky don't trust nobody. Hhmm, maybe this Garcia is a good ol' catholic, and maybe he ain't. Christ, maybe he's both. Hell, Santeriaism is Goddamn rampant in Puerto Rico, and there sure seems to be some sort of weird connection between it and Catholicism in these Latin and Caribbean countries.)

"Devin, Michael Garcia is a good man. He and a few other journalists have been the only ones willing to actually go down there, poke around, and try finding answers when nobody else will. One journalist told us, that their source informed them that word is, under no circumstances was Terry's case to be seriously investigated, or solved. Again, reasons are unknown as to why. Another journalist discovered that Guatemalan detectives did find Terry's cell phone taken on the night of his... death, and through phone records, they did have live leads, but were not going to pursue them. Devin, it's all so frustrating."

(Damn, she for-real, is not gettin' the picture here.) "Uh, Elaine, look, your brother and I more than likely did cross paths while down there; remember me tellin' you of the fire, ambulance, and emergency room? Well I made one hell of a big bang in Guatemala City, and it wasn't very far from where your brother lived; and since I'm American, well, it would have definitely been a story he would have went after. Elaine, what was Terry working on before his... uhm, death?"

Not surprisingly, she doesn't know, because most of Terry's recent works—writings, notes, photographs, etc.—had been ransacked. There were, however, some scattered photos, left behind in his apartment, of unearthed mass graves; though really, in Guatemala, photos as these, are anything but noteworthy.

Creating a pause, I gently clear my voice to get nerve up for asking an apologetic question, in most sensitive of manners, if such is even possible under circumstances. "Uhm, Elaine, please forgive me for asking, but were there any signs that Terry might have been tied to his bed?"

After some silence, she answers meekly, "Yes, Devin, now that you mention it, one of the journalists that was able to view the police crime scene photos, did say it looked like Terry had really struggled... and, there were what appeared to be rope burns around his ankles and wrists... Devin, he was... badly cut up... as you know."

Elaine, is now (understandably) havin' a really difficult time with this conversation. I refrain from askin' further questions, inquisitive in details, such as whether or not Terry's body had any evidence of torture by means other than brute force and knife, like perhaps multiple insect (or human) bites, scorpion stings, burning, genitalia maiming (or removal). No, these questions are not asked. Instead, the conversation becomes that of Sparky tryin' to gently persuade/convince this saddened grieving woman that the reason for her poor brother's death was result of my unintentional inciting escapades, so endured by circumstances surrounding. Elaine finally agrees, though solemnly claims believing the doomed fate not being a deliberate fault of mine. (But honestly, conscientiously, deep down, she must hate my guts!)

"Elaine, please understand, the man truly responsible for Terry's death will never be brought to legal justice. All we can hope for now, is that possibly journalists will get down there, stay alive long enough, and expose these atrocities, bringing forth attentions and warnings, so that pressure might be applied for at least making them not so damn commonplace. The corruption, mass murder, terror, and…, and these sick torture/snuff films have got to be exposed to the world, as does the voodoo Santeria cult thing! Jesus, they torture and eat people for Christ sakes!" (Eugh! Biting lower lip for some sort of calming. Man, where the fuck are those cigarettes?)

Elaine seems to sense the clinging-edge anxiety within. (Uh, gee, perhaps she can hear my knee playin' spazzy paddy-cake under bottom of desktop!) Her voice becomes almost a whispered hush, "Yes Devin, maybe you are right. I guess all those awful things we see in those horror movies Hollywood makes, the ideas must come from what really happens in places like Guatemala, huh?"

(Yeah sure, or the other way around.) "Yes, Elaine, it's very possible."

The conversation is over, this we both know; time for bringing it to a close. We do, by goin' through the (uncomfortable) customary motions, ending with "Bye… goodbye. Okay, bye."

Pushing the big white button, having blue stripe, I set the little phone down and stare up into the bright blue eyes of Angel Face, eating my wife's pussy. A feeling of sad, spooky gloom is flooding and it don't want to go away.

Pulling from ever magnetic erotic photograph, my hand is noticed, again clutching the little phone. Damn, these things are indeed a marvel. Who'd 'a ever thought? And-and, uh, how those sick bastards down there in Central America loved 'em. Aughg! It's all comin' back: the memories, visions, sounds, and even the stinkin' smells. Eyes dart back up for Angel Face… Wow, must halt this haunting onslaught. Seal off perimeter; lock and load! Withdraw, pull back, advance into friendly territory. Listen closely to river's night sounds; yes, chirping crickets, croakin' frogs, my boat gently bumping up against faithful dock, holding all that is tied, occasional squawk from startled Great Blue Heron, even vibrant massive muffled hum of passing barge. Oooh, it's not workin'... Poor Terry, poor Elaine, poor all those innocent people, and especially children, that died because... God, why, why, why? It's just so weird!

Oh fuck, mental perimeter has been breached... shit! Glancing up to my right, there is another framed photo. This one is of dead William Walker's headstone. During the 1800s William Walker had been an American adventurer, or rather, mercenary? He and his private army (financially backed by the United States government) went and seized Nicaragua for the taking; however, their success was short-lived due to the resilient militant ousting, whereupon William and boys decided it best for movin' on and tryin' hand with Honduras. There, they would have, without a doubt, triumphed, had not Britain intervened. Anyways, ol' Willy got himself captured in 1860, and was promptly executed by firing squad in the Honduran town, Trujillo (where for me, my real nightmare began). While there, before all hell broke loose, I took this photo of William Walker's grave. Why the thing has been enlarged, framed, and hangs from my corner writing station is a very good question. Geez, it's not like the guy is some deceased hero of mine or nothin', but still, guess the photo does have meaning—actin' as a reminder, reminding that, unlike William Walker, I did survive Trujillo. Admittedly, there are times when such trivial things are required, like now! Yeah well, tough luck, Willy! And Trujillo? God, mustn't look at the photo long.

Instead, drop eyes to nicely framed poem by dead poet and legionnaire, Alan Seeger. This too is hangin' as a reminder for, well, the living (and it's my very favorite poem in the whole wide world.) Unlike William Walker, Alan Seeger is a big time hero of mine.

He was an American serving in the French Foreign Legion during the Great War—WW1. Alan Seeger died in action, save not before writing this poem (while in the trenches): "Rendezvous with Death." Though memorized, the motions for reading the poem are put forth, but to no avail; my mind is now way too fuckin' creeped-out! Man, I need a cigarette, and Valium; it's gonna be one of those long, wide-eyed nights. Jumpin' up, startling even myself, I go and fetch both vices, along with a nice tall glass of diet coke having floating lime wedge and frosty ice. Sitting back down into the sweaty, butt stickin' chair, a 10 mg Valium tab gets popped, chased with big gulp of icy Coke and long drag from non-filtered Camel. Inhale deeply; follow by thick exhale for doubts as to whether or not one Valium will even be felt. Hhmm, maybe another should be swallowed?

Looking to my left, is yet another framed photo hanging. It's a beautiful one of my wife Nancy. She is topless, standing on a wondrous bright sunny beach holding two large exotic birds of color and character. The birds are Macaws, and though absolutely exquisite, they in no way equal my wife in either the exoticism, or beauty departments. Without exaggeration, my wife is remarkably stunning in visual excellence. The photo was taken during our stay at the four-star, all-inclusive resort. The place is top notch, Italian owned, and just two miles south from cool little town Playa del Carmen, in the southern Yucatan region, Mexico. My eyes lock onto Nancy. Yes, she is (when not bein' a hyperventilating bitch) positively intoxicating! The effect is somewhat calming, and so my gaze stays.

D espite bein' very full of anxieties concerning the journey that lay ahead, and some bickering between Nancy and myself—caused primarily because she too is sharing (and expressing) strong concern toward my going onwards south—we, as a family, have a wonderful ten day vacation. One like we'd never had before. The beach is beautiful as any could ever be, having clean deep fine sands, and calm translucent water, shimmering many hues, brilliant with luminous blues. The air is hot, and sun strong, burning through glorious vast skies. The resort itself was built for luxury, yet still managed integrating the natural beauty of region. Trees, foliage, and flowers are everywhere.

This place caters to mostly European guests, which makes us, like, the only Americans. This is cool because Europeans seem less loud and obnoxious than Americans, and, as a whole, not as fat! Here, there are very well mannered uninhibited attractive people; especially amongst the young Italians that work the resort. They are thin, beautiful, and lacking the disgusting body fat that seems so plaguing for our overfed, lazy American youths of today. Not to mention the entire American population as a whole. I hate fat! It's a Goddamn disgrace to the human race. Solution? New and improved miracle diets? Or how about the absurd bombardment of the one and only ten-minute-a-day workout gizmo? Guaranteed, or your money back! Christ, what a bunch of pork bellied bullshit! Why don't you just get off your fat jellied ass, and stop stuffing food into that spoiled rotten needy face! Hhmm, wasn't it Benjamin Franklin that said, "Eat to live, don't live to eat"? Yeah well, he was certainly one to talk. Now, wasn't he a little fat fucker himself?

Anyway, the resort is worthy of high recommendation. The boys have a blast! And are given much adoring attention by everyone, just how it should be for children. And Nancy? Well, she is a big hit, receiving much adoring attention herself. She, as usual, has her pick of playmates, and does choose two for sexual recreation, both bein' young, attractive, Italian, and male. All in all, our stay there is one very much enjoyed, and the ten days flow by way too fast.

Goodbye time comes. I must catch my bus for Cancun airport. This is sad, you bet, and very difficult. So much so, that doubts are presently flooding as to whether or not this, now seemingly foolish, blasted solo journey should even be actually attempted. Uh, the smart thing would definitely be to inform warm loving beautiful family that there has been a change in plans and head 'er on back home with them! Yep, that would be the smart thing to have done (despite the forever self-inflicting ass kickin' for doin' such). Honestly, this is the path that would have been chosen, if not for two annoying, persistently pesky women, bein' obviously overly sexually attracted to Nancy, even competing with me for her attentions, right at the very moment the bus is waiting, and we are tryin' to do the family goodbye thing. Selfish cunts! Damn, Nancy and the boys weren't leaving until later. These women knew this, and still... Jesus, if they'd just left us alone for only briefly, to say our goodbyes in private, maybe Nancy would have pleaded one last time "Please don't go; come home with us." And if she had? I seriously would not have been strong enough to refuse. Only, such was not the case. No, it was not.

On the bus, fighting back tears, I sadly wave goodbye to the family. My two, small, gorgeous sons, having deep golden brown tans and sun-bleached hair, and Nancy, who is now waving with big tears flowing—even during this, the two women, one on each side of her (all chipper like) are workin' for engaging a conversation. Geez, some people... Oh well, suck it up, man, wheels are in motion; time to clear the melancholy and think positive toward the adventure that lay ahead.

At the Cancun airport, because of personal physical semblance, resulting from humpin' an old French military backpack, red Converse high-top tennis shoes, baggy khaki shorts, and fishin'/travel vest—with no shirt—displayin' highly visible tattoos, and sportin' a hole in the right earlobe, bein' the size of a dime. (I had, before comin' down here, removed all gold bead rings and earlets from my ears. Still, the one earlet hole is greatly noticeable. A finger can fit completely through it; somethin' these people obviously are not accustomed seeing.) Also, there's the hair—blond, having natural white streaking, worn in usual two-foot-long tight ponytail—topping a body of skin—bronze, brown, baked—not many white people can tan as dark. My overall appearance is that very much of a hard rode *gringo* backpacker, havin' what must be assumed little money, and therefore, not worth the time of day. Treatment accordingly is received. Yeah well, fuck 'em! This will be to my advantage (or so is thought). The airport personnel (every one of 'em) give the run-around, while pretending *"no hablar ingles."* However, from their dung eating smirks, it's more than evident they can. This is Cancun after all. Sure wish my Spanish weren't so damn retarded.

The destination is San Pedro Sula, Honduras. But because seldom does anyone travel there from Cancun (shared tidbit from Playa del Carmen travel agent who looked at me as if I were outta my mind), Sparky must first land in Guatemala City. Then I can head 'er on for San Salvador (El Salvador), having a several hour layover, after which catchin' a flight onwards to San Pedro Sula.

Somehow, the correct boarding gate is finally found. Oddly, there is no gate number and no one present, not for long though. I take a seat and light a Camel. Soon, in comes a young Asian man, seating himself in a chair beside mine, politely askin' for a light. We, both smokin', immediately strike up conversation, where it is learnt the young man is Korean, and has just come in from Cuba, where he fulfilled a lifelong dream of paying homage to his hero, Che Guevara. The chatty Korean is now on route for Antigua, and will be gettin' off in Guatemala City.

We are sittin' there, smokin' and jokin' (nice thing about these Third World countries, you can smoke anywhere, and everywhere), when in comes a man who is obviously American. He's quite the sight, lookin' very much to be still buzzin' with big time cocaine high—his mannerism and speech, pretty much confirms this. From around the man's neck, swayin' to and fro, bending him forward, is a large leather travel bag. From each white knuckled grasping hand, dragging on the floor behind, he's got two (clearly heavy) duffle bags. Wild-eyed, seeing we are the only ones in the boarding gate waiting area, the animated American lets off some steam, hissing dislike for the "fucked up airport, Mexicans, and all of Mexico!"

Taking a seat directly across from us, he instantly begins asking speedy questions, through quivering jaw and teeth grindin': Who are we? Where we from? Where we goin'? Why? etc, etc. Then, with excited darting eyes, Mr. Twitchy shares he too had also just come from Cuba. There, he—"snicker, snicker"—bought cigars, and had himself, "one hell of a good time!" Proudly, Twitchy shows off his completely full duffle bags of fine Cuban cigars.

Now havin' a major fondness for cigars myself (dating back even to childhood), my interest is captured. The man understands, and takes out boxes for displaying prized loot. He shows box after box of Cohibas, and world famous Montecristos. Twitchy excitedly swears the Montecristo No. 2s are worth an easy $400 a box, once back in the States (of course). "Hee-hee! four hundred smackers! And look how many boxes are in these duffle bags—a fortune! Hee-hee! Snicker, snicker. It ain't drugs, just tobacco! Can't go to jail for that; huh? Haw, ha ha!"

As it turns out, this mid-thirty-somethin' guy, is from (all places) St. Louis, Missouri. He is (naturally) tryin' to get his cigars and himself back to St. Louis. Only the thing is, because he had just flown in from Havana, possessing Cuban contraband—uh, like two duffle bags full—Mexico wasn't allowing him departure for the United States, not with the cigars they weren't. One box, sure; two duffle bags, no way! However, they did hint that Guatemala would probably allow it; and so, they sold him a ticket for Guatemala City, thus leaving the guy flat broke. You see, Twitchy (or whatever the fuck his name is) had spent most of his money on cigars and having himself an exceptionally good time in Cuba!

Twitchy, bummin' a cigarette from the Korean, asks, "Where is Guatemala, anyways?" The Korean and I look to each other with eyes rollin'. Curbing a chuckle, clearin' my throat, "Uh, it's the next country down, bordering Belize."

Twitchy appears confused, and admits not knowing where Belize is, either. Before we can explain, he shrugs his shoulders exclaiming, "Hell, what does it matter! I've already bought my ticket, right? Eh, just so long as they have banks there. Dudes, I am broke: I've got to get some money wired to me, and like fast!"

Mr. Twitchy from St. Louis scoffs at my serious suggestion in having this transaction done here in Cancun Mexico, rather than Guatemala City. The guy declares (ignorantly) that he needs a real bank, not a Mexican bank! "Here, they will just give me the money in those pesos—fuck that!" Hey, what's the currency in Guatemala?'

"Quetzal."

"Quetzal? Never heard of it. Oh well, it's gotta be better than the Mexican peso, right?" Chewing on his bottom lip, while tappin' foot a hundred miles an hour, the guy looks to us for corroboration. We both just sorta stare back at him in silence, not knowing how to answer.

Holy cow, is this guy ever in for a trip! What, goin' into Guatemala, naïve, broke, not speakin' Spanish, and humpin' two duffels of very expensive Cuban cigars. Geez, Twitchy here, is just askin' to be jumped, robbed, or possibly worse. And he hates Mexico... Oh Christ, the dumb ass is gonna love Guatemala City! Poor guy.

Approaching Guatemala City, the view is vast miles of red hilltop clay and one gigantic mass of shanty-town slums. Welcome to a major Third World city. Wow, even from the air, the poverty below is clearly large scale evident. After landing, my two new friends get off. Mr. St. Louis Cigar Man ain't lookin' so good. He now seems notably afraid, again, poor guy.

San Salvador, El Salvador—here, after retrieving ol' backpack, armed security (soldiers) and custom officials come and confiscate my passport. I'm then led out of view from the general public, and placed in a three-walled cubicle, having benches, whereupon other people sit with their luggage. Most are young men, and all are silent, lookin' nervous and depressed, with eyes to the floor. The three-walled cubicle has a rope and standing guard for enforcing containment. Okay, what kind of set-up is this? Hhmm, just guessin'—it's most likely a mule (drug carrier) holding pen. Yeah well, my butt don't belong in here; no, it does not!

The standing armed guard is presenting himself a stance, standard for bad asses, sportin' sunglasses and all (including parkerized Mossberg twelve-gauge pump). After tolerating an hour or so of this weirdness, I've had enough. With a heave, heavy backpack gets slung over one shoulder. In doin', the guard becomes enraged, shoutin' orders in Spanish! Damn, this sure ain't no way for startin' a journey. Refusing to stand down, confronting the guard with verbal outburst of my own, his eyes betray somethin' amiss here. The guard's demeanor drops intimidation for uncertainty; out comes the walkie-talkie, into which he spews forth rapid Spanish, questioning?

Soon, a very attractive woman, dressed in airport attire (having obviously been tailored to include skirt shorter than standard issue) shows up holding my passport, sweetly apologizing, claiming they had innocently mistaken me for someone else. So sorry were they, that she had personally already processed my ticket for continuing onwards to San Pedro Sula. Motioning to follow, she hands over my passport, ticket, and even boarding pass. Following the young woman towards the upper level for departure gates, it's difficult not admiring her taut femme fatale form, downright sexy; and she, rightfully so, is greatly aware, carrying herself accordingly.

The intriguing woman points out my boarding gate, again apologizes, gives a mysterious smile, offers "Happy travels!" and walks away with a striking strut knowing herself to be watched. With her gone, my attention regains itself for full regrouping. Whew, gee-golly, wasn't that all quite strange! And, uh, where is everybody? The upper level is, for the most part, vacant—no people. Guess not many folks down here travel at this hour of night. There is still time to kill before my flight; it's spent sitting at an empty coffee counter, drinkin' espressos, smokin' and studying my Spanish for retards book.

Landing in San Pedro Sula, despite the standin', ugly, peerin', disordered, ill-uniformed soldiers, armed with an array of such weapons as Mossberg pumps, Mini 14s, AR-15s (or M-16s?), and even some variants of the AK-47s (not mentioning holstered side arms), all goes smoothly, no problems. It is very late, and after exchanging some US dollars with an old, foul smelling, half drunk man, sittin' in a wooden straight back chair, before some surrounding soldiers (the currency exchange rate is somethin' like thirteen to one). Fifty US dollars are swapped for a huge wad of rolled dirty lempiras. A long dark cab ride ensues, for a place called *Hotel Luna Creciente*. This place (printed up in a certain prominent travel guide book) is supposedly quite popular with the Peace Corps people, bein' low budget *cheap* and just a few blocks away from the central bus station.

Well, the place is indeed low budget, costing only a couple of bucks per night, but, what a dump! The lighting is poor wiring, and a few hangin' bare light bulbs. This filthy, stinkin', poorly lit place, is a concrete block compound, consisting of several floor levels, havin' gloomy narrow walkways. My room, bein' on an upper floor, is only a small damp cubicle, hardly big enough for accommodating a bed, while still obliging the door to (scarcely) open and close. There is no ventilation, uh, 'cept for the small corner fan, having timer switch. The room reeks strongly of overripe rot, urine, and feces. Yes, along with your typical graffiti, there is human shit smeared on the walls. Oh yippee. Damn, what's up with these Latins and their shit smearing? Geez, I'd stayed at several places like this in my travels through Mexico (though, none quite as bad), and all had feces smeared on the walls... Fuckin' weird.

Relieving shoulders of heavy backpack, watchin' it practically collapse the old frail bed, landing upon, without bounce. I will not be crawlin' into this bed tonight. Reaching down to hit the switch for the fan, seeing all the dead insects and whatnot littering the floor, pretty much confirms this decision.

Stepping out onto the narrow dim walkway, locking flimsy door behind, I head 'er on down to the bathroom for a much needed pee; Whew-wee! The bathroom is what one would expect from such a place. Afterwards, it's a quick jaunt down the dark stairwells for front desk. "Uhmm, *dos* Coca-Colas, *por favor... Gracias.*" Surprisingly both bottles of Coke are cold.

Back in filthy, cell-like room, sitting on the bed, it's a laugh how worn-thin the mattress really is, having bedspread thing matching, with many disgusting stains.

Using the bottom end of my plastic Bic lighter, off pops cap from sweating, wet Coca-Cola bottle. Sparky drains that sucker down, in like two big gulps! Boy, thirsty much? And gee, still am huh? Oh well, must nurse this second bottle; she's gotta last 'til mornin', 'cause Skippy Joe, there are no plans on this night for goin' back down those dark stairwells. Nope, not gonna be usin' the bathroom either.

So, adjusting my backpack on the bed for use as a backrest, I lay against it, with feet up on the door. Of course sleep does not come. Eyes open to light another cigarette, or allow a sip from fast becoming empty (remaining) Coke bottle.

Jesus, what a strange transition, goin' from the four-star, all-inclusive resort, to this squalor! And, leaving behind my family at that. My warm precious loving wife and sons... Aughg! Must not think of them; it will only bring on depression, and doubts. Doubts? No doubts! Doubts are for weak people. Man, gotta commit and do! March or die! And Skippy, the commitment has been made; therefore, make the best of it. Otherwise, this will be all for nothin', 'cept, uh, exposing great stupidity.

Listening to the ever-present, constant street noises, and now, that of boisterous, drunken men coming in from the bars, I take mental count of remaining Darvocet: only twenty. Ught, these will barely hold my need for two days. Fuck! How did it come to this? Who the hell needs ten Goddamn Darvocets a day? Oooh, if a substitute narcotic is not had within two days' time, Sparky is a-gonna be one serious unhappy *camper*! Hhmm, past experience traveling Mexico had taught that Darvocet would not be found in these parts. The Mexican pharmacists hadn't even known what Darvocet were. And despite popular belief, one cannot just walk into a local *farmacia* and purchase opiate painkillers, at least not in south Mexico anyways. It took one hundred US dollars for bribing a doctor into writing me a prescription (of considerable quantity, requiring contribution from several *farmacias*) for just codeine tablets. They were, however, literally the size equaling imagined horse pills; and yepper, those puppies did work! I am hoping for the same here, tomorrow, in La Ceiba, only without the hassles of having to go through a doctor. Shouldn't be all too difficult, right? Yeah, well, guess this will be seen tomorrow, after buyin' some *agua*, in one of those tall plastic liter bottles.

In the wee hours of the mornin', still dark, before sunrise, it's a quick silent tiptoe down the walkway for the bathroom—someone had just used. There is standing water, at least an inch deep on the broken tile floor, having come from the shower. In places as these, shower curtains, like toilet paper, are not considered bathroom essentials, and neither are well functioning drains. Without pause, the routine of vigorously brushing mouth and teeth goes into motion. I've always been sort of a ninny for teeth brushing. Back home, it's several times a day; using toothpaste, salt, and hydrogen peroxide. Anyway, with that task completed, time for next—must attempt the forced bowel movement thing.

Surprisingly, bowels cooperate. An even bigger surprise bein' that the toilet actually flushes—no floaters here. Also, no need for toilet paper, as I carry in my vest many individual wet wipe packets. One packet does the trick. A decision is made against the shower, opting instead for a cold water face wash. No need, yet, to shave.

Exiting the sloshing bathroom, and briskly walkin' back towards my room, feelin' refreshed, despite having no sleep. Several room doors open, with hung-over construction/laborer types emerging. From these men, very strange looks are received—strange looks indeed, to point of indicating that *gringos* are not a common sight here, nor a welcome one. My thinking now is not many (if any) Peace Corps volunteers actually intentionally stay at *Hotel Luna Creciente*. I had, over the years, met several Peace Corps folk while still on the job, and never would any of them have need, nor want, for stayin' in such a dump as this. A primitive hut? Sure. A shit smeared cell-like room? No way! Time to gear-up and split.

The sun is cresting, thus bringing life to the streets. Everywhere, there is much hustle and bustle! People are comin' and goin', busy opening businesses and setting up curbside street/sidewalk market stands for sellin' an array. Produce is bein' laid out, and fire pots for cookin'. Hand carts are pushed to and fro with hawkers, barkers, and bawlers shoutin' their calls.

Now, all this sudden activity can be very fascinating and even over-whelming, only I'd seen it all before, in other places—nothin' new here. Must find that bus station, and board the first bus headin' for La Ceiba… 'cept first, whoah, need a liter bottle of water. Actually, two get bought and in doin', directions asked.

The bus station turns out (for Sparky) not so easy to find. Third World countries are notorious for lacking street signs and addresses, but damn, that station should be right around here! Jesus Christ! How the hell am I missin' the main central bus station of San Pedro Sula?

Finally, after circling several block perimeters (and becoming increasingly frustrated), while politely declining persistent offers by many young (and not so young) vendors on foot, constantly approaching, peddling wares from boxes hung around the necks containing such goodies as candies, combs, ballpoint pens, cheap watches, sunglasses, cigarettes, tampons, whatever!

I recruit from these, an eager youngster for help. Purchasing a handful of Chiclets (chewing gum) from the small boy, and then offering him a couple to chew himself, he accepts, thanking with a big wondrous smile (a smile that only a child can give). I ask "Habla Ingles?"

The child's smile grows even broader, answering, "Si, yes, you are British or *Americano*?" Silently, my grinning shrug from shoulders answers him, "You guess." The great sparkling eyes of this beautiful boy convey he's keen to the game. Save first—in an instant—he has spun, waving arms and spewing a vicious (speedy Spanish) verbal outburst towards a steady growing number of street vendors, and the sorts, closing in, surrounding. Surprisingly, they all back off, giving space: and most are like way bigger and older than this young boy child; yet, (due to sub-culture street rule?) I am his catch, and so, they will hold and wait. The little guy satisfied, turning, resumes his enormous smile while softly tracing fingertip lightly over some of my tattoos, as if mesmerized. He answers, "I think you are *Americano*, and you are a soldier."

At this, I burst out laughing! The boy also laughs, noddin' his head exclaiming, "Si, yes, yes."

"No! No, no. Kid, I am American; but no soldier! Look! See?" My ponytail is quickly brought around, swishin' entire length for him to see (as if he, and everybody and their mangy dog on this block hadn't already noticed the long blond ponytail). "See? No soldier! Ha ha!" (Fuckin' haw.)

The little boy smiling, points to my *Marche ou Crève* tattoo, and (interestingly) several visible scars, as well. "You are soldier, private soldier!"

Ught-oh. Lookin' around, the gathered street crowd hearing, have begun mumbling, with eyes, scrutinizing. I am now becoming very self-conscious of my French military backpack, exposed US military olive green wool socks, khaki baggy shorts, and belt bein' obviously of military origin. Hell, even tan multi-pocket fishing/travel vest could be mistaken for military! However, these aren't the things the kid is pointing at. No, the boys assumed I'm a private soldier (mercenary) from only the tattoos and scars. And he appears quite confident with his assessment! Despite Sparky a-laughin' it off, pointin' down towards red Converse high-top tennis shoes, and swishin' ponytail, the kid ain't buyin'. This sucks! People down here can't be thinkin' I'm some sort of mercenary, and especially, not a red shoe wearin', long-haired one!

"No, no, no soldier. No *soldado*, no *militar*. *Soy turista*! Understand. *Comprender*, *entendido*? Hhmm, huh, a, look, *donde esta terminal*... Uh, um..." (Fuck it, the boy speaks English.) "Where's the bus station pal?"

The boy bursts into giggling laughter while mocking with enlightenment—we are practically standin' right beside the damn thing! Yepper, the place (and sign) is right here—hidden from view, within a one-block perimeter, fenced off by ever popular Third World rusty corrugated roofing panels.

Yeah well, the gate is now open, and the buses inside are beginning engine start-ups, idlin', passing exhaust from diesel. The young boy, askin' destination desired, quickly grabs hold of my hand, and leads the way through gate for bus, having only a number indicating route.

A large sweaty man is loading this bus, among many, midst a lively muster for beginning a new busy day, he stops upon glimpsing our approach. My little friend goes to him, speaking rapid Spanish. The man, meeting my eyes, nods acknowledgement. The boy informs that I must give this man some lempiras, and he will load my backpack, guarding against theft. (Uh, okey-dokey. Uhmm, wonder how many lempiras are required for such?) Pullin' achin' shoulders from backpack straps, without bounce, she lands at feet. (Whew, what a heavy bitch. Humpin' her is gonna take some gettin' used to.) And now for the lempiras.

I'm sorta carrying funds, spread out and about. US dollars and newly acquired credit cards (for emergency use) are in a folding wallet of right vest pocket. A separate, large leather-zippered trucker/biker wallet holds all traveler's checks and more US dollars, accommodated by left vest pocket. My passport is contained within yet another pocket. These chosen zipper pockets have been seam-stitched into interior of the vest itself. No sneaky fingers can get at without alerting. Right front baggy khaki shorts pocket keeps local currency. An extremely well made (large) COLD STEEL folding knife, having five inch sharp blade, rides clipped on inside left shorts pocket. Yeah okay, nothin' brilliant, but, what the fuck. It's the best that can be arranged considering. Only other option would be carryin' everything up my ass.

Out comes a wad of lempiras. Pullin' off a twenty, thinkin' the man's expression will tell if the amount is enough... It is; the man hurriedly reaches for the twenty, and grabs my backpack (showin' surprise towards the weight) and tosses it into the outer bottom side baggage/cargo compartment. Damn, twenty limps had indeed been enough. Geez, that's like not even equaling two US dollars!

My little friend then leads the way over to the garage-like entrance of the bus station house. Here, he informs, my ticket must be purchased, and the bus will be departing shortly. Looking into his big gleamin' brown eyes, I hand him two twenty US dollar bills, thanking him. "*Gracias*, my young friend." Not thinkin' the boy's smile could possibly get any bigger than what had already been seen—wrong—it explodes with surprised joy! He quickly snatches both twenties and hurriedly stuffs 'em into his pocket. With a wave, he's off sprintin'; from a short distance, he yells back, "See you, tattoo soldier Man!." Fuck! Little brat.

The buses are actually quite nice, comfortable, and exceptionally inexpensive. The bus ride for La Ceiba is long, eight hours or so. After popping five Darvocets, I settle in, and enjoy the relaxed ride, watching diverse beautiful landscape pass by. Just like driving the Caribbean coast along Mexico, the visual delights enthrall. This countryside is green-green, lushy green! Exuberant rolling hills a top cresting heights for even more. The narrow curvy road circles up, around and around, climbing, only to descend, weaving down into enchanting valleys of lowlands, crossing small rivers via bridges always unique. The bus pushes onwards, up, down, all around. Passing through small towns of character, people busy goin' about their day: children playin' in the road, men walking to and fro carrying machetes and other tools of labor, women totin' large baskets, workin' at chores, keepin' infants and toddlers close. Carts, lots of carts, are bein' pushed, pulled, dragged by man, beast, and/or child. These towns surroundings are, more often than not, fields—bananas, sugar, sparse corn, and just plain fields. Through these, the snaky ride winds back up lush rolling hills again, and again.

Every couple hours or so, the bus will pull over, stopping at rustic, extremely busy, roadside restaurante/rest areas. All bein' quite similar, providing outdoor latrines, and eating facility... not mentioning the many gathered vendors selling an array.

Arriving on the outskirts of La Ceiba, we are here. No station/terminal, just many taxis waiting. True to my young friend's word, my backpack was not stolen (probably because she's as ugly as all get-up, and heavy like a fat granny). Popping another five Darvocets, a taxi is taken to Hotel Europa. Why Hotel Europa? Well, a travel guide book claimed the place bein' a good deal: nice, clean, reasonably priced, and centrally located. Yes, after last night, an upgrade in lodging is needed. Plus, Sparky must be central (center city) for searching farmacias.

The place is indeed nice, and costs approximately ten US dollars per night. And here, Gustavo is met. He is a large, good-lookin', laid-back, friendly black Carib.

While paying, and thanking the cabby, Gustavo emerges from the big glass front of Hotel Europa and its adjoining restaurant. Introducing himself with a handshake and shouldering my backpack (course not without comment towards weight), he leads our way through the hotel's glass front entrance. In doin', Gustavo shares introductions to a nearby seated armed guard.

The hotel is a multi-level structure, formed around a small courtyard and garden pond, sportin' a quaint fountain and several chubby goldfish.

My room is on the upper level. It is clean and modern, having private bathroom, tidy bed, TV, and ceiling fan. Upon entering the room,

Gustavo asks, "Devon, from where in America is it, you live?"

With some amusement (knowing he had not seen my passport), "Gustavo, how do you know I'm American?"

Laughing he points to my tattoos and ponytail, "Devon, European men do not have such long hair and tattoos; only Americans, and maybe [tilting his head] Asians? I do not really know, Devon; Americans and Asians are not a common sight here. We see them mostly only on TV, and in the movies. Devon, you will be standin' out very much in this town; many eyes will be watchin'. Devon, you must be very careful, and not trust anyone. Understand, Devon? This is most important. There will be those that will attempt to trick you, and take advantage. But not me Devon; you can trust Gustavo. If there is anything you are needin' or desire—girls? Or marijuana, perhaps? Anything Devon, you come to Gustavo, me; I will get you whatever you wish for."

Gustavo then explains that the girls he knows are all very clean; and the hotel guards are friends, allowing Gustavo's girls discreet admittance onto the premises. Also, Gustavo has the best marijuana; he and long-time girlfriend bring it into La Ceiba themselves via lengthy bus ride, from some region famous for top quality weed. Every other week, they take this bus ride under pretense of visiting her cousin. On the trip back, Gustavo's girlfriend will have a pound taped high around her upper thigh. Reason bein'? the many military roadblock/checkpoints, where regularly, men are ordered off the bus and strip-searched. Women however, are, generally not publicly subjected to such sporadic systematic degradation.

"Uh yeah, hey man, Gustavo, right? Gotcha! I'll trust only you, okay? But my need is not for girls or *mota*."(Gustavo smiles at this acknowledged use of Mexican slang for marijuana.)

"What I need is painkillers, hhmm, or maybe *chieva* (heroin)"

Gustavo gives a strange look, asking, "Devon, what is painkillers and *chieva*?"

"Gustavo, pain pills! You know, for taking away pain?"

"Devon, you have pain?"

"Yes."

"Where?"

"In the head, Gustavo, in the head."

"Devon, perhaps you would like an aspirin?"

(Oh Jesus fuck!) "No Gustavo, I need real pain pills, very strong ones. Understand?"

"Aw, yes Devon, but for those, you need a doctor's permission slip." (Damn!) "This is no problem Devon. I have a doctor friend. Tomorrow

we will go see him. He will give you the required permission slip."
(Gosh, can't wait.) "As you see Devon, Gustavo is here for you. Yes?"

(Well, we will see tomorrow, now, won't we?) "Uh yes, Gustavo, you are the man!"

"Devon, what is this *chieva*?"

"It's heroin, Gustavo. Can you get any?"

Appearing quite surprised for such a request, no, this he can't do, though he does, however, profess having contacts for scorin' some very good *coca* (cocaine). Hhmm, tempting, but no. This cowboy needs opiates! And his pony is gettin' tuckered out.

I hold the door open for Gustavo to leave now. (He will receive his tip/*propina* tomorrow, after it's seen what his claimed doctor friend can do.)

"Devon, what is it you do for earning a living in the United States?"

Quickly, I tell him about owning Tattoo Blue. Gustavo thinks this is just great! He suggests perhaps I could help him acquire a US visa and work permit?

"Yes, possibly Gustavo. We will see."

Slowly closing the door on him, he asks "Devon, how long will you be staying here with us?"

"Not for long Gustavo, maybe only for tonight and tomorrow. After getting some pain pills, I'm going to the island of Utila. But from Utila, I will be returning back to here."

"Devon, this is good! Very good, you are goin' to Utila. Perhaps you will go to Roatan as well? Devon, you will like it there even better; plus I have a cousin that can—"

"Uhm, thank you, Gustavo! We will see each other tomorrow, in the morning? You will take me to meet your doctor friend, okay?"

"Yes Devon, okay. Bye bye!"

Following a shower, shave, and vigorous teeth brushin', the remainder of the night is spent lying in bed, tryin' to catch the evasive sleep mode, while suppressing thoughts depressing. It's a failed attempt, with sleep escaping.

In the new early mornin', it's a trip down for a little adjoining restaurante/cafeteria. I eat nothin', but do order coffee.

When the young cash register woman asks "Instant or brewed?" Sparky makes a funny face, mocking. Softly laughing, the young woman, game, pours hot rich brewed coffee. Upon receiving my decline for cream and sugar, she returns the silly funny face.

Sitting at a small window-side table, alone, sippin' wonderful strong black coffee, smokin' cigarettes, I watch the crowded street scene start its day; damn, these people sure are weird. Just like the Jamaicans and Mexicans, they grow some of the best coffees in the world, and yet, their populations mostly prefer instant coffee. Hhmm, wonder why? Man, I don't use instant coffee, even when out campin'.

As it turns out, Gustavo is exceedingly busy today, too busy for promised escort to doctor friend. And so, I'm on my own. Mission: find painkillers.

Here, city central is incredibly chaotic, reminiscent of areas similar to Kingston, Jamaica. The big difference here, though, is at every so-called modern store, selling large ticket items like jewelry, appliances, furniture, etc. (having price tags of fifty dollars and above), armed guards are standin' in and around the doorways. And these ain't no bored lookin' uniformed guards with old holstered revolvers. No, they are not! These guys look like goons, thugs, for-real bad-ass types. And most have that nervous, wild, red, swollen and runny eyed appearance, so common among those habitual with cocaine/crack consumption. It wouldn't be that bad, except these men are locked and loaded! Most have at-ready, pump shotguns, mini 14s, and AKs. All are wearin' standard military battle web-belts around their shabby t-shirts and blue jeans. Hangin' from their belts, are full ammo mag pouches; these guys ain't dickin' around, they are prepared for big time shoot outs! And the banks? Oh Skippy! The difference with them, is the banks (each and every one) has its very own squadron—all in black BDUs. The bank soldiers are (without question) pros, sportin' AR-15s or M-16s? (They're probably M-16s, 'cept fuck knows, 'cause there is no desire for gettin' so close as to determine the selective fire lever.) Now obviously, from lack of insignias on uniforms, these soldiers are not government, but private. And a vigilant eye they do keep on my (passing) presence.

Whoa Gustavo was right; around here, I stand out like a sore fuckin' thumb! Christ, even the street people and vendors are keepin' a distance and that's really odd.

On nearly every street corner, there is a *farmacia*, each pretty much the same, resembling old wooden general stores of a hundred years past, having a woman running it. What is up with this? Why women? All the pharmacists here seem to be women. I thought women in these parts didn't hold important positions. Guess it don't apply to the healing department, huh? The problem with women is they are like near impossible to bribe! And so, none will sell any opiate pain killers. "No! No, no, no, not without doctor's permission slip!"

Well, fuck me! Man, somewhere in this city, there must be a *farmacia* operated by a man! Problem is now, all these streets and city blocks are really lookin' alike. Time to backtrack, and take up new direction, this time though, really making the rounds—jotting down rough diagrams with pen and paper, mapping routes taken. It is amazing, and somewhat humorous, just how persistent a person becomes when workin' at scorin' his (or her) drugs.

Finally, down by the waterfront, a *farmacia* is found operated by a man. An elderly man he is, and though game, he cannot sell that which is sought, for he don't have any on the premises. No, none in stock. However, a few blocks away, there is a known *farmacia* owned and operated by a male doctor. The doctor/pharmacist will have there, certainly available, my, ahem, medication. Sparky! Now we are gettin' somewhere. Uh, 'cept the old man's directions for the place suck (or rather, my ability in *entendimiento* sucks). He acknowledges the confused struggle, and motions for a nearby young boy to come and lead the way.

Hey, this is a nice *farmacia*, quite modern, having glass store front. I hand the silent boy a twenty *lempira* note, and receive a delightful big smile. Inside, one is immediately hit with rushing cold from air conditioning. Good! This guy has himself some hefty overhead costs; he will know how to deal. There is an armed guard sitting in a chair… his appearance bein' that much tamer than those out on the streets. This guard is more like the ones back at the hotel, armed only with holstered revolver showing age.

From other side of waist high, floor length shop counter, there stands a lone female employee. Crap, she sure the fuck ain't needed. No, she is not! The doctor is, but Goddamn if this stern bitch has any intention of bringing him forth. Downright refusing she is, despite my repeated polite requests for his presence. Fortunately, without notice, the small boy (whom was thought gone) is at my side, brazenly barkin' Spanish (scolding) and demanding the woman fetch the doctor!

The smiling doctor turns out bein' a willing man of business. Oh yeah, he's sellin' the strongest pain medication in-house. The thing is, they're only codeine pills, and they are the size bigger than a pop top; thus for swallowing, they must first be dissolved in water (Alka-Seltzer style, 'cept *sans* fizz). The doctor assures they will indeed do the trick: "Much codeine in these."

Okey-dokey. "How many you got? Two hundred? Cool! How much—*cuanto es?*'

He begins the math, and in doin', I ask, "What about Valium?" Oh Skippy Joe, the doc's got Valium, and lots of 'em—two hundred 10 mg tabs—no problem. Hell, even if the horsey pills don't work, at least there will be Valium, and I do have a special fondness for Valium.

The doctor adds everything up with pencil and paper: he don't use the cash register, which indicates this sale won't be goin' on the books. Finally, he gives the total price in lempiras. It's a large sum; I try punchin' the numbers out on my pocket mini-calculator for determining exact cost in US dollars, but fail. The thing is too small, and a pain in the ass. Screw it!

"Tell you what doc, I'll give you one hundred dollars US for every-thing." After a moment's thought, he nods his head, smiling; it's a deal!

The grinning doctor quickly brings forth two boxes; these are how the pharmaceuticals come directly from the manufacturer. The tablets are individually sealed in long plastic bubble pack strands. One box codeine horse pills, and the other Valium. All very cool! The doc is happy; Sparky is happy; and so, this has been a notably good deal. We shake hands, with the doc giving his business card: which is greatly accepted, and kept, for traveling purposes, you know, with the pills and all? Golly Wally! We now have doctor's (sorta) permission slip, huh?

Stuffing the pharmaceutical boxes down into well-worn black shoulder bag that had been my book bag throughout college, then becoming a hunting game bag, presently bein' travel, go everywhere bag. This old bag, she seen a lot, that's for sure. Now bulgin', it's a fast haul back for the hotel, replenishing *agua* stock with two new, tall, plastic bottles, on the way.

Back inside my room, I pour half a glass of water, and drop in four big codeine tablets. They quickly dissolve—gulp—down the concoction goes. Yuck, the aftertaste is awful, and the kind that lingers, like all day (or night) long. Soon though, comes that warm codeine glow. The doc had not been lyin'. No, he had not! Feelin' pretty darn good, the rest of the evening is spent watchin' Spanish TV, while leisurely cutting open Valium bubble pack strands. The codeine pills stay kept in their sealed packs. Swallowing two Valiums, on this night, sleep does come.

Waking up early, refreshed, and feelin' great, it's a quickstep down for the front desk. No one is there yet; oh well, the restaurant is open. Rich black coffee is drunk, until the front desk girl arrives. Upon greeting, I ask (pay) her, to call, inquiring day's first hop-flight for Utila. Hhmm, two hours. Checking out, gearin' up, Gustavo ain't here yet... So, some money is placed with the front desk girl on promise, he will receive it.

A cab ride to the airport, board airbus, and with a hop, we have landed on Utila's short, dirt airstrip. The airport here is merely a weathered corrugated tin hanger shed, and rustic open-air concession stand. Waiting is a tractor pullin' a flatbed trailer (possibly a hay wagon.)

Exiting the small plane with some ten other people, the sky looks like rain. With everybody else hurriedly climbin' onto the hay wagon, this cowboy moseys on over to the concession stand. The tractor, hay wagon, and passengers drive off up the island's only road.

On request, the pretty young woman tending the concession stand gingerly hands over a disposable plastic cup. Grinning, she curiously watches, as I pour *agua* from a liter bottle (that now rides everywhere in my shoulder bag) into the cup, followed by four horse pills dissolving, then tossed back for swallowing. Eugh, the aftertaste is so bad that it's difficult keepin' the foul stuff down. Even their smell is bad! The pretty girl scrutinizes closely my funny face bein' made while workin' at seriously not pukin'. She suddenly bursts out laughin'! Down comes the rain. After regaining composure (and stomach), I laugh with her. We watch the rain, flirt, and sip the cold Cokes I buy for us.

The rain is short-lived, and my horse pills have kicked in. Up on the shoulders goes heavy backpack. "Uh, which way to the hotels?" She giggles, pointing towards the only road. The island is somethin' like two miles long, and not even a quarter wide. From the travel guide book, my chosen place for spendin' the night is at the other end of the island.

Utila is far from bein' your typical tropical paradise island; it's actually (except for one lone road, Main Street) only a low hump of marshy mangroves, harboring (seemingly) every hungry, hard bitin' insect in the world. Here, insect repellent/bug dope is indeed a necessity, twenty-four seven, even for us foul tasting people that can usually get by without. Garbage disposal is an evident continuous problem, as is human sewage, especially obvious at low tide. And like with most of the coastal regions, the recent hurricane has left its mark. There is some new development; however, it's only on a small scale. Everything else still retains that wonderful weather-worn, hundred-year-old flave. This whole dump of an island is very intriguing and picturing myself and family living here is not difficult.

My first night's stay is at the Ocean Side Inn. Despite its claim, the place is not oceanside. No, it is not! The inn should be called Road Side Inn. Upon revelation, the clouds let loose another drenching barrage. My shoulders are now really bitchin' to be free from the eighty-odd-pound backpack. (Boy-oh-boy, these shoulders of mine had better toughen up, 'cause they and this pack are gonna become very tight!) I decide to check into this (no oceanside) Ocean Side Inn, just for tonight.

The owners are Europeans, very nice, and seem genuinely surprised with my polite decline in joining them for tonight's fresh grilled fish supper. It does sound delicious, but really, since leaving that south Mexican four-star resort, the appetite has been *nil/desuet/perdido*, resulting in weight dropping fast, requiring belt needin' cinchin' tighter with each passing day.

Although missing out on the local tasty food samplings, I do enjoy not eating—the feeling of bein' lighter, faster, and more agile. Also, the look—no body fat—very cool; just lean sinewy muscle, how the human body was meant to be.

The rooms, for the most part, are constructed via two-by-fours and water damaged plywood, all painted a chalky white, having intricate wet stains, squashed bugs, and the sort. At least there is no human shit on the walls. Gosh, the budget backpackers compound/resort that I am gonna one day build, sure will be a lot nicer than this. Geez, it too is gonna be simple, rustic, and cheap, 'cept damn, there's no excuse for poor maintenance and filth like what is here at Ocean Side Inn.

The following mornin', pack goes up into place with heave: shoulders wince in moaning protest, as straps come down hard. Nevertheless, like a horse adjusting for cumbrous rider, calm ensues, accepting submission. The shoulders are indeed routing a toughening.

Today, unlike yesterday, the sky is clear, bright, and beautiful; and so, my march back down Main Street (only street) is not a march at all, but rather a leisurely stroll, absorbing the views. Also, I'm searching for a cool dive resort.

Now, since scuba diving is really the only reason most people come to Utila, there are many such places catering. The trick is which one. The want is seaside, on the ocean's shores, so, to hell with travel guide books. I start askin' the locals.

The other travelers on this island are, for the most part, budget-minded Europeans, who are quite clearly regarding my presence with much cautious suspicion. It's been a personal observation that European travelers, as a whole, are less loud, obnoxious, and rowdy than Americans; however, they are less friendly. Well, less friendly towards long-haired, tattooed American men anyways. They do seem always quite friendly (and eager) for makin' acquaintances with attractive American women; though really, who ain't?

Contrary, the locals are just plain downright some of the most friendliest people one could ever encounter. I talk with many, both young and old. Their warmth is admirable, as is their genuine dignity: the poverty is ever-present, yet there is no street begging or aggressive sales barking. Yes, these are indeed a proud people. And of course, they all have different opinions concerning which dive resort is best. Still, it's fun talkin' with 'em.

An old man, who asks that he be called Sheriff, for claimed official title holding, kindly invites me to come sit with him out on his simple wooden veranda overlooking the sea. Sipping fruit juice, sweet like thin syrup, we sit and talk—very little of each other, but rather mostly his *lancha* (boat) and the local fishing. Sheriff loves both. His boat is similar to the traditional, large dug-outs, in that it is long and narrow; however, like most boats I'm seein' around here, his *lancha* is made from plywood and fiberglass, modeled after the Mexican skiffs. Sheriff's is powered via small diesel. He explains on this island, diesel engines are preferred over gasoline outboards. Diesels, though slower, are—in saltwater—more reliable, require less maintenance, and are easier on fuel consumption.

When asked about the building of traditional hand carved Cayuco boats, the old man's expression goes sad, slowly shaking his head, explaining. Yes, long ago, Utila had been greatly known for building such sea-worthy, dug-out *lanchas*, but no more. Obviously, extremely large trees are essential. The island does not grow them, so, they must be floated over from the mainland. Clearly, this is costly, and no longer practical. Sheriff informs that for learning how such boats are built, I should search for simple country people in the Miskito region, inland, on remote rivers.

After a pause, his wrinkled face brings forth a wondrous grin, as he extends offer for us fishin' together, sometime soon, from his *lancha*. Sincerely grateful, shaking the kind old man's hand, while standin' to leave. Sheriff surprises by complimenting my visible tattoos. Seeing the shocked expression, he laughs, telling, "Aw Devon, here, we are islanders; we have seen many people from all over the world that come to visit us. We do not judge them by how they dress, or look; we judge them by the good inside. I see there is much good in you. I should know, I am Sheriff! Ha, ha! No one will bother you here Devon. Carry peace in your heart, and come back soon to visit me; we will go fishing!"

Wow, what a nice guy. Golly, all the islanders are nice, and both young and old seem genuinely impressed with my tattoos. Yep, these are some very cool people. And the police? Well, they too appear very laid-back, just mostly standin' around in their uniforms, having old holstered revolvers—no exposed serious weaponry here. There is much good-natured intermingling between police, street vendors, and shopkeepers. Occasionally, a policeman will shoo-off a bunch of kids that had been hangin' out for too long in front of a business, or somethin'; always though (from what little personally witnessed), this is followed by much laughter, including from the kids themselves.

A lone young man attracts my attention having weed for sale. After politely declining, ensuing casual conversation, I ask him if there is any heroin on the island? Of course, there is none. For the hell of it, "What about *coca* [cocaine]?"

The young man again shakes his head, answering, "No, only perhaps a very little; and it would be difficult to find. There is much in La Ceiba, and even Roatan. But here, most people only bring to Utila enough for themselves; not for selling. However, I will ask around and see what can be found. This is a small island; if any can be had, I will find you— okay?'

"Yeah sure. Okay, thanks." Geez, didn't really even want any cocaine; but hey, if it's cheap, why not? Besides, what harm could there be?

Along Main Street there are many waterfront/seaside dive resorts, each appearin' pretty much the same: low budget, basic, no frills, just serious scuba diving, and naturally, cheap PADI certification courses for which the island is noted. Everyone had forewarned that the charge rates for services from these places would be the same. There had been a recent price war amongst the dive resorts; rates dropped so low that none could turn a profit, and were actually losing money. The solution? A fixed price rate. Which made selecting one even more difficult. Finally after passing several, one instantly captures attention!

Like the others, this dive resort is down along the water. Unlike the others, this one has hammocks hangin' between palm trees. And in two of these hammocks, there are reclining semi-nude hot chicks! The place is called Aqua Vision. I sign on for a five-day open water PADI course, room accommodation included. Sparky never did learn if the hammock-lounging, topless beauties were for luring purposes; either way, they should have, 'cause you know it works!

My dive instructor is named Oliver; and, whatta ya know, he's American. Oliver is damn good-lookin', having golden tan, sun-bleached hair, and build similar to my own. You can bet ol' Oliver gets about all the pussy he wants on this here island. Lordy, under right circumstances, I'd suck his dick! He's also just an all-around nice guy; hhmm, Nancy would really like him.

Each instructor is assigned two novice greenhorns for teachin'. My fellow student just happens to be American as well! Coincidence much? Ught, we three are probably the only Americans on the island at present time (or so Oliver claims). My co-student actually lives in London with his English wife. We get along fine.

Just like with skydiving, scuba diving proves to be a bit disappointing. The small amount of classroom time required is (except for learning that underwater everything appears twenty-five percent larger, and sound travels four times faster) exceedingly boring. Thus, what little math (never a personal strong point) involved becomes unnecessarily difficult. My American dive buddy helps out here. We cheat on the exams—or rather, I do. And the actual diving? Well, breathin' underwater via forced air is nothin' new for this idiot. However, bein' sixty meters down and seeing is. Still, it's no big deal.

My eardrum fuckin' hates it! Skydiving, black water mussel diving, scuba diving, all puts serious intense pressure on the inner ear. At times, the pain is much like that of an imaginary ice pick bein' shoved through, right into the brain! Regardless, not ever wantin' to be a pussy, I stay the sport, and do try learning just what the hell everybody finds so fascinating with this here scuba divin'. Naw, nope, for Sparky, it ain't doin' much. Now maybe if we were hand feedin' sharks, or tearin' the shit outta the reef using heavy equipment in search of treasure! Oh Skippy, that might be a kick! But just to swim around down here, ooohin' and aaahin' at every fish or critter seen, or gettin' a boner from dropping over edge. Diving steep coral reef walls, interesting? Yes. Fascinating? A little (at first). Breathtaking? Hardly. Man, where are all the brilliant colors you see in photographs, books, and magazines? And where's the big fish? Gosh, bigger fish than these are caught from bait seines on the Mississippi River. And not even one shark (of any kind).

I much prefer snorkeling nude among warm, shallow, blue waters with hot sunshine beaming down from above, or bein' in a boat fishin', letting the imagination paint splendors of what might lie below.

The one good thing about this open water scuba course is we are usually finished each day by 10 A.M., leaving the rest of the day for doin' whatever. Always, I head 'er to the Old House Café. It is indeed simply an old house, having large front porch facing Main Street. The porch is set with weather-worn, small, round tables and straight back chairs. Inside the old house, in front room, there are more tables and chairs. A short ordering counter is on the right, and behind this, a standard kitchen from era long gone by. Back towards the front dining room and through, there is another room open to customers. This is a comfy area for loungin' about in greatly aged, overstuffed furniture. The walls surrounding are loaded with a shamble of bookshelves. A sign states "Read what you like. Trade what you got. Leave what you've brought."

I think it's a very cool gig. This Old House place is owned and operated by an attractive British couple having beautiful four-year-old son. They live upstairs, and are (seemingly) able to support themselves comfortably here with this business, only needin' to keep hours of 9 A.M.–2 P.M. Not bad, huh? The food they serve is fresh, simple, local staples, large in portions, at reasonable charge. Plus, this is the only place on the whole island that serves espresso coffee! This couple has it figured out! The thing is, is they are wanting to sell, yep, sell building and all; and only for $30,000 US. The reason, is their young son. They don't want the little guy growin' up here; plus, as a family unit, Third World living has become tiresome. Geez, wonder why?

Each mornin' after an exhilarating scuba dive (not), I sit out on the front porch of the Old House, gulp down four or five codeine horse pills, drink several double espressos, and smoke Camels. At some point during this ritual, a game must be played. The game is called "No fuckin' way am I gonna *puke* here!" It's a mean game my stomach enjoys. The stomach first recognizes the smell, and then the taste of the awful foul codeine water, and reacts with response for seriously pushin' to vomit it all up! ("All" bein' at this point nothin' but codeine, some water, espresso, cigarette resin, mucous, slime, whatever.) Now obviously, this is neither the time nor place for such a body function. Here I am, sitting surrounded by many other people, everyone enjoying their coffees, juices, and fresh breakfasts, not mentioning the morning's beauty, then outta the blue, some tattooed long-hair (me) ups and starts pukin' all over the place, followed by loud, gasping, eye bulgin', snot slingin' dry heaves! Get the picture? Embarrassment wouldn't even begin describin' such an act. Fortunately, I have had (due to a past involving many years having been a serious alcoholic) much experience playing this particular strange game between mind and body. The trick is relax, put out the damn nauseating cigarette, try breathin' a slow, deep (not too deep), steady rhythm. Oh, and always keep chin up, lookin' straight ahead (at nothin'), and when mouth does fill with gushing thick saliva; don't panic. Just keep 'er tightly clamped shut (mustn't drool), swallowing small amounts on timely exhales only; never on inhales, for if any air does by chance reach stomach—she'll *blow*!

Remember, with no hurry, diligent restraint, and controlled calm intake of fresh air, the need for barfing guts up will pass—thus the game. The real challenge, though, starts when the game is bein' played, and some person (or persons) sitting very near, tries engaging a conversation. Yepper, let the fun begin! Man, nothin' can be done 'cept smile, nod, and act like a deaf mute imbecile. Upon repelling stomach's assault— subduing resistance—relief is generally the feeling—whew! To celebrate such triumph, I order another double espresso, followed by lighting a Camel, followed by—Goddamn it! The game starts anew, with stomach rebelling on rebound! Oh, aren't addictions a fuckin' blast!

After the codeine has fully kicked in, with stomach settling (some-what) with espresso, I then take leave, walking to a spot on the other end of the island. The road greatly narrows, turning into deep rutted dirt. There are no beaches (not on the whole island); here though, at this one spot, there are flat concrete remains from some jutting pier, or somethin'. I come here for layin' out in the sun, and do so, stripping down—wearin' only a thong, or rather, G-string? Yes, it's for sure a G-string, and a tiny one at that. I had made the thing from one of my own designs, back when goin' through that whole sewing bit. This G-string is micro... having front that slides together, forming a pouch that just barely covers balls and top base of cock. Now, obviously to wear such a thing, it helps bein' thin, well hung, and smoothly shaven—no pubic hair. And if the shaved pubic region is golden tan, well, all the better, as this makes for sexy style both graceful and beautiful, complementing human form.

The next best thing, naturally, is total nudity—which is always tempting—but by not knowing local laws, and until seein' others as such, well, nudity (for a man) is best not pushed. Also, there is my big gold scrotum ring for considering; the less knowin' of it (reasons obvious) the better. Man, how I do personally get a kick wearin' these tiny G-stings. One, they are the next best thing to wearin' nothin'. Two, I find them very sexy on both men and women. (Those of my design for women are especially tiny, deliberately exposing sensuous outer labia curves, barely crowning clitoris hood.) Three, they evoke interesting conclusions from people, like the usual—since bein' a man, not wearin' standard, ever popular baggy swim shorts, hangin' below knees, makin' Sparky look (and feel) the stupid clown, add lack of visible pubic hair, exposing that indeed the entire genitalia region is shaved—assumption by most is that I am gay, consequently leaving only women and gay men comfortable placing their towels near mine. Uh-huh, most women are easeful laying close. Though they too, of course, believe I am gay, but in a tough-guy sorta way. They are not attracted to this *per se*, however do find security with the perceived assumption. Therefore, they have no aversion to bein' topless, wearin' only a thong (or pullin' bikini bottoms up between cheeks). Like myself, most women do like being nude as possible when sunning for the golden tan. What they do not appreciate is male gawkers, intruders, or whistling, catcalling assholes! Also, from these women, there is a sense of felt secure assurance that if by chance any harassment does befall them, this long-haired, G-string wearin', cock bulgin', tattooed scarred-up faggot will be there to intervene! Yes, he will! And occurrences of the likes have indeed, over the years, taken place. Yepper, sportin my tiny G-string can be quite interesting, you bet.

A peculiar thing about this sunning spot here on the island, is that I do have plenty of women sharing the concrete jetty, but no men—no men at all! This is very unusual, as I always attract gay men. Wonder where they are? Could it be there simply are no gay men on the island? How very strange. Hhmm, or is it? Let's see, dirty, little, bug infested Honduran island, havin' nothin' to do 'cept scuba dive and drink booze, damn, not real appealing draw for gay men, huh? Not like the nightlife is anything either. My second night on the island, I did go about exploring the local bar/club scene, yes, and the patrons were mostly Europeans— fuckin' cliquish bunch, they are. Keeping true to my long time sobriety (one can only drink just so many Coca-Colas, even with horsey pills), well, lonely and depressing the boring bars were. But hey, back in my drinkin' days—*wow*—Sparky woulda turned this sleepy little island, full o' sheepish Europeans, upside *down*! Hhmm, no wonder there aren't many (if any) gay men here.

However, after that night, I do find an alternative to the humdrum bars for nightly entertainment—fishin'! Yep, every evening, late into the night, fishin'.

There is a canal waterway cutting across through the island. Main Street passes over this swift-channel canal via old arched bridge. Below the intriguing bridge of stone is built concrete embankments. It is here, on these levied banks, that I and several others fish, the "others" bein' local islanders. They are men, usually the same faces every night.

Fishin' this is, though not the rod and reel fishin' with tackle box crammed plum full of gear that rarely gets used. No, but familiar with technique, I am all the same. It had been learnt, and used for catching salt water eels during my stays in Jamaica.

First, an empty can of mosquito repellent must be found. No shortage here, not on this island. Off cans work well because they are long and narrow. Next, monofilament line. After searching several stores and coming up (surprisingly) empty-handed, frustration sets in! Now, one would not think it difficult finding fishin' tackle on an island surrounded by water, would you? Uh, welcome to Utila! Goddamn, every store asked responded with the same expressed surprise for hearing request, "No, no not here. Try next store over." Finally, some nosey little boys catch on to my predicament, and offer assistance. These cute young midgets show the way to another very old (still standin') wooden general store type place. Uh-huh, this place has on the wall, behind cashier, up on top shelf, in corner, hidden from view, several spools containing cheap grade, fifty-pound test monofilament fishing line. Perfect! New hooks? "Oh no, not here. Sorry, no hooks, only de line."

Well slap my balls! (Personal aggravation must be apparent 'cause everyone is grinnin' ear to ear—some are even gigglin'.) Not to fret though, as my new, young, three-foot-tall friends eagerly lead the way for the only place on the island that sells fishin' hooks, and it ain't from no store. No, it's from an old weather-beaten man having warm eyes sparkling a fascinating jovial face, wrinkling numbers hundred times that equaling his years' antiquity. The old man carries himself a wicked limp, and does sell hooks (and only hooks) from the back of his home—bein' a large shack, half on land, and half (including deck porch colorful in character) out over water upon stilts. Attached, leading to back porch of spectacular ocean view, is narrow, rickety dock-walkway. Below, in the stinkin' mud, are caged fat pigs. They appear, at present, havin' themselves a very good time. However, we are now at low tide; damn, what do these critters do at high tide? Float? Hee, hee, hee! Man, I gotta come back here and photograph this; floating pigs, what a sight!

The old man graciously sells a box of hooks, and is all smiles wishing "Good fishing, my friend." Thanking him, and takin' leave, the young boys inform that I am (from what they know) the only tourist even to ask about buyin' hooks and line. Geez, this explains the sly grins from all the shopkeepers and such. The little boys then hurriedly set off in search for large lug nuts. You know, the kind from car and truck tires? In no time flat, the speedy guys are back, out a breath, but they got lug nuts! Also, each now has his very own empty Off can. Great! With them leadin' the way, we head 'er for the "best fishing spot" on the island. According to these little boys, the best fishin' is not the canal channel flowing under bridge across island. No, the best fishin' is, well, a secret spot known only by them. Yepper, so away we go! Around this shack and that, through dense foliage backyards, over rotting garbage trash heaps, onwards we weave an obstacle course of non-working, cast-a-side washin' machines, refrigerators, stoves, barrels, tires, parted-out cars, trucks, boats, your typical dump-junk, you name it. We walk atop decrepit sinking walkways, sucking at feet, while stepping over knurled, tentacled, tripping mangrove roots.

The boys' secret "Best fishing spot" turns out bein' a remote, lop-sided dock built from varied scrap lumber. Here, we huddle, squattin', makin' up our riggings. However, in doin', first a Camel is lit; and of course, each big-eyed midget wants one. (Eh, what the fuck. We are fishin', right? Little boys are allowed to smoke while fishin'. That's just part of bein' a boy and fishin'. Everybody knows this). Each one, now puffing away on a non-filtered Camel, is silently waiting—to watch how I make my rigging first. The little rascals are testin' to see if the funny long-haired, tattooed American knows what he's doin' or not. (Okey-dokey, watch this you little Hershey drops.) Quickly, a slipknot is pulled tight, followed by a bunch of monofilament line getting wound around empty Off can. Sufficient to my liking; out with a *snap* comes COLD STEEL folder cutting line, clippin'. Excited admiration encircles towards the blade, and it is requested anxiously to be held by all for closer marveling. Request denied. I then select the largest lug nut and tie it to the end of my line. A foot or so up, a loop knot is tied, and from this loop, a two-foot-long drop-line with hook. Perfect! The boys, however, disagree (little punks). They think my Off can has way too much line wrapped around, and they don't understand the loop-drop-line concept. No, in their strong opinion, the hook should be tied directly on-to main-line's end, with lug nut replacing loop knot. I am just about to argue defense for my riggin' bein' best, enabling greater sensitivity to feelin' any fish nibblin' on bait. Bait? "Shit! Hey man, guys, we forgot the bait!"

The boys laughin', quickly make up their own Off can fishing rigs; after which, for bait, small strips torn from plastic trash bags get knotted to hooks fluttering—essentially, simple lures. They begin jigging their artificial baits over the dock's side, workin' them around the submerged mangrove roots below.

Observing, I ask if they are tryin' to catch a small fish for bait (cut bait)? Chuckling, the answer is no. "Devon, it is the small ones most desirable. They be the sweetest for eatin'."

"Yeah sure, but not much fun in sport, huh? Plus, our plastic baits here, don't seem to be workin'."

"Aaaw Devon, this is due to the sea now bein' at low tide. Meet us back here this evening, before sunset. You will see then. Many fish we will catch, and perhaps you will catch a big one. Okay Devon?"

I promise a return meeting at this spot, later. (Honestly, there is no intention, for the little guys had become somewhat annoying: bummin' cigarettes left and right, askin' a hundred questions, continually bickering amongst themselves or showin' off, vying for my attentions etc., etc. Furthermore, their secret "Best fishing spot" don't appear bein' all that great—even pending a high tide). I gladly take leave, separating myself from them, and begin a search for purchasing fresh bait. A task, easier said than done. Yes, on this whole entire island, not one dead fish, squid, or shrimp can be had. No, not until this evening, when the fishermen return (in their slim long boats) with the day's catch.

The line of buyers waiting is long, and naturally, I am at the very end. All the fish get sold before my turn comes. Fortunately, an old man knowing, who had purchased himself a wheelbarrow load, wheels over.

Reaching in amongst the varied species, pulls forth one of the smaller, and gingerly offers it. The fish is a twelve-inch-long hard scaled, sharp forked tailed thing, having big eyes and a name I can't pronounce. The old man softly laughs at blundered attempts. He also laughs at my offer for payment. The old man puts the fish into my hand. While holding both with a firm grip, he declares the fish "but a simple gift. Cut it into small bits. The flesh is very sweet, and will catch for you many kinds of fish. Good fishing, young friend."

"Well thank you Sir!" Wow, these people are really somethin'.

Fishing the canal waterway channel that flows under the bridge crossing the island, I find a desired spot on the concrete embankment, further-most from bridge, and yet, still under dim pole, lighting way for guiding boats through. Here, narrow strips of flesh are cut from the given fish, and hook is baited accordingly. The lug nut (sinker), hook, and fresh bait, along with some line, get spun in tight circle above the head (much like swingin' a lasso rope). When fitting momentum and targeted objective has been obtained, fly baby, fly! The weight of attached lug nut rockets out over the dark water with line buzzin' from spooled Off can. My index finger determines the tension required for controlled cast. *Plop*! The lug nut splashes, hitting predetermined mark (well, close enough, anyways), and down she goes, with baited hook in tow. Down, down, down, damn, this canal waterway is deep! Now casting a hand-rig like this is fairly simple; the challenging part is setting the hook! See, your arm must take the place of what is typically (back home, in the States), a standard flexible graphite fishing rod. Using the arm in place of the fishin' rod is not nearly easy as what some might think. No, it is not! But man, like with trot lines, you sure can feel things good down there, every little bump and nibble.

Earlier in the week, I tried faxing and e-mailing my wife, from one of those computer/fax places. (Computer café?) And of course, for reasons unknown, neither fax or e-mail would go through. Hhmm, okay—let's try instead e-mailing an old lover/friend. A woman she is, and years ago, we did have ourselves a truly fiery, torrid affair while in Jamaica, where she lived at the time. This special friend is German, gorgeous, nine years older, and I fell madly in love with her. A love and passion still carried deeply in my heart. The elegant woman now lives on the Spanish island of Mallorca. We have not seen each other for over twelve years, but do correspond regularly. My e-mail to her, surprisingly, does get out; where within, amidst the usual lovey-dovey mush, information is given of present location, and sudden decision for goin' onwards to Cuba. My special friend, as asked, relays, from her own computer, travel route update to Nancy.

The very next day, word comes from Nancy (via computer café place); it's short, sweet, and depressing. "Devin, all is well here. The boys are fine. Be careful, take your time, enjoy yourself."

Damn, not one word in there about missin' me. Fuck, basically, it is "See ya when I see ya" sorta thing. Cold bitch! Regret now for even having reached out.

Cuba? Yeah, Cuba. This was decided while sittin' at the Old House Café, and often overhearing excited conversations about how cheap flights are from Honduras to Cuba. My interest is indeed captured, despite bein' an American citizen and therefore under obligation—patriotic duty—not to enter Cuba, for it is frowned upon, and theoretically forbidden, having ominous threats of repercussion through prosecution (which no one takes seriously). Cuba, on the other hand, was welcoming us (Americans) as tourists, for acquiring US dollars only. And why not? They needed money, real money. So be it. Besides, dead or alive, Che Guevara is still Che Guevara! And ol' Fidel Castro? Ha-ha! What a ballsy character. Yep, let's go have us a look-see.

My open water dive course is now over, and yes, Sparky is a certified diver. Eh, big deal. Well, at least I've done it, though not without cost. The price? One hellacious mean ass ear and sinus infection. The ear is constantly attempting to drain itself, discharging a rotting, putrid smelling liquid, adding a Goddamn loud popping and gurgling, followed by sensation similar to imagined small worm crawlin' about, all deep inside inner ear! And the nose? Uh, one minute the flarin' thing is clogged up good, and the next, it's runnin' like a pissin' race horse just lettin' loose, without warning—*splish*! From the nose, snot, mucus, whatever gushes out and down, across lips, over chin, and off— drippity, drip, drip! A real charmer indeed, talkin' with somebody, and right then and there, out of the blue, Mr. Nose decides to let 'er go with the flow! Whew, good thing my kit includes several red cloth oil rags used for hankies (snot-rags, and whatnot). I go nowhere without one right handy; usually tucked in, and hangin' out from khaki shorts waistband. This, combined with ever-present bandana rolled and tied about forehead or neck, pretty much completes overall image of who-the-fuck-knows!

Tonight is the last night to be fishin' here on Utila. This island will be missed. Geez, if nothin' better is found during my travels, I am most definitely gonna be comin' back here. Hell, who knows, maybe even consider buying the Old House Café, or some waterfront property. My desired backpacker retreat/compound resort would work quite well here, even without a beach. A sturdy pier, havin' large deck built out over the ocean, would take place of a fine sand beach. From this, people could swim and lounge about in a strong warming sun. And no reason why a sleeping hammock shelter couldn't be built alongside, it too bein' out over the ocean's waters. Fuckin'-A! All very cool, huh? Yes, it could be! But where the money will come for such, who knows; one step at a time.

Standin' here in the warm night, I fish, deep in thought, listening to the night sounds surrounding, and hearing those from the street, houses, bars, and clubs. Though neither close nor far, their oh-so varied sounds travel, reverberating off calm shimmering dark waters and everything within, on, and around. Occasionally, small boats will cruise by, some havin' running lights on, others will not. My envy goes out to them, followed with a wave, saluting their passing presence, and what lay ahead.

The spool-wrapped Off can stays in right hand, as left, workin' with attached arm at-ready, acts the fishin' rod. A mental lightless, laser-beam-like telepathy radar is constantly transmitted through monofilament line, down, down, down deep to the baited hook dancing along bottom, by rhythm forced current (or so is fancied, played, pretended, forming sporadic glimpses, hinting a rare gift we humans have yet to evolve). Shish, I feel ya, little rascal. Come on, you can do better than that. Stop nibbling and just gulp the nice sweet bait—and run! Setting the hook, another lively fish is added to my catch.

This waterway attracts local fishermen nightly. And fished it is from both sides, end to end, while still remaining uncrowded. The dim pole lighting enables us all to see and watch the others. The canal itself, is not so wide for preventing one from recognizing another fishing across. Most faces have become familiar, and greetings are exchanged on arrivals of the regulars here. My name, "Devon," is already known; and address accordingly, they do, with a gentle respect, earned from bein' a tourist and fishin' down here, along the water, with them, rather than drinkin' up there, in the bars. Plus, my catches are always equal, if not more so, than those of these fellow fishermen.

The fish we catch most often are of two different species, yet not so different where it matters much. Both fish grow to size equaling a man's hand only. And like with so many "sweet fish" (pan fish), what they lack in size, they make up for in flavorful tastiness (or so is always confirmed by those loyal to the pursuit). The other night, however, I did hook into somethin' a bit different. Got the ol' adrenalin goin' this one did for sure; a big boy he was. With hook set, he threw his weight into it, cruising along the deep bottom, refusing to surface, thus the "play" began, or rather, for him, "run for life." And just such, the big fish gave marvelous resistance, power thrusting, what surely must be a massive tail, to push stubborn unyielding head in imitation of spirited horse, rebelling against forced bit and rein, for direction not wanting. Monofilament line burned between fingers humming abuzz, tight with gleeful strain, while like a big Mississippi River catfish zigzaggin' to and fro, cutting water, leaving wake, then... shit! *Slack*. Mr. Big Fish has turned, altering tactics, for charging! Slack must be taken up, and Skippy, it is! Hand over hand, limp line is brought in, keeping speed with big fish. Rising from bottom he comes, but break surface he does not! As all fish do throughout the world when in similar predicament, while not yet exhausted, he turns on impulse, diving steadfast for the bottom, slamming full weight and force into the detestable hook and line that has so deceived. Again and again, this tactical maneuver for freedom is fiercely applied, for what else is a big fish to do? The struggle does not go unnoticed. No it does not. Every fisherman (on both sides of the canal) stopped, watched, and saw. Yep, for twenty minutes or so, then... *whammy*! Jesus fuck, the line is weightless—big boy is gone; he won his freedom, earning it with one helluva good fight! As frustrating as this can be, one should never be too disappointed in losing to such an admirable opponent. But Goddamn! From the other fishermen, sympathetic words are mumbled. Winding up the fishless line, coming to the hook, or what's left. He broke it! Well spank my ass and call me Judy! Good goin', Mr. Big Fish, and may you break many more.

The light of mornin' comes... my backpack is heaved and shoulders thrown into. Geared-up, a brisk march to the little dirt runway airstrip, catching airbus (hop flight) for La Ceiba, then on to San Pedro Sula... ensuing long layovers, and eventual flight for Cuba.

A rriving late in the night, nothing much at Cuban customs goes well. Right off the bat, I am singled out, pulled aside, separated from the other arriving passengers, who obviously are together as some sorta small traveling tour group. A giggling lot, all Europeans excited to be entering wonderful Cuba, and treated with welcome accordance they are. But oh Skippy, not me. Nope, no-sirree-bob! Guards and officials, wearin' dorky lookin', ill-fitting brown uniforms, take serious charge actin' the bad ass role. They lead way over to a long, lone, narrow table. Orders are barked—lay out all possessions for a searching inspection. Naturally, in complete compliance, everything is unloaded onto the table, opened up, and spread out nice and neat, for the convenience of aiding (and speeding) their dutiful job of rummaging through all my stuff. Meticulous (seemingly greedy) little fingers do just this. My glance turns to watch the small tour group pass through custom booths, gettin' passports joyfully stamped. No problem, no delay, and gone they soon are. It's now just Sparky and the Cuban airport authorities. My passport is bein' passed from one scrutinizing official to the next.

Of course, profiling single men traveling alone, lookin' as myself, is to be expected at airports, including Miami airport, where I have been, each and every time, pulled aside while coming in from Jamaica, and made subject for search (even once stripped searched in a private room). Here, though, we seem to be havin' a wee-bit difference in attitude. American officials treat fellow Americans not quite the same as Cuban officials treat Americans. Tactics are similar; however, demeanor for execution differs greatly. A Cuban security team of six (one individual bein' a large ugly woman, for-real lookin' just like somethin' from a movie portraying some beefed up commie bitch living in her uniform twenty-four seven, throwin' shot-put for sport) stand positions surrounding, and are tryin' to somewhat intimidate, while interrogate. A couple barks—remove this, open that, etc., etc.—while at the same time, others ask questions, barraging. To which, answers they do receive, in simple, civil, and polite form. Still, inner thoughts chime a different tune.

"You! You are American citizen?"

"Yes Sir!" (Fuckin' ass-wipe greaser. Can't you read the Goddamn passport?)

"Your name? Where are you coming from? Why were you there? How long were you there? Where did you stay? Where did you go while there? Remove your vest, and all contents, now!" Exaggerating murmurings, disapproving wonderment, loathing scoffs towards my tattoos (weird). "Remove your shoes and socks. Why are you wanting to enter Cuba? Now remove your shorts."

"Uh, okay, but fair warning, I don't wear any underwear; and that is a lady there holding my passport right?" Undoing my belt buckle, holdin' it open, "Also, there ain't no hair down there, it's all shaved off; and I got a big ring pierced through my balls." (Hee, hee!)

As if flabbergasted, each is lookin' to the other, questioning, what now? A whammy had just been thrown into their whole bad ass routine. The big gal in uniform holding my passport is wide-eyed, flushed, and keeps glancin' about, perspiring profusely.

My shorts ride so big that now with the belt undone, all that need happen is for right fingers to let go, and these puppies will drop for ankles, they will! (Yes, I am gettin' a genuine kick from this.) Ooops! Shorts slip, stoppin' right at bare base of cock. And what follows is funny as all get-up! Yellin' there is, commands, with much hand and arm waving! "No, no! You, you, pull them up. Up! Do the buckle, buckle now! You, you, do not do that again. Keep your shorts on!"

Loud high speed Spanish is immediately spoken amongst themselves with much animated exaggerated jaw flappin', head noddin', hand waving and looks of exacerbated disgust (how very strange).

Stern orders are shouted, "Okay, you, you, now pack everything back up!"

(Uh, okey-dokey Mr. euw, euw, Cuban man.) Fuck, repackin' everything ain't as easy a task as what one might think (or what ought-a perhaps be). My travel mode to regions intended, required much stuff. Obviously, for such kit to ride on my person, it required bein' rolled, folded, tucked, and, well, damn organized. The bullying airport security become bored during the process, and so disperse, leaving behind two (one bein' the big sweaty gal) for overseein' my repacking.

Upon completion, turning, two men and a woman stroll from across the room. Their strides are that having much arrogance and authority. The woman (like big ugly gal) is in what must be standard issue brown uniform. Unlike the big gal, she is of petite frame, tryin' hard to appear menacing. (Christ, small women actin' tough; you never know whether to laugh, or entertain amusing mental picture—throwin' 'em across the knee for a good bare bottom spankin'!) The two men with her are not in uniform, but rather outdated civilian office attire cut from a style, two decades old. The three stop short, and give pretentious glares presenting intimidation. *Chica mujer* can-o-whoop ass (without lookin') holds palm out flat, for big ugly gal to hand over my passport. Still sweating, the big gal complies, though not without noticeable resentment towards the smaller. (Whoa, big gal looks anguished, as if retaining some serious gas, needin' release, 'cept not daring.)

One of the civilian dressed men breaks the uncomfortable silence by sharply barkin' orders, "Unpack everything—yes, again, including the vest, and all contents."

(Well, fuck me! We get to play the game all over again.) "Uh, gee, okay, and the shorts? Y'all want me to drop them too?" Golly, guess not. A bit snarly, this bunch is. Of course, once every little thing is unpacked (again), laid out, spread before them, they don't bother searching; no, because the Goddamn commie assholes know a search has already been done! They are just doin' this to push my fuckin' cock suckin' buttons! (Man, just calm down; don't lose temper, not here, not with these guys. You know how it's going to be played.) *Chica* bitch, holdin' my passport, starts the questioning, using sharp, girly tones. "Your name is Devon L. Murfon? Correct?"

"Yep, yes Ma'am, 'cept it's Devin, not Devon. And the last name is Murfin, not Murfon."

The man nearest quickly demands (over dramatically), "Why do you wish to enter Cuba?"

(Uh, hhmm.) "I am a tourist backpacker, wanting to travel the famous route of Che Guevara. It's sorta been a life-long dream of mine." (Yepper, you bet. Viva ol' Che! Hee, hee!)

The other man, not to be out done in theatrics, fires "And is the United States aware of your attempts to enter Cuba?"

"Uh, no, no sir. Don't think my country really approves of such visits, you know?"

And so Ricky Ricardo with Comarade and Lucy Chiquita continue the silly annoying questioning. Each take turns, snappin' out questions (almost before answers can even be given). Where in the US do I live? What state? City? My occupation? Past criminal record? Parents' names? Grandparents' names? Married? Wife's name? Maiden name? Children? How many? Sons… ages… names… etc., etc.

During the provoking badgering, one or the other will, of course, order pull this, or that, from spread-out kit, open or unfold, on pretense for closer inspection, save really, this is just routine interrogation 101. A simple tactic to distract, break train of thought for those not fully rehearsed in possible, shall we say, storytelling? Likewise with the questions themselves, answers are demanded over and over, 'cept in sequence always different from the last. Predictable it all is. Still, agitating this has become; plus, they won't allow smokin'. Finally, the questions stop, and we are back to the silent bad ass glaring/staring. They are watchin' for any nervous body language, perhaps revealing. What they get, is my best dumbfounded ignoramus look. Then it comes: "Do you work for the CIA?" Dumbfounded is no longer an act: first mouth drops, then outright laughter! Pointing to tattoos and swishin' long ponytail, "Man, do I look like someone who works for the CIA?" This convinces—game over. I'm told to repack, and enjoy my stay in Cuba.

Big gal (still appearin' very much like she's paining from inner flatulent gas) now has my passport again, and she, with passport, are behind a booth that has been open for my passing. All other custom booths and counters have been long closed. Hell, this whole section of the airport is (except for guards, security, and whatnot officials etc.) like shut down. Obviously, they are expecting no more arrivals on this night. Grimacing, (Helga) big gal was supposed to stamp the passport and return it. But nooo! More problems there are.

Up 'til now, the plan had been pretty much have no plan (concerning my travels here in Cuba). You know, sorta just wing it? Get through customs, catch a cab, go to a cheap hotel, somethin' popular with backpackers and the sort. In the mornin', buy a map, visit the Revolution Museum, and then bus 'er around the coast. Really, I could give two shits about the interior of this Cuba. It's the small coastal towns and beaches that have my interest.

However, this plan turns out bein' a plan ol' Cuba officials don't like, and won't allow. No, not without first meeting the required mandatory three day/night stay here in Havana, that all visitors need first endure. Thus, before getting passport stamped, proof must first be obliged by providing customs with name of a Havana hotel having reservations for registration showing (at least) a three day/night occupancy.

Hey, is this some commie bullshit, or what? Quite loudly, my protest is expressed, along with an outright refusal. Of course, such behavior from an American entering Cuba is probably not a real bright move. Again, security is surrounding. Walkie-talkies are squelching over excited Spanish and English.

Pushing herself through the angry huff of conferring huddle comes a bleached blond, middle-aged woman, wearing too much poorly applied make-up around big, fake, chipper smile. She is holding a clipboard, and speaks English like an American, having southern east coast accent. (Hhmm, spend much time in south Florida, lady?) The woman, blabbering—blab, blab, blab—latching arms, ushers us out from growing cluster fuck hubbub. Two guards follow, persistently jabbing my ribs. Demanding questions concerning current problem, the woman insists I ignore them, for instead hearing her overzealous pitch, abiding Cuba's policy, requiring all visitors a mandatory three day/night stay in Havana. "It is no big deal." she claims, while herself personally owning several hotels here in the city, one bein' quite affordable, center city, and popular with traveling backpacker types...

However, the two guards... Goddamn it, if you little Beaners poke me one more time. *Poke!* "Sons o' bitches!" Spinnin', with fists clinched, "What? What the fuck do you want? I am not C-I-fuckin'-A! And I'm not carrying any contraband!" (This is true. My machete and COLD STEEL folder was not considered illegal; and hell, even all the packed Valium and codeine horse pills, they had thought nothing of, after seein' the doctor/pharmacist business card with signature.) 'So leave me the fuck alone! Please, at least until the lady is done speakin'!"

Both guards, take a quick, defensive jump backwards, pointing to my shoulder bag.

"Yeah, so... What about it?"

Grinnin' like turd eatin' rats, "We must search the cameras."

"What? Man, everything has already been searched twice!"

"No, not camera, *cavidad!*"

"*Cavidad?* Cavity? You want to search the inside of my cameras?" Lookin' to the bleach blond, hotel owning, clown face woman. She's motor-mouthing, "Yes, yes, correct. It's standard procedure. Hand them your cameras; they will search them, and then leave us alone. Now back to what I was saying about my hotel for you..."

Oh fuck me! Reluctantly, both cameras are pulled from shoulder bag and handed over. The outcome is predictable—and they are Nikon cameras! Ignoring the hotel lady's incessant babblings, I grind teeth, watching the two monkeys' fumbled attempts for removing the lenses from expensive cameras. Of course they won't allow my assistance. No, they will not! Both cameras are handled with intentional roughness, point bein' obvious that they will not survive ordeal without damage. One though, I do manage to save, by physically seizing. The other don't fare as well. No, it does not! The poor thing is handed back with pieces from broken lens mount dropping. My blood is boilin' mad, pushin' muscles twitchin' for action! The inner growing rage is clashin' against small (very small) section of cornered brain that prides itself on bein' the logical, now screamin' for restraint. Warning, ambuscade, set up in provocation. American tourist attacks Cuban airport security! (Jesus, look at 'em—logic is right. They are all just waitin', watchin', and ready. Even yackety-yak lady, her eyes are wide, and mouth is open, having lost voice). Uh, okay, how to recover from this while still retaining some dignity? Hhmm, hee, hee! Smile, calmly put away broken camera, and coolly light a Camel.

Inhalin' deeply, oh boy, that hits the spot—what the fuck! Goddamn if another greasy haired guard don't come a-runnin', yellin', "You! You go back to where you came from! We do not want you here!"

Throwin' my hands up, "Fine! When's the next fuckin' flight back to Honduras?"

The hotel lady again quickly takes hold of my arm. Motioning for the guards to stay back, she steps us a few feet, and, in doin', explains there won't be anymore flights out until morning. Yes, I'd have to spend the night sitting here in the airport. But why? When she has at this very moment, a nice hotel room waiting. "What do you have to lose? After all, it's only for three days and nights. Why come all this way, only to turn around, leaving, having not even seen the many splendors of Cuba?"

"Okay, okay! Does the room have a shower? Alright."

The smiling hotel lady hands over her clipboard, informing the special price is only fifty dollars US per night, which must be paid in full before my passport will be stamped and given back. (Christ, Sparky shoulda stayed in Honduras. Everything here is gonna be in US dollars; and not cheap.) I sign, pay, and get ol' Helga to stamp the passport. They certainly had their fun with this American for the evening. Fuckin' pricks!)

Yackety-yak has a car, and drives us to her downtown hotel. Gosh, Communism sure seems to be doin' right by this woman. Geez, here she is, living in Cuba, personally owning several hotels, and this car? Well, it ain't no classic jalopy, that's for sure. This puppy is a full size, brand spankin' new, American made car. Hhmm, wonder how she got it over here?

The hour is late and, 'cept for lights streamin' from windows and the likes, very dark. The city appears bein' in some blackout state. But then remembrance comes from somethin' read about how Cuba don't use public streetlights and such, not even in Havana. Damn, what an eerie lookin' place (at night, anyways). Man, the moment ol' Helga stamped the passport, it was regretted. I shoulda just sat down right in the airport chair, waitin' 'til mornin', and caught the first available flight out to anywhere! Oh well, the decision has been made, so make the most of it. Dummy!

Clown Face steers the big new car, pulling up in front of her hotel. She don't bother gettin' out. Nope, "Bye bye", away her and car do go! The street is dark, narrow, and definitely has that Third World inner city feel about. The only light is glowin' from the hotel's large, glass front, revealing street activity, mostly in silhouette form, exposing people leisurely strolling, lingering, hangin' about, seemingly doin' nothin'. Shadow-like, they do appear.

The hotel front desk man is a big guy (Mandingo black), whose name is one difficult in pronouncing, and therefore in retaining. Nice enough he seems to be, pointin' out the hotel's small cafeteria—now closed. However, the building does have an open-air roof top bar and lounge, keepin' hours all night long. "A good place, with reasonable prices, nice for entertaining ladies." Also, he informs his house rule, bein' that if by want I do decide bringing a lady back to the room, he must be paid ten dollars, on the side, for each visit.

"The way to the roof top, is out the front, next door over." (Okey-dokey buck.) To my room we go, up one flight, first door on the left. The room is of low budget standards. Though not bad, it sure ain't worth fifty US dollars. Buck (or whatever the fuck his name is) points out the small open toilet and shower (open except for cheap, plastic privacy curtain). Also, there is the now classic dial-a-number black telephone, sitting on top an old short narrow wall mount desk, havin' two straight back chairs; all parallel with bed, making for some cramped close quarters. "Devon, the phone is for in-house calls only. For calls going out, you must come down to the front desk. Okay? And Devon, let me know when you need anything—pot, coke, girls, anything— okay?"

"Uh, how about heroin?"

Shaking his head, "No Devon, heroin will be very difficult to find here in Cuba. But there is plenty of very good cocaine. It is everywhere, seriously, Devon."

With Buck gone, and the door closed, I remove steel twenty-inch MAGLITE flashlight and pull standard room search of every nook and cranny—not bad, no surprises. Then the floor-pacing starts. Damn, that whole scene at the airport had really got my ol' blood level a pumpin'. The smart thing to do would be to swallow a few Valium and go nighty-night. But nooo, for whatever reason, the codeine is chosen over Valium. Plop-plop, no fizz, *gulp*, down the throat they go! Eugh-yuck. Time for a smoke. Ught-o, last cigarette from last pack. Must go out and buy some more; just guessin', American brands won't be had here in Cuba. And Camel non-filters? Forget it! Can't find those puppies, not even in south Mexico. Hhmm, wonder what Cuban cigarettes taste like? Well, let's go find out! Down the stairs, noddin' a passing acknowledgment towards front desk Buck (or whatever the fuck). On the sidewalk, next door over, steep dark steps goin' up, up, up; music from simple sound system grows louder *en avant, arriver*. The roof top is a dimly lit, open-air, tiki-type bar, presently slow with business.

The bartender is a friendly enough sort; we both laugh at my silly request for Camel non-filters. He tosses over two packs of what (in his opinion) is the next best thing. The cigarettes are filtered, having been packaged to appear almost identical to Marlboro (Marlboro Reds). Oh well, filters are for snappin'. "Uh, and Coca-Cola?" Ha ha! More laughter! A cola can, very much resembling the trade mark design Coca-Cola, is opened and slid across the bar. Damn, for a communist, American-hating country, imitation sure seems the makings for its products. This Coca-Cola wannabe, might look like the real thing, but it's not. Nope, tastes cheap, sweet, and strong with aluminum. Don't matter though; in two swallows the cola is drained. Geez, thirsty much?

Back on the street (or rather, sidewalk), just off the side (in shadows) of hotel's lit glass front, I lean up against a wall and open my new brand of cigarettes. Snap! Filter thumbs to fly. Turning cig around, lighting end where filter was, deep inhale, firing tip. Eh, not bad—better than most Mexican cigarettes, that's for sure.

Being out here alone, on this dark sidewalk at such an hour, doin' nothin' 'cept smokin' and standing around, must seem very much to present the impression (understandably) of a man in want for somethin'. You know? Action, drugs, girls, boys—boys? Lordy, does Cuba even have a gay scene? Hhmm, I think such things got outlawed after the revolution. Aaaw, don't matter, 'cause my hangin' out here is only for fresh air, and curiosity—watchin' the stealthy movements of white-eyed shadows fleeting about—or so one half of the brain tells the other. The other half, however, knows different, and ain't buyin'.

Obviously, the feelings are anything but positive in coming here (Cuba). Also, gosh, traveling solo can be a, um, lonely business. And Bubba, lonely this cowboy has become. Honestly, some company might be nice, 'cept... As expected, whimsical shadows do approach for revealing passing acquaintances. Greetings are exchanged in usual fashion, fitting such circumstances. After which, young men ask to sell pot, and/or cocaine. The women offer services—themselves, their bodies—and enticing some are indeed! Especially one, having exquisite beauty, yet still unlearnt in the ways for using it to full advantage (no one likes a pushy sales pitch, does not matter the product). Taking the polite rejection as insult, she moves on.

Exhaling, flicking out the de-filtered, fast burning cheap grade Cuban tobacco cigarette, and thinkin' it time for goin' on back up to my room… *swish*! (What the fuck?) From seemingly nowhere, a rush of warm air is felt, ensuing presence of a fairly attractive young black woman. She leans herself against the same wall, so close as having arm and shoulder lightly touchin' mine. No pick up line, just silent playful nudge, and sensual giggle. She feels warm, having scent perfumed with only herself—fresh clean earthy musk—very womanly, thus seductive and captivating. Without speakin' a word, we (for quite some time) just stand there, pressed against each other. This is a game of course, which I do find charming. Lookin' down to red Converse high-tops, the young, frolicsome woman shoulders a bump, almost causing my feet to trip themselves. Gentle laughter and our eyes meet, finding gleaming magnetic sparkle. Holding her chin high, she knows I'm soaking in the presented dignified stature. Politely, the temptress asks for a cigarette.

Inhaling freshly lit, stale cigarettes, we introduce ourselves; her name is Carla. "Devon, you are American? Why do you come here, to Cuba?"

(Hhmm) "Uh, Carla, you see, I am a freelance photo journalist. Yes, really. (Uh-huh.) My work goes to a magazine called *Bizarre, Bizarre*."

(Yeah yeah, a little lie; big deal. What can it hurt? Besides, this just might be fun. My guise is believable enough; with several people having already asked on assumption. You know—the vest, cameras, appearance? Hell, who knows, but fuck, it's gotta be more interesting and informative than traveling about as simply a backpacking tourist, or private soldier, like the kid had thought back at San Pedro Sula's bus station. Yepper, from now 'til reachin' orphanage Casa del Corazone, I'm gonna be a photo journalist. Sure, you bet—and why not?).

"Carla, my assignment is to travel Central America, and Cuba, documenting as much as possible through the eyes of a touring back-packer, a mode quite popular with young people…" Blah, blah, blah…

Listening with interest, Carla comments how having such a job must be nice. She then, lookin' about with noticeable alertness, strongly suggests we should be moving along, "Devon, here in Cuba, it is not wise to be standin' on the street for long. Perhaps we can go to your room? Do you desire any pot, or coke? If so, Devon, this is no problem." Room? Coke? Carla? Hhmm, well, it would certainly shake up these hollow, lonely blues so persistent for osmotic filtration. I confess that a gram of coke and some company might indeed be nice. Nodding understanding, we agree to meet in my room. First though, I must give her twenty dollars and five minutes for fetching the *grama*.

Having doubts, surprisingly, within five minutes, there is a knock at my door! 'Cept it ain't Carla. No, it's Buck (or whatever the fuck). "Devon, Carla is downstairs, but before I send her up, you must first pay me ten dollars—remember?"

"Yes, I remember."

"Thank you Devon. Devon, Carla is a good choice. She has a great ass, is very clean, and can fuck all night long. You will enjoy her."

Carla and I sit side by side at the little wall mounted desk. Opening the small, string tied, clear, plastic containing *coca grama*, emptying contents out onto compact travel mirror, it's noticed that besides bein' a bit short of an actual gram, this stuff is texture and color unlike any Sparky's ever seen. (In the late eighties you see, after discharge from the army, and havin' myself one helluva good time in Jamaica, I briefly, back in the States, got into the cocaine sellin' business. My partner and I, unlike most that sold, never did really personally enjoy consuming the drug much; still, we sure did like the money and girls that came along with the selling. So, we sold our share. Rarely would we sell anything under an ounce at a time; and on what occasions we did, it was an eight-ball weight. Never gram this, gram that. We weren't big time, and we weren't small time, we were just middle dumb time. So, even though cocaine was far from bein' my drug of choice, I do know a thing or two about it, such as selling, weighing, cutting, etc.)

The coke Carla has brought is light yellow, and almost flakey damp. The mini-rocks are more like soft clumps, bein' all too easily broken down (chopped) via edge of ATM card.

Glancing over to Carla, who is now lightly rubbing my thigh, she sees the questionable look, and softly assures, "Do not worry Devon, the *coca* is very fresh; you will be pleased." (Hhmm.) Man, what the hell did they cut this shit with to give such color and texture? Eh, my head hurts. Despite the horse pills, a headache (*me tengo dolor de cabeza*) has been dancin' all day, and now into the night; also, the ol' stomach ulcers have (naturally) for last several days been making themselves known (though not too bad). From dip of finger, tongue tip immediately goes numb. This means nothing, as the coke could easily have been cut with powder-based prilocaine or the equivalent. That's what we always used. Yeah okay, but the yellowish color? Who knows. Oh-hoh! Saliva rushes forth, as does the distinct flave, distinguishing cocaine, and Skippy, she ain't shy! No, she is not! My curiosity concerning the strange color and texture becomes less and less, as the whole *grama* gets quickly chopped, laid out, and plowed into big fat flakey lines.

Carla, watching, comments with a grin and inquisitive eyes, "Devon, you do lines that big?"

Smiling, "Yes Ma'am."

However, first turning from her and the cocaine, I bring forth a red hanky, and strongly blow out all possible snot and mucus. Blushing, I apologize to Carla, and explain how scuba diving had screwed up my ears and nose (sinuses). Her right elbow is now propped on small desktop with weight of head resting in palm. She is looking very relaxed, having big, long, lazy lashes, adorning understanding eyes. Carla's sensuous smile never leaves her attractive face; and the soft hand continues its warm rubbing caress, as if assuring, yes, it is all okay.

With that, I roll a dollar bill, lean forward, and sssnnort! One flakey long fatty disappears up the ol' left nostril. Tapping the rolled bill on spot where fat line had just been, but ain't no more, head tilts back, eyes roll close, and throat gently constricts for inviting the savory drip. And there it is—that good, top quality cocaine RUSH! Hubba-Bubba, hot damn! Sinuses are numb, head don't hurt, body is alive with vibrant tingle. And you know Carla's warm velvet hand massaging so seductively is feelin' really, really nice! Opening my eyes in glazing approval, the rolled bill goes to right nostril for sucking up another fat line. 'Cept it clogs halfway through the line. Fuckin' thing (right nostril) has always been this way; even with heroin, and having no sinus infection. Oh well, that's why we have left nostrils, right? Without pause, the left finishes what the right cannot, and while still flarin' afire, vacuum pulls yet even another fatty. WOW-WEE-KA-ZOWEE. SHAZZAM! Now, this is some *good* cocaine! Glowing with a rush, swallowin' drippity-drips, I open legs, lean back into the chair, and slide mirror containing coke over to Carla. Smiling, she shakes her head, silently declining. The cuffed leggings of khaki baggy shorts are (shall we say) generously agape. It is nothing to direct Carla's caressing hand up inner thigh for fondling bare cock and balls. Though only semi-erect, the sensation is indeed wondrous! Time for a cigarette. Offering Carla one, lighting it for her, then my own, I inhale deeply, thoroughly enjoying the moment. Carla, squeezing and strokin', smokes her cigarette, asking knowingly, "Devon, are you enjoying yourself?"

"Yes Carla, very much. Thank you."

She, now lookin' sexier than ever, coolly smokes while still shaft strokin', milking it to stretch and grow. "Devon, is there anything else I can do for you tonight?" Then adding, as if embarrassed, "Devon, I must go home with some money; if you don't want any more of me, I must leave."

Now, the thing about cocaine (for most men anyways) is that doing any amount worth doin' (which, *pour moi*, is at least a gram at a time), it usually (much like heroin) means no standin' hard erection. The damn blood flow seems to be crankin' throughout every part of the body except the dick! So, a tad frustrating this can be, 'cause the coke makes Sparky horny as a mother fuck! And though the dick ain't fully erect, whoa, it is incredibly sensitive—entire body is. Oral sex? Well, a lap lickin' suck fiend I do become! Carla is informed of this, and invitation for long oral play is extended for hopeful granting.

"Carla, how much?"

Smiling, she slyly answers, "For you Devon, twenty dollars. Okay?"

"Okay" snuffing glow from hot stub of cigarette. Carla giggles, askin' why I break the filters off? Licking my fingers "Uh, because they taste better that way." Standing up, removing vest, handing Carla a twenty dollar bill, undoing belt buckle, letting shorts fall to the floor.

Putting the bill in her pocket, stubbing out her own cigarette, she reaches for the gold scrotum ring, lightly touching, "Devon, this is beautiful. We do not see this here in Cuba. Did it hurt?"

Opening legs, and sitting back down on edge of chair, "Yes Carla, very much, but not anymore. See?" A gentle pulling on the ring is demonstrated. Her hand drops, picking up the ATM card—she cuts herself a very skinny line. With a quick snort, followed by a sip from the water bottle, Carla stands, becomes nude, slipping from tight jeans and top. She is thin, shapely, having narrow hips and firm, round breasts, with large dark nipples riding high. Not surprisingly her pubic hair isn't shaven or even trimmed; ungainly it appears, bein' much out of place with smooth, graceful, elegant female form. (I never liked pubic hair; and even way before it had become common practice to do so, my girlfriends were always made to shave.) Oh well, it's still pussy.

Lightly brushing fingertip through crevice of moist entanglement, "Carla, do you ever shave this?"

"No Devon, here in Cuba, it is not popular. In the States it is?"

"Yes."

"Why?"

"Because it looks prettier, feels better for sex, and is cleaner."

"Do not worry Devon, I am very clean."

"I know Carla. You look beautiful."

"Thank you Devon." With that, she comes forth, dropping to knees, cupping my balls in one hand for massaging pull from kneading fingers; with other hand, long fingers raise engorging shaft, flute fluffing, bulbous bulging. Carla lowers her head, engulfing cock with soft, warm, wet, sucking mouth. Ohh Skippy, boy-oh-boy! This surely does beat the hell outta skydivin' any day! Plus (hee, hee) it's cheaper! With Carla down, suckin' away, I reach over, and send another fat line up greedy nose.

Leaning back in the chair, the face tilted upwards, eyes closed, illuminating rushing flush, for Carla's oral massaging (in which, she is skilled, and taking time). Soon, Carla has my dick (surprisingly) standin' tall, proud, and fully erect. Ensuing enthusiastic deep-throating, whereupon a good show of determination is set.

On the bed she lays. With gentle guiding, her knees are pushed up, spread wide. Parting mass of pubic hair for exposing that desired, lowering my mouth to work the larger than average clitoris, Carla stiffens, betraying uneasiness. "Carla, are you okay?" Holding hands over her blushing face, she timidly informs that such is not customary here in Cuba. Women are very much expected to give oral pleasure, but not to receive.

"What?"

"Devon, here in Cuba, it is not a popular practice."

"What? Why? Wait a minute. Carla, are you tellin' me that Cuban men don't go down on women?"

"Yes Devon, it is not a popular practice for Cuban men to do... Here, they just like to fuck."

"Uh, and get their cocks sucked, right?"

Giggling, with her head nodding, "Yes Devon, Cuban men like to fuck, and very much get their cocks sucked."

"But Carla, you have surely had your pussy licked before, right?"

Sheepishly, "Yes Devon, but only by other women for paying customers that request it."

Clearly embarrassed, she does admit having enjoyed it. And when asked if I may, her hips rise, offering pussy for answer.

My mouth works her clit similar to how one might suck a tiny dick. Fingers stay gently pull-massagin' swelling pussy lips. (Goddamn these fuckin' pubic hairs; one is already felt bein' stuck halfway down the throat. Hhmm, oh well, this is indeed still pussy, and squeaky clean Carla does smell and taste. Whew-boy, eatin' pussy while high on good coke is like super cool!) Carla does give the desired response, so much so she surprises us both! Whoa, man, how fuckin' neat this truly is, orally pleasuring a woman to level which Carla has now risen—yeah!

She is all sincere deep heavy breathin', long drawn out moaning, hips rollin' rhythmic waves, sporadically breaking for face buckin' spasms. Thumbing her clit (getting a real kick from what's to come), I, without revealing intent, dart tongue (in full) right up her rectum. With startled shriek, Carla almost sends herself through the headboard! My tongue follows with unyielding persistence. Submitting, she relaxes, catching breath, rubs pussy using one hand, while holding legs bent to chest with other, for aiding in the tongue ass fucking. All very cool. Gushing wetness. Carla is rolled over onto her stomach, and after caressing those high firm, round butt cheeks, they are spread wide for more deep tonguing. Carla grinds her pussy hard with cupped hands workin' below. The girl is enjoying herself, and it ain't no act. By the time I've stopped the tongue diving to blow nose, and snort up another line, Carla is glossy eyed, sweaty, and breathin' hotly. She shyly confesses—no one had ever performed such a thing on her before. (Yeah well, who don't enjoy a fine rim job, eh?)

Reaching over and retrieving the mirror having remaining two fat lines, Carla is (of course) offered some, but politely declines. On hands and knees facing bed's end, backside, hanging cock and balls are facing Carla. I go down on elbows for snorting a line. In doin', Carla does what had been hoped. She, from behind, begins stroking and lightly licking (super sensitive) scrotum, softly whispering "Devon, please promise to never tell anybody I do this, okay? Because this is not popular here in Cuba."

"Yes Carla, I promise."

Left nostril flares to suck up a line fitting for Devin! At very moment, Carla buries her long, thick tongue deeply into my anticipating rectum. Feel good? Oh Skippy Joe! This is the best, man, the best! Big line up the nose, big tongue up the asshole! WOW! Engorged, and fully erect the cock now is. Carla, still tonguing, has increased hand pressure stroking. One last remaining line of coke; and mercy, it's a real Mamma! I snort that big bad boy right up, straight to the brain! Carla, knowing, thrusts her tongue deeper and deeper! Rolling over, she withdraws tongue, licking over balls, up throbbing shaft, mouth opens to come around and down. Carla's blow job is indeed good, using hand in unison. Fingers stroke that which mouth cannot, while the other kneads balls. Working walking fingers—havin' first one, then two—glide smoothly up into anus. Sparky's head is a-spinnin' with sexual euphoria The cum is mustering for ejaculation (somethin' personally not a common occurrence while on coke). Blast-off is now pressing. Raising Carla's pumping mouth, ploppin' free from quivering cock... she nods understanding, shoving buried fingers even deeper, while hand-jacking shaft for igniting charged elation! With toes a curlin', I do cum, and cum, and cum! Carla, smiling, keeps right on milking, squeezing out every last drop. (Oh, you sweet-sweet girl.) And brother, we're talkin' heavy load—by anybody's standards.

After cleaning ourselves, we sit nude at the little wall desk, smoke cigarettes, and talk. Carla asks if I like both boys and girls?

"Yes Carla, sometimes, but I like women best. Why, do you know any men that do other men?"

She tilts her head thinking, then answers, "No, it is not…"

"Yeah-yeah, it is not very popular here in Cuba. Damn Carla, Cuba sure is big on what's popular, and what's not, huh?"

Giggling, "Welcome to Cuba, Devon." Putting out her cigarette, and taking a sip from the water bottle, "Devon, here everyone needs money; and they do not mind selling their sex to make it. It is a job, you know? If you would like a boy, I could probably find you one; but Devon, you would have to be very discreet."

"Thank you Carla, but no, that won't be necessary." Kidding around, "Though Carla, doin' some more of this good *coca* and having you suck me while we watch another couple might be nice; or perhaps, having you and another thin attractive woman? Threesome, foursome, what the hell. Ha ha! Right?" Surprisingly, she answers, "OK Devon, I will see what can be arranged; tomorrow night, yes?"

"Uh, hum, Carla, I wasn't—"

"Devon, want to go up to the roof top for a drink?"

Still buzzin' from the sex and good cocaine, "Uh, yeah, sure, you bet."

Carla shows a way of getting to the roof top via stairs within the building. We don't stay long; shortly it will be light. A kiss goodnight, thanking her for the evening—we depart. In my room, locking the door, I pop four Valiums and go to bed. Sleep comes quickly.

In the morning (despite having had little sleep), I awaken feelin' good! A vigorous shower, spirited shave, ardent teeth brushin', and this cowboy is ready to ride! Ride, that is, on bouncin' red Converse high tops, down to the small (now open) cafeteria, orderin' coffee, coffee, *coffee*! Whoa hoss! This here is some strong, darn tasty coffee; plus, it's hot, soothing throat and sinuses, which, considering, are in pretty decent shape. Thinking about last night, man, though thoroughly enjoyed, a repeat is not desired (or so is thought). While pondering, an English fellow approaches the mini-table, introduces himself, and pulls up a chair.

Being similar in age, we both smoke, drink black coffee, and shoot the general shit. It is learnt this man from England has one more day left of the required stay in Havana. Concerning Havana, he has nothin' positive to say. The weather has been lousy, and he's considering flying out, possibly today, leaving Cuba altogether. To where? The man answers only, "There are other places to go, offering the same as Cuba, having better weather, at a tenth of the cost." He also advises caution for watchin' myself while here. From what? The man won't say. And yes, he has been to the Museum of the Revolution. Impressed, he wasn't. "Not much there. A lot of write-ups and some bits of personal possessions carried and worn by a few that fought. Be ready for some reading." Rising, he scribbles down directions for the museum. We shake hands, wishing each other "Goodbye, and good luck."

Steppin' out from the hotel onto sidewalk, I am immediately approached by two young men, seemingly there for no other reason than becoming my new best Cuban buddies. They introduce themselves as Ramiro and Paulo. Ramiro is obviously the "Idea Man," while Paulo is the "Sidekick." They both know Carla, and share: she had told them "all very good things" such as I am a real nice American, open to new ideas, working as a journalist for an unusual American magazine, with desire to see and report the "Real Cuba," etc., etc. Fortunately, these young men are at service for showin' the "Real Havana" (Oh goody gumdrops.) First though, they want my thoughts on Fidel Castro and Cuban politics. Now, lookin' at them both, this street, and thus havin' a general idea how they live, it requires no genius for guessin' what position they take towards such. However…

"Um, hhmm, Ramiro… and Paulo, right? Okay, look guys, you are aware that most of the world views Cuba with charmed idealism, and that old Fidel is looked upon as a hero whom his people, en masse, love very much"—quickly adding—"and that those of the world blame America for Cuba's present state. You know, the whole trade embargo thing?"

Hearing this, both boys (young men) begin a rant and rave, clenching fists, spitting and stompin', while whole time cussin' Fidel Castro! (Damn, these guys sincerely hate the fucker.) After they've finished their brief venting display, both search my approving countenance.

"Okay! Well guys, I agree with you, and so does my magazine, *Bizarre, Bizarre*. We are a very controversial magazine, covering such topics as… hhmm… huh, basically anything clashing with views. You know, we write what the others won't. We seek the truth and usually have a pretty good time doin' it. Most of us working freelance have tattoos, body piercings, and truly enjoy meeting notably interesting people, such as yourselves."

Ramiro and Paulo are both happily sold! And are urging, at very moment, that I should follow them into their "block" to see and document the real way of life here, under Fidel Castro.

"Devon, living in Cuba is most difficult. Because of Fidel, there are no jobs; so we must resort to selling drugs, prostitution, and at times, even stealing! But, we know you must already understand all of this, right Devon? You have seen this before, right? We know you pay for girls, and use drugs; it's okay! We all do. Devon, you do not appear to come from a rich American home. Spoiled Americans do not have such tattoos and scars like you, do they?"

Smiling, "No Ramiro, not usually."

"See? So we trust you Devon. You must come witness how we live, and hear our life stories. You will document the truth, the real truth about Cuba, Havana, and life under Fidel Castro…" He spits.

"Yeah sure, okay guys, but first, I must go and visit the Museum of the Revolution."

"Aw, Devon, why do you desire to go there? The place is nothing! There is nothing to see. It is all junk put together for tourists—"

Paulo intercepts, "And it is all lies, lies, lies!"

Ramiro nods agreement, "Yes Devon, he is correct. Very little you will read there is the truth. All Cubans know this. Why waste the time Devon, when it can better be spent with us, showing you the real Cuba?"

Oh boy, even though I had taken my horsey pills this morning, Mr. Headache has overridden, makin' himself known. Aughg, maybe some food should be eaten today, huh? Damn, when was the last time I ate anything? It would have had to of been that grilled fish, beans, and rice, back in Utila. Yep, eating might be a good idea.

"Hey guys, man, there's no doubt you are right, but I still gotta check the museum out. You understand—part of my job."

"Okay Devon, we will walk you to the square. It is not wise here in Havana to stand in one spot for long, too many eyes watching, you know, Devon?"

Walkin' the street together, I look over to Ramiro and ask, "Eyes? What kind of eyes?"

Paulo answers, hissing, "Narks, nark eyes!"

Ramiro confirms, "Yes Devon, they are narks, you know? Informers working with the *policia,* and government. Around here, there will usually be one spying on every street block. See, Devon, there is one standing on the corner, over there."

Glancin' toward the direction of Ramiro's nod, I see a guy standin' around, doin' nothing 'cept watching. The man is goin' with the eighties nerd look: tan polyester pants—too short in length—tucked in and belted tight, short sleeved button shirt— having sleeves too long. Gosh, he even has a shirt pocket full of writing pens and note pad. Ha ha! What really makes him cool though is his sunglasses. The nerd nark is actually wearin' sunglasses and it's an ugly overcast day— no sun!

"Yes Devon, the narks mostly all look similar to him. They are easy to spot after you know what to look for. They will not bother us if they think you are but a tourist, and we are simply showing you around. We just cannot stand about for too long on the street, and you cannot be seen leaving the street to enter a block, for going inside our homes and learning how we truly live. Understand Devon? This is very important. It is not allowed. If the narks see you doing this, they will come search the homes they suspect you have been in. This is not good, many families will be hurt if their homes are searched, understand?"

"Uh, yeah!" Man, I don't need this type of responsibility. No-sirree-bob! Ramiro, seeing my expression, breaks out laughin', "Don't worry Devon! We can get you in and out of everywhere with the narks not seeing. This is our block! You would not believe what we can do... all under the noses of those unknowing pigs!"

After some distance we stop; before us is a long strip of center street set up much like a park. The young men point the direction for the museum.

"Devon, when will we see you again?"

"Uh, I don't know, Ramiro. Maybe in a couple of hours?"

"Okay Devon, we will meet up with you in front of the hotel, okay? Oh Devon, this is very important, listen. Some guys, perhaps just like us, might approach you and ask to sell you something, you know, like what you had last night—*coca,* girls, does not matter. Devon, do not listen to them. You will not be able to trust anyone here. Just us—me and Paulo only, okay? Because of Carla and because we have spoken together, we trust you, so you know you can trust us, okay? We can get for you anything anyone else can, anything, and cheaper.'

With a look of skepticism, asking, "Huh, anything? How 'bout some heroin?" Thinkin' to have them stumped, they pull a surprise.

Ramiro, without hesitation, answers, "No, no heroin, but perhaps you would like *morphino*—morphine?"

Goddamn, seeing he's serious, "Ramiro, how? And how much?"

Ramiro explains there is a pharmacist who sells it by the vial. "Devon, it might cost twenty or thirty dollars per vial. If you want, I will check for you, but I should have the money with me. The man selling is very busy and we do not want to bother him unnecessarily, understand? It is okay, Devon. I will not run with your money. We trust each other, right?"

"Hhmm, right. Ramiro, do you get your coke from the same source as Carla?"

"No Devon, but the *coca* of our block is all the same. It is very good, Yes? What did you think of the *coca* last night?"

"Uh, it was okay." (I had no intention of revealing it had been the tastiest cocaine ever to go up this nose.) "However, I think the gram was a little small."

"Devon, from now on, you will buy all your *coca* from just me, okay? It will be the best in Havana, and the *grammas* will be big! Right, Paulo?" Paulo nods his head in accord.

Yeah well, we will see. Reaching around for my shoulder bag, while at the same time unzipping vest pocket (discreetly), lettin' chosen wallet slip down into bag. Inside the shoulder bag, out of sight from all 'cept myself, I rummage, to appear bringin' forth a camera. While doin' so, five twenties are quickly removed from wallet and folded tightly.

The camera is then handed over to Ramiro, and thus, the "Money Slip." Smiling, he pretends, taking my picture. (Strike a pose!) Retrieving the camera, I inform Ramiro the folded bills equal one hundred dollars. He's to purchase a vial of morphine, and spend the remainder on coke.

"Get me the best deal, and if I think the money has been spent wisely, you know, good deals, then we will do coke together tonight, my treat. We will get high, and you guys can tell me all about Cuba. Tomorrow we will do some more business, okay, Ramiro? This is a show of trust, understand?"

"Yes Devon, trust. We will meet later, after you've seen all the bull-shit junk of the great Revolution! Bye bye."

"Yep, bye bye, adios." Whew, glad bein' rid of those guys, but must admit, there is some tingling anticipation for what, if anything, they might have later.

Alone, my walk for the museum takes on a slower pace, as I stop here and there to snap some photos of the once fancy and ornate, now dilapidated, architecture. Also, a few shots are of children playing, old folks sitting on benches, and naturally, the museum itself, including the American tank parked in front as conquest. The weather is indeed lousy, and so the photos will be the same—dreary. The museum inside is interesting, but hardly impressive. The English fella had been right—not much to see, but a lot to read.

And what is displayed in print, really, I'd already read from books: different format, same information (nothin' much new). Still, the Cuban revolution was one cool ass revolution. But man, if there had ever been a little island ripe for government overthrow, it was Cuba, and bubba, what a ride it must have been.

From the museum, it's a walk around Havana in search of subjects for the camera. Geez, where are all the old classic American cars one is always hearing about? The fuckin' city is supposed to be full of 'em, right? Well, not today it ain't. Same goes for the street musicians and soarin' Latin music. And even the street vendors and large open Third World marketplaces, always bursting with energetic activity. Havana must certainly have all these things. Hhmm, perhaps it's the lousy weather? Yeah sure. I bet on a bright sunny day, everything is different. Today, this is an ugly depressing lookin' city, not worth wasting film on.

Back at the hotel, I am met in front by Ramiro and Paulo. Other young men are nearby, all doin' nothing, yet appearing to be movin'— you know, hangin' out, though never stayin' in any one spot for too long. Their eyes do keep dartin' from one end of the street to the next, clearly bein' on look-out, a habit applied full-time. During greeting handshake, Ramiro discreetly slips a small packet of assumed promised goodies, askin', "Devon, did you enjoy the museum, and your walk?"

"Hey man, Ramiro, you were right about the museum, and also about the many narks. Damn, there is a lot of 'em, ain't there."

Laughing, slapping my shoulder, Ramiro's eyes sparkle. "See, I told you Devon! But you have not seen anything yet, just wait... Devon, where are you going?"

"Ramiro, man, I must go up to my room for a little bit, you know, get my thoughts together for writing down some notes. I won't be long friend, promise."

"How long, Devon? You did not forget about sharing your *coca* tonight with us? I got you very good deals."

"No, of course not Ramiro. I will be back down shortly."

"Devon, perhaps tonight, after we show you around, you will like to go to a real Cuban disco? No tourists go there. This disco is just for us Cubans that live mostly right here, in these few blocks. We do not have to stay long, but you should see, and perhaps write a little something of it. Many will be there tonight. Good for your magazine story, okay?"

"Uh, yeah sure Ramiro, we'll see, why not. Give me a half hour, okay?"

"Yes Devon, one half hour, no more, okay? We will not be here—it is not safe—but we will see when you come out, and meet up with you, okay?"

'Yes Ramiro, okey-dokey!'

Oooh, a coffee is needed. Buying two cups from the small cafeteria, coffee and I quickly go up to the room. Locking door behind, taking a seat at the wall mount desk, hot coffee scalds its way down throat, pressure steamin' sinuses.

Now let's see what ol' Ramiro scored. Well, whatta ya know—four grams, and a small ampoule vial of brown liquid morphine. The only way for opening the vial is by snappin' its glass top. Hee, hee! Gonna wait on that. Now though, let's taste this cocaine! Uh-huh, a little top grade coke at the moment will really hit the spot! Just the ticket for chasing those bluesy down in the dump feelin's. All four grams appear bein' the same size as last night. Opening plastic, one gram is poured out onto little compact travel mirror. Same yellowish color, but seems even damper. This is where they are gettin' the weight! Eh, who cares, it's the quality that counts.

Some quick chops, and the gram is cut into fat-boy lines. Blowing nose, and sssnnort! Oh-ho, Skippy, yes-sirree-bob! This here is most definitely the same Grade-A as last night. A hot swig of coffee followed by another line, and then another. WOW! Opening second cup, lighting a cigarette, snort-snort! Well, there goes that gram! Only three left. Geez, feelin' good much? Oh, you better believe! Let's go interview us some Cuban folks. (Man, this journalist thing is gonna be a real trip!)

Stepping out onto the sidewalk with tasty coke dripping down throat's backside, I snap a filter from cigarette and light it, while at the same time, doin' best for inconspicuously scannin' the length of the street, especially corners, where the narks are known (or so told) to be at times posted. Hee, hee! The ol' look-out bug is indeed lickety-split contagious. Hhmm, wonder about the tall building's rooftops. Wouldn't posting positions from these, up high, with binoculars be more efficient for the nark informers, to observe street activity below? Hhmm, I'll have to ask Ramiro this. Ught, from across the street, here he comes now, with Paulo and another guy. Also now emerging out on to both ends of street are more young men, block residents, actin' self-appointed network for observing and distracting ever watching eyes of Big Brother.

Obviously, drug induced elation is evident. Ramiro, laughin', asks "Devon, you get much thoughts together for writing notes? Ha ha" He taps my nose, adding, "What I got for you is all very good, right? You trust us now?"

"Yes Ramiro, it is good, and you know I trust you. We are cool."

"And the *morphino*, Devon, have you sampled it?"

"No, that is being saved for later."

"Devon, you will be needing a syringe and needle?"

"No, I don't use 'em."

"Devon, how then do you take the *morphino*?"

Smiling, "Sometime my friend, I will show you."

Paulo introduces their companion, sharing that his mother works rolling Cuba's finest cigars. She steals them by the box for selling very cheap.

"Really? Are the boxes sealed? Does she have Montecristo No. 2s?"

"Yes Devon, she has all the very best brands. You are interested then?"

"Hhmm, maybe… how much?"

"This I do not know Devon, but if we go see, I will tell her how you are a good friend to us all; she will then give you a very good deal, okay?"

Ramiro, smiling, slaps my shoulder, "Come Devon, you will enjoy this; also it is near where we want to show you."

"Uh, okey-dokey! Lead the way guys." All three turn glancin' towards both ends of the street. Receiving distant "all clear" nods from those posted, Ramiro hisses, "Hurry Devon, let's go!"

Quickly, we skedaddle, slippin' into one of the many narrow walkways within forbidden block sector. These separate one dilapidated building from the next (sorta). Some are sectioned, interconnecting, grid-like, while others simply branch off, becoming filthy dead ends. It's all like some big intricate, cluttered maze! Jesus Christ. Sure as shit wouldn't be hard getting lost in here. And makin' matters worse, the inner block maze is not a single level affair. No, it is not! You see, these once elaborate center city commercial buildings have now become (crowded) squatting conversions for poverty-stricken residential dwellings.

Old iron fire escapes act as heavily trafficked stairwells, and where these are not, shabby wooden ones are. All about, there are sections of brick and concrete busted out from structural walls, for creating doorways. Where salvaged doors don't hang, tarps, curtains, blankets, sheets (whatever) do. And where these fabricated barriers are not hung? Well, that indicates open passage walkway.

On the upper levels, makeshift catwalks get used for bridging gaps from building to building, forming their own aerial maze, criss-crossing that below. Fuck, it's not yet dark, but sure will be soon. Whew, how the hell do children and elderly get about without lights? The scene is just like somethin' right out of a Hollywood post-doomsday movie.

Seemingly everywhere, there are people, young and old, curiously peering at us, from this window (hole), doorway, corner, or up above—lookin' down watchin'. The guys (my Cuban pals) will greet kindly a few in passing, however, most they ignore. Surprisingly, other than many sounds from television sets and the occasional radio, all is very quiet. No loud yelling or verbal noises so common within many stairwell living environments. But, then again, this is not your typical stairwell living. No, it is not! Damn, people have made use of the space by hastily partitioning themselves cubicle apartments so often housing packed families, consisting not only of parents and children, but children's children, close relatives, grandparents, and even great-grandparents. Gosh, I'd go fuckin' crazy livin' like this! A life of crime? Skippy, this cowboy wouldn't even think twice! Anything for getting' outta this economic mayhem. Man, no point askin' Ramiro why narks aren't posted in here, up on the rooftops. Christ, no way they could ever get inside these block compounds unnoticed, and once on the roof? Well, you get the picture.

Making our way single-file through the seemingly never-ending maze, stepping over this, turning to go around that, watchin' careful footing, crossing, climbing, ascending, rickety whatevers, etc. Ramiro (smiling) keeps glancing back for a quick study of my absorbing expression. (Whoa, and this is only a one city block perimeter!) On upper levels, we do stop here and there for select introductions. Handshakes received are warm and welcoming, as are the insistent invites into cramped cubicle homes for meeting all occupying habitants. Once inside, lifestyle deemed necessary becomes exposed for presentation in trustworthy manner. Word concerning this American (throughout the block) has indeed spread.

My entrance into such places—interrupting families, scrunched together, usually around a black and white television set—creates delighted distractions. Most do speak English. Within each cubicle visited, after seeing and hearing (briefly, for thankfully Ramiro is expounding the evident unjust hardships that must be endured living under Fidel Castro's rule) I am then shown proudly (from those that have and sell) large amounts of cocaine on hand. A demonstration is even provided, accompanying explanation: due to the local *coca's* fresh purity, it must be further dried in a pan via electric hotplate, before bein' weighed and wrapped in little gram-size, plastic, string-tied ball-packets.

Now, obviously, not all family cubicles visited deal in cocaine; no, there are some that prefer the marijuana trade, while others deal in stolen (hot) merchandise. And for those having young, attractive female family members, I am introduced with special attention.

Finally, we reach the cigar Mom's hold for an apartment. Babies crawlin' around feet too many. Boxes of cigars (hundreds) are stacked along every wall bein' several rows deep, and some so high as reachin' the ceiling. After meeting everybody, a box of the famous Cuban Montecristo No. 2s materialize. Because I am a friend, writing about the "Real Cuba," only thirty dollars. Paying, putting precious cigars into black, trusty shoulder bag, while politely declining the persistent insistence for purchasing more. It's *gracias,* thank you, nice meetin' y'all, bye bye. We are outta there! Well, Ramiro, Paulo, and myself anyways. The other guy stays behind with his cigar Mom, to help watch that big pot of tasty smellin', bubblin' stew on top a hotplate. (Goddamn—I forgot to eat, again.)

Dark it has become, and so keepin' up close, not darin' to fall back: "Hey man, Ramiro, where we goin' now?"

"We are goin' to my home Devon. It should be empty tonight. Maybe just my sister will be there. Perhaps you will like her, right, Devon?"

Both guys laugh, with Paulo adding, "My aunt, he will like! Devon, you will meet her later, okay?"

"Yeah okay, but really guys, tonight I'm not lookin' for any women."

More laughter, "Aw Devon, that will change after we have a little *coca* and smoke. And after you have seen all the sexy *chicas* at the disco!" Oh crap, that's right, the disco. I'd forgot all about that. Fuckin' hate discos, always have. Can't dance, never could, not even back in the drinkin' days. "Watch your step Devon, this one is not well made."

As it turns out, Ramiro's home is ground level, on a dead end within the block, bein' near street fronting my hotel. The cubicle apartment inside has a high ceiling, which they have taken advantage of by building an upper floor/loft, having roughly built wooden stairs, enabling accessibility. The loft above is obviously for sleeping. Down here, the dwelling hasn't the room. Old overstuffed furniture makes for tight quarters. On a stand beside the door is a black and white TV from the sixties. Cheap poster art is on the walls, candles here and there, and colorful cloth drapings cover all furnishings. The back wall is used for the kitchen having short counter, electric hotplates, old refrigerator, and small sink.

"Ramiro, I gotta pee."

"Yes, sure Devon, it is right over there." He and Paulo have knelt down to the center coffee table, and are in the process of de-seeding weed, and rollin' a joint. Ramiro, glancing up, points toward the small kitchen sink. Stepping over him, Paulo, and the coffee table, adjoining sink, left, is the refrigerator, and diagonal hangin' shower curtain partitioning makeshift shower, having a toilet damn near in the shower itself.

After a long, very much needed pee, I re-emerge a new man!

The guys, passing a now lit joint, make offer for sharing. "Uh, no thanks. I never smoke the stuff." Reachin' in pocket, out comes little brass pill box containing two of the remaining three grams. (Third had been deliberately left back at the hotel room.) Ramiro is handed one string tied gram; whereupon, biting a tear, he empties contents onto same magazine cover havin' been used for the weed. A playin' card— chop, chop, chop! Three quarters gets cut into equal size lines, which we expeditiously snort, snort, snort! Feelin' good and chatty... suddenly, movement is heard from loft above!

"It is only my sister. Here Devon, hand me three cigarettes, please." Giving Ramiro the requested cigarettes, descending steps turn our heads for seeing. There stands the sister, wearing only a loosely wrapped sheet. She had come halfway down before stopping. The woman is (guessing) early twenties, and quite notably attractive. Ramiro addresses her via speedy Spanish. She, acknowledging, uses free hand pushing long black hair from pretty face, smiling seductively. Ramiro turns back to the cigarettes as his sister's eyes command mine for locking, "Hi Devon."

"Uh, uh, hello!"

With a nod, she turns, and gracefully goes back up the steps, letting wrap around sheet drop, exposing elegant bare back and almost that lovely convex below.

Meanwhile, Ramiro taps out tobacco bits from three cigarettes, and into them, he puts equal amounts of remaining coke from the gram. Twisting ends, he hands us each one. Ramiro, fires his up with deep long inhale; Paulo and I follow suit. Getty-up GO! Thare's cocaine in that thare cigarette! Whew-wee! Rushin' glow of exuberance soarin' throughout... Shit! Abruptly, unexpectedly, a man opens the door, and walks right on in.

"Lucas!"

"Hey Ramiro, Paulo, is this Devon? Hello Devon, my name is Lucas. I have been hearing about you all day! So, you want to document the real Cuba? Good! Very good. We need more Americans to come here and see what is really going on. Maybe then the American government will kill the pig Castro, and finally liberate us! But first Devon, let's party! Ha ha!"

Lucas slaps down a bag of weed, which Ramiro and Paulo attack with rolling papers. Lucas is broad-shouldered, tall, and, as a man, gorgeous, having glossy, wavy, black hair. He himself is not black, not white, and not brown Latin, but rather a mix of all three, gettin' the best from the cocktail gene pool. Also, he is extremely likable. Lucas lives in another nearby block, where later tonight he wants to take me for meeting his family, and showing off their pride and joy rooftop garden. However, first, Lucas has some relatives living here in this block, presently having a birthday party for a small child. He thinks the party should be photo- graphed for purpose, documenting the Cuban people's strong sense of family, "Okay?"

"Yeah, sure Lucas. Why not."

Ramiro suggests we do my other *grama* first. Sounds good! Fortunately Lucas don't do coke. Nope, he had a professed problem with the stuff awhile back, and so, well, it's pot smokin' and drinkin' only. The gram goes quickly, and feelin' quite spry, we all make our way, single file, through block's eerie-ass maze for the child's birthday party.

The great-grandmother meets us at dwelling's entrance. She is a bent, cackling old lady, obviously a serious alcoholic, who has been drinkin'. She speaks no English, yet, her eyes betray our arrival was expected. Upon greeting, the old gal embraces, hangin' from my neck with hands rubbing and fondling (yes, even crotch), though it is blond ponytail that seemingly has her most intrigued. The guys (naturally) are finding this greatly amusing. Lucas (after havin' a laugh) gently pulls the frail, drunken old lady off. In doing, she caresses his face, warmly cooing Spanish. Lucas, acknowledging, looks over, almost apologetic, saying, "Devon, she wants to know if you have a single dollar to give, so that she may buy a bottle of rum." Handing her the dollar, she accepts, beaming *la timide gracias*; her worn wrinkled face is trying oh-so hard to be that it surely once was—soft, smooth, femme fatale... but those days are long gone. Turning, without warning, the little, old great-grandmother *barks* Spanish! A young boy comes a-runnin'; the dollar is passed on to him, and away he goes for purchasing rum.

Inside, there is indeed a child's birthday party goin' on. Despite the cramped space, it is all very adorable, sweet, and charming. There are no men present (except for some little boys). A table, taking up most of the room, is covered with bright ornate tablecloth, laden with treats and candies, surrounding a beautiful multicolored birthday cake, proudly sportin' five candles. The birthday girl has turned five years old, and like the other children (most anyways), she is all dressed up in a darling party dress, having much Latin flave. The mother turns out bein' the sexy prostitute—or rather working girl—that I had rejected last night; the one that was really hot, but just a bit too pushy. Anyway, other than having the exquisite face for recognition, it would be difficult even knowin' this the same woman. She too, is in an elaborate (traditionally conservative) party dress, even wearing a festive, bright conical party hat. My presence, without question, has broken the wholesome, merry mood of this celebration. Yes it has! The children and women are eyeing with much suspicion (even maybe fear), especially the birthday girl's young mom. She now most definitely is not soliciting my company: the resentment concerning us having crashed her daughter's birthday party is more than evident. And Jesus, who could blame? Somethin' very precious here is being violated. I want to leave. Sharing this with Lucas, he understands, yet insists some photos be taken before we go.

From shoulder bag, out comes my camera. Giving a look apologizing, I ask the pretty young mother permission to photograph? She, removing her party hat, silently nods a yes. With camera in hand, a few shots are quickly snapped, although really, in such close quarters, and by not havin' a wide angle lens, what should be captured is not. Thanking the young mother, and wishing her little girl happy birthday, it's time to get the fuck outta here!

Lucas leads the way through a curtain into another room. Here there is the standard old couches, coffee table, and cloth-draped overstuffed chair; which now has cackling old granny sitting, sippin' from her clear white rum pint bottle, lacking label. Ramiro and Paulo take a kneeling squat at the coffee table to sift through their bag of weed for rollin' joints. Lucas walks over, shuts off the black and white TV, sits down, and begins speaking rapid soft Spanish to the old lady.

Taking a seat across from both (not understanding a word bein' said), I snap a filter, light cig, and return the old woman's constant smile. Lucas, nodding his head, turns. "Devon, she wants to know what kind of girl you want." He's all grins, and really getting' a kick from this.

"Girl? Lucas, I don't want a girl."

Lucas and the old woman share some words, then he turns explaining, "Devon, it is common knowledge you like girls. Tonight, you must choose one from our family. If you do not, it will be considered an insult. Devon." Patting now menacing grandmother on knee, "She has much influence around here. It will be wise, having her think well of you. Devon, this is a serious matter. You do not want her angry with you. No one does."

"Oh man, Lucas, what have you gotten me into? I thought we were going to be good friends."

"We are Devon, and I must apologize; I did not know she was going to do this, but after what she heard of you last night... Aaaw, she thinks you are a *blondo* stallion, that must like the girls all the time! Ha ha!"

(Damn, just what the fuck did Carla tell these people?)

"Seriously Devon, friend, what is the big deal? We have many girls in our family, all very good looking hot *chicas*! Those stairs behind you go up to a private bedroom, just for this purpose. I can have a girl here, in say, ten minutes? They are my cousins, and wild sexy. They will do anything you like. Devon, please, it is just business; it helps to buy food for the small children and yet costs you so little. Ha ha! See how we must live life under Fidel Castro! But, seriously Devon, the girls do not mind this type of work when it is with friends like you. All of the women in Cuba will be crazy for you."

(Oh yeah, that was evident with warm reception received from next room over.)

"Really Devon, they think you are very attractive; and they love your long *blondo* hair and tattoos. You are an exotic American! They love you. Ha ha!"

"Okay, okay Lucas, enough with the shit." Grinnin', trying hard to keep this light, and on joking friendly terms "Man, Lucas, you tricked me into this!"

"No Devon, honest, I did not know. But what is the big deal? I promise you Devon, you will enjoy yourself; and afterwards, we will get you some more *coca* if you like, and go party. Okay? Ha ha! Now Devon, how would you like a nice, beautiful fifteen-year-old girl that has only been fucked once before? She is the next best thing to a virgin—still an angel!"

"Lucas, no, no kids!"

"Devon, here in Cuba, age fifteen is woman. This is the age they start working."

"Yeah well, Lucas, that's still a little young for me, you know?"

"Aw, I understand Devon, see? The women of Cuba will now love you even more for this way of thinking. Perhaps then, you want her older sister? She is eighteen, and even better looking, having more experience."

Whoa, glancin' over to the old hag, who is now most definitely sending an eye-piercin' warning for not refusing, "Eighteen, huh? Lucas, you promise?"

Grinnin' like a Cheshire cat, he answers, "Yes Devon, of course. Don't worry, here this is no big deal. Just enjoy yourself."

"The thing is Lucas, I've been doin' coke; and this makes for me, getting' an erection, hard-on, very difficult. Hmm, unless I do some coke just before, or during sex. Understand?"

Lucas, softly laughin', understanding, "Yes Devon, the same is for me. This is the reason I stopped doing the *coca*. Aaah, I like to fuck too much! Ha ha! So, you need to buy some more *coca* now, or you have some in your pocket?"

"No, there is a gram back in my room, also condoms."

"Yes, Devon, we use condoms as well. Good. Okay, so you will go to the hotel, get what you need, and I will send a boy for my eighteen-year-old cousin. Okay?"

Yepper! Ramiro and Paulo lead escort through darkness toward street. Lookin' up and down, hand signals are given and received from corner posted, white-eyed shadows, indicating a green light crossing.

Alone in my room, after two quick lines, a cigarette, sip from water bottle, and long piss, thoughts are seriously considered for stayin' put here in the room. Yes, but this will only provoke angered resentment from those waiting. Somethin' definitely not good. No, I still have required time in Havana, during which these people could make trouble, uh, only a hundred different ways. Yes, it's best playin' by their rules, so long as nothing gets out of hand.

Back inside old granny's home, the girl (young woman) is already waiting. Lucas had not been lyin', this chick is hot! Really hot—uh, and young. How young? Beats the fuck outta Sparky! She might be eighteen, then again... However, she is old enough for havin' nicely rounded, high pointing, developed breasts. They are not large by any means, though this, of course, means nothing, as the girl herself is merely a *petite jeune dame*. Yes she is. Having long dark hair, olive skin, big brown eyes, and delicate facial features. She is wearin' skin-tight jeans, sandals, and sheer, gauzy halter top. Her abdomen is slim, narrow and firm. The beauty, with head held high, is quiet, and clearly a bit nervous, having smile, sweet and shy. No veteran working woman here. Oh boy, I'm feelin' just like a dirty old man, about to molest somethin' that should be gazed upon for its exquisite beauty, and not touched! (Must re-think this.) Hhmm, upstairs, alone, we just won't do nothin'. I will pay her, but tell Lucas, that because of the coke, the ol' cock just wouldn't rise. (No *blondo* stallion here.) Yeah, that's the ticket!

A wave from Lucas sends us both up the rickety stairs *estrecho*, for a loft room, simple, clean, and having two beds. The enticing young woman does speak English, only we don't say much. I take a seat, pull forth compact travel mirror and remaining gram. Chop, chop, chop, into nice fat lines. Turning around to face the bed, holy mother of God, sweet Virgin Mary, slap my balls and make me giggle, the one on the right is ready to wiggle! Young beauty has herself completely nude, and is sprawled out across the bed with head resting on elbowed hand. One knee is pulled up, placing sleek feminine foot against inner thigh of other. Luscious? Oh you better believe! Eighteen? Wouldn't bet the farm. But child, she is not! Hhmm, or is she? Damn, don't know why I'm makin' such a big deal over the age issue; fifteen, eighteen, is there a big difference? So long as it's consensual, right? A couple years back I had a young mistress/girlfriend who professed bein' eighteen, when really she was only sixteen. Yep, sixteen and more mature mentally than most within my own age group, and that's no lie! Still, is it right? Probably not; however, when in Rome... Aw, fuck that shit! Although— *wow*! The girl is absolutely, gloriously stunning!

Gently patting the bed, hushed whispers convey having heard (via Carla) about last night's oral play. She purrs suggestions for us to do the same.

"Uh, okay, no problem."

With that settled, the sleek beauty crawls to bed's end for compact travel mirror, and cuts herself a small line from one of the big ones. She is down on elbows with one hand holding gorgeous, long, black hair back. Her knees are spread wide with alluring little ass arched open—winking. Reaching, I begin caressing, gently finger pulling on parted pouting pussy lips, while at the same time lightly running little circles around pretty rectum. Her narrow hips sway with the rhythm, inviting a call for mouth drawn invitation. Beauty snorts her line, and in doing receives a tongue worming deep into wanting anus. Though making no verbal sound, her heavy breathing and body language conveys pleasure is indeed bein' received. So much so, that she goes for another line, and more anal rim-reaming.

All goes pretty much as last night had, 'cept, with this sexual darling, standin' erection is sustained for rollin' on a condom and fuckin' us both to ridged orgasm. Man, it must be the quality of this coke, uh, and the young lady herself—grade A, super-fine! After cumming, and with the last remnants of coke dripping in our throats, we sixty-nine each other until the guys from below begin yellin' for us to hurry. Time up! Thanking beauty with a salty kiss and extra twenty-dollar tip, we stop and get dressed. Everybody is now happy.

Before leaving, old hag granny gives a big drunken hug. Ramiro takes off to fetch four more grams. He will meet us over at Lucas's home. Out on the street, while walking together, Lucas explains that if we are stopped by narks or *policia*, not to worry, they will not harass. "Devon, just simply tell them the name of the hotel you are staying, and that we are with you to show the way for discos and nightclubs. Okay?"

Lucas's block is a bit nicer than Ramiro and Paulo's, but not by much. His family does, however, have a top floor apartment with an adjoining open roof space, in which they (the family) have taken great pride in creating a wonderful setting, containing many potted tropical plants, hanging lanterns, Tiki lights, a small bench here and there, and hell, they even got a small round table with chairs and umbrella! I meet the entire family, all of whom are seated, packed tightly, in the cubicle apartment, watching TV. Nice and polite they are, extending warm greetings while hastily making room for Lucas to lead the way through, for showing rooftop garden. Out under the stars, taking a seat on a bench, lighting a cigarette, pretending interest for Lucas's political opinions concerning Cuba and what he thinks would make good writing, I drift, pondering... Damn Carla, thought you wanted to keep the whole oral/anal thing secret. Hhmm, yeah well, just again proves most people can't keep a secret for nothin', no matter how much they might want. Lordy, probably all of Havana knows about Sparky by now. And this probably ain't a good thing.

Ramiro has arrived claiming the *coca* is so fresh, we are gonna need a hotplate for further dryin' it. Hhmm, wonder what's up with this wet cocaine? Inside (the kitchen area), the coke gets dried via pan and electric hotplate. Naturally, this must be done before full family view, and yet, no one appears thinkin' anything of it. We might as well be boilin' water for tea! Afterwards, we go back out on the roof garden, and do a gram. Like before, a bit gets topped off in cigarettes. This wet coke is out-fuckin'-standing! And yepper, it is quite easy seein' how perhaps such quality might become a wee bit addictive.

Before leaving for the disco—the real Cuban disco favored by locals—we do up another gram (a gram don't go far split three ways). Then to the disco, we go! Down this street and up that street, turn right here, left there, etc., etc. Whoa, I got no idea where... Ught, here we are, down by the waterfront (for whatever that's worth). The disco is an aging warehouse building. It's big, loud, and jammin'-packed!

Interior, the place is one huge dance floor, flooded with rolling waves of gyrating young people movin' to music blastin'! There is most definitely no shortage of super sexy women, all dressed in their chosen attire for advertising finest assets. Many are wanting my attention, vying for a dance, or return of provocative body rubbing. I hardly mind, but, it is somewhat overwhelming. Lucas is very popular, and tryin' to set us up with two cuties, both wearin' skin-tight, white pants, ever so diaphanous. Still, the allurement is not working. "I gotta get outta here!"

Lucas, groovin' to the sub-sonic Latin club music with a girl under each arm, nods acknowledgement, shouting, he's gonna stay "for the pussy, ha ha! See you tomorrow Devon!"

Paulo is also staying (good), though unfortunately, Ramiro is not, and comin' with. Ramiro (it is obvious) loves the *coca*. He's hangin' for as long as I might have, or might be wanting, any. On the way back to his place, he surprises by leading us a short cut, from off the street through one of the many block sectors. Eugh, it is fuckin' spooky dark in here. There is however, some glowing light streamin' from drapings and makeshift doors (some open and some not). Stayin' tight on Ramiro's heels and watchin' step, we come to an iron fire escape, at some sort of intersection within maze-like, narrow, trash-strewn, cluttered walkway.

Lookin' up, then down, for goin' around… Ramiro? Hey, where is he? Turning about, on verge for callin' out his name— *What the fuck*! I am grabbed from behind and violently thrown into cornered entrance of unknown!

Now, the thing about bein' suddenly hit or grabbed from behind is that it surprises very much. And if you are already jumpy, walkin' in amongst a creepy-ass area of zero familiarity and the person guiding you has abruptly up and disappeared, well, you just react! Some freeze, some scream, Sparky pulls his knife! I'm yanked backwards and slammed hard against a wall. The man is upon, facing, having hold of my vest, ready to slam again… it's all so fucking fast! He says no words, only snarls a heavy grunt. In that split instant, the man becomes visible through the nothing light. He is in filthy t-shirt reeking with booze and sweat, having stubbled, oily, mean lookin' face and slicked back thin hair. A short bulldog of a man—all chest, shoulders, and gut, with a thick bulging neck, bloodshot wild eyes. (Incredible what little light is needed for seein' such details when pumpin' pure adrenaline and fear.) My COLD STEEL folder is *snapped* open, and with body acting on absolute impulse two steps ahead of brain, I stab deeply into the man's right eye, cutting hard and outwards! He screams like a girl, throwin' both hands up, cupping face, while flinging weight to the right, tripping a stumbling collapse. The fucker is down, 'cept not quiet. No, he is not! The man is shriekin', thrashing about, yellin' loud, panic stricken, wailing cries for help! His noise is deafening, everything is getting brighter and brighter, my eyes can see clear as day, and the brain has (somewhat) caught up with the situation. My heart is poundin' like no tomorrow! Can't swallow, can't breathe! What am I gonna do? Man, the only thing you can do: turn and run. *Run mother fucker* and hope like hell for findin' a way outta this hideous block in one piece… Must get to the street; figure the next step from there. But, but ohh, just—go! Spinnin' on heels to do just that, *whoa*, Ramiro? So startled I am by his sudden presence, I almost stab him!

"Ramiro! Man, we gotta get outta here!"

"No, Devon, shut up!" Grabbing hold of my vest, hissing "…Devon, kill him and do it now! Look, Devon, you must. If he lives, he will tell the *policia* that you attacked him. Devon, why are you here? What are you doing here? Buying drugs, prostitutes? You are American, they will love to find you guilty, they will make you guilty, and you will never get out of prison, never! Not even your country's government will be able to help. You must kill him. Quick, kill him! It is no big deal! No one will talk, and the *policia* do not care who gets killed in here, they won't even investigate. Devon, he must not live. If you do not kill him, then all of our homes will be searched, and we, your friends, will be taken away, put in prison and tortured, understand? Now kill him please! I will get you out of here, and there will be no questions asked, but you must kill him and shut him up, now!"

Oh fuck me! Ramiro is talking so fast, and everything he's sayin' sounds the truth. Okay, gotta kill the guy, sure, this makes sense—just another murder in the ghetto. Who cares, right? No one, that's who. Hell, it even works this way back in the United States. Man, got no choice, here goes... Quick! We've been through this sort of thing before, right? Try stayin' out of the blood... Uh, okay, no problem there—not!

The man is now up on all fours, workin' at crawlin' away. (Commit and do, mother fucker!) Rushin' him, I throw one leg over and quickly straddle the man from above. The bloody face lifts for determining.

Knowing it takes more force than most think, all my strength is put forth—reachin' under, and cutting the throat, pulling wide semi-circle—lightning fast! Not just once, but twice! Must jump free, sliding in blood from bucking kicks, a rolling. A horrible gasping sound of air-sucking blood through rasping gurgling, ensuing spasmodic convulsion seizure like twitching..., then quiet. And he's dead (or soon will be). The blade was felt slicing his windpipe (trachea) on both cuts, plus, if blood force squirting is any indication, it's a fair assumption both carotids got it as well.

Oooh, I am strangely intrigued by the calmness from within. Everything is so placidly surreal. Muscles relax, breathing slows, and feet feel light as a feather, almost floating, steppin' backwards, avoiding ever-growin' pools of blood. Ramiro, grabbing my arm, barks, "Devon! We must go. Now!"

Like a slap to the face, his urgent words hit home. I spin and follow him the hell outta there! And go we do, fast, without trippin' or stumbling on whatever the fuck! People are wide-eyed, peering at us from around doors, draping cloths, and window openings. Our presence and actions have indeed been noted, heard, and seen. Yet, no one calls out in protest or alarm. Still, we haul ass! Yes we do.

Entering Ramiro's place, we swiftly close the door behind us and just sorta stare wide-eyed at each other, breathin' hard; that is until Ramiro literally bursts out laughin'!

(Uh, uh, wonder what's so fuckin' funny?) Lighting cigarettes, he sees the tense confusion, and is patting my shoulder, actually praising with compliments, while reassuring all is gonna be okay. What I did happens often in the block to those that are deserving, and never is it a big deal! Everyone has heard I am a very cool American, one that thinks and understands the same as they (or so Ramiro is pitchin').

"Devon, relax. You are safe! No one will talk. You have seen too much of the block, too many homes and what people have in their homes. No one will want you to get the blame for this. If so, they fear you will talk and tell on us all..." As if reading my mind, "Aw Devon, do not think of that! No one will attempt to kill you. You are American; your death would bring an entire army of investigators down on these blocks! That pig—" he spits "—back there was not trying to kill you, just only rob you." Ramiro slaps my back, encouragingly, "Devon, you did only what you had to. Be proud of this, do not worry."

Uh, okey-dokey. God, why does shit always seem a *fatidique qui de la chance pour moi*? Hearing a noise from above, Sparky nearly jumps through the wall! "Aaah Devon, it is only my sister. You are safe, Here, sit down. Perhaps we should do some more of your *coca*? You will feel better."

Trance-like, I pass him a gram.

Just as we are about to snort lines, the pretty sister descends the loft steps. Upon seeing, her eyes go wide with alarm! Noting the fact, I look to my legs. They are splattered greatly with itchy, drying blood—splashing off-color patterns, chaotic with intricacy, a fusion of blood, sweat, and dirt—as are the arms (especially left one). Glancin' to her, questioning, "Is there any on my face?"

Nodding a silent affirmative, she goes to the little sink and wets a washcloth. Despite everything, it can't be helped noticing how sexy she is—now wearing a very short thin slip dress. Ironically, it's red, blood red.

With a line of coke just sent up the nose, eyes close as head leans back for pulsing drip, cool wetness is felt. The sister is now kneeling down beside on the couch, gently wiping blood from my face. In doing, she asks Ramiro what happened. Tenderly, she works the washcloth from my face to arms, then thighs. For the legs she must go back to the sink, wringing bloody washcloth for more fresh water. On her return, Ramiro answers with soulful laughing, enjoying the feel of a new line up his own nose, "Devon here, killed a man tonight..." Glancing over, through glazed eyes, 'Devon, this is not the first man you have killed, right?"

Trying to appear calm and collected, I lie, answering with a long sigh, "No, this is not the first. There have been others."

Ramiro suddenly claps loudly, startling a jump! The sister's warm hand swiftly comes to neck and shoulder for soothing. Ramiro shouts, "I knew it Devon, you worked the knife very fast! I knew you would kill him when instructed. Aaaw-haw! Very cool Devon. It is good you killed that pig."

The sweet caring sister, with an assuring squeeze, slides off the couch for resuming the grimy blood removal from lower legs. Softly she asks, "Who did he kill?"

Ramiro, intently watching his sister, answers, using speedy Spanish (which of course I can't follow, but do know more is bein' said than just the man's name). The sister acknowledging, looking sly, responds back with quick converse. Ramiro, having mischievous glint, and knowing I don't speak the rapid Spanish, informs, "Do not worry Devon. We are just discussing how the man you killed is only a pig. No one likes him. He is nothing to nobody. A thief, who it is good you killed."

The pretty sister, now nodding agreement, uses intense, glowing, sensual, brown eyes for locking on to mine, directing alluring gaze, hinting. She slowly presses elegant cheek against my inner right thigh, with magnetic attention goin' straight up wide, bloody shorts leggings. So sexy, (for visual effect) deliberately tongue glistens, full luscious lips bein' only inches from beckoning cock and balls.

Caressing her cascading hair, I lean forward, and do up another line. Settling back into the couch, with eyes rolling under closed lids, a warmth of moist panted pussy is felt straddling shinbone for sensual erotic rhythmic pelvic presses. Long fingertips walk (spider-like), pushing up legging, freeing erect standin' cock. Yes, it is indeed hard, throbbing' hard! Goosebumps have surfaced, tingling a shiver! A wet tongue follows, licking to guide pulsing cock between coaxing lips. With maned hair flouncing forward, the pretty face lowers, making gliding introductions to back of wondrous gripping throat so receptive. Sucking hard and slow, while keeping in time with pussy riding shinbone, this sexual performance is enhanced by seemingly amplified sounds—heavy breathing, salvia slurpin', lip smacking, and self-inflicted, gagging, deep throat constrictions. A well rehearsed, splendidly polished orchestration it is, ensuing a slow determined pull. Disengaging her power sucking to catch air, while tongue toying saliva strands, she coyly asks "Devon, are you feeling more relaxed?"

Shifting my gaze, eyes answer "Yes", as Ramiro is now noticed having large elongated cock out, stroking while watching. His expression is glassy eyed, and a smirk devious in arousal. The sister aware, giggles, explaining her brother enjoys watching her pleasure other men. "Devon, maybe you do too, eh?"

Now thinkin' that surely the night can't possibly become any more bizarre ('cept for perhaps Cuban cops bustin' down that there door), the answer managed is a silent smile only. She accepts the smile, and pivots on knees, swishing her short slip dress to settle in small of back, fully exposing lean calves and fine ass, having matching red thong bridled between tautly firm cheeks. The sister crawls around the old coffee table to her brother. Taking hold of his hard dick, she glances back, sending a wicked sexy grin, before lowering her head and performing the slow, sucking blow job number on her brother!

Ramiro, clutches tight his sister's hair for controlling, while, with the other hand, he lights a coke-laced cigarette. Inhaling deeply, his eyes search mine, approving.

Strokin' a handful of throbbin' boner, I light my own coke-topped cig, and can't help bein' thoroughly captivated by this strange erotic act—so taboo—*wow*!

Suddenly, the door swings open and in walks Paulo! Fuckin' A! Sparky damn near jumps outta his skin!

Paulo is boisterous upon entrance, "Hey Ramiro! You fucking the sister again? Aaw-haw! I see she is sucking cock! Here, I have some!" Pulling out his dick, he begins wavin' it, a-floppin'. Laughing, he is quite enjoying himself. Ramiro and I both put away our own cocks. The sister is finding no humor in Paulo's joking; she stands, straightens the short slip dress, and without a word, tenderly brushes red-nailed fingertips across her brother's cheek. Turning and stepping around coffee table, she bends for doing the same to mine, before picking up the bloody washcloth, tossin' it into the sink, en route back up the stairs for loft above.

Fortunately Paulo is alone, and obviously feelin' quite good from his drinking. Ramiro, at first, appears agitated by the interruption, however, he quickly gets over it, for tellin' Paulo about the killing. Paulo listens wide-eyed, glancin' approving nods and grins. With story complete, he gives praising congratulations and asks to see my knife. I oblige, bringing forth the COLD STEEL folder from shorts' front left pocket. In doin', I notice it is covered with dried blood. There is much blood also on shorts, vest, chest—Jesus, what a mess! After Paulo has oohed and ahhed over the knife, I take it to the sink for washin'. Steppin' from shorts and vest, the same is attempted with them. Luckily, both are stout construction, tan in color, thus don't announce the staining as bein' blood (much). Ramiro and Paulo, while busy cleaning weed for joints, are talkin' between themselves. They act as if it is nothin' for me to be standin' here, nude, before this sink, scrubbing at blood from a murdered man.

Stepping back into the damp spotty vest and shorts, despite a serious urge for gettin' outta here, it's time to take a seat with the guys, play along, acting the same as them. This is no Goddamn big deal; I kill men everyday, right? Oh fuck me! What have I done? Man, forget what you've done. Instead, concentrate on what you're gonna do! Christ, must stay calm and cool, and hope to hell for protection. Protection in form of silence, which is, in itself, impossible; but maybe, just maybe, word concerning my action will be kept to the underground world only, and not reach those that can easily inflict life imprisonment. Crap, silence is never lasting. Must live by the moment only. A plan will come later (hopefully).

Ramiro suggests doing my last *grama*. (Uh, okay.) After snorting, we each smoke a coke-topped cigarette. Feeling spirited, Paulo jokes around, asking whether or not some mention of tonight's killing should be included in my magazine article. His thinking is "yes" but not to disclose any incriminating details. Ramiro strongly disagrees—voicing no mention should be made. His sister, yelling down from the loft, sides with him.

Clearing my throat, "Augh-hem, uh, Paulo, before I leave Havana, there will be much in my article for revealing the real Cuba without having to mention any negative that, uh, might have occurred on this night."

Ramiro agrees, adding, "Devon, there is much more for you to see, plus you have not yet heard the stories. Tomorrow we, and Lucas, are going to show you other parts of Havana; and Lucas has people for you to meet for telling what terrible things the pig Castro and his regime have done. These are people that endured prison and torture. Their families have suffered greatly. So Devon, you are right, there will be much for your magazine story. As for tonight, the man you killed; me, you, my sister, speak nothing of this. It will be all okay. We trust you Devon. You are one of us now. We will look out for you. When it is time, we want you to go safely back to the States so that your magazine may have our story. This is our mission, but Devon, we can still have fun, right? Right Devon?"

"Yes, of course! (Rightio) But for now, guys, I must take leave." Waving off over-dramatic protests, explanation is given concerning need in returning back to my hotel room—notes are requiring attention for the article, and some serious sleep must be had. "Killing is exhausting!"

Laughter ensues, with understanding nods. "Good night, and sweet dreams, Devon," floats down from the loft above.

Entering the (seemingly) brightly lit hotel, it's noted that front desk Buck (or whatever the fuck) ain't there. No, he is not. Another man is workin' the desk. Passing greetings are exchanged with nods acknowledging.

Up in the room, locking door… Oh fuck, fuck, fuck! What shit have I gotten into now? Goddamn murder, and in Cuba, of all places!

Turning on the shower… Scrubba-dub-scrub hair, body, knife, watch and fingernails. Wool OD socks are rinsed out after bein' used for wipin' down brown blood splattered, red Converse high-tops. And shorts and vest? Jesus, not much more can be done with them.

Sitting down to ponder all options… Suddenly, knock, knock! "Devon, Devon are you there? It is me Carla. Let me in, I have something for you." Her voice sounds its sweet self, lacking any hint of trouble. With a long exhale, forcing calm from the startling surprised knock, I open the door and see Carla is not alone. Nope, with her is a very attractive young woman bein' all dolled up, in high heels and fishnet stockings, having hint of garter showin' from beneath a micro-mini dress. Yeah Skippy, this chick is hot! But still, the mood for such, after this night? Forget it! 'Cept how? Obviously Carla hasn't heard yet about tonight's killing. She must be handled with tactful sensitivity. I need her for a friend, and an ally. She mustn't be made to lose face. Carla gives a warm kiss, lightly caressing my cheek, cooing, "Devon, you look tired. You have been out partying, yes? Devon, this is my friend, I have brought her for you, like we discussed last night."

Shaking the lovely friend's hand (whew, she even smells good, they both do), stepping Carla aside, I cautiously try to worm out of this sexual engagement. Carla, smiling, waves the excuses off as bein' trivial—same with the pleading suggestion to do this tomorrow night instead. "Nooo Devon." Brushing up close, she cups my crotch, kneading with massaging fingers. "My friend has tonight only. See how she is all dressed? Just for you. Devon please, I promised her. She does not speak very good English. Tomorrow she must leave for her family's home outside the city. I told her what we did last night—" (Of course you did Carla, her and about a hundred other people. Geez, what's the big deal with eatin' pussy, tonguing ass, and snortin' coke? Eh, so much for your great Latin lovers.) "—and she is very excited to try it. Devooon pleassse, we even cut our pussy hairs for you."

"That's great Carla, but, uh, really? Hhmm, did you shave them?"

Giggling, "No, not all, but we did shave each other's to look very small, and cut the hairs to almost nothing. You are going to enjoy them very much Devon. And look what I brought for you!'

She brings forth two grams of coke, dangling from fingertips. (Fuckin' temptress! What a gem.) "Please, Devon. She needs to make some more money for taking home to her family. We will stay for only one hour. Plus, you get these." (She holds two dancin' *grammas*.)

Aughg, coke is not what is needed right now. However, if refused, Carla will be offended. Look at her, after goin' to all this trouble. Anger will surely ensue, if gratitude is not shown; and this cowboy can't afford enemies right now. So, to oblige and not hurt feelings... enthusiastic sex must be performed (and of course bought). And Skippy, to do this even halfway, cocaine will be required. Eugh!

Sighing, as if defeated, "Carla, how much—*cuanto es?*"

Seductively smiling, having triumphed, she answers, using voice lusty "For you Devon, only forty dollars and that includes these."

Wow, Carla really is giving a deal; two girls and two grams of top grade coke for such a low price. Man, here in Cuba, this is one helluva deal! Carla can't be makin' nothing. She must only be doin' this from kindness, kindness for her friend, and possibly Sparky?

"Okay Carla, you win. Let's do it." Taking seats at the small wall desk, Carla turns, speaking Spanish to her still standing friend. The girlfriend is smiling, though clearly a bit nervous; she's been intently staring at the tattoo work on my bare torso. (I had only bothered putting on shorts before answering the door.) Carla's words are reassuring, thus putting at ease *sirène timide*. Biting into the little plastics, Carla pours both *grammas* out onto my mirror and begins chopping. From the yellowish clumps, she cuts two small lines, nodding to her friend an offer. Holding long black hair back, the sexy woman in micro mini dress, leans forward and snorts up a line. Carla follows suit, then begins making big Devon lines. Oh yeah, Devin-Devon likes his lines big, long, and fat!

Undoing belt buckle, letting shorts drop, I vacuum snort not one, but two big fatties, igniting inner nasal blast off. Beam me up Scotty! Carla, knowing, goes to her knees for a throat stuffing of cock swelling.

The *chava buena*, slipping from micro mini, adorned only by garter belt, fishnets, and high heels, slowly crawls onto the bed, coming upright with knees spread wide and ass settling down on heels. She finger plays her pouting pussy while keeping eyes locked to mine. Well-well, the girl does have my attention. Her pussy is a succulence for outstanding beauty, having long protruding butterfly labia. Carla had done a wonderful job manicuring the little remaining cropped pubes. Uh, yeah! She looks good enough to eat... and like an oyster bein' slurped, that pink clam is goin' down!

Standing with throbbin' boner flopping from Carla's lip smackin' suckling, I move to the bed, intent on sliding between open funneled fishnets for swallowing greedily the offering so appetizing. However, in doing, the tantalizing femme fatale quickly rolls over onto the hands and knees, with butt arched and cheeks open, clearly exposing targeted objective—enchanting rectum. Carla, on cue, places *coca* mirror down before her friend, offering a snort; after complying, Carla's eyes meet mine, nodding green light to proceed the obvious. Oh boy, talk about teachin' a new trick. I've never seen anything like it—fantastic! My tongue goes to work, deep diving into the dank, rousing realms of quivering sphincter so accessibly responsive. The erotic pretty is moaning low sweet soft sounds, while pushing crevice for wanting tongue worming.

Carla strips nude, proudly sporting a fresh manicured pussy. I return her smile, very much nodding the desired approval. Carla motions for the stirred girlfriend to roll over onto her back. She, obeying, effortlessly spreads wide her long agile legs encased in fishnets and heels. Between these, it is now my ass arched up in the air... with mouth workin' a clit from face bucking pubis! Carla gives instructions, using Spanish, and sprawled squirmin' flushed face playmate stops to lay still. Looking up, Carla pours a small pile of coke on the tight sweaty abdomen. With a rolled bill in hand, I quickly snort that flakey powder heap, licking remnants sticking. In doin', Carla's long tongue is felt wiggling a probe into my own anus. Oh mercy me!

And this is pretty much how it all goes. Basically we just do lines, and tongue-fuck each other's rectums. Yes, the main course is indeed ass, with pussy and cock bein' side dishes. Though my dick maintains (more or less) a cavalier erect standing, I do not (cannot) cum. No matter, as both young women sincerely cum enough for us all, especially while workin' each other, in which clearly they are well practiced.

Carla, pullin' up skin-tight jeans, receives payment, puts my hand to her bare breast, gives a warm kiss, asking, "Tomorrow night?"

Giving the strong nipple a playful tug, "Yes Carla, of course, tomorrow night."

"Okay Devon, tomorrow night I will bring the same, plus another friend. Devon, we are going to the rooftop now. You are most welcome to join us, but I think you should get some sleep."

Agreeing with her, kissing both lovelies a good night, I close the door, locking. Okay, what now? Ha ha! That's a funny—what now! And the sooner the better. It's gotta be tonight. Commit and do, mother fucker! Uh, but how? The airport. If lucky, the first flight to anywhere can be had before word or investigation comes down. Yeah right, gotta go now! No, must wait a couple of hours, just before sunrise. Most of the city will be home sleeping, thus least expecting. Yes, that's the plan. Get everything ready. Oh shit! The morphine. Sure as Christ ain't gonna travel with that. Valium and horsey pills are one thing, morphine? Whole 'nother story. So, what to do with it? Hhmm, there's still a couple of hours to kill.

Snapping off the small morphine vial, I dip a skinny coffee straw down into thick brownish liquid; with fingertip capping straw's top, acting as a holding vacuum, I withdraw some for a taste-test lick. Yep, this is morphine all right! You see, I've had a little experience with pharmaceutical morphine. A good friend of mine, had a father dying from lung cancer. He was on the Die at Home program. Anyway, for awhile there, before the old man died, my friend was able to keep both his father and Sparky fucked-up on morphine. Trust me, the father did not go without. Hell, he had a whole case of the little vials. Even after he died, there were leftovers. So morphine it is. Tipping head back, placing straw into left nostril, lifting capping finger tip—*snort*! Shot-gunnin' morphine up the nose! Much unlike cocaine, the back-drip of this stuff is terrible! Lordy, the methods people will use to get their high… And to think back as a wild teenager, we used to do this with whisky—for fun! And burn? Oh you better believe! But not morphine; it don't burn—just makes you wanna puke! Now some might ask why I don't simply inject via syringe and needle? A good question which can only be answered with—such things for me, are simply way too intriguing. We all need principles, you know, lines (for whatever reasons) that can't be crossed? Injecting dope is one of mine.

The vial of morphine is now half gone, and I do feel a bit calmer, but still sharp. The morphine has balanced out the coke very nicely. No more. Must maintain this keen edge. Can't afford to overdo, resulting in dopey morphine euphoria (also can't be pukin' all over the place). Crunching vial under foot, it's time to go! Double-checking everything again for blood stains: red Converse high-tops, green army socks, tan shorts, vest, belt, and black shoulder bag. Yeah, the stains are there, but really, they now are only the appearance of bein' most anything you know—coffee, dirt grime, whatever. Best just to wear them in hopes of passing off as a well traveled backpacker for whom laundry is not a top priority. Damn, what a ballsy move, here goes nothin'. Tucking my COLD STEEL folding knife (like always when going to an airport) down deep into my backpack, I shoulder the old gal of a pack. Double-checking the room, blow my nose, close the door, and down the stairs for checkout. The front desk man (not surprisingly) is very surprised in seeing me all packed, handing over the key.

"The airport—*aeropuerto*—it is open all night long?"

"*Si*—yes sir, but why are you wishing to check out at this hour?"

Slapping myself on the forehead, in mimic of exaggerated Latin form, "Ah, just thirty minutes ago, I remember that only two days from now is my son's—*hijos*—birthday, understand—*entiende usted*? Uh, me *hijo* uh, umm, *cumpleaños!*' Obviously the man speaks English, and just as obviously, he knows I know he speaks English—still my retard attempts in Spanish is a show of respect, and always an icebreaker followed by (more often than not) warm smiles and/or laughter.

With a broad smile, he chuckles, answering, "Yes, I understand, it will be your son's birthday in two days. This is very important!"

"Yes—*si*! I must go at this very moment to the *aeropuerto* and try to find a way back to the United States. I will never forgive myself for missing such a special day..." Blah, blah.

The front desk man, never dropping his smile, checks me out while dialing a taxi cab. Daylight is quickly approaching. Taking a seat in the taxi, the street is fortunately empty; no one anywhere. One of my big fears had been that a nark guy or informer would be out to spot me leaving; none are seen. The morphine had offered calmness which is accepted and leaned upon as crutch in aiding for much hopeful success. (Jesus fuck, just get my ass the hell outta Cuba!).

Tipping the kind cabby, slinging pack onto shoulders... Well (again), here goes nothin'! Entering the Havana Airport, all ticket counters are closed, not yet open; however, there are various employees milling all about (including behind the counters) in preparations for hectic day soon to begin. Spotting a small-framed, attractive, immaculate young man, making ready his obvious station behind one of the ticket counters, our eyes quickly meet (betting my left nut him bein' gay). I approach, holding his increasingly seductive gaze. Introductions are made while the eyes convey sexual energy of wanting—wanting him—his cock in my mouth, etc. The young man is responsive, and thus (discreetly) flirting. His voice is lusty soft, almost cooing, "All flights begin departing in one hour. What is your destination and which flight are you booked?" I quietly tell him that there are no bookings or reservations for me. However, an emergency has arose and there is urgent need to catch one of the first flights departing Cuba; preferably for Honduras, but any flight to any destination will suffice as well. With eyes never leaving his, I allow for some of the true panic to surface, damn near coming to tears. And Skippy, this ain't no act. (No it is not!). The young man's face drops its flirting, with eyes goin' from seductive to genuine concerned. He sees mine are of sincere despair—swelling for crying, but fighting to not. Keeping the desperation between us only, I decide to risk it, explaining in whisper, that earlier tonight bad men had attacked me, and, in defending myself, a man was severely hurt. If I do not get out of Cuba soon, I will be blamed for an act that was not my fault. The punishment will surely be a very long prison sentence, where who knows the outcome.

Turning on heels, acting the professional his job calls for, he begins to punch keys of a computer, whole while sending me secret darting looks of sympathy. After viewing the screen, "I am sorry sir, there are no open seats at this time available for Honduras. If you would like to be put on standby, we will gladly make note, perhaps there will be a last minute cancellation, one never knows." Quickly adding in hushed undertone, "Do not worry, I will get you on this flight. Just wait over there, at the refreshment stand where I can see you. Stay right there. Do not leave for any reason. I will come and get you boarded moments before departure, okay?" (Uh, hell yes!) With a nod, my eyes project hope and whole-hearted thanks. He gives a wink, busying himself for the order of the day.

Following instruction—stepping over to the small circular island of refreshment stand, I order an espresso and light a cig; yes indeed, how the airport is now coming to life. People are milling all about and the noise level is increasing accordingly. Man, shut the brain down—don't think. Just smile, appear harmless, tip the refreshment guy well, and look straight ahead. Yeah, read all the different labels of the liquor and coffee flavoring bottles out on display. Time goes by, and the need to pee is so extreme that it be for-real painful to hold. But still, leaving this spot for doing such is not an option. No it is not! (Christ, enough already with the fuckin' espressos!) Don't think, just stay put. Then from the corner of eye, he is seen approaching. Oooh, let this go smoothly.

"If you will, please follow me sir." Slinging my pack up on shoulder, I follow the young attractive man. He leads me to a closed lane counter. Here, he asks for and receives all the required necessities: passport and payment. He works quickly, backpack is tagged and sent to go its own course. In no time, I'm following my new best friend. We are kickin' to a brisk pace. With him in lead, escorting, we are able to bypass all the long lines and even security boarding checks. At the gate, a woman takes my ticket and urges me to follow quickly. I do, but not before looking back and thanking my Cuban friend with words of no sound. He smiles a wink, and is gone. As am I! The plane begins rolling almost as soon as I get seated. *Goodbye Cuba!* And thank you sweet airport counter man. For duration of flight, the mind is allowed to ponder nothin' but great relief. No dwelling on coulda-shouldas, and whew, no lookin' back; 'cept, for maybe, Cuba can kiss my ass!

With plane touching down in La Ceiba Honduras, this grateful cowboy gets off. Fuck, almost forgot how scruffy-ugly these bad-ass acting, heavily armed guards and soldiers are here. Oh well, anything is better than Cuba, right? Not surprising in the least, my backpack does not come off the line. No it does not! I'm told to come back tomorrow. Fortunately there is a jolly fellow who is in the same boat, luggage wise. We had both flown in from Cuba on the same flight, lacking our luggage. He speaks very good English, telling me that he and his brother own a cigar shop here in La Ceiba; he must fly regularly to Cuba for purchasing cigars. "They always do this Devon, they fuck up the luggage all the time! Where are you staying Devon?" I answer, "Hotel Europa."

"Come Devon, come with me. I know the direction. My auto is parked here, I will give you a ride." His auto turns out to be a small pickup truck. The jolly fellow is very nice and talkative. Pulling up in front of Hotel Europa, he offers to pick me up tomorrow, here in front at eight o'clock in the morning for going to the airport together, in search of our misplaced luggage. Thanking him, his offer is greatly accepted. Checking into Hotel Europa, I get the same room as before, and answer the questions concerning my no luggage (backpack) situation. Thankfully, bein' in no mood for any more company or conversation, Gustavo is gone for the day.

From the little cafeteria I purchase two hot black coffees and large icy lemonade to take up to my room. Inside the room, after locking the door and turning on the TV, I sit on the edge of the bed and blankly sip hot coffee. Goddamn Skippy, that had been cutting things a bit close! Fuckin' A, too close! Cuba, boy-o-boy, talk about your strange… Jesus Christ, I was only there for two nights! And like a meteorite slamming! Impacts of thoughts, visual memories, and emotions: relief, fear, thrill, happiness, sadness, depression, the rush, shame, arrogance, guilt, self-pity, stupidity, exhilaration, etc. It's like a hundred different ingredients all thrown into a blender at high speed, becoming mixture of ugly colored gunk! And pieces of the man murdered are amongst it all spinning, but refusing to blend. Eee-Yuck, gotta get this garbage outta my head! The son-a-bitch attacked me, and so got killed. Cuba can't touch me now even if they wanted... end of stinkin' story. Missing my wife and sons, there is strong desire to head 'er on back home, but defiant stubbornness won't allow for such, no it will not! The mission is still a go. Cuba is not going to ruin this trip for me, no sirree-bob! Fuck Cuba! Damn, I need some sleep.

Draining second cup of coffee with four Valiums and taking a hot shower, my missing backpack is longed for. It carries my kit including toiletry bag, and now also COLD STEEL knife. Needless to say, vulnerable nakedness is felt without the blade. The Valiums kick in, and doing, sleep inevitably overcomes.

Waking early, after fetching fresh coffee, Gustavo is at my door, seemingly very glad to see me. Sympathetic to my luggage situation, but assuring that it will come, he wants to know if I want some *coca*? His friend has just come across a large quantity of very good quality. He tells me I can have ten *grammas* for eighty dollars US. (Gosh, that's eight dollars a gram! Now how can that be passed up.) Handing Gustavo one hundred dollars and telling him to keep the change, I hurry to the hotel's front for catching my ride to the airport. Of course, my jolly friend's large bags are there, but not mine. The ugly dog face soldier guards are eyein' me like you wouldn't believe, and it ain't just me bein' paranoid either. Man, you just know these guys gotta hear everything comin' and goin' from all over the place, including Cuba! Aughg, they give me the creeps. Back at Hotel Europa, I do eat some rice, beans, and these delicious sausage things. Gustavo meets me up in my room and gives ten grams of cocaine. (Gee, this is needed like a fuckin' hole in the head.) The coke turns out to be not like the Cuban coke. No, this stuff is more how cocaine is supposed to be: white, dry, and rocky hard. Chopping for doing a line—WOW! She packs a bit of a nasal burn. Also, the quality is not equal to that of Cuba's; still, it's much better than what most can be had back in the States.

On the third day my backpack finally comes in. The thing has gone all over the place—El Salvador, Nicaragua—stupid retards! Golly wolly, maybe it's time for this cowboy to get a-gallopin' outta these cities, huh? But first, a visit to my favorite doctor/pharmacist. He is all smiles and very happy to see me; yep, just arrived is some very good codeine pills. "These are just as strong, maybe even stronger, but are smaller in size and do not need to be dissolved in water." Yeah, the tabs are smaller, but not by much—horse pills they still are! Okay, 200 of them, and 200 of the ten milligram Valium; and all at the same price as before. Good— *mucho gracias!*

Saying my goodbyes to those nice at Hotel Europa, a taxi ride takes me to the bus terminal, where a small bus is caught, headin' for the small port town of Trujillo. Trujillo, of Trujillo bay: despite its very fascinating history and supposed thirty-seven miles of white sand beach, Trujillo is (in my opinion) anything but charming. It is nothing more than an old raggedy-ass shithole of a deep water port town! However, one travel book declared it as being "one of the great untapped tourist sites of the Caribbean." Man, whoever wrote this must of been high as all get-up while stayin' here, because I sure don't see it. Further reading, though, does tell some interesting tid-bits concerning the old port town. Trujillo is where that wild and crazy guy Christopher Columbus himself made his very first step upon America's mainland. The town was to become Honduras's first capital, being a major port for shipments of silver, gold, and other goodies goin' back to Spain. The infamous pirate, Henry Morgan, attacked and successfully pillaged the town. American William Walker was executed here via firing squad. American short story writer, O. Henry, is rumored to have hidden out here while running from the law, and while doing so, wrote his book, *Cabbages and Kings*. Warships of US and Allies were kept on hold (hidden) here during WW2. Good ol' Ollie North (another American) reportedly spent long periods of time here, plotting the whole contra war mess against the Sandinistas during the eighties. And it is common knowledge (at least in Trujillo) that CIA and American Special OPS teams are frequently seen hangin' out, drinkin', and contriving their Central American mischief, right here in Trujillo!

Garifuna black Caribs appear to make the majority of the population, and understandably, the general atmosphere (contrary to what's written in certain travel books) is one of mistrust and suspicion, almost to the point of bein' hostile! Not by all of course, but... You know the type of town—full of scowling faces, forming aura of negative vibes. Damn, I hate towns like these. There are thousands of such (little redneck) towns back in the United States. Despite popular belief, most of these (in my experience as a pierced, tattooed, long-haired white man) is not in the deep south, but rather up north, where the people are as cold as the icy winters themselves. Still, sometimes all it takes is just a little time for warming; perhaps Trujillo requires the same.

I spend four days in a low budget strip hotel along the coast, east of town. The miles of (not) white sand beach would and could be very beautiful if anyone ever bothered to clean 'em up. This however, is not priority, thus trashed-out they are. A man is befriended, that I really do like (and believe the fondness is mutual). His name is Martin (pronounced Marteen). He is sincerely nice, having a warm laid back personality. Martin wears his hair in semi-long dreadlocks, and works here at the simple hotel doin' whatever.

The hotel (and all those closely neighboring), much like the beaches, could be nice, but seem to suffer the same fate: a debilitation of deterioration due to obvious decay in an already poor economy. Tourism would help, but promotion for such doesn't deem all too popular, or even much in want. The rooms aren't bad though, facing the Caribbean Ocean, each having their own corner toilet and shower with privacy curtain. To stay is cheap, costing only a few bucks per night. Down near the beach there is a small open-air, thatched palm Tiki bar with assorted tables and chairs. Here, such rustic seaside watering holes are numerous, all being pretty much the same, dotting the long unkempt coastline up and down.

My second day in Trujillo, after stopping at the first *farmacia* to buy some nasal sinus spray and liquid ear drop stuff for my now very infected ear, I go exploring about the town. My wandering with camera in hand leads me for a tour through the ancient fort of Santa Barbara, and then on to ol' Willy Walker's grave site. In doing, while whole time walkin' around sightseein' and the likes, a very strange feeling of bein' watched and followed is on me strong, and it ain't from coke or haunting Cuba heebie-jeebies. No it is not! Too many of the same faces keep poppin' up. These faces are both male and female, all young adults and in considerable number. They're working to be blending for incognito, but failing horribly. Swinging my camera to zoom in on a few, they (every time) quickly turn to dart out of view. Yeah Skippy, we are bein' followed! But why? Hhmm, they could be cruisin' for determining possible worthwhile prey in easy mugging, or the sort. Eh, then again, it could just be out of bored curiosity. Man, in these parts my character is more than a little unique. Even the few Anglo tourists (all in small sparse groups, not a one is solo), are viewing me with awe and bewildered skepticism. And everyone stays clear, as if I'm carrying the fuckin' plague or somethin'.

However, on the road heading back toward the east end, two men do approach me. I had spotted them from way off, and knew them instantly to be Americans. How this is known from such distance? Who knows, but it is; and so invited acquaintances are had. The men are Bill and John from Minnesota; both appear to be in age of mid-to-late-forties. They are long-time best friends and own together, back in the States, a small construction company, which hadn't been doing all that well. So ol' Bill gets on the computer and quickly sees there's a great need for volunteer work down here in Central America. He contacts some US government agency department that just happens to be heading a project of building modern, low-income housing compounds somewhere in Guatemala. Further correspondence (and according to both men "a mountain of paperwork") somehow lands these two best friends jobs, via not volunteer but rather paid US dollar salaries to oversee the (soon to start) building projects from beginning to end. Gee, what a set-up! Almost not believable.

Now, having had some personal experience in the construction field—both large and small—I am quite able to ask questions that ol' Bill and John seem to be right on top of. Both men are indeed very knowledgeable of the construction/building trade. Why are they here though if their project is in Guatemala? Well, they explain that the equipment and materials are to arrive in Guatemala any day now (which is good because they are almost broke) and that once the project gets started, there will be much government monitoring and they (of course) will have to be good boys, so they want to party a bit beforehand. You know, smoke a little weed, sample some of the great Central American cocaine that everyone hears so much about? And girls, these guys want young girls! Well, not children, but teenage girls. They read in some travel book that this is very common here in Trujillo (older tourist men with young teenage girls); and everything is very cheap here (cheaper than even Guatemala). So they figure the weed, coke, and girls must be cheap as well. "Uh gee guys, can't help you with the girls, but the coke is damn cheap and very good."

Martin had told me he can get me *coca* for only five dollars a *grama*! Martin is a true Rasta, so he doesn't do coke, only "de weed," but like everyone here (according to him), he does sell it. He also informs that the abundance of cocaine is like it has never been before. Those that used to grow only marijuana are now growing *coca;* those that used to traffic only marijuana are now trafficking the *coca*. The reason being? One, the profit for coke is much greater. Two, the penalties for getting caught in dealings of either drug has become now (theoretically) the same, thus resulting in a very serious problem. There is now so much cocaine being produced, more than can ever be trafficked, that (according to Martin) everybody has become "*coca loco*" (coke crazy). Martin believes this is a very bad thing and truly blames the American CIA. He explains it is common knowledge that the CIA sets up the drug routes, giving permission for the big drug families to produce and traffic; consequently, these drug families become even more rich and powerful, therefore literally determining how life is lived here. "Devon, never before have there been so many powerful families, and they are all very ruthless and corrupt. Also, never have they all been connected. They all work together now. The American CIA has created this and controls them all! If the CIA had not done this, then there would be less drug families and life would be easier." Hhmm, interesting, and hardly a surprise—it all makes sense. Everyone and their mangy dog knows that Central America has been the CIA's dirty playground for like ever!

Anyway, as things turn out, Bill and John are stayin' at the smaller (cheaper) hotel next door to mine. The two Americans confide they had just scored some pot and are headed for their room to smoke some. They invite me to join them. Geez, these guys look so square, and after Martin's talk of CIA... Eh, let's tag along and see if they actually smoke the stuff. They do, and both seem to be on the up and up, concerning who they are and what they are doin' down here, etc. Damn, if they are CIA, then they are doin' a hell of a good job acting. Both men have the pale white skin of those flyin' in from the north this time of year, also they've got the Minnesota accent down. They claim this is their first time traveling outside the States, and act accordingly they do. But then Bill inquires about my *Marche ou Crève* tattoo. Not wanting to go into detail, I reply simply, "It's a military thing." Both men claiming to have never served, ask what branch? Allowing pause to observe, I sigh, answering, "None that you guys are familiar with." The subject gets dropped with Bill and John squinting eyes as if tryin' to recall some inner data. (Hhmm, bet my left nut these guys have served in the US military and are not admitting... Wonder why?) They then give me some money for getting them some coke. Okay, why not? Let's see what the two are made of.

Alone, back in my room, I take the remaining coke bought in La Ceiba, chop it all, opening the small plastic nasal/sinus container and pouring half out to be replaced with cocaine. Recapping, shake, shake, shake! Now here's some real liquid nasal spray! Let's give 'er a test squeeze. Squirt, snort! Yepper, that does feel good, soothing both the sinuses and fucked-up ear. When this is all used up, no more cocaine for me. Time to jump this pony ride. No coke, no girls, no trouble! Must continue onwards, explore the Mosquito Coast a bit, check out its people and possible boat builders, do some fishing and photography, and then head 'er back up for the Rio Dulce region of Guatemala to sign on for Casa del Corazone orphanage. Yes sir, that's the plan. But first, let's get these Minnesota boys some local *coca*. Why? Good question, that can only be answered: they have me very curious. Also, after Cuba, some American comradeship is greatly tempting. Even if they by chance aren't on the up and up, they are still Americans, right?

Finding Martin, he's informed of the two American *gringos* next door wanting some coke. Martin saw them, and suspiciously doesn't want anything to do with them. Even after I share with him their story, Martin thinks they are most likely CIA, and has no plans of goin' anywhere near 'em. He does, however, have me deliver two *grammas* with promise of never revealing the source of where it came.

The two guys from Minnesota chop up a gram and start snorting. Just as predicted, they are very impressed with the quality. Their offer for me to join them in tasting is politely declined with excuse of for-real sinus/ear infection. Eh, all the more for them! Ha ha! Afterwards, they are all sparked up to go out lookin' for girls! As for me? It's becoming evening with shadowed dusky glow. I go to an old wooden shack that Martin tells me about, and buy a sack of firecrackers. Whoa, these puppies are more like little black powder bombs! The American M-80 ain't even in the same league. When these things go off, it's a big time loud KA-BOOM! You'd almost swear there was a pinch of C-4 in 'em. The Hondurans are crazy over them; but geez, wonder how many little kids lose fingers to these short fused, mega crackers!

Just around the corner, and back, in between the two hotels, there, on the curb of the street, is a small family operated, open-air refreshment snack counter. Here I buy a cold bottle of Coca-Cola, and shoot the shit with the couple that own the place. At first, they aren't very friendly, but after buying them and all their cute kids cold soda pops and handin' out firecracker mini bombs, well, in no time, my popularity is one of delight. BOOM! BOOM! KA-BOOM! BOOM! Yep, you can imagine, little friends I do have! And the numbers keep growin'! This is mostly how my evenings are spent here in Trujillo. Drinkin' Coca-Cola, lightin' off sonic firecrackers in the street with a hundred little kids, and there's the time spent in the ocean's shallows, wading out, shining my flashlight down and catching crabs. This is just for sport, as after bein' caught, they'd get set back free.

Martin thinks I'm crazy for attempting to travel and explore the Mosquito Region, as does the owner of the small hotel. Like Martin, he's a nice guy, similar in age to myself, and living with his wife upstairs. Now, a drawback of letting people know you own a business back in the States is that often certain individuals will want to befriend you, exchanging addresses and such, in hopes of obtaining a US work permit and visa for entering the "land of opportunity." The owner of this hotel is such a person. When I ask him why he wants to go to the United States for work when he has this great set-up here—a beachfront hotel and all—he exclaims, "Aw Devon, you do not understand. I share ownership with my brother. We can make no money with this. The *policia* here are very corrupt, and the gangs are ruthless. They take most of what little money we are able to make. It is not just us; they do the same with all the businesses here, and we must do as they say. The *consecuencia*—consequence—is more terrible than you can imagine. And not only do they take my money, I must also provide a room at no cost for their *puta*—" (he spits) "—*del rejuego*, whore! She lives in my hotel, and I see no money." Martin interjects to the owner, "Yes, except this is not her fault. They force her." The owner, looking disgusted, silently nods. Well damn (not surprising), guess good ol' Trujillo can get crossed off as a possible location for a backpackers' travel station. Anyway, Martin and the hotel owner strongly advise against me traveling into the Mosquito Region, though neither had ever been there (nor ever intend to go). They do express their reasons for being fearful. According to them, it is a wild frontier that will swallow a being up, to never be seen again. The region is full of man-eating crocodiles and jaguar cats. There are venomous snakes, reptiles, insects, and even the plants are deadly! Both men, seeing that I'm not bein' persuaded for detour, change their tones and reasons. Lowering voices, they explain the biggest and most deadly dangers for a man such as myself are truly the very powerful drug families; they control the entire region. These families of Moskito (Mosquito) are direct descendants of savage, warring tribes that had, due to their aggressive violent nature, dominated, through terror, the region for centuries. The descendants terrorize to this day, having complete domination; plus, they control all trafficking and production of the cocaine that comes up through the Mosquito Coast region. Thus, they are very rich and powerful, having *violento* strong-arm influences extending far and wide! Also (again according to Martin and the hotel owner), these powerful drug families of the Moskito still practice the beliefs and religions of their savage ancestors, which include human sacrifices, head hunting, and even cannibalism!

"Yes Devon, it is all true; and because so, they are the most feared of all the drug families. They kill and torture without mercy. These families of Moskito do what they have always done, except now they are modern. Nobody dares to oppose them, not even the American CIA. They are *diablo satanicos*, practicing their savage ritual killings wherever they please. Devon it could very easy one night be here at my hotel; and I can do nothing to stop them—nothing but pray not to offend them, and pray to God! Devon, do you understand now why I want to leave here for America? And why you must not go to the Moskito?"

Uh-huh, okay, it certainly is some shit to think about. But come on, headhunting? Cannibalism? Give me a break! Jeppers, trying to picture some wealthy-ass drug cartel, lounging beside his elaborate swimming pool, chewing on some dismembered human body part—it's a laugh! However, I am getting the general idea that perhaps goin' to explore the Mosquito Coast alone might not be the smartest move in the world.

Still, what the hell, I'm gonna go at least to Puerto Lempira. If the atmosphere there is anything like it is here, or worse, we'll do a turn around, getty-up-go, and head 'er for Casa del Corazone! A two-mile walk down the trash-strewn beach takes me to the town's port pier (now nothing more than a small concrete jetty). Docked, with two men unloading, is a stripped down wooden shrimpin' boat made to be used as a supply freight boat. This boat runs regularly, hauling supplies to and from Trujillo and Puerto Lempira. I make arrangements to catch a ride with the two man crew for Puerto Lempira tomorrow morning at 7 A.M. sharp. Cool! It's now Saturday.

The sun is sinking, leaving evening to trail; time to go say goodbyes, and inform of my early morning departure. Martin seems to be genuinely concerned. He not only shakes my hand, but also gives a strong embracing hug (a very rare thing for a Rasta to do, huggin' a man, especially a white man). The act deeply touches, and my eyes convey such, which Martin acknowledges. The hotel owner comes down, bringing with him his wife. They both together wish me good luck, safe travels, etc. We exchange addresses and a promise is made to write for staying in touch. Now to go seek out the two Americans, Bill and John. These two characters have discovered that it's cheaper here in Trujillo to stay high on cocaine than what it is to drink beer. They have been bingin' on the stuff ever since our first meeting. My own personal stash is now gone; there is no want for more, and I honestly do not miss it. The codeine horse pills and Valium have helped immensely with the kickin' come-down. Bill and John, however, are chompin' at the bit (with teeth a-grindin') to be gettin' on with the promised Guatemala project; but they have (or so claim) just received word (from whoever) that the project is running a bit behind schedule. Not even the blue-prints or surveying equipment have arrived yet. Their personal housing needs have not been determined, and more importantly, no money has been received. But both men are assured that the project is a go. It's just gonna take longer than expected to get off the ground—maybe a week, or even longer. Bill and John have decided to stay put right here in Trujillo for wait of green light. They like Trujillo, it's all very cheap, the coke is good, plus they've found girls to screw. These Minnesota boys are meeting their girls tonight, down the road at a small, open-air Tiki bar on the beach. The guys invite me to come along for a farewell drink. Both know I don't drink, and so they offer to buy me a Coca-Cola. Sure, why not!

Saturday night in Trujillo, the town is hoppin', mostly with young Garifuna black Caribs out to party. Amongst the boomin' loud music, there is much energetic activity surrounding the string of open-air beach bars and gathering spots. We have two young Garifuna men (these are Bill and John's new friends) walking with us down the dark unpaved waterfront road leading to where the girls are. Both of these Caribs are askin' me questions non-stop with annoying persistent aggressiveness. Their faces are recognized from bein' of the bunch watchin' and following me two days earlier. Needless to say, I do not like or trust them. Arriving, this place is indeed a young person's hang-out. My appearance immediately brings about much attention—to point of bein' center of attention! Overwhelming, completely surrounded with many fingers touching my hair and tracing outlines of exposed tattoo, with much exaggerated compliments, ooohin' and aaahin'! (Man, with so many so close upon, all with touchy-feely fingers, must guard black shoulder bag and zippered side vest pockets.) Damn, where did Bill and John go? Christ, there they are. Oblivious to my predicament, they both are sitting at a small picnic table, engaged in flirty conversation with two very young girls. The girls, though all dolled up to be sexy women, are, however, not. Geez, their tiny breasts have barely even budded! Hhmm, since getting out of Cuba, I've had zero sex drive, but even if not, these girls are way too young for such business. Pulling myself away from the groping attention, a good lookin' bartender having nice smile sells me a wet bottle of Coca-Cola. There is though, this persistent male Carib that will not leave me alone, and is really getting on my nerves. He is aggressively insisting I buy him a drink. Thanking the bartender while shouldering Buckwheat the fuck outta my way, I pass Bill and John's table, informing them that I will be only a few yards away standin' down by the water. I want them to know; just in case any backup is needed. We Americans need to look out for each other in places like this, right? They both smile nodding affirmative.

With calm ocean casually playin' footsy with my dirty red Converse high-tops, I pat down all pockets to make sure everything is still in place. Oh shit, the zipper to big, back pouch of vest is down, and my COLD STEEL folding knife is gone! Goddamn it! While back there surrounded by all those fingers touching under pretense of admiring my tattoo work, some mother fuckin' monkey swiped my COLD STEEL knife! Aughg, how stupid! Especially since I've had some experience with pick pocketing, and pickpockets. And to think, an inner voice had gave warning that the knife was gonna be targeted here; that's why it was moved from the front pocket of my shorts where the knife rides clipped inside for quick easy access, and put in back zipper pouch of my vest. Fuck, fuck, fuck! Too many pockets to keep secure with so many fingers touching, all at the same time. Oh you idiot! That's no excuse. God, our knife, what are we gonna do? (Snap out of it man, we'll buy a new one, first thing; of course quality such as COLD STEEL will not be had here in these parts, but still, we should have no problem in finding a big cheap folding knife. Yeah sure, okay buddy, guess we got no choice huh? Ught! Buddy, looky who's comin'. Man, pull yourself together, we now have no blade.) Approaching, with strides of swaggering confidence, is Buckwheat the asshole. Glancin' to the table for Bill and John... Well, fuck me! Guess who ain't there? Come on, guess, guess, guess! The Minnesota dick wads left without even tellin' me. Without even a word, no goodbye, no nothin'. And no wonder Mr. Buckwheat is all cocky, full of himself. (Buddy!)

The asshole strolls right up, knuckle thumpin' my chest, and demands money. The body just reacts; a quick left punch to his neck drops him to roll in the sand gasping for air. In doing (stupidly) I yell, "Don't fuck with me mother fucker!" Of course everybody hears and turns to see. (Should we search him buddy, for our knife? Hell no, get out of here!) Holding the Coke bottle in such a manner to bash upside any head that messes with me, I march up to the bar, deliberately unzipping my right pocket (for all to see) as if appearing to have unseen weapon perhaps at ready. Somebody here does have my knife, and heart is pumpin' for fear it's gonna be pulled and used on me. (My own knife! Stinkin' shit monkeys!) However, without incident, the now silent crowd parts, allowing me to pass unchallenged.

Down the dark road I do march, lickety-split, nervous as all get up of bein' followed and jumped, it takes about everything within to keep from runnin'!

The hotel is reached without incident; in my room (leaning against the door), catching my breath, eyes close with shuddering visions of Cuba flashin'! (Aw man, fuck Cuba! The son-of-a-bitch had it coming. And so did Buckwheat back there. Soon you will get another carry knife. Meanwhile, we still have our little pocket knife and short machete; both are razor sharp, and no one knows about them, well, except for Cuban customs. But hey, that doesn't mean anything. All you need is to spend some serious time on a tropical river, soaking in deep serenity of nature living life as it does from such. Yeah okay buddy, that sounds nice—Goddamn nice. By the way, buddy, why do I know you? And why are you now surfacing? Man, don't be silly. You already know the answers to both questions. Uh, I do? Buddy? Buddy! Aw crap.) Now, much too pumped for sleepin', I ready kit and (tryin' to think of nothin') wait, wait for sunrise, to catch that 7 A.M. boat outta here.

The time passes slowly, but does pass. In doing, from up and down the beach strip, the local clubs and Tiki bars are heard first, lowering their boom music, then no music; they are shutting down for the night. However, this hotel's prostitute (workin' girl), just two doors down, has been, and still is, a very busy girl. Wow, she really works it on a Saturday night! Wonder how many men she can do in a night? With there now bein' no music, I can clearly hear her with customers: talkin', laughin', agreeing on price, suckin', and fuckin'. The woman averages fifteen to twenty minutes per man, one right after another. I even hear a mother pull up in a car, dropping off her son to be serviced (his first time). The mother calls out asking to make sure he has his protection (condoms). Thinking this quite funny and peering out the window to see... Ught-o, I see somethin' not so funny. No it is not!

There are small groups of young people—male and female (teens and adults)—sitting on the ground, discreetly congregating to blend in, with backs against trees, and lying in shadows of leafy foliage only a few yards from my window. Some are cuddling couples, others are solo. Obviously though, they are all together, knowing each other and speaking in hushed quiet tones. Also, just as obvious, they are all seriously watchin' my window! Fuckin' weird. A chill worms up the spine. (Buddy, we gotta get out of this town!)

With the early light of morning, pack and bag get shouldered, and out the door I go. Young people are still hanging about watching my window (most are asleep); none follow. Humpin' the two-mile beach trek at double time, tossin' heavy ol' pack up onto the jutting concrete pier and heavin' myself up behind for re-shouldering, I am greeted by a small group of little boys fishin' the pier. Ornery cusses they are, full of innocent curiosity, askin' the usual hundred questions, while admiring my tattoos. Joking around with the grinnin' midgets, handing them requested cigarettes, the time is noted and I am seriously concerned. There is no boat docked, nor is there any even in sight, approaching. (Where's my Goddamn boat?) Asking the boys, they laugh, answering it is Sunday, "No boat will come dis day. De captains and crew use Sunday for sleepin'." An old man, stepping from his bicycle, overhears and confirms. The elderly wrinkled man carries himself admirably: squared shoulders, back straight, and long strides of dignified confidence. His smile is warm and genuine; though it does turn to concern upon hearing about my boat arrangements made yesterday. "This is most unusual young man. Tomorrow there will be boats, but not today."

Like the boys, this man with gentle eyes had come to the pier for fishing, but found conversation with me to be more interesting. During which (after all the usual questions asked of those traveling) his voice drops into a tone having sadness, giving warning for serious caution concerning bad times that have befallen the region. The *policia*, he explains, are now very corrupt; and most of the town's young people are in street gangs and *loco* from smoking so much *coca* and crack.

"Crack?"

"Yes young man, crack—crack rock." (He also adds another term for it I don't fully catch... *Bosco? Busca?*) "So many are smoking this these days that they cannot be reasoned with. Aw, here come two such now; do not trust them. They are no good and most likely just coming to get information of you for the *policia*."

The two young men approach on bicycles. They are acting overly friendly and (of course) askin' the usual hundred questions. The old man will have nothing to do with them, but does stay at my side. I act the nice traveling backpacker, giving them each a cigarette and answering their questions with polite short answers.

It's now past noon and I gotta piss like a bowlegged race horse! Oh boy, what to do—what to do? Obviously no boat is comin' today. Going back to the hotel is out, goodbyes have already been said, it would be embarrassing. How to get to Puerto Lempira? A bus? Huh, that's funny, since, through lack of road, there is no direct route. A bus would take me to almost Nicaragua before even getting turned for direction wanted. Fuck that! It will be quicker to wait the time out here and leave by boat in the morning. Hhmm, what about a hop flight? There is a small private charter company that does daily flights from here to Puerto Lempira—daily, except for Sundays.

The old man quietly asks what I'm gonna do. Shouldering my pack, I tell him of my plan to go check with the private charter company for inquiring if perhaps a pilot might be persuaded in flying me the hop jump to Puerto Lempira. The two young men, hearing, step up and take off on their bikes with pedals a-kickin'! The old man shakes his head, looking concerned. Grasping my shoulder, he whispers to be cautious. Nodding affirmative, I thank him and turn to the little boys and holler goodbye and good fishin'!

Marchin' down length of pier from water to where beach is below, a jump lands feet upon sand. Here a much needed long pee is had—whew wee! Shakin' my dick dry and tucking it back under shorts' legging, a man is seen from corner of eye approaching. He is in uniform, claiming to be some sort of port official. The man demands to see my passport, and orders me to open backpack and shoulder bag, which I do; but surprisingly, he only glances without search. Handing back my passport, a silent nod indicates for me to be movin' along. And so move along I do! Humpin' it all the way mostly up hill for the center of town where the private charter flight company's office is located. The backpack, though still heavy as ever, does not feel to be. The ol' body is toughening.

The charter flight office is indeed closed, having only a sour faced cleaning woman on premises grumbling for me to come back tomorrow morning, 8 A.M. Fuck, this sucks, but what choice? Uh, a hotel for the night? Yeah okay. There's one up the street looking nice, quiet, and in need of business.

Entering via the glass front, a short reception desk is to the left. Here two snooty women check me in with an attitude as if resenting my business. And, they are almost hostile! Plus the cost for the room betrays obvious overcharging. And telling them so I do, but still they get their price. Yep, they get their price, and sell me two bottles of Coca-Cola from a refreshment counter across the room, but will not give me a pitcher of filtered tap water. Why, when there is in plain sight a water filtering tap above a row of cheap plastic pitchers? Also the hotel's large dining room restaurant is partially seen bein' just the next room over. Answer: "It is not permissible."

"Oh bullshit!" And so an argument ensues, but to no prevail. The two hard glarin' bitches, with arms crossed, hold their ground unbending. No pitcher of filtered water for me. Aughg, screw 'em!

Entering the room, an immediate sensation overcomes with somethin' not bein' right. And what is that smell? Bleach. Bleach and what else? Eee-yuck, euw, it could just be my own infected sinuses. Yeah sure, that's probably the other smell. Still, the red warning light inside my head keeps a-flashin'. Wonder why? The room looks nice enough: right of the door is a closet having its own trifold wooden sliding open slat (louver) door, and adjacent is a real bathroom having also a door, toilet, and shower. Passing the bathroom, there is a bed against each wall. Two beds? Why two beds, when only one was requested? Strange; a small nightstand holding a lamp is between the heads of both beds. The one bed is parallel against the far back wall, being one long picture window of glass. Damn near the entire wall is glass window. And on both ends of the great rectangle window there is the standard type horizontal section slat glass jalousie windows that open and close in unison, via small hand crank. A curtain hangs from all this glass, but it's so sheer as to be semi see-through. Silhouettes of leafy tropical plants can be seen swaying on outer perimeter. Pushing aside the sheer draping to see my view... Ught, here we are at ground level and the view is that of only shabby trash-strewn walkway separating the backside of this hotel from an adjacent ugly rundown apartment building. This walkway is obviously a service/delivery entrance for the hotel and its restaurant. Visible, are overflowing trash cans and a dumpster. Gosh, why so much glass for a view like this? Makes no sense.

Closing the gauzy drape curtain and turning, looking up—holy crap! The front of drop ceiling, spanning from bathroom across room to wherever, is not enclosed. No it is not! Pulling out my twenty-inch black steel MAGLITE flashlight and shining. Jesus, up there it looks like an attic storage loft that hasn't been finished off. Hell, the damn thing could run across every room in the place. A little creepy? Uh, just a bit. The bathroom, too; in the ceiling there's an open section as well. My light reveals a box on it's side stacked full with lempiras (Honduran currency). Thousands of bills in bundles neatly placed almost as if someone intended for them to be found? Ught-oh! Quickly lookin' under the beds, nightstand and closet, guess what is found? Come on guess! Oh fuck me... cocaine! Bags of cocaine, tucked here and there! Lots of 'em, each appearing to be approximately half an ounce in size. Aw, it sure don't take no genius to figure out what's goin' on here. This is a Goddamn mother fuckin' set-up room, for framing people! The placement of it all is simply too obvious. Shit, shit, shit! (Buddy what are we gonna do—what are we gonna do? Buddy? Buddy! Man, just calm down; stay cool and think. Yeah, yeah right; think—gotta think.) Hhmm, the room is what it is... Okay, but perhaps this has nothin' to do with me. Why would it? My semblance is that of not having much money... Ught, someone is knocking! Taking a deep breath, opening the door, there is a woman, different from the two that had checked me in; this one is thirty-ish and all smiles. The woman informs me that she is the hotel's manager and has just heard about my earlier request for a pitcher of filtered water. Smiling, she hands over a full pitcher of water while asking if everything is now okay?

"Uh, hhmm, *gracias por agua*, but perhaps I can be placed in a different room?"

"But why? This room is not satisfactory?"

The woman is invited to come in, for showing the exposed dark upper loft attic. She waves this off as being nothing, apologizes and explains that all the rooms have this, due to the hotel presently undergoing a remodeling; and (of course) this is the only room available "at this time" for me. She smiles; I smile; and we both pretend everything now is hunky-dory. (Believe her? Fuck no. Buddy should we show her we know of the coke and the money? Fuck no!)

Closing the door behind the woman manager, a sensing for trouble bein' just around the corner is strong. Still, what to do? Grab my kit and leave? Maybe, but possibly this would offend the manager, inciting her to call the police, claiming I had checked in, then (abruptly and without reason) left, leaving behind all this *coca* in her hotel's room. Damn, what to do—what to do? Oh fuck it! If I've been targeted then there ain't a lot that can be done. If it's gonna go down, this is as good a place as any—right? Blasted hotel doors down here; never a deadbolt (cross-slide bar) or even a chain latch for locking, only the door knob. Hell, if anyone wants to come in, all they need do (if they don't already have one) is go get a key. Real security, to be assured.

After some serious floor pacing, a hot shower, teeth brushin', and shave are in order. For some reason, shaving my face and genitalia has always had a calming effect. Sitting nude on end of the bed (furthest from opposing big window), bent working a towel for drying out my long hair, there is a distinct sound and feel of plastic bein' over the mattress, under sheets and bedding. The plastic is not like a fitted protective mattress cover, but rather simply thick plastic sheathing. Uh, without a doubt, further assessing the predicament at hand must be pondered. However, in doing, thoughts of my wife and sons keep surfacing. I miss them very much, but try hard to not think of them. They are beautiful, clean, pure, and all that is good. Thinking about them only weakens the ugly steel in my core. Yes it does! Oh shit, especially now at this very moment when a glance towards the sheer curtain draping large window reveals, suddenly, way more plant foliage silhouettes than what had been out there before. Now how can this be? Fuck me, it's not plants, but Goddamn people! People outside up against my window, just a-gawkin' in. They have been watchin' me the whole time while sittin' here nude, deep in thought, idly drying and brushing out my hair. They are young adult Garifuna Caribs (male and female), and seem delighted in my discovery of them. More keep coming up to my window, with talk and giggles easily heard. Stupid weirdo gawkin' sons-a-bitches!

Now, for whatever reason, my anger boils, overriding caution and fear. It is felt important to exhibit such. Standing up with back straight and shoulders squared, I walk to the bathroom and back again. (There, are you all getting' a good look-see? You wretched monkeys). Standing before them nude, flexing, as if challenging. Their chattering comments to one another concerning my overall mien would, under quite different circumstances, be accepted as extreme compliment; but not now, nope, no sir. This is indeed a violation of privacy and with stern tone they are told. Stepping into my shorts, flinging aside the sheer curtain drape, all the gathered gawking idiots spring to scatter. My shouting for them to "Stay the fuck away from my window!" is cut short upon spotting a cop leisurely sitting a few yards to the left on lower steps of stairwell to adjacent apartment building. Whoa! This ain't good. "Wow, he's lookin' just like somethin' right out of a low budget movie: tan uniform, sunglasses, slicked back black hair, little Beaner mustache, and one evil ass grin directed at me! Okay, maybe it's best to keep mouth shut, pants on, and hope to hell this ain't the bad sign it must surely be.

Before letting draped curtain fall closed, mental note is taken for counting the approximate numbers of those now huddled and giggling in and around various half-hidden spots within the walkway. Christ, there appear to be at least twenty (give or take).

Sitting back down on the bed's end, plastic sheathing under sheets seems to crinkle with amplified alarm. Six bungee bands quickly go around hair for tight, two-foot ponytail. Oooh, what to do—what to do? A cop, a Goddamn Central American cop with a street gang of Garifuna Caribs, right outside my window; and here I sit, in a hotel room littered with cocaine that is not even mine. Oh why, why, why? Listening, it is learnt that this cop is a sergeant, and goes by the name of Sergeant Lobo. He is in charge of this show, whatever that may be.

A young man comes to my window, his fingers reach through the slat glass of side jalousie window to pull open some nothing drape for clear viewing. "Psst, Devon? Devon, do you have any money? Want to buy anything? Maybe some *coca,* marijuana, sex? It is okay, have no worry of Sergeant Lobo; he is lookin' out for you Devon, givin' permission for you to have whatever might be desired—all very cheap."

Ught-o, Sparky's in a pickle now. Is this Sergeant Lobo setting me up to be arrested, or is he just tryin' to make a little cash? Is it best to verbalize polite decline for all offers or simply remain silent? Is remaining silent gonna offend him? Geez, does it matter? Either way the Sergeant has been revealed as bein' a crooked cop, and I'm not an appreciating participant, a big time no-no. Maybe he will just go away (yeah right). The decision is made to remain silent; only because not one intelligent thing can be thought (under circumstances) to say. Wonder how they know my name? Uh, lordy, that's a no-brainer huh? The hotel's register. Also, more than likely, there are those out there that have known of me since the first day of my arrival to this town.

The young man at my window repeats his offers. Upon receiving no reply, he steps from view for report to Sergeant Lobo. Quickly a different young man appears, and stands there holding out a baggy of what looks to be a half ounce of coke. In his other hand he is lightly tossin' up and down several individually wrapped grams, "Devon, you want *coca*? crack? I have both, all very good, the best; and for you—a most reasonable price—very cheap." After a while, this sort of becomes a sales pitch chant. A song he's made up, with strong inclusion of my name repeated as fitting. Then, a friend holding a large bag of weed comes to stand beside him, for joining in on the ridiculous chant song. They do this for quite some time before movin' on, only to be replaced with a very attractive petite young woman. She too begins calling my name, except her voice is cooing and seductive: she is offering herself for sale, describing in detail all the pleasures that can be had from her services—of which there seem to be no limits. The young woman has unbuttoned her shirt and has it open for me to watch her caress the small breasts while pulling on nipples, stretching. She wiggles, dropping pants for exhibiting a finger play of exposed pussy, slowly gyrating to music unheard; this, admittedly, is a bit hard to ignore. But stay put—and silent—I do.

Receiving no response, she acts offended, pulls up pants, and steps aside. An older man comes forward trying to sell trinkets. They look like wooden and tin boxes of the sort. However, his time is short, due to bein' pushed out of view by the first Garifuna having spoke to me. He's back, and this time his cock is in his hand bein' stroked to full length. The guy in doing is telling how much he had enjoyed seeing my body, how it had excited him, and what fun we could have with each other, etc. Damn, they are definitely workin' to cover all areas of potential interest. The cock is long and thick, bein' stroked slow and deliberate. He brings it to full erection, and an impressive dick it is indeed! The girl then returns with blouse still open. Her hand replaces his, as she takes over the cock stroking. Cooing on about how she would like to be doin' this to me, her mouth lowers for excellent display of throating the big thing.

Jesus, normally a show such as this would have me a boner the size of Montana, but not here, no not now, not like this. Honestly, I'm too scared for sexual arousal, wishing very much for them all to just go away;

they (of course) do not. No, instead, another older man appears, standing beside the bent bobbing *chica*; with him in tow are three pre-pubescent girls, each a head taller than the other and guessin' to be in ages of five to ten years old. They are dressed in colorful peasant dresses. Adorable these girls are; yet heart sinks as the man is offering them for sale. He reaches for the youngest, holding her up with skirt raised for revealing the bare little girl genitalia. The man then lowers the child back to her feet and has her call out my name in a tone that only a child can. Bobbing *chica* has stopped slurping to hold forth the massive dick for offering to the *joven niña*. The little girl grabs hold and tries with her own mouth, while being playfully encouraged by those around. For them, she is doin' something very cute and acting the "big girl." And me? Shocked, disbelieving, I yell (uncontrollably) "God no! Stop! Stop! Please… stop! Go away—go away!' They stop, and look at me as if surprised. Then the voice of Sergeant Lobo is heard, ordering them to leave my window.

The sound of a key unlocking and turning the door knob jumps my heart a-poundin'! Grinning, Sergeant Lobo has opened my door, and with him is another cop. This one is a mean lookin', tall black Carib. Sergeant Lobo tells him my name, then asks me if everything is okay? Clearing my throat, "Yes."

"Devon, were they bothering you? The street vendors?"

"Uhm, they were a bit distracting."

Sergeant Lobo nods his head with menacing smile, "Not to worry Devon, I will keep them away from you now on."

"Uh, *gracias*—thank you."

The black cop silently stares a glaring message of pure unwavering hatred towards me. They leave, closing the door unlocked. (Oh, buddy, we are in a pit of some serious weird shit.) Walking over to relock the door, in hopes that at least the sound of someone unlocking will give notice. Sitting back down on bed's end, tapping foot and lighting cigarette, draining last swallow from my second bottle of warm Coca-Cola (there is no intention for even sampling the water in the pitcher), yearning thoughts go out wantingly for missed COLD STEEL folding knife. The knowledge of it bein' in some punk Garifuna's hands is indeed frustrating, yet such distraction serves no purpose. So thinking is switched instead to my machete, standing with handle up, riding discreetly in my backpack which leans against the nightstand.

The machete is positioned for quick easy access (if the pack's flap is unbuckled, as it now is), being centered among the pack's other contents, with rolled clothing covering the handle. At a glance, no one would even know of its existence. The little machete is far from bein' a four-star quality blade. Like with most machetes, mine is cheaply made of soft grey carbon steel that dulls easily, but is quick to re-sharpen, hence they do usually get the job done (if handle rivets don't break). My machete has a sixteen-inch blade with a five-inch white handle, having thick brass rivets. The edge I threw on the blade is a good half inch in width (on both sides) tapering to a razor sharp cutting edge running up the entire length of the blade. I had even created the same edge for the topside running four inches down to sharper than need be point. These edges of gleaming, bright, sharp bare steel contrast greatly with the dark grey blade itself, resulting in the little machete now bein' showy in design of a wicked sharp weapon rather than a simple chopping tool. Despite the present circumstances, I have to laugh, thinking damn, the machete hadn't even cost me five dollars and here I am considering it to be my top secret weapon! Why this is funny? Who knows, other than hey, sometimes you just gotta laugh over somethin'.

Hearing my name, Garifuna Big Dick is back. Again his dick is out flopping as he strokes it to erection, while babbling how nice it would be to come into my room. I tell him to go away. Looking insulted and angry, he does, but only to return shortly, hissing, "Devon, you are in big trouble."

"Why?"

"Devon, you have angered Sergeant Lobo. Tonight you are goin' to get it!"

"How?"

"You will see. Ha ha!"

Where he had stood is now darkness of night. Big Dick is gone, but his words are still ringing, "You have angered Sergeant Lobo. Tonight you are goin' to get it!" Christ, why is this no surprise? Whew, guessing, here at any moment or sometime during this night, Sergeant Lobo and pals will storm through that door, arrest me on bullshit charges and off to a Honduran jail this tattooed long-hair will go! Geez, can hardly wait. God, I'm almost too depressed to be afraid (almost)

In the bathroom, shakin' my cock from a pee, the key turning door knob and footsteps of people quietly entering my room is heard. Well crap, here goes nothin', time to march or die! Stepping from the bathroom… What the fuck? Two young men with a gunny sack are scurrying under the bed; the sheer curtain drapes have been drawn completely open with outside walkway lit up from lights. And there, standing in the walkway, almost against my window, is the grinnin' Sergeant Lobo. Beside him is a *gringo* having blond curly hair, white skin, and bein' of age (guessin') mid-to-late-thirties. He must be American or European. On his shoulder is a large video camera. (Ught oh, why the camera?) Behind Lobo and this *gringo* is the street gang seen earlier (their numbers have increased); they are jokin' and smokin', hangin' out, comin' and goin'. Turning for a quick scan of the room, people are hiding in here; their presence can be heard and felt; plus the two with gunny sack were seen goin' under the bed. Aw, what are they doin' in here, what's with the gunny sack, and why does *gringo* there have a video camera? (Buddy, deep down we already know—don't we? Don't we buddy? Man, just hold it together and be strong. Don't show weakness—unless it's for baiting. You must play this shit—however it might come. Tonight my friend the time will come to march. Or die? Oh no fuckin' doubt buddy, but I think we are gonna die.) Chin up, chest puffed, shoulders squared, be the man that ain't afraid of nothin'.

Standing before Sergeant Lobo and camera totin' *gringo* with the glass of window between us, I respectfully ask, "Sergeant Lobo, sir, *como sta*, Boss, what's up?" (Can't disrespect these Latin macho pricks. Gotta let 'em think they're always in charge. But, must not show fear.)

No longer wearing sunglasses, his eyes squint a maliciousness matching ever-bearing grin. Waiting for answer, my own eyes glance at the lively walkway and activity now taking place up on the low flat roof of the apartments across. People—men, women, and children—are getting situated (even opening cheap lawn chairs and the likes), all getting ready for some sort of show. And obviously this show is gonna take place in my hotel room. Fuck me.

Sergeant Lobo finally answers, "There is cocaine under your beds. Maybe it is yours and maybe it is not. You must be arrested all the same. In jail you will wait for the judge to decide. Here, this is a very long procedure; such cases require many months before one even sees the judge." Grinning for pause, "Is this what you want Devon?" His tone is hinting strongly that there is an alternative. Acting game to the situation and eager for the hint of alternative, I answer loud enough for all to hear, including the spectators up on the roof, in hopes of some having a little compassion (which, considering, is highly doubtful). "No, no Boss! That is not what I want. My poor wife, *esposa,* and two, *dos,* young *hijos* will be very sad and heavy with burden of no income if I get into trouble here. Boss, what can be done to correct this?"

Lobo, nodding approval, turns to the *gringo* and motions for him to speak. With some brief hesitation the blond cameraman does. "He—" (referring to Sergeant Lobo) "—will look the other way and not arrest you if you do him a favor. Pay the fine so to speak." (The *gringo*'s accent reveals him bein' from good ol' California! Bet my left nut on it.)

"Uh, sure okay. What's the favor?"

"We want to make a video starring you. Down here you are considered to be an extreme exotic. The film will sell very well and thus your fine will be paid. In other words, you won't have to go to jail."

(Buddy? Hold it together man.) Turning to look at both beds, while forcing a smile, "Let me guess, this movie is to be a porno, right?" (Lobo is silent, but absorbing every word.) The *gringo* only nods. "Hhmm, and not only is it to be a porno, but a gay porno at that, right?" (Yeah, just keep on noddin' you California puke!) "Hey, that's cool! I've made pornos before, lots of times!" Then turning toward Lobo, "So Boss, if I do this for you then everything is cool between us? *No problemas?*" (With a very sly ominous smile, the sergeant nods.)

Now, in a situation like this, one's mind immediately begins to race a hundred fuckin' miles an hour, goin' nowhere! I am cornered, trapped, and no matter what, somethin' very bad is about to go down! But to what degree? Murdered, tortured, gang raped, jail? My head is spinning with guts feelin' like they've been pulled inside out. Heart is doin' the THUMP, THUMP, THUMP number as if tryin' to beat itself right up through and out of rib cage, runnin' off leavin' rest of me behind! My lungs are constricting in attempts for hiding somewhere within the spleen. Oh fuck. Some weird-ass shit is about to hit the fan! What to do—what to do? (Buddy? Buddy!) Gotta think—gotta think! Worse case scenario: death by prolonged torture (snuff film). Best case scenario: sexual violation, gang raped, followed by being left alone to lick my wounds for getting the hell outta here! Under no circumstances though can jail be an option. Jesus, if they are ballsy enough to pull this crap here in my hotel room in front of all these people, imagine the horrors of a Trujillo jail! Damn, these feet (along with heart) want to run, but jail will be certain if they do. Once on the streets, I will be arrested and Sergeant Lobo will be most definitely pissed. The dwelling thoughts of his repercussions can not at this time be afforded. Must think, think and buy time... need time... more time!

Surprising even myself, I loudly clap my hands together and begin rubbing them. "Goody! We are gonna make a porno! Hey guys, let's make this one the best ever! If we are gonna do it—let's do it right! I love makin' pornos! Hey Boss, how do you want this one to go? Lots of cock sucking and ass fucking, right? That's cool Boss. Only one problem though, look...' Undoing belt and letting shorts fall to the floor I begin to tug on my very flaccid cock. A murmur of awe is heard concerning the all too visible large, shiny, gold scrotum ring and lack of pubic hair.

Gringo hurriedly puts his face into the camera with red indicator light on. "See Boss, it is all soft. Normally my cock is nice and big, great for pornos, but now? Well, now, because I haven't slept in a couple days, it won't go hard. Maybe Boss, you know of something to help me out with this? The porno will be a lot better if my big cock is hard! Also Boss, we should bring in a lady. Yeah, a hot *chica*! Bisexual videos, they sell the best making the most money. Hell, we can do threesomes, foursomes, and moresomes! What do you think Boss?"

Sergeant Lobo appears briefly perplexed at my display of excited eagerness in making this porno. After a moment, his grin broadens with head nodding as if an inner light had blinked on. He answers, "Crack! Smoking crack will make your cock get hard. I will get you crack."

"Really Boss? Crack will make it get hard?" (He's all nods and grins.) My act becomes that of a silly giggling idiot, yet harmless, thus truly amusing Sergeant Lobo and those spectating. The general mood, overall (for now—at this moment), isn't quite so threatening or extreme. Maybe if I can keep them all humored, and believing this tattooed, ball-pierced, long-haired American is more than a little nuts, they won't come down on me quite so hard. But still, come down they are gonna. This is only the calm before the storm. In any case, somethin' has got to be done with all this pumping fear and adrenaline. So let's do some bed jumpin' with cock and balls a floppin'! The crowd outside loves it. Chanting encouragements, along with my own for those under the beds to "Come out, come out, come out, and play! We are gonna make a porno!" Sergeant Lobo, seemingly genuinely pleased, turns and leaves. A bounce leads me to stand before the filming *gringo* to ask where the Sergeant is goin'? Through the glass, he answers, to go get me crack and a woman for the video.

Music is heard coming from the hotel's restaurant. Despite being close, it hardly sounds so. Catching my attention is another sound, very familiar but never so amplified. Deep, low slow croaking. Looking, I can see toads hiding here and there, in the various shadows of cover along the walkway. Croaking toads—giant, croaking toads! Toads literally the size of semi-deflated basketballs! And that's no lie! Who knew such things even existed? Damn, their big eyes are bulgin', as bellies and throats swell and un-swell for eerie, long, drawn-out croaking. These giant toads know what's about to go down here. Just like all the people waitin' and watchin', they have all seen this before. 'Cept, tonight, things are gonna go a little different. Sparky now knows the purpose for all the plastic sheathing under the sheets.

Pulling my eyes from the toads, I try to engage the American camera-man in small talk; he is leery hesitant and responds very little, but does

178

listen. And so I tell some things deemed very important for him (and all those nearby listening) to know. He hears of my tattoo businesses, Tattoo Blue—how they are famous, being represented and advertised in all the major tattoo magazines—and me too. As a tattoo artist and a body piercer, my reputation is renowned with acclaimed world-wide recognition. I tell him of the various film crews that have flown in (two from Europe even) to document me doing the O-Kee-Pa hangings. On my chest and back the scars made from the quarter-inch-thick steel hooks are proudly pointed out while explaining in brief detail just what an O-Kee-Pa hanging is and the entailing for doing such. The cameraman is listening intently to every word and, of course, he is not the only one. There are many ears perked. All of this self-revealing babbling is in major effort for conveying bragging comfort of bein' in front of a camera. Of course, the real reason for this pretense is for all those listening to understand—I am no John Doe! If anything should happen to me, or by chance my body just ups and disappears, there will be serious investigations with much attention paid. I tell that while serving in the US army infantry, my squad of Recon (reconnaissance) company was filmed demonstrating certain tactical combat maneuvers, and later, (here a whopper of a lie) while serving in the Foreign Legion of France, I was actually interviewed by Sixty Minutes. (Hearing this, the cameraman's eyebrows raise.) Taking notice, laughing, while pointing to my *Marche ou Crève* tattoo, I ask (hoping like hell he does not, because my French is even worse than my Spanish), "*Parlez-vous français? Ou? Non?*" The asshole just blinks, giving no indication whether he does or not. Oh well, on with the charade. "*Comprende? Legion étrangère, troisième regiment infanterie. Guyane Français, cinq ans.*" (Buddy, no way did that come out sounding right. Man, who cares, just so long as it sounds French.) "Understand? I did five years in the Legion, most of it was in Guyana." He stares blankly, giving no answer, as do the others hearing. Hopefully, they are all thinking me to be a half-crazed American with a very documented, adventurous past—consequently, no easy prey, maybe not worth the hassles of fucking with. You know the whole cat and dog thing? Most dogs can kill a cornered cat, but more often than not, they don't, simply because it's not worth getting their snoots shredded in the process. I have always tried to fight like a cornered cat—despite the odds, inflict as much pain and damage as feasibly possible.

The scene in and around my hotel room is becoming weirder and weirder by the minute. Here I am, nude, standin' before a huge lit-up window, rambling on and on about myself to a fellow American about to film the obscene violence to come. Behind him are these monster size toads, croaking a language as eerie as the present situation is bizarre. A street gang and local spectators are milling about, hanging out, and leisurely waiting—watching, and listening. They all seem to be in genuine awe of me. (Fuck knows if this is good or bad.) Sergeant Lobo has returned and is now in my room arguing with a stern old woman. She seems to have some authority, but not enough to override that of Sergeant Lobo. The old woman is bitching about him taking all of her crack; he hasn't left enough for the girls to work tonight. A few Garifuna gang members are shuffling about the room setting up—here and there, little piles of four to five plastic wrapped crack rocks; with each pile, there is a red striped white straw of stout paper upon some aluminum foil. This must be how they smoke the stuff, "chasin' the dragon." Also there are little black mesh bags all about. Some are the size equaling a pack of cigarettes, while others are half that size. Wonder what's in 'em? The old woman stops her arguing with Sergeant Lobo to stare long and hard with eyes piercing.

Turning back to the *gringo*, "Hey man, what are the other hotel guests goin' to think of all this noise and activity goin' on here in this room and outside?"

He hesitates for answering, then in hushed tone, "The other guests on this floor will think nothing of it, as they are all prostitutes that live here in the rooms."

Without blinking an eye, my expression drops to cold seriousness, and in tone just as quiet but hissing, "You are aware that if this turns out to be a snuff film, nobody is going to gain a Goddamn thing from it. My death will be bad business for everyone." The puke doesn't answer—says nothing, thus, sending one eerie chill. The door closes, and the room appears to be empty, but it's not. No, Caribs are still in here—hiding; plus there is somethin' else… Uh, what is it?

Sergeant Lobo is again back out on the walkway. He's standin' off to the left, and with him is that mean ass lookin' black cop; they are bent in discussion. Whoa, if Sparky was spooked before, he's sure spooked big time now! Must get somethin' in my hands; a weapon. Of course mind is racing for machete tucked in backpack, but Christ, that is a bit extreme. Not quite ready for committing to that. Once the machete is pulled, all holy hell is gonna break—giving these cop fucker sons-a-bitches just the excuse for blowin' my brains out! Hhmm, my flashlight—twenty-inch steel black MAGLITE! It's discreetly standin' upright over there beside my pack, in front of the nightstand between the two beds. The need for getting my hands on it is feeling urgent; but how? How to justify having such a thing in hand without these monkeys assuming it's for defense purposes—a weapon? Aughg, the dreadful solution becomes obvious. Oh well—show time! "Hey cameraman! If we are gonna make a kick-ass porno, we need condoms! Yeah, also wet-wipes!' Bouncing over to my vest, folded over nightstand, I open one of the small side pockets and pull out a few individually sealed wet-wipe packets. "See, wet-wipes! Never leave home without 'em! Ha ha!" (Yeah, keep right on smilin' you sick weirdos.) "And now for condoms…" The backpack's top flap gets unzipped for condoms within. "Here! Here they are, condoms, rubbers! He he! They are magnums! For *mucho grande* cock! Can't have ass fucking without 'em! Hey you guys under the bed, when are you going to come out and play? Yeah, let's get this porno party started! Look at all this crack rock! I've never smoked crack before." (A lie: years ago back in Key West when crack was new to the scene, I once gave it a taste, and ended up smokin' ten rocks, one right after another, then started pukin' blood. Haven't touched the shit since.) "Bet it's a blast, especially if it makes the cock big and hard!" Looking, both beds have scooted closer together allowing for a gap between both walls and beds. (Buddy, they are under both beds, and are gonna spring anytime. Buddy!) Also noticed is the contents of all these little black meshed bags. Oh Sparky no… Guess what's in 'em? Guess! They are full of Goddamn, live, creepy crawlin' critters of the nasty insect variety. Packed in they are, all squirmin' to get out. Some bags are alive with hundreds of tiny black spiders, others small black scorpions, and at least one is noticed to contain centipedes. Fuck. (Buddy are we seein' this right? Yes; but don't let on to such. Yeah, okay).

"Hey cameraman, looky here, bet these guys under the beds can't do this!" In a blink of the eye, my steel MAGLITE flashlight is in hand. Spitting liberally on its blunt end for exaggerating lubing, a performance ensues with me appearing to slowly insert the damn end of huge flashlight up my own rectum… (ouch). But what the hell—it's buyin' desperate time, and the crowd outside is lovin' it! More importantly, this has given me my excuse for having a good solid weapon in hand (way better than my scared to death flaccid cock). Retracting flashlight from strained bung-hole, stepping up to the window for bowing in mock grace to applauding audience, I see Sergeant Lobo and the black cop still in huddle, 'cept now they are with a young woman wearing nothing but a thin robe about herself. She is nodding as if receiving detailed instructions. Lowering my voice and changing tone, I quietly ask the *gringo*, "Man what's up with all the spiders and scorpions?" The camera's indicator light goes off, and the guy does a quick discreet look about before answering in almost whisper explaining that this is not to be just a porno, but also what he calls a "shock film." (What the fuck?) "All those creepy biting insects are gonna be let loose to crawl and do whatever, over some poor soul? Uh let me guess, since I am the star of this video, the poor person would be me, right?" The American cameraman, having no expression, simply nods his head - yes. And now I can't breathe! Glancing to the cops, the black one is seen handing the young woman a knife; it's a medium size butcher knife, having thin curved blade and long angled point. The two then step through a side door, entering the building, while Lobo comes to join the *gringo* cameraman. I turn to walk for my pack. The time has come to die…

Just then, all hell breaks loose! From seemingly nowhere, yet everywhere, I am rushed, hit from behind, with Garifuna Caribs grabbing both arms, tossing me onto the bed furthest from the window, all gang piling, pinning my arms and legs, for spreading wide! Everything seems to go into some sort of surreal slow motion, despite knowing it to be not; this strange mode has engulfed me before while enduring traumatic experiences. Why? Who the fuck knows! My flashlight is clutched tightly in right hand (being mostly left handed it had been deliberately kept free for making that unsuccessful reach for machete). Someone is twisting and yanking trying to seize the flashlight from unwavering grip. Teeth are soon felt biting down hard on my index finger. Goddamn if it seriously don't feel like the finger is bein' bit off. Bone is struck and flashlight is surrendered with agony. A yell of triumph goes up for the victor now wielding the prized flashlight!

Everything must surely be goin' super fast, but the charged struggling commotion all seems a blur. A feeling of being in a rubber bag, suffocating, enfolds panic, horror, yet still I do feel them trying to force the flashlight up my ass. Fortunately, my pulsating adrenaline is overriding the pain, however, it is registering that they are having a time succeeding in penetrating the depth desired. So occupied these retard baboons have become, even the ones holding down my arms and attempting to tie my wrists to the bed's headboard. Despite the shocking haze, I sense they have become overly confident, and are at present, more interested in watching the flashlight go up my ass. There is now one primary thing on my mind: must not allow hands to be tied. Then a vision flashes: it's of a catfish. I had over the years witnessed the clever fish do this instinctual trick, and way more often than not, just about everybody one time or another—including myself—falls for it. The catfish—when put on the skinning table under firm grasp of captor, or when having a hook removed, after an admirable fight—will go completely limp, as if lifeless, and then right when the captor is confident of complete dominance, the slippery cunning fish will start violently thrashin', a-struggle with lightning speed of everything within, resulting in many a fisherman receiving deep painful wound. And sometimes, if out in a boat, the great catfish will occasionally—through steadfast, determined, aerial acrobatics—succeed a splash water landing, thus escaping! After witnessing the young woman being given the knife, I am (obviously) facing sure death. I'm nude, slippery with sweat, and have nothing to lose; so a catfish I become.

Suddenly my body goes completely limp—limp, like wet noodle limp—no breathing, no nothing, even heart stops. Everyone on me senses this and eases up somewhat on firm grasping grips. One even lets go of my left arm to adjust strap (short rope) for tying... Like a firing pin striking primer, I explode to life! With everything now in fast forward mode, I spin on my back, a-kickin' and lashin' out at everybody and everything! Frantic screams of surprise: "Grab him! Grab him! Hold him down!"

Too late—Sparky is upright with flashlight out of bloody recturm and in my hands. It's swingin', impacting hard against the side of Carib's head on my right. He bounces to slip down between the wall and bed. Large numbers of crabs rain down upon the bed! They are now scurrying all over. My oh-so-brave Garifuna attackers are now haulin' to get away from yours truly and the crabs that had obviously been tossed upon us—me. The crabs and (now) complete chaos only increase my ignited, flaming adrenaline! Sparky is usin' this energy of blasting velocity to full max! Oh yeah!

Off that bed I do fly—while at the same time reachin' into my pack pullin' out my sweet machete! (Oh—come to Daddy! Come to Daddy!) Spinning, standing before me is the cunt with the butcher knife. Like me, she too is now nude, and also like me, she has her blade. But in the instant, her eyes betray a loss of nerve and she begins motions telegraphing retreat. Too fucking late you skinny Garifuna *bitch*! My machete comes down chopping her at the neck where it meets with the collarbone! The blade vibrates as it strikes into the bone. The impact flings her onto the far side of the bed nearest the window. The young woman's neck is gashed open so wide as to look as if it just might lose the flopping head entirely. Blood is pumping, spraying gushes! Her hands go up for the head, as if tryin' to keep from losin' it, in jerky, spastic fashion. The dying woman rolls to slide down between wall and bed leaving behind so much blood, resembling buckets splashing! It is everywhere and brilliant!

I'm now pumped, with my own blood pulsating throughout a hundred miles an hour! Bloody machete is in left hand and flashlight is in bloody right hand (my index finger is bleedin' good from the bite). I'm ready for battle! I want battle—need battle! Need to kill more—MORE! But now the room is empty, well except for those hiding under the beds and (guessing) in closet and, more than likely, bathroom. Dumb buckwheat mother fuckers! If they had any brains they'd have all gotten the hell outta here, 'cause Sparky's gonna kill any that shows! Try rushin' me now you sick puke Garifunas! Glancing to the window—just on the other side, *gringo* and Sergeant Lobo are standin' side by side. The camera indicator light is on, and Lobo is grinnin' like he's getting' a blowjob! Mother fucker! A bit of a twist has been thrown into his little shock/snuff film, and he's diggin' it!

Yeah well, dig this dog face! I begin to yell and holler at the top of my lungs a continuous stream of "HELP! HELP! AMERICAN CITIZEN BEING ATTACKED! AMERICAN CITIZEN, HELP! HELP! *SOCORRO! AYÚDAME POR FAVOR! AYÚDAME! SOCORRO! SOCORRO!* PLEASE HELP! AMERICAN CITIZEN BEING ATTACKED!" Of course no help comes; and really none was expected. However, a voice such as my own, though most always gentle and soft, can, when called upon, rise forth to levels equaling that of any hyper-ventilating drill instructor of any military corps. And drama? He he! Whether it's for intimidating or pleading, Sparky can be dramatic! Thus the unseen, but very much heard, distress signal flare broadcasting position has been sent up for any that might want to take notice. Also, my sudden booming calls for help announcing an American being under attack, has (momentarily) wiped that sinister mocking grin from Lobo's arrogant Beaner face!

The sergeant begins to glance nervously all around, revealing that he don't want this becoming a big news story. No he does not! And me? Christ, here I am cornered in this stinkin' hell hole of a bloody hotel room, littered with cocaine, crack, hundreds of live crabs, and meshed bags of hideous biting insects. Not to mention the corpse of a nude young prostitute viciously murdered by me. (Buddy we are dead, dead, dead! But, we are gonna go down fightin'! And maybe, just maybe, when after we are dead and gone, talk about what really did happen on this night will reach the American Embassy, and well, at least they will know; and perhaps an investigation will ensue.) And so, covered in blood with machete in left hand and twenty-inch steel MAGLITE in other, I'm jumpin' and bellowin'! Never before have my senses been so more alive! Door, bathroom, closet, window, beds! Door, bathroom, closet, window, beds! Come on puke monkeys, rush me now!

"HELP, HELP! AMERICAN CITIZEN BEING ATTACKED!

HELP! *SOCORRO, AYÚDEME, AYÚDEME!'* (Aughg, what's the right call for help in Spanish? Uh, like it really matters). The old woman re-emerges outside, and she seems to be pissed as all get up and even scolding Sergeant Lobo. Her arms are waving before him with feet a-stompin'! The reasonable guess for such anger (other than Lobo earlier taking all her crack) would be to assume that she's understandably concerned with all the noise I'm making. Sergeant Lobo is again grinnin'; this time the smirk is directed toward the old woman. She must have some clout, but still, Lobo is in charge and so cannot seriously take an ass-chewin', not from an old woman, not in front of all these people. He will lose face. However, despite his cool demeanor of suave machismo before this old woman, he cannot totally ignore her either. I stop my howlin' to hear what's bein' said, but upon my silence, she turns and marches off. Lordy, it's time to flee this hell hole of a room; let 'em kill me out on the streets. (Yeah, more publicity that way, thus guaranteeing an investigation—and my dead body.) It's now or never! Must get my pack, vest, shorts and dirty red Converse high-tops on.

Jesus, even through fucked up sinuses, the smell—God the smell—is thick of blood, human blood, and shit: shit, blood, and death! Movies always leave out the shitting part of killing. Wonder why? The bed where the young woman landed before sliding down wall to go under... Oh Christ, looky at all that blood and loose feces. (Man, stop it! If you don't get out of this room, like soon, the next bed over is going to look the same—except it's goin' to be your blood and shit. At least dying out on the streets will be more dignified than in here as they are wanting. Must make it to the street. Okay buddy, you're right.) Blood! Blood is now coming from underneath the bed; crabs too. The Garifunas hiding under there (now with that hideous corpse) are stayin' put, but are pushin' and tossin' out live crabs that are seeking dark refuge amongst them. Quick and cautious, I step over and slide my pack toward the end of the beds. The ever growing pool of blood had almost reached it. The grout lines between tiles are already filling. Now for my Converse high-tops.

"HELP! HELP! AMERICAN CITIZEN BEING ATTACKED!" Glancing, there just on the other side of the window stands Sergeant Lobo; he has resumed his sinister grin towards me, conveying my shouting is having no effect. The *gringo* is standing beside him with camera rollin'. Oh well, time to shut up anyways. Gotta listen for all movement, especially there at the door, where the deadly grand exit will be attempted. But first, need to get shoes on, and for this, time must be bought. Buy time? How? Talk... Yes, must start talkin' to Lobo (make it loud enough for all to hear). "Boss! Boss Man, why'd you do this to me? I would have cooperated in making this porno. It would have been a good porno— the best! Boss, you would have made money... lots of it! But nooo, you had to pull this sick crap! And why Boss? Why? What did I do to you, except for, uh, minding my own damn business?' (Must get these shoes on quick!)

Aw fuck! The monkeys have put an open mesh bag of black tiny spiders in the toe of each shoe. Now the little leggy bastards are crawlin' all over inside and about the dirty red high-tops. Normally this would have been a real creep-out for me, since I've always sorta had a slight thing for spiders. (You know, not a phobia, but more of a, uh, understanding. They stay clear of me and Sparky stays clear of them, an arrangement that has, for the most part, worked well for both parties.) But, compared to this Sergeant Lobo and tonight's weird violence and that surely to come, these scurrying critters ain't jack squat—hardly worth noting. Yet, for benefit of buyin' time, for sake of camera still rollin', in attempts of capturing what was—and is to be—a shock rape, torture, snuff film. (\Mercy, the atrocious things man is capable of!) A bit of a show is put forward concerning the leggy nuisances.

"Aughg, SPIDERS! Who the hell put spiders in my shoes! You mother fuckers—I hate spiders!"

Laying steel MAGLITE down on top of pack (machete never leaves left hand, nor is guard dropped), shaking spiders from blood-sticking, dirty red Converse high-tops, while doin' an exaggerated dance of paranoia spinnin', as if bein' snuck up from locations obvious (no hard act to follow considering). With shoes on, bending for quick tying, it is noticed just how much of the young woman's blood has splattered on me. Also my bitten index finger is bleeding profusely, and, of course, this blood dripping from my balls must be from violated rectum. (Man, ignore it. Show no pain. You are a lean, mean killing machine—ex-Legionnaire!) Now for my shorts. Socks are muddled in the growing pool of thick ghastly blood, but shorts? Where are they? "Where are my Goddamn shorts?" Ught-O, also, my vest is missing with passport, wallets, traveler checks, and money! "And where is my vest? You mother fuckers toss out my shorts and vest NOW? And if you've even touched my passport or wallets I'm gonna flip those beds and start choppin'!" Instantly, the shorts come flyin' out from underneath the bloody bed, and my vest comes from the other.

The shorts are saturated in blood and a small snake is hastily crawlin' out from front left pocket. The tip from the machete's blade sends wiggling serpent for a lopsided hurl. Also in the blood soaked shorts there is a black meshed bag, full of squirmin' whatevers. Tryin' hard to ignore them, but noticing they are small scorpions freeing themselves; amongst them I put my foot down on shorts and reach—pulling needed belt. The shorts are stayin' right where they are. Another pair is rolled in my pack up toward the top. Without looking, they are felt and pulled forth.

"Why Boss? Why did you have to go and do this? I never did nothin' to you! I'm a husband and a father, a good man! *Soy Padre de familia*! My *familia* needs me *muy* much!' The fresh shorts are now on; but of course, way too big and keep wanting to fall back down, presenting a very comical spectacle that Lobo is finding great humor in. (Yeah, keep laughin' you sick puke.) With machete at ready and jumpin' to everything and anything, I am urgently attempting to get this belt through too-tight belt loops of khaki shorts… (Goddamn confounded French equipment). Fuck it. Using top waist line of over sized shorts to roll down over, the belt is cinched tight, without goin' through loops. A serious sense of time running out is upon. "Boss, I'm a Christian" (not). "A God-fearin' Christian! And you, you can do this to me? And on a Sunday! The day of the Lord!" A murmur is heard goin' around from some of the observing rooftop spectators. (Hhmm, is this good or bad? Who the fuck knows. One would think that all those Bible thumpin' missionaries from the last couple hundred years would have had some impact—yes? Yeah well, geez, obviously they missed a few huh?) Now for vest; I must quickly go through all pockets of importance. It doesn't take long to discover that they didn't take anything out, but did put things in. Things like many bags of cocaine, ranging in weight bein' mostly individual grams to that equaling quarter ounce. Along with the dope, they put in black meshed bags having the various creepy insects now crawlin' freely throughout the vest. My wallets are in discreet zippered inside pockets. The monkeys obviously hadn't the time to find these. There is a total of eighteen pockets after all. My passport has been removed, but replaced. So now my hands are left spazzin' with instinctual jerks for pullin' out cocaine and meshed bags, still containing some nasty critters.

With shoes and shorts now on, and bein' confident that wallets and passport are in place, I change tone with Sergeant Lobo and begin to ramble on and on about how I came to Central America for doing some volunteer work for a Guatemalan orphanage, but wanted to first visit Honduras because of its beauty and rumored friendly people. "I just loved Utila; the people there are great. Uh, by the way, you are aware that I've just flown in from Cuba? Well, my travels are now bein' tracked by the American Embassy!" (Jesus, buddy, is this last blurt a gamble or what? Oh like there's really anything to lose at this point.) "Tell him cameraman, tell Boss how it is for Americans goin' to Cuba!" Fuck it, roll the vest up, spiders and all, tossing it into the pack while very quickly runnin' straps through buckles, but not cinching tight.

"Boss! Whatta you say Boss? Forget and forgive? Think about it Boss... Let's just chalk this whole thing off like it never happened. Let me walk out of here Boss, and I won't look back, won't breath a word of this to anyone. Hell Boss, you can trust me. I have nothing to gain by speaking of tonight. Besides, you are a very important man, I don't want you for an enemy! Before God I swear never to speak of this night to anyone—on the lives of my wife and *dos hijos* I swear. Please, just let me walk out of here in peace. Boss?" From the corner of my eye, my red cotton oil rag hanky is noticed there on the floor. While bending for snatchin' it up, a Garifuna is revealed attempting to slide out from under the bed. (The fuckers are still whisking persistent crabs out.) My eyes meet his and back under the bed he slides.

Grinnin' Sergeant Lobo, for answer, sarcastically shakes his head for a silent no.

"No? Why Boss? This doesn't make any sense! What do you have to gain... from any of this? Please, please Boss: let me walk outta here!"

The asshole only hisses, "No!"

Gringo clicks off the camera's light and leans toward the Sergeant for speaking quietly as if not to be overheard, but overheard he is. "We will not be able to sell any of this film in the US or Europe. He is too well known and has been documented too much. Tattoo artists are now very popular. See the scars on his back? They are from doing an ancient American Indian ritual where he hung from hooks pierced through his skin. It is very probable that he is famous for this. He is also an ex-soldier, both American and French. See the tattoo on his right upper arm? It's French military, Foreign Legion. He claims to of been interviewed by Sixty Minutes while he was serving. I believe him. It's not common for Americans to join the Legion; he would be considered unique for doing so. Also if he was in Cuba before arriving here?" The cameraman shrugs his shoulders, adding, "He does speak French and has the markings."

Lobo coolly waves this information off like it has no meaning and changes nothing. But standing behind him, to the left and slightly in the shadows, is the old woman; she too overheard the *gringo*, and upon now seeing the Sergeant's unheeding response, she throws her arms up in disgust and again leaves.

Well now, wasn't that interesting. Goddamn Latin macho prick! He's like the Beaner from hell! Must get some of this blood off and make for a breakout! Urgently, my red hanky is bein' spit on and used to somewhat wipe blood (mostly succeeding in only smearing). Again the camera light is on and Lobo seems to be amused with my actions. A few wet-wipe packets are seen bein' within reach. The hanky rag, after bein' used for quickly wiping rectum from up under shorts' wide leggings (and noting it's no longer bleeding much), goes to bitten index finger. (Human bites bleed good.) Wrapping the rag tightly around the bleeding finger of right hand while whole time keeping machete at ready in left, reaching for the wet wipe packets and tearing open with teeth, I put 'em to work. (Fuckin' blood!) In doing, a giant toad is noticed crouching from the corner. Gosh, how many different critters did they bring into this room? The bizarre toad is just staring, staring at me.

Suddenly a noise is heard coming from up in the ceiling loft. Oh, how stupid! The brain had spaced-out the ceiling loft. Sparky forgot to look up. Bad, bad, bad! A gun could be pointing down at this very moment! In a blink of an eye, right hand is thumbing the MAGLITE's on/off button, but the damn thing won't turn on! Shake, shake, shake, click, click: light abruptly bursts forth shinin' bright! Up in the loft, there is no one with a gun. No there is not, but there are two little girls. They are nude and their big hollow eyes are looking down, conveying their purpose. My heart sinks, but only to bounce with a surge of anger not to be controlled! Spinning: "You sick, SICK MOTHER FUCKERS! You use children! CHILDREN! For these sick videos! Baby children… Jesus GOD! How do you people out there let them do this sort of thing! I pray you all BURN IN HELL!"

At that very moment, the same Garifuna as before slides halfway out from under the bed and throws a good-size snake at me! The snake's flight is easily blocked (chopped) with machete, that in swing cannot be stopped there. Pouncing the bed's side, I begin to hack into the unseen, snake-throwin' bastard underneath! The impact from the stabbin' is felt hitting human flesh and bone. He is screamin', pleading cries of pain, shock, and fear! The bed is heavin' up and down as those under are now desperately struggling to get as far away as possible. Swinging and thrusting with repeated flash speed, the blade works a bloody mess. During this, above the shrieking screams, I'm yellin', "FUCKER! FUCKER! MOTHER FUCKER! Were you gonna hurt those little girls! Like hurting people, huh? Huh? Who's gettin' hurt now MOTHER FUCKER!" The blade withdraws, cutting through two clutching hands, a final thrust strikes skull. His limp, wheezing gurglings convey death. From out of corner, my eye catches movement. There, across the room, two Garifunas are in strides for rushin' me!

In a heartbeat, I am upright to take 'em on, with machete a-swingin'! However, they quickly change their minds and dart back for the closet from where they had come. Springing after them to kill, I am now insane with rage, adrenaline and blood lust! KILL! KILL! KILL! In pursuit, flyin' around the end of the beds...WHOA-SHIT! To a halting stop I do come! The room's door now has a hole through it bein' the size of a baseball. It had been discreetly covered by an unnoticed panel plate before, but not anymore. The panel plate is now lying on the tiled floor. And fuck me! From this hole, there is a stainless steel rifle barrel pointed right at you know who! By the distinct front sight, diameter, and shape of barrel, the gun is easily recognized as bein' a Ruger Mini 14. And behind this rifle? Well, obviously it's that mean ass black cop. Now, ain't this just the wretched icing on the cake!

"Boss? Boss Man! Call him off! Think about this... It don't have to go down this way!" Turning sideways with legs apart ready, back is to the long wall, but not touching, leaving space for unhindered spinning. Before me are (more or less) the ends of the two beds, right of these are (adjacent) bathroom and closet. My right arm is raised at ready, pointing black twenty-inch steel MAGLITE towards room's door with rifle targeting me at distance of perhaps twelve feet. My left hand holds bloody machete toward window fronting Sergeant Lobo, *gringo* camera-man, and spectators. My chest is heavin' (having most probably doubled in size), muscles are corded, visibly twitching with veins surfaced, bulgin' from blood surgin' throughout like never before! As with all cornered creatures, my eyes are darting at lightning speed to and fro! Door, closet, bathroom, beds, window! Sometimes in this order, sometimes not, but alert and darting they are. Must keep 'em movin'! Do not fix eyes upon anything. Blood is now spreading out from under both beds—ignore it. Pay no attention to blood, crabs, snakes, spiders, whatevers—only people! Kill any that move! To hell with the rifle.

The cornered giant toad nips at a brown crab that has scurried too close. For surreal micro instant I feel a strange sorta kinship with this bizarre creature. Maybe I can put him in my pack and we can both go for this sure to be suicidal break-out. (Man, snap the fuck out of it! Stay sharp—frosty sharp!) "Boss please! I'm begging you please, please let me walk outta here! You have the respect of the people; you have this place with the girls working for you, and here you make your sick movies! A lot of money is made here. Cameraman, tell him! Tell him he's got some good shock film of me; and because of what has happened here and it all bein' on video, I'll never talk. Tell him cameraman. Tell him! Tell him what will happen if he kills me." (My voice is now boomin'!) "Cameraman remind Boss that I've just come in from Cuba! The US government is trackin' my every move down here. They know where I am. My wife and *familia* know where I am. Hell, even the French government knows I'm here! If Boss Man kills me, the investigation will be so big that everybody's operation will have to stop! Boss, it's bad business, just bad business! Please let me walk out of here in peace and go home to my family!"

The cameraman leans over for sayin' something to Lobo. At the same time, the old woman is again in sight, with hands on hips, looking both concerned and angry. A rooftop spectator yells down in a sincere tone, "Let him go! Let the American go home!" Lobo's grin drops as he turns to see who yelled that. The old woman has come up close to the window and is eyein' me as if she is lookin' at pure trouble. (Good okay, now talk to her, get the bitch to feel sorry for us.)

"Ma'am, please Ma'am, I didn't want any of this. I wanted no girls, no boys, no *drugo*. I just wanted to be left in peace! But they just came in. Please advise the good Sergeant that this is bad business. All businesses will suffer from my death tonight. Please Ma'am, please, I just want to go home to my *esposa* and *dos hijos*. Please Ma'am, surely you are a lady of business, therefore understand the logic in letting me go free. All will benefit. My death, though, who will benefit? Only bad business and investigations. Ma'am please, my *familia*…!"

She turns to Lobo and says something. He responds by grinnin' and shruggin' his shoulders. The old woman, again looking pissed, takes leave. The Sergeant then speaks to me, "Drop the machete and you can leave. No one will harm you and you can go home to your family in the US."

"Boss, let me get this straight, if I drop my machete you will let me go? Just walk right on out of here a free man? No one will attack me?" His sinister grinnin' nod betrays him bein' full of shit. I'm dead. With my own mocking sinister grin, "Boss, how about me keeping my machete and you get Deputy Dog there to back the fuck off, and tell your boys to stay put, and I'll just walk out of here and you won't ever hear from me again. How 'bout that?"

Grinnin' his evil ass grin, he shakes his head—no—then steps out of view. Fuck, fuck, fuck! "Hey Deputy Dog! Whatcha got in that Ruger Mini 14? It's a Mini 14, right?" The muzzle nods up and down answering yes. "Yeah, see I'm kind of familiar with firearms. Let me guess, you don't have hollow points, but rather NATO full metal jacket 5.56 or in civilian language .223, right?" This babbling is for desperately buyin' some time, while waitin' to see just what it is that is gonna be comin' through that door: a bullet, or Lobo and boys chargin'! The Sergeant is back again to the window. With him are Garifunas holding a blanket up to prevent watching bystanders and rooftop spectators from seeing what is about to take place. My time is up; I'm gonna be shot and they (for whatever reason) don't want any witnesses. Sucking in a big breath, and just about to *charge* that door with a last-ditch battle cry for *death*, I'm hoping to take the bullets in the chest and head for a quick death before the torturing baboons can have their fun with me. Then... what the hell? They've brought out a little girl of (guessin') five years in age. She is nude, gagged, and her hands are tied behind her back. (Oh my God, NO!) The Sergeant steps back and cameraman zooms in. A big Garifuna grasps the terror stricken child by bound arms and hoists her up. Two other Caribs each grab hold of her legs and spreads them wide. (Buddy? Man, don't look, don't watch this sick shit. Most likely they are just doin' this to distract for the charge attack! Watch the door, bathroom, closet, beds!) "Devon, oh Devon, drop the machete, or else..." Looking, I see there is a nude taunting teenage Garifuna bitch holding a Bic lighter up to the little girl's vagina. White fucking teeth are gleamin' in menacing contrast to the dark skin of those grouped, participating in this child torture. Of course the young lighter wielding woman is recognized as bein' the same that had earlier been out there exposing herself and blowing big dick; she continues the insane staged demands of threatening, "Or else... Devon, drop the machete."

Think, must think! "Uh, If you hurt that child I will KILL everybody in this room!"

Oh Lordy! Oh God! The baby girl is squirming, with eyes clenched tight and face bright red in strain from intense pain. She has urinated and there are still droplets. The torturing bitch has flicked the Bic and a flame is now burning the little bucking girl—burning her privates! The flesh is turning colors. The sick bastards are laughin' while bracing to hold the tortured, struggling child; her screams are muffled, gagged, breathless. The tormenting laughter continues until the little girl defecates; this brings a stop to the laughing and they all behave in deranged mannerism as if the child had done something bad, disgusting, intolerable. And now she must really be punished (Oh Goddamn! The floor is moving, it seems like the tiles are rolling into waves of four-legged snakes shaped like the tiles themselves... O-huh-whoa... Man, snap out of it! Do not go into a freak-out, shock mode! This is just what they are wanting. Breathe, breathe, and remember, four-legged snakes will not hurt you; only the two-legged ones can. So breathe; shake it off, and stand strong. They must not detect any weakness. Yeah, yeah, you're right buddy; whew! Buddy we have seen the light, we have been in the know all along: there is no God, none. Looky what they are doing to that poor baby girl.)

"You sick MOTHER FUCKERS!" Screamin' at the top of my lungs, "HELP, HELP, HELP! They are hurting BABIES! HURTING BABIES! *Malo hombres* HURTING *LA NINA'S!* Help! *AYUDA, AYÚDEME, AU SECOURS, SOCCORO, AID-AIDEZ, SECOURS, ATORMENTAR LA NIÑAS HELP! MEURTRE LA ENFANTS, ASESINATO-MURERTE-HOMICIDA! AU SECOURS! MEURTRE LA ENFANTS—NIÑAS! HELP!"* (Geez, I don't know if I'm yellin' Spanish, French, or what? But it is workin'.) The old woman is back, and despite Lobo, she is obviously ordering the torturing Caribs to wrap the child in the blanket and take her away. The old woman speaks a language I've never heard before (but that ain't sayin' much). My booming hollerin' stops to catch breath, listen, and save energy. However refrainment is short lived for sounding off "Hey Deputy Dog, if you're gonna shoot me then squeeze that fuckin' trigger! And you—Sergeant Lobo—that's some sick shit you do. I'm outta here—gone!" Sarcastically he snarls, "And how is it, Devon, you think you are going to leave, eh?"

"I'm gonna charge right through that window! Have fun explaining that one asshole!" And *charge* I do, stopping just short of busting through the glass. Everybody scatters, and like *fast!* These sons-a-bitches are now thoroughly convinced Sparky is goin' down fightin'! The oh so brave Sergeant Lobo bolts a run, taking up hiding there around the end of the dumpster, thus exposing to everyone just what a punk-ass chicken whimp he actually is; and all have seen. And still, Deputy Dog has not yet fired (The expected slammin' bullets are compounding adrenalin like can't be believed.) Sergeant Lobo quickly realizes my charge was only a bluff, generating much humiliation on to himself. He tries to regain his old machismo demeanor. Rises from his squatting hiding spot, acting cool, calm, collected, and once again in command. Straightening out his uniform, he pulls the six-inch barreled revolver (an older colt or Smith and Wesson, in .38 special), and approaches the window with entourage emerging from shadows. I step back and take up my room defense position. Lobo, looking furious, aims the .38 right at me.

Now for some reason there is a strange confidence the shot ain't gonna come from him. No, it's gonna come from the Mini 14 pointin' through the door. He he! That black bastard better not miss or he just might take-out ol' Lobo himself! The humor is very short-lived. Fuckin' terrified I am, but this they are no longer seein' in me. No, my seeming mien is now that of wild, blood lust, loco crazy. Lobo lowers the revolver. (My God, why are they prolonging this horror show?) The music from downstairs is again heard and floats to me in answer. Hhmm, Maybe and maybe not. Could it be that they are waiting for the night's hour to grow later, for the restaurant below to close? Obviously, people are down there. People perhaps Lobo would rather not have hear the blasting of a gunshot echoing within the hotel. Bet my left nut he isn't wanting a gunshot—not at this point in time.

"Sergeant, Boss, my friend, with no disrespect, I am outta here! Hey Deputy Dog, whatcha got in that Mini 14, a twenty—or thirty—round magazine? No matter, whatever's in there, you better empty 'em all into me, 'cause I'm comin' through that door and if you don't drop me, I'm gonna make you dead! Goddamn I am pumped!" The old woman is heard on the other side of the door, speakin' that strange Garifuna tongue to Deputy Dog.

Fuck it! With speed of fluidity impressing even myself, twenty-inch steel black MAGLITE is drop-shoved down into pack, shoulder bag is slung over neck, and right arm slides into both straps of heavy backpack (now seeming almost weightless). Up it comes, acting as a shield for my chest and face. Machete raises. (Boy-oh-boy, the suicidal surreal reality of chargin' a deranged, gun pointin', Central American cop with a bloody machete is at best an electrified, gut wrenching, breath-taking fusion of beginning and end.) "MARCH OR DIE MOTHER FUCKER!" And I charge!

But not a shot is fired. The rifle quickly withdraws as my pack slams into the door! At the same time, my left foot flies up to brace close the trifold wooden slat (louver) closet doors. Between the wide gaps of the horizontal slats, I can see the whites of eyes and teeth against dark skin. There's three of them in there. One moves, causing my pumped self to react on automatic impulse. Flash thrust the machete through a gap of the slats deep into the soft lower abdomen. He grabs the blade with both hands while letting out a long hollow gush of agonizing moan. His comrades (one on each side) work to hold him up before them as they do their best to become one with the furthest wall of the closet. Blood is pooling at my feet and mental note is taken, for footing must not slip.

"Any of you fuckers even try comin' out of there, you're dead— DEAD! And the same goes for those of you in the bathroom! Lobo! Sergeant Lobo! You even try stopping me out on the street, be prepared to gun me down, 'cause I ain't gonna be taken alive! And mother fucker, someone will talk, and tell the real story of what went down in this room. The Americans investigating this mess will be payin' money—cash money—for information concerning facts of what lead up to my death! Tell him cameraman—tell him, someone will talk!"

Out the door I go, swingin' pack out first! Surely here, in the hall, bullets will start rippin'! However, they don't. No, no they do not. Why? Where is that black Carib cop? Spinning—oh Jesus Christ—the next room over has its door (obviously purposely) wide open. There upon the bed, lying on her back, sprawled, gagged, and tied, staring straight at me, is the nude little girl they had tortured with the lighter (or so it's guessed to be the same little girl). This child is literally covered in blood from what looks to be multiple cuts, in the hundreds. Her chest is slightly heaving (she's still alive), dark specks of whatever are crawlin' all over her. (Snap out of it—MOVE! Yeah, buddy, right!) With straps riding crook of arm raising pack for shield and machete at ready for battle, I fly down those stairs, expecting a waiting firing squad. Landing at the bottom in crouched position, there is no such thing. Bright lights and loud music. To my right is the short front desk; behind it are standing two very big-eyed, innocent teenagers (one male, the other female). They freeze at the sight of me. To my left (across the room) is the small refreshment counter; behind it is one of the two bitches that had checked me into this hell hole. Beyond this counter and slightly out of view is the lively loud restaurant dining area. Before me is the big glass front. No one at present is out on the sidewalk, but there sure will be—and like soon! Glancin' again to the left, and expectin' the bitchy woman to start screamin' for help or somethin', she doesn't. No; instead she quickly nods urgency toward the two teenagers, while motioning with frantic silent gestures for me to get goin' out the front door! The woman then swishes from around her counter to stand with arms crossed as if monitoring the dining crowd, but really the purpose of this position is for blocking view. Jesus, I'm shirtless with blood all over me, my eyes are crazed for killing and machete is at ready! In a flash, my pack is dropped to the floor and machete is thrust down into with handle protruding for quick pulling. A leap has me and pack to land before the front desk of the two teenagers. "Taxicab?" (Breathing hard.) "Where can I catch a taxicab? Understand—*entiende usted*?"

Both youngsters snap out of their dazed stupor. The girl shoots a hand pointing to the left, while in hurried low tone answers, "They park there—town's central—but you must not go that way; they will search for you there!" Swingin' her arm to the right, "Go that way, to the sea. There are always many taxicabs driving along those streets, you can catch one there. Find a dark street, hide and wait for a taxicab." The boy tosses me a very wet rag (possibly an old cotton diaper). He has others that he is fast wetting down with big squirt bottle, retrieved from behind the counter. I immediately begin to wipe down my legs, torso, arms, and hands. The right index finger is still bleeding, but not as bad.

From finger to front pocket red hanky goes while using the diaper for the speed wipe-down. (Blood is very hard to make go away.) Fuck, it must be doin' some good because the girl points to my neck and face, nodding for me to wipe. I can smell and feel the bleach cleaning solution. The boy swiftly goes about scrubbing my bloody footprints from the floor. Reaching for now bloodstained diaper rag, the girl waves frantically for me to go! Tossin' my pack up, throwin' arms into the straps, out that door I do go! Three steps has legs a-pumpin'! The mouth of (now dark) walkway separating back hotel from apartment complex is instantly spotted. (Ambush?) No choice, must cross deserted street to avoid the more than likely possibility. In flyin' past, sure as shit Skippy, two Garifunas dash out from the suspected ambush site and are in hot pursuit! Fortunately, this is a downhill run; houses have lights on but there is no traffic; also there appear (at the moment) to be no people out—uh, except for the two persistent sons-a-bitches on my heels! Darkness is a few blocks ahead and this is guessed to be the seaside road.

The two Caribs are gainin'. Goddamn, they are comin' down fast! Reachin' up and back, out comes the machete while at the same time red high-tops skid for a turn-about and a charge ensues with me now chasin' them! However, the stupidity of such action is quickly realized; so another turn-about kicks gears for haulin' ass down that street into looming darkness calling. Bounding across the seaside road and plowing through thick entangling scrub brush foliage paralleling, sand is felt under foot and the lapping sea is before me. Halting, bending to catch air for breath… Whoa! What now? Bad idea, bad idea! Yes, it is dark, but not that dark. The moon, though not full, is shinin', creating an ocean of glimmerings, thus giving off way more light than needed or wanted; plus now the ocean has just become one big, long, unyielding wall that cannot be climbed. Fuck, fuck, fuck!

Gotta keep movin'. Can't hide here on the beach; the chasing Garifunas are most likely now reporting to Lobo my position. Must avoid the sure to come flanking. In both directions up and down the beach, there are distant lights and music from various scattered seaside open cabana Tiki bars and the likes. Aughg, it sucks not being able to blend in with the general population. Hhmm, this must have been how it felt bein' a black man back in the States during the South's not-so-long-ago lynching period. Wretched Klu Klux Klaners. Geez, maybe in my last life I had been one of those sick crackers out to hang me a nigger, and this is my payback. (Buddy whatcha think? Man, enough! Get moving, and think—think of nothing but escape. March or die! okay, right.) Escape; but how? The ocean? No, will never be able to swim the required distance and can't waste the energy even tryin'. Must conserve strength and energy for fighting and running. (Then do it—RUN!).

Backing away from the lapping water's edge and taking my shadow silhouette with me, running along the sparse cover of trash-strewn overgrown scrub brush of knurly knotted bush, saw grasses, vines and dwarfed palms, mangroves—whatever! Rocks! There's some rock pilings up ahead, big ones that run from this line of cover down to the water's edge. Damn, the ocean's noise is seriously interfering with my fear induced ultra acute hearing. It's decided to use the rocks' cover for again goin' back down to the water. There is a need to wash up better before taking on the now decided course of my run.

I'm gonna play rabbit! You know? Run a big circle—circling back. They will be all down here lookin' for me and I'll be back up there tryin' like hell to stay hidden and catch a taxicab. But first, I want the blood out of these shorts and off the machete. (Man, just make it fast!) Tryin' hard not to cast a silhouette, sliding shoulders from pack and shoulder bag, I wade out into the water with machete in one hand and red hanky rag in the other. Fast as can be, a scrub down ensues, including the dunking of face, head, and hair in banded ponytail. Also, I gotta pee. Raising sopping wet short legging for emptying bladder, it won't come; though full, the bladder is too uptight—scared for releasing contents. Gosh, I thought people were supposed to piss themselves when overly afraid? Fuck this, there's no time! Reaching for my pack and shoulder bag, my heart *slams* the chest! From corner of eye, the whites of another's eyes. He's to my left, lying on his side, down in between a long crevice of the rocks. He is bent with back arched and torso forward to discreetly conform with rocks concealing. It would have worked too had not the whites of his eyes betrayed him. With the second beat of my heart, I'm up on him, using both hands to shove the machete through his upper rib cage! Despite the blade's sharpness and my adrenaline speed and strength, there is some brief resistance and horrific screaming (from him) before the blade punches through for cutting vital organs and shutting him up! Christ, the shrieking screams are echoing! Backing away, my heart is poundin' and lungs are constricting. I can't fuckin' breathe! Dropping to knees and crawlin' for my pack, the inner head is whirlin' with brilliant colors flashin' within. (Come on man, you've been through this before. Don't pass out! Remember, breathe, make yourself breathe. That's it, nice and easy. In and out—in and out. Okay, now open your eyes, shake it off, gear up, and move—*run*!)

Getting to feet, wiping blade, pack and shoulder bag on, breathin' heavy with last of fleeting tracers clearing head (somewhat), hunched forward with red Converse high-tops sloshing, *I run!*

After letting a slow non taxicab car pass, I shoot across that road making use of any and all possible cover for getting myself back towards town's *centro*. At first this is not too bad, but then backyards become smaller and more fenced off; also dogs are barking. Having no choice, it's haul ass time, up one street, down another, jumpin' yards for barrelin' out across this street and that... Ught, there goes a taxicab! Zippin' to the middle of the street I go, chasin' after the passing taxicab, but it doesn't stop. No, but I must... Bent for sucking in much needed air, lungs are screamin' with strained knees trembling. Gotta keep movin', get out from the middle of this blasted street. But to where? There now ain't jack shit for cover. A sound—"Sphsisst!" It's from a little old woman. She is on her veranda porch, sitting in a rocking chair motioning for my approach. I do, stopping at the four-foot block wall that seems to be now spanning the bordered front of most every property along these streets. The low rod-iron gate used for accessing the few feet of yard before veranda steps and this block wall is now (like everyone else's) closed. The woman's eyes and smile appear warm, calm, and genuinely kind. She asks if I'm in trouble.

"Yes, yes Ma'am!" And rapidly my story spills forth (of course leavin' out all the parts of me *killin'*). My body lowers, pushing into the block wall, tryin' to blend with only head peering above. My tale ends with the blurting of urgent need for a taxicab. She just rocks the chair gently, listens and looks upon me with sad sympathetic eyes. Nodding, the old woman remarks, "Yes, the *policia* here are very bad. They pay or force young people to do their dirty work. It is all very bad now."

"Ma'am, are all the police in Trujillo this way?"

"No young man, not all, but so many are that it is most difficult for those that are not."

I now very, very much want to be on the other side of her low concrete wall and hide. You better believe;and she could be my look-out for a taxicab. However, upon politely asking, she, looking heavy-hearted, answers, "No, my husband is away and it is not permissible for anyone to come through my gate when he is gone."

Oh damn—can't blame her, after what has been seen and experienced tonight. (Jesus, she probably doesn't even have a living husband.) Geez, if they found out that she had let me hide on her property, they would for sure kill her. Seeing my anxiety-ridden despair, the old woman tries soothing, "Do not worry young man, a taxicab will soon come. They drive up this street very often; one after the other. You will see. Just stand right there. No one will hurt you while you are in front of my gate."

Yeah, okey-dokey; there's real security in those words. If a fuckin' taxicab don't get here like quick, all hell is gonna break loose! On feet jumpin', I begin to tell the old woman about my wife and sons. Repeating their names and town and state where they live, I ask her, if she should hear of my death or imprisonment, would she share this information with someone that might be able to pass it along to the American Embassy people? Gently rocking her chair, she answers, using voice and eyes hinting, that here in Trujillo, this is no absurd request. The kind woman promises to do what I ask.

Shit! Here comes a taxicab! Oooh, please stop! My frantic waving · stops him. "Thank you Ma'am! Please remember—my name is Devin, Devin Murfin!"

"Yes young man, I will remember; and may God be with you so that you may return home safely to your *familia*!"

(Yeah, well God can kiss my ass.) I dash for the taxicab. Machete is, and has been, in hand, but with blade riding somewhat discreetly up inner arm against side of pack.

O pening the front passenger door, tossing pack and machete to floor board, I jump in on top with door a-slammin'. The frail aging cabby glances at the machete but of it remains silent, asking only "Destination?" Not wanting to frighten him, my answer is calm, serious, yet urgent: "There is a street gang of very bad people trying to hurt me, I must get out of town immediately; can you, sir, drive me to the next town... Please?" The cabby, upon hearing, nods and looks concerned, with a willingness to help, but explains that the nearest town is no short drive and will be expensive.

"No problem, I can pay in US dollars; just get me outta here and there will be a big tip—*mucho grande propina!*" His eyes light up with the prospect, but first (guess what?) he must drive to the *centro* square and leave word as to where the vehicle is bein' driven. (No, no, no!)

"No, please, please! I will pay extra! Let's just drive—please! No one must know where I am going. They will come for me!"

"I understand young man, have no fear; our destination will be very discreet. I must only inform my employer; he is understanding with such matters and will say nothing. It will be okay, you will see, one *momento* only; a quick stop, and we will be going!"

Fuck me! The old cabby is insistent, and so to town *centro* we go! And of course it's hoppin' with activity. Not one American or European tourist is seen (little damn good they'd do anyways). However, there are several open jeeps full of cops and soldiers wearin' either brown or black uniforms. These jeeps have row bar mounted strobe lights and are patrolling. The cabby, after pulling up to a curb and parking, quickly exits the vehicle and walks towards many parked taxi cabs, all side by side, with cabbies standin' around. I am scrunching down best as possible, while still keepin' eyes above dash. Suddenly bright flashing blue lights appear; a jeep has pulled up behind. I am strongly ordered out at anxious gun point! The machete now is not even an option... Hhmm, or is it? A move for the blade will surely bring instant death, thus ending this nightmare. Four have exited the jeep, two are in brown uniforms and haven't even drawn their weapons, which appear to be older revolvers. But the other two—wearin' black military BDUs—are locked and loaded! One has advanced swiftly, to have me starin' up into the barrel of his twelve gauge pump. The other is covering with a 9 mm Beretta.

The old cabby comes running over to excitedly ask the problem. Fuck, though my death will be quick, with a body for sending back home, I just can't do it, not here, not out in the open like this while there is still a possible chance that this cabby and all the now gathering witnessing people might provide. My arms slowly raise and from the taxicab I am pulled, along with the machete and kit (pack and shoulder bag). The cabby is persistently repeating his question as to the problem? Finally, one of the brown-uniformed cops explains I'm being put under arrest for possession of a machete. The cabby respectfully argues that there is no law forbidding machetes. The cop calmly declares that there is: "One can not freely go about town possessing a machete with blade exposed. His machete has no [some word used to mean sheath]. This is a very serious violation." The cabby and others passively express their muttered opinions concerning the charge as being ridiculous.

Finding my voice: "A sheath? I have a sheath for the machete! Here, it's in my backpack…" Reaching to open the pack, both guns instantly go to my head. Whoa, the bladder is quiverin' now!

After bein' ordered into the jeep, I'm driven around the circular square for the police station/jail. The two brown-uniformed cops escort me (one on each side) through the station house door and lead me to cross the room toward the long old wooden front counter desk. My head is whirlin' but still registering. There are several cops behind and around the desk; they are brown Latinos and, ironically, they are wearing brown uniforms, whereas the black Caribs are clad in solid black military BDUs. My approach is now being watched with silent, intense curiosity. (None appear least bit surprised. Quite the contrary, they seem to have been expecting.) A few feet from the front desk when SLAM, a combat boot lands a kick into my center back, sending me to fly, bouncing onto and off the front desk, buckling knees for dropping to filthy floor. Gasping and desperately struggling to regain footing, I am amazed at the instant barrage of (seemingly) sincere verbal protests that are now bein' directed towards the black Carib in black uniform that had kicked me. I am even helped to my feet by two brown cops escorting. The Caribs, in their black BDUs, just smile a glarin' smirk. They then take up positions beside the door, where they can watch both me and the street, as if waiting for somebody. Oh God, please don't let it be Sergeant Lobo and his black Deputy Dog sidekick! In their hands… Fuuuckk.

The cop on the right passes my machete across the desk, handing it to an older cop having Sergeant stripes with ranking rockers; he is holding himself to be (for now at least) the one here in charge. The sight of my machete brings about excited murmurs of interest. Every brown uniform in the place is now eager for a chance at handling the blade, almost as if they were in respecting awe. Damn, it is more than obvious that these guys know all about what went down back in that hotel room, but somethin's missin'—there seems to be little if no hostility towards me. No, not from these browns. Their eyes betray them to be cops crooked as corkscrews, but lacking that spark of blood-curdling cruelty, the whole loose wire, I'm a-gonna torture for sport look. These guys aren't like Lobo, Deputy Dog, the *gringo*, Garifuna street gang, and two black Carib soldier thugs now behind, covering the door, or so is assumed. (Right buddy? Buddy? Buddy! Crap.) The ranking desk sergeant inspects the machete while sending searching glances toward me as if for some sort of determining. After a minute or so, he passes the blade to others waiting. (Play it man, play it. Let's see what happens. Okay-buddy, besides, it ain't like we got nothin' to lose, right?) Frantically lookin' deeply into the ranking desk sergeant's eyes, I let it out!

Trembling, heaving, spasmodic gulps for breath and even some tears, a Goddamn nervous breakdown ensues! Yep, I turn into fuckin' jell-O and begin weeping out my frightful tale of how two bad imposters dressed like policemen, and a street gang of young people, terrorized me in my hotel room. And the children—little children—*pequeno niñas*! They hurt the *niñas*, severely burning them and sexually violating—raping and forcing sex—while the whole time filming it all on video camera!" (Blah, blah, blah!) The mentioning of children and video filming does seem to strike home! And from the expressions now surrounding, it is guessed these cops know all about the torture/snuff films and do not approve. I add that I am a serious Christian with a loving wife and two young sons; and my purpose for coming to Central America was for volunteer work at an orphanage in Guatemala and...

The ranking desk sergeant interrupts my ramblings to ask how it is I know the two men dressed in police uniforms are not really police? My mouth drops, with eyes glancin' from one cop to the next, "Uh, well because! Because real policemen could never do such things. It is not possible. The community would never allow it. And neither would God. Only very evil men are capable of such hideous atrocities!" (Of course, this is all bullshit. Lobo and Deputy Dog are both very real cops, and everybody here knows it. Still, they seem more than satisfied with my answer.) They are all nodding agreement and looking at me with some understanding and even sympathy?

A jeep pulls up and in comes more cops wearin' brown uniforms. My heart freezes for fear that Lobo might be with 'em; he is not. Now there is much excited news sharing concerning me and my tale. The newcomers act shocked that there are "bad evil men disguised as policemen" making torture videos involving children. Their acting is greatly exaggerated, but so is mine. I am asked to describe the imposters. I cannot "for they were wearing sunglasses. Only their uniforms, appearing to be those of policemen, can be identified, but really, they had no distinguishing rank or insignias." And the man filming with the video camera? "No, the camera light was always shining and his face he kept hidden behind the camera." (I keep lookin' to the ranking desk sergeant to see if my answers are correct. His eyes nod, telling me they are.) I am also asked what color these imposters were, "black, brown, white?" My answer comes as a stupid blank of not bein' able to remember. The ranking desk sergeant continues nodding encouragement for the dumb act. His eyes dart towards the two black uniforms standing post at the door intently listening to every word. Taking a risk, I do add (mostly because everyone in the room is Latin brown) that "I do know that the street gang members were for the most part black Caribs and the *niñas*—children—they tortured were brown— big brown-eyed, baby girls!" My eyes tear up for genuine sobbing cry.

The whole mood of this station house changes. Everyone just sorta becomes quiet like, while lookin' around as if not knowin' what to do next. That is, until another jeep pulls up. Both black uniforms dash out the door, speak some fast unknown language and jump into the back of the already full jeep of black uniformed Caribs and drive off. After their departure, it is more than obvious that those guys are not liked by these now here in the station house. Not only are they not liked but also they are feared. The black uniform Caribs are considered to be (understandably) very dangerous. The old ranking desk sergeant (looking glad to see those two gone) calmly asks to see my passport. (Gee, wonder why no one has ever asked what hotel I was stayin' at.) Reaching to open my pack, an arm gently, and almost apologetically, nudges me aside.

Two cops pull loose straps from buckles and flip top flap, opening the backpack. I tell them my passport is in a pocket of the vest. My rolled vest is pulled and placed up on top of the desk, as is my shoulder bag. The old ranking sergeant slowly goes through the motions for searching the shoulder bag, as if really having no interest. His eyes instead are more to my blood-stained filthy vest, now bein' unrolled, as other cops are gathering to snoop out my backpack for possible goodies. However, this all comes to a very quick halt when the cop goin' through my vest's pockets jumps back, loudly announcing, "Bugs! Bugs!" Despite my predicament, I do find their recoiling reaction somewhat humorous, but to let on such would be stupid. With expression of hollow resignation, "Yes—*si*—they put many bugs on me, and in my pack and pockets: spiders, scorpions, and snakes—*cullers!*' All cops but the ranking desk sergeant flinch in disgust! Motions are made for me to remove contents from the vest myself. Little black spiders are now scurrying about the desktop which doesn't bother the old ranking sergeant in the least. Those within reach, he casually squashes with his hand. On this night, the spiders here are (at the moment) nothing to me; ignoring them, while handing over my passport, there is still terrible concern for previously planted cocaine or crack bein' now discovered. Emptying all the vest's pockets (much to my relief), none come out. Only possessions and of course some meshed bags the spiders had come from. Turning, I vigorously shake the vest free from any remaining spiders, out over the floor and squash 'em with sole of damp, dirty, red high-tops. The cops watch this with cringing dismay, especially after I put the vest on and zip it. Reachin' for my wallet (the one containing some photos), I begin to show everyone pictures of my wife and sons, of course bragging them up, proudly putting much emphasis on missing and longing to be with them. My finger is again bleeding good, thus requiring to be rewrapped with red hanky. When asked how the finger got cut? Looking to the ranking desk sergeant for cue, my answer is that of dumb—not knowing. The ranking sergeant nods approval.

With head hung low and tears swelling: "What's gonna happen to me now?" All of the police look to each other. The ranking desk sergeant sighs and tells me not to worry, "No one will hurt you tonight. We are going to protect you. We will take you to a nice, big, American-owned hotel. You will be safe there."

Desperately not wanting to sound ungrateful—after all, this night (considering) has so far, gone better than expected—"Uh, is this hotel here in Trujillo?"

"*Si*, yes, more or less; only a short drive."

"Uh, maybe it's possible for me to take a taxicab to another town and stay the night there?"

"No, that is not possible. You will be better protected with us taking you to the American hotel. You have no choice in this matter, and should be grateful."

"Oh yes Sergeant, I am very grateful, and will do whatever you think is best!" (Eugh, wonder what's really to come? How can they possibly sweep aside everything that has happened? No way can even these guys let me live, not after tonight, not after what I've seen and done. And they are gonna take me to an American-owned hotel? Mercy, Americans here in Trujillo have so far proved to be anything but good fellow Americans. And, what if the American cameraman stays there? Or owns the place? Or more than likely, is friends with the owner? Oh fuck, realistically I won't even survive the ride to this American hotel.) Looking to the ranking desk sergeant, I ask in almost whisper that perhaps only he would hear, "Phone call?" His head discreetly shakes with eyes silently answering, "No, not a good idea."

The desk sergeant then speaks, suggesting that I should show appreciation for their help by giving contributions. "Like you, all of us here have families to provide for, and we get very little pay. Perhaps you can help this one time?"

"Uh, yeah, yeah sure! You bet, how much—*cuanto es?*"

"We are all fair men, and we are very upset at your misfortunes here in our town, so we require only a small amount, perhaps twenty? Twenty US each?"

"Yes, *si*, sure! I am most grateful for your help. You are all very good policemen. My wife and sons would thank you as well. You have all been very kind and understanding with me."

Everything goes back into vest's pockets, except for the one wallet from which I hand out single twenties to each waiting cop. Suddenly the door opens and in comes a whole new bunch of cops—blacks and browns— and these guys appear to be all business, with the blacks looking pissed! Upon their entry, every man in the place stiffens, including myself after hurriedly putting my wallet away. Leading these newcomers are two men side by side, one brown and one black. The brown uniform is sporting captain's bars and acts accordingly. Beside him is a black Carib in black military BDUs with no visible rank or insignias, but carries himself to be equal in rank as that of the Captain; and he's glarin' as if he wants to *kill me*!

The old desk sergeant is now standing and speakin' rapid Spanish (guessing he's telling my story) to the Captain, who listens without interruption; finally the Captain turns to me, asking if this is true—all the facts? Not understanding a Goddamn thing the desk sergeant has said to him, I glance to the old sergeant, who discreetly nods for me to answer yes.

"Uh yes, yes sir! They were bad evil men! A street gang, and two were imposters dressed to be policemen, but I know they are not real policemen. They tortured the little girls—*pequeno niñas*! They burned and cut them, and sexually violated them just for the purpose of making a movie with a video camera!" The Captain's eyes dart back towards the glarin' black Carib; his look reveals much anger and disgust. It is clear the Captain does not approve of these videos, or of this Carib in black uniform. "Uh sir, this is how I know they were not real policemen. No *policia* would be capable of such atrocity—*atrocidad*—and most certainly not towards their own people! One day those men will have to face God and he will strike them down for the crimes committed to his children!" There is silence and the room has become thick with tension. (Damn bladder is quiverin' in reminder of bein' full; also, there is a huge cravin' for a cigarette, but the time is hardly right.) It is becoming more than obvious that the browns strongly resent the blacks and vice versa. The brown uniforms are the actual police, and the black uniforms a military unit; for whatever reason, the two must work together, and as would be natural, there is probably a constant power struggle between the two.

The blacks do have the upper hand in firepower though (at least in this room). They have automatic side arms, pump shotguns and seasoned M-16s. The browns (police) mostly have side arms appearing to be of the older revolver variety. The Captain breaks the silence by sternly informing me that they had just come from the hotel I was staying at. There they were told by the manager that a street gang was witnessed gathered outside my room's window. "They frightened you, and you ran away! Yes?" He gives a long questionable look waiting for an answer.

My eyes glance to the desk sergeant for searching answer to this strange question, so deliberately omitting of detail; his signal is to play along. "Uh, yes, yes Sir!"

The desk sergeant, again speaking rapid Spanish to the Captain, quickly reaches from behind the desk to raise a partial view of my machete for the Captain to see, and then returns it out of sight. The Captain nods.

In doing, the black military Captain (or whatever his rank) barks, "The pack! It must be searched; open it!" Stepping over to begin pulling items from the backpack, two browns jump to my defense, aggressively arguing that there is no point as they had already searched it (they had not), and found nothing illegal, "All is in order!" They aren't standing down. Tensions are rising, when the door opens and upon turning— complete silence. In walks one man; beyond him out on the sidewalk, there are black uniformed soldier guards posted with M-16s. The man, though dressed in casual buttoned blue striped short sleeve shirt and tan slacks, is all big time authority! Everyone stiffens.

This man is not tall, but is stocky. He is brown-skinned, yet has black features. His hair is cut short and is beginning to grey. The man stares upon me with menacing eyes of mild amusement. He approaches, stopping to stand beside the police Captain. The Captain speaks quietly and respectfully to him in a long slew of Spanish. I just stand there, tryin' my best to look the dumb innocent tourist that just happened to be in the wrong place at the wrong time. With a wave from his hand, the civilian dressed man announces that he would like to speak to me personally, in private. The Captain gives a nod, looks to the floor and takes a step back. I quickly glance at the old desk sergeant who now avoids eye contact and just stares at my black shoulder bag.

The man roughly grabs hold of my arm, "You, come! We will have a private talk." Everyone makes way as I am led around the long front desk and through a doorless doorway leading into another room. He motions for one of the black uniforms to come and stand guard in the entryway. The soldier does, with his back to us. The room is barren, small, and dark, dark except for light streaming a glow around posted guard's eerie silhouette (Buddy, we are in some deep shit now.) I begin to desperately glance about for possible means of escape. Of course there are none. To the far end, some muffled sounds of men are heard coming from an adjacent corridor leading to (guessing) jail cells. AUGHG! A hard push from the man slams me to bounce from the wall. Recoiling a spin for instinctual counter strike, but logical side of brain seizes control and instantly lowers the fist to drop and hang passively. (Oooh, must not fight, not this man, not if he's only wanting to hit, torment and humiliate. Let 'im. However, if it looks like torture and death are a certainty, well, then tear his fuckin' face off and go down fightin'! But first, must be sure—play it). The man seeing my reaction, is now all up on me, pushing his big chest into mine, squashing me against the wall. His breath is hot, foul, smelling of booze and whatever. He hisses, "So you are a fighter. I know you are a fighter, but you will not fight me will you? Ha ha!" His hand goes to my crotch where he squeezes down hard. "Aw, I really know what happened in the hotel room; we all know. You Devon, you are an actor and fighter! I can have you easily executed for the killings you have committed on this night. Your acting has convinced them—" (his head nods toward the police now out of view in the station front from where we had come) "—to take pity on you. They ask for me to overlook your crimes and allow you to go to the nice American hotel. Hhmm, possibly I will feel generous and allow for this, and possibly I will not. You understand—your life is in my hands?" His head is nodding yes, and my head is nodding yes. The fucker releases his vice-like grip from my crotch and has slid it up my wide loose short legging and is now roughly fondling my cock and balls. His breathing increases with sexual excitement. "Aw, there it is. They told me you had a ring here. Tell me, is it real gold?"

Slowly shaking my head, whispering, "No, it is fake gold. I know of no one that would spend money for real gold to put there." The man considers for a moment, then nods his head as if concluding my words made logical sense. While stroking my cock he whispers, "It is said that you are a faggot, but you also like girls; this is true?" Oh Christ, how do I answer this one? These macho Latin pricks are so Goddamn weird with bein' homophobic. Yet, here he is sexually forcing himself on me and becoming more than a little aroused in doing. If I answer yes, will the pig feign disgust and become merciless? But geez, if I answer no, will this expose him then as bein' the fag-gay, bisexual, and me the one straight? Jesus, this sinister bastard will probably have me tortured and killed in revelation of this alone. In all reality he is most likely just a rape anything freak... but still, how to answer? Shrugging my shoulders, an answer comes, "I do what I must."

He seems satisfied with the answer, and hisses "Make it hard!" I tell him quietly, "I can't, I have had very little sleep, also I need to pee. A push sends me into a very dark corner with orders given to pee. Turning to raise my short legging, and despite his groping hand on my ass with finger worming around very sore rectum, bladder complies to let loose forced stream spraying the wall and pooling at our feet. Whew! Shakin' the last drops, my face goes to the wall with the pig burying his finger up my ass! Withstanding the intensity of present pain and humiliation, a big worry now is my rectum bleeding again. How will this degenerate react to my blood getting on him under such circumstances? With these rape fucks one never knows. No matter, must not anger him by pullin' away, and yet, can not pretend to enjoy either. He withdraws his finger and I'm seriously expecting to be ordered to drop shorts for an ass fucking. However, I'm spun to face him. His cock is out and my hand is directed to stroke it; and of course, after a bit of this, my head is pushed down. (Going to my knees), his cock slides between lips, filling mouth. Fortunately the dick, though thick, ain't very long. Uh, nothin' quite like having to give your enemy a blow job! The pig of course has hold of my head for a humpin' deep throating.

While this is goin' on, thoughts go out to ol' Clint Eastwood, Arnold Schwarzenegger, Sylvester Stallone and all those other macho Hollywood action stars. No way would any of them suck dick to save their lives. No, they would rather be slowly tortured to death! Or somehow heroically fight their way outta this mess, killing the deserving bad guy and escaping right on through those heavily armed soldiers and cops! Yepper, that's just what would happen. Yeah well, maybe in the movies, but here? Right now? Damn, if givin' head is gonna save my head. Sparky is all for it! Yeah, here's the throbbing quiverin'. Oh goody fuckin' goody. His cock starts jackhammerin', so guess what's a-cummin'. Swallowing while gettin' the back of my head bucked into the wall, the blow job is over. Gee golly, wonder what's to come next? This night has been just plum full of surprises, and it ain't over yet.

Rising from my knees, the pig zips up, warns I'm to never speak of this to anyone—ever! (Well duh!) And also, guess what? He must now slap me around so that the others out front will think he's been back here questioning me instead of forcin' a blow job from me—a man. Oh, and also, with each slap I must moan and beg for mercy. Christ this is more humiliating than sucking his cock (and more painful). The degenerate has his fun slapping hard and often. My face swells with stinging tears and it's not difficult to act in accordance of ordered instruction.

Finally the pig fuck (out of breath) has had enough. Back to the front of the station house we go. Mr. Big Shot is struttin' with chest all puffed out, actin' the macho almighty one in charge! "Okay, now you can take him to the American hotel. Take him in the jeep with my man in it!" He marches for the door and out, with the black soldiers following. Wow, the lights are seemingly now very bright. My face (knowingly) is swollen red and tear streaked. From around the room looks of sympathy are received from the police—even the Captain himself. Clearing my throat, permission is asked to smoke? Encouraging answers come immediately from several "Oh yes—si—yes, please!" The Captain gives some brief instructions to the front desk sergeant and then he too leaves. From vest's pocket, out comes pack, and a cigarette is offered to every cop here; they all graciously accept while going about lighting each other's, including mine. I inhale deeply and try to swallow down the foul salty taste of forced cum, still lingering.

It's now time to go. The ranking desk sergeant barks out some orders, one cop (with cig still dangling from one corner of mouth) picks up my backpack; another hands me my shoulder bag. The old desk sergeant pulls forth a rag, wiping the blood smear from his desk top—left from the bag. I politely ask him for my machete, and as expected, he slowly shakes his head, answering no. I quietly thank him anyway for all his help. Sparky ain't outta the woods yet, but, it sure had been nice havin' this old sergeant here.

Exiting the station house, orders are given for me to climb into the back of a jeep already crowded with four cops, and—fuck me—a black uniformed soldier wearin' a full face ski mask. He's got a Mini 14, and hunched in front of him is a German shepherd dog. Scrunching myself in, the feelin' is strong that this ride is gonna be only to some remote spot of the boonies for execution. The soldier in the ski mask keeps smilin' at me as if reading my mind (and yes, even when they are wearin' full face ski masks, you can tell when they're grinning and smilin'.) Now for whatever reason, we slowly drive around the lively circular central square several times. This is done as if purposely for showing me off. It works; everybody hangin' about (there are many) has stopped their doings to point and gawk. Nobody seems to even look twice at the armed black uniformed soldier having no identity but the black death squad mask (obviously a common sight in these parts, more common than that of myself). Lordy, I feel just like a caged circus freak bein' paraded. Ught, is this good or bad? The police are doing this intentionally, but for what purpose? The travel books never mention anything about crap like this. "Trujillo, one of the great untapped tourist sites of the Caribbean." My ass! Oh fuck, fuck, fuck; we are now driving out of town. The dog (unlike its handler) is not interested in me. No, he's more interested in vacuum sniffin' my backpack. Goddamn, hope it's just the blood he's smellin' and not planted cocaine. (Yeah, like it would really matter at this point.) The road is rural, unpaved, curvy, narrow, deep rutted, and dark, seeming to be goin' all uphill. On either side there is dense overgrown tropical foliage. At any moment this jeep in all likelihood will pull over; I will be ordered out, led off the road and shot dead, or worse, be taken to a waiting Sergeant Lobo and friends. The excuse for my disappearance could be simply they were kindly driving me to the nice big American hotel when all off a sudden I went *loco*, running off, to never be seen again. Geez, out here with no witnesses they can concoct any number of stories. In any case, just as soon as this jeep does pull to a stop, or things begin to appear a little too questionable (or whenever buddy says), Sparky here is gonna jump and run! Meanwhile the time is spent feelin' out the mood of this jeep, while pondering how best to deal with this dog, if need be. You know? Even if somehow bullets do get dodged… there will still be the blasted dog on my heels! Quick logic concludes that if distance is made between me and the jeep full of shooters, it will be stupid and costly to try and kill this dog. No, best course will be inflicting a disabling wound. Easier said though than done; fighting a dog of German shepherd caliber is much like goin' into a knife fight. No matter what, you are gonna get bit, cut, hurt! The question is, how bad? Hhmm, just fight the toothy canine harder than he fights you, and do it early on; can't waste energy tryin' to outrun the four-legged, brush bustin' beast. He will go for my feet, legs, throat, and face. I must go for his feet, legs, nose, and eyes. Oh fun-fun! Hey, what's this? Lights! Hotel lights! They lead to a hotel that is big and quite fancy! Oh fuckin' Skippy! Are we really gonna survive this night? Can't hardly contain myself as we pull up the front drive; but then remembrance comes of the American cameraman, and this settles my ass right down. Sparky, this night ain't over 'til it's over.

We all pile out of the jeep, all, except for the grinnin' masked soldier and the dog. They stay where they are. The older cop instructs me to try and make myself more presentable. Seeing my questioned look for how and him not having the answer, he just shrugs, changes tone, and asks for more money, explaining that after all, they did not have to help me like this. They did so because they are very good policemen, and so, should be rewarded as such. Damn, sure glad I have plenty of small bills.

While handing out five, tens, and twenties, also cigarettes, a black Rasta with dreadlocks appears from the entranceway, for inquiring our wants and needs. Seeing him reminds me of Martin, whom at the moment is missed very much. The hotel is, for the most part, not including the rooms themselves, all an open-air affair sheltered mostly with high overhead roofing of various materials like galvanized panels, reed thatching, and red clay tiles. Different areas of setting, utilizing different roofing and surroundings. The Rasta suspiciously asks us to wait at the front desk, while he goes for "de lady." We do, and in doing, more money and cigarettes are asked and received. Jesus, why don't they just take it all? Instead they seem very satisfied with the petty scraps. The lady appears and quickly puts a stop to this grubby badgering. The woman looks to be fifty-ish, in good shape, and at one time very pretty. Now though, her face betrays many years of hard partying, you know, more lines and wrinkles than what should be on a woman her age? But hell, who knows. She could very well be way older than my guess. I've never been any good at guessin' a woman's years. Her eyes look deep and reveal they have seen some things. While keenly observing me up and down, the woman warmly greets each cop by name. They in turn greet her likewise with polite respect.

Placing herself behind the front desk she asks the older cop what's going on? And how can she be of service? Much to my surprise they (the cops) begin to excitedly tell her! They do however leave out me fighting, killing, bein' sodomized with a flashlight and having to blow some important big shot. But they do tell of the street gang, imposters dressed as police, torturing of children, and the video camera. As the woman listens, she gazes upon me with eyes softening, growing more and more sympathetic. The woman just keeps nodding as if this were a very sad unfortunate thing to have happened. But it's obviously not shocking or even appearing to surprise her. After hearing, she speaks, trying to sound gentle and understanding. (Her English is indeed American.) "Well young man, you must be terrified! Of course I want to help you. However, we are presently all booked up; we have no vacancies at this time." My heart sinks, and mouth drops. She sees this and her smile broadens. "I think though we can fix something up for you. It won't be one of our guest rooms, but it should fit your need for tonight. It will be a room at least, a place for you to shower and comfortably sleep, which young man, you look like you are desperately needing! So, should I have the room made up for you?"

"Uh, oh, yes Ma'am! Please! Yes, please anything. I'll take anything!"

Nodding with prediction of answer and reaction, she adds, "Okay but I must tell you right here and now—"(a brief pause to roam her eyes again over me and backpack) "—we are not normally considered to be in a backpacker's budget. We are an upscale, high-end hotel, can you afford us?" Holy crap! Is this woman serious? What the hell is up with Americans in this country? Here I am, a fellow American, having just survived unimaginable atrocities. I'm in trouble with the police, military, street gang, and fuck knows who else. This woman is in a position to help and she wants to know if I can afford it! Suppressing the secret flash desire for reachin' over that counter and throttling her Goddamn greedy American throat (whoa hoss, shake it off), I smile sweet as pie, "Oh yes Ma'am. You bet!" Seeing behind her the postings for the major credit cards accepted, I proudly whip out one of my platinum select VISA cards. (The card even has my picture on it, so there!) With eyebrows raised, she holds the card and slyly murmurs somethin' on the order of there being more to me than what meets the eye. The woman turns to process account data; as she does, the police linger. The younger ones keep asking if I could tattoo them, and all are nudging for more money. The woman catches on—warning "I certainly hope you guys aren't taking money from this young man? I think it's now time for you all to leave. I will take over from here. Thank you for escorting Mr. Murfin to our hotel. Bye now, go on, bye bye!"

With big smiles, handshakes, and even pats on the back and shoulders, the police all leave. The woman calls for the Rasta and has him go instruct so-and-so to prepare my room. Meanwhile we make small talk. I tell her where I'm from, why I'm down here, what I do for a living, and give information concerning my wife and sons (just in case). The woman tells me that she has been down here for a very long time, but is originally from one of the western states—Nevada? Utah? Fuck, I don't know. At this point, retaining information like names and numbers is proving difficult. Uh, Sparky is still tryin' to process the fact that he made it outta that hell hole of a hotel room. Outta the police station, and standin' here—still alive! The woman mentions somethin' about how she and her husband own this place and just love it here, etc. (Did she say her husband was Honduran? Don't matter, he's not here, gone—went somewhere, won't be back.) Whew, my head is fillin' with rush of a million things right now!

The woman instructs me to wait while she goes to check on the progress of my room. Nodding affirmative, I step over and sit down on three top steps leading down to a lower tiled floor level, which is set up as a large open-air dining, drinking, lounging area. In other words, it's full of outdoor round tables and chairs. Directly across from me is a thatched roof Tiki Cabana bar, presently without patrons. People (hotel guests) are sitting about, but they are down toward the other end. Lighting a cig, inhaling deeply, their voices are heard excitedly asking the passing woman proprietor of this hotel what's goin' on? Some sound to be obviously American, while others are distinctively British. Surprisingly, the woman stops and tells them all what the police had said about my terrifying ordeal experienced at an in-town hotel. People (guests) are gasping, horrified at such shocking news! (Buddy this is good, good that the woman is tellin' them all. It's a sign she's not in on it. Which means—for tonight we are probably safe. Damn, could this be possible? Buddy?)

Looking about, my heart leaps! Strewn here and there, littering the ground, are many little torn baggy plastics like those used for coke and crack. Fuck me! Is the stuff bein' used to this degree, here, right out in the open like this? I need to make a phone call—must call my wife. The woman comes back motioning for me to follow; my room has been prepared. When I ask to use the telephone she apologizes, informing that they are all down—out of service—for the night. This happens often here, but they should be up and working tomorrow. (Geez, why is this no surprise.)

The rooms are to the other end of the grounds. Following the woman, we pass many sitting guests. They all (understandably) stare at me wild-eyed as if I had just crawled up from the netherworld. (Yeah well, if you only knew the whole story… No matter, chin up, shoulders squared, avoid eye contact, but do glance for any sign of malicious hostiles—like the cameraman! No, none among these.) However, the smell of pot bein' openly smoked is strong. Once out of earshot of the guests I ask the woman about all the little empty little plastics strewn about. "Are they all from cocaine?" She gives a nervous, silly laugh, answering somethin' on the order of those being not from cocaine but rather some special medicinal Navajo Indian powder. (Navajo Indian powder? Here in Honduras? What the fuck!)

The hotel rooms themselves are of multi-level concrete block structure, seemingly a bit out of place and not fitting with the general setting of this resort as a whole. And it's big too. Damn, they do have a lot of rooms here! How is it that they could be all booked full—no vacancy—when there appears to be so little noise and activity? (Christ man, remember how late the hour is. Everybody is probably asleep.) Goin' up some open steps, my room from the outside (though the lighting is poor) looks to be the same as all others. There are neighboring doors on both sides of mine. I was expecting to be placed in some sort of service/closet type room or the such. The woman opens my door and Goddamn! It's a regular hotel room, and it's got two beds to boot! No wonder the woman had charged me one hundred dollars US. Yeah but, why did she earlier say they were all booked-up with no guest rooms available? This room ain't no different than any of the others; just look at it. Wait a minute, what's this? The far wall is all window, and there is a screen door, a weathered, old, flimsy one at that. The only source for locking it is a very simple, small hook and eye latch. Eugh, real fuckin' security here!

As the woman stands, holding the key while closely watching me, I go over to the screen door and with fingertip lightly touching, lift the nothing hook from the little eye screw. Opening the door, it leads out to a shared roofless patio. Though from the front we are two stories up, here to the back, the ground elevates sharply with the patio only bein' now four feet (if even that) above a vast field of bush and tall grasses. (Aw, why? Why? Why?) Turning, I quickly go (stepping around the eyeing woman) to the front door, and of course, no deadbolt! Putting on my best just been kicked puppy dog look, "Uh, Ma'am, is there any chance you might have another room available? One with a deadbolt lock, or at least no back door?"

As expected, she answers no. "No Devin, this is the only available room. Listen young man, you are perfectly safe here. You have guests all around you, American and European. If by chance anyone was to bother you, they will hear; but son, no one will. That's a guaranteed promise! Look, I personally know all of the local police around here, plus I know very important town officials. Nobody has ever bothered me or my place, ever! And especially not any of my guests. Devin, you are in the region's most luxurious hotel; you are not in some low budget dump. Come on young man, no one would dare come here to harass international tourists! Plus, if it makes you feel any better, the hotel does have night security, and [whatever she calls him, Rasta-man] is awake all night watching the bar, okay? Now please, I understand how you must be feeling after what you have been through tonight, but really son, you are now safe. All you need is a hot shower and some serious sleep. Alright?"

Having absolutely no choice, head reluctantly nods in agreement and key is accepted. Looking deeply into her eyes, "Thank you Ma'am, thank you so very much." She gives a warm smile, turns to leave, but stops as if remembering something, "Devin if by chance you do hear voices out on the balcony, don't fret son, as it will only be from neighboring guests. They use it often for sitting in the porch swing and enjoying the night air; okay?" Okay. She leaves.

Now alone, I open the backpack and pull out my twenty-inch steel MAGLITE flashlight and begin searching the room from top to bottom. Fuck! Tucked here and there are little tied baggies of pure white powder! (Buddy, is it cocaine or just that Navajo Indian stuff the woman had spoken of? Man, who knows, just don't touch any of it.) The bathroom door is a wooden horizontal slat louver door. A bit unusual for a room having two beds (not offering much in bathroom privacy). And the beds? Well, they appear to be nice, clean, and comfy, but damn, underneath, the bottom fabric of both box springs have indeed seen better days—they are stained and frayed, with several holes and tears.

Removing my vest and laying it on the end of the bed nearest the bathroom and furthest from screen door patio and wall of window, I enter the bathroom. Leaving door wide open, I contemplate a shower, but just can't get up the nerve—still too fuckin' spooked. No, instead settle for a piss and quick body scrub from vanity sink. Desperately wanting to brush mouth and teeth but needing toiletry bag, I go to backpack standing upright near vest. Oooh, entire pack is gonna have to be emptied and searched for creepy-crawlies, and (more importantly) coke and crack. Sliding the pack away from the bed... voices! Out on the patio. They are American, a man and woman couple, sitting on the porch swing, softly talking, smoking, and being intimate. Must stay on-guard and alert. Start goin' through this pack. In the mornin', Sparky is leavin' to be haulin' ass for getting out of this sick country! Pulling items from backpack, everything is—as expected—an infestation of mostly black spiders with a small number of defiant scorpions. Shaking 'em out, dirty red Converse high-tops squash all but a few that manage to get away. The act is mesmerizing and mechanical, until an emotional tidal wave slams me down to knees with an onslaught of visual remembrance from all that had been done and endured. The children, God, those poor beautiful children, and… and the young girl child… They burned and cut her… and… and… and they… they were laughing, filming, enjoying themselves. Oh Goddamn, how can there be such people? A flooding from tears swell to level of no holding back, so gush they do! Spilling forth with sobbing heaves and constricting chest pulling tense, spazzin' every fiber of being. The couple out on the patio can hear and see me. Their pathetic comments are heard between gut-wrenching sobs. Plus, their astounded eyes are felt—I don't care. One cannot cry forever, and of course, this is no exception. Eventually, like an abrupt rain downpour, the tears just stop. Blowing my nose with ensuing hollow exhaustion, reachin' for a cigarette, it's noticed that the couple are now gone, as are all of my cigarettes! I hadn't even realized the pack was empty. Fuck me, gonna have to go buy some. Sparky needs a smoke!

Geez, it's late. The woman had better been tellin' the truth about the Rasta bein' at the bar all night. Not bothering to put on the vest, but grabbing both wallets and room key, I double time it out the door, down gloomy corridor and stairs, crossing grounds. (Damn, it sure is dark; COLD STEEL knife is missed like you wouldn't believe.) Entering the perimeter of light, walking on tile flooring, I step through the now empty maze of table and chairs, empty except for two Carib women sitting at a table up towards the Tiki bar. The Rasta man from behind the bar watches my approach. Passing the two women sitting at the table, it is very much noticed that they have before them what appears to be a kilo of cocaine, a scale, plastic wrap, scissors, spoon, and string. Their busy fingers are workin' fast at tying many gram-size balls for adding to an already impressive pyramid pile. (Oh buddy, sure wish we hadn't seen this! Man, just walk on by, this is all normal as pie; right? Right.) My greeting of "*Hola*" they return with cold silent stare only. At the bar the Rasta's eyes look tired and very bloodshot (a common look for Rastas). Much to my great disappointment, he informs me that they are completely sold out of cigarettes; they will not have any more until "de lady" goes to town tomorrow. Okay, now what are the odds of this? Dumb question. What are the odds of anything that has taken place on this bizarre night?

"Uh, how about loose cigarettes? Any for sale?"

"No."

Bummer! Time for getting back to my room! Quickly retracing steps, entering room, locking door behind, a thought comes to mind for a possible quick fix. Crossing the room and stepping out onto the patio, the ashtray is noticed having a good size cig butt. Firing it up for a deep inhale of stale hot smoke, ensuing long exhale while eyes glance across vast moonlit bush field... What the fuck? My heart jumps a thump, thump, thump number. Just below me, camouflaging himself very well, is a soldier. He is lying flat, blending in with the weeds and grasses, having much foliage tuft deliberately attached to his black uniform. I wouldn't have even spotted him had not somethin' from within gave warning. Looking hard, sure enough, there they are; the whites of his eyes. Dirty bastard! Glancing to the left another soldier is detected. Both are wearin' full face black ski masks. My eyes dart back to the first one. He now knows he's been spotted. Surprising myself, acting cool as spiked punch, flicking cherry-red cig butt out toward the ground hugging soldier, "Hey man, don't you guys get hot in those face masks? What, no answer? Hhmm, well tell me this, are you here for me?" His head is silently nodding yes. "Are you here to kill me?" Oh yeah, with a grinning nod, he raises and takes mock aim with his M-16. "Well then, do me a favor, one shot, one kill! And be a man about it and not some fuckin' torturing street punk!"

Spinning, light feet fly my ass back into the room—locking flimsy screen door with stupid hook and eye latch. A leap sends me over the first bed, bending to grab twenty-inch-long steel MAGLITE flashlight, before spin-rollin' over the other bed, to kick a hurling mid-air jump for slammin' back and shoulders into the locked front door! Oh, no, no. Shit fuck! Shit, shit, shit! Not again! Not again! What to do? Think, *think*! My first brilliant course for action had been to exit this door while screamin' bloody murder! However, somewhere between soarin' from back screen door and this here front door, logic comes concluding— duh! If the back is covered, then obviously so will the front be... aughg, bet both left and right nut that they are just outside this door waitin' to pounce! Yeah well screw that! Sparky ain't goin' nowhere this time— except to hell! And here they come! The back patio is fillin' up fast with black uniformed soldiers, all locked and loaded, wearin' full face ski masks.

Like all creatures when cornered, eyes are desperately darting for a means... On my left, the bathroom door is closed. Uh, I never closed it. Glancing—oh crap! Through the horizontal slats of the louver door, a big Goddamn black Carib soldier is in there, and what the fuck? He is stringing up what looks to be monofilament fishing line all around the inside of the bathroom. He's got it so as to ensnarl me for if and when I did run in there, the line would entangle, thus enabling a quick easy prey for him!

Without hesitation, I begin to *scream* at the top of my lungs! Yep, like a squelchin' bull horn: "HELP, HELP, HELP! American citizen! American citizen—Bein' ATTACKED! SOLDIERS in my room—HELP!" In doing, left hand is bangin' the hell outta the door with butt of steel, MAGLITE flashlight. And at the same time, edge of right fist is literally bashin' in the dancin' hollow core closet door! (Strangely, the right fist is also clenching my little pocket knife—now open. How and when the tiny knife got there, only the body knows, for it acted on its own—without brain knowing or realizing. The knife's size, considering the circumstances, is almost humorous; still, Sparky is glad havin' it—one small sharp claw is better than no claw.) In any case, the amount of noise now bein' made is deafening with reverberation, sounding alarm! The soldiers grouping out on the patio have stopped their advance and are now lookin' to each other as if asking—what now? The black fucker in the bathroom has also stopped his line stringing and is now just watchin' me through the slats. Sucking in much needed breath and lowering voice (somewhat), "Come on you mother fuckin', sick, mask-wearin' cowards! Come on, all of ya! Come on! Come get me! Pussy sons-a-bitches! HELP, HELP, HELP! AMERICAN CITIZEN! SOLDIERS ATTACKING—HELP!"

Whoa, must conserve some energy for fighting. In between long bouts of frantic hollerin' for help and beatin' on doors, short breaks are had for catching breath, listening, surveying. Somebody is on the other side of this door and is tryin' to turn its knob.

Of the soldiers grouped on the back patio, one is teasing—wiggling the pathetic screen door. The soldier is a stocky baboon and his black ski mask contrasts greatly with his huge gleamin' white teeth. The screen door would be nothin' for him or anybody else to (if wanted) kick down. Obviously they are holding tight, awaiting orders for advancing—a charge! "HELP, HELP! AMERICAN CITIZEN! SOLDIERS ATTACKING ROOM!" Yes, the hotel guests are awakening, and in frightened voices are heard calling out to each other from room to room. Word is spreading!

From the other side of the door, Rasta man is heard hissin' to someone or someones "Whatcha doin' here mon? Ah, soldiers comin' roun' in te middle of de night! Mon, all dis hotel is now awake, you must go. Your plan has failed."

The Rasta is now knockin' on my door callin', "Devon! Devon mon, whatcha be doin' yellin' an bangin' all dis racket in de middle of te night?

Come Devon, open de door and tell me! Please Devon!" Oh yeah Skippy, let's open this door for a little chat with the Rasta… I don't fuckin' think so! "Rasta! Rasta man, go get the lady! Get the lady!" But Goddamn if the dreadlock dick don't respond, "No Devon, quiet mon, you be still! Open te door. You can tell me de problem. Trust me Devon, everyting will be irite!"

"Bullshit Rasta man, I know you got soldiers out there with you. Now go get the lady right the fuck now! HELP, HELP, AMERICAN CITIZEN! SOLDIERS ATTACKING ROOM! Help, oh God please help! You saw! You all saw! The police brought me here for sanctuary and now soldiers are here to take me away! HELP!"

Catching my breath, the Rasta is heard again hissing to whoever, "Mon, I know it was not goin' to work! Go now—quickly!" He then speaks through the door, "Okay Devon, be still now! I will go fetch de lady."

"Hurry Rasta! Must hurry—HELP!" Oh-hoo, is this nightmare of a night ever gonna end? Out on the patio, to the left of grouped masked soldiers, there are now several men distinct of bein' greatly important and having much authority. There is one in civilian attire, a couple in high ranking Honduran military officer uniforms, another looks to be an officer of the police, and shit, there is even a black Carib sportin' a spanking white naval officer uniform. Holy fuckin' Mary, mother of sweet baby Jesus—what the hell have you gotten me into now? The masked soldiers are leisurely amusing themselves jiggling the door, tapping on the glass window, and pointing their rifles at me. They do this while the important men discuss the situation, and my fate! These officers keep glancin' at me, but when my eyes go to meet theirs, they quickly look away as if they'd prefer not to be in any way recognized.

A strange dim ringing sound is heard coming from the bathroom; the black Carib soldier inside pulls forth a cell phone and speaks into it briefly and quietly. Afterwards, he hurriedly busies himself with taking down all the monofilament fishing line, wrapping it around a short piece of wood. Is this a good sign or bad?

The hotel guests are now creating quite a commotion, loudly calling out for each other, the Rasta, and the lady. From their tone, they are afraid! Yeah well, y'all oughta be in my shoes! Finally the lady is heard approaching, assuring all the guests that everything is all right! "Go back to bed. The soldiers won't be taking anybody away. No harm will come to Devin. Go back to bed. It's all being taken care of; there has been a misunderstanding that's all. Go back to your beds."

The woman then knocks on my door calling, "Devin, Devin, are you in there? Devin, I'm going to unlock the door now. I have a friend with me and we are going to come in and use your bathroom for discussing this unique situation. Devin, I need you to move away from the door and go sit quietly on your bed, okay? Can you do this for me? Don't worry young man, nobody is going to hurt or take you away; not while you are on my property they won't! But Devin, I really need for you to go sit on your bed and be calm and quiet while my friend and I solve this misunderstanding, okay?"

"Uh, okay Yes Ma'am."

"Alright, good, Devin. We are coming in now. Are you sitting on the bed?"

"Uh yes, yes Ma'am." The door is bein' unlocked and I'm jumpy as all get-up for a rush attack. It doesn't come.

From sitting position on bed's end, their entrance into the room cannot be seen, but, true to her word, they do go straight for the bathroom. The woman's friend gives orders for the Carib soldier to stand guard outside the closed bathroom door. Well spank my fuckin' ass! I recognize that voice! Guess who the woman's friend is? Come on guess? Why it's Mr. Big Shot—give me a blow job, let me slap you around and you can go free—himself! Looking to the patio, everyone is now gone except for two soldiers simply standin' guard. The darkness of night has also been replaced with a hazy morning glow that will quickly turn sharp and bright. (Goddamn, buddy, we did it—fucking did it—we survived the night. But wonder what we survived it for?)

With my fate bein' discussed in the bathroom, ears perk to hear. The woman is heard calmly, matter of fact, asking "So what's it going to take for this young man to be left alone so that he can safely return home to his family? And what is this I hear about children being used for your videos? I honestly hope this is not true. You know it would destroy are very long friendship if it is." The pig laughs, claiming the accusations ridiculous! He goes on to tell her that it had simply been a "faggot porno" of me with another man. Ironically, the other man just happens to be the big Carib soldier standin' guard at the bathroom door. (Ught, this is downright retarded!) The woman is heard giggling, exclaiming, "Oh how I would love seeing those two together!" Weird… Obviously the woman personally knows the big Carib standin' guard and is very attracted to him. Anyway, the pig scoffs her remark as being disgusting, "They were really going at it when this Devon suddenly became *loco*, running out of the hotel with this wild story of pornos involving children being tortured and murdered. Of course it is all lies. I could never allow for such things; you know this." Blah, blah, blah!

The woman is wholeheartedly expressing assurance that she does indeed know that he could never be capable of such a thing. She then repeats her question—what is it going to take for me to be left alone? Hhmm, a very clever move on her part, see? If the insane fucker makes any sort of big deal to-do concerning me, after spewing forth that line of shit, it will surely draw suspicion towards his self-proclaimed integrity in the eyes of this woman. So, he shrugs her question off as if it were only trivial. Mr. Big Shot has himself a kilo of cocaine—if she buys it for his asking price, he will forget all about me, but only on the condition I leave Trujillo and Honduras today. Agreed! Now with that aside, he wants her to sample the cocaine she is buying. Soon there is chopping, snorting, giggling small talk (which goes on and on) and then it sounds as if she is sucking his dick.

Enlightened by this overheard news, I stand—stepping for sliding my backpack over to the bed. The job of ridding it of all creepy-crawlies, planted coke and crack must be completed before my departure from this wretched country. In doing, I come face to face with the big Carib soldier. Despite his intimidating mien, he is very handsome and it is easily understood how the woman could be attracted to him. He sternly waves me back to the bed. I oblige, dragging my kit with me. First, the vest—let's get the wallets back in place and everything organized. Fuck me! There's cocaine in the pockets! How the hell did coke get into my vest pockets—again? Hhmm, let's see, the vest was left here in the room while I left in attempt of buyin' cigarettes. That's when Carib soldier man there must have simply shimmied the screen door hook and eye latch (believe me, nothin' difficult), came in, re-latched door hook, planted cocaine in my vest pockets so vulnerable. (Buddy, I'm pullin' out rolled half ounce bags here, and geez, how many gram size balls?). He then must have hurried, goin' into the bathroom and begun stringing up ensnarling monofilament fishing line. Obviously my return from the Tiki bar had been quicker than expected. Also, they probably did not anticipate me spotting the concealed soldiers in the field, thus hauling ass across the room grabbin' twenty-inch steel MAGLITE and pocket knife while bellowing alarm, screamin' bloody helter-skelter! The Carib soldier in the bathroom by this time had more than likely strung up so much monofilament line as to hinder his own charging exit from the bathroom to silence me, and really, it had all happened so fast that in no time, hotel guests were awake, alerted, and calling out questions. And the Rasta man? Whether he wanted to be or not, Rasta had been in on it as well. So, you see, in a sick funny way, smokin' had sorta saved my life.

Ught, looky who's at the window now! Why it's my ol' pal Sergeant

Lobo, wearin' a black ski mask, yes it's him; one can't mistake those cruel eyes and matching grin. Also, he's brought along his punk ass Garifuna street gang—what's left of 'em anyways. Scooching for sitting down on the floor between bed and outer bathroom wall, I busy myself with task at hand, while keepin' one eye on Lobo and gang. Lobo is amusing himself tryin' to intimidate by play-shooting at me with his stupid finger. Receiving no reaction, he soon grows bored and leaves. His Garifunas, however, stay and can be heard making plans for slipping into the room to steal my stuff. Also, they are threatening revenge for the deaths of their comrades last night. Fortunately, a posted soldier, hearing, sends them away.

The woman must be finished sucking Mr. Big Shot, because instead of such sounds, they are now again engaged in small talk. Meanwhile, a small snake has captured my attention; from under the bed, through the box spring's many worn and torn holes, the snake, a dark striped blunt-nosed thing, gracefully lowers itself to the floor and quickly slithers across the room, disappearing under a dresser. Damn, snakes living in box springs! Fuckin' weird, but hey, why not? I wonder how he gets back up there though. Geez, that's quite a reach for a snake his size. He would need the ability to stiffen and raise more than half of his body up off the ground for re-entering that hole in the bed. Can a snake even do this—raise so much of itself mid-air? Fuck, pretty soon here he comes a-slitherin'—paying absolutely no never-mind to my presence—raises himself, stretchin' up as if it were nothin' at all and back into the mattress box springs he goes. Wow! Sparky is impressed, but uh, this does shed some new light on beds unfamiliar, that's for sure!

Suddenly, Mr. Big Shot and the woman are saying their goodbyes and out the door they go! However, the big Carib soldier is still here, he is back again in the bathroom. I ask him tryin' to sound strong, confident and militant, "Hey troop! What now soldier?"

He answers I must stay put and wait, "wait for the lady." Then softening his tone, he asks, "Devon? I want to *bailar*. You *bailar* with men; you will *bailar* with me—Yes?" (Oh good God, *bailar* is Spanish for dance, right? Yeah well, somehow I don't think it's dancing this soldier is meaning—or wanting! Christ, why me?) "Uh, troop, you must ask the lady. She must give permission first." And so he does! Out the door he goes—yellin' down to the woman asking her if he can *bailar* me? Thankfully, she answers a loud no! But then offers up that she will *bailar* him. He asks how much? They settle on a nothing formality price bein' equivalent to two US dollars, and so off they go (guessing) to *bailar*!

Stepping back from the now open front door and… What the fuck!

The street gang has returned and a little Garifuna brat is seen dashing out the back screen door! Goddamn it, the midget prick took all the collected cocaine and my pocket knife. My father had given me that knife! Aughg! I wanta kill the little son-a-bitch! Whoa there hoss, settle 'er on down; he was just a kid, some poor little street kid. Can't be blamin' him for stealin' your shit. Just be glad you had your vest on containing wallets, money, and passport! Time to gear-up, wait for the "lady" and get the hell outta here. Hopefully she and Big Boy will *bailar* quickly.

Yeah well, I'm glad the scrawny snot stole the coke, but not the pocket knife. My father had given me that knife and now he is dead—dead! Reacting on delayed impulse of rerun thought processing, twenty-inch steel black MAGLITE is in hand and a screamin' charge ensues, leapin' both beds, out the screen door: "Give me back my pocket knife you mother fuckers!" Of course the big, bad, brave Garifunas haul ass! This in turn only feeds my fury, finding myself out on the patio with nobody to fight (fortunately the posted soldiers are gone). Head clears itself from rage and allows logical thought to conclude, uh, perhaps this ain't the smartest of moves. Still it does act in rekindling the weary energy back to alert action mode. Also again, the street gang—without armed official back-up support—are exposed as bein' quite fearful of Devon.

Looking to the ashtrays, they've been picked clean having no smokable cig butts. Sparky could sure use a cigarette. Oh crap, there's the sound of a vehicle starting and the woman calling out to the big Carib soldier just how much fun she had with their *bailar*. She's leaving—driving off! Darting for the front door—sure enough there she goes with truck a-bouncin'! Fuck, now I gotta wait for her return. Sparky ain't goin' nowhere without talkin' to the woman first. I need to know what's goin' on, and how much money is owed to her for saving my life. She did save my life last night, right? Yeah she did, but only after her entire hotel had been awakened. Hhmm, it could just be para-fuckin'-noia, but there is most definitely somethin' concerning her that's not on the up and up. Still, without her I would be dead. She bought me time, and that means no matter how it came to be—the woman saved my life, and therefore is owed. Now whether or not she calls me on this, is what's to be seen. No matter, I can't leave until she returns, it would be stupid and disrespectful; Sparky cannot afford any more damn enemies.

Standing there in the open front doorway I wait and wait. Yep, just wait, passing time with ears perked, listening to the hotel's guests excited chatter. They are down below, across the grounds, eating, drinking, hangin' out. All are loudly discussing the startling goings-on of last night. My name is a constant mention.

Eventually, the woman does return, stepping from her truck. I dash into the bathroom and drain my lizard (don't know when there will be another opportune chance for such). Heavin' backpack up, throwin' shoulders into straps, slingin' shoulder bag across, down those stairs I do go! Crossing the grounds, all heads turn to watch (fuck 'em). Chin up, back straight, shoulders squared, and heavy backpack straps digging into both shoulders thus exaggerating corded arm and chest muscles. Bulging veins surface to quiver a pulse from surging blood flow, exhibiting sharp tattoos glistening with sweat. Long tight ponytail swishing, I march. I march like a man ready to kick ass and take names!

Despite the irony of this, the people seem to be falling for it. Passing along the many tables and chairs filled with guests, there is complete silence, almost like everybody momentarily freezes (forks and glasses have been put on hold, stopped mid-route). Mouths are agape hanging stupidly. My passing ensues a tailing domino effect of order, regained for low buzz murmuring. Okee-dokey, all of you get a look-see, and remember, remember my name.

The "lady" quickly notices and motions for me to follow her around a private corner. She appears to be coming down from the coke high and in dire need of a jump-start. Fucking coke! With that drug it's always more, more, more! Wouldn't be so bad if the high lasted longer. But unlike heroin, cocaine is a short-lived pleasure demanding frequent intakes. The woman is tryin' hard to act cool, like everything's hunky-dory. She asks how I am doing today and if I'm ready to check out? (Chompin' at the bit to be goin'.) "Yes Ma'am, I am fine, and ready, thank you." The woman, nodding, tries to engage in some meaningless small talk acting like nothing unusual had even happened last night. Not having the patience, "Ma'am, uh, what do I owe you for saving my life last night?" She laughs this off, claiming I owe her nothing. It had all been a simple misunderstanding. A misunderstanding that she had worked out with her good old friend Colonel Charlie. (Did she call him Charlie? Fuck, who knows.) The woman goes on to tell how he is the most influential man in the region, and really a sweet guy... Her words fade out, replaced with visions of bein' forced to suck his cock, endure slappings, and..., and, and the poor, poor children and torturing videos. Enough of this woman's bullshit! Interrupting her, "Uh Ma'am, I know about your friendship with the man. I overheard your conversations while you were in that bathroom." Her smile does a quick drop. She clears her throat. "Well Mr. Devin, you know the deal; you must leave Trujillo and Honduras as soon as possible, and young man, I would very seriously make that today if I were you." Nodding in acknowledgement, the woman's smile returns, "Well then, let's check you out! Shall we?"

Signing out, the woman sells me two fresh packs of cigarettes from cartons just purchased in town. In no time flat, a pack is opened, cig is out, filter snapped, and that puppy is lit. Inhaling deeply—oh my goodness—whew! Boy-o-boy! Talk about needin' a smoke! The woman watches intently; I ask her which way to town. She points. "Uh, and the phones?" No, they are still down. She asks me my plans. My answer is curt, "Walk to town, catch a bus for San Pedro Sula, and fly the fuck outta Honduras for ever!" The woman nods approval, offering that she does have a cell phone, would I like for her to call the American Embassy and let them know of my name and route? "Uh, yes please. Thank you."

A—haulin', ass-marchin' rural road at double time—sharp, while on red alert. The midday sun is high, bright, and hot. Sweatin' like a hard rode horse, my mouth is as dry as the dust now being kicked from dirty red Converse high-tops. (Buddy, when was the last time we had anything to drink? The two bottles of Coca-Cola yesterday at Hotel Hell. Yesterday, Goddamn, talk about havin' a long night!) So far, so good. No vehicles, no pedestrians, and no ambushes!

Arriving on the outskirts of town, a turn for dirt road not familiar is decided and taken. Why? Because instincts command, and they don't give reason; and really, at this point, none are needed. Sparky is just following and hopin' they (instincts) know somethin' I do not. The road leads through a section of shanty town neighborhood. Whole families gather to watch my passing. I can see in their eyes that they have heard of me and last night. Also, surprisingly, there appears to be sympathy? The way they are silently watchin', I feel like the perfect candidate for a dead man walkin'! Must stay on alert. And even though lungs are workin' overtime with backpack straps feelin' very much like they are intent on separating my arms from torso... sweat is burnin' eyes, and legs are twitchin' from strain due to demand placed upon them for speed of march... however, mustn't reveal this. Chin up, back straight (not such an easy feat when humpin' some eighty-odd-pound pack, while on verge of complete exhaustion), stop breathin' so damn hard! Must not show weakness—weakness of any kind. Lean mean fightin' machine! (Geez, all I really want to do is find true safety, curl into fetal position, and *cry*! Sparky is scared, tired and don't want to fight *no more*!) Hey, I know this road. This road will lead me right to the beachfront hotel where Martin works. I must go tell him about last night and inform him of my route. There ain't a whole lot of faith in the hotel woman calling the American Embassy. But Martin? He will do this for me. Rounding a bend, and passing a sheltered, tucked away spot, young Garifunas and Rastas are hanging out; these men are familiar to me and I to them. They are Martin's friends, and sell drugs. According to Martin, they are much like himself, in that they despise the local street gangs, police, and military. They are not into violence or strong-arming. This disassociation from the very cruel mainstream underworld sorta makes these guys popular local underdogs of the underground (they are the good guys). Needless to say, life for them is very dangerous. Upon seeing, several discreetly wave, anxious for me to come over. Acknowledging, I point towards the hotel where Martin works; adding a hand signal indicating urgency and quick return.

Across the street, diagonally, is the open-air refreshment stand. The man that owns it is there alone. He does a darting glance both up and down the street, then sends me a big warm smile and a short fast wave. Nodding to him, I hurry on to the hotel in hopes of finding Martin. The hotel owner's wife is up some stairs sweeping the landing. Noticing me, she begins to frantically wave, calling out for her husband, "Come quick, come quick, Devon is here! He is here! He made it to come back!"

The owner dashes out the door. Looking down at me, he is one big kind grin, silently nodding his head back and forth as if in disbelief. Before he can say anything, I breathlessly ask for Martin. The owner's smile goes to serious for telling that Martin is gone—on an errand—but he will be back shortly. "I'm in big trouble and can't wait for him!" The owner nods, sharing they are aware of my trouble; also he agrees it's best for me to get out of town as quickly as possible. He asks my route and upon hearing concludes, "San Pedro is very far from Trujillo, it will be good to fly out from there." I ask if he still has my address? He does, and agrees to contact my wife and the American Embassy if by chance word comes of anything happening to me. Martin will do the same. "Devon, we have all been greatly saddened by your situation, especially Martin. You see now how things are here? It is very bad—Yes? You must go now Devon. Buses leave everyday from town's centro for San Pedro. The next one to depart is at two o'clock. You can catch that one, Devon."

The wife now has her hands together as if in prayer position; tears are streamin' down cheeks while murmuring, 'God be with you Devon, may God be with you." The husband adds, "If you do make it back to your home, remember us and how things are here!" With a promise, good bye, and thank you, I spin on heels to march 'er straight for corner refreshment stand. In doing, thoughts come concerning the hotel owner's wife. Wow, her true colors had certainly surfaced. Always before, she had been cold as ice towards me.

Rounding the bend for the refreshment stand, the proprietor sees me comin' and, with eyes, indicates a warning to take notice of a teenager squatting on the curb across from where Martin's (good guys) drug dealing friends are. I, of course, recognize the squatting prick. He is a street punk in the gang working for Sergeant Lobo. The refreshment stand man greets me warmly. (Gosh, wonder where his wife and kids are? They're always here with him.) I order a cold Coca-Cola and a liter of water. Thumbing the filter off from cig and lighting it, a glance reveals one of Martin's friends crossing the street, approaching. The Coke bottle is emptied with two burning swallows cutting through dry phlegm, mucus, and dust. Plus, my throat is raspy and cracked from the night's yellin' and screamin'.

The refreshment stand man, using hushed tone, is complimenting—even congratulating—me on last night's success, especially the killings! (Shivers burst and goose bumps crawl.) Martin's friend steps up to the counter and orders a couple of local soft drinks. Without looking my way, he informs, "Devon, you have a follower." Knowing him to be referring to the squatting prick, my head nods knowingly. I then ask the whereabouts of the two Americans. Martin's friend bends to spit loudly on the ground. "Devon, those two left yesterday morning. As you know, we guessed them bein' CIA. They are no good. Only bad comes from those kind. Devon, what is your plan?" I tell him. He urges me to go now. He will have some children follow me as if playing. With them around, and in daylight like this, chances are good I will not be attacked on my way to town *centro*.

I hiss, "No! No children. They will hurt and kill them!"

"Devon, do not worry about this. We have all grown up here. We know how things are better than you. Go now and be quick or you'll miss the bus for San Pedro!"

Shoving the tall plastic bottle of water down into shoulder bag, it's again haul ass time! From corner of eye, the squatting street punk is seen darting off to wherever; but it takes no genius to figure out he's gone to report. The beach seaside road is giving me the major creeps, and poor legs are a-bitchin' up a storm, but stop or slow down they do not; no-sirree-bob they don't! Soon the joyous sounds of little boys on bicycles are clearly heard. They are following, but holdin' a right smart distance. They have done this sort of thing before, and are actin' just like normal loud, chattering little boys. Even though I do protest their involvement, I gotta admit, yes, it's nice havin' 'em back there! I'm bein' shown that even here in a psychotic place like Trujillo, there are still good people, people with true goodness in them. Those guys (Martin's friends) didn't have to do this. They are on constant red alert themselves. The Goddamn torture hammer can come down on them at any time, any place, for suspicion or spite alone! Geez, I am truly grateful. The fuckin' American bitch back at the fancy hotel, she coulda offered a drive into town, but no-ooo-oo! Not Miss *Bailar* Queeny!

And how 'bout those two Americans: very fishy they turned out to be. They left yesterday morning? Yet both had said they were gonna stay put here in Trujillo for at least another week or so. Hhmm, somethin' inside keeps suggesting those two personally knew Lobo's *gringo* cameraman. Of course there is no proof, but the cameraman seemed to know some things concerning me before even bein' told. Aaw, it's probably just paranoia. Right now Sparky is seriously on edge with everything seeming suspicious. Veering a turn, oh yippee, town *centro*. At least the little boys are still following. Oh looky here! Look what Sparky gets to walk past? Why it's Hotel Hell! Street gang members are grouping and spewing threats. Oh and here we get to pass the police station. The police and black uniformed Carib soldiers are standing out and around brandishing various weapons, looking intimidating and/or sportin' fun with cruel remarks and sneering laughter. Eyes forward, to the buses I march. Seeing the bus marked San Pedro Sula, and that it is boarding passengers for departure, Sparky double times it! The bus's baggage man hustles over to hurriedly assist with my boarding. There are now four black soldiers standing in front of the bus's door. All four are armed with M-16s and bad-ass attitudes. The sweaty baggage man relieves my shoulders from the heavy backpack. (With weight lifted, Sparky feels light as a feather, and jumpy as a mother fuck.) The baggage man senses this, whispering, "Devon, be calm, just do as they say. They are under orders to let you pass, but are here to frighten you and have their fun. Understand? Now be still and follow me." I do and of course the soldiers surround me, demanding passport and information concerning destination, etc. It's all bullshit, but scary bullshit all the same. The bus driver pleads that he is running behind schedule. "The bus needs to go!" A soldier hands back my passport; the baggage man squeezes through the soldiers and takes hold of my left arm; we turn to board the bus when BAM! Everything goes black with brilliant white tracers burstin' every which way from beneath (now scrunched closed) eyelids; my head is a poundin'!

Though not being able to see, I am still standin' and still conscious. Yeah but now what? The hands! Can't let 'em get hold of my hands. Need sight! I feel just like a goofy cartoon character that has just gotten its head *bopped*, to disappear down into chest cavity. Sparky desperately needs his head to pop back up! Goddamn, how I hate bein' hit from behind! Between the loud ringing sounds accompanying the streamin' inner fireworks display, there is sinister laughter, but also, wow, some people are actually openly verbally protesting the assault.

My hands fly to face in attempts of literally forcing eyelids open (and to keep 'em from bein' grabbed), but there is no time. Baggage man has dragged me up into the rumbling bus and with door quickly closing, away we go! Baggage man's grip remains firm, helping me keep balance midst unsteady motion of moving bus. He even pats my back until I'm able to open eyes and regain senses. Finally, vision comes to focus on his smiling face. Eugh, it's not just the head that hurts, in so much as the neck. What the fuck did they hit me with? Toward the back section of the bus, which is not very full at all, the nice baggage man motions for me to take a seat. I do, getting both seats to myself, rasping out, "Thank you Sir. Thank you very much." With a silent nod, he turns to go take a seat, up behind the driver.

Leaning my face into the window, and rubbing aching neck, conclusion comes that they must have hit me with a sock of sand or somethin' similar. The neck feels like it's been whip-lashed. Oh well, at least my ass made it (thanks to the baggage man) onto this bus, and we are out of Trujillo! Now let's hope the military road blocks and check points won't be harassing... Fuck it, one thing at a time. Eyelids lower, not for sleep (wouldn't dare), but rather to relax, becoming one with the inviting drift of bus in motion.

However, this is not to be; for no sooner is rhythm saddled than two Garifuna street punks move to take up the seat directly behind mine. And of the two, one is easily recognized as having been my "follower" from in town. Christ! "Sphsisst, Devon, Devon, how is the head, Devon? Ha ha! You got whacked good Devon. We were all watchin' to see if you fall down, but you stayed standin'! Tough man Devon is—ha, ha!" Damn, this is gonna be a very long trip. It will be nothing for one (or both) of these monkeys to step up, lean forward, and cut my throat. "Devon, hey Devon, for a white man you manage the machete very good. You hurt the gang very badly. You killed how many last night—four? Ha ha! Plus Devon killed the *puta* too. Aaaha! And Sergeant Lobo has now much humiliation. You tricked him, makin' him look the fool!

Aaah! He now has no respect. He is very angry! Sphsisst, Sphsisst! Hey Devon, how is it you learn the machete so well? You been in the American army?"

Growling, "Yes."

"And Devon, you have also been in that other army, the difficult one in France?"

Exhaling deeply, "It's called the French Foreign Legion. And yes, I served with them."

"Tich, tich, tich Devon the *mercenario*! Hey Devon, this Foreign Legion, it teach you killing with the machete?" (God, the way he's pronouncing "Kill" and "Killing" is giving me the fucking creeps! Also I'm confused; he's claiming that I killed four plus the prostitute? There was the one on the beach, closet, and bed! If he is right, then it means not one, but two men had died from my stabbings and hackings under the bed. Aughg, mustn't think about this right now.) "Uhm, Devon, and did this Legion Army also teach you to put the big torch light in your ass! Aaah, and teach you to yell like a woman when you have no machete? Ha hah, ha!"

From bottom of my core rises forth a stern hollow tone, "It taught me to do what I must to kill as many of the enemy as possible." Well, that certainly shut 'em up.

After a while though, they again start up: "Devon, sphsisst! Devon, no hard feelings, okay? We know you did what you had to. The whole town knows this."

(Yeah, whatever. Now with a crankin' headache, the codeine horse pills are briefly considered, but decided against.) "Hey man, what did they hit me with back there?"

"Devon, they whacked you with a special glove. It is made very heavy with lead powder." (A fuckin' SAP glove.) "Hey Devon, want to buy some coke? Buy this *coca*, I will give you a very good price."

To my feet, a plastic wrapped gram size ball is slid. Left dirty red Converse high-top heel kicks it back, with a blunt answer—no. But again he slides the cocaine to my feet, and this time there are three grams. (Hhmm, Sparky could really use a little jump-start pick-me-up! But, no way! These assholes probably put ground glass in it. Martin had warned of such practices.) With a kick the grams disappear! And despite my now painfully sore stiff neck—body spins round (almost over top of seat to lunge), hissing, "No, Goddamn it! You fucking slide any more of that shit near me again, and I'm gonna break both your mother fuckin' necks!"

They remain silent and un-harassing for the duration of the ride. My eyes are open, but not seeing. My head is full, but not computing; well, except for that of bein' on guard, red alert, mostly concentrated to that on this bus, and those in the seat behind. The ride is long and the sun has gone down to be replaced with darkness of heart, soul, and night. It is late when the bus reaches destination.

The baggage man carries my backpack to a taxicab. Handing him a roll of lempiras, I again thank him. With a big smile and a pat on my back he is gone. The taxicab driver informs me that the airport is closed for the night, no flights until morning. And no, it is not permissible to wait inside the airport throughout the night. For security purposes, all doors will be locked and no one is allowed on airport grounds after closing hours. Crap, this sucks! So much for my plan of hangin' out in a brightly-lit airport, in wait for catchin' the first flight out. Well, at least Trujillo is a long ways away, and that's the most important thing right? The cabby knows of a nice, safe, affordable hotel located in town *centro*, Yep, he sure does, so to town *centro* we go.

J esus, what an ugly city (at least this part). The streets are basically empty of people, but Skippy, they are full of trash. And dark? Oh better believe! (Buddy what's this reminding us of?) The hotel appears to be a fairly good-sized simple block structure. Its glass front is, however, very narrow and small, bein' not much more than an old short desk in a recess cubby space adjoining steep dark stairs goin' up. Two men, looking very much like east Indians, are tending the front desk. For some reason the glass door entrance is locked. Both men see me and their expressions regarding are indeed strange, almost as if frightened and nervous. One cautiously approaches, unlocking the door. They both check me in as if it pains them to do so. My room is on the second floor halfway down a center hall separating rows of rooms on both sides. The room is small but somewhat clean. Its door seems sturdy enough but of course lacking dead-bolt lock. The bed parallels length wise with the big glass window—so close to be practically butting. Ten minutes upon entering my room, all hall lights, 'cept for a few dimmers glowing, go out. You can still see, but whew, is it ever eerie. Fuck, please don't let this be what I think it is. Not again. It can't be!

Hearing many hushed voices and activity, I quickly flick off the room's light and, in darkness, sit on the bed facing the big window while thumbing twenty-inch steel black MAGLITE and desperately hopin' to all holy hell that my fears of what's to come are wrong. Well, guess what? They aren't. No they are not! The walls are thin and horizontal slat glass jalousie windows bein' on both ends of room's large window are (since there is no air conditioning) permanently open. And Skippy, if a pin were to drop anywhere near, Sparky would hear! Fear has a way for given one such an ability.

A cell phone rings and a man is answering. The voice sounds to be comin' from the room behind mine. The man speaks a Caribbean accent of Rastafarian. I hear my name mentioned often and it is evident the man is receiving instructions concerning me via cell phone. However, there is a strong hint of reluctance toward the task bein' ordered. Little good it does though, for in the end he (this Rasta or whatever) complies, agreeing to do it. (Gee, can we possibly guess what "It" is? Buddy!) With

232

phone conversation over, the man explains the instructions to a woman, obviously his girlfriend. And I'll be Goddamned, if the woman isn't American! Believe you me, in a foreign country, under conditions such as mine, one can indeed spot an American by voice alone. She sounds young, early twenties. And upon hearing, she is appalled, repeating over and over, "Kill him, scalp him? Kill him, scalp him?" Yepper! Seems like whoever is ordering my death is also desiring my hair as a trophy. Oh ain't this just great! Can paradise possibly get any more fun than this? Now they not only want to kill and torture me, they want my scalp! Jesus fuckin' Christ—who the hell scalps people in this day and age? Ught, don't even try answering that. (Buddy, we must be payin' some dues for serious atrocities committed in previous lives. Aughg! How are we gonna get out of this one, buddy?)

The couple are now arguing. The man is trying to persuade the young woman that I am a homo, fag, child molesting, murdering mercenary that had in Trujillo killed many innocent people, etc. The young woman, however, ain't buyin' it, retorting she had seen me coming up the stairs. "He is nothing more than an American backpacker with long hair and tattoos. If he did kill anybody it was probably in self defense. You know I'm right. Think about it! If he really is and did what you are saying, why was he allowed to leave Trujillo to come here? Why? Tell me why? And now we must kill him? Oh, and not only kill him but cut him up and scalp him! Are you out of your mind! I can't be a part of this! I won't, and neither will you! It's a set-up! You know it is! We will never be able to leave this country!"

The boyfriend sternly orders her to shut up. Then, with his own voice lowered, admits she is most likely right, but what is he to do? If they don't follow orders then they will be next—themselves being tortured, scalped, and murdered. He reminds her of the videos that are made in this region. After a long silent pause, the boyfriend gently suggests she should smoke some coke. He, then, as if coming up with a compromise, offers that if she helps to get them inside my room, my death will be very quick and there will be no cutting for torture or scalping. "De scalpin' Captain Matrix himself can be doin' on Devon. Irite?" (Hey, did he say Captain Matrix? Who the fuck is this Matrix?) With a long exhale of smoke, as if she is considering, "Wait a minute! They told you he was gay right? Well, duh, if he's gay why then would he let me into his room? Especially if he's already suspicious and just coming out of Lord knows what they put him through down in Trujillo. God, how I hate that town!"

Her Rasta boyfriend explains that according to what had been told to him, I am indeed a faggot, but also fuck women and children. I had raped many of both while traveling. The young woman snaps, "Bullshit! You don't believe any of that!"

He hisses, "It makes no difference what I believe. 'Tis his misfortune. All we con do 'tis try and help 'im cross over to de next world quickly and wit' out much pain; now come, we will work te hotel in our usual fashion. When we get to his room, he will let you inside; you will have no clothes, he 'twill be comfortable. Inside, you must leave the door unlocked, get 'im on the bed and crawl up on 'im like a very good piece of ass. De whole time tell 'im how you too are American and you miss American men. Aaah tell 'im anyting, just get 'im to lay flat; din hard as you can, hit 'im! Right on de nose. Dis will make his eyes water and prevent 'em from seein' well. Do dis, din quickly roll off de bed an' hide under it, all te while yellin' for me. We will din come in fast an' beat 'im wit our clubs. Devon will die quickly crossin' over to de better world."

After a pause, she is heard asking, "Are you insane? Oh God, this isn't happening." (Buddy, what are we gonna do? What are we gonna do? No fuckin' way are we lettin' this chick into our room. Thus they will simply get a room key and charge in! Buddy what are we gonna do? Buddy! Aw crap.)

Hhmm, let's see, think—think! Do I start up the whole bloody murder screamin' thing now—or wait? My voice is so cracked and hoarse. Perhaps it would be best to haul ass out this door and run! Like NOW! But Goddamn, run to where? They will surely have the stairs guarded; can't go that way. No will have to make for the other end of this hall, which was noticed to lead out onto an open walk-around walkway. From there, a jumping leap for ground. This is only the second floor after all. Sparky has sure made higher free jumps than this—that's for sure! But, once on the ground, where to then? My appearance bein' such as it is, there's no blasted way of blendin' into the general population, and by not knowin' anything—*anything*—of urban surroundings, I will be spotted quickly by street gangs, hoods, police and/or military, and Sparky can't deal with another police station. No, no, he can not! Plus, unlike last night, I now have this Captain Matrix guy for-real wanting my scalp! Lordy. And what kinda name is "Matrix"? Damn, who gives a flyin' fuck… What's it gonna be? Run? Or hole up for last stand fight? Gotta decide—now! Ught, too late; they have entered the hall. Time to die soon! Well, at least the boyfriend promised to kill quick without torturing. That is sayin' a lot, believe you me. And the chick? Hhmm, if I've a wild card, it's gonna be her.

From down the hall a tape is popped into a portable cassette player to float low soft music. Several rooms from mine there is tapping on glass (window) with the young woman seductively asking room's occupant if they would like her company or perhaps just a show. Obviously this is what was meant about "workin' the hotel in usual fashion." One room she does get invited into while the boyfriend is heard waiting in the hall with cassette player. I use this time to light a cig and drain bladder, pissin' in the sink so as not to make (seemingly) amplified sounds of urine hitting water in toilet bowl. In no time Sparky is back to hunched springing position from bed's end with MAGLITE flashlight at ready for battle. All too soon, the window next to mine is bein' tapped. Receiving no response, they are about to come to my window when a tapping sound on glass from a room directly across the hall from mine diverts their attention for approaching.

Crouching down low, with only one eye peering, the couple are now in full view. Despite dim lighting, eyes have adjusted for absorbing much detail. The boyfriend is a good looking Rasta of late twenties or early thirties. He places a wooden box down in front of the window across from mine while assisting his girl—a gorgeous petite thing with long falling blond hair—up onto the box for her to groove a sensual flow, to that matching music softly playing. Money is slid out from under the door; the blond beauty lets drop the short sheer slip camisole. Her balance is good and she knows all the moves. Obviously the girl has had experience as a pro stripper. The box top dance keeps Blondie turning to face me as she bends, enticingly spreading butt cheeks for paying customer. The boyfriend is heard whispering, encouraging her to keep turning for facing my way. "Devon is watchin', he must be. Let 'im see you good, dis will make 'im desire you all de more."

Well, even in this grey light, there is no question that the girl is desirable. She is golden tan with a very sexy face, and, unlike others I have seen while down here, her pussy is shaved. The femme fatale seductively asks the customer/occupant if he would like for her to come inside. The man answers no, not tonight; he only desires a sex show. More money is slid from under the door, and the boyfriend is heard whispering, "Good, we must make dis look sweet for Devon. He will be crazy for you."

With that, Blondie steps down from the box, and Rasta boyfriend steps up on it. With much showmanship, she undoes his pants, lowering them for a big cock to spring forth. The girl takes her time fondling, massaging, stroking its full length before using tonguing licks and deep sucking with slurping saliva dripping, following the occasional, standard constricting reflex gag. This is a damn good show; or would be under very different circumstances. Right now my dick is shriveled limp and, like me, just wants to hide! Sparky does watch, but mostly I'm tryin' to pick up on any clues as to the positions of where waiting charging others might be.

After gettin' his cock sucked nice and hard, the Rasta steps down from the box; he turns beauty to face the customer's window, lifts her so that tan bare feet can rest on window's narrow ledge. She bends her limber spread knees to lower pussy down onto her beau's standin' erection for some interesting cock riding. Wow, down here this gorgeous little blond would be a real prize for anyone. Keeping her must be a full-time worry for Rasta boyfriend. Oh shit! The show is over and here they are approaching my window. Obviously, the Rasta does not allow himself to cum for these shows 'cause his cock is still jutting proud. Not bothering with the short slip camisole, nude beauty steps on the box now in front of my window, and begins her erotic swaying with revealing bends exposing. Without hesitation, my urgent whispering freezes her in mid-motion. "Please help me, God, please help me. My name is Devin Murfin. I'm from Illinois. I have a wife and two young sons. I came down here to do volunteer work for an orphanage. Everything they are saying about me is a lie." (My voice is shaking). "In Trujillo the police, military and street gang charged into my room. They raped me and I had to fight; all the while there was a video camera filming. They tortured and killed children for these sick snuff films. I barely got out of there alive. I just want to go back home to my family. Please help me! There must be somethin' that you can do. I am truly a good man. My wife and sons need me. You are good people, I know you are. I don't want to hurt any of you, but just like in Trujillo, I will be forced to fight if you attack me. I must survive to get back home for my family. It will be bloody, it's always bloody. This is bad business, bad business for everyone. Please help me! I do not want to fight you people!" (With that I unscrew the end of my MAGLITE and sharply rack the metal together to sound very much like a gun's slide chambering a round. In any case it does announce that I do have steel in here for fighting.)

"Please help me, I beg you. Don't let this night become a bloodbath."

Stepping down from the box, giving it a kick, the tart answers, "I'll see what I can do!" With her hair tossed back and ass in motion, she stomps down the hall with Rasta boyfriend on her heels demanding, "Whatcha doin'? Ay, whatcha doin'?" Back in their room, they are heard again arguing. Blondie is loudly pointing out the stupidity of attacking me here in the hotel. "Look, it wasn't his fault. None of it. In Trujillo they attacked him. He has a wife and children. He came down here to do volunteer work with orphans, for Christ sakes! He's ready for you. Go ahead—charge his room. He is going to fight to the death to get back to his home and family! I bet you anything he will kill two of you before you can get him down. How the hell do you think he made it out of Trujillo to get this far? Huh? How? I know guys like him. They don't die easy. He will have the entire block awake before this is all over. His family will demand an American Embassy investigation, with international news coverage and everything. And guess who's going be stuck taking the rap for his murder? We are! Goddamn it, everybody knows we live here and what we do. I told you this was a set-up! Why else would they be throwing this shit in our laps? We don't do this sort of thing! I don't care, call whoever you have to; tell them that this plan is off! Tell them the entire hotel is now awake and we can't get to him without a million witnesses. Tell them whatever, but just get us out of this mess!"

Following a long silent pause, the Rasta does as he is told. It is obvious that he agrees with the logic. On the phone to whomever, he explains the situation. The Rasta then suggests that instead of killing me right off, I could be used as a mule (to carry drugs). "Ya mon, we use 'im several times to mule de *coca* an' din you do as you like wit 'im. You will tink about it? Okay, good, let me know back soon."

A few minutes later, movement in the hall; and a sheet is quickly tossed up and tacked in place, completely covering my window. Those doin' this can only be seen in silhouette form. There are four of them out there. Oh fuck—*fuck*! This is not a good sign. No it is not! And why are they doin' this now? The Rasta is still waiting with Blondie for that return phone call confirming further instruction. Sparky, it's now or never—before the phone call does come. (Buddy? Man, do it! Out in the hall where there will be witnesses from the windows watching and hearing. Obviously the sheet was hung to prevent us from seeing how and when they are going to charge in. This time we take the fight to them, while they are still unsure of exact orders—now! Jesus Christ buddy, feelin' a bit brazen are we? Damn, okay.) Aughg, Sparky, get ready—once we unlock and open this door, most likely all holy hell is gonna break loose with a whole lotta *hurt*!

Standing, recreating loud steel on steel racking sound. The four workin' the sheet split. And out that door me and twenty-inch steel black MAGLITE do fly! What the fuck! There to the end of the gloomy hall are eight black men, blocking, standin' side by side with legs slightly open and arms crossed. They are all grinnin' at me through some of the most bizarre masks this idiot has ever seen. Behind the grinnin' barricade of masked men there is stacked, as if ready for shipment, what surely must be, at very least, a hundred kilos of cocaine. Fuckin' A! Squaring myself for battle, I nod towards the sheet and loudly ask with words bouncin' an echo along corridor hall, "Is this for me?" The biggest one in the line silently nods his head. "Are you going to try and kill me tonight?" Again the big one nods. The baboon is all grins, and those masks! Damn evil lookin' things. Some are feathered and colored, while others resemble more of a Roman God thing. Tryin' desperately to sound cool, determined, and fearless, "I have done only what you would have done in my place. Police and military attacked me without proper cause. They killed and tortured children before my eyes. I kill only those that try to hurt or kill me; same as you."

A lone man then steps from around the corner. He is wearin' a brilliant silver mask, and somehow this man is just known to be Blondie's boyfriend and thus in-charge of this crew. Looking to him, I ask, "You are the man in charge here, right? Top Man! Well, Top Man, I have a family and must get home to them; maybe there is some work for me to help in accomplishing this, Yes? No?" The silver masked man silently shrugs his shoulders. "Yeah well, either way I'm outta here! Tell your boss or whoever, Devin-Devon went to the airport. They can have me killed there, or they can send me on a job. No matter, it's still way better than bloodying up this hotel, right? Besides—" (I point to the large stacked bundles of cocaine.) "—it appears you men have more important work to be doin' on this night."

With a flashing sidestep, my backpack and shoulder bag are slid from the room and slung over right shoulder, leaving free left side of body for swingin' twenty-inch steel black MAGLITE. Fortunately, the use of such is not required, because surprisingly, the masked human barrier opens up to let me pass. It is then their weaponry of AKs, M-16s, and pumps are spotted leaning up against the long row of stacked cocaine. Goddamn, obviously they don't want any reporting gun shots, and/or possibly also, they had heard about me charging the aimed Mini 14 and Sergeant Lobo's revolver head-on. Who knows—and who cares! The silver mask man has again disappeared around the corner and can be heard speakin' into the cell phone, "Ya mon, he be goin' to de airport—now! Says we con kill 'im der if we like…'

Once on those stairs, Sparky does fly—landing at the bottom lookin' up at two very surprised East Indians. Their jaws are literally hangin' open, speechless. My eyes are on them big. Their eyes are on me big. I dart a glance to the stairs. They (in unison) dart a glance to the stairs. I look scared; they look scared. Jesus, at this point I don't know who is more frightened, them or me! Seriously, they both look terrified! For some reason, Sparky finds this a bit amusing. (Yeah well, under conditions such as these? One's sense of humor does have a tendency to become dry. And boy, oh boy, mine is becomin' drier and drier.) Snapping out of it, clearing my throat, "Taxicab! *Nececidad* taxicab! *Donde?*" They both turn and look at each other, then one finds voice to answer, "Yes Devon, taxicab. Come quickly, come!" The other has rushed around and unlocked the door, holding it open for us. Out the door we run, crossing the street for an intersection. Here, he waves down a taxicab, while excitedly asking my destination. I answer him, "The airport." The East Indian's excitement drops as he warns, "It is a trap; they will be waiting for you there." Nodding my head in agreement, "Yes, but it is a chance that must be taken." Opening the taxi door, he pats me warmly on the shoulder, breathing, "Thank you Devon, thank you." and is gone, running back to his hotel.

En route for the airport, I light a cigarette—offering one to the old cabby. He accepts and we silently smoke. Yepper, just another fun-filled night in Honduras! Hhmm, why did that East Indian guy thank me? Geez, thank me for what? Not getting myself butchered in his hotel? The drive to the airport is dark and dismal to say the least. Thoughts are torn between whether or not to actually attempt playing this night out at the airport or have this cabby pull over, letting me out for takin' a chance at running terrain of now bush, woods, and fields. Yeah but, where to run? The American Embassy of Honduras is in Tegucigalpa, uh, nowhere near here. Traveling that distance undetected is not even a possibility. Naw, Sparky's just gonna have to play this out at the airport, and hope for the best.

Damn, was that a lot of cocaine back there at the hotel or what? Kilos and kilos all taped together into big rectangle bundles the size of feed sacks. That's some serious cocaine to be trafficking through that hotel. There's no doubt the two East Indians have no say in the matter whatsoever. The Rasta, his crew, and American girlfriend are obviously in charge of movin' the shit through the hotel, yet there can't be much profit in doin', not if they have to hustle her little ass for cash, there can't be. Guess, like the East Indians, they too have no choice and are bein' forced. Well Blondie, I owe you one. Okay Sparky, get it together; here's the airport. (Buddy, any clues on how this should be played? Buddy? Buddy! Crap.) The place looks as if it's undergoing some construction. The cabby pulls up to the small, enclosed, guard-station post. A soldier comes out and peers into the taxicab. Seeing me, he waves us through. Huddled here and there are heavily armed men. Some are wearin' black uniforms, while others are not; some have dreadlocks, and some are even sportin' the very evil looking black full face masks. (God, how I hate those things!) My arrival is of course expected, and to greet me is one lone man, one that is strapped with a shoulder holstered 9 mm Berretta. He is not in uniform, but looks very much like a clean cut undercover cop.

He opens the door and silently motions for me to get out. I do, while making a big show of kindly thanking the old cabby and paying him—adding a big tip and another cigarette. I'm wanting the cop or whatever he is to begin suspecting this tattooed long-hair of a backpacker is not the bad killing, raping monster that seems to be so ever popular in rumor. Stepping with him inside the brightly lit airport, the man turns and relocks the glass doors while indicating for me to take a seat beside his. These seats are near the entrance and are the standard molded fiberglass jobs, bolted to the floor, and bein' equally spaced one to the other in a series of several rows. We are seated in the first seats of the front row. This cop, or whatever, has obviously been given orders (for present time) to be my watchful keeper. On the end seat to his right is a folded newspaper and (get this) open baggy of approximately one quarter ounce of chopped powder coke with straw sticking out. On the man's (my keeper's) left is myself, and on my left (of course) is backpack and shoulder bag. And that's it. From our seated position the entire spacious ground floor before us can be observed, as can the activity outside, just beyond the all glass front. This is not a big airport; however, this part appears to be mostly new, and in process of expansion. Due to the late hour, everything—airline counters, small shops, and stands are closed. There are stairs leading to the second floor and here a big windowed office is noted. The office window blinds keep opening and closing, plus assorted people keep stepping out to look down at me. Some of these people are PRISA International Airlines employees. Others are soldiers, police and important civilians.

Outside too, from through the glass, it's now noticed that more and more armed men are approaching to peer in for a good look-see of Devin-Devon. Their expressions and body language are mocking, cruel, and full of mean. Some are even pointing their guns at me. There is evidence of three dug-in main bunkers spread out evenly before the ground level glass front. They have attempted to make the shallow bunkers blend in with the job site construction material of work in progress, but the stacked, arranged sandbags are pretty much hard to miss. Approximately five or six men are hunkered in and around each bunker. Plus, there are men patrolling on foot, while a few are even up in the stout, short trees. Now why would they be up in those trees? It's not as if they are concealed, camouflaged, or nothin'. On the contrary, they look just like armed, dangling monkeys. And why are most of the troops positioned to be facing inwards rather than outwards? Hhmm, either they are all really fuckin' stupid, or there is, on this night, one big-ass deal goin' down inside the place; thus, if trouble is to break out, it will be from within. Aaw, who knows!

My keeper seems completely at ease, having distinction of bein' very serious, but not hostile or menacing. He is an attractive man, maybe a couple years older than myself. He is Ladino: light brown skin with Latin features. (For some reason these people aren't Latinos, but rather Ladinos. Sparky can't even remember the reason for this.) His hair is glossy black and, despite its shortness, wavy ringlets are evident, similar to that of how my father's had once been. The keeper, feeling my eyes on him, closes his newspaper, leans to the right, and sucks up a big snoot of cocaine from the baggy. Holding fingers to nose, he looks over. Sensing the feel good snort, I begin.

In a very earnest, somber tone, Sparky spills forth entire poor mis-fortunes, with much emphasis on loving family and of course the whole orphanage volunteer thing. There's tellings of the hotel attack, torturing of children and the video filming. In a macho sorta way I even allow myself to cry a bit. Keeper man's attention is fully had now. He even reaches over for a couple more good snorts. His eyes are wide and have grown sympathetic; he's all ears and slightly nodding agreement while listening to the absurdity in the lies bein' told about me. I then ask him straight out "Are you goin' to be the one to kill me?" Keeper man answers, "No." It won't be him. It might be someone else, but not him—he won't do it. "They are deciding at this moment what to do with you." He reaches for another snort. I ask him about this—the cocaine he is so openly doing, as if it were nothing more than sipping hot coffee. He offers some, explaining that it is permissible during "closed hours." Damn, as much as it pains to do so, Sparky politely declines. Just what I need—to be seen snorting cocaine here at the airport. Cameras! The airport has to have security cameras all about. They more than likely are not on now, but they gotta come on sometime! Must hold it together until morning.

Upon closer observation, several young people—white backpackers (male and female)—are noticed sleeping on the floor behind a series of seats up toward the other end of this main level. I'm guessin' them to be Europeans, and presume, since their being is as it is, they must be forced mules. Also noted, outside, more thug troops have arrived. Why it's the Rasta and crew from the hotel. A few are still wearing the strange-looking masks. Blondie is even with 'em. She glances in, our eyes meet, and then she's off, skippin' away with skirt a-flappin'. The crew brought some coke in a large clear plastic zipper bag, and they are goin' from one bunker to the next, offering it to the men for filling huge rolled aluminum foiled pipes with a cocaine ganja-weed mixture. Now Sparky has seen, made, and used aluminum foiled pipes, but, nothin' on the scale as these. It must have surely taken up an entire roll of aluminum foil to make such pipes; they are that big!

Sitting, watching the big aluminum foil pipes get filled, fired, and passed around, a grinnin' masked baboon is noticed watching me watch them. Damn, against the black mask his teeth look like Chiclets. He shoulders his AK, holding mocking aim. *Fuck him*! Raising to my feet, taking a couple steps forward, spreading arms wide, a stare down ensues. I am—in full view—openly daring him through the glass front to do it: *shoot*! And everyone is seeing it all. His comrades are now teasing, laughin', and eggin' him on. The baboon's smile drops to an evil grimace. Vibes are reporting his finger is a-twitchin', in want of pulling that trigger, oh so bad! Myself unable to resist, and obviously not thinkin', smile a taunting ridicule callin' his bluff while makin' him look the fool! Stupid move? Yeah probably, but so what! I am so tired of this shit you wouldn't believe! Also, rebelling and stirrin' up trouble must be a large part of my nature. Plus, Sparky is now just mostly listening to instincts; and they are tellin' that it is, at this very moment, very, very important to show *no fear*!

A crackling comes across my keeper man's walkie-talkie. With an acknowledging nod he mumbles into the thing, then tells me to sit back down. I do, lookin' up toward the office. There, two PRISA International Airline people in uniform are glaring down at me. One is a Ladino woman with walkie-talkie in hand. The other is a vicious lookin' black Carib. Mercy, if looks could kill—loose wire much? The woman holds herself to have substantial authority.

They both turn, going back inside the office while others keep peering down from through the window blinds. Whoa, without a doubt, at any moment, they are going to summon a command for me to go up into that office where I will surely be tortured, murdered, or forced to mule. Muling will only buy some time. It takes no fuckin' genius to figure out that when bein' forced to mule for a major airline such as PRISA International, your life is gonna be short. No way can they allow you to live and tell. (Buddy, what are we gonna do? Man, live for the moment only, and act cool as a cucumber. We'll play it as it comes, but for now be cool and show no fear! Uh, okay.) And so I begin to whistle a tune with legs crossed, rockin' in my seat as if out on the front porch of

Mayberry with ol' Andy Griffith, Aunt Bee, and little Opie himself. How this is bein' so smoothly pulled off—fuck only knows.

Soldiers and thug-troops are now movin' out. Also the light of mornin' is pushin' on backside of dark night. I ask my newspaper reading, coke snortin' keeper man where all the troops are goin'. Lookin' up to see and then down to his watch, he answers, "They are cold and moving around back to come inside for getting warm." Yeah right, Sparky believes that one. Smokin' coke in this heat and getting' cold? Don't think so! That stuff heats you up inside-out. Naw, more likely they have gone around back to start loading planes with stow-away cargo.

Pretty soon the office blinds open wide, and standin' up there is the grinnin', Chiclet-toothed, masked baboon, holdin' forth for me to see a cocaine crack rock literally the size of a duffle bag! And Sparky ain't lyin'—the thing is huge! Obviously, they are doin' this to observe my reaction. I smile, wave and give the thumbs up! (Yeah, just keep smilin' you crack-head retard.) The blinds close and my keeper man's walkie-talkie squawks. He then tells me they are wanting him upstairs, but I'm to stay put. Yeah, sure!

Just as soon as he leaves, Sparky is up and walkin' straight for the center of this main floor, with objective for learning locations of security cameras and to be noticed as not havin' a fear in the world. Just a typical backpacker, bored, waiting to catch the first flight out. Glancing up and around, security cameras are spotted, but there's no way of knowin' if they are on or not. What the hell! Up high in the shadows among curved steel rafters are some strange lookin' critters. They appear to be similar to possums, yet different. Wonder what they are? (Uh, who gives a fuck? There is no time for this. Must keep moving. Yeah, okay). Near the young white backpackers laying on the floor, I loudly slam my foot down onto bolted fiberglass seat, while bending forward in pretense of tying red Converse high-tops. Eyes pop open, and Goddamn how there is the look of doom within these young people. Removing my vest, slowly turning to be seen from all angles, I pretend to shake dirt from the filthy vest. Topless, my tattoo work is very visible, which is the intent. Lighting a cigarette, inhaling deeply, casually swinging vest in hand, Sparky is makin' quite the spectacle, while (on pins and needles) leisurely strollin' past various small closed shops and stands. Much to my delight, there are a few people now inside. They are busy in preparation of opening for a new hectic business day. Janitors are also starting to emerge. With these few workers, I do try engaging in light conversation. They, however, avoid me like the fuckin' plague, movin' away to keep distance and avoid eye contact. But oh how the attempted introductions do announce my name. And they do see; they all see. A phone booth is noticed… (Buddy? No, man, not yet. The time isn't right. Must wait and stay toward the center of the floor).

From the upper office landing, the PRISA International she-bitch is again glarin' down, and with her is the same vicious lookin' black Carib. Damn, the only way Sparky is goin' up into that office is a-kickin', screamin' and bleedin'! My plan (not bein' able to think of anything better) is that of a retard. If and when they do come for me, I'm a-gonna call forth everything from within and *run, slammin'* into the big glass front! Hopefully the glass will break cutting severely enough for bleeding to death. Either way, it will surely be a surprise attention getter. Must go out with a bang! You know, shake things up a bit to where questions are asked and hopefully an investigation. I am not endin' up like these young backpackers here. Christ, they are the breathin' dead, and by their looks—blank hollow eyes—they know it.

Keeper man is now hurrying down the stairs from the office. He looks to be quite disgusted and frustrated (not with me, but rather with those upstairs). I quickly go to him asking, "What's up Boss?" Grabbing his baggy of coke and newspaper, he informs his shift is over and must go home now; also, I'm to go upstairs (oh fuck). "Uh, upstairs? But why Boss?" Shaking his head and not meeting my eyes, he answers simply "*Droga!*" And with that, my keeper unlocks the glass doors and is gone.

Droga, huh? Well that's one way of puttin' it. Still, Sparky ain't goin' up them stairs, no-sirree-bob! With heart a-pumpin' as if on an all out run, I march over to the other side of the floor to where a closed coffee counter is. Despite the thing being closed, there are two people now inside working to ready it for business. Lighting another cigarette, a hot coffee is really craved—yep, a coffee and a couple of grenades! A little greasy lookin' piss-ant of a PRISA International Airline employee comes down the stairs. All cocky like, he crosses the wide floor to inform the young white backpackers that they are needed upstairs. Zombie-like, they silently rise, getting their packs together, and away to the office they go with heads bowed low. The greasy Beaner then approaches, ordering me to go upstairs as well. Lookin' him straight in the eyes, my face slowly beams a broad grin for bursting forth an obnoxious laugh, and then yells, "BULLSHIT! I know what you're up to! I bet you aren't even a real PRISA Airline worker are you?" The greaseball is takin' cautious steps backwards, lookin' more than a little rattled. "My name is Devin Murfin. I came down here as an American volunteer for a Guatemala orphanage! Guess what? The American Embassy knows I'm here to catch the first flight out for Guatemala City. Why do you think I'm flyin' out from here instead of catchin' the flight from La Ceiba? Huh? Why?" (Jesus, where did all that come from?) The little, bug-eyed prick spins on his heels and almost runs for the stairs! Lookin' up, and around, many had indeed seen and heard.

Sparky marches back across the floor with an overflow of showy confidence; slinging backpack and shoulder bag over right shoulder only, the PRISA International Airline woman is heard screaming, "If the embassy knows he's here then it's off! We cannot use him... and why wouldn't they know he's here? It seems to be now common knowledge. He is much too popular! We will just get someone else... No, we must let him go, we cannot afford the risk..."

Almost unable to contain myself—to that phone booth I do go! The morning light is streaking in as are now many various employees, shopkeepers and such. My AT&T phone card is out and Sparky is a-punchin' numbers! (Man, calm down, just calm down; you never get these numbers right first time around. Can't afford not to this time.) Punching in password—I'm through! Oh-hoh, the call is actually goin' through! Come on Nancy wake up—wake the fuck up! Oh well, if nothing else, the answering machine will at least pick up and record my message of instructions, location, and route. "Hello—Hello!" (Oh thank the gods, space aliens and this here telephone.) The sound of her voice makes me want to laugh, cry, and literally gush with a million different emotions all at once. But only one can be afforded right now, and that's instructional command. "It's me, Devin. Don't say anything, just listen and write. I'm at the airport of San Pedro Sula, Honduras. My hotel room was attacked, I'm in big ass trouble. PRISA Airlines might be trying to force me to mule coke for them; I'm goin' to try and catch the first flight out for Guatemala City." A glance reveals the airport is now open with people and passengers flooding in. Also, those from the upper office are watching me with glaring hatred. "Nancy look, the first flight out of here is in one hour. I will call you if they let me pass through to the boarding gates. Just as soon as I hang up, call the American Embassy. Have them contact the embassy in Tegucigalpa, Honduras, and the embassy in Guatemala City. Tell them everything I've told you. If you don't hear back from me, call the major newspapers and my mother in California. She will know how to help with this." Nancy keeps tryin' to get questions in, and she's sounding confused and frightened. I keep cutting her short and demanding, "Do you understand? Nancy do you understand? Baby, do not fuck this up!" I then quickly repeat all instructions, and against her protests, tell her, "I love you!" and hang up.

Stepping away from the phone as if just havin' had myself a very pleasant good morning conversation with my wife, I go to the ticket counter. The vicious lookin' Carib himself comes down to personally sell me a ticket and check my pack. He then motions me over to a podium where an exit tax must be paid. Yepper, a tax for having had the privilege of stayin' in friendly, warm Honduras. The Carib aggressively stamps my receipt, hissing, "Devon, your tricks do not fool me!"

On upper level of boarding gates, a refreshment stand is now open. Here, a hot coffee, liter of water and two packs of cigarettes are bought. At a nearby payphone, the coffee scalds its way down parched, cracked throat. Cig is snapped free of filter and lit for exquisite inhale, while punching numbers. Nancy is again reached. I inform her that it looks like they are going to allow me to board. She is given my approximate arrival time for landing in Guatemala City. Her voice is understandably shaken, hyper, and full of questions. However, for such, there is no time. Also there is suspicion that the call is bein' monitored. She keeps repeating, "Just come home. Oh God, please just come home!" I remind her again to follow earlier instructions. "I love you, and will call upon landing in Guatemala City." But Nancy is (like always) bein' persistent, so Sparky must regretfully hang the phone up on her.

At the gate, I stand and wait, watching some pretty teenage Ladina princess puke her guts up, right there on the floor in front of everybody. She is makin' a big show of it, just sittin' there, bent forward and barfing. There is a small group of people gathered around her, all over-acting as if she were dyin' or somethin'. A well dressed man comes over to her behaving very much like a doctor (and probably is), pats pukin' beauty on the back while encouraging her to keep right on doin' what she is doin'. He then announces to everyone that it is simply a case of nervous anxiety. She will be fine after her stomach is emptied. The girl is getting much sympathetic attention by all and it is obvious she is milkin' it. Oh how I do want out of this fucked-up country!

On the plane, seated and feeling its glorious lift off, a long exhale ensues, one that has been hidden in reserve for the last two days and two nights. Goddamn, is that all it's been? Whew, in a span of less than forty-eight hours they had… I had… Oh Lordy-Lordy, mustn't think about it. We made it; we made it out. And that's all that matters, right? (Buddy, right? We will just put all this shit behind us and move on with journey as planned, right? Buddy? Man, you need to listen to your wife; it's time to go home now. Isn't that what you kept telling yourself and everyone that would listen throughout this whole nightmare? In Guatemala City you will board the first flight to anywhere USA, yes? Devin, Devin! Hey man, have you forgot Cuba? Fuck no buddy, how the hell can anybody ever forget that? It's just—buddy, you know! Know what man? Buddy if we go home, it will mean they have won! Won, huh? Yeah buddy, they will have won! Man, you are mad with anger! All of that fear is being replaced with pure *rage*! What if they come after us in Guatemala? Huh? What then? Let 'em come, the sick bastards! Oh, we are tough guy now? Indestructible, is that it? No, buddy, quit bein' an asshole. Those sick fuckers hurt me way down deep inside, and they stole somethin', a piece of my being. They took it! How am I ever going to get it back? How-how-how? Mother fuckers! And how do I live with myself, running home now with my tail between my legs! Huh? How? Buddy, I gotta make somethin' good come from this trip. Besides, Guatemala ain't Cuba or Honduras. It's a completely different country. One travel book declared Guatemala as now bein' one of the safer countries of Latin America. And the Americans back in the States having experience with the orphanage had all confirmed this, so there! Man, haven't you learned anything? Oh shut up! If all goes well, we should be at the little orphanage on the big jungle river tonight. We will be surrounded by wonderful children and international volunteers. And we will sleep. Buddy I need sleep... Man, when was the last time you slept? I don't remember exactly. I bet though when we do sleep, the dreams are gonna be a real blast—nightmare city! Maybe you are in a dream now? Christ buddy, I wish! Man, you need to eat. When was the last time you ate anything? I don't remember exactly. Now go away, my bladder is about to explode and I've an orphanage to get to.)

Guatemala City airport is big, bright, and lively! Full of many friendly, smiling faces, indeed, a very welcome contrast to that just left. Here, everything goes smooth as punch; everything except for ability in reaching Nancy. After several tries with her phone buzzin' with busy tone, Sparky must give up. The bus ride for the Rio Dulce region will be an all-day affair. Cash is exchanged for local currency of quetzals. A taxicab is caught for the city's bus terminal where, as if right on cue, a bus is boarded headed straight for Rio Dulce, well, Puerto Barrios, to be exact. From there it's a thirty-minute boat ride to the town of Livingston. Livingston is a small Carib town of Garifunas. It is reached only by boat and is situated at the mouth of the huge Rio Dulce waterway. Here, another boat must be caught for going further upriver to where the orphanage, Casa del Corazone, is located.

A speedboat fleet does most of the transporting of people and supplies. These boats are actually long, narrow, deep-water skiffs (Mexican launches) powered via outboards. I am just able to catch the last one departing for the day to Livingston.

The boat ride is exhilarating and renews my sense for positiveness. The air is brisk and cool. There is a familiar smell of outboard engine exhaust, with gas/oil mixture accompanying the unfamiliar scent of freshwater mixing with saltwater. It is very wondrous for me. This boat has no tourists on board, just a few warm smiling local passengers; and she's heavily burdened with tarp-covered supplies. This is big water here, and the spray comin' from over the bow is almost chilly. Sparky hardly minds; it feels refreshing. But just like back home on the Mississippi River I can understand how this might become a bit annoying during early morning hours when the air temperatures are much cooler than those of the long hot balmy nights spent on land. The view is spectacular with distant banks of tropical, lush, sprawling greenery. Needless to say, my mood is up—feelin' confident with the decision in continuing onwards with the journey.

A rope is thrown and the boat is tied off beside many others. We have arrived at Livingston's town dock. It is evident that the docks here are (during the day) a lively center for activity with much hustle and bustle.

But now with the day drawing to a close, the activity is following suit. Street vendors are loading up their carts, stands, and wares for callin' it a day; as are the dock workers themselves. A few though do hang back to unload our boat, as does a uniformed official customs inspector. He waves me aside asking to see my passport, why I'm here, for how long, etc. This customs officer is polite and professional, but Sparky can't help feeling the guy already knows somethin' concerning me and he thinks it to be quite humorous. The man, now having a sly mischievous grin and no interest whatsoever in contents of my backpack or shoulder bag, hands back the passport, with wave to be movin' on. Thanking him, I turn and am greeted by a gorgeous little boy.

He is all big brown eyes, bright toothy smile, and appears to be about ten or eleven years old. This boy works the docks every day, doin' what he can for passengers, boatmen, and whoever. He's full of questions, you know, the usual ones, and even asks if I will tattoo him just like the ones on myself (cute kid). Surprising the boy with a few quetzals, I inform him of my need for a boat in goin' further up the river to orphanage Casa del Corazone. He, of course, knows right where the little orphanage is and will personally tag along on the trip to ensure my guaranteed arrival.. Only problem is that there will be no more boats leaving on this night. "No Devon, not even if you offer to pay more. You must spend the night here in Livingston and catch the proper boat when they start runnin' in the mornin'." Oh damn it to hell! I almost made it. The little guy knows of a hotel, so up the road we walk.

Everywhere, it is noticed that the ground it littered with torn tiny baggies used for gram size crack and coke. There is no doubt whatsoever as to the extent the shit is bein' used in this town. What does this mean to me? Fuck only knows. But, I gotta get to a phone. The hotel turns out to be more like a small, short, single strip two-story roadside motel, except there are no cars parked, nor is there even space or need for such.

A nice big Carib woman checks me in. She and her husband own the place and live here at the hotel, as do their adult son and daughter. The big woman appears to be around sixty years old and asks to be called "Mum." She and her husband, "Pop," live here on this end of the hotel. My room is the furthest—on opposite end. Wow, it's trash-strewn and secluded here on this end. Also noticed are the many vacant rooms, and so I ask Mum if it might be possible to get a different room—perhaps one closer to hers and Pop's? Mum gives a suspicious, questioning look. And so, an explanation is given—she is told briefly (and without details) how I had experienced in the past some harassment from bad people while staying at other hotels. Mum, with hands on big hips, sternly informs that this is the only room presently made up. After a moment though, her searching eyes, as if reading my true character, soften and with much pride she states how never in the some twenty-odd years that she and Pop have owned this place has any of their guests ever been harassed, molested, or harmed. "Devon, this is a very respectable hotel. All of our guests have safe pleasant stays here. And the same will be for you as well. I give you my word." (Ught, Sparky's heard this line before.)

Surprisingly, the room, once inside, is much nicer than expected: simple and very clean. These people do take pride in keepin' their rooms clean (hopefully a good sign). There are two single beds divided by a nightstand. Both beds run parallel to the standard wall size hotel window. And of course on each end of the big window there are horizontal slat-glass, jalousie windows that open and close via hand crank. God, how I am really hating this window set-up! Across from foot of beds, against the opposing wall, is a cheap dresser and to its left is a door leading into the room's small private bathroom. Above the toilet is another glass jalousie window. (Oh yippee.) Mum hands over the key while kindly informing that their restaurant is just up the stairs above my room and that the food is very fresh and always good. If I need anything, anything at all, she and Pop are down at the other end. I thank her, she leaves, and Sparky pulls out his twenty-inch steel black MAGLITE for routine room search. The room is indeed clean—from top to bottom. Stepping outside, locking the door, and walking for other end, I see Mum sittin' at an old outdoor table workin' a small paring knife for peeling yams or the sort. Mid-distance from my room to her, I hear it! An all too familiar chill shoots right up the spine. Fuck, fuck, fuck! Looking up above to narrow second floor walkway terrace, is, guessing, Mum's son; he is a good-lookin' young man of late twenties. While leisurely sitting back in a simple white molded plastic chair, and talkin' on a cell phone. The young man is heard mentioning my name several times, laughing, repeating things like "This Devon stuck it up his ass… and he killed how many… Ha ha! Yes, he is here now… How much? Okay, we can do that…" Mum's son then notices me standin' below listening, and so moves on into his room closing the door.

Like a meteorite slammin', realization comes exposing the stupidity in coming here. Goddamn, why wasn't buddy listened to. Red alert, red alert! Adrenaline is once again pumpin'! Sparky's gotta become real good friends with Mum, and like fast! Also, a phone is desperately needed. Nancy must surely be crazy-sick with worry. A payphone is mounted on the outside wall near where Mum is seated at her table. Putting the phone to ear, there is no surprise in finding it dead—not working—out of order. Mum, without raising eyes from chore at hand, casually informs that the phones are down at the moment. The power too. No phones, no electricity. "They both just went down. Happens often here." Well crap, ain't this a coincidence! What are the fuckin' odds? Acting all sweet and sincere, while taking a seat beside Mum at the table, I apologize for appearance, then go into great lengths telling her of my loving family, while pulling forth wallet and proudly showing off pictures of two adorable young sons and attractive devoted wife. Of course I explain to Mum the reason for my being here—the volunteer orphanage work. "This is my way of tryin' to thank God for blessing me with such a wonderful family." Mum, is even told about my mother and sisters with much emphasis put on my stepfather and baby sister both bein' black, and how we are all such a close loving family etc. "*Familia* is very important Mum. It is the most important thing in life." Mum, with busy hands, looks pleasantly surprised, nodding "Hmm-hmm, hmm-hmm... Yes Devon, you are correct. Family is very important. You sound to be a very good man."

The sun is going down and nightfall is formin' around us. Pop emerges and Mum introduces us. Pop is a little gray-haired man, having light brown skin. He looks to be Ladino, whereas Mum is black Carib. Pop acknowledges me with a simple nod. His eyes betray concern for my presence here to be that of bad news—trouble. Grumbling, he walks away to start the gasoline generator. I ask Mum when she thinks the phones might be back up and working? "It is very important Mum, that I contact my wife. Of course she knows I am here, but I promised her that I would call to say good night. She will be very worried if I do not." Mum suggests going down the street and trying the bars and clubs. "Some have private phones that work when ours do not."

Rising from my seat to leave, I ask, not bein' able to resist, "Mum, what are all these little plastic wrappings littering the ground?"

"Hmm... Devon, they are all from the *coca*. It has become a very big problem with our young people these days. They smoke it as you smoke your cigarettes. They do not care what it does to them."

Back in my room, leaving door open, I reach for my MAGLITE flashlight and sit on the bed's end, while rubbing eyes, wondering just what chances are for getting hold of a working phone, and (more importantly), what chances are of this night not becoming another living nightmare. Fuck, over the sound of working generator, croaking toads, buzzin' insects, and night whatnot critters, there is conversation. The son has come downstairs and is sitting with Mum. They are talking.

There is also a young woman's voice, guessed to be Mum's daughter. I cannot hear the entire conversation, but do catch bits and pieces—enough. My name is mentioned often and then Mum responds, "Yes, that is a very good price for the *coca,* but I do not like this business concerning Devon. He is not, as they say... No, we must just leave 'im be, to go on his way in the morning." Shit—*shit!* Time to look for that phone. If nothin' else, maybe Sparky can find some friendly Americans or Europeans that will help—yeah right, but must try all the same.

The road is gloomy-dark with long, wavering shadows. The bars, clubs, and nightspots are lit, some with generators while others only candles and lanterns. They are all serving a rowdy drunk crowd. There is no luck in finding a phone or friendly people. I am, though, attracting attention, and it's all the wrong kind. This is crazy. Sparky must get off this street and back to the hotel, at least the mum is there. Ught-o, why does everybody seem to know my name? Passing various small groups of young people hangin' out in shadows along the road, they hiss my name, "Devon," while making an array of verbal threats. I keep twenty-inch steel black MAGLITE at combat ready position and go into act for confident tough guy mode. Despite the vicious threats, Sparky makes it back to the hotel physically unchallenged.

Unlocking my door, clicking on MAGLITE flashlight for a quick room sweep. All clear! Door is closed and locked, and of course there is no deadbolt. Whew! Boy-o-boy, well, that certainly was fun—my ass! Pacing the floor while thinking how worried Nancy must be, I glance out the window. Oh fuck me! Looky what's seen from my window. Why if it ain't several Garifuna black Caribs—whatever the hell they are called. There they are, young men hangin' out only a few feet away, intently watchin' my room, which is, of course, the hotel's furthest most end room. To the left is a battered, pieced together privacy fence with much overgrown greenery, weeds, and trash. Also, my room is practically under the stairwell leading up to second floor and restaurant, which by the way, is closed due to the power outage. No open restaurant, no customers, no witnesses. How Goddamn convenient! Oh well, it's doubted that this restaurant does much business anyway. And where are the other hotel guests? Could it possibly be I am the only hotel guest presently stayin' here?

"Devon, Devon can you hear me?" The voice is recognized as bein' that of Mum's daughter. She is tapping on the glass window and speakin' in hushed tone. "Devon, do you want to buy some *coca*? Open the door Devon. I will give you a small amount to sample for free. If you like it, we will sell you some more. All at a very reasonable price. Come Devon, we do not wish to harm you, we only desire to do a little business." I stay silent, hunched down low, knowing they can't see me through the pitch-black darkness of my room. "He will not answer!" A man's voice whispers for her to try the sex. "Devon, perhaps you prefer some company? Sex? I saw you earlier. You are a very handsome man with your long *blondo* hair and wild American tattoos. You make me very hot. Look Devon, look. Can you see me?" (Fuck, not again.) Yeah, Sparky can see her. She has her shirt open, exposing bare breasts. While fondling, she pushes them together, using fingertips to pull on long nipples. She does, however, seem a bit wary of getting' up too close with the glass, almost as if afraid.

There is a sudden shout from Mum; the girl quickly closes her shirt and turns away. The others jump as well! Mum is shooing them away. "You all go from here! Leave Devon alone. He wants nothing from you. Go now, be gone from my property!" Mum then starts scolding her daughter in some language, I haven't a clue. The young men do disperse; somewhat, mostly just leapin' to the left for hunkering down into the overgrowth of weeds and trash runnin' along the still standin' dilapidated privacy fence. Sparky takes notice of two giant toads doin' their eerie low chants of puffed up swellings. (Oooh, buddy, it's happening again. Man, of course it is, you dumb ass. What did you expect? Thought just by leaving Honduras for Guatemala that the bad guys would leave us alone—after what you did? Why didn't you catch a flight for the US when you had a chance? Huh? Why? Buddy, shut up! Who says they would have even allowed us to board a US-bound flight anyways, huh? Did you think of that? Man, you still should have tried. Well duh, no shit, dummy! Man, don't call me dummy, dummy! You were the one so up on himself getting out of Honduras alive, while full of bizarre rage, not thinking clearly. Man, hope your head is clear now, because if it isn't, don't come whining to me. Buddy what are we gonna do? What are we gonna do?)

Let's see. Hhmm, the Mum seems to be, at the moment, on my side. The son, daughter, and friends are not. However, the daughter is obviously fearful and thus bein' directed—used. So far, no guns, soldiers, or police. Also these people, though assumed quite capable and intimidating, are—just guessing here—lackin' the whole kill, maim, torture for fun spark. There is a sense of no hardened experience among them. Terrorizing is not their specialty. But there is a price on my head, and this is not good. No it is not!

The generator shuts down, and thus, so does the outside lighting.

Darkness of night is all about, but Sparky can see. Damn well better believe! And hear? Oh Skippy, how I can hear! Mum and Pop are heard briefly arguing from their living quarters down from the other end. Then, there are only normal night sounds of the region. Ught! The door to the room neighboring mine is bein' opened, and now occupied with Mum's son and pals. They seem to be using the room for a hangout and since they are making plans for attacking and killing me, gee, guess the room could be classified as their retard command post as well! Stupid idiots, I can hear everything.

First, they all agree the money bein' offered is too good for passing up and therefore must do what is required—kill Devon. Mum's son is obviously the one in charge, with the sister's boyfriend acting as right-hand man. All are in the room, smoking coke/crack, drinkin', and discussing the mission before them. Green novices to this sort of work they indeed are. At first there is much gung-ho bravado, that is until the son warns that I have had combat experience in both the American army and a special European mercenary army. To this, he adds a greatly exaggerated telling of the killings in Trujillo, where I had (according to him) single-handedly, using a machete, wiped out an entire gang, killing both men and women. A murmur of concern and disbelief goes about the room. Some ain't so gung-ho no more. Funny how exaggerated bullshit, combined with cocaine, has this sort of effect on people.

Most of them do agree that this can't all be completely true, but still… What is needed is more information. It's decided they need to learn for themselves more about me. And really, since it is rumored that besides bein' a crazed murderer, I am also an uncontrollable sex maniac that fucks both men and women, they conclude who better to get the desired intel than the very attractive sister.

So to my window, the sister comes, again softly tapping on the glass while seductively callin' for my attention. This time Sparky thinks it's best to chat. Hunkering down low, using gentlest voice possible, I give her the short sympathetic version of my side of the story. Of course much emphasis is put on my wife, sons, orphanage Casa del Corazone, and God. She listens, and wants to know more concerning the killings in Trujillo. (There is someone else out there goin' back and forth from her to the next room reporting all that is bein' said.) Without hesitation, she is given detailed account with focus on how soldiers, police, and a street gang had attacked my room and how they tortured and murdered children for the sake of making cruel sick videos. "I fought and killed only for purpose of defending myself. Like any man, I will fight to the death in order to return back home to my family." (This last, Sparky menacingly hisses, and generally likes as bein' a nice touch.)

After a pause, the sister asks if it is true that I had been a soldier in "those armies" and did I also "kill for them" I'm now grinnin' to myself. (Yeah okay, one would think under such circumstances that finding humor of any kind to be not possible. Adrenaline, though, has many different faces, almost acting as a bizarre drug unto itself.) I ask, "Armies? How do you know anything about the armies I served in?" (Sparky don't want her, or them, knowin' he can hear damn near everything bein' said from the next room.)

Following brief hesitation, Mum's daughter answers, "It is rumored. There are many rumors following you." Then she whispers, "Cell phones, understand?"

(Yes! The girl has exposed sympathy! Maybe between her and Mum…) With a long sigh for her to hear, the answer comes, "Yes, it is true; I served in special units of those armies. And yes, there was killing, but we fought only other soldiers. Never did we police or kill civilians. I would have never been apart of such action. Please understand, all of that had been a very long time ago. Now I am a family man and want only peace, and to work with those in need. Do you understand? Please do not believe the horrible rumors."

I allow a moment for silence. She breaks it, quietly responding "Yes Devon, I understand. I will be back." With that, Mum's daughter leaves to go inside the next room. Inside, there is much commotion heard as she shares her learnings and expresses the strong desire in wanting nothing to do with any of this business. However, the brother and boyfriend think that since she and I had gotten along so nicely, their best bet still lay with her persuadin' me to open the door. (Yeah, right.)

All are in agreement that I am more than just a little bit dangerous, but they have a gun! And by the remarks concerning, Sparky is confident the gun is a revolver. The sister is given instructions on how to use this handgun; she is to sweet-talk me, gain my trust, offer sex, get me to open the door, and *start shootin'*! Understandably she is quite unnerved. After all, it does sound as if they are placing the entire task of mission on her. Whimpering, she outright refuses. The brother, adamant, orders his sister to be taken outside and persuaded.

Outside, the boyfriend begins to slap her around. She is crying and pleadin' her frightened fears! The boyfriend argues: does she want to wait tables and clean rooms for the rest of her life? He reminds her that this favor has been requested by very important people. (Basically he is tellin' her that if they can succeed in killin' me, he and her brother will be given other jobs; thus, she won't have to work the family hotel

255

anymore). In between sobs, the girl justifies her fears by reminding him of their own little son. "This Devon is very experienced; he will surely take the gun from me, then what? He will kill us all! Who then will care for our son? Please—please do not make me go before him without a door between us!"

There is a brief silence; obviously the girl has made a very good point, one worthy of serious consideration. They both quietly go back inside the command post to rethink things with the brother. Whereupon, revelation of the logic concludes a change in plans. It is decided that the sister should not have the gun after all. She should try getting me to open the door, but not go inside. And if I absolutely will not open the door, then she must lure me to come up close to the window for presenting a quick easy target. "We will shoot Devon right through the glass! Meanwhile, [so-and-so] will be around back opening the bathroom window, okay? And if you must, fuck her in the ass! That will get the freak stickin' his head up to watch; then we shoot him right between the eyes!"

The bathroom window is heard squeaking with strain from glass cracking. Thumbing the MAGLITE flashlight for split-second only beam of light, it reveals a double prong tool is bein' used from outside to open the jalousie horizontal glass slats. Pieces of chipped glass are now evident on the floor below. Oh shit! It's now or never; a man's gotta do what a man's gotta do. Time to wake up the Goddamn neighborhood! "HELP! HELP! AMERICAN CITIZEN BEIN' ATTACKED! MUM, POP, HELP, HELP! AMERICAN CITIZEN—DEVIN MURFIN! DEVIN MURFIN! THEY ARE ATTACKIN' MY ROOM! HELP, MUM, POP! HELP!" Suckin' in more deep breaths for more yellin' to come, local dwellers from over the other side of the fence are heard stirrin'. It's a commotion fitting for excited, nosy, concerned neighbors. Dogs are barkin' and people are loudly callin' out from house to house, askin' the obvious.

"HELP! MUM, POP! HELP! DEVIN MURFIN—AMERICAN CITIZEN BEIN' ATTACKED!" (Now Sparky ain't sure whether this is—at this point—the smartest move or not. I mean Christ, it's sorta like pushin' the big red button with no turning back!) The hooligans have, for the moment, scattered. Pop is bitchin' and Mum is comin' with her own small flashlight beam dancin'. "Devon, Devon! What is the problem?" (As if she don't know; deceit is in the nervous voice.)

For her, I open the door, using tone and eyes accusing betrayal. "Mum, you promised! You gave your word, your word, Mum. You said I would be safe here. See, see Mum? They are tryin' to break into my room. They have chipped and cracked your glass—see?" Lookin' past her as she steps inside to personally inspect the window, two cops are seen approaching, walkin' in from the street. (Buddy, is this good or bad? Man, who knows!) Soon they are standin' beside Pop and wanting an explanation to the problem. Both cops look old, tired, and genuinely ignorant of that concerning my situation. Pop is expressing anger toward the damage done to his window. Mum is patting my back, pretending to give caring comfort. The son, daughter, and boyfriend are seen standin' together some distance away. They are hangin' back to hear what is bein' said. Sparky makes no mention of them; instead I tell that it had been a group of unknown young men. "They came sneakin' around outside, then they started forcing open the bathroom window."

Mum, Pop, and the two aging cops step out of earshot for whispering conference. Mum then hurriedly leaves for fetching somethin'. Upon returning, she announces how everything now will be all right, "All that is needed for our Devon here, is for 'im to get some nice peaceful sleep." Is this woman serious? Oh yeah, she sure is! So much so, that she has even brought sleeping pills! And of course everyone but me thinks Mum's hit the nail right on the head. I'm sternly ordered to take the white pills, be quiet, and go to sleep! The door is then literally slammed in my face!

Fuck me! Spittin' out the sleeping pills, while somewhat hurriedly re-closing the bathroom window, I then dash back to my spot for peering out the big front window. Mum walks the two old cops (whom she seems to know personally, and vice versa) across the narrow grounds to the street. Seeing them off, she turns on her adult children, scolding. They retort in defensive argument, but Mum shrieks, "No! Devon is no longer like that. His wife has made 'im change his ways. She has given 'im sons! He is now a family man; and I believe 'im to be a good man! Trujillo, ay, do not tell me anything of that place. I do not care what is bein' said of 'im. I know what I know. We must leave 'im be. It makes no difference how much they offer for 'im." Mum's words trail off to follow her back down to the other end of hotel. Sparky paces the room wondering—wondering if there is any chance in hell of Mum havin' the power to hold back the dogs (at least for this night).

My pacing slows to that of stealth mode when, after only a short time, occupants are again heard bein' in the adjacent room. And by the sound of things, the gang is all there! The son is speaking to someone via cell phone. He sounds to be updating the other person with current events. After this, the son receives further instructions. Clicking off, he repeats what had been said. "We are to continue with the job. This

Devon must die—tonight. The police have been ordered not to interfere." After some silent moments, this crew of misfits seem anything but
enthusiastic. The reasoning for this could be one of several, or all of
several: perhaps they are not into killing (or possibly bein' killed),
perhaps they deep down agree with Mum, perhaps they want no
involvement whatsoever with whomever is really the one in charge of
this insanity. Realistically, though, it is probably simply due to them now
bein' all very high, a bit paranoid, and greatly unmotivated. I mean,
really, who in their right mind would want to attack a known dangerous
man in a dark hotel room when nicely high and jumpy as all get-up on
coke/crack/whatever?

The boyfriend, however, is still very gung-ho (even more so now
than Mum's son). He reminds them all how I had screamed like a
frightened *niña*! Mum's son counters, "Yes, but this is his strategy
technique for bringing about as much attention as possible to himself
while informing all that can hear, he is American, named Devon, and
bein' attacked here, on this spot." Several in the room quickly come up
with various lame excuses and split, with the boyfriend cursing after
them. The sister now sounds giddy and high herself. And soon she is
back to my window whispering for attention. "Sphsisst! Devon, Devon,
did you swallow your sleeping pills?" I answer "No." She giggles,
"Devon, I am sorry if you were frightened. It was not our intention. We
just wanted to do some business, and Devon… I have been smoking
crack. It makes me always very hot and horny. Devon, my coochi is wet
for you… Devon, will you not let me come inside your room? Please
Devon… Please? No? Okay… Devon, I understand. You are still very
frightened. Devon, no bad feelings, okay? I want to prove to you that we
have no bad feelings for you. I have a friend here with me and we want
to give you a free sex show, okay? You will enjoy it very much, Devon, I
promise. This show will help to relax you. Look Devon, look out your
window and see me. Watch what I am going to do for you."

With my backpack and shoulder bag, Sparky is hunkered down low
in between the two beds, at their footing. From here, both the big front
window and the small bathroom window can be watched while still
maintaining position unknown to those outside. Even their short burst
of searching flashlights (which they use sparingly) can not reveal me.
Despite the pitch-black darkness within, I now know this room like the
back of my hand. How far are these retards willing to take this? (Buddy,
when should we start up the whole screamin' bloody murder bit? Man,
just hold back on that for now. Let's see what their next move is going to
be, okay.) Geez, when they do finally realize that there will be no easy

head shot through the glass window, are these idiots actually capable of gettin' it together for busting down the door and charging in? Jesus, it must seriously be assumed yes! But, no way is Sparky gonna be the only one to go down here. No-sirree-bob! Yep, a plan is definitely needed. Must prepare inside perimeter for battle.

Take inventory... Weapons? Hhmm, of course trusty twenty-inch black steel MAGLITE flashlight. What else? Cameras? Possibly, if the straps hold up for swingin' impact. (Good thing before departing on this journey Sparky had replaced the wimpy original straps with thick canvas military shoulder straps.) On the room's nightstand, there's a ceramic table light. A quick silent slide sends me under the bed for retrieving the lamp. What else, what else? My rope! I have rope! Fifty feet of it, all rolled nicely in such a manner to allow for fast, smooth, knot-free deployment. Okay, so Sparky's got rope. What to do with it? Hhmm, must use it somethin' on the order of how that big *bailarin'* Carib soldier attempted with the monofilament fishin' line. String it about to slow, trip, add confused chaos. Whatever, just keep the rope out handy.

Following hissing instructions from the boyfriend, Mum's daughter has been doin' her seductive best to lure me to the window. The girl is verbally goin' into great detail describing the sex bein' performed. Despite the boyfriend's roughness, she does seem to be enjoying herself! That is until the boyfriend insists on buttbangin' her, and with much encouragement from others about watchin', he does just that. In between straining moans, gasping breaths, and stern reprimands, she continues to call out while describing how she is now bein' fucked in the ass, etc. Through the darkness of the window, I can easily make out their forms. They both for eyes now have strange little green lights. These lights, I assume, are those cheap eyeglass things. You know, plastic glasses having tiny lights affixed on each end? In any case, under these circumstances, they are creepy and weird lookin' to say the least.

There, right outside my window, are two sets of little bright green alien eyes, peerin' in toward me. Oh, and the one alien, the female, is bent forward supported by a simple straight back chair with a dick up her ass! And, and, the other, the male, doin' the rump pumpin', has his Flash Gordon laser-beam gun pointed right at me! But then the mother ship sends down a signal and the Mum's son is heard answering the cell phone. He gives (whoever) a brief summary of the situation in progress. It sounds as though he is actually tryin' delicately to convince (whoever) that this might not be such a good idea. The son is now sounding very much like his mother—Mum. Much to my obvious disappointment, (the other person) does not agree. Thus, end of phone conversation. The son calls for the sister's boyfriend and others to come back into the room. With a last deep thrust, and spanking butt slap, the Mum's daughter is left clinging to the chair, breathing as if tryin' to catch breath. (Yeah Skippy, those green-eyed aliens sure know how to fuck, don't they?)

Back in the room adjacent to mine, the son is now informing them all that the Boss (whoever) is on his way over here. Oh shit! This ain't good. No it is not! An effortless slide has me under the bed and up to the window, urgently whispering, "Hey you, Mum's daughter." She is now knelt down with head resting in seat of chair. The girl, still wearin' those ridiculous glasses, sees me; quickly she looks around for the others, but they are now all inside. Turning the chair, she takes a seat and with knees up spread wide while finger playin' with her pussy asks, "Devon, could you see? Did you know I was getting fucked in the ass? Does that make you hot and horny? Would you like to do the same to me? Oh Devon, how I would love to feel your cock in my ass. It would feel so—" My voice stops her to listen.

"Hush now! I told you not to believe the rumors about me. I do not have sex with anyone but my wife. Look, I know what you people are tryin' to do. Remember, I have been trained for this sort of thing. You must convince your brother and boyfriend not to go through with this. The price, no matter how great, is not worth it. Understand, this night will become a bloodbath—just like in Trujillo. And young lady, I do not need a weapon to kill! Understand? Think about it. Have you any idea how this room is gonna look in the morning? Blood, blood everywhere, all over the floors and walls—everywhere! Blood, entrails, and pulpy bits of human flesh, and it won't be all from me. I do promise you that." The daughter has brought her knees together with arms crossing breasts. Sparky has her full attention, but must hurry. "And who will clean this room tomorrow? Huh? You must think of all this. Is this what you and your family want? Will this be good for the family business? American citizen violently attacked and murdered right here in your hotel! Look, I respect your Mum and Pop very much. They are good family people, same as I am now. You, Mum, and Pop must stop this. Mum knows; she understands that such things as these do not go unpunished. God is watchin'. Now go! Go tell Mum and Pop! The blood from this night will be on the hands of those cleanin' this room in the mornin'!"

In an instant, the girl is outta that chair, pickin' up her clothes and is gone—runnin' to other end of hotel! And with a swish, I am back under bed to my spot. The daughter wastes no time in relaying the message. Pop is soon heard entering the adjacent room, ordering everyone except for his son out. With only the two now in the room, Pop drops his tone to one of sad understanding. He confesses to his son how when he was a young man, he too had once done somethin' similar to that which the son is about to do, and how to this day he is still haunted with the memory. Pop pleads for his son not to do this. "The family business is not doing so well as it is, and after tonight, with news of what you are attempting, there will be no business. Who will want to stay at our place after an American has been killed here? All will know that we, the family, were the ones who killed him. Son, this man Devon is not how they say. Word is spreading rapidly that he is not. He is ex-military yes, but now he is a family man. They assaulted him unjustly in Trujillo. Please, son, reconsider this act you are about to do. One day, like me, you will have your own family and you will have to live with this. It will come to you at night, in your dreams. I do not want this for you. Think of my words. You are a man now and so must decide for yourself. I can say no more." The son remains silent and Pop leaves.

A good sign? Yes, but Sparky does not allow for much hope. There is still the boss man (whoever) comin'. And all too soon he is here. This man sounds to be very similar in age, power, and position as that mother fuckin' pig I had to blow back in Trujillo. He is in a hurry and very agitated. In the room, he addresses the son, boyfriend, and those remaining of the crew. "Listen, I know what is being said and what you are now all thinking. You are thinking this Devon is a nice guy, good family man that was wronged in Trujillo and did his killings only to defend himself. I am here to tell you to forget Trujillo. Devon is a very bad man. Do any of you know that before Trujillo he had been in Cuba? Yes, there he and some old friends of his did as they pleased. Like animals they stayed drunk on rum and smoking crack, they raped and terrorized the poor people of Cuba. Devon, to amuse his friends, cut out a man's eyes before cutting his throat to kill him. That poor man had been the good family man, not Devon. So you understand now why Devon has angered so many important people? He is a bad man, a killer, and so must be punished for his crimes. I am leaving two shotguns for you to use; this is how they work..." (Fuck me, shotguns!) They are pumps. The shells bein' fed into a tube followed by the racking of slide for chambering a round are clearly heard, echoing! Shit-fuck! (Sparky is dead—dead!) The man continues, "After I leave, you must allow for some time to pass. You know what to do then. And if you still do not wish to kill him, eh, then simply wound him, but it must be severely. Shoot off his arm or leg, I do not care. Remember, important people are wanting this Devon punished. They have even ordered the town's power

261

to be shut down just for this purpose. Also, as you are aware, I was never here, and have no involvement in any of this matter." With that, the man goes, leaving behind two pump shotguns, and a room of murmuring soon-to-be-killers!

Sparky, it is time to put balls to the wall and move! With my rope in hand I fly into action. Both beds get flipped up onto their sides. One is slid over to and up against the big front window; a slip knot lassos corner window hand crank. Rope is then wrapped around the bed frame, down its length to the door knob, and quickly pulled up tight. Around the door knob a clove hitch type knot is cinched. The other bed gets slid, butting end up to bathroom door. Here, the rope is brought down and tied right tight to bathroom door knob and end of bed. The existing length of rope is quickly run back and forth, zigzaggin' from bed to bed, while securing mattresses upright with bed frames for some—barely better than nothin'—cover against shotguns. However, the room is, at least, one big trippin' obstacle. Within the center of this mess is the dresser and nightstand.

My speed in accomplishing this is even surprising me. It is almost as if the hands and body are operating on automatic pilot while brain just keeps thinkin' shotguns, shotguns, shotguns! They're gonna be bustin' in here with shotguns a-blazin'! Goddamn, is it ever gonna be loud! And oh boy, what a bloody fuckin' mess. Sparky does surely know what shotguns can do. Yes he does! Slidin' to the far corner of the room, behind second bed, I take up my position.

Those from the adjacent room had certainly heard the noise of my abrupt commotion. They are now out and about—front and back—for look-see. Without any further ado, I begin to yell my heart and lungs out, literally like there is no tomorrow! This time though, the yellin' and hollering is a-pleading to Mum and Pop directly (with of course the whole damn neighborhood listening as well). "MUM, POP, HELP, HELP! THEY'RE COMIN' IN WITH SHOTGUNS! THIS IS MURDER MUM! COLD BLOODED MURDER! IN THE NAME OF GOD, PLEASE HELP! HELP!" Takin' no time to catch breath or for listenin', I bellow out my pleading beggings while describing in detail what a bloodbath this is gonna be and how this room is gonna look in the morning, and how their business will suffer. I then again bring up my family—wife and young sons. Sentiments are poured forth with such examples as my sons will have no father to play ball with them. And who will teach them to swim and fish? A family needs a father, husband, and provider, etc., etc. Thoroughly (for the moment) out of breath, I suck in much needed breath. (Goddamn it! Mum ain't comin', meaning her and

Pop are gonna do nothin' to stop this.) Yeah well, fuck it! Sparky is sick and tired of this sissy bitch beggin' for mercy bit. Time to change tune to bad-ass last stand defiant challenge! But then a new thought slams into brain—Money! "Mum! MONEY! I got lots of it: CASH, TRAVELER'S CHECKS. And more importantly—CREDIT CARDS! I have VISA, DISCOVER, and two MASTER CARDS! All are PLATINUM! Brand new with FULL CREDIT LINES! MUM, POP, a lot of money here! You know, you are good business people, you have knowledge of how much such credit cards as mine are worth. But you need me ALIVE to draw the money from them! Mum, whatever they are payin' you, I will pay more. First thing in the mornin' we can go to the bank. Okay? Or— or Mum! Call the boss man and tell him of my traveler's checks and big PLATINUM credit cards. Mum, it's better to have good money than an innocent American murdered on your property! Bad business! Everyone knows I'm here and what's happening to me. There will be a big American Embassy investigation. Someone will talk. American Embassy investigators pay cash. Cash, US dollars, for information concerning the murder of a fellow American!" Sparky has no idea if this is true or not. Guessing though, I'd say it's not. But it does sound believable. "Pop, people will talk, and then no more hotel business. And Mum, who do you think will be blamed for my murder? Yes, this will be very sad for your *familia*. Mum! Call the boss man—NOW!"

Suckin' in air as if having been underwater for at least ten minutes and just surfaced, I hear it! Mum is next door demanding the cell phone. In no time she is speakin' into it. "He will pay! He has many new credit cards, all are platinum... Yes, that is very big credit lines! Also he claims to have traveler's checks. With his money you can use 'im to make more money. Money is much better than a dead body! No! We cannot do as you ask. He has made so much noise, the whole town is now aware of what you are askin'... No! The Americans will be all over us... No! We are not goin' to be responsible... I do not care! We will have nothin' to do with any of this... Yes! He claims to have the cards! Okay, bye."

Well, slap my balls! Looks like a little time has been bought for Sparky. But for what? Who the hell knows! Must just stay alive from one moment to the next. (Buddy? Man, they are probably going to come and take us away. Keep yelling, for all to hear, your name and citizenship. Okay.) And so I do. Soon, however, the son is heard hissing loudly from the adjacent room, "Shut up, shut up now! We are not going to kill you. Here they come."

Mum is now poundin' on the door, and in a loud but sweet, con-cerned voice is sayin', "Devon, Devon honey, I heard you. I heard you all the long. Mum did not give up on you. I am here now. No harm will come to you. I took care of all that. You are safe. Now quiet down, be calm. It is goin' to be all okay. Open the door, honey." Then, lowering her voice, "Devon, honey, I did as you asked. I told 'em of your credit cards. They have allowed for the police to come and keep you safe. You must go with 'em, and do as they say. It makes no difference what is asked, honey, you must do it. This is very important, understand?" Then, raising her voice with more door poundin', "Come now Devon, open the door. The nice police are here. You must now go with them, they will keep you safe."

Having absolutely no choice (fuck, buddy you were right), "Uh, yes Mum, in a minute, I'll be right there!" Oh well, here goes nothin'! Flashlights from the police are shinin' beams of lights into the dark room. Sparky is hurriedly undoing knots, wrappin' up rope and tryin' to (somewhat) get the room back to how it was, but there is no time; the cops are growling impatience and Mum has serious urgency in her voice; so, squinting eyes for lights to come, I open the door. Sure enough, all flashlights point directly into my face. "Uh, hi Mum. Sorry about your room."

Pop's generator kicks on, and with it, all outside lights to the grounds. Mum, putting' on quite the show, is now all hugs and wanting to know if I'm okay? She has been so worried, etc. Directly behind her are the same old cops as before, and of course, there is the son, daughter, and angry lookin' boyfriend, standin' together a few yards to the right. Pop is nowhere to be seen. With Mum leadin', we walk across the narrow grounds to the street. Here, we are met by two more cops. These are wearin' brown uniforms, whereas the other elderly two are wearin' olive green. The browns look to be more Ladino than Carib, and are standin', waitin', beside their squad car. It's an ATV golf cart sorta thing.

They order me to put my backpack into the open back of this ATV vehicle, then they (the browns) demand to see my passport and credit cards. Mum does not recognize or know these browns. Right away she asks them, in suspicious tone, if they are Guatemalan or Honduran police. (Wha-wha-what? Honduras? Buddy how can Honduran police be workin' here in Guatemala? Man, come on, after what we've been through, does this really surprise you? No, guess not, especially after hearing that boss man (whoever) tell of me killin' a man in Cuba, and how this had pissed off some very important people. Crap, buddy, it's like jumpin' from one sizzlin' fry pan to the next.) Both cops answer Mum, "Guatemala." With hands firmly on big hips, Mum informs how she personally knows all the local police, even the young ones that are not real police but work as such. The browns confess they are not Livingston police, but rather Guatemala City police. They are down here on temporary assignment. Mum buys this, then asks where it is they are goin' to be taking "Devon". They answer her a place of name Sparky can't catch. Mum excitedly puffs up, askin', "Why there? Why must he go there?" One of the browns casually shrugs his shoulders, answering, "It is ordered." Mum gives a slight protest but knows it's to no avail. She turns to me, gives a big strong hug, while whispering, "Devon, remember, you must do as they say. Does not matter what it is, just do exactly what they say, and make no trouble." I'm then ordered into the back of the ATV cart, and away we go, passing the two old green uniformed cops walkin'. By Mum's reaction, Sparky is guessin' the destination to be jail. Fuck, what to do? Jump and *run*? (Buddy? No, we must first see what the credit cards and traveler's checks buy us. Okey-dokey.)

T he little ATV cart is slow. The road, leading direction unknown, is narrow, dreary, dark, and rough with rutting bumps, much like the inside of my head. Realizing, lungs bellow fresh air in, rechargin' on guard, red alert mode. Must be ready for anything! Offering both cops each a cigarette, smiling they accept. Inhaling deeply on my own, thoughts of what might lay ahead swirl to pulsate blood within for sharpness.

Whoa, what is this place? Through the moon's dim lighting, it does not appear to be a police station or a jail. It just looks to be a lone one-story building of ancient concrete that had probably, a hundred years ago, been quite elaborate, but now is just another stinking shithole. Seriously, ripe stench is oozing from the place. Even from outside, there is strong smell of damp decay and human rot. Our arrival is expected, and the door is opened for us. Inside is a group of waiting police. Through the glowing lantern light, my eyes search, tryin' to meet those of the cops for learning the mood, which, surprisingly, seems to be that of great curiosity. With as much dignity as can be mustered, I march across the room to an old wooden office desk. Here, my backpack, shoulder bag and vest are laid out for searching. As several busy themselves with the task, I look around the room. Up against the walls are low, long benches, on which layin', seemingly passed out, are men. Their manner of dress and filthiness presents them to be drunk, homeless men (but who knows). God, the smell! An embalming prep room smells less foul than this place. The walls are crumbling with multilayered peeling paint splattered and smudged with human feces, blood, vomit, and the likes. There, movin' about in the shadows with a mop and bucket, is a man (or what's left of him). He is thin, frail, and bent like a broken man. His eyes are bugged, but will not meet mine. One of the younger cops taps my shoulder. Not expecting, I jump—spinnin'! This makes the other cops jump, with a few even throwin' hands to holstered side arms! I quickly calm myself, smile and shrug my shoulders as if apologizing.

The police seeing, all relax, and there is even laughter. Laughing with them, Sparky understands the reason for the tap had been the young cop simply wanted to ask for a cigarette. Impressed that they would even bother asking, I more than oblige, passing around cigs to those that want one. Most of these guys are in the police green uniforms and are diverse in age, skin color, and rank: the youngest—early twenties—havin' no rank, to the oldest—sixty-ish—with sergeant's rank, havin' two rockers beneath his stripes. The four brown uniforms present seem to be Ladino and in their thirties. One brown, ranking above everyone here in this room, is an officer sportin' a Lieutenant bar. For obvious reasons, and because they are all making it easy to do so, I'm tryin' my damndest to get on the good side of these guys. It seems to be workin'; we are a-smokin' and a-jokin'! Sparky is in the middle of explaining the tattooing process to some of the younger ones, when the Lieutenant's cell phone rings.

He answers it speakin' speedy Spanish with tone turnin' serious. A hushed silence goes about the room with sympathetic looks targeting you know who. The Lieutenant ends the call, turns to the bug-eyed-zombie and orders him to wake up the doctor. Soon an old, half-awake, irritable man emerges, demanding to know why he has been awakened. The Lieutenant speaks rapid Spanish to him. Grumbling, the old doctor nods and roughly begins to examine me. Using a mini flashlight he looks into my eyes, mouth, and nose. From the old desk he retrieves a small steel dental-pick-like tool, shoves it up my nose and (Goddamn it!) scrapes out a big bloody scab. With blood now runnin' freely down my nose, the doctor is sternly demanding while waving the speared bloody bugger scab so close as to make me cross-eyed, "Why this? Why do you have this? *Coca*? Cocaine, yes?"

(Fuckin' A, what a nut!) "Uh-uh, no sir! It's only a simple sinus infection from scuba diving. I went down too deep too fast! The pressure was too much; understand? Sir?" Growling, the old fucker shrugs his shoulders, like okay. The Lieutenant then shows him my big plastic zipper bag of Valium and codeine horse pills. The cranky doctor just waves these away as if they are nothin'. The Lieutenant then hands him my little brass pill box containing two Zantac tablets for my stomach ulcers. For whatever reason, there has been little need of them; thus the tablets have suffered from sweating humidity and sorta melted into a white cakey powder. The doctor holds a lighter under the pill box to cook down the substance while smelling. Claiming it to be nothing, he does however take a liking to my brass pill box, and so keeps it. Yep, just ups and sticks it in his pocket. (Aughg! My baby sister had given me that pill box!) The quack of a doctor then quickly checks my inner arms for needle track marks and declares me fit for work.

The Lieutenant reminds him of the "other thing." Agitated, the old doctor looks around to all the passed-out men on the benches and points to one across the room on the end: "He can have that one. Come get me when he is finished." The doctor then leaves the room. Hey, what's he talkin' about—I can have that one? That one? That one, for what? Oh, please don't be for what I think it to be! No, no! Just then the door opens and in walks another old sergeant wearing a green uniform, followed by two attractive young men. One has brown hair, the other, black. Hell, they both are Ladino, but barely. They could easily pass for bein' white, and their English is flawless. As if very excited to be finally meeting me, they (the Bobsey twins) act like they are my new best pals. The strange thing is, I actually see sincerity in their eyes. These guys aren't acting. After vigorous handshakes, warm smiling introductions, and a lighting of cigarettes (of course from my pack), they begin explaining (my) current situation.

First of all, even though they (the Bobsey twins) are not in uniform, they are police. They had broken the law, got caught, and were fortunate enough to be deemed fit to best serve out their time by working for the police as police. This is a very common and accepted practice, not only here in Guatemala, but also most of Central America, including Mexico. They then ask if I would like such a job? Sparky thinks they are jokin' and so I laugh in attempts of playin' along. "Me? A job as a cop? Ha ha! Yeah sure, why not! I've always wanted to be a cop. How much does it pay? Where will I live, and what exactly is it I'll be doin'?" Immediately, their eyes betray they are serious (oh shit).

Again, the Lieutenant's cell phone rings; after receiving brief orders, he announces, "If he—", referring to me, "—is going to do it, then it must be now. They want him at the station as soon as possible for deciding what is to be done with him." The Lieutenant turns to me, explaining very dryly, "If you want the job being offered, then you must prove yourself." He motions towards the passed-out drunk man that the evil doctor had indicated that I could have. The Lieutenant, smiling, adds, "And since it is rumored that you can, you must do it with bare hands only." (Oh fuck me! No, no, no!) Playing dumb, "Uh, do what with my bare hands?" Several answer as one, "Kill him!" Wha-wha-what? Lookin' desperately to my new best pals (the Bobsey twins), hoping for support, "Is—is—he serious? Why? How? No, I can't, it's against the law! You are all police. It's a set-up, you will arrest me! This is a trick! No! Oh, why? Why can't I do somethin' else to prove myself?" (Uh, man, you might want to rethink that last one. As has been seen, there can be far worse things than being asked to kill an innocent adult drunk, uh, like hurting a woman, or—child! Goddamn, buddy, doesn't human life have any value down here?) Sparky is stuttering and becomin' confused. What to do, what to do? Think! What if I just up and refuse? Christ, this whole rottin' place is full of cops! Cops just waiting to watch me murder a man! (Hey, calm down, breathe, in-out, in-out. That's it; must not panic, hyperventilate, or lose it!)

The Bobsey twins come up close, and one even puts his arm around my shoulder. With soft voices, they both begin to explain that this is the required procedure for acquiring the offered job, considering circumstances. No one is going to arrest me, they both themselves had to do the same thing, as did half the men in this room. The only difference being, they had all got to use a ball bat or club of sorts. "Devon, without the job, you are dead! It has been instructed to hand you over to Captain Matrix. Matrix is wanting you very badly. He is the sort of man that is evil—sick in the head. He has his own private army, plus many followers. It is their religion to torture and kill men, women, and children, even eating their flesh. Yes, Devon, they are *satanico* cannibals. They believe such acts make them stronger. Also, they now do it for the movies they make and sell. Devon, do not forget Trujillo. Sergeant Lobo works for Captain Matrix. Imagine what they will do to you." (My head is spinnin' with a voice other than buddy's, screamin' RUN—RUN mother fucker—RUN! But I don't.) "Your only hope, Devon, is to take the job. Become valuable by making important people money and they, in return, will protect you. We too, can protect you once you begin working with us and prove your loyalty. Understand? Besides, Devon, you have killed before. This will be easy for a man such as yourself. You have been trained for this sort of thing. Devon, you have no choice, just do it, get it over with and then we can all go to the station; our Captain will make necessary arrangements with the important people and you can still get some sleep tonight!"

(Oh, fuck me! Fuck, fuck, fuck! How the hell am I gonna kill this poor bastard usin' only my bare hands?) In the movies they always make it look so damn easy. But in reality it's hard. I know—once during my later teen years, I had tried killing my elder sister's junkie boyfriend with only bare hands. He was, of course, much older and bigger than myself; however, Sparky was able to come out on top with fingers wrapped around the man's windpipe, where I squeezed with all my might while even pushin' the back of his head into it; still, that thing would not break (it sure flexed and constricted a lot). Also, despite him turnin' colors, goin' from red to bluish pale white, with neck veins, arteries corded, bulging and twitchin', snot pourin' out of nose, mucus and saliva hangin' from his gasping rigid mouth locked open quivering, the prick would not die! He was just about to pass out though, when unfortunately his two pals came bustin' in and jumped me off him. Lucky bitch! And now I must kill this poor drunken soul without use of any weapon. He is laying upon the bench in fetal position, with his hands and palms together for cushioning his face from the hard wood. The man's mouth is open and he is snoring loudly, gulping air in fits the way drunks do. Sparky looks around to the other benches and notices that not all wretched occupants are passed out asleep. Some are awake, just layin' there, watchin'. Fuck, is this weird or what?

My mind is racin', tryin' to recall all info I have concerning killing a human using only bare hands. Damn, all methods now seem completely ridiculous. Plus, Sparky has got to make this look good. It cannot turn out to be embarrassing, wrestling around here on the floor with this poor drunk guy. His death must be quick and somewhat impressive. But how? The mood of the room is now one of much silent anticipation. They are all expectin' a show and I'm the star attraction. Having no choice, I cautiously approach my poor stinkin' filthy victim. In doing, it is noticed that he is not as old, or small as he had appeared from across the room. No he is not!

The man has pissed himself and the floor is wet where it has pooled. The man is Ladino having a large, yet, gaunt face. Thick saliva is dripping from the corner of his mouth. His hair is balding, and oily black. The man is guessed to be late forties or early fifties. It is apparent that in his prime, he had been strong, stocky and barrel-chested, but not anymore. Now he is only a pot-bellied, withered wretch. Or is he? Why am I getting the strong feelin' that this being is probably a really nice guy with an interesting tale to tell and Oooh, just don't think. Don't think of nothin' 'cept how best to kill him quickly! Goddamn, hope to hell he is as drunk as he smells. Please Mister, do not wake up, and please forgive me.

Steppin' lightly into the thin puddle of urine, Sparky instinctively tests it for slipping. The old floor is tiled but my red (not so red any-more), Converse high-tops still have plenty of rubber. Footing should be fine. Hey, you know all that hand to hand combat crap they teach in the military? Well for most of us, it is downright worthless! I mean, it looks impressive, and works good on stuffed canvas dummies, and it's a blast to practice with on your pals and/or sparring partner, but in reality, up against a pumped, high octane, adrenaline charged opponent? Forget it! You're better off just usin' the normal, boy-learnt, street fighting skills, the ones that have proved effective time and time again. These are the methods the body best knows and is able to throw into action the quickest, without the brain even needin' to be there.

Yeah, yeah, but this is different. This is not a fight. This is me needin' to kill a passed-out drunk man. (Buddy? Hhmm, remember that one move the army taught you? The one for taking out a posted sentry? Sneaking up from behind the lone enemy, a headlock is thrown, and with forearm under chin, he is dropped backwards to the ground while at the same time your upper body weight hammers down into back of his head; this is supposed to separate and break the neck vertebras, thus quickly killing? Yes, I remember that one, and yes, it just might work.) First though, this poor drunken bastard's torso and head must be brought upright. Then Sparky will simply drop him backwards while in headlock, throwin' weight for snappin' neck. Easy, right? Yeah, no problem (fuck). Quietly I bend down to the man and gently slide my left hand and arm under his cradled arms, neck, and head. He must be leaned upright without waking. Huggin' him closely, putting my face to his awful foul face, having sharp, oily whiskers, his rasping snorts and wheezing snoring is deafening to my left eardrum. With my right arm now also around him, our chests are pressed together; Sparky has full embrace of the man. Straining with knees buckled, all strength within is summoned forth to bring the wretched man upright. (Aughg, please mister, please, for the sake of us both—do not wake up.) With him now sittin' upright, and me strugglin' to keep him so, a much needed deep breath is sucked in. Despite doin' so with nose closed, the man's rancid smell of stale booze and human stink enters strong. My head is becoming light with vision ghosting—everything is turnin' black and white with grey shades dancin' in and out of the lines. This Sparky snaps the fuck out of when the drunk man begins to mumble affectionately and tries to reach for me as if I were a lover or the sort. Pullin' my face away, his eyes leisurely open with a contented smile.

I fucking lose it—*lose it*! Forgetting all about the army neck breaking move, Sparky instead instantly goes into desperate street fighting mode, slammin' the back of the guy's head against the solid, rock-hard wall! SLAM! SLAM! SLAM! MOTHER FUCKER, MOTHER FUCKER! DIE, DIE, DIE! God, oh Goddamn, please fuckin' die! I felt his head whip on limp neck to strike against the wall bashing in the backside of his skull, thus killing, and still Sparky kept a-slammin', even after my foot slipped, bringing shin bone down hard on bench's edge. If the poor drunken man spazzed a last departing grip for life, I did not feel it, nor was the blood, pulpy matter splattering hands, arms, face, and hair felt. After the first killing slam, nothin' was felt, and—except for the insane screamin' inside my head—nothin' was heard. And still, the murdering slammin' continued for grotesque overkill.

But then, as if an invisible hand had come down to rest itself on my shoulder, I just stop. With mind completely blank, my arms gently slide the dead man against the wall for laying his torso back down on the bench. Sparky gazes upon the open hollow eyes, gaping mouth, and sagging bloody mess of pulverized skull. Colors return, and they are brilliant and bright! My God, looky what I've done! The wall! Oh, Jesus! My hands, arms! I now feel the blood on my face and body as if it were insects crawling. (Buddy? Man, don't look; turn your back to the corpse, wall, and bench. You did what you had to. Pull it together, the march continues. Yeah, okay.) Gulping in air with veins surgin', I square off shoulders and turn to face the silent spectating audience. Lookin' from face to face, they are all gawkin' at me strangely. Why do I feel like they were all expectin' a show of some sorta quick fancy karate chop or somethin'?

The Bobsey twins are the first to recover. Coming over with big smiles and congratulations, they are even patting me on the back—bein' careful not to get blood on themselves. Their example ensues other cops to follow suit, and there is even clapping, applause! (Yep, Yee-fuckin'-haw!) I walk over to the old wooden desk and with bloody, shaky hands, reach for my cigarettes. Snapping a filter, one of the Bobsey twins lights the cig for me (of course using my Bic lighter, while helpin' himself to a cigarette from my pack as well). There is now a big loud commotion. Everyone is excited and apparently very happy. Many have gone over to get a closer look at my handiwork. (Oh aren't I proud!)

The doctor comes out with a glance, and declares the man dead! After this, he approaches me while sternly demanding to be paid. Paid? Paid for what? The Bobsey twins are all smiles as the Lieutenant explains that the doctor must be paid a fee of one hundred US dollars, for services rendered. This is his place after all. The bug-eyed, broken man, is ordered to clean up the mess. I, of course, pay the crazy doctor, and then receive orders myself to gear up; we're goin' to the station now. Wanting to wash some of this crawlin' pulpy blood off first, my request is denied. The Lieutenant wants me to stay as I am, for the Captain to see. (Sure, you bet.)

Outside, with my backpack, shoulder bag, and vest, Sparky breathes in deeply while bein' ordered into the back of the ATV cart vehicle. But before jumpin' in, an old sergeant informs that now since I will be working with them, I must salute him every time I come into his presence—like right now. Sparky reminds him that I'm not in uniform.

This however, doesn't seem to matter. Uh, okey-dokey! I throw him a snappy salute. The old fuck actually returns it (weird). The Lieutenant nudges me to get in. He sits up front, as does the old sergeant—behind the wheel—and away we go! Slowly we pass walking cops en route (guessing) to the station. (Yippee! Christ, wonder what kind of fun is to be had at the station!)

Down the dark road we go, headed in the direction known to lead toward town's small main district, centered a block or so up from the waterfront docks. We are met by the Captain himself at the bottom of some wide stone semicircle steps that lead up to the police station's long, narrow veranda. At the Captain's side is another Lieutenant—a little wormy greaseball—who barks for me to come stand before the Captain. I do, coming to attention and throwin' the Captain a snappy salute. Both Lieutenants and old Sergeant burst out snickering chuckles! The Captain does not. Instead, he spins on them and, in Spanish, sternly scolds. Instantly they are silenced. The Captain then, as if himself embarrassed, motions for the ridiculous salute to be dropped.

With flashlight spotlighting, the Captain quickly looks me over, and then gives instructions in Spanish. The light clicks off, and the Lieutenant barks for me to get my gear and follow the Captain up to the veranda. Ascending the steps, a shooting pain from shin bone makes itself known. And with it, visions of how the hurt came to be. Fortunately, we do not go inside this police station. The large front door of the place is open and within is pitch-black darkness. They don't even have a lantern burning, and Sparky don't want to go into no more stinkin' buildings! We all stay out here on the flat open veranda. I'm ordered to drop my backpack and shoulder bag down beside a long lone wooden bench and empty all contents; again it all must be searched. Many of the cops on foot that had been up at that crazy doctor's place are now arriving. The Bobsey twins are here. They are now standin' at my side, actin' like we are best pals. To be honest, Sparky is glad as all get-up to have 'em. The men address the Captain with much respect, and always in Spanish only. Obviously, the Captain does not speak English, at least, not very well. This is indeed rare in these parts. He must not be from the coast; he is Latin, Ladino, whatever. He is fifty-ish, brown-skinned, with curly, glossy black hair. By light of flashlights being used to search my stuff, I can see in the Captain's eyes a keen intelligence, a kind of intense, sad understanding. This man knows good from bad. He seems to be looking upon me with much pity.

The Captain lets the men search through my stuff, with many askin' if they can have this or that? They know I won't say no. But when they

273

spring forth my condoms, showin' them off as bein' Magnum size and comparing this with much theatrical re-enactment of how I had killed, the Captain tolerates no more. He sternly orders them all to stop! His Lieutenant then barks for me to repack everything. I do, and most of the cops disperse; some leave, others spread out, sitting on the dark steps, while others go to stand down beside the street. Just when Sparky gets everything repacked, a civilian-dressed man, older than the Captain, arrives with four armed black uniformed Carib soldiers. And Skippy, how the voice is recognized… recognized as bein' the same as the man's who had come to Mum and Pop's hotel, given the son pump shotguns with a bullshit story of "Devon" bein' a bad man goin' on a rapin', murdering rampage while in Cuba. A flashlight beam goes to my eyes, and the civilian man demands my credit cards (for whatever reason, he has no interest in the traveler's checks). Also, I must again unpack everything for another searching (Eugh!).

The important civilian is in discussion with the Captain, but because it is all in Spanish, I do not know what is bein' said, yet the general gist (like most always) can be understood. The name Matrix is brought up often, and Sparky does comprehend that this Matrix is indeed wanting me very much. The civilian man is in a nervous hurry, almost like he does not want to be seen here. His soldiers have casually spread-out, taking up positions on the veranda to watch outwards. The Captain's Lieutenant is now standin' at my side, listening in on the conversation. All other cops, including the Bobsey twins, are keeping their distance from the present goings-on of this veranda.

The Captain is nodding to the civilian man, but he does not look pleased. He keeps lookin' to me as if tryin' to decide somethin'. Mr. Civilian Man quickly whips out his cell phone and is speaking to— guess who—Matrix! There is some hissing and bickering, but the civilian man is sternly insistent, and in a hurry. The call is brief; he turns to the Captain, who nods understanding. And with that, Mr. Civilian Man and soldiers are gone! The Captain makes a quick call on his own cell phone, after which he calmly motions for me to repack my stuff— again. With my wallets in hand, it is obvious that he is waiting for the summoned somebody to arrive. The Bobsey twins return to the veranda to hear the little punk Lieutenant explain what is going on.

Evidently, the Captain has sent for somebody that is gonna come and call in my credit card numbers to good ol' PRISA International Airlines. PRISA Airlines is going to max out my credit cards by booking me flights from Bogotá, Columbia to Mexico City, and everywhere in between. Snickering, the greaseball Lieutenant adds, "After he has made the mule runs he is to go back to Trujillo, beg forgiveness and work for Sergeant Lobo. If he does not cooperate, or if he tries any of his tricks, then he is to be immediately handed over to Matrix." (Fuck me!) Damn, muling is no way surprising. It makes sense, what with the credit cards and all. But goin' back to Trujillo? Begging forgiveness? I murdered a man in cold blood for this? Sparky is dead, dead, dead! (Buddy! Man, are you really that surprised? What did you think? That we could serve out our time alongside the Bobsey twins here as corrupt cops and then after time served, just up and head back home? Man, get a grip. You killed that drunk for one reason only—to buy time. March the march, mother fucker, and do not get detoured!) Spinning on the Bobsey twins with look of panic stricken betrayal, "No, no please! You said, you both said, if I proved myself I could have a job! I thought you meant a job here in Livingston. Here, in Livingston! Livingston is now my new home! I will go and faithfully mule the airlines, but I must be allowed to come back here and work in Livingston!" Now shouting, "My loyalty is to our Captain here! You guys, Livingston, Guatemala. I'm one of you now. Turning to the Captain, "You will see, my loyalty will make you very proud. Please Captain! Captain please, Sir, please don't let them send me to Honduras!" The Captain is now looking upon me with sad tired eyes. Both Bobsey twins are looking towards him as if silently pleading on my behalf. "Captain, in Honduras they will torture me to death. Sir, you know this is true. I won't stand a chance and will be valueless, but here, working for you—Sir, American and European tourists will trust me— think of the many ways I can make you and important people much money!" The Captain uses his hand for motioning me to calm down and be still. Sparky does, becoming silent. The Bobsey twins step over to him for hushed discussion in Spanish. The one having brown hair breaks out into a smile, and informs that they just told the Captain everything I had been saying; he understands, and is going to try and arrange for me to stay here in Livingston and work for him, after the muling of course. First though, before all else, the credit cards must be settled and here's the man now.

The other Lieutenant has brought him. The man is fat, out of breath, and bitching about having been awakened in the middle of the night like this. He is carrying a briefcase. Several cops gather around and shine their flashlights so he can see. He is handed my credit cards, and via cell phone, calls PRISA International Airlines. In no time the fat man has all my cards maxed out with detailed flight schedules written down. Everyone seems quite impressed with the amounts my cards are capable of purchasing. Yes, Sparky will be doing a lot of flying—big time *coca* mule! (Lucky, lucky me.) The fat man stands, hands the Captain back my credit cards and all the written flight info, looks over to me, slowly shakes his head, and leaves. The Captain gets on his own cell phone and gives report; a heated debate ensues. In the end the Captain wins out. The Bobsey twins are all smiles, happily patting me on the back, helping themselves to more of my cigarettes while explaining that after my muling, I can indeed come back here to live and work. The Captain has declared me his responsibility. This is a great honor, and so I must not let him down or allow him to lose face.

Also, one day soon, Sergeant Lobo will be arriving here to receive a personal apology from me, but I am not to worry because the Captain does not like Lobo and especially does not like Matrix. So, now that I've been officially declared the Captain's responsibility, no one can harm me without his permission. (Cool, cool, cool!) Sparky is literally becomin' giddy! This night is turnin' out way better than expected. And guess what? The Captain is gonna give me a few days to get settled in here (Livingston) working the boats before having to mule for PRISA International Airlines. Tomorrow my job on the boats will start. The same boats that transport people and supplies back and forth from Puerto Barrios and Livingston, also transport drugs—large quantities of drugs. These boats bring the coke and crack over from Puerto Barrios; and from Livingston to Puerto Barrios goes the marijuana.

The Captain steps over. Lookin' me up and down, he kindly hands over my wallets and credit cards. With a sigh, he turns and gives instructions to the Bobsey twins. They both nod understanding and motion for Sparky to follow. With their flashlight beam bouncin', we walk through the dark station house. (Damn, this is a bit creepy; but then again, what the hell isn't these days.) Eventually, we reach a damp filthy bathroom—of sorts. The Bobsey twins explain that the Captain has ordered for me to clean myself up. He can't have people seeing me look this way. Ignoring the large cockroach-type bugs scurrying to hide from surprise lighting, I step up to the grimy, copper-stained sink. In it is an old galvanized bucket full of water. This is the only available water right now. The Bobsey twins both stand in the narrow doorway, providing light from their flashlight. I pull forth my semi-red hanky rag, and dip it into the water bucket. On the wall is a cracked mirror. My God! Would you look at me... Sparky looks just like he's stepped from the movie *Night of the Living Dead*! Oooh, you mother fuckers! Black sunken eyes. Brown sweaty blood, smeared all over, especially around nose and mouth, where it has caked heavily, due to the crazy doctor pullin' out scabby clot from nasal passage. Sparky's been swallowing the drippity drip of blood ever since. (Buddy? Man, don't look, don't think, just scrub! And be quick.) And so, I haul ass—scrubbin' fast and hard! Of course, the deep bite on my right index finger reopens to add fresh blood to caked dirty blood. And now noticed is some skin torn from left hand's knuckles, guessed to have occurred while bashin' the poor drunk's skull against stone/concrete wall. My shin bone, though very sore and bruised, is not cut deeply. (Man, just scrub!) Rolling wet red hanky and wrappin' it tightly around bleeding bit finger, slide off the elastic hair bands used for keeping hair in tight ponytail. I do a quick hair-flip while vigorously using my fingertips to scratch and rake through sweaty itchy scalp and filthy oily hair. Sparky can feel bits of dried pulp and blood in there. Realizing just how long my hair must appear in this state, I quickly re-flip it back, and in no time have those bungee bands on a tight ponytail. There! Ught, no not yet; bladder is full—quiverin'! Lookin' to the toilet, of course there is no lid or seat; and despite lack of water, it has been grossly used. Raising wide short legging, Sparky pisses like there's no tomorrow! Whew-wee! Chuckling with the Bobsey twins, despite everything, I'm feelin' pretty damn good!

On the way out through the door leadin' on to the veranda, the black-haired Bobsey twin stops and shines his flashlight just to the right of the door frame; there, stuck all over the place, in between the cracked mortar of the bricks that are missing huge sections of stucco plaster (long gone), are many little gram-size plastics containing cocaine. "Devon, this is one of the ways we make money with the tourists." He pulls a mini-ball of coke from the wall, and places it between his fingers hidden. "See, like this Devon. Keep it between your fingers, and when you search the tourists, magic! They have been caught possessing cocaine, a very serious offense. They must now pay a fine, or spend a long time in jail! Ha ha! Devon, wait until you see their faces! Of course you can not do this to just anyone. Never to people who look important. Also, you must never make the fine too big. Twenty dollars US or equivalent, is the usual amount, just enough to give them a sting and yet put a little something in your pocket. Devon, we have many such methods for making money, you will learn."

It is now very late. People are coming out from closed bars and clubs, walking the streets to wherever. Many are drunken, loud tourists in small groups, while others are quietly staggering solo. Some are locals, drunk themselves, or hurriedly pushin' home vending carts. Either way, it's now fun money makin' time for the cops. Most are down along the street stopping people to search them and collect fines. I ask my Bobsey pals if there are always this many cops here in Livingston? The answer is no, and they explain that most of these guys (police) are from Puerto Barrios. "Devon, it all depends on how much product the boats bring over. Also, many had heard you were coming, so they too came to see what would happen. You have become very popular."

My pals leave to go join their comrades down the street. It's now just me, the Captain, and his worm of a Lieutenant up here on the veranda. I light a cigarette and observe. In between the harassing, searching, and fining of people, the cops are becoming increasingly rowdy, pullin' big swigs from bottles of rum they now have openly out on the steps. Every fine demanded, they receive without resistance. Most people are—for good reason—terrified of Third World cops. These guys are especially enjoying searching the women. Needless to say, all women get felt-up good, and if they are wearing a skirt or dress, like most are in this heat, they are ordered to raise the garment. There is very little protest, just sobering fear and obedience. One woman, however, an attractive blond in a white gauze dress, is pulled aside away from her friends. She is of course felt-up, and it is excitedly announced that she is wearing no panties! All flashlights turn toward her, and she is ordered to raise her dress. She does, and even opens her legs, while coolly hissing in an English accent, "Getting off are you? Fucking pervert!" Then with much dignity, the suave woman strolls back to her friends. The cop yells, "You, you should be wearing panties!" In mid-stride the blond flips back her long hair to retort, "And why is that? I'm no child; I can control my body functions! Obviously the same cannot be said for yourself!" Damn, that chick's got some balls! Grinnin', I watch the asshole call after her a slew of insults on the order of *puta*, whore, *del rejue*, etc. Receiving no reaction, he turns, proudly holding up his two fingers bragging how they are still wet from her coochi. Goochy? Whatever the hell these morons down here call it.

The Captain, noticing my amusement, turns to the Lieutenant and has him tell me to lay down on the bench and go to sleep. It will be daylight soon, and I must be up early to work the boats. Feelin' somewhat confident of actually surviving this night, Sparky lays down upon the bench, rollin' over onto my side for better viewing the street activity below. Really though, now there's not much to see. The brief pre-dawn rush is over, once again leaving the street dark and empty. Even most of the cops are now gone, including the Bobsey twins. Those that do remain are drinkin' and loudly bullshitting. Still, they are however, able to nab one last staggering tourist. He is a young man, a backpacker type. He has no money, claiming to have spent it all in the bars. So with watch and ring, the young backpacker pays his fine and receives a kick in the ass to be movin' on! He of course does; and soon following is a young local woman quickly pushing a vending cart. The cops know her by name, and she too is fined. The young woman expresses surprise in finding the police still on the street at such a late hour. They laugh; she laughs! She is then led over to the steps to pay the fine. She bends forward to blow one cop as another flips her skirt to fuck her from behind. The young woman is being a sport, and it is obvious that she has paid this fine often in such a manner. The remaining cops gather around to watch and wait their turn.

The Captain notices me observing this strange spectacle and has his Lieutenant scold a command, "You, you! Look the other way; and go to sleep. Captain's orders!"

"Yes Sir!" Rolling onto my back, with left arm resting across oily forehead, ears are perked, and eyes are only partially closed. Sparky tries to relax and not think of wife and sons. Must keep mind clear from everything but stayin' alive and getting the hell outta this mess! Damn, at the moment, remembrance isn't there for how all of this came to be. Hazy dawn is surrounding and with it comes persistent visions of my sons. I can actually smell them, the warmth of their heads and perfect little bodies. Of course it's a trick; my mind is screwin' with me. Struggling to fight it, I fail. My sons' enchantment is just too alluring, intoxicating... The drift encases, floating me towards them... "DEVON!" Off that bench I do jump! Comin' face to face with the grinnin' punk of a Lieutenant.

He's actin' the big shot, barking out orders. It's time for me to go work the boats. Seein' the Captain standin' off to the right, but not seein' anyone else, I look at my watch; it's 6 A.M. Fuck me! I cannot believe I actually allowed myself to fall asleep, and for almost a whole hour at that! Yeah well, that's what Sparky gets for lettin' guard down for even a split second. Can't Goddamn afford it. Must stay sharp, alert, focused—AWAKE! Now, because of the brief shutdown (sleep), I feel groggy, sluggish, and metabolism, or somethin', has dropped 'cause Sparky is now cold, shiverin' cold! And bladder is again full.

The greaseball Lieutenant is in my face, badgering me to hurry, hurry! I must get ready for work, but first, I must come to atten-tion and salute him. Doin' as told—throwin' him a snappy salute—the little Beaner cracks up laughin'. The Captain sees, and turns to the Lieutenant, giving stern silent reprimand while motioning me to drop the salute and relax. Respectfully I share my need for using the *bano*. Before the Captain can give answer, the worm of a Lieutenant spits a tongue biting "No!" The Captain however, appearing more than a little annoyed with his Lieutenant, answers in English, "Yes," and waves for me to go do what must be done. In lickety-split time, Sparky is in the disgusting bathroom, pissin' and again scrubbin' myself down with the same water from the same bucket. The water stinks of foul whatever and it makes me even colder. Back on the veranda I open my backpack and pull out a long sleeved, cotton, olive green, pullover shirt and a pair of French military camo pants. Of course the Lieutenant strongly objects, but the Captain, speaking in very broken English, expresses the warmer clothing to be a very good idea—working the boats at this early hour will be cold. Looking tired, he motions for me to step inside the station house for dressing. The Lieutenant follows to watch. His eyes betray he wants to see my dick, not for sexual purposes, but rather (guessing) curiosity. Gold scrotum ring, no pubic hair, magnum condoms? Who knows. I turn so he can only see my ass. In doing, I'm only inches from the wall with cracks full of gram-size balls of cocaine. Jesus, do these guys really think Sparky is gonna use this shit to frame fellow American and European tourists? Fuck that! And, and Sergeant Lobo will be comin' here to receive his personal apology from me. Oh Goddamn, it sure takes no genius to figure out that even with the Captain's protection, I will surely be ordered to perform some sort of sick torturing murderous act for proving my sincerity. Hell, look what had to be done just to survive last night; and that was for the nice Captain here. Whoa, Lobo, I just know, is gonna want me to do what he knows I will not ever do—torture and kill a child! Aughg! If the Captain wasn't just outside there, I would spin on this puke of a Lieutenant, kill him, and with his revolver and ammo, try to make a run for it. But to where? It's always the same fuckin' dilemma.

Must figure somethin' out; and it's gotta be before bein' sent to do the airline muling. Hhmm, the boats? Sparky is damn good at handling outboard motors and boats; but again, even if by chance I do seize control of one, where to go? Sure can't go up river to orphanage Casa del Corazone. That madman Captain Matrix and his army will be let loose, and guess where they will go a-lookin' first? Geez, even if they know I am not at the orphanage, it will just be an excuse for them to go there, perform their unspeakable atrocities on the children, and instill terror while making an example. So where does an American run for help down here? The American Embassy? Christ, that's in Guatemala City. Sure the fuck can't get there by boat. Gotta figure somethin' out, and like soon!

Dressed now in long sleeved shirt and French camo pants, I feel better, well, warmer anyways. I'm ordered to shoulder gear and follow.

The punk Lieutenant is full of teasing, half of which is incomprehensible. With much sarcasm, he informs that we are going first to my new home for dropping off my stuff, then it's on to the waterfront, where I will start my new job. Down the steps we go, stopping at the little ATV cart vehicle. Tossing my backpack into the back—*smack!* The Beaner Lieutenant smacks me upside the head! Spinnin' on confronting reflex, Mr. Slappy backs a few steps away with hand on holstered revolver. Seeing I'm not gonna spring on him, he laughs—hissing for me to re-shoulder the pack. The batteries to the cart are down; it won't start. The Captain immediately approaches, and in Spanish, lashes the Lieutenant with a royal ass chewin'! Afterwards, the Lieutenant is made to apologize in English, to both me and the Captain. He does—looking pathetic—and is sent away.

With the Lieutenant gone, and the Captain now walkin' the lead, guess where we go? Guess where's to be my new home? Golly Wally, it's back to Mum and Pop's hotel! As we enter the narrow grounds, Mum and daughter are seen busy cleaning my old room. Needless to say Mum is not one bit happy in seein' us, and even less so upon learning I'm to be stayin' here. Yep, my new home! Mum wants nothing to do with any of this business concerning me. Clutching cleaning supplies, she uses Spanish for venting out stern protests to the standing, quiet, tired-looking Captain. In doing, Mum becomes more and more flustered with frustration—even glancin' to me, as if I might be of some help with this matter. Uh, Mum, don't look at me. Sparky sure as all holy hell didn't ask to be a part of this shit. However, a thought does come to mind, but wow, it's a whammy! Yeah well, fuck it! For better or worse, I must keep tossin' monkey wrenches into the works. Clearing my very hoarse throat, and quickly getting everyone's attention, I begin tellin' Mum how last night they maxed out all of my credit cards with PRISA Airlines. "This is all okay by me Mum, but very soon the credit card companies are going to become suspicious and will be contacting my wife. Of course my wife will know immediately that somethin' is very wrong. She will share her concern with the credit card companies. They will cancel all the charges and send investigators. Credit card fraud is a very serious offense, an international offense! The American FBI will come. Also, when my wife does not receive word from me soon, like today soon, she will start contacting American embassies and other important officials to have me reported as a missing person. This, of course, will involve many more investigators, and since my wife knows I'm supposed to be here in Livingston, well, here is where they will all come to start their big investigation. Understand?" Oh yeah Skippy! Every damn word

Mum understands—and with big eyes at that!

Excitedly, she turns and rapidly translates to the Captain all that I just said. The Captain absorbs it with a long sigh. He silently looks down to his feet as if in serious thought. Mum watches with her big arms crossed, and me? Well, I'm feelin' really, really doomed. They warned me no more tricks. In their eyes, Sparky has just pulled a big one! They, all those behind this insanity (with numbers growing daily), will most certainly be thinkin' I've deliberately set out to make 'em look the fool! But Goddamn, what do they expect? And why didn't they figure this out themselves? Did they actually forget about "Devon" having a wife at home? Forget about how credit card companies check up on unusual charging? Or are these people simply ignorant when it comes to credit cards? No matter—either way, this is really gonna big time piss off some very important assholes!

The Captain looks up and, without expression or word, motions for me to follow him. I do, leaving Mum and daughter both waving bye bye! Obviously, all deals made last night are now off. No workin' the boats, no stayin' in Livingston, and no protection. The Captain is washing his hands of me. In silence we walk to the waterfront docks. Here amongst the general hustle and bustle of the new business day, the Captain points out a boat and motions for me to go wait to board it. Seeing that I understand—truly understand—he stands back to watch. Many eyes are on us: vendors, dock workers, boatmen, and local passengers waiting to board. They see, and give plenty of room. Hell, once again, Sparky is a dead man walkin'.

The adorable little boy from yesterday suddenly runs up to me and excitedly asks if I'm ready to board the boat with him for Casa del Corazone? The little guy remembers my name, but has not yet heard of my predicament, nor had he noticed the Captain over there. Looking down into his sparkling, big brown eyes, I fight back tears. The child picks up on this, taking a full step back. I glance over to the Captain, who is now trying to just blend in by casually leaning up against a rustic power pole with cell phone in hand. The Captain's eyes meet mine as he slowly nods his head conveying no, I cannot go upriver with this child to the orphanage. Well, duh! Like that hadn't already been figured out. Sparky wouldn't even dare try.

The little boy follows the direction of my glance. He sees the Captain and turns, softly asking, "Devon, you are in big trouble?"

"Yes."

"They are not allowing you to go upriver?"

"No."

"But they are allowing you to go to Puerto Barrios?"

"Yes."

"Devon, they will be waiting for you there. If you do get away, trust no one. Try to find the white Christian people, they will help you the best. Sorry you are in such big trouble Devon. Bye bye."

With that, the boy is gone, and a boatman comes. He directs me on to a boat. Stepping down into the long, narrow boat, Sparky attempts to take a seat towards the stern for bein' near the boats outboard motor. (Who knows, maybe buddy will decide to pull a fast-one and seize this boat after all.) The boatman, however, as if readin' my mind, uses strong, corded, black arms and powerful gripping hands to seat me up in the very foremost front of the bow. With the boat now full of passengers and tarp-covered cargo, the outboard fires up and is thrown into reverse with familiar gas/oil mixture wafting. As we back up for getting the bow turned outwards, I look up and over, to see the Captain now talking into his cell phone. Our eyes lock for a very strange goodbye. I'm supposed to now be handed over to this Matrix guy, and he's probably waiting for me in Puerto Barrios. (Buddy? Man, gonna have to play it as it comes. Can't fuckin' wait.)

Damn, thirsty much? Wish to hell I had some water left, but that got drained long ago. Other than bein' thirsty, I feel very hollow, void of just about everything, including fear. This however, is quite understood to be a short-lived thing. The whole fear factor will be kickin' in again soon enough. But for now? Sparky is just enjoyin' the escapism of this hollow shell phenomenon so uniquely odd. Hhmm, a cigarette though, would be nice, but they're all gone. Imagine that; blasted cops, they cleaned me out.

T he boat ride is of course, under the circumstances, way too short. As the boat idles down to dock at Puerto Barrios, I immediately spot the man waiting for me. He is without soldiers or police. The man is Ladino, Latino, whatever. He is my age and of similar build, except not near as lean or sinewy as I now am. His hair is glossy black and, of course, he's sportin' the standard issue caterpillar mustache. He is dressed casually in a t-shirt, blue jeans, and tennis shoes. Also, the snap sheath encasing a large cheap folding knife riding on his belt is hard not to notice. The man is all smiles as he introduces himself, even offering his hand for a handshake greeting. His name is Pio, and he is my new friend who is gonna help by driving me to an airport so that I may safely fly home to my family. (Sure you are Pio, and you're gonna suck my dick as well, right?) My eyes do a glance around. Jesus, how everyone is indeed watchin' us! And if their expressions are bein' read correctly (which they easily are), I am soon to be dead, and Pio here is a hired man (thug), a gang punk who has grown up to be a gangster of the underworld in organized crime. He's here to pick me up for delivering (guessing) to Matrix. I know; he knows; everybody knows; but what to do about it? Ain't (even if possible) a Goddamn place to run to!

Pio sees my distrust and increases his exaggerated new best friend act, even patting me on the back for that special touch of added reassurance, after which he reaches for my backpack as if to carry it for me. But upon realizing it's weight, he passes on the idea, and so I shoulder it. The busy crowd opens before us. Pio, while directing the way through, is at the same time right on me. He clearly has been forewarned and is alert, ready for any running escape attempt. As we approach his small parked car, I'm half surprised to see that it is a taxicab. "Pio, you are a taxicab driver?"

"Yes, Devon, yes! You see now? You have nothing to fear. With me, you can relax. I am your friend. No harm will come to you; I give you my word."

Once seated in the front seat of the small car, he pats my knee, asking what airport? San Pedro Sula or Guatemala City? (Fuck me!) San Pedro Sula? That's Honduras. Aughg! This is hardly a surprise, but Goddamn it. Even though it was more than evident from the very start that this guy is full of shit—Latins, when speaking English, are lousy liars—a small pathetic part of me had, way down deep, slipped through the grasp of logic, and had hoped. A lie is hard to deflect entirely when it is so wanted to be true. Yeah well, there's no doubts now, huh?

"Pio, man, San Pedro Sula is in Honduras."

"Yes Devon, yes. You want to go to Honduras then?"

"No—no, please! Pio, I do not want to go to Honduras! Very bad men are there! I did nothing, nothing, and still they attacked me and tortured poor little children for the…, the horrible cruel sick movie videos that they make. I had to fight to defend myself…, and…, and run! Oh God, the poor children they hurt!" (Choking up, Sparky is givin' his best just kicked, whimpering puppy performance). And in doing, Pio's eyes change slightly. They have for-real softened from their trickery sparkle to that of maybe, possibly, understanding. Sympathy? Hhmm, there is some good in there. I'm gonna have to keep playin' on this.

"Devon, Devon, it is okay. I understand."

(Damn straight you understand! You already know the whole story! Hhmm, or does he? Maybe this guy doesn't know the whole, real story. But he's gonna.) "Devon, you don't wish to go back to Honduras. No matter, we will simply go to Guatemala City." His big smile betrays that Guatemala City had been known to be my preferred destination all along. "Devon, you see now, I am here to help you. I am your friend, you can trust me. Relax Devon, and do not worry. I will drive you to Guatemala City airport. This time tomorrow, Devon, you will be home safe with your family…" He gives a big smile. "Good? Good! But now Devon, you must give me money for gasoline and *cerveza* (beer). It is a very long hot drive to Guatemala City."

"Pio, last night they took all my money, but I do have traveler's checks, many of them. If we go to a bank, I will cash as many as you need."

He wants to see my traveler's checks. Impressed by the amount, with a grin, he helps himself only to a fifty, declaring, "This is enough, Devon. And we do not need to bother with a bank; I have a friend here in town."

Unable to resist asking, "Pio, are you sent here from Honduras?"

His mouth drops open, and in a micro split second the eyes expose betrayal that yes—yes, he is indeed. However, he quickly recovers, laughs this off with Latin exaggeration of "No, no, of course not Devon. I am Guatemalan, a taxicab driver! Here, Devon, look, see?" From his wallet, Pio pulls forth his supposedly valid Guatemala taxi permit. The thing is the size of a standard fishing license, folded, unlaminated, and in such condition to be almost illegible. Also, the print is from an outdated typewriter. To make or forge such a simple document would be nothing. Pio points to the faded inking of Guatemala and his name. Sparky smiles and acts assuredly convinced. (I'm not, and Pio knows it.) The fake license is put away and off we go to find the check-cashing friend.

After circling the very busy, large open-air outdoor marketplace of the town's *centro* several times, we find the man. He is a fat black Carib, and his weight greatly burdens him as he waddles up to Pio's car. Greetings and such are exchanged, as is my traveler's check for cash. I don't even need to sign the thing. The transaction is brief, and in no time we have the car's tank full of gas, and Pio has his six pack of *cerveza*. He seems genuinely surprised in learning I do not drink alcohol. No not even beer! Instead, I now have a much needed tall liter bottle of water and two packs of cigarettes. Despite the thirsty urge to guzzle the *agua*, only sparing small sips are allowed. Can't afford any need to pee. A funny thing is that Pio informs we won't be taking his taxicab car after all. (Well, actually it's not that funny; and really, it doesn't surprise me.) Nope, for whatever reason (I don't even bother asking), we can't take his now full-of-gas car. We need a different car, and Pio needs a friend to come along for the drive. (Yeah, whatever you say Pio, just don't take my water or cigarettes away, okay?)

Pio's cell phone has rung a couple of times already. The conversations have been brief and in rapid Spanish. Pio has also made several calls, again, speakin' only Spanish. Obviously it is common knowledge to all, that I do not speak Spanish, because everyone seems quite confident in assuming that I can't follow what is bein' said. Well, they are half right and half wrong. For example, right now, Sparky knows that ol' Pio here is havin' a not so easy time finding a driving partner for this trip. His friends are either not answering their cell phones, or they are comin' up with lame excuses. Hhmm, is this a good sign or bad? Well, hell, guessin', it must be reckoned to be bad! Especially after we drive up to a guy's house where Pio begins yellin' for him to "Come, come! Good money is to be made from this simple job…" etc. The man, however, is quite hesitant, looking to be wanting nothing to do with this simple job. And also, his wife isn't allowing it; she yells back how her husband cannot today come. "Visiting *familia* is soon arriving! He is needed here at home." Pio, cussing, gets back on the cell phone and eventually reaches a friend willing to come along "on this simple job." At the willing friend's house, we switch cars. From Pio's taxicab, we all climb into the friend's taxicab. Yep, both men have their very own taxicabs.

The friend/driving partner gets behind the wheel, Pio takes the front passenger seat, and me, I get the back seat, with shoulder bag at feet and backpack nudging close on my left. Pio introduces me to his old friend/new partner. The man is large and seemingly of quiet, laid-back nature (though this means nothing). And his name? Fuck if it is caught, much less retained.

With car now in motion, the two men begin to converse in Spanish; with Pio of course doin' most of the talkin'. Despite the Spanish, I am able to pick up on some very important key words and their meaning in reference; such as many mentions of Matrix, video camera, hotel room (*cuarto*), knife (*cuchillo*), cutting (*cortada*), Devon, *chica*, torture, killing (*matar*), and a lot more of the *cortada* crap! Sparky is fucked! It is easy to comprehend that they are discussing not what has been done, but rather what is soon to be done. To me! The driving partner guy mumbles somethin' on the order that most likely the freak (me) will *gusto* the pain very much. Pio glances back to see if I have understood any of what has been spoken. My response is to inhale deeply on a cigarette, while lookin' clueless.

But Pio ain't buyin' it, so he reverts back to speaking English mixed with a little Spanish. He shares with Partner how he doesn't believe I am as they say; he believes the other rumors—the good ones. The partner shrugs his shoulders, replying, "Yes, it is possible, but a job is a job, and the money for this one is very good."

Upon stopping briefly to fill this car too with gas, Pio has his Partner pull up curbside. On the corner, sitting in a simple wooden straight back chair, is a Garifuna boy. Under his chair are clear plastic wrapped balls of white powder the size of a fist; they are stacked neatly in pyramid fashion. Pio, turning in his seat, informs me that he is going to buy some *coca* for the drive, and asks if I want any? (*Coca*—cocaine? Hhmm, so tempting. Buddy, should we? Hell no! Man, you know a clear head must be kept at all times – idiot.)"No thank you Pio."

He looks at me very surprised and again asks—to make sure. "Yes Pio, I'm sure. No *coca* for me, but thank you very much for asking." Partner also declines. Pio just shakes his head toward us as if we were a couple of pussies. He jumps out of the taxicab car, then sticks his head back in through the window, reminding Partner to keep his hand on it! Partner retorts assurance, "Yes, yes, I have my hand on it now, see?" His right hand is tucked down between seat and crotch. I can't see what "it" is, but just guessin', hand gun at ready would definitely be at the top of the list. Pio again reminds him, warning to be ready, and not to hesitate! Partner, now seeming very annoyed and impatient, scoffs, telling Pio to "just be quick. We have a very long drive before meeting Matrix."

Pio quickly glances back to see if I had heard. Well, duh! He then looks to Partner as if silently asking, "Man, what'd you have to go and say that for?" Partner just shrugs his shoulders, with eyes fixed forward. Pio, looking perturbed, leaves for the boy in the chair. I ask Partner if that is really all cocaine that the boy is so openly sitting on? Partner glances up at me via rear-view mirror and calmly answers, "Yes."

"But isn't it illegal, and won't the boy get arrested?" Of course Sparky already knows the answer, but the goal here is to engage this Partner guy into some sort of conversation. You know, try to get him comfortable with me? Evidently it's gonna be a long ride, perhaps Partner can be persuaded first in at least understanding I am no murdering freak, but instead a nice guy, good family man, with fault of only having long *blondo* hair and tattoos. And this is just one big fucked-up mess! (Yeah well, gotta try.)

He answers in surprisingly soft tone, "Yes, it is illegal, but not for everyone. The boy will not be arrested because it is permitted and has been instructed for him to do this. All by very important people, understand? He is protected."

"Yes, I understand. Thank you." Pio quickly returns, not with a fist size plastic of coke, but rather several grams the size of marbles. He takes one, crunches it up between fingers, opens the plastic, inserts a rolled bill; big snorts ensue. Holding his nose, he turns and offers me some. (My mouth is literally salivating.) "Uh, no thank you Pio." Shrugging his shoulders, swallowing deeply from his bottle of *cerveza*, he motions for Partner to drive.

Out of Puerto Barrios and on the open road, Pio is now feelin' pretty damn good and like real chatty. So we talk, with subject bein' mostly of myself. Pio is sincerely interested in all I have to tell. Sparky speaks in tone of polite respect, yet, it ain't the kiss-ass kind.

Soon both men are intently listening to my personal tellings, and I tell 'em lots, including details of my close bonds once had with recently dead father and grandfather. (Both Pio and Partner add, they too had been very close with their own fathers and grandfathers, who are also now dead.) These guys hear about my days living on the river working as a commercial fisherman and a mussel diver, etc., but, it's the mention of owning tattoo and body piercing studios that has them most intrigued. So elaboration for such (as requested) is brought forth. Their interest here, of course, is in wanting to hear all about the "wild American women" that get the tattoos and piercings. And so, these become the topic of choice in relation to owning tattoo/body piercing studios.

Quickly these two men are laughing and giggling in boyish, fascination!

It is good hearing Partner laughing. They especially enjoy the stories about how on rare occasions certain hot chicks would climax with orgasm while getting nipples or genitalia pierced. One such lady actually ejaculated after getting her clitoris pierced. The woman did have the largest clit this cowboy has ever seen; it was for-real the size of my thumb tip, and that's no lie! More common, however, is simple nervousness, followed by hyperventilation, followed by sometimes passing out, puking, and even farting. "Yep, farting! And one young pretty, while I was piercing her pussy lip (labia) just up and lets loose a gush of pee, spraying me right in the face!" (This is exaggerated. The girl did urinate, but it certainly wasn't a gush to the face. The poor, sweet thing was terribly embarrassed, still, admirably she stayed and saw the piercing through.)

The stories get both men convulsing with belly laughs! And Sparky is laughin' right along with 'em. Pio (chuckling) again offers me some coke. Geez, I'm more than half tempted, but we ain't on no joy ride here. No we are not! This is a Goddamn death ride! Sparky is just humoring these fucks to feel 'em out, and because I haven't decided it yet best to start bashin' in the backs of their heads with twenty-inch black steel MAGLITE flashlight. This will be easy enough to accomplish, even with Partner having a handgun. My MAGLITE is in close reach (inches) from my left hand casually resting on top of backpack, with cover flap now loosely (discreetly) unbuckled to allow speedy grabbing of unseen flashlight club, riding upright inside. But wow, this is one hell of a drastic move! Once committed, amongst the bludgeoning close quarters, there will be a crashing car wreck; and if by chance Sparky does survive, well Jesus Christ, cops and military are gonna be all over me! Must save this course of action for last ditch, suicide mode. Also, right at the moment, These guys are bein' non-threatening, and so, I really, really do not want to tear into their heads! This, however, in all likelihood, will, of course, quickly change but for now...

Pio informs Partner that a military checkpoint is coming up. He asks if the number is still the same. Partner, nodding, answers "Yes." And so Pio gets on his cell phone, punches in numbers, and speaking Spanish gives a password or the likes. After this, he turns to me, informing we will not have to stop for the checkpoint. Sure enough, without having even to slow down, we are waved around and through the mass of busy soldiers and long lines of stopped traffic. Amongst the soldiers, I see two white American soldiers wearing their American military issued camo BDUs. And they do appear to be in charge of this cluster fuck!

Uh-ooh, my heart sinks as we speed past. Hey, they would have helped me. Wouldn't they? American soldiers would surely help a fellow American in trouble on foreign soil, right? Gee, what a silly man I've become, learning nothin', huh? (Buddy? Who knows; what does it matter? They are back there, and you are here. Stay focused. Yeah, okay.) Still, the sight of American soldiers does increase inner frustration, big time. But the show must go on!

Pio, as if seeing my despair, asks if rumors concerning my soldiering past are true? Giving him a sad look, I answer, sighing a solemn tone, "All of that had been a very long time ago. Now I am a family man that only wants a life of peace." For added effect, I pull forth my wallet and begin showing off all the photos carried of my wife and sons. Each photo shown is accompanied with sincere, proud, unabashed (Latin style) bragging. Pio and Partner view the photos, and give the customary complimentary comments. Both men spend extra time gazing deeply into the one of my wife, who is sitting, looking very sexy, with her white blouse unbuttoned displaying (thanks to breast implants) one hell of a lot of very enticing cleavage. Her large nippled areolas are just oh so close to bein' exposed, but they aren't. Pio and Partner both politely compliment my wife's beauty, and do so carefully so as not to offend. (Yes! Buddy, they are showin' respect. This is good. Man, just keep workin' the whole loving father/husband act and be glad they can't find the one nude photo of Nancy there, hidden in between the others.)

The telling of my family though is for-real bringing tears to surface, tears that are becoming very difficult to hold back, they are wantin' out! Goddamn, it would take nothin' to break into chest-heavin' sobs. Pio notices, and, appearing sad for me, hands back the photos while softly sharing that he too has two young sons. Partner announce that he has two daughters and one son (*hijo*). Both men also proudly claim to have very good wives waiting for them back home. And we all agree *familia* is very special and very important.

Upon such conclusion, the mood within the car becomes one of withdrawn silence. Obviously, all thoughts now are on the very real bizarre magnitude of that awaiting us. After some time, Pio breaks the quiet to have Partner pull over; he has to piss. Stepping from the car, Pio does just this. On completion, he discreetly takes out his large cheap folding knife, opens it, and tests the edge—thumbing for sharpness. Then our eyes meet. Quickly, he closes the knife, re-snaps the sheath, and jumps back into the car. With a couple more good snorts of coke, and the car again up to speed, Pio turns to Partner and attempts to speak quietly (using both English and Spanish). But just like with their lying, speaking quietly is not this people's strongest point. And so, heard they indeed are. Also, the Spanish is understood enough to know they are discussing the hotel I'm being taken to.

Matrix, the *gringo* with video camera and a *chica* will be there waiting for us. Partner is more informed on the details of my fate than Pio is. He tells Pio that it is going to be done in a bathtub, with the *puta* doing all the *cortada*. Matrix wants the cutting to be *prolongar* and *muy* bloody. He has a real thing for this Devon; it has now become a personal obsession. Pio asks what *cuchillo* is to be used? His own has no edge. Partner, nodding his head back towards me, answers, "They will have his machete there. Matrix wants all to see that Devon gets it from his own machete." Fuck me! Whoa, talk about your deranged psychos. Matrix, Matrix, Matrix! Why the hell does this sick son-a-bitch have it out for me so bad? Huh? Why? Damn, even in the eyes of a madman, one would think his anger would be more directed toward that fool Sergeant Lobo; he's the one that started all this, not me. I did only what was necessary under conditions confronted. How is it that Sergeant Lobo comes out of this bein' the victim, having lost face from insult, while Sparky is the fuckin' bad guy! Insane degenerates, these people are! Pio slowly shakes his head, commenting, "Matrix—he is *satanico loco*!" Pio then glances back and sees I've been following the conversation and do know my fate. I try very hard not to expose the imminent fear that is about to erupt into violent action, by masking with restraining surface of sad—so sad—expression of doomed despair, which Pio acknowledges.

Clearing my throat in finding voice for passive somber tone, "Pio, you are not taking me to the airport in Guatemala City, are you?' After a moment's pause, Pio slowly shakes his head back and forth, indicating silent answer of no. "Pio, you are taking me to a hotel where Matrix is going to have me tortured to death and…, and the *gringo* will be there with his video camera filming, right?"

Pio softly answers, "Yes." Partner immediately hisses disapproval towards Pio for answering. Pio spins to justify, "Eh, look at him! See how sad he is? And what does it matter? He knows already anyway. He is a nice guy; I like him. We owe him at least to inform him on how it is he is to die."

Partner answers, "Yes, but now he will attempt his tricks, make trouble and try to escape. They warned us of this. Now he will be very difficult."

Pio glances to see my response. Of course he sees only the (presented) very tired vacant man, broken into yielding submission (hardly a difficult act, considering). With a long defeated sigh, Sparky answers,

"No, I knew from the start that you guys were driving me to Matrix. They told me in Livingston that this had been ordered. Believe me, there are no hard feelings toward you guys. I know you are only doing your job as instructed. You are both good men, good family men, and I like you. If things had been different, we three would be good friends. I will not make any trouble for you, or try to escape. Besides, there is nowhere to run. And even if there were, I am much too *triste* and too tired for such an attempt. Also, it would accomplish nothing, other than to anger important people into possibly bringing harm to yourselves and *familias*. And this I will not be responsible for. Enough innocent people have already been hurt and murdered by those evil that want me dead. I know I am to die, here in Guatemala, and I accept this. It's just that, well, I have been a soldier and have had to fight seemingly my whole life. I just want to die, to go to my death with some dignity." (Tears are swelling and voice is cracking.) "I do not want to be tortured to death and especially have it be on video. Understand? Please, that is no way for a man to die. I would not wish that on my worst enemy."

Pio's eyes were already bloodshot red from the coke, but now they are like more so, tenfold, yet wide and somber. "Devon, Devon, we will talk to Matrix on your behalf. We will plead for him to kill you quickly and not do it as he is wanting. Devon, he will listen to us, you will see. Many people think as we do. We do not agree with the methods of Matrix. He is *satanico* and the movies he makes are the work of the *diablo*…" Partner interrupts to inform of an upcoming military checkpoint. Pio punches in numbers, same as before. "Now no tricks, Devon, okay?"

"Yes, Pio: no tricks, no trouble. I give you my word. On the lives of my wife and sons, and under God's eyes, my word is given."

Pio seems more than a little impressed in the extremity of my oath. We speed through the roadblock checkpoint. With Pio closely watching, Sparky lights a cigarette and stares down at dirty red Converse high-tops. If there are American soldiers at this checkpoint, I don't even want to see 'em.

Must think of somethin' and like fast! No way is Matrix gonna listen to these guys. Hell, if anything, he will just be all the more evil and prolong the torturing for spite. The landscape now is turning from lush green to hilly parched earth of mostly red clay. My two companions (or whatever you want to call 'em) are sweating heavily from the heat, as is Sparky, what with the French camo pants, long-sleeved shirt, vest, and all, but really, who cares? Certainly not me. Not while bein' faced with the hideous torturing death awaiting. And my poor wife will never even know. After Matrix has had his psychotic fun with me, my body (or what's still remaining) will be disposed of, and simply disappear, never to be seen again. Knowledge and acceptance is more than clear. There is no way for ever gettin' out of this fucked-up country alive, but damn, if only there was a means of dyin' in such a manner for news to reach back home. Nancy would then at least know. And Skippy, this is a huge importance! (Buddy? Man, you should have started bashin' heads with the MAGLITE while in proximity of the last military checkpoint. At least there, it would have probably become public, international news and… Yeah, yeah, but too late now. Maybe there will be another. Christ, unless Pio and Partner change disposition, it's gonna be tough to hurt 'em like that. Man, stay focused. Can't afford sentimentalism. Okay.)

Sparky has become a personal obsession for this sick mother fucker Matrix, right? Yeah well, kiss my ass, Matrix! With loose wires now snappin' all inside the head, determination sets in like never before. Matrix will not get the satisfaction he so desires by getting hands on me. No he will not! Oh death is gonna come to me, but it won't be on Matrix's terms. "Uh, Pio, why must I die by Matrix's hand?"

After some thought, he answers, "Because Devon, it has been ordered."

"Yes Pio, but ordered by who?" He hesitates, showing reluctance in giving the name. (Yeah like Sparky is really gonna live to tell.) "Pio, it has been ordered by someone even more important than Captain Matrix, right?"

"Yes Devon, there are many that are more important than Matrix. Matrix operates mostly as he pleases, but there are those that he must answer to."

"Pio, we both know that you will not be able to convince Matrix not to have his sick bloody fun, cutting and torturing me to death, right?" There is no answer. "Pio, be truthful, do you really want to be a part of this? Having to hold me down in that bathtub with Matrix laughing and that *puta* cutting on me as the *gringo* makes his video movie? Is this really something you want to do? And do you believe I deserve this? Especially when it is all common knowledge that it was Sergeant Lobo who attacked me first, and without proper cause? Pio, I did only what was necessary: fight for my life and stay alive. I am no homosexual. That is just ridiculous! You have both seen the pictures of my wife. She is very beautiful, yes? So how could a man be a faggot with a wife like her? Sergeant Lobo is only calling me such because I left him looking like the fool he is. And the rumors of me while in Cuba, you have heard these, right? They are not true. Have either of you guys been to Cuba? No.

Well, let me tell you: Pio, in Cuba they are very suspicious of Americans. They have secret police that watch very closely and follow us everywhere. It would not even be possible for me to behave and kill as rumored. You must know Cuba would never allow for an American to do such things. It is all rumors and lies told only because of how I look. See? My tattoos and long *blondo* hair. Matrix and Sergeant Lobo started all of this mess. And yet, they rape, torture, and kill young *niños* and *niñas* for the sick sadistic videos. You both have *familias*. It is not right. It is bad, very bad, and here I am, the one that must pay. But that's okay, I will pay for the offenses accused. I offer to make amends—restitution. They can have one of my fingers, I will cut it off myself. Plus, I will buy a small house on the island of Utila. I will live there, mule whatever is asked of me. There I will make a lot of money for the very important people. Utila has no *coca* route, yet there are many tourists going there. Many would buy cocaine, but there is none available. I know, I was on Utila before going to Cuba—"

Pio interrupts to inform that very soon they will have a *coca* route going directly to Utila just for this very reason. One already goes to the neighboring island of Roatan. Pio, also reveals that he and Partner (or whatever the guy's name is) are both really Honduran, but they live and work mostly in Guatemala, under pretense of bein' taxicab drivers.

(Yeah, whatever Pio, like tell me somethin' not already obvious.) "Pio, many Americans and Europeans are now liking the crystal meth better than the coke or crack because the high lasts longer and the women love it for sex."(Sparky is now just bullshitting for a direction.) "Pio, I can make crystal meth…"

He seems surprised, but quickly interjects, "Devon, we make crystal meth here too!"

(Well, goody for you, Pio.) "The cost of living in the United States is very expensive, and the tattoo/piercing business does not cover all expenses, so I do what I must. I make the best fluffy crystal meth there is. Man, Pio it's the best—the best! I could live on Utila, make crystal meth, help operate the new *coca* route (God, those poor people of Utila) and from there, be very valuable in many other ways. Dead, I have no value—worth nothing. The video that Matrix will make from torturing me will make no money. It can not be sold in the United States or Europe. My tattoos and such are too recognizable. And the price now bein' offered for my head? That is small pocket money compared to what can be made keeping me alive. So Pio, for good business, maybe you might want to call someone important, and ask them to consider this new proposition. No tricks. Just a proposed business arrangement."

The wheels in ol' Pio's head are now spinnin', as are Partner's. Obviously, these two men do not want to do what they know Matrix will command. Geez, if Sparky can just buy some Goddamn time! Time to figure out how to leave this life with a bang, big enough to be heard all the way back in the United States! And, of course, also to deny Matrix his sport with me.

"Devon, the only problem is that you have been offered jobs before, and you always pull tricks, making everybody look foolish. Devon, if this proposition is allowed, and you buy your house on Utila, you will also send for your wife and sons to come live with you?"

"Yes, yes, of course, Pio!" (Yeah, over my dead body.) "See Pio? This will prove my loyal sincerity. I would never try any tricks for fear of harm coming to my family. What man could? You have seen pictures of my wife and sons; how could I ever risk their safety? They will love living on Utila. My young sons will go fishing every day! You will see, it is a very good deal—good business."

Pio glances to Partner, commenting, "It might work. It is possible if he does send for his *familia* to come and live with him. He is correct about being valuable alive. We must just get around Matrix, that is all."

Partner considers, shrugs his shoulder, answering, "It is worth trying. I do not want to be in that room when Matrix starts on him."

Pio spins, asking, "Devon, do you have a pen and paper?" Oh yeah, damn straight I do. He instructs me to write letters in detail: first apologizing to Captain Matrix, and then offering to make restitution for offenses. Pio especially likes the part about me cutting off my own finger, but more importantly, the sending for my *familia* to come live with me. "Devon, this is the most important part. If your *familia* does not come then all will know this to be another one of your tricks."

And so Sparky begins to write down everything that is instructed by Pio. He sees how I've spelled Matrix's name, and has a fuckin' fit, demanding correction to spelling in no way resembling pronunciation. Pio regains calm, admitting understanding, "Yes, yes, but in Spanish this is how it is spelled. If they see you have spelled his name wrong, they will perceive it as an insult."

My penmanship, under normal circumstances, has always been that resembling a retard's. But now? With hand shaking and this car bouncin' like it is? Somehow the letter gets written, and is legible. Pio, reading, approves with a nod, adding, "Devon, just in case they do not accept, write your wife a letter saying your own personal goodbye. I will give you my word that we will send it." He glances over to Partner, who nods in agreement.

Crap, Sparky wasn't expecting this, and by the way Pio is lookin' at me? It must show. He again expresses assurance in promising to send the letter. His word has been given, okay, but... Fighting back the big tears now swelling, thoughts of just how the hell to put such a thing into words—on paper. Jesus Christ! My dear wife hears nothin' from me for like ever, then one day, outta the fucking blue, she reaches into the mailbox and, voila, the letter of all letters! How does one even compose such a letter? How to even begin? Must hold it together, hold it together! Cannot let them see me lose it, crying, or in a state of confusion... or can I?

"Pio, I am very grateful for this generous, kind gesture. I truly am. Back during my soldiering days, they would have us write similar letters before going out on missions; but Pio, that had all been so long ago. I had no wife or sons then. Pio, I don't know what to write. How do I tell my family that I am dead and they will never see me again? My sons will never again have me—their father—to play ball or go fishing. Pio, what am I to write? What would you write to your *esposa* and *hijos* if you were in my position?" (Obviously, the goal here is to involve him, get ol' Pio seriously, for-real, to feel from the inside. His sympathy is needed one hundred percent.)

Pio, avoiding my tear-filled eyes, gives a sad look, answering in soft solemn tone, "Devon, I do not know." He glances to Partner for possible suggestion, but Partner shakes his head, wanting no part of this discussion.

Pio gets on his cell phone and calls somebody important. To this person, he confirms that they do have me, and gives present location. Pio asks to meet with him. The man agrees. Ending the call, Pio turns to me, informing that in the next town coming up, we will be stopping briefly to speak with this very important man. There, Pio will ask for my life and show the man my letters. He is also wanting the man to personally see what I look like in hopes that this might aid in persuading him to take pity on me, thus consider my offered proposition. Pio then commands me to be quick with the goodbye letter to my wife, and to make no mention of it to anyone.

Oh gosh, with tears streamin' and hand a-shakin', so comes a pathetic scribble:

To my beloved wife,

By receiving this, you will know that these are my last words in this life. I will be dead. Please raise my sons as we have discussed. Be strong my love. I have always loved you and I always will. My sons, *you know how I feel about them. I am sorry for leaving you with so many bills. I was proud to have had you for a wife. This is a short last letter, but I am finding it hard to think. I love you so very much. Tell my family the same.*

Goodbye my wife and sons.

On the bottom, I write our address. Revealing the address thing scares me, but only briefly. Hell, it's on my passport, driver's license, etc. For anyone wanting to find out my home it would be anything but difficult.

Pio reads the letter and seems genuinely moved. I think the letter is absolutely dreadful, but it's really the best Sparky can come up with, considering. Pio hands it back to me, but keeps the other two, consisting of personal apology to Matrix, cutting off my finger, and a proposal for relocating my family to live on Utila, while working at whatever.

Slowing to enter the town, both men seem to know where we are goin', but neither appears all that thrilled about it. Partner keeps askin' Pio, "You are sure Matrix is not here? You are sure?" Pio answers, "Yes, yes, Matrix has already left. He will be at the hotel waiting." Turning in his seat, "Devon, do not worry, the hotel is not in this town. It is in a town not far from Guatemala City. We will still have a little time."

Partner steers the car down into a narrow vacant alley snaking through an old, decrepit, run down district. Rolling to a stop, he does not want to get out. No he does not! Partner thinks it's best that he and I wait in the car while Pio goes and talks to, this Mr. Big Shot (whoever) granting audience. Pio, however, is insistent; he wants us with him. Reluctantly, Partner complies.

It feels strange to be getting out of the car. Both men are up on me close. Pio opens a back alley door; looking past him, I can see that instead of this leading into a business such as a shop or a store, it leads down some steps for a narrow gloomy basement walkway of sorts. The smell comes up strong: moldy, damp, rotting garbage, urine, excrement, and other things, such as death—death of plant, animal, and human. Aughg, Sparky does not want to go down there. Taking a step back, I bump into big Partner. He sternly nods for me to follow Pio, and so I do.

Down the dank steps we go in single file. Hanging bare light bulbs havin' low wattage show the way. At the bottom of the steps, in the eerie-ass hall of stink and filth, we three stop. All of my senses are screamin'. Red alert! Red alert! Other than this and the sound of my two escorts breathing, I hear nothing. Well, nothin' except for the dull hum of electricity flowing throughout the building in unison with erratic scratchy scuttles from scurrying critters, large insects, mice, rats?

Without warning, Pio suddenly calls out our presence. This just about jumps me right the fuck outta my skin! The calling sound echoes with reverberation off the putrid walls of damp decaying, crumbling plaster and bricks, (somewhat) covered with a hundred years of a hundred layers of cracked, peeling paint, grimed heavily with living, unearthly, thriving infestation of bacteria not to be (willingly) touched. There is no answer to Pio's call except for a momentary ceasing of activity from all busy nearby creepy-crawlin' vermin. Partner whispers, "They are not here; we should go!"

Noting the nervous urgency within Partner's tone, it is more than evident he wants to get outta here; and, so does Sparky! Down the rancid, malodorous corridor stacked with produce crates, liquor boxes, and even fifty-five gallon steel drums, there is a door partially open with light coming forth. Pio, with a "Shsssh!", waves for Partner to be silent. We all listen, hearing only again that the vermin have re-busied themselves. Pio motions for us to follow; he is stepping slowly and cautiously as if not to make any sound; so, Partner and I do the same. It's weird as all get up; the tension is thick, almost like we three are tiptoeing into some place that is forbidden.

Pio is obviously leading us toward the lit room not having door completely closed. Looking down into the once block-tiled flooring now thick with so much filth incrustation of soiled overlay, that it could be considered...What the fuck? Shoe prints and many of 'em, all leading out from that room. Hhmm, to leave such distinctive footprints on flooring as this, would take stepping into some kind of thick liquid. And these prints look somewhat fresh, not wet fresh; but no one has yet disturbed them. A tracking expert Sparky is not, but deep down I know what the substance is that so defines these distinctive prints for tracks. Yes, it is indeed known, as is the strong new form of dominant stink now surrounding us. Once smelled, it can never be forgotten—the revolting odor from burnt human flesh. Here, also wafting, are traces of acetylene gas, the kind used for welding and torch-cutting steel. I should know, because one of my many, many past jobs was as an iron worker. Sparky has torch-cut a lot of steel, and has burn scars to prove it.

The fuckers have burnt somebody in that room there, and they have used an acetylene torch to do it. Eugh! The stench has now become nauseatingly thick; and there is a sound coming from the room, sound of little critter feet scurrying upon crinkled plastic. Pio, with a darting, unsure thrust, pushes the door all the way open, while at the same time taking a retreating step back! Partner steps to stand beside him, guiding to position me before them both. There we three just fuckin' freeze! Confronting us is a sight the brain does not want to register.

Rats are fleeing every which way. The floor and bed are covered in plastic sheathing. Blood is everywhere! Copper color blood; thick, coagulated, bluish burgundy viscera; blood; shit; blood; and smeared, smudged, splattered, pooled everywhere blood! There on the bed—on the bed! Oh my God, looky what they have done. A nude woman and two young girls (what is left of them anyways) are on that bed positioned so obscenely that one would think it not humanly possible. The woman is sprawled out flat on her back. Her face and hair are burnt off. Lying there, as if to be attached to her shoulders, are two little girl's severed heads, one placed on each side of the woman's grotesquely charred, skeletal, blackened features of all teeth and large eye sockets... The eyes! The little girl faces have not been burnt. Ooh God, the eyes! Fuck me— O— FUCK ME! They are staring right at me. Movement! Rats, determined loathsome rodents trying to conceal themselves somewhat, while they gnaw on the far side of the mutilated corpses. The woman's breasts have been cut off, hands too. Where these are supposed to be is just black burnt flesh! Her abdomen and thighs have been criss-crossed, slash cut, and the entire pubic region has been burnt to a smoldering cavity. Her feet, the woman's feet, God they too are gone, now just gross burnt stumps. And where her feet were supposed to be, at the foot of the bed, there, slumped, leaning as if in a propped up position, are the two little girls' headless bodies! Though their youth made them too young for breasts, their small chests are severely burnt, as are their abdomens, and Goddamn (guessing) genitals as well. God, God, God, please let it be that these poor innocent beings were quickly killed before this mutilating torture took place.

Bloody wheel tracks lead to the corner of the room; there it stands: the welding cart containing the tall eighty-pound cylinders, one of CO_2 oxygen and the other acetylene. Hanging from it are, of course, the hoses, nozzles, spark lighter, etc. and also a number of bloody cords of braided rope, used for tying these people down. The woman and two girl children had been tortured and mutilated while still alive! And I just know the *gringo* was here with video camera filming this, this sick decadent atrocity! There is no God! No God – No God, oh fuck me... My head is whirlin'. The color tube has blown, leaving only black and white. Lines are ghosting, heart is beating too hard, but in slow motion. Breaths are quick, short—can't get enough air! Sparky is on the verge of passing out. (Buddy! Come on man, we've been through this before. Slow the breathing, but do bring in air, lots of it, nice and steady, in rhythm. Look but don't see. No! Do not close eyes; you will fall over. Look up, look down, look all around—shake it off and breathe. No, idiot! Not through the nose! Oooh buddy, the smell from burnt flesh, hair, plastic, feces, blood, acetylene… Man, hey! Snap out of it! Uh, okay, okay!) With some quick spazz shakes of my head, I turn to look first at Pio, then Partner. Both men are still as I was: frozen in place with jaws hangin' open and eyes fixed in shocked disbelief. Pio recovers, spinning quickly to put hands on the shoulders of both me and Partner while barking "Go! We must go—now!" He actually prods us as if we need it. We do not! The entire corridor is now seeming to shrink down on us as if it were some long dark tunnel that, if we don't get the fuck out of, will constrict us to death. Partner breaks into an all out run, with me right behind. Sparky could easily pass him and run baby, run! But with Pio on my heels, I don't.

Outside, beside the car, we all three breathe in long gulps of fresh air, and we look at each other. Not a word is spoken. What the hell does a person say after such a thing? I light a cigarette, handing it to Partner, and then another for myself. We both inhale deeply as Pio gets on his cell phone. He has no conversation, just asks this Mr. Important Big Shot, whoever, where he is. Then, with a nod, we all three get back into the car and drive out of this alley to a nearby café with outdoor curbside tables.

There, sitting at a table only a few yards away from where we have parked, is the man that Pio wants to persuade for letting me live. Pio approaches the man's table with my letters in hand. Partner and I stay put in the car. The man is dressed in a suit and tie; sitting with him is a hot number *chica*. Her attire is that of an upscale prostitute. They are in conversation while eating.

The man does not show Pio the respect or courtesy of even looking at him, not even when they speak. He does, however, shoot me a quick, glaring once-over. I see immediately that the fucker hates me and this is a wasted effort. Hhmm, or is it? This Latin prick pig and his bitch are acting so damn arrogant. The *chica* won't look at Pio either, and when she does glance toward me, it's with much airs while deliberately forking food into her mouth. Their rude arrogance is insulting to say the least. Not for me so much, my life is hangin' by a rapidly fraying thread. Sparky is pretty much beyond all insult, but Pio? Uh, this is not going over well with Pio at all! For men such as him, in countries such as Honduras, Guatemala, etc., a man's machismo is, more often than not, *fanático*! Though Pio is acting all humble, I can literally see the hairs on the back of his neck standin' on end. Mr. Important Big Shot, not bothering to look up (or stop eating) does extend his hand for the letters. He reads them quickly, grunting sarcastically; the letters get thrust back to Pio with verbal retort, "Eh, this Devon has made such promises before. These are nothing more than another one of his tricks. He has seen what we have left down in the room? Good, good, now go! Take him to Matrix, and give him plenty of *coca*. Matrix wants him lively and alert." (Big wink goes to the *chica* cunt who responds with a gleaming smile.) "Ha ha! Now, go!"

On the road again, Pio vents his anger and frustration, using both Spanish and English. Partner listens, nodding understanding. Pio did not appreciate how the arrogant Mr. Big Shot had acted towards him. No he did not! Also, he really did not like how we had been tricked to go down into that basement place for viewing the atrocity so deliberately left for us to see. After a few big snorts of coke, Pio does settle, becomes quiet and stares out the window.

And me? Well, Sparky is anything but settled! I mean, on the outside, the shell appears to be calm and collected, but on the inside? It is fuckin' helter-skelter! My mind is racin'. Gotta figure somethin' out, and like fast, but I can't think, plan or concentrate. Cannot keep brain on course. Visions, visions of that room… What had been done to the poor woman and two little girls, and how it had been set up for me to see. Why? Why? Why? What was the point? To scare me? Disorient? Confuse? Make me lively and alert like the sicko Big Shot had said? Geez, if so, it is workin', all of it! Without even thinkin', Sparky blurts, "Pio, that man back there I do not like. He did not treat you with respect." Pio gives a grumbling mutter of acknowledgment and slumps even further into the seat. "And Pio, why did he trick you into goin' down into that room to see? Why do they do these terrible atrocities to innocent women and children? It is so evil, bad, and *perverso*. The money made from the videos cannot be all that great. There must be only a small market for such horrible things. Surely there is much more money to be made with the *coca drugo* routes. Really, most everybody loves drugs. There is no dishonor in that business; it has become very respected—" (Sparky is now just rolling out words. I haven't a clue where they are comin' from) "—Pio, do you believe in God? Are you a Christian?"

Spinning in his seat with eyes wide, he answers strongly, "*Si*—yes, of course!" My gaze goes to Partner for asking the same. Pio sees and answers for him, "Yes Devon, we are both Christians. We are not *satanico*!" Partner nods his head, confirming.

Pio's eyes lock into mine, they convey understanding of where this is going. Sighing, he turns back around, resting foot up on dash, and comments, "Yes, Devon this has become a very bad business we are now in, very bad." Partner silently nods in agreement.

"Pio, I have another—different business proposition for you guys." He turns, looking sadly skeptical. "Pio, this is a very good proposition. See, I have offended very important people and so I must die. It is that simple; and I have accepted this. I'm guessing these important people, not Matrix, are for the most part pretty smart and really don't care how I die, just as long as I die soon, today, right?" Sparky now has both men's full attention. "Pio, as you know, I have many traveler's checks. They are worth over $4,000 US. I want you to have them before Matrix gets them. And all I ask in return is that you simply pull over here, on one of these deserted dirt roads where no one can see, let me get out of the car to sit in the sunshine for a few moments of quiet peace so that I may think loving thoughts of my dear wife and sons; and then you kill me. Just shoot me in the back of the head! I will be dead and all you guys have to explain is that I pulled one of my tricks and attempted escape, so you had to, of course, kill me. You had no other choice! No one will doubt your word on this. Everybody has heard of my tricks before. Pio, this is a very good deal. Think about it! The important people will be pleased that I am dead, and I will get to die like a man, with dignity, at the hands of friends, instead of that torturing monster, Matrix. We three will have denied him of at least one of his satanic rituals. This will look very good in the eyes of God. Plus, you guys will have done your job by not allowing me to escape and live. Also, you won't have to, well, you know, be a part of what Matrix wants to do with me. And, and, you will have all my money! Just think what you can do with that!" (Oh Skippy-Joe, they are thinkin'!)

After a moment, Pio looks to Partner, then asks for my traveler's checks. He quickly counts them up, and shows Partner the amount, while informing, "We will not be able to keep them all. They know he has these. If there is very much missing they will become suspicious…"

Sparky interrupts, "Yes, but they do not know how many I have. In Trujillo, they were mostly concerned with the charge capability of my credit cards. And of course my cash, which they took."

Pio hearing, suggests to Partner, "We could very easily keep three thousand, leaving the remainder on his possession. Three thousand is still a lot of money."

Partner is nodding big time agreement and answers, "Yes, but to make possible cashing that amount we must go to a *banco* in Guatemala City."

Pio considers this and after a moment of thought, responds, "Okay, we will drive into Guatemala City; he will cash the checks at the bank, then we will bring him back to the country, kill him and take his body to Matrix with the story that he did his trick, went *loco* trying to escape, and we had to kill him."

Partner thinks, shrugs his shoulders and asks, "Okay, but how do we kill him?"

I eagerly suggest, "Just shoot me! Or let me shoot myself!" Pio glances to Partner, and in doubtful tone asks, "You have a gun in the car?" Partner shakes his head, sighing, "No, I have not had a gun in this car for a very long time now."

(What? What? No gun? Hey, what was all the "Keep your hand on it" shit? You know, back in Puerto Barrios? Pio had told Partner to keep his "hand on it." On what? Sparky thought it was a gun! Fuck me!) "Uh, guys, you don't have a gun? No? Do you have any weapons? No! What if I had tried to escape?" They explain that the car has a push button thing for quick-locking the car's doors. Also, they were to use their cell phones. I would be caught no matter what. "Pio, your *cuchillo*! You can kill me with that!"

Partner and Pio look to one another. Partner shakes his head; no, he's not doin' it. Pio turns to me, sorrowfully stressing, "Devon, it has no edge, and now that we know you, we cannot use the *cuchillo* on you. No, we cannot do that. You are the type that will not die easily in such a manner."

Aughg! "Yes I am, Pio! Look, all you have to do is shove the blade right here... in my carotid artery. It is easy! I will die by bleeding to death. No pain! It will be peaceful to die this way while thinking of my warm loving wife and sons."

Pio motions his head no. They won't do it. What is up with these guys? They will partake in holding me down for a slow, obscenely cruel death, but won't fuckin' stab me? Weird, weird, weird! Christ, gotta keep this goin'. Cannot let them fall back from doubts.

"Okay okay, then give me the *cuchillo* and I'll do it myself. Hell, anything is better than going to Matrix."

Pio sighs, "Devon, it will not be possible for you to do this. No one can cut their own throat."

(Oh bubba, you just watch me! Hhmm, from seemingly nowhere, a new idea comes.) "Uh, okay, okay, Pio, listen, I have a new plan. You will like it. Lets buy some *coca*! Lots of it, enough for me to overdose and die. Yes, yes! See? You guys will then not have to kill me; and you can tell Matrix and all the important people that you had given me only the usual amount to keep me alert and lively, as had been instructed from the Mr. Important Man. You were only following orders; but just like that, much to your surprise, I upped and died! Probably my heart was not able to withstand all the stress and fear, and the small amount of coke was just enough to give me an unintentional heart attack. Pio, it happens all the time with people!"

Both men, listening, nod, glance to each other, and Skippy, this plan they do like! Pio even comments, "Yes, Devon, this is a good plan. Yes, very good plan. It makes better sense this way, much more so than the other plan. And it will be no problem getting the *coca* in Guatemala City, but only after we first go to the *banco* and cash the traveler's checks, yes, okay?"

"Yes, Pio of course! You let me die like a man and send my wife the letter and I will give you everything with full cooperation."

All of a sudden, Pio yells for Partner to pull over! Partner does, and Pio jumps from the car and runs across the street to where an old bus has just driven off from a stop. There, standing in the dust of the bus, wearing sweat soaked, starched white shirts, buttoned all the way up to the neck, are two American missionaries. Mormons they are; here to teach the ways of the Church of Latter Day Saints (or some crap like that). They hesitantly follow Pio back across the street, to the car, where he shows them me. Pio has them read my goodbye letter to my wife. After quickly reading the letter, they ask me my name? "Uh, uh, uh…" Shaking myself from the state of disbelief, I, of course, respectfully answer. Pio hurriedly tells them to take me! Partner adds, if they do not, I will be killed.

Hearing this, both white shirts missionaries take a step back as if the car held the fuckin' plague or somethin'. One of the American Mormons cautiously questions, "Who is going to kill him, and why?" Partner answers flat out and straight up, "We are. It has been ordered by very important people." The missionaries take another full step back, their eyes growing wide. Pio sees, exclaims, "No, no we want to forget the orders. We want to help him. Look, he is a nice guy, good family man! Devon, show them your *familia*, the *fotografías*." I do, now wishing the photo of my wife wasn't quite so provocative. Aw screw it. Sparky already knows that these Bible bangers ain't gonna help. It can be seen in their eyes.

One is looking at my photos while the other explains to Pio how it is impossible for them to take me, reason being they live and work in a very small poor village; there is no phone, no auto, no nothing for helping me. "If it is as you said, his death has been ordered, then we cannot even take him back with us to the village. If we did, you know word would quickly spread. Soldiers will come and not only kill him, but also many innocent villagers as well." (Damn, he's right! The visions of horrors that would be inflicted on poor innocent villagers, and me the cause, brings tears streamin' down my cheeks.)

"If you truly want to help this man, drive him to the American Embassy in Guatemala City. We have no means of helping him here."

Pio considers. "Okay, okay, where in the city is the American Embassy?" The one white shirt answers somethin' like "Avenida la reformat, Zona 10? Calle-what?"(Sparky is really tryin' to pick up on this address, but...)

The other white shirt hands me back my photos and letter, adding, "Look, I think these men are going to try and help you. But I will warn you, if you are involved with drugs, have any drugs on you, or even high on drugs, the embassy will not help you. They at the embassy practice a zero tolerance position concerning drugs. It does not matter if you are American or not; do you understand?"

Whoa, is this Jesus prick for real or what? I'm on a death ride to hell and it looks like, possibly, perhaps maybe, there just might be a chance, a chance that I might be taken to the American Embassy instead of to Matrix. I could avoid havin' to die from a cocaine-induced overdose seizure. All this, and this Bible bangin' bung hole is standin' here givin' me a drug lecture; and his eyes betray—he's actually getting' off on it! (Fuckin' A—weird.) Uh, this is a matter of life and death here, my life or death! Who gives a flyin' fuck about drugs! Is every American down here out of their Goddamn mind? Whatever happened to Americans helpin' out fellow Americans? Shit, does this patriotic camaraderie only exist in the movies and books of fiction? With tears streamin' from a flood burst of frustration and other things, I thank him for the advice, and quickly write down my name and address on a piece of paper. "Please, remember I was here. Please, my name is Devin Murfin, from Illinois!" The white shirt pockets the note, while promising to do just that. Driving off, there is little faith in his word (square headed, God-fearin' worm).

With car up to speed, Pio turns in his seat. "See Devon, now that the Christian men know of you, and your story, we must now take you to the American Embassy. You do not need to die, okay?" Pio is smiling proudly of this great deed he has just done. And Sparky is, of course, returning the smile, looking to be grateful beyond all belief. But on the inside? Well, we ain't there until we are there. Must refrain from allowing for too much hope. Hope, however, is a funny thing that, when desperate, will jump eagerly to any optimistic seduction.

Pio looks to Partner and explains the new plan. "We will go to the *banco* and cash his traveler's checks, then let him out at the embassy, okay? We will simply tell them that we had to go into Guatemala City to cash one of his traveler's checks to acquire money for the *coca* to give him as instructed. Once we were in the city, he went *loco,* escaping. Of course we drove after him, but he ran straight for the embassy. For proof, we will have him leave some of his belongings here in the car for them to see."

Partner considers the plan for the moment, then, shrugging his shoulders, answers, "Yes, okay, whatever you think; I am with you. All the same, no matter what the story is, they are going to be very pissed off. Especially Matrix. I do not want to be the one to explain this to him. Still, perhaps after now, they will not give us any more jobs such as this. That will be good, but we also must make it worth our while. The money that Devon has given us we should use for buying *drugo* to sell and start our own small business. It must though be very *discreto*, yes?"

Pio excitedly agrees and pulls forth his cell phone, asking Partner what he thinks are the best prices going now, "*coca* or marijuana?" Partner shrugs his shoulders, answering, "Call for the price. *Coca* was going for the best price, but it changes daily."

With cell phone in hand, Pio punches in some numbers for listening to an automated voice listing the current price rate of both *coca* and marijuana. I can actually hear it; the recorded voice is that of a woman's. Lordy, a drug market with continuous fluctuating prices determined by supply and demand, bought, sold, and traded by various brokers of all degrees seeking the best deals. Pio confirms to Partner, "*coca* is the best rate going."

Another military checkpoint is comin' up. Pio calls us in, and again we are quickly waved through and around the thing. Looking, I can make out at least one American. He's clad in issued camo BDUs, having no visible rank or insignia, but he is white and American; just as sure as Sparky has a gold ring through the scrotum he is. Fuck it! War on drugs? Yeah, right, more like let's come up with some bogus excuse for suckin' millions of US tax dollars to be sent down here with our organized man power and get a flow on drugs! Christ, people learn nothing from history. Prohibition of alcohol basically created the organized crime operative methods. And now we have a war on drugs. Good God, is there even a description for what this has created?

Partner informs Pio of an upcoming town with a hotel that houses very good prostitutes. "They are not crack-skinny like how most now are." He wants to stop and get laid. But fortunately Pio says no (quietly,

Sparky lets out a long exhale). "There is no time. We must get to Guatemala City before the closing of the *bancos*." Partner realizes that Pio is correct and nods accordingly.

Pio then announces that he is going to take a nap. And just like that, he falls asleep soon, snoring. Oooh, this cannot be good. Nap? Sleep? What's Pio gonna be like when he wakes up? Moody, grouchy, hung over from coke and *cerveza*? Will he have second thoughts about everything? Change his mind and have Partner drive me to Matrix? Whew, how does anyone sleep on that much coke? No way is Pio gonna wake up feelin' good. Fuck, fuck, fuck!

Staring out the window, with jagged barren desolate landscape whizzin' past, I smoke cigarettes, sip water, and think. Think what it is that Sparky is gonna do when Pio wakes up having a change of mind. Really though, the means of action has already been decided. Yeah, if Pio wakes from his nappy-nap, and even looks half cock-eyed with doubts of continuing onwards to the bank and American Embassy, well guess what? It's gonna be a berserker time for me, buddy, and Sparky! Berserker, as in I think the term was once used long ago as title for Scottish warriors of certain rare individuality that would charge into battle, crazed for nothing but killing the enemy—complete, total aggressive assault! No consideration what so ever for their own survival, which was, as one can easily assume, very short-lived. Still, you gotta admire such commitment. Hhmm, I *think* it was the Scots that had the berserkers. Hell, basically the description applies to all that have found themselves in such desperate position for deciding to go down that path. Damn, Sparky sure ain't lookin' forward to hurting these guys. They have both (so far) been more than decent to me.

Passing through a town, Partner quietly announces, "Here is where Matrix is waiting." Partner slowly shakes his head as if he is now seriously having some second thoughts. And me? A fuckin' chill is corkscrewin' up my spine. With left hand resting on backpack cover flap, now way looser than what had even been at the beginning of this ride, I am like a cat ready to pounce! Literally, and just like a cat at ready, my haunches too are quivering in anticipation. Partner, oh chum, oh pal, just keep a-drivin', keep a-drivin'. Don't slow down, don't look back, and please do not try turnin' this car around. Watching him closely, there is a moment when his silent body language does betray that the very thought had more than just a little bit, indeed crossed his mind. But good ol' Partner stays the course, and soon the traffic begins to increase very rapidly, showing we are entering Guatemala City.

Partner nudges Pio awake and informs him of our arrival to the city.

Pio, gathering himself to sit upright, is briefly disoriented, moody, and complaining of bein' hungry. The road now is a multi-lane freeway of Third World conditions with heavy traffic comin' and goin'—fast! Partner has his hands full of steering wheel, swerving in and out, passing with horn a-blarin'!

Sparky is watchin' Pio closely; if I gotta go berserker here, the result will be auto wreckage of grand finale! Major collision pile-up. Geez, it's gonna be goin' out with one hell of a bang, hopefully loud enough to reach the United States with news of my death. Rubbing his eyes, Pio turns to me. His eyes are bloodshot red while still retaining a gleaming twinkle. Smiling he asks, "Devon, still want to go to the embassy?" Knowing full well the answer, he adds, "Okay, but first we go to the *banco*, and then we go to a nice restaurant for sitting at a table and getting some good food to eat, okay?"

(Oh no—shit, shit, shit! The bank will be bad enough, but now a restaurant? Are these guys dickin' around... tryin' to trick me?) "Uh, Pio, you still are going to take me to the American Embassy, right?"

"Yes, of course, Devon! Only we will eat first."

(Red alert, red alert!) "Pio, is this wise? Maybe we should not be seen together so much if you're going to take me to the embassy. What happens if we're spotted and word gets back to Matrix?" (Whoa, perhaps that shouldn't have even been brought up, but damn! Right now Sparky can't afford police—or really, anybody for that matter—even seein' me. If I am to make it to the embassy, it's gotta be fast, quick-fast! And I'm not even sure we are gonna be able to pull this crap off at the bank. What with me lookin' the walkin' dead, wantin' to cash all these traveler's checks, with this more than obvious gangster hood, hovering. No fuckin' way can we do this without raising suspicion. Not even down here in psycho-land. My raging fear, now, is that we will be stopped, questioned, and held long enough for word to reach police, soldiers, Matrix, and all big shots wanting me dead.)

Partner adds, "Devon has a good point. We are past the time for meeting Matrix. He will be making calls, getting the word out. I am very surprised he has not yet called us on your cell phone." Pio, rubbing his forehead as if he has a headache, holds up the cell phone showing that it has been turned off. (Oh yeah, like that's gonna put Matrix right at ease!)

"Pio. Please, let's just go to the bank, cash the checks, drop me off at the embassy, and then you guys can go eat without worry." Now for some fucked-up reason, ol' Pio here doesn't like this idea and expresses objection in form of exposing his childish side by havin' a bit of a temper tantrum. "No! I am hungry. I am hungry now! We do it my way. We go to the *banco* then we go sit at a nice table and eat! Then Devon, we will take you to the embassy! It is settled! Understand?"

(Uh, okay, but why? Why is Pio wanting to do it this way? It's got to be a trick or somethin', especially if we are already way late in meeting Matrix. You know that monster is chompin' at the bit and makin' phone calls. Pio must be stalling for time, but why? Partner seems to be just as ignorant to Pio's reasoning. What are you up to, Pio?)

After a moment, Pio calms himself and glances back. He sees my expression of desperate uneasiness. "Aw, do not worry Devon. We will go to the *banco*, then we will go to a very nice restaurant." Turning to Partner for gaining mutual agreement, Pio suggests, "We will go to Restaurante Americas. Yes?" Partner nods, and Pio continues his assuring pitch, "Devon, this restaurant is very safe. Many Americans go there. Nobody will recognize us. You will see; no police, no calls to Matrix." He gives a warm smile, which, of course, is returned. Then Partner blurts to Pio as if it had just occurred to him, "We cannot drive to the American Embassy! They will see my car with its taxicab numbers." Sparky quickly leans forward offering, "Just get me near the embassy and I will run for it! That way it will be better for you guys. I do not want you to get into trouble." (Trouble? Lordy, if they actually do go through with this promised attempt, and are caught, which they surely will be, they are in for more than just trouble. Mercy, they are dead! More than dead! They are like grueling dead from a slow, obscenely torturous, agonizing death. No way are they gonna go through with this! But what to do? Can't do nothin' 'cept play along until it is known for sure. Besides, we probably won't even make it out of the bank without bein' caught.)

Pio and Partner discuss where exactly they think the American Embassy is. Neither one has ever been there, but both seem to agree that it is near the Restaurante Americas. Pio instructs me to start pulling some keep-safe stuff from my backpack and to put it into my shoulder bag. I will be escaping with shoulder bag only. The heavy backpack will be left behind to help make their story believable. Not yet wanting Pio to see my twenty-inch black steel MAGLITE flashlight, Sparky nonchalantly waves this off, as if there were nothing worth taking from the backpack. Pio exclaims, "No?" This he must see for himself, and of course in doing, quickly discovers the long steel black flashlight. Of the find, Pio is overjoyed; so much so that he must turn and show it off to Partner. The twenty-inch black steel MAGLITE flashlight now belongs to Pio, and he caresses it appraisingly, while mumbling how he had thought certainly they would have confiscated this in Livingston. (It sure doesn't bother ol' Pio that the damn thing's been up my ass. No it does not!) Partner draws Pio's attention from the flashlight to inform him we are approaching a *banco*, but thinks it is closed.

The traffic is that of rush hour traffic, except worse; it's Third World rush hour traffic! How does Partner navigate in this shit? Cars, cars, and more cars! Trucks, buses, bicycles, pushcarts, and pedestrians all goin' lickety-split every which way, seemingly without order. Partner pulls an impressive U-turn and double parks for Pio to jump out and run to the bank's doors. Yep, closed it is; but Pio knows of another. Partner, driving like a true cabby, works the car in keeping with Pio's uncertain directions.

"There! There it is! And it's open. Let us out, then keep driving around the block. Be ready for us when we come back out of the *banco*. Okay? okay! Come, Devon, quickly!"

We dodge cars and people to run across the dividing boulevard for the bank. Before reaching earshot of two armed soldiers guarding the entrance, Pio instructs me to just "act natural." (Uh, okey-dokey! Here we go!)

Pio, with hand on my shoulder, is guiding the way as if I were a child, and he is doing so at a very fast pace! (Oh, this looks real natural!) Right on through the metal detector we go, which immediately starts beeping. Pio smiles to the alerted soldiers and guards while pointing down to his encased folding knife. Acknowledging, they return his smile and nod us the okay; we are in.

The bank is big, semi-modern, and busy. People turn for seeing us and all seem to instantly understand what is goin' on. High mounted security cameras are noticed. Knowing it makes no difference, I still try to avoid lookin' in their directions. Sparky does not want recognition here. All it will take is just one call from any of the many surrounding cell phones, and orders will be given, thus detaining me for Matrix.

With Pio pushing me forward, we cut in on one of several long lines of people standin'. No, cut in is not the correct description, but rather, we just march right up to a female teller's cashier window as if there were no line at all! And the waiting people not only make way, giving us plenty of room, but do in hushed silence without protest, to which Pio appears to be indifferent. Obviously this is the norm for him and his type. He is, however, sweating profusely, with eyes darting shifty alertness. His nervous urgency is more than a little noticeable. Discreet he is not. This is compounding my own fears ten fold! Whoa, for as jumpy as I now am, we might just as well be robbin' this bank! What a sight we must make, Pio and me.

The young cashier lady's expression, wide eyes and mouth hanging half open as if frozen, confirms my speculation. If this were a movie, the scenario would be funny, but this ain't no movie. No it is not! Clearing my throat, and tryin' like holy hell to keep controlled steady voice, I ask, using tone soft and gentle, "*Hola... Habla Ingles?*" Yes. Upon hearing my request to cash $3,000 US worth of traveler's checks, she timidly, cautiously, politely, informs, for this, approval from a superior is required.

Pio responds with a short burst of speedy Spanish! The young cashier lady spins on heels and in no time at all, we are off to the far wall standing in a small glass enclosed office dealing with another woman. She is a superior, and quite attractive, in a very dignified sorta way. Sparky guesses her to be forty-ish. The woman is all business. And it is more than obvious she understands full well what is goin' on here. And really, who wouldn't? Geez, Pio is holding my checks as if they were already his. He is also in not such polite manner, barking how we are in a hurry and she needs to be quick with the approval requirement. Mostly, this just consists of her personally witnessing me signing the checks, and then her filling out, in (whatever) an official bank form. Holding her head high, the woman does as Pio insists; she hurries, pronto like. After this, she then calls in her superior, a man to approve her approval.

Though the process is going quite quickly by Third World bank standards (gosh, by any World Bank standards) it is seemingly (in contrast to my heart poundin' a hundred fuckin' miles an hour!) going painstakingly slow! Pio's beads of sweat are now dripping from the end of his nose and he is ceaselessly and nervously fidgeting with a hand spazzin' to his eyes for clearing stinging sweat. The small glass office of cubicle is in plain view for all to see, and boy is everybody seein'! The whole damn bank is watchin' us. I can hardly stand it! At any moment, I just know soldiers, guards, police are gonna come for me! But they don't.

After everything is finally approved, with Pio getting the cash from the checks, we are outta there! On the sidewalk, glancing up, down, all around, we break into a run up the block. We don't see Partner's car so we run back down again, stop, turn, and there he is! Partner pops the curb for fetching us. In a blink of an eye, we are in that car and a-goin'!

Restaurante Americas turns out to be an upscale Chinese restaurant (if you want to call it that). The place appears to be Asian owned and operated, having the tacky décor of all such establishments. It is super clean, very nice, and for most Guatemalans, on the expensive side. And so, looking the way we do in this fancy restaurant, we three stand there, like fish out of water,. Fortunately, there is no crowd. Actually, we are the only customers presently wanting service; and still (for obvious reasons), they seat us clear in the far back corner where one would have to look the place over pretty good to spot us, which is more than fine by me! Pio, however, takes it as an insult; but because now he is in such a great mood, what with a wad of cash in his pocket big enough to choke a horse, he only briefly mumbles his objections, which are quickly forgotten as he takes a seat, slowly glancing around, absorbing the surrounding grand décor (indeed grand in his eyes anyways). Pio's eyes are sparkling like that of a child's gazing upon wonderment! Partner, too, is looking around as if in breath-taking awe! These two men are most definitely not accustomed to eating at (or even being in) such a place. And to think, back home in the United States a place as this wouldn't even be considered all that upscale. For some strange reason, this sorta makes me feel a little shamed.

Our waiter is a young good-looking Asian man carrying himself to be very formal and respectful. His body language does though betray a hint of cautious alert toward both Pio and Partner. He keeps a polite, yet wary distance from the two, never approaching nearer than need be. Handing us each the large menus (surprisingly, they are in English), the young waiter and I momentarily lock eyes, and it is made clear that he somewhat understands my predicament, and is sympathetic. Pio orders some sort of fish plate special and then leans over to help Partner with his order. Partner is havin' a difficult time reading the menu. They decide Partner should have the duck. And me? Well, against greatly exaggerated objections, I order only coffee—hot! With the waiter gone, Pio decides he will now go and find the restroom and do his last remaining *grama* of *coca*.

Now it is just me and Partner; we sit in silence. He is closely examining the silverware as if it were real ornate silver. I'm gnawin' on my bottom lip, while tryin' to keep the knees from doin' the whole knockety-knock table thing. And whew, my guts are screamin with frustrating anticipation. Fuck! It's maddening! Sparky made it out of everything, surviving to arrive here in Guatemala City, so close, so close to the American Embassy, and here I must sit, sit and wait, wait for these retards to eat this absurd meal! Again the question is why? Why had Pio been so insistent on us coming here to eat before dropping me off at the embassy? Christ, by now Matrix must be foaming at the mouth with fury, and you know word is spreadin' throughout the long reaching, massive grapevine. Oh yeah, no doubts about that. And here we are sitting… Stupid, stupid, stupid!

Why, why, why? Are Pio and Partner just bein' reckless? Or is it somethin' else? I mean, if they do make it possible for me to reach the American Embassy, no way is Matrix gonna take that lightly. He's gonna have their heads (literally). Aughg, what to do?

The waiter arrives with *cervezas* and coffee; before leaving, our eyes again meet and his are sad, sad for me! Oooh shit. If I'm gonna run, now—at this very moment—is the time to go, what with Pio in the restroom and all. But Goddamn, once out those doors, having no clue what so ever as to even which direction the American Embassy is, to just run aimlessly in this densely populated city is nuts—desperate, crazy nuts! In broad daylight like this, Sparky might just as well be a red flag runnin' in the streets! Down here, I do stand out that much. (Buddy! What to do, what to do? Should we bolt! Now this very instant? We might not get a better chance. Man, just hold tight and keep playin' it. Try to learn more of direction and distance to the embassy. Yeah, okay.)

Pio returns lookin' like he is feelin' really, very good! And he is giggling to Partner about how nice a place he thinks this restaurant is, etc. Soup arrives for Pio, as does Partner's duck. Evidently, Partner's duck plate was meant to be an appetizer, because that is all it is. Pio finds this greatly funny and looks to me for joining in on the laughing. Patting Partner on the shoulder, Pio informs him he is no longer hungry (surprise, sur-fucking-prise) and that Partner can now have his soup and fish plate. (Oh Skippy, it's takin' just about all Sparky's got to refrain from jumpin' up and runnin' the hell outta here!) In one gulp I send half a cup of steamin' hot coffee down my throat. Partner, bein' a sport, accepts the soup, but the fish plate he will have only on condition of sharing half with me. Pio, thinking the gesture outstanding, exclaims insistence, "Yes! Devon, you must eat. Eat! If you want to go to the embassy, then you must eat. Ha ha ha!" (Uh, that is funny, Pio.) However, his eyes do reveal hint of earnest truism within this jesting statement. He wants me to eat. And so eat Sparky does. Slowly at first, but then the eating sensors kick-in, becoming very much alive. The smell is wondrous; saliva is flowing; and stomach is kneading itself with constrictions for the food to come. Jesus, how long had it been since last eating anything? Hhmm, can't remember, and really, what does it matter? Wow! This fish, rice, and beans are fuckin' *bon—délicieux!* (Man, slow down. Must not let them see how hungry you actually are.) Ooops, too late. Pio and Partner have, of course, taken notice; they are watchin' intently with satisfied amusement. The nice looking young waiter has noticed as well. He is right there pouring more fresh hot coffee, smiling, and even patting me (discreetly) affectionately on the back. His warm closeness is very much felt and appreciated. The young man (I just know) is gay. I like him immensely. His eyes are on Sparky constantly as if protecting. And it is known, that if within his power, he would do just that—protect.

With the meal finished and another round of *cervezas* ordered (more hot coffee and a soft touch to the back of the neck for me), Pio asks the gentle waiter for the location of the American Embassy and how best to get there? Without hesitation, the waiter jumps into action giving directions, even drawing out the route on a napkin; after which, very brazenly, he asks, using tone surprisingly stern, "You are, then, going to be taking this man from here directly to the American Embassy? Safely and unharmed?" Pio appears to be half insulted, but before he can respond, Partner grunts, "We are going to try." The waiter quickly fires, "So then you will not mind that I telephone the American Embassy to inform them of your very soon arrival?" He nudges me, silently communicating. In no time flat, my small notepad is out and I've written down my full name and address. Handing the info up to the waiter, we both look to Pio and Partner, who in turn look to each other and silently shrug shoulders. The waiter, accepting this for an answer, hurries off to go make that damn good idea phone call.

In the time span of a cigarette smoke, the young waiter is back, excitedly informing that he had indeed made the phone call, giving the American Embassy my name and present location. "They are expecting his arrival anytime now!"

Questioning unsure blank glances go around the table. We rise to pay *la cuenta* and leave. The waiter briefly pulls me to the side while very closely whispering how he had tried to get the embassy people to come pick me up, but they had refused, claiming it was not allowed. I must come in on my own. (Yeah, well no surprise there) "Devon, if you must get away—" his eyes dart towards Pio and Partner "—run in that direction." (East?) "Keep running; stop only briefly if you must ask direction. People will know why you are running, and will point out the way. Good luck!" Our eyes lock. I want to hug him, but don't dare. His hand quickly squeezes my shoulder in sad understanding.

Outside, with the sun beaming, we are again in the car with Pio giving charged directions, as Partner somehow navigates us through the dense onslaught jumble of erratic traffic. Sparky is on fuckin' pins and needles! Is it possible? For real possible that I'm gonna actually make it to the American Embassy?

Oh Momma! There it is! That's it! Sparky can see flags! But... hey, where's the American flag? Where the hell is ol' glory? There is a large building, though nothing impressive. The compound and surrounding grounds are barricaded, but only with a wall of brick perhaps three to four foot in height, hardly towering that's for sure. Geez, a person could step right over that wall. Soldiers are patrolling and standing guard within—on the grounds of the perimeter which acts as a *sequester* consisting of perhaps one city block. A guarded island boulevard midst a sea of big city asphalt chaos, especially during rush hour. The soldiers are all wearin' camo BDUs with the powdered blue UN berets, and yep, there's the UN insignia; but, the troops are all Central American... And where is my Goddamn flag?

Partner floors it, circling around to the other side of this official perimeter. And there she is! The wondrous American flag! Oh Skippy Joe, just let me reach that flag pole! So close, so close, need only to get my ass over that ridiculously low wall and Sparky will be safe, safe, safe, on American Embassy soil! Once there nobody can touch me, right? Nobody but authorized Americans, right? Pio is screamin' for Partner to "Pull over, stop! Stop!" And I'm practically crawlin' right out through the car's window. Partner hits the brakes, thus double parking (sorta). Pio instantly is on his cell phone, excitedly informing Mr. Big Shot, whoever, of my escape. There is hostile speedy Spanish, Pio tosses the cell phone to a now fumbling Partner, then jumps from the car, swinging open my door, quietly urging, "Quickly!" Uh, no problem there. With shoulder bag in hand, I'm outta that car and about to fly, but whoa! It's then noticed all the people, huge lines of 'em waiting to get inside that building. Surprisingly Pio has grabbed my heavy backpack and leads the way at a hobbled run. Eugh, other than that there American flag, this sure don't look like no American Embassy. No it does not! And ught, the soldiers have now of course taken notice of us, and are closely watching—alerted—bringing up arms to chest level as if prepared to take aim, take aim on me! Shit, shit, shit! If this truly is the American Embassy then why aren't American marines guarding it? Huh, why? Maybe this ain't the American Embassy after all. Aughg, fuck it! Let's just stay right close to ol' Pio here. He's doin' his best to run fast with my heavy backpack. On this sidewalk paralleling the grounds perimeter wall, I refrain from just jumpin' the damn thing to follow Pio for one of the wide guarded entrances.

Hundreds of waiting people are now watching our approach with much curious interest. Several Latin UN soldiers abruptly stop us at the entrance. Pio, huffin' and puffin' for breath, asks a gasping, "American

Embassy?" Heads nod, and we are allowed to enter the yard grounds of the compound. Pio again sets off at a hobbled run, this time heading for the large building itself. However, upon almost reaching, we are brought to a halt; this time by a lone older sergeant having rocker bars under his stripe. Again Pio anxiously asks, "American Embassy?" The old sergeant calmly answers, "*Si*—yes, yes, it is here." He casually swings, pointing past the sizable, ascending stone half curve flaring steps that lead up to grand doors, allowing no admittance. The finger points to adjacent ground level glass revolving doors where long lines of people are waiting in turn to enter. Pio drops my backpack, declaring, "This is Devon. He is an American; protect him!" With that, Pio slaps me on the back, and takes off a-runnin'—gettin' the hell outta there! My head is whirlin' and Pio is gone before words can be found to thank him, or even say goodbye. Christ, now what? Confusion is flooding. (Buddy, is this for real the American Embassy, and we are alive? Buddy? Buddy!)

The old Sergeant observes my confusion, and smiling as if almost understanding, gently asks for my passport. Into his walkie-talkie he sends out the passport information to whoever. After this, he motions me to follow him. I do, to the front of the massive line of people, being many several abreast, waiting in turn to enter the building via revolving glass doors. We stop. Here, perhaps twenty feet distance from the glass revolving door entrance is a designated painted line that no one is allowed to cross without authorized approval. Obviously they let inside only a few at a time in intervals of order fitting; thus the line of waiting people moves very slowly. Also here, there is a waist high independent standing L-shaped brick wall, guessed to be used as a small fire wall. The position allows me to see through the glass revolving doors. There, just inside, are airport-like metal detectors, a baggage x-ray machine, and of course soldiers for standing guard and searching, etc. They presently are allowing no waiting persons to enter; and Sparky can't help but wonder if I'm the cause. A soldier emerges, is handed my passport, and disappears.

With the lines no longer moving, guess who is the main topic? And quiet these people are not, no they are not! Bunching up, pushing to the front for a better look-see, they are all chattering their stupid-ass exaggerated talk of me, using both English and Spanish. Fuckin' Beaners, they can care less if I hear 'em or not. Sparky has learned that this is pretty much the norm in these parts. Hell, the only time they even attempt showing marked restraint for speaking is when in fear, or tryin' to sneak up on you. Wow, they are now really comin' in on me close! Many have broken the multi-column formation and...and, if not stopped, they will have me encircled, surrounded! Oh shit! Sparky don't like this, not one bit he don't! And, there ain't one American in the lot! Aughg! You stupid, Latin, dog-faced baboons, keep the fuck away from me! This is my embassy... Mine! Ught-O, think I'll just hop 'er on close to the old Sarge here. Much to my relief, he loudly blows his whistle, getting all soldiers' attentions. Many start slowly advancing towards the ever growing crowd. The old Sarge, with whistle in mouth, has taken hold of my shoulder for stepping a few retreating steps back while his right hand drops to wooden grip of holstered revolver appearing to be as old as himself. Another soldier, an intimidating, tall, lean black Carib having squinty eyes and absolutely no facial expression, his post being obviously the revolving doors, steps forward with palm of hand resting on his own sidearm—a very modern Glock 9 mm—riding in a new, molded plastic holster. He, without a word, begins to stare down those at the foremost head of this blundering, painted line crossing herd of fools. Thus order is regained without incident, and back to the ever long multi-columned formation all monkeys go to stand, hot and bored.

A squelching comes across the Sarge's walkie-talkie and I'm led through the revolving doors. Inside, the air is cool and clean. Soldiers instruct me to put backpack and shoulder bag onto the x-ray machine's short conveyer belt. Also, all of my pockets are to be emptied. Sparky is in the process of doin' as told, when a distinctive American voice announces, "He's okay, let him through." A tall, very white, American man strolls over to stand before (and above) me. He is all smiles, smartly dressed in casual clothing, and has my passport in left hand. This smiling American, with sandy brown hair cropped short in buzz-cut fashion, introduces himself as American Ambassador Todd Boil. He extends his hand (not without noticeable reluctance) for handshake greetings, afterwards keeping hand out away from himself as if it might now be contaminated or somethin'. And really, due to my present filthy appearance, who can blame him? "What can we do for you Mr. Murfin?"

"Uh, uhm, uh—"(Jesus Christ, answer the man.) "—Uh, I need help! Protection! People are tryin' to kill me, very important people! I must get out of this country. There is a price on my head! I need embassy protection. They attacked my hotel room! They torture and kill women and children for snuff videos. They… They… I need help! They…"

The Ambassador's hand motions for calm, while interrupting, "Okay, okay, Mr. Murfin. Hhmm…" Glancing down to my open passport, "Devin? Is that the correct pronunciation? Yes, okay, very good. Devin before we can go any further here, I must ask are you carrying any drugs? Any on your possession, any at all? No? Devin are you presently high on drugs, or rather, have you recently before coming here partook in any form of drug consumption—any at all? No? Are you sure? Devin, if you have, right here and now, is the time to tell me. Because if it is discovered that you are lying, well, then we here at the embassy will not be able to help you with whatever problems you may or may not be having. You will be sent right back out that door, and I will personally have the marines escort you off the grounds. Devin, do we have an understanding?"

(Fuckin' A, is this dork serious? I'm a Goddamn American! Have me escorted off the grounds by marines. What marines! These guys sure as shit ain't no American marines. Lordy, how Sparky does wish they were… To be surrounded by good ol' American marines…)

"Uh, Mr. Ambassador, sir, understanding? Uh, yeah—yes, no! Ught, I mean yes! Yes, we have an understanding; no, I do not have any drugs on me; and no I have not been doing any drugs. But wait, yes! I did do some cocaine, but—but, that had been a long time ago! I'm clean! Here, look! Look, at my arms—no track marks. And I'll take a blood test, urine test, anything! But please, you can't throw me out on the street. It will be my death sentence. Oh God, please; it took me so long to get here. I have a wife and two young sons; they haven't heard from me since this nightmare began. They don't even know if I'm dead or alive. I need to go home. I need protection!" (Frantic my voice has become, and needless to say, many ears are pricked for hearin'.)

"Okay, okay, calm down Devin. Hey, if you're clean and not carrying, then we're here to help. Let's go upstairs and talk, shall we? You can tell me all about everything." Sparky hurriedly re-shoulders kit for following the Ambassador across a large, shiny bright floor… "So Devin, you mentioned having a wife and two sons? Aw, and here is our lovely Ms. Laura Simms."

Looking up, a young woman is seen standing on a broad landing of ascending stairs, leading to a second level. Ambassador Todd Boil lowers his voice for asking up to her if what she is holding is "the file" Laura Simms answers that it is. (Sparky is guessin' that "the file" is my file?) Laura, smiling sweetly, reveals that she already knows my name by greeting a warm "Hello Devin." Geez, the woman looks to be way too innocent for working this job in such a country as Guatemala. White American she is; having a soft plain Jane face and sparkling eyes that seem to be acting as façade for fear and nervousness within. (Hhmm, yep, there is trepidation there, behind those eyes, but why?)

"Devin, Laura here is my intern; she will one day be taking over my position as Ambassador. Isn't that right Laura? Devin, Laura will be joining us for our little talk; you don't mind do you? No? Good man." Holding his empty right hand out, as if it now contained invisible dog crap, he raises it for Laura to see, while in very exaggerated mouthing of tone quiet, announces, "Devin has been smoking. A lot!"

Sparky blurts, "Uh, uh, only cigarettes! I've only been smoking cigarettes. No drugs! I don't smoke drugs!" (Man, settle down. Yeah, right, okay buddy.) "Uh, Ma'am, please excuse my appearance. I can imagine how I must look. It's been a hard time gettin' here."

Laura gives a kind, gentle smile, as Ambassador Todd Boil, now acting all chipper, assures me not to worry; after our little talk he will see to it that I get a hot shower, nice meal, and clean bed, etc. (Damn, why is this sounding a bit too good to be true?)

After following the Ambassador up the stairs, we enter a large room, presently vacant of people, that for-real resembles a waiting room for an out-dated Department of Motor Vehicle office. There are rows of aging wooden benches, assorted mismatched straight back chairs, and even (get this) several antiquated school desk units. And it is to one of these, in the far back corner, that the Ambassador directs me to go and sit. Gosh, Sparky hasn't sat in one of these things for like ever! Fond memories of these, there are not. Dropping my backpack and shoulder bag to the floor, I slide into the silly wooden chair having attached mini writing top. My arms dangle over its edge. Ambassador Todd then abruptly announces, "Well, this is it! Welcome to the American Embassy of Guatemala." Smiling, he watches my face for the anticipated response, and of course he receives it. My mouth drops! This is just a waiting room, a place for people to sit, fill out forms, then stand in lines up there at the front counter, bein' almost the length of the room itself, now having closed wooden rolled-down reception windows, thus creating a view blocking divider wall. A divider wall with a door that must lead to official offices and such, yes? (Oh boy, why does everything gotta be a mind-fuck in this wretched country?)

Clearing my throat, "Uh, uhm, uh, Mr. Ambassador, Sir, surely you're kidding, right? I mean there's got to be more to the American Embassy than just this, right?"

"No, not really Devin; this is pretty much it. We share the building and grounds with other embassies and consulates; so this is pretty much all there is for us... Not what you were expecting?"

"Uhmm, uh, hhmm. No, not really. I sorta thought American embassies were kinda how you see 'em in the movies. You know—big grand places with elaborate furnishings and lots of elegant art." He remains silent, but his eyes are mocking. Therefore, Sparky can't resist adding, "One would think that our great country would take more pride in its embassy than this."

"Hey Devin, if you don't like it, you can leave, right now. Just go! You won't be hurting my feelings, nor anybody else's. Here, I'll even hold the door open for you."

(Oh shit, fuck me, stupid, stupid, stupid!) "Uh, no—no! Mr. Ambassador, please, you misunderstood; I do like it! I like it here very much—a lot!" With ever piercing eyes, his cocky grin broadens. He smiles, Laura smiles, I smile; we all smile! (Weird.) "Devin, Laura and I are going to step into the next room, for only a minute… and then we will be right back, okay?"

Closing the door, they disappear behind the long counter divider wall. Though they can't be seen, they sure as hell can be heard. Yes they can! In hushed tone, the Ambassador is asking to see the file. Papers are heard shuffling, then a phone call is made. "Yes, it's me. We have him. He is here right now… Okay…" (Buddy, what the fuck is goin' on? Buddy? Buddy!) Ught, the Ambassador is now speaking to Laura. "Okay, we will question him, hear his story, and you watch how he responds, all right. Ready?" Ughgt-O, what's this crap about? Watch how I respond? Respond to what? The door swings open, and here comes Ambassador Todd Boil and Laura Simms; she has in her hands the same file of papers, and now also a pen and a note pad. Before even reaching straight back chairs for sitting directly across from me, the Ambassador sternly barks, "Mr. Murfin! Have you been muling drugs?"

Again, my mouth drops, "Uh, wh-wha-what? Christ no! But, but, they did try forcing me to—to mule crack and coke.'

"Who did Mr. Murfin?"

"PRISA Airlines! That's who. And they were in their uniforms and everything. It was at the airport, and during closed hours!"

The Ambassador doesn't even bat an eye, asking, "And at what airport did this occur?"

"San Pedro Sula, Honduras!" I try to explain the events in detail, but Goddamn if this Ambassador will let me. He keeps interrupting—firing questions completely not relevant to that of which is tryin' to be told. Obviously, this guy must already know about the activities of PRISA Airlines because, unlike any normal person, he ain't even curious in hearing. No he is not! Instead, his goal at present seems to be simply interrogation 101, phase one: confuse, disorientate, and break all train of thought. Or so Sparky concludes, but why? Why is the American Ambassador doin' this? I interrupt one of his meaningless shotgun questions to ask him if the embassy had received a phone call from a waiter working at Restaurante Americas informing that I was coming and in need of help?

After a moment's pause, he answers sharply, "No! No Devin, sorry, but we did not receive any phone call concerning you." Aughg! This asshole is lyin'! Sparky can see it in his eyes. (Buddy? Man, give this guy as little info as possible. Especially, no matter what, do not confess to killing or hurting anybody. My eyes lock on to the Ambassador's; he sees that I know him to be lyin'. However, this does nothing for deterring him from pursuing his persistent insidious questioning, allowing none to be fully answered. Maddening it is becoming, and Sparky is doin' all that is within powers to keep from seein' red—and scrambled my brain is. Finally, the Ambassador softens his voice and asks, "Okay Devin, so you left your wife and sons in Mexico, and from there, you went where?" Now he is all ears, letting me tell the story from the very beginning, 'cept now my head is all jumbled. I can't keep nothin' in order. Sequences of events are temporarily muddled. I'm finding myself talking like a stuttering retard full of contradictions, and those listening (Ambassador Todd Boil and Laura Simms) are lookin' upon me as if I were just that—outta my mind! "Uh, uh, look, uh, it doesn't matter. Everything started at this hotel of horrors in Trujillo, Honduras."

"Devin you claim that two police officers and a Caucasian American with a video camera asked you to make a porno movie?"

"No! They came to my room and told me there was cocaine in the room..."

"And was there?"

"Yes. Lots of it, stashed all about the place. Also bundles of cash. None of it was mine! How could it be? I'd just gotten the room; there's no way I could be backpacking around with that much dope. It wouldn't even be possible. You don't understand how this room was setup! The hotel people said it was under construction, and they wouldn't give me another room! And, and..."

"Devin, Devin, hey! Back to the police officers and making the porn movie. You said..."

"I told you, they came to my room and said there was cocaine in the room. They said maybe it was mine, and maybe it was not. Either way though, I was going to be spending a long time in jail unless I participated in making their porno movie; but it wasn't a porno movie at all! It was a Goddamn—"

The Ambassador interrupts to ask, "Devin, have you ever been in a porno movie before?"

"Wh—what? Uh, only a few amateur videos, you know, just for fun."

Hearing this, the very square, clean-cut American Ambassador confesses that he too, back in his younger days, had also done some amateur porn. Wow, is this guy full of crap or what? Geez, it takes about all Sparky's got to keep from burstin' out laughin'. "Yeah well, this wasn't no fun porno amongst friends." No it was not! The very short-lived humor is replaced with anger, and then overwhelming sadness. I break down into for-real sobs while telling details of the torture and what was to be my true intended purpose within that God awful room.

322

Of course, nothing is mentioned of the machete and its use. No, only the flashlight is, the twenty-inch black steel MAGLITE flashlight, now belonging to Pio. Interestingly though, Ambassador Todd here, seems to now only have interest for hearing details about the creepy-crawlin' critters: crabs, spiders, scorpions, and snakes, etc. Of these, he is quite intrigued and upon hearing... What the fuck? The son-a-bitch is actually grinnin'! Grinnin' and nudgin' Laura to start writin' notes, which she rapidly is. Everything I tell thereafter, the Ambassador just waves off. He seriously doesn't want to hear any more. No, but he does want my (sorta prescribed) Valium and codeine tablets. The mention of these had been casually revealed in hopes that possibly, like everyone else down here, they would be considered nothing. And really, at the time of their being noted, the Ambassador hadn't even raised an eyebrow, but now? Now he wants them. All of them. Upon receiving the bulging plastic zip-lock baggy, Mr. Ambassador lets out a long whistle to express his exaggerated surprise for its size and the amount within. Sparky tells him, "I haven't taken any for days now!" But the Ambassador pretends not to hear, and strongly declares the pharmaceuticals confiscated. "Uh, no problem." And so, we three sit there. Ambassador Todd Boil and Laura Simms are both eying me intently. Every time I go to say somethin', a hand is raised indicating silence. These two do not want to hear any more of my tale. No, instead they want to play this sheep-headed game of silence, in attempts (guessin') to make Sparky feel uncomfortable and watch his body language? Yeah well, you all just go right on ahead. After what I've been through, we can do this all night long and it won't bother me—just so long as we stay here in the embassy. As if reading my deliberations, they both excuse themselves and disappear into the next room.

Sitting here alone to ponder, my bladder sends report that it has not been emptied since early this morning (now seeming like a lifetime ago). It is in dire need of a draining. Also, a cigarette sure would be nice. However, glancing about the room for unlikely ashtrays, my eyes even search the floors, and in doin', lock upon filthy, once bright red Converse high-tops. Damn, to think these puppies had been brand spankin' new at the beginning of this regrettable nightmare for a journey. Geez, now look at 'em. Whoa—ah! Head is spinnin' with flashin' visions and remembrance! Just like at the American lady's hotel in Trujillo, emotions are rushing in upon realizing acceptance of what had been experienced—and survived. My God! Chest heaves for breaths cut short and tears are gushin'! My first instinct is to clamp down and keep this emotional onslaught of weakness silent and hidden, but in doing, I hear Ambassador Todd and Laura whispering shared comments while secretly observing me from the other room. They are just on the other side of a closed, rolled-down reception window of divider counter. Clearly, they are psychoanalyzing my (thought to be) private break down. Ol' Todd Boil can be heard instructing good little intern Laura on how to interpret my *reveille* of inner bouts. Well well, aren't you the sneaky shrink; who'da thought ambassadors were trained in such. What the hell! Mention of Matrix is made. My heart freezes! Ambassador Todd is now sharing his concern with Laura on how Matrix should be handled. Stepping away from the rolled-down reception window, a cell phone call is made to whoever; both my name and Matrix's are mentioned before moving out from ear shot, becoming completely inaudible.

Oh fuck me! Matrix? Sparky didn't mention nothin' to them of Matrix. No he did not! Not one single thing! So that means they (Ambassador Todd Boil and Laura Simms) already know of Matrix. Damn straight they do. And really, how could they not? But uh, ught-O, they then must also know all about me. Sure, that would explain why Ambassador Todd hadn't wanted to hear the details. He's already heard everything. Hhmm, yeah, but which version? The one of me bein' a drug crazed, murdering, rapin' pervert, or the real one? Either way, this is not good. No it is not! This means he knows things that he most definitely should not, like me brutally killin' people! Self defense or not, it's my word against important big shots. (What to do buddy, what to do buddy? Buddy? Aw, Goddamn you buddy!)

Blowin' my nose into dirty, once red rag hanky, and wiping eyes, the door opens and Ambassador Todd emerges, but no Laura. He is acting to be in a very good mood, informing me that it is "Closing time. Laura went home." He is pretending not to notice that I've been cryin'. The chipper Ambassador, holding his mini cell phone up wiggling, informs how we are going to first call my wife. (Yeah Skippy Joe!) Then, after that, he's going to take me to a nice hotel: Mr. Benny's bed and breakfast. (No fuckin' way!) Following a moment of complete disbelief, Sparky closes his mouth, clears throat, and as calm as can be managed, asks, "Uh, Mr. Ambassador, sir, surely you can't be serious?" But oh, he is, almost sarcastically exclaiming how, "Mr. Benny and his wife own and operate the place. It's nice, clean, and very affordable Devin; and it's only a few blocks from the embassy. Isn't that great Devin? And Mr. Benny's wife cooks the best…"

"No! No please, Mr. Ambassador, please, you don't understand. I cannot go to a hotel! They will kill me there! Please hear me… If I'm there, the place will be attacked!" The Ambassador is softly grinnin' a mocking laugh, while expressing how ridiculous this thinking is.

(Ridiculous my ass!) Sparky begs him to let me stay here, at the embassy. "Mr. Ambassador, please, the embassy must have some sorta safe room, or, or—a holding cell! Surely there is somethin' like that here, right? Anything, anything at all? There has got to be a way for me to stay here—at least for the night!"

"No, sorry Devin, but there's nothing like that here Ha ha! I think you've seen too many movies." Still grinning, he goes on to add that since they (the American Embassy) share the building with other embassies and the likes. For security purposes, everyone, excluding the so-called marines, must be out of the building and off the grounds by eight o'clock. No exceptions.

"Uh-uh, political asylum! Mr. Ambassador, sir, I'm requesting political asylum! Hell, this whole damn government down here is wanting me dead! You can't not grant me political asylum. Please, I'm an American!"

The answer, however, is basically, "Nope, no can do." The only person they ever did such a thing for here in Guatemala City, was for some drug cartel in need of protection because he was rolling over and squealing. And that had been over ten years ago. (Oh fuck me!) "Man, Mr. Ambassador, you mean to tell me that a non-American drug cartel can receive protection from the American Embassy, but an American tourist such as myself cannot?"

Laughing, he answers, "Yes, Devin, it would appear so. But hey, I don't make the rules. Devin look, you will be more than safe at Mr. Benny's. I will walk you there; we will get you checked in for the night. You can take a hmm, very needed hot shower; and I'm sure if you ask Mr. Benny, he will have his wife cook you up something. Devin, she is a very good cook—trust me. After which, of course, you will get some sleep, in a nice, clean, soft bed. Now how does that sound, huh?" (Uh, gee, let me think; sounds like a fuckin' nightmare!) "In the morning, first thing, you will walk yourself back here to the embassy and I will personally process your paperwork and see to it that you are on a flight for the United States. Devin, by this time tomorrow, you will be home with your wife and sons!"

"Uh, Mr. Ambassador, sir, that sounds great; but please, not another hotel. Please, you don't understand…"

"Hey, Devin, I'm going out of my way here to help. If you don't want it, you are more than free to go and find your own lodging for the night, and I'll see you back here in the morning; it's that simple. But, Devin, you must be off these grounds by eight o'clock. Are we clear?" Glancing down to his watch, "Devin, hey, let's make that phone call to your wife, shall we?"

"Uh, yeah sure." After giving the phone number, which seriously, the Ambassador seems to have known all along, Sparky really needs to pee, like right now! Sharing this urgency with Ambassador Todd, he, punching numbers on his mini cell phone, tells me the bathroom is out the door and down the hall.

Staring at the shiny bright wall tiles, I stand at a urinal, and drain my lizard while drifting into thought of what the real chances are for surviving another night, in yet another hotel. Jesus Christ! Hhmm, Devin-Devon, somehow managed to divert himself once again from the sternly instructed path of his demise; no *problema* though, because the funny looking American Ambassador is going to take Devon to a nice, low budget, Guatemalan hotel. Wow, something is really not right here. This Ambassador Todd Boil is all act. He knows of Matrix, and therefore he has got to know somewhat of me and my predicament and recent past acts of, uh, bloody desperation, and yet he is playin' ignorance. Why? What's he up to? Shaking my dick, it goes back into the zipper fly of French camo BDUs. Glancing into the mirror, oh yeah, Sparky is lookin' good! Lordy-lordy, I look like a blondie-haired Charlie-fuckin'-Manson wannabe!

After vigorously scrubbing my hands and face, and retying long ponytail, I head 'er on back to the room Todd Boil calls the "American Embassy". He is on his mini cell phone, just chattin' away. "Why speak of the devil; here he is now! Hold on Nancy, and you can talk to him yourself." Cupping the cell phone with hand so Nancy can't hear, he whispers, "Devin, she is understandably quite upset. She has been very worried and has had little sleep." (Gee, guess that makes two of us.) "I have assured her that I am personally taking you to a nice clean safe hotel, and that tomorrow we will have you on a flight for home. Devin, make the conversation as brief as possible, and know, that these cell phones are not secure lines. Anyone could be listening in. Do not say anything that you might not want overheard. Understood? Okay, good. Now say hello to your wife." I receive the mini cell phone. (Hell, I don't think Sparky's ever even talked on one of these things before. Damn, what does a man say to his wife when in a situation such as this?) "Uh, hello?"

"Devin—Devin! Are you all right? Why haven't you called me! You call from a Honduran airport telling me that you are in trouble, people tried to kill you, make you mule drugs… I'm supposed to contact your mother and American embassies… and then you tell me you are going into Guatemala! Devin, that's the last I heard from you!" Her voice is ultra loud and hyper. Holding the tiny, nothing of a phone out away from my ear, Ambassador Todd hears her as well. He is all grins and nods, as if in approval. "Devin, I haven't slept since. I've called embassies and newspapers. Nobody can do anything! Nobody understands what you are even into! What's going on! Todd Boil tells me you look like shit, smell like alcohol and thinks you've started drinking again? We both know you've been doing drugs!" (Aughg! If Sparky hears one more thing about drugs!)

"Uh, uh… No dear, I haven't started drinkin', and my drug use has not been all that much… I haven't done any for days…"

"Yeah right, Devin. I know you… You don't do anything in moderation. I don't even know why you went on this crazy trip. You know this was all your idea! Your idea! You up and leave your family…"

"Uh, hon, the Ambassador here is motioning for us to make this call brief." He is too, lookin' like some tall, grinnin', slack-jawed idiot. "Look, Nancy, he wants to put me into a hotel. I have been hit at every hotel I've gone to. They know where I am. If the Ambassador puts me into a hotel, they will simply come and kill me. I have used up all my playing cards. Tonight, I will not be able to get away." (Oh fuck you Todd! I'm hurrying.) "Sweetheart, please understand, I cannot go to a hotel—" (Sparky is very much aware of how his dry hollow sounding voice must be coming across, but really the only other alternative is much angered hysteria, which must stay checked-in.) "—Please dear, tell the Ambassador not to put me in a hotel."

"Devin, Devin! Todd Boil has assured me that the hotel is safe. He personally knows the couple that own the place; and it's only blocks from the embassy. Devin, he also told me that it's right across the street from a Korean military base. Devin, you will be fine. Just go with Todd, stay calm and get some sleep. Tomorrow you will be home. Thank God!" Ambassador Todd can hear her every word. My wife is anything but quiet; very excitable, she is. The Ambassador is now insisting we end the call. Sparky informs Nancy of this, and she shrieks, "Devin! Just lock your hotel door and stay there! Nothing is going to happen to you. Whatever you do, do not leave the hotel. Dev—"

"Nancy. Nancy! Here's the Ambassador. I love you. Bye…"

Ambassador Todd snatches up the mini phone, and acting as if everything is peachy, he gives Nancy some light-hearted assurance that everything will be fine, and not to worry, etc. And that is that.

Reluctantly, Sparky gears up and follows the Ambassador out of the soon to be closing embassy building… Across the outside grounds we go. Fuck me! The sidewalk! We are no longer on embassy soil! Here Ambassador Todd instructs me to wait; wait for him to fetch his bicycle. Yep, he rides his bicycle to and from work, but he's gonna walk the bike while escorting me to this great hotel. The idiot won't shut up about the place. Oh and it's right across the street from a Korean military base! Hhmm, what's up with a Korean military base bein' here in Guatemala City? Who knows, but I do know that for it to actually be here, on Guatemala soil, their power of rule is within the confines of the designated compound only. No way, even if wanted, could any Korean troops advance into the streets for interfering with anything—including stopping crimes or atrocities.

Standing alone, on the sidewalk, Sparky is feelin' very much like a rabbit finding itself exposed in the open, knowing that at any moment he's gonna be pounced upon. Despite this, a stance is presented to appear otherwise. Legs are open, back straight, shoulders squared. Shake out a cig, snap filter, and fire that baby up! Look, everybody look and see, this tattooed long-haired *gringo* ain't afraid of nothin'! (Though empty, my bladder is quivering.) The positioned UN troops, standin' and patrollin' along the inside of very low block wall bordering the compound's perimeter grounds and running parallel with outer side-walks surrounding, are all intently eyein' me; as are passers-by and groups of young adults just hangin' around watchin', watchin' me! One such group from across the street, sneer loudly, "Devon! Devon, you think you are so smart, eh? Tonight you will not be so smart!" Two within the group, I recognize from... Trujillo! What the fuck? Oh shit.

Hazy dusk is setting in. The street traffic has slowed drastically. There are, of course, no more lines of people on the guarded embassy grounds, just UN soldiers and a few authorized personnel exiting the premises. One such person is a small-framed, gray-haired man carrying himself with much authority; he stomps across the grounds to a nearby soldier standing guard along the short wall. Speaking English, the man barks to the soldier, "You! Did you see the taxicab that brought him here?" ("Him" bein' me! Jesus, the little old fucker is pointin' right at me!) The soldier nods affirmative. "Did you see the cab number?" Again the soldier nods, and sounds off the number. Mr. Barky writes the number down, spins on his heels, stomps back across the grounds, and disappears into the building. Oh no, poor Pio and Partner, and poor me.

From the far end of the embassy compound, my eyes catch sight of a white soldier, a for-real American soldier! He is wearin' standard issue American camo BDUs and a ranger cap, not the UN beret. His strides are hurried; also, he's goin' the other way. Sparky is tempted to run after him, but... Ught, here comes Ambassador Todd now, whistling a tune while steering his bicycle. I excitedly tell him about the now gone group of young people, and what they had said, and how two were recognized bein' from Trujillo. Also, I tell him about the older man coming out from the building, demanding to know the taxicab number that had dropped me off here. Ambassador Todd, shrugging shoulders, could give two shits. His mood changes to that of agitated impatience while denouncing these observations as being nothing more than delusional paranoia. And again my options are sternly reminded: I can stay out here on the streets and find my own lodging for the night, or follow him to Mr. Benny's bed and breakfast. It's completely my choice. The Ambassador, personally, does not care, but he does feel obligated in divulging how because of me, he is now going to be very late in meeting with his soon to be ex-wife and lawyer. (Well, excusez-fuckin'-moi, Toddy!)

During the walk for Mr. Benny's bed and breakfast—which turns out bein' a bit further away than what ol' Ambassador Todd had made it sound—he babbles non-stop, on and on, about his wife and coming divorce. Sparky listens as if interested, but really, the only true interest (at present) is observing urban surroundings and noting direction back for the embassy. And in doing... Fuck me! We are bein' followed by the same group having two from Trujillo. Sharing this observational fact with the Ambassador, he abruptly stops, turns on me, shouting for all nearby to hear, how I am suffering from "mental breakdown! A psychotic disorder of paranoia and hallucinations!" Bla, bla, bla. If I don't stop badgering him with this "absurd nonsense", he's gonna leave me right here and now. (Aughg, what an asshole! This guy is obviously puttin' on a show, but why?)

Of course, I apologize, but damn, can't help thinkin', Okay, if this American Ambassador truly believes his professed diagnosis, then why, oh why is he checkin' Sparky into a hotel? Especially since he knows the mere thought of goin' to such a place is flippin' the crap outta me! Geez, admittedly, there's no question I'm paranoid. Who wouldn't be, after bein' in my shoes? Besides, the paranoia that's now carried within is not a distorted reality. No it is not! I prefer to view it as keeping the edge— gross suspicion combined with red alert mode of readiness. The American Embassy had been a hope beyond all hope, but for what? To be taken back out on the street and be put into another stinkin' hotel! Oooh, you dirty son-a-bitch! If Sparky is hit tonight, killed, and body disappears, ol' Ambassador Todd here will just claim I was suffering from psychotic hallucinations and simply ran off, never to be found. And, of course, the owners of this Mr. Benny's bed and breakfast will only confirm, make somethin' up, or play ignorance. My one and only chance now is that possibly, just possibly, I'm wrong about everything, and the asinine Ambassador is right. Hhmm, at least there is some consolation that my wife knows I made it this far. (Yes, but now she is convinced, thanks to the Ambassador, that you are lost in a mindless haze of alcohol and drug bingeing. Not a good ticket to go out on. Yeah, no shit buddy, but what to do? Man, just stay sharp, focused, and assume nothing. Well, duh!)

The Korean military base is pointed out as if it were somethin' I might find comfort in knowing. By military standards, it is small—tiny small. Why is it here? What is the Korean troops' objective? Ambassador Todd professes to have "no idea." Yeah right! The American Ambassador doesn't know why the Koreans have a military base in the middle of Guatemala City? Give me a break. Damn, this guy won't give a straight answer for nothin'.

Crossing the street, we turn and enter through an open gate of the high stone-walled courtyard of Mr. Benny's bed and breakfast. The place is simple, basic, and overpriced. Just another wretched hotel. And Mr. Benny is another little gray-haired man of approximately sixty years in age. The front desk is also the so-called lounge:having some old chairs, couches, small end tables, and an obsolete Coca-Cola machine. After introductions, Ambassador Todd explains to Mr. Benny that I have had some problems in the past with people bothering me during my stays at certain hotels. Very boisterously, Ambassador Todd adds, "And under no circumstances is Devin here to be bothered, disturbed, or even visited! Devin, you don't want any visitors do you?" I look at him like he's outta his fuckin' mind. "Okay, so no visitors. Is that understood Mr. Benny?" Mr. Benny, with eyes growing wide, silently nods. "Not even from any of the other guests. I do not want this man disturbed. Devin here just wants to be left in peace, take a hot shower, and get a good night's rest of serious sleep. Is that understood Mr. Benny? Good. You have my phone number: I want to be called immediately if Devin is bothered in any way or form. Agreed? Okay."

Mr. Benny is still nodding from the overacted instructions received. He clears his throat, and begins his own line of bull. He goes into the whole spiel about how he and his wife have both owned this place for some twenty-odd years now, and never in that time has a guest ever not had a pleasant peaceful stay. (Yeah right, Sparky's heard this before.) "Rest assured, no one will be bothering this young man. Not here. This is the safest hotel in all of Guatemala City! We have the Korean military across the street for our neighbors! Ha ha!" The hotel's registry is slid over for signing. Ambassador Todd glances to his watch again, comments on bein' late for the appointment with ex-wife, lawyer, etc.

He confirms our meeting in the morning,—eight o'clock sharp, at the embassy—and with that, he's gone.

Mr. Benny plucks a key from a row of several hanging. He walks straight across the floor to a room closest to the short walkway entrance. Opening the door, he declares this one being mine. The room is a bit unusual in that it has large wall windows to both the front and back. One such glass set-up is facing the outside courtyard, and the other is facing the inside front desk area (strange). Also, against the left wall are bunk beds. (Bunk beds?) The right wall has a protruding closet type thing. Beyond is the tiny bathroom consisting of toilet and vanity sink; no showers here. Mr. Benny informs that the showers are shared and located across the lounge area and down the hall (fuck).

I follow Mr. Benny back out into the front desk lounge area, and ask him politely for some money to buy two bottles of Coca-Cola. He knows my credit is good. With two frosty cold bottles of Coke in hand, I head 'er for my room, and in doing, notice to the left a service-type door leading into another part of this hotel. The door has a solid sliding panel—now open—and a woman near the same age as Mr. Benny is on the other side sneakily glarin' through at me. Our eyes meet, and immediately the panel slams shut (Christ).

Once inside my room, the door is quickly locked; surprisingly, there is a deadbolt lock on this door (sorta). Well, at least it's better than nothin'. Glancing about, I have the strong desire to pull my standard room check, but I've no flashlight. Pio has it, and (guessin') now also has no life. Hitting the light switch, details of the room are absorbed. Goddamn glass slat jalousie windows are to the front and back, also one is above the toilet, for drawing air in from the hotel's entrance walkway. There is a typical hotel floor mounted A/C unit underneath the room's courtyard windows. It is presently not on, nor will it be. The windows facing the front desk lounge area are between the door and the heads of the bunk beds, centering a short nightstand with small desk light. The mattresses to the bunk beds are held in place, supported with removable one-by-three boards. Also there is a silly little hook ladder for getting up to the top bunk. My weapons of defense if attacked are, once again, pretty obvious—and limited.

Looking through the windows facing the front desk and lounge, Sparky's eyes go to the service door with sliding panel. Again, it is open with the same woman gawking, and with her is a dark boy of (guessin') twelve to thirteen years of age. Mr. Benny sees me noticing, and yells for them to close the panel and stay away from the door! His tone reveals the woman and boy to be his wife and son. Mr. Benny himself then disappears for joining them in the room beyond the panel door. An argument of sorts ensues. The wife starts shrieking how she does not mind Todd Boil bringing people here to stay, but not people "like this—this, Devon! Not for purposes as this one. I do not like it! Do you hear? This is not right. He should not be here. I do not want him here!"

Mr. Benny whines, "Aw, what can I do? Todd Boil brings him here, I must give him a room. I have no choice. This is just how it is. Eh, it is now getting dark; I am going to close the gates."

Gee, guess leaving the room for that hot shower, is, well… No way! Also, somethin' is strongly suggesting that it is now time to kill the light and adjust all drapes. I must be able to see out while still bein' hid. Sparky silently walks the soon to be pitch-black dark room for learning its familiarity. Meanwhile, Mr. Benny closes the gates, enters the lounge area, locks the short front desk, and shuts off all but one glowing light. He glances to my room, walks past, and takes exit via server door. From the other room, he is heard informing his wife how my lights are out, and more than likely, I am already asleep. This, however, does little in calming the irate Mrs. Benny: her ranting begins anew with protests for my being here. And from within the woman's high-pitched yelling, more than a hint of Carib accent comes to surface. This, combined with noted skin color and facial structure, pretty much confirms the woman bein' of Garifuna descent. Mrs. Benny, after a bit, finally quiets down the venting, but does keep repeating, "This is all bad—all very bad." Oh boy, this night oughta prove real fuckin' interesting.

Two swallows drain the first bottle of pop (Coke). The other is uncapped using end of Bic lighter, but though still thirsty, restraint is called for not drinking. It's gonna be a very long night. Setting the bottle down, I then go and piss. During this, the front gate's buzzer is heard. Mr. Benny, grumbling, goes to see who it is. A young woman's voice is heard askin' for—guess who? Fuck me! She is askin' to see Devon. Devon has invited her; and she is expected. Fortunately, Mr. Benny sternly tells her that there is no one here by the name Devon. The young woman leaves, and Mr. Benny returns to the room beyond the server door. By the sounds within, this is likely to be the kitchen. He is softly swearing, and his wife is verbally attacking. Her tone is that of anxious fear and desperation. She is wanting her husband to call Todd Boil right now—this very moment—and have him come and get me out of here. "If this is so important to Todd Boil, then he should have this Devon stay at his house, not ours!" Damn straight lady! You tell him. Come on Mr. Benny, listen to your wife and call Ambassador Todd Boil. Sliding under the bunk bed to test for amount of space and silence to do such, then rolling out in one fluent move, go onto lower bunk, then top. Surprisingly, this can be accomplished with smooth speed of almost complete silence.

The front gate's buzzer is again heard. This time it's a man's voice having grim authority claiming to be *policia secreto* asking for me. Mr. Benny answers him that there is no guest by the name of Devon: "Only the European tourists are here." And this, admirably, Mr. Benny firmly sticks to, even when the man growls that I had been observed entering the property with Todd Boil. Still, ol' Mr. Benny holds his ground, denying any knowledge of a Devon. (Buddy, the shit's a-buildin' with net closing in. What should we do—what should we do? Buddy? Buddy! Goddamn you buddy. And Goddamn you Todd Boil! FUCK!) Hhmm, Sparky notices that this *policia secreto* does not refer to Todd Boil as bein' American Ambassador Todd Boil; hell, come to think of it, neither has Mr. Benny or his wife ever once been overheard using the title. Odd, ain't it? Aren't Latins notorious for bein' big on titles? And Ambassador is, without a doubt, an impressive title. Ught, the man claiming to be *policia secreto* is gone. I slide silently off the top bunk and take up position in an upright space tucked away between room's door and standing closet thing. From here, I can see (somewhat) through the large courtyard window and lounge window.

Mr. Benny is now back inside trying to calm his wife. She is again shrieking for her husband to call Todd Boil and get me out of here! Also, she is askin' if he does not, "How are we to hide Devon? They are going to be all around this night!" Mr. Benny shushes his wife, demanding she stop using my name. He does not want the other guests to hear. His voice then drops to quietly convince, "Devon is in his room; no lights, he is asleep. You saw, he is a very tired man. He will sleep through it all. Do not worry, no one will know he is here—" Mrs. Benny loudly interrupts to point out the absurdity of this, since people are already comin' and askin' for me. Footsteps are then heard up on the roof. People are noisily walkin' about on the roof! Mr. Benny rushes out to confront them. He is met with jeering mockery from a group of young people up on his roof taunting, and demanding Devon be brought out! Mr. Benny puts on a good show, loudly retorting, "There is no Devon here! Devon, Devon, Devon! Everybody wants this Devon, but there is no Devon here!" Mr. Benny then spins on heels, stomps away, declaring how he is going to start setting up more outside lights!

Yeah, you go Mr. Benny. Get some more outside lights. Like that's really gonna make a difference. Dumb ass retard! (Buddy, how come he's not calling Todd Boil? Why, why, why? Buddy? Buddy! Crap.)

Young people, male and female, are movin' about freely up on the roof. They are talking and giggling. The Carib accent of most is indeed noted. Lordy, how to get out of this one? Maybe I should make a run for it! Run for the oh so safe, protecting Korean military base across the street. Actually, the thing is a bit further than just across the street. Yes it is, having many obstacles from here to there. And of course, with the lingering street gang up on the roof, there is no possibility for sneakin' out. No, it will have to be an all out dash! Which will surely bring down a prompt pursuit, from the entire outside perimeter (guessin') to be now literally swarmin' with waiting murderin' hoods! Gosh, assuming that Sparky, by fluke of sheer luck does succeed in gettin' up and over Mr. Benny's tall gated stone wall, dodges those surely waitin', and arrives (still alive) at the guarded compound of Korean military base, there is no guarantee (and a whole lotta doubt) that they can protect or give asylum, especially if the Guatemalan police are involved. (Buddy, is it worth it? Worth the risk? Buddy buddy! Man, don't be a fool. The time for that is too late.) Those up on the roof have been joined by many others, others that are now on the ground, spreading out and forming into chatty groups. Numbers are growing rapidly, my name "Devon" is bein' mentioned all over the place. Goddamn you to hell, Todd Boil.

Aughg-oh, whoa. What the fuck? Oh nooo! It's my bowels. My bowels are full from the food Pio made me eat earlier. Now contents are wanting seriously to evacuate, and like bad! Sphincter and abdominal muscles constrict for holding back the assaulting force. Not now—not now! Hunched over clutching stomach, beads of sweat are drippin'. Three heads appear with hands cupped for tryin' to look into the room's courtyard window. My room is blacker than black, and so they cannot see me. Still, this does nothin' in swaying the persistent bowels so determined. Once the three heads move on, Sparky hurriedly waddles for the bathroom. Just as I'm about to sit on the toilet for that oh so needed blast of relief, the hotel's entrance walkway door opens and in come several giggling, whispering young monsters! They are, of course, in search of me. So much for defecating now; the bloated, insistent bowels are just gonna have to wait. Yes they are!

Goddamn these fuckin' street gangs! How many are there—how big are they? Jesus, it's impossible to get away from 'em. They know I'm here, but don't know which room.

Time for getting back to my posted position beside the closet. Sounds of a man and woman frolicking are heard coming from the showers. The couple have a distinct British accent. Some from the gang go to check the couple out. They return, confirming that the showering occupants are not me, but rather "English tourists here for the *fiesta*." One petite gang bitch coos, "Yes, tonight will be a great party. The angels will be about us all." Someone tries my door knob, but the lock holds true. Uh, *fiesta*, party, angels? What kind of shit is this? And with Brits partaking? Aughg-oh, bowels again remind of their needs, but to accommodate is not possible. No it is not! The way they are rumbling and crampin', this is gonna be one intense bowel movement with some loud amplified noise sounding off! Aaw, euw, wow, must be doin' somethin'. Move— step lightly about the room—but do not make a sound. And so, buckled over, in stealthy silence (silence, except for the squashing grumblings of pressurized activity within lower abdomen), I cautiously pace from window to window. Even in breathing, Sparky has pretty much mastered the art of hyperventilating in silence.

From all windows, I can see and hear more and more gang members arriving and milling about. The ones in the lounge are going through the front desk. They've broke it open and now have the hotel's registry book out, 'cept none can read. And so a runner is sent for fetching someone that can. Meanwhile, others have opened the old Coca-Cola machine and are helpin' themselves. Obviously, Mr. Benny and wife are layin' low. Why isn't she stoppin' this? And more importantly, why ain't she callin' Ambassador Todd Boil? All too soon, a non-illiterate shows up, and my room becomes sur-fuckin'-rounded. A cell phone is used to report the finding. Orders are instructed back, and loudly relayed amongst all: to hold tight position around my room, but not to attack until Matrix the Orc arrives. Gee-golly, Matrix is comin'. Mercy, no surprise there, but Matrix the Orc? What the hell is an Orc? Hhmm, It's gotta be short for Oracle. Oh boy, right, the sick psycho is head of a satanic cult (or so everyone's been tellin' me), and has many followers from as far away as Europe. And yet there are English tourists now here—here at this very hotel for a party with angels that include these street gangers and Matrix. Matrix the Orc? Good God Almighty, what a mind fuck. Ught, here comes a vehicle slowly driving into the courtyard via rear entrance. Oh please, oh please be Ambassador Todd Boil. *Please*! Oh fuck me! It's soldiers—black Caribs, wearin' solid black BDUs—and these guys look serious as a heart attack! And more and more just keep comin'. Their weaponry is mostly M16s and Mossberg pumps havin' black synthetic stocks. Many are also sportin' modern sidearms as well. This private army is indeed locked and loaded; and they ain't here to help me. No they are not! Their objective is in taking up positions here, there, and on top block walls of the courtyard. More vehicles, soldiers, and young street gangers arrive. Also, Mr. Benny is back, directing the set-up of outdoor lighting, and lighting it is. In no time at all, they've got the whole courtyard lit up like a small football field. Geez, the whole city must be able to see the glow. Gas generators are supplying the power, and... What the fuck? Scaffolding is being assembled across the courtyard.

A great big tarpaulin is laid directly on the ground, a few yards from my window. A gloss black Chevy blazer slowly pulls up, driving over the ground tarp. It stops to allow a select number of street gangers to bring out kilo after kilo of cocaine, which is immediately cut open and dumped onto the tarp. Then gasoline cans are brought forth with liquid from 'em bein' deliberately splashed, wetting the piles of cocaine. The smell is outrageously strong. It does not smell like gasoline, but rather ether? The cocaine takes to it as if alive, pulling itself up and toward the gasoline/ether/whatever. A welding cart appears, containing two eighty-pound cylinders: one oxygen, and the other acetylene. A soldier spark-lights a flame and adjusts it to very low; he then begins to slowly run glowing flame back and forth, allowing the heat to pull the cocaine even more—forming it into hard solid rocks. When Torching Soldier gives orders, the Chevy blazer is then cautiously backed over the big crack rocks to compact them even more. The desired size seems to be that of fireplace logs. More and more kilos are bein' brought and stacked; this process is going to be goin' on for a while. An odd thing noticed is that they have installed on this two wheel welding cart a caution warning beeper device, just like large trucks have for when backing up. While the torch is in use, the beeper beep, beep, beeps! (Weird.)

Most everyone now is smoking the freshly made crack cocaine, and needless to say (for most), the mood is becoming festive. I gotta keep moving. Cannot stay in any one part of the room for too long. The lounge has a small group of gangers positioned just on the other side of my window. They are smokin' crack and discussing "Devon," how best to flush me out, etc. Sparky learns from listening that this street gang is from Trujillo, and it has been ordered by Matrix, that I be gang raped, tied to a tire, and dick cut off. "Te Orc be wantin' Devon's cock and balls wit te gold ring true dim. He he!" Also, it is learnt that some old honcho heading a very important family is desiring my tattooed skin for his wall; and, of course, I'm to be scalped with face burnt off, while still alive! (Just another fun-filled night in Central America.)

Mr. Benny and his wife are arguing in the next room beyond the panel door, assumed to be the kitchen. Mrs. Benny is again shrieking for her husband to call Todd Boil. Mr. Benny, however, stoutly refuses, and so on.

The group hangin' around the lounge window has among them a young, very attractive woman, who is obviously girlfriend to the big young man that's been instructed to lead the charging gang rape. Well, she's not one bit happy with this news of what her boyfriend must do. No she is not! She fears I will have AIDS. The boyfriend confides that he also is not keen on the idea; reason being? It is rumored Devon is a junkie, and it is common knowledge "all junkies are constipated—filled wit' shit. Yuck!" Damn, what a weird-ass fuckin' joke, and to think, Sparky is doin' all within his powers to keep from shitting my brains out! Oh how that Mandingo buck is gonna love rapin' me. Surprise surprise! Aughg, oh, can't think about it. No, must instead concentrate on removing gold scrotum ring. Matrix might end up tonight getting' my cock and balls, but Goddamn if Sparky is gonna let him get my gold scrotum bead ring.

Silently I begin working on the ring using only fingers. Whew, to open a ring this thick is difficult enough when one has pliers designed for just such. Tryin' to do so without, under normal conditions, would surely be impossible. Yes it would. But this ain't no normal condition. No it is not. And fear does give adrenaline strength of exceeding measures. Filthy red hanky rag is brought forth for aiding in securing grip. Straining determination sets in, and somehow that thick gold ring reluctantly surrenders its solid gold bead (the size of a plump pea), enabling me to slide the ring free from two harnessing skin flaps.

Without a sound, Sparky tucks the weighty gold ring and bead way down into the crevice of backpack that would be very difficult for anyone to ever find. Now, for the old lordship wanting my tattooed hide… Well, there ain't much that can be done about that. Hhmm, except for perhaps getting 'em to blast me with shotguns and such during the sure to be last-ditch throw down bayonet charge. Yeah right, wish I had a bayonet. Not sure that such a weapon would save my life, but it sure would guarantee me not bein' taken alive to endure the torturing, mutilating sport that is intended to be my fate.

To the lounge window, it is noticed that the alpha couple from this barrel of monkeys have started fucking. They are nude, her hands are up against the glass, and she is facing into my pitch-black room. He is working her from behind. The thrusting is slow and rhythmical, to the loud beat of drumming now bein' heard out over the courtyard. Sparky can see them, but they can't see me; and of course, they know this. The alpha couple (unlike previous others) really don't seem to be doin' this for purposes of attempting to lure me, although the woman is cooing my name. No, they appear to be fuckin' pretty much just for the pleasure.

They are, however, receiving gleeful support and encouragement from their surrounding crack smoking peers. A large hand-rolled tin foiled pipe smoldering with fresh crack cocaine is handed up to the couple; they, without missing a beat/stroke/whatever take turns on the pipe.

Meanwhile, headlights from another vehicle appear. Someone from the group smoking near the alpha couple asks who it is that has just arrived. A runner dashes into the lounge announcing that the Orc and witch are now here! A beefy hand comes sliding through the glass horizontal slat window. The idiot has succeeded in removing one of the glass panels and is inserting his hand into my room. Dumb ass, he doesn't realize I'm standin' right above his sneaky hand. (Christ, talk about your timing.) Matrix pulls into the courtyard, and a moment later, I slam an empty Coke bottle down (hard) onto retard's wrist! Glass shatters! The impact hammers the wrist down—through splintering glass panels below, thus cutting him very deeply—with blood a-gushin'! The severity of the cut leaves nothin' to guess; and still, his gang comrades burst into mocking laughter. The buffoon screams like a pussy, and runs down the walkway and out, toward the newly arrived Matrix.

Sparky glides across the dark room to the courtyard window for seeing; and see I do. Holy shit! There, finally, stands Matrix. He is a tall, lean black Carib, approximately fifty years old. He carries himself in a stance blazin' with relentless authority. His eyes are a livid gleam from snappin' inner loose wires, set seemingly convexed upon sharp, high cheekbones and squared jaw jutting with cruel determination. Captain Matrix is clad in black BDUs and he's even sportin' a pair of American jump boots, having shine equal to that of any drill sergeant's.

The whimpering, bloody-armed idiot runs up to Matrix for report. Matrix, however, is not the least bit interested. He roughly pushes the bleeding ganger aside, approaches my window, and just stands there, glarin' into my pitch-black room. I can feel the evil hatred, and see the set resolution. Tonight is the night that he gets his way with me. An assured confident menacing grin forms; he then spins, barkin' orders. And people do jump! Now there are two shiny black Chevy blazers parked (more or less) in front of my courtyard window. The witch turns out to be, uh, guess who? Why it's the same old woman from the Hotel of Horrors back in good ol' Trujillo. And guess who else is with 'em? No, not our pal Sergeant Lobo (though it would hardly be surprising), but rather, it's the American *gringo* cameraman. He is presently setting up video equipment. And the witch? She is tending to the young man's bloody cradled arm. He is carrying on, whimpering to point that even the old witch scolds him to shut up. Matrix the Orc is checking the progress of the crack bein' made. Also, he's stepping about, firing off orders. He wants everything to be just right for this ceremonial whatever.

There! (My heart leaps.) Over there—white people! Real white people are forming into a group out in the center of the courtyard. White men, women, and couples... They are smokin' crack from several big tinfoil pipes. And excited they are, gettin' really high. Matrix goes to greet them. They are a-smokin', jokin', and steppin' to the rhythm of (prerecorded) primitive drummings reverberating from large speakers. Upon spotting Matrix approaching, they all put hands together and do silly, giggling, playful bows. Matrix the Orc laughs along with 'em, even returning the animated bowing. Aw, no way are these tweaked out imbecile tourists gonna be able to help me. What is their purpose for bein' here anyways? Young, nude, very attractive, light-brown-skinned gangers gather to start helping the white tourists out of their clothing. While at the same time, elaborately costumed (Mardi Gras type) figures ascend the scaffoldings and begin a dance exotic.

Matrix marches back between the two Chevy blazers parked in front of my windows. He barks orders: no British visitor is allowed to approach this area without his personal invite. Also, I am not to be pulled from the room while the Brits are here. Matrix does demand that my room stay closely surrounded, and he wants to know where within the room I am at all times. "We will give the Brits their ceremony over there; and we will have our own right here. Ha ha!" It is suggested to him from one of his troops, that perhaps they should simply light up my room with one of the bright lights? Matrix answers, "No, it will only make the visiting British curious. Use the snake lights and NODs.'

NODs? NODs, short for Night Observation Devices. The US military are the only folks I know that used this abbreviation for such illuminating optics and damn, last heard, it wasn't even bein' used by them anymore. Hhmm, bet my left nut ol' Matrix here has received some military training at Fort Benning back in the day Sparky did. During that period, we were sharing the base with a whole lotta Central Americans brought in for learning tactics: mostly catering to the Nicaragua mess, but there were others.

Heroin is then suggested; Matrix considers a moment, gives approval, but warns, "I do not want him too doped up. I want Devon able to feel everything I am going to have done to him. Ha ha!" (Ught, earlier today he wanted me on coke. And now, it's heroin? Go figure.) Matrix the Orc is tonight a very busy man. Many are requesting his attention, including the American *gringo* cameraman, old witch, and of course, the absurd British, who are now calling for his presence. And me? Well, Sparky is doin' his best to play ghost, tryin' desperately to float about this room undetected and yet, still watch all flanks. Yep, Casper the ghost, just about to literally shit his brains out!

Two soldiers, who appear to be Matrix's personal shotgun guards, bring forth from the vehicle, twin sets of NODs and snake lights. They begin to demonstrate the How-To operations of the equipment to several select male street gangers. It is more than evident that although the young men are very excited in bein' privileged to use such high-tech gear, they really aren't up to following the instructions required. Damn, they are high as a mother fuck off that bizarre crack bein' made and smoked. Hell, the fumes alone… Wow, strong it is, even in my room. The soldiers hasten the demonstrations to get back to their post of covering Matrix's every move. He is now strutting around all over the place, barking out orders, demanding this or that, seeing to it that everything is how he wants. Of course, his demeanor when dealing with the ludicrous Brits is that of humble being, wanting only to please. Sorta like playin' host to a big party; and Skippy, this is his party!

The giggling ganger monkeys, havin' big white teeth gleamin', begin to fumble adolescently with what they obviously consider impressive equipment. Snake lights worm their way through pried glass slats of jalousie windows, and NODs are clumsily slid onto heads and pressed up to the glass.

Not knowing what else to do, I swiftly move about the room, stopping here and then there; with each location, Sparky flicks his Bic. Though only a brief snap of flame, it does, due to darkness of the room, seem very bright. And my reason for doin' this? Mostly it's just to shake things up a bit. I do remember how when back in the army, we had used large mounted NOD scopes while on certain night maneuvers; from only light of the stars and or moon, you could identify troop movement from a mile away. If anyone lit a cigarette, blinding bright it would seem; and if an illumination flare went up—forget it! But that had all been a long time ago, in big terrain of the outdoors. I really have no idea how these little NODs respond to such light when bein' used in close quarter situations—such as viewing into gloomy pitch-black hotel rooms, having heavy lighting in the rear. However, each time Sparky does flick the Bic, there is much excited commotion. "Ter! Ter he is! Over de ter! No, he over here now! He keep movin' about!"

The alpha couple are softly giggling, at the back lounge window. The male whispers, "Devon? Sphsisst—Devon! Dat is very good. You keep dim runnin' about. Devon, grab te snake light and pull it from dim; it will make the Orc very angry wit dim." The girl coos, "Yes Devon, do this. He he! We want to watch you trick dim. Te Orc will not be pleased if dey lose his special *militar instrumentos*." The boyfriend shushes her, cautioning not to be so loud.

Gliding over to see: yep, they are still fucking up against the lounge window. However, they are now presently the only ones inside guarding this position so close.

Okay, so these two want communication; let's briefly appease and see what comes. Swallowing thick bitter dryness, surprisingly, voice of smooth, quiet, cool calm is found.

"Hey, how you two doin'?"

"He he! We be better den you Devon."

"Man, ain't that the truth."

"Ay Devon, you see what we doin' here?"

"Yeah—yeah, I see, it looks good. Your woman is very attractive. Same as my wife back home. Man, sure wish I was home now with her, instead of bein' trapped here, in this room. Is there any way you guys can get me outta this mess?"

"Ha ha! No mon, Devon, you are to die dis night. But first, you will be hurt severely." The young woman interjects, "Devon, he must rape you. It is how te Orc orders. Possibly you will do a trick to prevent dis?"

"Gee, lady I sure wish I could; believe me. But I'm all out of tricks."

The big buck flatly states, "Aw Devon, you are never out of tricks." Then, lowering his voice even more, "Devon, when te time comes, der will be many of us chargin' you. Perhaps when fighting, you will watch for me? If you allow, I will kill you quickly. Dis will benefit us both greatly; understand? Dis will be only our secret. Okay?"

"Yeah sure, sounds like a plan; I'll try." Time to change locations.

Catching the movement of a snake light worming in from the front courtyard… eh, fuck it, let's see what happens. YANK! Surprisingly, the monkey feeding it in has a very firm grip; his hands are pulled through the jalousie slat, shattering glass! And still he don't let go. No he does not! And thus ensues a very, very brief sorta tug o' war, with much rousing chaos of shouting. Knowing there is no time for such crap, I urgently attempt to snap the thing, but it won't snap; it does however, bend to a crunching kink before bein' let go, by me. The snake light has been broken. Matrix is there howling anger! Also, it sounds as if he is physically hurting the young man. The NODs and snake lights are then ordered to be put away.

The heroin has arrived and command is given to have spears readied.

(Spears?) A peek reveals a soldier approaching, holding a jumbo zip-lock baggy. Damn, the thing must certainly contain at least a full pound of brown powdered heroin. Jesus, and to think, everybody and their mangy dog had said there was no heroin in this region. Yeah well, guess there is now! Matrix again gives strict reminder of not too much. He does not want me doped up. Just enough to slow my reaction time for when they do rush the room. Several monkeys begin to work on long stout poles. Attached via duct tape looks to be somethin' long and sharp. The heroin is instructed to go to the rear (lounge area).

Alpha couple again want my attention: "Sphsisst—Devon. Devon, you der? Devon, you like heroin? Come see. Come see what we have for you. Can you see?"

Whispering, while gliding, never staying in any one spot for reasons obvious (need to keep body racking bowels from having way), "Yes, I can see. That's a lot of heroin."

"Devon, dat was very funny what you did to te snaky-light. He he! You like heroin?"

"Yes, yes, I like it very much—*muy gusto*."

"He he! *Muy gusto*… Devon, you are very funny. Come, we will give you heroin."

"Uh, okay, can I have it all?"

"No Devon, but you can have as much as you desire."

"Can I have it in a syringe loaded with enough to overdose and quickly die? If so, you will not have to rape, fight, or kill me. It will be easy. The Orc won't care. I will be dead and everyone will be happy."

"No Devon, sorry; we have no syringe. We can only blow te smoke to you."

I give no response. The alpha couple stop fucking long enough to fill one of the huge aluminum tin foil pipes with powdered brown heroin. Soon it is fired up—lit—and again the two are back at it while puffin' sucks from the jumbo pipe. After which, the buck turns the pipe around with stem entering room through busted slats of jalousie window. Covers the bowl with hands and mouth for blowing in long streams of room-filling smoke. Of course Sparky recognizes the distinct aroma. It is indeed heroin—uncut top grade heroin. The young woman herself even comments on how good this heroin is. The male, bellowing lungs for blowing, quietly bitches about how he can no longer feel his dick. The young woman lifts petite hindquarters up off his monster size boner, drops to her knees and starts throating. And erect he still is! Geez, how is this even possible, what with all the crack and now heroin bein' smoked?

Mrs. Benny is heard again shrieking in the kitchen for her husband to do something. Something to stop this. "They are goin' to kill him! This should never be! Never be! Not here! Do somethin'. Go out there and help him! It is said he has a wife and sons... Oh look! They are now fillin' his room with that *drugo* smoke. He will not be able to defend himself. You must stop this!"

Mr. Benny whines, "Aw, what is it you want me to do? I can do nothing. I did not bring him here. He is now in God's hands. Besides, Devon is doing okay. They have not succeeded in getting him. He is fine. He will figure something out. You will see."

Mrs. Benny screams, "How can he figure somethin' out! They have 'im surrounded! They are druggin' him! Oh how I hate that Todd Boil! He should be in Devon's position at this very moment; maybe then, he would not think himself so smart. I hate him. I hate Todd Boil for bringing this to our home!"

There must be more heroin, because now there are two more pipe blowers at the front courtyard windows sendin' in streams of smoke. I'm actually quite impressed that so much smoke can be pumped into a room via such a simple method. At first, attempts are made not to breathe any, but this is impossible. Plus, since my heart's a-thumpin' a hundred miles an hour—sendin' blood surgin' throughout my entire body, almost too much for needed extreme stealth and keeping of calm head. Eh, a little heroin might just work to my advantage. (Yeah yeah, sounds like goofy logic, but until you've been here...)

The hunched down posted monkeys with crude spears at my now busted open courtyard jalousie windows are easy to avoid; and so avoid I do. Out beyond the two parked Chevy blazers, there in the center of the overly-lit courtyard, the Brits have each partnered off with attractive young gangers, bein' both male and female. They have formed a huge circle and all are nude, bent fucking—humpin' and bumpin'—gyrating to the loud bass of rhythmic drumming, blarin' from large speakers stacked. Soldiers are about, holding their posts—most bein' positioned atop the high block walls of ground's perimeter—their guard of course bein' that within.

The process for makin' the outrageous amounts of strange crack is still at full-throttle. And the *gringo* cameraman is now set up for the filming of something. Whatever it is, it ain't for the stupid Brits, that's for damn sure. No, he's hangin' back beside the black Chevy blazers, waiting for somethin'.

Mr. Benny is again heard: he is demanding his wife be quick with the food preparations. His voice softens to add, "Perhaps feeding them, will help take away their intentions from Devon." Mrs. Benny, in tone near hysteria, shrieks protest. She does not like cooking and serving good food to the likes of these people! Mr. Benny shushes her, claiming understanding, "Yes, yes, but it is important *tradicion*." She retorts, '*Tradicion*? You do not tell me of *tradicion*! What they are doin' here is not *tradicion*! There, they are... Is that your *tradicion*? They have begun doin' it—*satanico sacrificio*! Here! Here in our home. I will not observe this. This is all wrong—wrong!" Loud clanking from pots and pans inform that she has busied herself with cooking.

Sparky, cautious to stay clear of hunkered spear chuckers, glides toward the courtyard windows. I gotta see what Mrs. Benny is referring to... *Satanico sacrificio*? God, oh God, please don't let it be children. Two soldiers have laid a middle-aged woman down on the ground near the black Chevy blazers. This is taking place out of view from the fucking, fucked-up British tourists. The woman is small, Indianish, and garbed in traditional peasant dress having bright colors. She is completely passive, giving no resistance. Laying flat on her back, looking dreadfully doomed, trembling with fright, and surely burdened with a sadness that only those bein' in her shoes could even possibly comprehend. Having hands tied, she does the Catholic cross motion over her chest, tightly scrunches face, not daring to open eyes. It's guessed the poor old woman is doin' her best to think last thoughts of loving *familia* only. The old witch is there, and she has brought with her a very attractive, young teenage nude girl, who in her hand, has a wicked looking butcher's boning knife. The witch is instructing the young girl on where and how to make the cut. The girl is all smiles, nodding understanding. The American cameraman is standing above, ready to start filming. He gives some instructions of his own before stepping back and motioning the girl to begin. The nude teenager sprawls out on the ground beside the peasant woman, and she—in acting form—softly caresses the trembling woman's wrinkled face, as if it were her beloved mother or somethin'. After a dramatic kiss goodbye, the little naked bitch raises forth the knife, and using both hands—throwing her weight into it—slices the poor victim's throat! Even above the loud rhythm of constant drumming beats and maddening beep-beep-beep from that torch, I can hear the woman's gurgled gasp for air that does not come from her mouth, but rather, the incredibly large gaping gash that just a moment before, had been her throat. The woman arches, buckles in spasmodic reflex, then lays still.

The knife wielding little cunt is giggling with exhilarated intoxication. She is splattered with bright thick blood. *Gringo* cameraman reminds her of somethin'. The girl understands and obeys; she performs an extreme gross decadence of sensually rubbing the murdered woman's still warm pumping blood all over her nudity, even smearing it around her mouth and leisurely licking it from fingers. She then bends forward for using long tongue to lap at the blood spilling from the poor woman's neck. The bitch looks to be that of some sorta feeding animal or somethin'. And this the cameraman is all over! Being sure to get the shots from both front and rear... Blood smeared little ass wiggling, and young pretty face buried, feeding on... My God—Jesus fucking Christ! This is a horror movie of extreme proportions without special effects, and..., and Sparky's stuck right in the middle of the wretched thing, and it's no movie. No it is not!

I need some air! Well Judy, there ain't no air, not in here. No, just heroin smoke and crack fumes. Ught-oh, aughg, ow-ee, arrrgh; my bowels again. Goddamn enough already. Give me a break—please Mr. Bowels, please. We can't defecate right now, can't you see? Aughg! You stupid shit bag! The persistent bowels are wanting to explode, and has body bent in painful rigid determination for containing that within and not submit to this internal bullying. Hearing my name, I waddle/glide over to the fucking, sucking, heroin blowing alpha couple. Just then, word spreads that Mrs. Benny is serving food: "Good eats!" Most of the surrounding gangers—including the monkey spear chuckers—dash for the kitchen. Clearly, heavy crack smoking does very little in acting as an appetite suppressant for these hungry monsters.

The alpha couple, however, have declined to join the others for "Good eats." They are quite content right where they are. And whew, who can blame 'em? The *petite chica* is indeed a femme fatale, having mouth and hands still wrapped around walloping whopper of hard dick. Plus, they have at reach all the heroin and crack that anyone could possibly want for a night of consuming—and then some! That pipe, much like their sex, never seems to stop. (Buddy, should we risk smokin' a bit of that heroin to stiffen up these bowels that are about to turbo blast contents all over the place? Buddy, we gotta do somethin'. Christ, they ain't lettin' up. It's gettin' worse and worse—can't hardly stand it. Should we, buddy? Should we ask to smoke some heroin? Yes, but man, only a small amount. You must keep head clear and reflexes sharp. Okay buddy, promise.) "Hi guys! Can I have some?"

"Aw Devon... He he! Devon is back. Whatcha be needin' Devon? Pussy or heroin?"

"Uh, mostly I'm needing a safe way out of here..." They both giggle non-menacingly. "But obviously that isn't gonna happen. So how bout some of that heroin smoke?"

"Sure Devon, I will give you both pussy and smoke. Push your cock true te window. She will suck you te same time I blow you all the shotgun smoke you can manage, okay? Dis will be my gift for you before I must kill you. Remember te deal Devon? You watch for me, make it look good, and let me kill you quickly. Dis will benefit us both, yes?"

"Yes, it's a good deal, but I ain't stickin' my dick out there. Not even for your pretty lady. Besides it's too busy thinkin' of other things."

After a moment's pause, "Okay, Devon, I understand. Come, come closer." He reloads the enormous pipe with powdered brown heroin, fires it with bellowing puffs, then inserts stem through broken-out jalousie slats. From the stem comes a shooting steady stream of thick rich smoke. Taking the risk, I expose my head, bend forward, and suck that distinguished smoke in long gulps, much how a dehydrated man would water. The alpha couple are impressed with my enduring enthusiasm, and are given encouragement; the petite pretty, while still strokin' a double handful of cock is whispering chant, "Go Devon, go, go, go, go! Devon, go…" Finally, Sparky can't hold no more, and eyeballs are about to pop from head. A coughing fit wants to come, but for obvious reasons, this is not allowed. So snot and tears start pouring. Time to relocate. "Uh, thanks guys. I'll be back." Straightening my back, the bowels are now settled and seem quite content. Yeah, you liked that, didn't you? And you want more. Yeah well, me too, but it ain't gonna happen. Sparky must keep a clear head. Damn, I sure could use a cigarette.

The murdered peasant woman's body has been removed, and now, in its place, is the torch wielding soldier, busy scorching the ground for burning all traces of blood. Mrs. Benny is then heard in the kitchen talking on the telephone! Oooh could she possibly be talkin' to Ambassador Todd Boil? Could it possibly be? Has she finally called Todd Boil to come get my ass the hell outta here? Please be so! But then it's noticed that she is speaking in very strong Carib patois dialect. Fuck, she ain't talkin' to Todd Boil. No, probably some neighbor or somethin. Suddenly, though, over the noisy chatter of rude table guests eating, Mrs. Benny deliberately drops Carib tongue to speak loud English, as if wanting all to hear. "You know Devon from Trujillo? He has a *familia*… a wife and two young sons. He is a businessman… Tattoos? He is famous for them? Movies have been made about him from around the world! He hung from hooks to show respect to the American Indian… Yes… Yes. His step pappy and baby sister are black? Yes. Yes. Devon is a good man. His death will be bad for all… I know—I know! But you see we have this Todd Boil. We can do nothing…" (Buddy, who is she talkin' to? Ught!) Matrix is heard taking the phone away from her. In no time, he is standin' with it out in front of my courtyard windows. In

346

tone cruel of ridicule, he teases, "Oh Devon! Devon, you have a phone call. It is your old friend Martin, from Trujillo! He is begging we spare your life. Devon, you really should come out here and speak with him. He is very worried for you." Matrix's voice lowers to a ruthless growl. "I do not understand why, when it should be his own life he should be worried for. Devon, after I'm finished with you, I am slowly going to cut your friend Martin into little pieces. He will regret the day he ever met you. Oh, so sorry Devon; Martin is no longer available for phone conversation. Guess he didn't want to speak to you after all. Eh, no matter. Devon, you just stay in there and watch. Watch what is to be only a small taste of your fate this night."

A bound and gagged black man is laid to the ground. He is nude, having very visible torture burn welt marks on his body. His struggles are, of course, to no avail, and he keeps glancing to my window as if I might be some help. The man's eyes are huge with fright. The tight gag prevents him from speech or sound—just gurgled nostril flaring grunts. A soldier, laughing, lands a hard kick into his rib cage. The American cameraman and witch are there, and so is another naked knife wielding cunt. The witch is bent forward, instructing the girl where to make the cut, and how it should then be put in her mouth for the camera, etc. My God, they are gonna cut the poor man's penis off, while he's still alive! The witch wants a slow sawing-type action. It is then suggested by the cameraman that perhaps for this shoot, two girls should be used. Matrix nods approval, and so another nude giggling girl is brought. The bound gagged man begins to struggle frantically, rolling side to side. Matrix sends a kick, with shiny American jump boots shattering the man's jaw line; still, he struggles. The soldier operating the torch is called in, and as calm as can be, the torch wielder bends forward, and begins to burn the top of the doomed man's head. Singeing hair sizzles and flesh is charred, floating nauseous malodorous reeking horror. The victim goes into convulsions of rigid trembling seizure. Obviously, the torch wielder is intent on burning a hole right through the skull's crown. "Enough!" Matrix waves him off, motioning for the others to proceed. In doing, it is noticed that the crotch of Matrix's black BDUs is flag-poling with an erection. This brutal sick shit has him sexually aroused! Jesus Christ! What could possibly make people like this Matrix? Uh, gee-golly, guess that would have to be God! God the creator, creator of all. Hey God, you can kiss my atheist ass! And while you're at it, send in the Goddamn cavalry!

(Hhmm, buddy, wonder how many times over the years we've seen goofy cartoons where there is some white folks all crammed into a big-ass pot atop a fire; and always, there is a bunch of knappy-headed, bone nosed cannibals dancin' around. It's supposed to be funny; but buddy, that ain't funny, is it? Buddy? Buddy! Crap)

Both nude girls drop down to hands and knees beside the tortured man; one on either side. They reach for each other across the man's abdomen, whereupon they begin to kiss and sexually fondle each other. In doing, giggling ensues. Matrix barks a scolding threat! Needless to say, both girls stop giggling, and get to doin' what has been instructed. They bend to lick and suck the poor man's limp shriveled penis. The curved boning knife is handed to one. They both turn and smile into the camera, behaving how those do when thrilled being in front of the camera and wanting all the camera time to be on themselves. The American cameraman is losing patience and turns to Matrix. Matrix, however, is already on it; sharply slapping one girl's face, while pulling the hair of the other, hissing, "Get on with it." And so they do. After the one wipes away stinging tears and re-fluffs her hair, she and the other begin pulling and sawing off the poor, oh so poor, man's genitals: penis, scrotum sac, and testes. The victim struggles, and flame is applied to his face. His back arches for a spazzing slump of deep rasping. His face is no longer a face at all. The girls are allowed to giggle, and giggle they do, while holding up the bloody genitals as if a trophy; but they have not succeeded in severing all the attached entrails, looking much like long tentacle organ membrane, gland septa tubes and—and, stuff. Fuck me! Now both girls are licking at the bloody mess and using teeth in attempts for biting off chewable chunks; even goin' so far as to each take a bite hold of the genitalia flesh, growling, pulling at it from each other, pretending to be wild animals doin' tug o' war with the flesh. Cameraman is all over this action, not wanting to miss any of it.

Whoa, talk about your for-real grisly sights! The brain can't hardly register it. One girl loses the biting grip to bend forward and start lapping at the mangled bloody hole that had once been this man's groin region. She palms pooled blood up to her face and drinks! The other, with mouth full of penis flesh and entrails, is chewing, slowly shaking her head while deliberately making strange animal noises.

My God—Jesus—my God. And this is only a taste of what they have planned for me? No fuckin' way! Oh, Sparky will die all right, but not like that. Gotta think of somethin'. Damn, just gotta!

I glide 'er over to the fornicating alpha couple. They give me more heroin smoke. Mr. and Mrs. Benny are heard arguing with the table of loud rude guests. Mr. Benny is now speaking up, shouting how "Devon" is hard-working, a good family man; and they are nothing but lazy murdering hooligans that sleep all day, etc. Mrs. Benny then reminds them all how very attractive "Devon" is, with his long *blondo* hair. (Oh boy, wish she hadn't mentioned that.) Now the boisterous table guests are jeering how she will not be thinkin' "Devon" bein' so attractive after they have gang raped me, skinned me, and burnt my hair and face off! But remembrance comes to some at the table how "Devon's" hair is not to be burnt. No, it is to be scalped. This, shared, brings about raucous enthusiastic approval from those seated. Mrs. Benny shrieks, "No! No, I will not listen to anymore. Leave! Leave my table at once. No! Do not come near my son! He is not one of you! He will never be! Go now. I have fed you; now go!"

Taking in another big blast of heroin smoke and thanking my accommodating hosts, I step away. From the walkway there comes the sound of giggling, hyena she-bitches, skipping their way to the showers. Glancing out the courtyard windows, men are now dragging off the poor, mutilated man's corpse. They must be puttin' the bodies into a vehicle. Suddenly, Matrix spins. Staring into the darkness of my room, and he seems to know exactly where I am. "Yes Devon, keep watching. Soon it will be you. On this night you are to be my prize; and I do claim it. Bring me the *niñas*!"

(*Niñas… Niñas.* Oh God, no… Children!) Stepping back (fuck it), reach for a cigarette, snap filter, cup with hands and light. Inhaling deeply while fidgeting with Bic lighter, a thought of an idea comes to mind; and I do like it. Smoking my cupped cig and givin' my new idea further consideration, Sparky watches the monsters bring forth a nude infant baby girl. They lay her to the ground. She is loudly bawling out as only infants do. A quick torch flame to the face quiets the throaty crying; baby cannot breathe. Again, one of the naked bitches is there, still wet from the shower; and in her hand is that wretched boning knife. She sprawls down beside the quivering burnt baby. Cameraman is, of course, filming, as the cunt goes into acting mode for tenderly caressing the infant as if it were her own. Moments later, it is the tip of the boning knife doing the caressing. The cutting edge is inserted cross-wise into the infant's mouth, and, suddenly—cuts! Baby's mouth just became ten times larger! Bloody knife point then goes to infant's privates. More cutting, followed by more burning. (Lordy, how the smell of burnt human flesh is strong. Even above all the crack and heroin, burnt human flesh dominates.)

That's it! I've made up my mind. In the bathroom, cig butt goes into toilet and large handfuls of toilet paper come off a nice full roll (at least this dump has toilet paper). I use it all, silently goin' about the room tucking in gobs of the stuff here and there (mostly in the thin bedspreads, pillows, and around the old frayed curtains). As last resort, Sparky is going to burn this stinking hell hole to the ground! The alpha couple, watching, have a general idea of my intent. Clearly, their eyes (like my own) too have adjusted for seein' through the darkness. The male is encouraging, whispering, "Devon, sphsisst. Devon, dat is very good. A good trick. It is most probable to work." Sparky is gonna burn himself up! It Goddamn better work! Fuck me... What a way to go... Still, it's better than Matrix gettin' his hands on me. Besides, they say, the carbon poison (smoke) kills you before the flames do. Well, let's fuckin' hope. Whew, I just hope the flames grow fast enough to keep the baboons out so that I may die.

Hearing now that all the monkeys have left Mrs. Benny's kitchen, I call out to her, "Mrs. Benny—Mrs. Benny! Call Todd Boil. Call Ambassador Todd Boil! Even if he won't answer, your call will surely be recorded, and you and your family will not be held responsible for this night. Please call! Please try—you must or else, the American Embassy and authorities will blame you for allowing all of this to take place on your property. People talk, they always talk, and it is no secret what is going on here tonight. Christ look at the lights and music. The truth will be told!"

Mrs. Benny shrieks hysterically to her husband, "He is correct. Devon is correct! You will do nothin', but I must. I must try! This is our home—our home. This must not be allowed to continue!" Mr. Benny, sounding very small and scared, shushingly begs her not to interfere.

Entering the front desk lounge area via panel server door, Mrs. Benny ignores the posted alpha couple and others, now leisurely hangin' about. All appear to be quite comfortable, unmotivated, and wasted. They ignore her as she does them. "Do not worry Devon, I am callin' that Todd Boil right at this very moment. This should have been done from de very beginning. You just stay in your room der Devon, and keep doin' what you're doin'. Fight dim off; do not let dim in. Help will soon come." It is evident Mrs. Benny is exceedingly frightened; her patois dialect is coming out.

Hey, how is it that Martin from Trujillo got a call through? How did he even know where I am? He is in Honduras! Hhmm, with all the damn cell phones around constantly ringin' and bein used, it's pretty obvious that my predicament here is an event of quite widespread knowledge. And really, how could it not be? Subtle, this insanity is not. So then, how is it that Ambassador Todd Boil and the American Embassy folks don't know about this? Huh, how?

From the old front desk, Mrs. Benny picks up a phone and begins dialing... Matrix storms in, holding a traditionally dressed peasant girl of (guessing) only perhaps five or six years old. His big hand is over the little girl's face, squeezing hard, preventing her from crying out. The panel server door opens, and in comes a soldier dragging Mrs. Benny's very terrified son. Matrix hisses, "Drop the phone or we'll chop your son's hands off. And won't that be nice... to watch your son grow to be a man, having no hands? Ha ha!"

The phone is instantly dropped! Mrs. Benny rushes to her son for pulling him from the soldier. Receiving the nod from Matrix, the boy is released to his mother. Mrs. Benny, now having firm grip on son's wrist, slowly approaches Matrix. Big sad tears are streaming down her wrinkled face as she—with unsure hand—reaches out for the young girl. Matrix, however, has no intention of releasing the child to Mrs. Benny. Instead, he spins, facing my window, removes his hand from the girl's face, and shoves it up under the child's dress, hurting her privates, while commanding she says what has been instructed. Racked with fear and pain, the small child squeaks meekly, "Please Devon... Come out... out te room..." She then bursts into heart-breaking sobs. The little face scrunches up, gushing big tear droplets that only a baby child can produce. Matrix, without so much even battin' an eye, violates the girl's privates some more (his erection growing beneath the BDUs). He insists she tells what is to be done to her if "Devon" does not come out of his room. "Dey..., dey gonna rape me, cut me, din burn me..." The words turn to weeping cries of confusion and pain. Matrix is indeed hurting this child.

Tears are rollin' down my own face. Fuck me! What can I do—what can I do? That little girl is dead no matter what. And now, Martin is probably dead, as are Pio and Partner. Aughg, how many people must die because of me? How did it ever come to this? Sparky don't know and don't care. Mrs. Benny is now frantically pleading for the whimpering young girl. Matrix, ignoring, is bitching about the time; he is behind schedule, growling, "Let's get on with it. There is very little time left."

Out the walkway he and others go. Between the two black Chevy blazers and my courtyard windows, the girl child is laid to the ground. Of course, the American cameraman, old witch, and torch wielder are there waiting. After all, the sick show must go on, right? Lordy, here it never seems to end.

Mrs. Benny is back in the kitchen, loudly hyperventilating. Mr. Benny is tryin' to calm her. I light another cupped cigarette, inhale deeply, and watch as a nude ganger couple, male and female, approach the poor frightened little girl. (Hey man, sure hope you are feeling

351

strong. Why are you watching this? The monster's erection out there confirms what is about to take place. So why watch? Buddy, I don't know. Maybe it will help make burning this hell hole to the ground easier. It's gonna be a trip with no return ticket. You know? Yes.) The nude young woman drops to her knees and begins to undress the now wailing child. The cameraman is zooming in… Billowing skirt of colors is removed, the nude child appears to be teeny-tiny, still just a baby really. With the young woman pinning the little girl baby's shoulders down, the stocky, big faced, young man lowers to his knees, and impales baby. After one terrifying piercing shriek, there is no more crying from little girl baby—no more tears. Little girl baby is convulsing in body shut down from physical and mental shock! Not to mention internal mutilation. The big faced man's penis is gigantic in comparison to the tiny child's body. Like a rag doll bleeding profusely she is. Still Big Face keeps on raping, impaling, mutilating, whatever. He withdraws his cock every so often for added sick effect of havin' the woman lick and suck blood from murdering shaft. Big Face even continues the ruthless impaling while torch wielder steps in for applying flame to little girl baby's head, neck, and face. By the time Big Face ejaculates, the torch wielder has charred all tiny upper torso; no face, no hair, no skin, leaving only smoldering mess of what had not so long ago, been a beautiful baby child… a little girl.

Big Face, bein' all smiles, rises to his feet and acts to be proud as punch. Matrix barks at him to drag away the body and bring forth an infant. Big Face is harshly reminded to be quick." "Time is running out!" Soon, Big Face is back with a dangling, screeching infant girl.

Sparky lights another cigarette. (Hey man, are you all right? No buddy, I'm not. Man, just be ready to fire this hell hole to the ground. The cavalry is not coming tonight for Devin-Devon. No it is not. And if you keep watching this shit, to be honest, I'm not sure you will be up for doing the task required before the natives charge in here. Don't worry about that, buddy. I'm sharp—frosty sharp! They ain't gonna get us; not like how they want, they ain't.)

The infant is dropped to the ground, and the giggling couple lie down on either side of it. These snickering tormentors are then each handed a fork. (My God, what's with the forks?) Torch Wielder approaches, bends forward, and bathes wailing infant's baby face lightly with flame. Baby is shocked, and silently struggling for breath. The infant's privates are torched, as is little belly and chest. The desired effect, besides burning, seems to be for inducing spazzing jerks of convulsions. Why? I'm guessin' to prove that the infant is still indeed alive? Who the fuck knows! After much of the baby infant is blackened, the monster couple, giggling, begin using their forks for picking at flesh and eating baby, while it is still quivering—alive! American cameraman, of course, is right there—filming it all. Matrix then orders them all to be quick and clean up. It is past time, and he must still bring over the British.

"Sphsisst! Hey Devon, you der?" It's alpha couple whispering for my attention.

"Yeah, I'm here; what's up?"

"He he! Devon tinks he is one of us now. One of te gang. Devon, you no longer fear us?"

"No, not anymore. There is no percentage in it. Fear will only inter-fere with my battle strategy. Can't afford fear, understand?" Sparky can make out their look of puzzlement.

"Devon, you have forgot our deal?"

"No, but before I allow you to kill me, others will die first—understand?"

"Devon, you watch what dey be doin' out front, and still you make yourself not know fear so you can better fight?"

"Yes."

"Devon, dis is very admirable. Most are not so strong to do such. Devon, needin' some more smoke?"

"Yeah sure, why not." Soon the heroin smoke is shootin' in, and Sparky is again suckin' it up, inhaling with eyeballs a-bulgin'...

"Devon, have you checked te pilots?"

"Uh, the pilots?"

"Yes, te pilots. Dey must be all readied to go. After te English tourists leave, te Orc will order many of us to pull you out from der. Te pilots must be readied for rapid lighting. Devon, I do not much feel like fighting dis night. Go stand ready by te pilots, okay?"

"Yeah sure." Sparky will be right over here—ready to flick Bic to "pilots."

Just outside the courtyard window, there is a small gathering of Brits. They are pale, white, nude, laughin', and high as kites. They are each gettin' to have a turn with the torch for burning somethin'. And this is thrilling them no end! Finally, I am able to make out what it is that these British retards are torchin'. They are burnin' the hell outta a bunch of little guinea pig type critters; all alive, yet individually encased in clear, plastic wrap. With each poor creature the giggling Brits get to char, they beg, pleading, for another, and another, exclaiming gleeful delight, how yes—yes, they can feel the angels! etc.

Eugh, give me a break. How Sparky would like to put that torch to their British bare asses and see then, how they "feel the angels!" I hear one Brit ask another, why my window area is off limits to them? The other answers, it's due to some Bible thumpin' American opposing their rite to religious choice (what idiots). The elaborately costumed dancers are no longer up on the scaffolding platforms, and the scaffolding framework itself is bein' quickly disassembled.

After the poor rodent burning spree, it is fire suit time (with some fucking and sucking on the side). Yep, fire suit! Each Brit gets his and her very own turn to climb into a for-real, silvery fire suit, and have the psychotic torch wielder apply flame to their genitalia regions. Just what is the thrill here? I haven't a clue. Believe me it ain't burnin' or hurtin' 'em. (Wish it was.) Fire suit play comes to an end, and so all British tourists/followers/whatevers are respectively rounded up and headed off to somewhere. For them, the party here is over. For me? He he! It's just gettin' started.

Matrix is now in a genuine great hurry. The cocaine/crack logs are bein' quickly loaded into the black Chevy blazers. Soldiers are descending from top wall posts and dispersing. The two soldiers always guarding Matrix have brought forth a steel battering ram for bustin' down my door. Matrix is givin' instructions to a group of larger male street gangers. Evidently, Matrix the Orc has overextended his party time; thus, he must take leave to deliver the freshly made crack. Matrix growls out orders: "Devon" is to be gang raped if possible, "but do not waste much time with this." Now, what is most important is that I be dragged from the room, tied to a tire, and carefully skinned and scalped. Great care must be taken here. Both scalp and skin must be removed cleanly. Matrix has very important people waiting for them. Also, Matrix, for himself, he wants my cock and balls with gold ring handed to him before the sun's rising. "Is this understood? Wait until I am gone; then drag our American John Wayne out from that room! When you are finished with him, smash his head using the battering rams; then put what is left of him in [so-and-so]'s car. Drive Devon up to the hills and bury him where he will never be found! Is this understood? And if Benny and his big mouth wife try to interfere, eh, grab the son and bring him to me." Big white toothy grins nod understanding. The gangers are getting' themselves all pumped up. (Oh shit!) The old witch is waiting, sitting in the front passenger seat of a black Chevy blazer. American cameraman is holdin' back, with equipment at ready. (It's guessed he's there for filming the butchery of me!) Torch Wielder is gone, having taken with him that welding cart with maddening beep, beep, beep, beeper.

Matrix, glancing to his wristwatch and cussing the time, climbs in behind the wheel of the black Chevy blazer having seated old witch waiting. But upon spotting one of the nude pretty brown girls walking past, he steps out, grabs her by the hair and puts her to the ground. He himself goes to his knees and roughly forces the girl to blow him. And, of course, the young pretty is obliging without protest.

Sparky hurriedly glides over to the alpha couple, "Hey man, if by chance this does not work, please don't bury my body. Please just drop it off in front of the American Embassy, so that my wife may have it sent back home. Please, I beg you!"

Low urgent whisper, "Devon, forget 'bout dat. Look, Matrix is leavin'. You have no time. Get to te pilots!"

Mrs. Benny is now screaming at the top of her lungs, "Devon, Devon! Dey comin'! Comin' fer you—dis very moment! Fight Devon! Fight dim wit everything you have—fight! Oh fight! Fight!"

Fuck me Skippy, the time has come to flick Bic! Burn you sons-a-bitches, Burn! With all the pilots (clumps of strategically placed toilet paper) lit and spitting flame, the room is now bright with fire! And smoke. (Buddy, we got smoke!) Black, grey, and white clouds of the swirlin' stuff billowing to life faster than what could have been thought or hoped. And ow-ee! How it does burn, scorching inner nose, throat, and lungs. Like thick mass of dooming airborne acid it is... BAM—BAM—crash! Above the roar of the furiously intense hungry fire feeding ferociously and growing to size for engulfing all... I can hear windows shattering, and ganger monkeys outside excitedly shouting.

Inner adrenaline is pumpin' to near insanity as Sparky loudly laughs and yells, "Yee-haw! Ha ha! Come on you sick mother fuckers! Come and get Devin-Devon now!" Ught-oh... (cough, cough, choke, gag)... Both upper and lower respiratory tracts are constricting and screamin' in protest! The scorching acid smoke is burnin' the holy crap from 'em. Fuck, can't breathe... don't want to breathe! The chest is heaving in confused panic. I'm drowning in this harsh biting strangling smoke. Tears, snot, and mucus are gushin' forth, makin' a day training with military CS gas (Tear gas) seem like child's play. No longer bein' able to see, I back step into the bathroom, close door and lock it. Down goes the vanity sink stopper and on comes the water—full blast. A towel is grabbed and thrust into the sink. (Man, you must get to the floor. Okay, buddy). With drenched towel, Sparky drops flat to the floor, wrapping head and face. Entire body is racking convulsions in want for air. Shoulder and arm wedge, blocking bottom gap of door. Water (now feeling very cold) has overfilled the vanity sink and is spilling over to flood the tile flooring (so cold—so damn cold).

Thoughts of people drowning come. (Hey man, breathe. Just relax and breathe it all in. Let's get this over with. Yeah, okay buddy.) Despite the searing burn and choking gags, I do get the lungs to suck in short, sharp breaths.

Light-headedness ensues with a spinning. Sparky is about to pass out and die. And in doing, I allow the inviting state of euphoria to engulf, and it takes me deep into mind, no longer associated with body. My beautiful wife and precious young sons are before me. Their being, is that lovingly clinging. And as if miraculously, the wondrous smell of each is presented for intoxication. But then they dissipate, and are gone! Nooo! I'm not ready yet. I didn't even get to say goodbye to them. (Man, fuck it! You are dying. Be grateful they are very, very far away from this gruesome world of insane torture, mutilation, and murder. Yeah, okay buddy, guess you're right. But now what? Ught, looky! It's the big bright light that everyone's supposed to see during the cross-over for death. Buddy, this is good, huh? It means we won; we have succeeded in dying before Matrix and his monkeys could get hands on us. Ya-hoo!) The now embracing light, is caressingly warm, incredibly comforting, pure elation of enlightenment. What the... Dad? Dad, is that you? (Look buddy, it's Dad! He's all draped in white light, lookin' happy as can be!) "Son, how have you been? I'm glad you are here. I've missed you. Can you walk?" Hell yes, I can Dad! Where are we goin'? Dad? Dad! Wait, I can't keep up... The light! Where's the light? DAD! It's gettin' dark... "Hey boy, whatcha doin' here? Damn it boy, this is not your time! When are you gonna stop screwin' around?" Murf? Grandpa Murf? It is you! Aw Murf, don't be mad. I've missed you. I have missed you so much. Murf, I saw Dad! Come on, he went this way... We gotta catch up with Dad. Murf, come on! We can catch him. Here, I'll help you. "Go home boy. It's time for you to go home." But Murf! Murf, don't leave. I want to come... Murf? MURF! We gotta find Dad! Murf? What the fuck? (Buddy, who's got hold of us? Don't they know we gotta find Murf and Dad? Buddy, Oh shit! Buddy! No, no, no! Buddy, we are bein' brought back! They ain't gonna let us die. Nooo! Buddy... Man, fight!)

There's my arms, but they won't move. Up down—up down… Sparky is off the floor and bein' bounced. Oooh, is it ever cold again… I can't breathe, somebody is behind me performing a jarring diaphragm racking Heimlich type maneuver. Oomph-ug, oomph-ug, the lungs are tryin' to jump-start for working order, while at the same time, stomach is constricting to puke; stomach and lungs are in a state of panic competition. (Buddy this sucks the big one. Christ we were so close, so very close. Fuck, how did they ever get through that burning inferno of a fire to even reach us? Sparky should be dead, dead, dead!)

The cold water covered tiled floor comes into vision of criss-cross lines. From my mouth, out comes big globs of thick foul tar substance; followed by chest-sucking bellows for long drawn lungs full of hot rancid air. Everything comin' and goin' within the body is scorchin'! Eyes begin to focus… The bathroom door has been busted down, water is everywhere, and from outside flashing colored lights. (Whoa, we really burnt the hell outta this place, didn't we buddy?) The man holding me up, still doin' the Heimlich type maneuver must obviously be a paramedic-fireman, or the sorts. His arms are sleeved in a heavy black and yellow, coat, covered in dark ash and muddied soot from the fire.

The sound of Mrs. Benny's shrill voice comes through. "Is he alive— is he alive? Oh—he is alive! Devon, Devon, can you hear me?"

My head is throbbin' with lungs and throat full of hurt. Plus, body don't know whether to puke again, or defecate. Ught, it's then realized, I've already shat myself, and bowels are giving rumbling bloated notice that there is still more to come! Aughg, why didn't they just let Devin-Devon die? Now Matrix is gonna for sure be all over me.

As Mrs. Benny shrieks in excited delight, the fireman/paramedic still holding firm, turns me to face him. (Buddy, what's happened to our neck muscles? They ain't there no more. The head is slumpin' around much like that of a newborn baby's.) The clutching paramedic uses one gloved hand to lift my chin for directing rolling eyes to focus on to his. The man is thirty-ish, having kind face and eyes of genuine concern. He is asking my full name, nationality, date of birth, etc. Finding voice, the answers come out in drunken, like proud blurt! The nice paramedic man smiles, nodding, but then turns serious, urgently exclaiming, "We must go now, before Matrix comes back! Devon, Captain Matrix is going to put you in jail if we do not get out of here. Devon, do you understand?" Oh boy, do I ever! Mrs. Benny and son both rush over to me for giving big hugs. She has tears streaming down her wrinkled face, while shriekin', "Devon, oh Devon, you did it—you did it! You did everything just right. You tricked dim, tricked dim all. You are truly as they say—El Zorro!"

The bowels pull a fast one and send a squirt of liquid feces down the inner leg. (Yeah well, right now ol' El Zorro needs to take a dump.) Pulling myself free from the nice paramedic, I fall for the toilet, slipping to tiled floor of standing water.

The paramedic, though very understanding, is urgently insisting there is no time! And of course, he is absolutely correct; but still, the toilet is right here. They denied me the very hard-earned, cross-over for a fairly pleasant death. Sparky should be with his Murf and Dad; but nooo! So Matrix or no Matrix... this cowboy, having already fallen from the saddle, is gonna lighten the load. Indians be damned!

Undoing belt buckle, lowering soaking wet, shit soiled, French camo BDUs, sincerely apologizing to those standing around, I climb to take porcelain seat, and let 'er BLAST! Finally, with nothing more than rotten gas sputtering, the tolerant paramedic pulls me up and helps with my pants and belt buckle. Upon inquiring, he learns my passport and wallets are bein' kept in now wet vest. The vest is removed and handed over to Mrs. Benny for safe keeping. There is deep concern: they do not want Captain Matrix to get it. Mrs. Benny, clutching the vest, excitedly babbles on and on, how after this night, they will be changin' the name of their hotel to "El Zorro!" (Wow, she's losin' it.) Again, the cold sets in, racking body with spazzin' shakes and shivers—and it won't stop!

Another fireman/paramedic, looking anxious with worried alarm, enters, and quietly announces that Captain Matrix is now here—out front. My paramedic nods, tosses his thick fireman's coat sleeved arm around to hold me upright for walking. (And to be honest, if he were to let go, I'd fall!) In tone low and dead serious, he instructs, "Devon, act like you are all fucked-up. To protect you, we must take you to a hospital. This will require convincing Matrix that you are in condition of near death. By law, Matrix cannot interfere if you are in such serious condition. Understand?"

"Yes sir. Yep, uh-huh, you bet." (Buddy, what a sight we must be: shaking uncontrollably, dripping wet, covered in smelly shit and black soot... Man, just concentrate on regrouping the formation of body's motor skills. We are about to come face to face with Matrix!)

As if to give support and added validity, Mrs. Benny and son both grab a hold of me for assisting the paramedic in leading the way out. We pass Mr. Benny standing amongst the smoldering ruins; he is just shaking his head, looking stupid.

With muscle groups quickly returning for duty, Sparky looks to Mrs. Benny, and tries to convey apology for burning up their hotel room. She shushes me, whispering assurance that it is all right: "Devon, you are alive. You tricked dim. Dat is all dat is important. Hush now; and be very sick."

Outside, Captain Matrix is steamin' mad, ordering "Devon" immediately be released to him! The paramedics, Mrs. Benny, and son hold tight, preventing Matrix from physically dragging me away. My shaking has just increased tenfold! The paramedics are bravely outright refusing to hand me over. Thus, fierce arguing ensues. Both paramedics are shouting that I have serious carbon poisoning! "If Devon is not treated at-once, he will die. Look for yourself. See his condition; and the shaking, that is the sign. He must have hospital treatment now! You cannot interfere. It is against international law!"

Captain Matrix's two soldiers raise weapons, pointing. The other paramedic quickly pulls forth his cell phone in show of defiant retaliation. And to help out, I recall some gruesome scenes witnessed earlier, and begin to puke up globs of thick burning black tar stuff, and it just keeps comin'! Again, breathing constricts. Eventually head slumps backwards; Sparky is about to pass out. My paramedic jumps to examine, our eyes meet—I discreetly wink.

Matrix, now stompin' around with much hostile frustration, has his men stand down. In doing, I am hurriedly dragged to the ambulance van. Inside, laid flat on a gurney, oxygen mask is slid over my face, except hardly no oxygen is bein' fed through. The reason? Uh, guess the paramedics have done this purposely to make certain that Sparky does indeed stay fucked-up. Mrs. Benny's son slides in beside the gurney and clings to me. Mumbling, I warn him of my unsanitary condition. Quietly the boy declares he does not care; I am his hero. (Hero? Jesus Christ, I'm not worthy of bein' anyone's hero. Least of all, this poor sweet kid's.) Matrix jumps into the van, shoving the boy aside, growling question, demanding answer, "Who lit the fire and why?" (Yeah, like you don't know mother fucker.) Sparky just stares at him with glazed eyes, and pretends not to understand. Captain Matrix's face is grimaced with twitching hatred. Unable to contain, he suddenly throttles my throat for strangling while repeating the questions. All but his soldiers jump in to pull him off.

Removing the mask, Sparky finds voice to shout answer: "I did! I started the fire. There was no choice. The room was surrounded by this *satanico* cult group. They had British tourists with them. They were torturing and raping baby girls! They were burning and cutting people up. They were eating them! *Satanico* cannibals! And, and, there was an American cameraman there filming it all! They started to break into my room to do the same sick stuff to me; orders were given to skin and scalp me. I had no choice—there were too many to fight." Sparky deliberately leaves out the mention of Matrix himself bein' the one responsible. But by how everybody is now lookin' at him, they all know, know him to be the monster he is. Matrix responds by lashing out, slapping me hard across the face, barking, "Liar!" (Yeah, boo-hoo, sticks and stones may break my bones. Man, knock it off! Stay sharp. And stop dickin' with this psychotic maniac.) The paramedics intervene, nudging Matrix out of the van. The non-pumping oxygen mask is again placed over my face; after which, the paramedics exit to argue more with Matrix outside the ambulance van.

A vehicle is heard pulling up, stopping; car doors open and close. Mrs. Benny shrieks with disgust, announcing the arrival of Todd Boil. He is completely ignoring her accusations. Also, it sounds like Mr. Benny is tryin' to hold her back for hushing. Matrix is hissing somethin' to Todd Boil. My paramedic quickly crawls in to kneel beside me, quietly he whispers, "Devon, Todd Boil is here." (He says this as if it has little to do with anything. Catching his drift, I nod understanding.) "Devon, we must take you to see a certain doctor for deciding if you need hospitalization. Matrix will have it no other way. Devon, this doctor is a very important man, but he is ruthless evil. He and Matrix are close friends, and of the same *satanico* belief. Yes, sadly, there are many as such. Devon, you must act very sick, understand? This is your only hope. You cannot trust anyone. Be very sick Devon, okay?' Hearing my "Affirmative," he gives my arm a squeeze, then backs out of the van to make room for Todd Boil and friend.

Todd Boil slides in, actin' all concerned, but careful to keep his distance. "Hey Devin, how are you holding up?" Searching his eyes, I give no answer. Christ, what does one say? "Devin, this is my friend [so-and-so]; he's a journalist." Not catching the name, I look past Todd to his friend, who, obviously, is American or European. The man's features are almost delicate, having big sad eyes. His hair is dark, cut short and neat. However, somethin' about him… His clothes, though casual, are…, well, you just know. This man is conscious of every single button and wrinkle. A journalist, huh? He appears too damn petite, soft and sensitive to be a journalist in this hard core Third World city.

Unexpectedly, a wave of emotional overload comes crashing. Tears surface, triggering much coughing up of big, harsh burning, black, tar-like-gunk goobers. Between the sobbing gasps for breath, "Todd, I told you! I told you they would come. They came! I told you they would, and you didn't listen; you laughed at me. Well, they came—they came! And, oh God, you should have seen what they did to…, to those poor people! Those poor, poor children and babies! Oh! Oh God, why did you put me through that? Why… Why? I told you, but you put me in there anyways, to be a fuckin' lamb for the slaughter! And the British! Why were the Briti—"

Calm as can be, he looks to his silent, sad-eyed friend before interrupting, "Devin, Devin! Hey pal, you were right! I didn't know. Honestly, I did not know. Look, relax, just relax. It's all over now. Nobody is going to come after you anymore. Hey pal, promise—give you my word—okay? Tell you what…" Glancing to his watch, "Aw, it's too late now, but first thing in the morning, I'm going to request that a marine be personally assigned for protecting you. Your very own marine body guard! How about that? Not bad, I'd say. They won't even assign me a personal marine body guard." (Buddy, this guy is so full of crap! His friend over there don't even believe him. Yes, but he's all we have. Oh buddy, why didn't they just let us die!)

"Todd, Todd!" (To hell with the Ambassador title. Nobody else refers to him as such.) "Todd, they say I gotta go to a doctor. This doctor's approval is needed before I can be admitted to a hospital. Todd, they say—"

"Yes, yes, Devin, that's right. It's no big deal. Don't worry pal, I personally know this doctor. He's a real good one—nice guy. Devin, stop worrying. Hey, you're alive! You survived!" (Yeah, no thanks to you—prick.) "So, let's put this all behind us, okay? They will drive you to the doctor, he will give you a quick once-over, and then have you sent to a nice safe hospital with a clean bed and sheets just waiting. Now, how does that sound? Pretty good huh? I'm going over to speak to the doctor personally. You won't see me, but I'll be there. Uh, actually pal, you won't see me again until tomorrow morning. Well—" turning to his quiet friend "—we better get going if I'm to talk to the old doc. Devin, everything will be fine—trust me. I will see you first thing in the morning." And just like that, he and friend are backing out of the van, and are gone.

Sparky is now shaking violently from inner cold chills, and teeth are chatterin' hard. A blanket is needed. The boy (Mrs. Benny's son) quickly goes to report this. Soon he returns with my paramedic, who discreetly explains the reluctance for giving a blanket. He does not want me warm. Despite Todd Boil's words, the paramedic is deeply concerned that they will not be allowed to take me on to the hospital. No, he fears I will be handed over to Matrix, thus taken to jail for torturing interrogation, rapings, and then murder. Maybe Sparky don't need that blanket after all. But Goddamn, biting bottom lip, back involuntarily goes into a series of arching, spazzing tremors! Mrs. Benny, glimpsing my predicament and understanding why "Devon" should not have a blanket, still, she loudly insists on one. Goin' so far as to threaten fetching one of her own! The paramedic sighs, and from the side of his ambulance van, he pulls out a blanket of sorts and wraps me in it. But does so only after receiving promise that I stay very sick, and not allow myself to become completely warm. (Oh Skippy, this we can do. No *problemo*! Especially with this blanket thing.)

The blanket, or what's left of it anyways, has been used at one time or another to put out a fire on a burning person. Half of it has been burnt away, and its charred remains smell strongly from scorched human flesh. The brain now registers this distinct odor very well. I want to puke, but the jaw and stomach muscles are too busy playin' slappety-slap tug o' war with each other.

My paramedic wants Mrs. Benny and her son to ride along with me in the ambulance van. "It will be the best for Devon if he has local support for him. This doctor is an evil man, and very unpredictable." Against Mr. Benny's protests, Mrs. Benny and son take up seats, and away we go! I am truly grateful having Mrs. Benny and son riding along. To say their presence is a comfort would be a big time understatement. During the short ride, my breathing is done through a cracked seal of the oxygen mask. The paramedics have turned off the oxygen completely. Without a doubt, they sure are wanting "Devon" all fucked-up for what sounds to be another quack of a Nazi-type doctor. (Buddy, the fun never seems to end in these parts, huh?)

Arriving at our destination, Mrs. Benny is now noticeably all nervous and fidgety. Her head is turnin' every which way, and she's chewin' on fingernails. The loving son, with big brown eyes, pats her knee for calming. He then leans forward to do the same to my arm. Aughg, if anything happens to these two… Oh why, oh why didn't they just let me die? The ambulance van is now parked, and again the paramedics are heard outside in heated argument with Matrix and others. Matrix is insisting I be removed from the vehicle for examination. However, the paramedics, protesting, want the doctor to come to me. But this ain't gonna happen; so cussing, they swing open the back doors and help Mrs. Benny and son to exit, then it's my turn. Supported by paramedics (one on either side) for standing, I see we are in the front parking lot of what looks to be a closed private clinic or the likes. Matrix and his two soldiers, now with company of several plain clothes cops—*policia secreto*—are gathered about, leaning against their cars, for taunting with smirking stupid comments. Still, they do let us pass.

Upon entering the clinic's front, a light comes on, seeming very bright. From around the corner steps the doctor: and I'll be damned if it's not the same little gray haired man seen earlier at the embassy, questioning a marine as to what the taxicab number was that dropped me off. God, wonder if he's had Pio and Partner killed yet? Of course, there is no sign of Todd Boil. Bet the sneaky prick hasn't even been here.

Matrix stops the grim, frowning doctor's approach to quietly speak with him. Sparky can't hear what is bein' said, but fear is causing the body to shake and convulse even more. The doctor takes notice of this, waves Matrix aside, and comes up close. With firm grasp of jaw, he shines his small light into my eyes, while asking (in demanding growls) my name, nationality, date of birth, etc. I'm tryin' to answer, but the mini-light is piercing my brain. Eyes are rollin' and whole body is spazzin with jerking. Knees have given out, and neck muscles are now nothing more than quivering noodles (or so it should appear). Matrix ain't buyin' it, hissing, "He is faking! Faking it all. Our American John Wayne is merely acting. He is attempting to make us look like fools! I know him. I know all of his tricks. I need him for questioning. He must come with me!"

Again, the paramedics and Mrs. Benny are in argument with Matrix. The doctor ignores them, squeezing my jaw even harder. He is trying to see into my brain. Must keep him out—keep the wretched bastard out! I'm just about to make myself start puking when he releases my jaw with a push. Against Matrix's protests, the doctor glares to the paramedics and orders them to take me to *centro* (wherever). The paramedics waste no time draggin' Sparky to the ambulance van. In doing, the doctor is overheard informing Matrix, "There is no choice, we can deal with this Devon from *centro*. I will put Doctor [so-and-so] on him. This Devon won't live to see tomorrow." (Fuck me!)

My paramedic explains that he must take me to the city's emergency center, which acts like an emergency room for those having no means of payment. "It is for the very poor. Do you understand Devon? It is not a very nice place. Many of Matrix's people will be there. Devon, you must be on your guard. Be extremely careful and do not trust anyone. Stay as you are—very sick—but do not fall asleep, not there. Try to stay alert, but be very sick. We will not be allowed to stay with you, understand?"

"Yes, I understand. What about Todd Boil? Will he be there?" Sparky already knows the answer.

Following a long sigh, "Devon, I do not think so. As you have seen tonight, Todd Boil can not be relied upon."

Mrs. Benny blurts, "Devon, Devon do not worry. We will be right der wit you. We will look after you. Oh, how you need sleep, so bad. And still very cold; I will make dim give you a proper blanket." With her arm around her son's shoulder, she begins to hum a tune—cheery?

From the ambulance van I am helped down some big concrete steps leading to the open emergency room for indigents. Wow, what a sight! The middle of the floor is filled with waist high gurneys. Most are occupied with moaning, wailing, ailing, injured people. Some are hooked up to IV tubes. Most are laying in blood and/or pusy discharge permeating ugly discoloration and foul smelling rot. Up against the far walls—and facing in toward the floor of gurneys supporting the unwell—are a mismatched assortment of simple chairs and short benches. In these, worried family members sit to watch over their hurt ones, or are waiting hurt themselves, etc.

My entrance creates quite a stir, to be assured! There is much murmuring, finger-pointing, and not so quiet whispering. Whoa, you'd think I was somebody frightfully famous! Even the so-called nurses behave this way toward me; none approach. After a very long moment of absorbing just what a true shithole this place is, the frowning gray-haired doctor arrives, without Matrix. On command, we follow him down a filthy narrow hall, passing the small nursery of newly born infants. They are all very loud, bawling in distress, and howling throaty whimpers, all as if in sad protest of having been born into this world.

The doctor has a fun treat for "Devon." He opens the door to a cluttered janitor's type closet; there in the corner, on the floor, is a concrete basin for rinsing out mops and the sorts. Pulling me from the arms of the paramedics, and ordering them to leave, he roughly shoves, demanding I remove the mops and buckets from the filthy concrete basin. And no! He will not let Mrs. Benny and son help. (Yeah well, screw you doc!) Mostly just to piss him off, Sparky deliberately falls, crashing and landing amongst the mops, brooms, buckets, etc. (Oh darn, I've fallen and I can't get up!) The little psycho is now so mad, he's thrown a bucket to have the thing bounce off my head! He's spittin' out verbal threats, barkin' commands, and kickin' stuff all around! (Eugh, this guy is fucking insane—a Goddamn Nazi doctor!) With thump on head, my ears are now ringin' a background theme to the infants' ceaseless wailing protests against life. I am spinnin', not knowing what's up or what's down, but do know, that this crazed Nazi doctor (against Mrs. Benny's shrieks of anguish) is now kickin' me, and like hard! To get away from his kicks of fury, Sparky crawls into the corner of concrete basin. The Nazi doctor, stopping for breath, and looking quite pleased with himself reaches, and turns the water on full blast! Of course it's bitter cold. Thrusting a stiff bristle scrub brush towards me, he orders my clothes removed; I am to scrub clean my French BDU pants, and myself. Oooh, this is freezin'! The teeth are clankering so uncontrollably hard that the jaw aches. And body is shakin' to point of almost uncontrolled, for-real seizure. I can't stand it! Can't stand this fuckin' cold water. (Buddy! Man, scrub! It's the only way this sadistic Nazi doctor is going to let us out of this cold, oh so cold, water! Yeah, okay.)

And so scrub—with sharp bristles from brush biting streaks of red—Sparky does. In doing, it is noticed that the Nazi doctor obviously has an interest in my genitals. The reason for this is guessed: he's lookin' for the rumored big gold scrotum ring. Aaa-haw! It ain't there! Gee, golly Wally, wonder where it went? Well, it ain't here, you sick son-a-bitch! So why don't you run along now, and inform your ol' cult pal Matrix of this news? Oh, won't Matrix be disappointed. Holy hell, just get me outta this fridgid water! Finally, the insane asshole reaches down and shuts off the water.

Despite bein' barely able to walk, the Nazi doctor has intended for me (nude, dripping wet, and freezing) to follow him as is. Yep, parade my nudity across the room of gurney-bound patients and seated, waiting people. And really, I couldn't give two shits. Mrs. Benny, however, throws a screamin' fit, demanding I be given a towel and a hospital gown before bein' led out to where others can see. The Nazi doctor spins on her glaring. He then calls for a nurse. A gown is brought but no towel. Mrs. Benny, holding my wet clothes, has her son help me into the tie-string backless gown; after which, we cross the *centro's* main floor. People, including nurses, are pointing and making fun of my exposed buttocks. Some are trying to get "Devon's" attention by callin' out, "El Zorro, El Zorro, Hey Devon, El Zorro!" Mrs. Benny gives my shoulder a squeeze, while whispering encouragement to ignore them all. I can't do that, but strength is returning, thus back straightens, shoulders square, and legs push, finding balance.

(Hey buddy, do you see him? Yes, I see. Buddy, that must be Doctor So-and-so that the Nazi doc told Matrix about. Geez, what a little worm he presents. Buddy, he don't appear old enough even to be a doctor. I bet he's an intern. Buddy, does he look Guatemalan to you? No, man, he does not. No is right. Just guessin', he's Puerto Rican, here to serve an internship. We had lots of good Puerto Rican pals while in the army, didn't we buddy? Yes. Hhmm, but no way would any of them be like this guy, that's for sure. Look buddy, see his shifty beady eyes of arrogance. The rat is high on somethin'. Watch how he fidgets; hell, he can't even stand still. See how the side of his face is quivering? And still, the Beaner has the holier-than-thou smirk. Oh yeah, we can picture this one bein' our final executioner for the night. Huh, buddy? Buddy! Aw crap.)

In a doorless doorway of a small cubicle room, facing the *centro's* main floor, and bein' right next to the very stairs we took for descending down to this Third World shithole of an emergency room, stands the arrogant prick. He is impatiently tapping his foot while tryin' hard to act the bad-ass, motioning for us to hurry, as if we were bein' deliberate with our slowness. (Hhmm, buddy, are you in any rush to get to that room? No, not really. We can smell it from here, huh? Excrement, urine, blood, pain, human rot. The entire hospital smells of this, but whew, how it is strong comin' from that room! Buddy? Yes? We are gonna need a blanket soon. I'm not sure how much longer Sparky can hold out bein' cold like this. Man, hang in there. We will get a blanket.)

The young Doctor So-and-so, having nose lifted poised with airs, orders Mrs. Benny to lay my bundle of wet clothes on the disgusting floor in far corner of the room; he then roughly grabs hold, and pushes me down into a wheelchair. Immediately, the leather arm straps are noticed. He attempts to strap in one of my arms (get ready buddy! I don't know what's gonna go down here, but this mother fucker ain't strappin' our arms!) and, of course a struggle ensues! Mrs. Benny, seeing, understands, but her attempts at intervening are to no avail. She and son are pushed from the room, with threatened consequences if they should return.

Sparky kicks the chair to spin, scanning the room for a possible weapon (while hoping like hell such will not be required). On my left is a nearby counter; upon it, as if asleep, is a blanketed old whiskered man. (Hey, he's got a blanket!) Behind me, against the wall facing outside, is another counter top. Above it is a row of half open windows, leading to upper ground level landing. Whoa! Fuck me. The ganger monkeys from the hotel are up there! All side by side, having big snarling white toothy evil grins. Matrix is right there amongst 'em. They are now clothed, scrunched together, looking in, watching, obviously enjoying the show.

The worm of a doctor is frantically shouting for assistance! A young nurse comes a-trottin'! She is a Guatemalan, having short black hair and an evident dislike for me. The young woman nurse is a bit unusual for this region in that she's got herself a big fat ass, with a mouth to match! The cunt is more than eager to jump in on the arm strapping challenge. And in doing, the prick doctor—since he is a tough guy and all, and possibly in part because it's known Matrix and monkeys are watchin'— pulls back and lands a hard smarting *smack* across my face! Mrs. Benny, standing outside the doorless doorway, lets out a shriek! Jeering laughter comes from the windows of gawking gangers. And Nurse Fat Ass barks threat: "Now do as you are told, or you will get another!"

On reflex—not thinking, just reacting—both arms shoot out for taking hold. The left catches her hand to bend it at the wrist, thus forcing the bitch's head down almost to lap. And the right, grabs Mr. Slappy by the neck of doctor's smock to yank his face down to mine. (Man, what the hell are you doing? I don't know buddy, we are dead— dead!) While Nurse Fat Ass screams in (exaggerated) pain, the rat doc and I momentarily stare into each other's eyes. His are lit with nervous fear. And mine must surely be wild with seemingly nothin' to lose. Now, not having a clue as to what should be done next, Sparky just loudly growls "NO!" and releases them both with a push. In walks a woman doctor and the old Nazi doctor. Of course, they are demanding to know what is going on. The nurse immediately begins to loudly run at the mouth; that is until the Nazi doctor sternly orders her out of the room. The young rat doctor then quickly whines how I had become violent, and therefore required restraining…

Looking to the woman doctor, I clear my throat to find voice for interrupting. "He is lying. Just go ask Mrs. Benny. He and the nurse attempted to strap my arms without proper cause. Plus, he slapped my face. See, look at the mark he left."

The woman doctor, taking notice of the swelling welt, turns and glares at the young doctor for explanation. And of course he stutters to find one justified. The lady doctor, ignoring him, leans forward and shines a small light into my eyes, mouth, nose, ears, etc. During the (welcomed) gentle examination, she softly asks, "So, you are the one we have all heard so much about?" As if perplexed, I silently look to her questioningly. She only nods her head, as if slightly sad, giving no further comment. Before taking my pulse, both inner arms are closely inspected, with her thumbs even kneading, as if massaging, into the knurled veins. Sparky knows what she is lookin' for. And of course there are none.

Without looking up from my arms, the lady doctor sternly addresses the young rat doctor "Doctor [so-and-so], you are here from Puerto Rico—" Haw! I knew the little hyper prick was Puerto Rican! "—by invitation only. You are a guest to this country, and being such, you are never to strike or deliberately harm a patient—for any reason. Is this understood doctor?" The gray Nazi doctor barks, "That is enough! I am the one in charge here! I will do the reprimanding. This is a problematic patient; his actions and reputation precede him. We must therefore handle him accordingly. Doctor [so-and-so, Puerto Rican] what is your diagnosis?" The Puerto Rican rat, now having fully regained his snooty Beaner impudent composure, quickly babbles out something on the order that since "the patient" is obviously a junkie and needing sleep [such and such] gas should be administered. (What? Gas—gas? Sparky ain't no junkie! Buddy, they are gonna gas us! Buddy? Man, stay calm, all we can do is play along. Play along? Buddy, how the hell does one play along with gas? Buddy? Buddy! Crap.)

The gray Nazi Doctor thinks the gas is a dandy idea and gives the go-ahead. The nice lady doctor seems not to be believin' what she is hearing, boldly blurting, "You can not be serious! Have you two even examined this patient? He is not a junkie. Look! Look at his arms—no needle tracks. This man is seriously suffering from carbon poisoning. He is literally full of it. Gas is the last thing he needs!" Teeth clankin' without mercy, I interrupt politely, "Uh, Ma'am, please, I really need a blanket; and please, no gas." She pats my arm, understanding. With that, the Nazi doctor snarls, ordering her out of the room! She, leaving, loudly announces how her objections are going on record!

In rolls the tall cylinder of whatever gas. The hyper Puerto Rican sharply snaps the mask onto my face, warning that if I make any attempt at removing it, he will have no alternative but to use the restraining straps. Grinnin' like a nervous little puke lapdog that has just killed the neighbors' kittens, he then spins the wheelchair around adding, "Here Devon, some good friends of yours have come to see you. Why don't you greet them." From the window, Matrix and his monkeys wave, joke, and give verbal teasing meant to torment. Sparky, not knowing what else to do, smiles, and does a Forrest Gump wave. This brings about much laughter and giggling, from all but Matrix the Orc, who hisses, "Devon, you didn't think you were going home now did you? Home for those big hugs and kisses from your wife and kids? Thought just because you made it to the American Embassy, that Todd Boil was going to let you go home? Ha ha! You will never get home Devon, never! You are mine!"

My body racks with a hard shiver! God, how Sparky hates that sick mother fucker! Also, he scares the piss outta me big time. (Man, just stay determined—determined in not letting him get his hands on us. Must use the fear to feed the determination. Hey man, you are with me on this, right? Man! Yeah buddy, I'm here—somewhere—but I'm so cold, and wow, this gas is like liquid nitrogen! I hate bein' cold! Buddy, who the hell would have ever thought it possible to freeze to death in central America? Huh? Buddy, who? Yes, well, it's still better than bein' in Matrix's hands. Buddy, what is the gas supposed to do to us? Uh, besides freeze us to death? Man, you heard them; it's supposed to make us go nighty-night! Which, as you know, must not happen. So man, breathe in as little as possible; we are not going to fall asleep. You know the drill. Yeah, okay.)

Mrs. Benny yells in, asking if I'm okay? Also, she informs that Mr. Benny is now here, and they will be just down the hall, singing to the *niños*. Yeah well, sounds as if those infants could use some singin' too. Soon, Mr. and Mrs. Benny are heard singing, but it does nothin' to quiet the poor little ones.

The nice lady doctor returns, and in her arms is a blanket! Well, sorta. Actually, it's more like one of those little thin things that the airlines hand out to passengers—not quite cozy. Also, she has brought threadbare old swim shorts, having shit stained mesh lining, accompanied with a button-up short sleeve shirt. Both are way too big in size, but, Sparky ain't complainin'. Gently, she helps me to stand, unties the gown strings and lets it drop; and of course, the monkey gallery from the windows above immediately start hootin', cheering, and laughin' toward my nudity. The nice lady doctor is appalled! She had no idea they were up there. Hurriedly getting me dressed, her eyes glare to the smirking Puerto Rican prick. "Doctor, you knew—you knew they were there? And you allowed for this despite them being known followers of the *satanico* [such and such] cult?"

The grinning Puerto Rican answers in swaggering tone, "Actually, we are hardly a cult. We are worshippers of a religion far older than your Christianity."

She blurts as if flabbergasted, "You are one of them?" His answer is that of silent smiling only. "You cannot be serious! This poor man has just barely escaped these people with his life! And now he has been handed over to a doctor that is actually one of them? This cannot be! It is not right! It is not ethically right. This man needs another doctor. He needs one now! And you, and those *satanicos* must leave! Leave this hospital at once!"

As if waiting for just such a cue, Mr. Beaner Boy from Puerto fuckin'

Rico begins to jump up and down, excitedly spewing forth questions for justification. "Why, Why, why do you say this? I am deeply insulted! I am a professional, a doctor! I would never allow for my personal religious beliefs to interfere with the well-being of a patient; just as I assume and hope you would not. And as for Devon's concerned visitors here, why do you say they must leave? Is this not a public facility? Are they not the public? I am quite positive they are. Therefore, I feel they have as much right to be here as anyone. Besides, they are visiting with our nice Captain Matrix. Surely, you are not suggesting that he leave as well?"

Following an uncertain gaze up towards Matrix, who is now all evil grins, she stutters as if seriously frightened. "Ye-yes, yes, yes I do. This patient needs undisturbed rest. He should not be having visitors of any kind at this time."

The impudent Puerto Rican sarcastically whines, "Devon, oh Devon, are your concerned visitors preventing you from getting the rest that you so desperately need?" Knowing it to be pointless (and probably stupid) to give any other answer, "Uhm-uh-uhm, no. No, I'm just cold, and this gas is only making me feel worse." (Sparky had removed the mask to give an answer. Matrix loses temper for barking.) "Get that mask back on—now! And you had better start breathing it in. All of it! You think I don't know what you are doing?' Matrix's attention turns to Rico the Rat. "Our Devon is not breathing in the gas; he hasn't been since you hooked him up. I want him sucking that gas—now!" Directing glaring gaze back, "Keep it up Devon. I know what you are doing. If you waste any more of the gas, I will have you brought to this window in straps and personally cover you with so many scorpions that you won't be able to breathe. Is that understood!" The nice lady doctor screams, "No! No it is not. This is insanity. This, this, this is a hospital! My God—I do not believe this!" And out from the room, she stomps, leaving Sparky to exaggerate the sucking in of icy cold gas.

Mrs. Benny briefly pokes her head through the doorless doorway to cheerfully announce that she and family are now leaving for the night, but they will be back first thing in the morning. Also, good news! She has just heard that US documents containing all my legal records are arriving here in the morning. "Important American officials are person-ally bringin' te documents dimselves!" Mrs. Benny is convinced that this is very good news. According to her, the documents will prove that I am a very good man, "Good *familia* man, and not te crazed, loco criminal dat some be tryin' to make you out to be." She instructs me not to worry anymore, and to get some sleep. Her tone, however, changes drastically though, when she and family, once up the stairs and outside, are confronted by Matrix the Orc, and gang. Mrs. Benny is heard shrieking a gasp! Matrix is hissing threats he will take the son, if the Bennys ever speak of what really did take place at their hotel.

What the fuck? There is a commotion out in *centro's* main floor. Reporters are here, and are wanting to see "Devon." Matrix sends his two soldiers down for persuading against. Several, however, do succeed in getting a quick glance before bein' roughly pushed back. One, I instantly recognize as the humble looking journalist friend of Todd Boil's. Our eyes briefly lock. (Hey, is Todd here? Is Todd Boil out there with you?) A black Carib soldier uses his Mossberg pump to push the journalist away before questions can be verbalized. Hhmm, again thoughts come how there is somethin' about this journalist making him stand out different. Whatever it is, his brown tan indicates he's been down here for some time. While the other reporters and journalists are loudly asking questions, excitedly tryin' to get the story on "Devon" and how he, the American, had bravely made a last stand against *satanicos* by setting fire to his own hotel room rather than be taken alive etc., I hear Matrix hiss upon spotting Todd Boil's friend. "There! There goes that fag American journalist! After we take care of our Devon here, I am going to have some fun with that faggot; then I am going to kill him." The ganger monkeys laugh and giggle with one asking, "Orc, what of Todd Boil? Whatcha gonna do wit' him?" Matrix rolls his eyes and answers, "Eh, Todd Boil? Todd Boil is nothing. He will get his soon enough. First though, he must be made to understand, that I can kill any American of my choosing. It is a game Todd Boil and I play, a game I do not like to ever lose, especially when it comes to the likes of our Devon here." Another ganger monkey asks, "Orc, why you be hatin' Devon so much?" Matrix the Orc leisurely shrugs his shoulders while answering, "I hate all Americans; especially the ones that think they are John Wayne and will not play by the rules, like our Devon here. Isn't that right Devon? With your long hair, tattoos, and faggot ring in your dick, and still you think you are American hero John Wayne. John Wayne does not have to play by the rules, does he Devon? Just like you; but you will, Devon. You will play by the rules—my rules! Look at me!"

Uh, don't think so! Sparky ain't lookin' up at him no more. No, instead, it's bounce the ol' wheelchair around to have back facing, thus brazenly defying. Of course the Puerto Rican prick hurriedly spins me back around—even pullin' my hair—forcing me to look up for facing Matrix's verbal wrath of threatening vengeance. In walks the gray Nazi doctor. The Puerto Rican lets go of my hair. The Nazi doctor instructs (not caring whether I hear or not), that if "Devon's" files arrive revealing the wrong things, then he (the satanic cult worshipping doctor from Puerto fuckin' Rico) is to give "Devon" an injection of (whatever) into each kidney. The Nazi doctor even forces my torso forward so that he can point out the exact location within the kidneys he wants the injections to go. "It will kill him quietly and quickly, and there will be no trace, not by the time his body makes it to the autopsy table. Understand?"

The Puerto Rican nods understanding, but in doing, his eyes betray a loss of menacing sparkle. He's afraid! (Hey buddy, check it out, Rico the Rat is afraid. Sure as shit, he is! I bet our young bad-ass doctor here don't like getting' stuck bein' the lone executioner. Just think buddy; if by chance the old Nazi doctor is wrong, guess who's gonna be held responsible for our death? And he will be all by himself, so far from home, while everybody else in his sick voodoo cult—older than Christianity—is off murderin' and torturing, generally having themselves a bloody good ol' time. Geez, the prick almost looks to be depressed. Aw, poor bummed out beaner. Hhmm, hey buddy, what the fuck you think is up with this John Wayne crap that Matrix keeps referring to? He he! The psychotic maniac acts like he don't even know John Wayne is dead. Buddy, I would have to say we are most definitely not at all like John Wayne, but rather, more like the character Dustin Hoffman played in *Marathon Man*. Whatcha think buddy? Man, please shut up. This gas is really becoming hard to stay on top of; so enough with the ramblings. Yeah, okay buddy.)

Following the old Nazi doctor out of the room, the Puerto Rican prick bolts up the stairs and outside, for speaking with Matrix the Orc, who calmly assures the young doctor that he will not have to give me the fatal injections. No, Matrix does not want my death being so boring. He wants some deserving fun with "Devon" first. "I have plans for our Devon. Go turn him back around again for facing us. Force him to watch the small surprise I have for him. Go, it is getting late!"

Before the Puerto Rican puke can trot his butt back down the stairs, two unfamiliar paramedics arrive, pulling a wheeled gurney having legs folded up, hence, the thing is only inches above the floor. Upon it lays the little peasant woman that had earlier performed the Catholic cross thing before passively letting a naked she-bitch slice her throat. Matrix's two soldiers order the paramedic guys to leave the gurney (with corpse) right in front of my doorless doorway. They are appalled, giving brief protest before seeing just how serious the soldiers truly are. So, there the poor woman is left, uncovered and in full view. And with rigor mortis setting in, the gaping gash of a once throat has pulled itself open for width and depth lookin' extremely surreal.

Young Doctor Rico, now again bein' all arrogant smiles, casually steps over the corpse, grabs a handful of my hair while spinning the wheelchair around, forcing Sparky to look up at the grinning, white toothed monsters. In doing, the big gas cylinder sputters to a stop. It is empty. Aaaw-haw! I drained the whole thing! Unfortunately, Rico the Rat takes notice and begins calling out for another cylinder. But before one can be brought, in walks the nice lady doctor shouting, "Enough—enough! No more gas. This patient is seriously suffering from carbon poisoning. He needs liquids, sleep, and an IV of antibiotics. I will not allow for you to force more gas into him!" Of course an argument ensues, attracting the old Nazi doctor, who again, sternly orders the nice lady doctor from the room, while giving the okay for administering more gas, before leaving himself.

With a fresh tank of bone-chilling gas replaced, Doctor Rico the Rat resumes the hair pulling, forcing "Devon" to watch the window monkey gallery. Matrix now has before him a frightened nude little girl. And off to the sides are two young Garifuna voodoo bitches, each holding a struggling infant crying out in throaty desperate manner that only infants can. (Buddy? They are dead, man, dead. You know it, I know it, hey, even the babies themselves know it.) The infants are squirming, while bawling, spine-chilling alarm of despair. And even though their cries cannot be distinguished or heard much above the many loud newborns in the hospital's infant ward, the voodoo bitches are both working to keep covered the mouths of the hard to hold babies, having flailing little legs and feet flinging up toward chests as tiny hands and fingers grasp and claw. (Buddy? Yes? What if we were to start screamin' bloody murder? Think that might help to save the little girl and these babies? Hhmm, no. Matrix and gang would simply slip away long enough for our Puerto Rican doctor to convince everyone that we are indeed insane, suffering from hallucinations or the sorts. After which, Matrix will return more pissed off than ever, and the whole hellish ordeal will simply start anew, understand? Yeah—fuck.)

And so Sparky sits, freezing my ass off, tryin' not to breathe in much of this noxious gas, while at the same time hopin' to appear as if I were. Also, brain is rushing to reinforce fortification for defense toward the oncoming maddening assault of sick atrocities in advancing motion from outside.

The little girl, in frightened little girl voice, is forced to plead repeatedly my name for attention. (Buddy! Man, just hang in there. Be strong—march or die. Remember? Yeah, but Goddamn.) Not receiving the desired reaction from "Devon," Matrix forces the little girl's head forward, and a Bic lighter is applied to angelic face. There is, of course, a brief scream and instinctive struggle, but Matrix is strong. The flame from the lighter is small, yet it's enough to steal her breath and do despicable, flesh charring damage. Matrix must keep raising the girl's face up for me to witness the progressing results; also, time is needed for cooling down the Bic lighter. The one actually holding the lighter and doing the burning, is a stocky grinnin' baboon, complainin' mockingly how the lighter is hot and burning his fingers. The little girl's face is all burnt in pock-marked blotching of swelled up second and third degree burns. Her mouth, lips, nose, and eyes are a blistering mass of brutal ugliness. She is quivering with mouth gaping as if locked into place.

Despite having my hair pulled, eyes are able to roll themselves up and back, for seeing that the Puerto Rican rat holding me, is not watching the child's torture. No he is not! He is deliberately lookin' the other way. What's the matter doc? Don't have much stomach for this part of your satanic voodoo religion? I bet you are just mostly into this shit for the young pussy, drugs, and position. Hhmm, but whew, this guy is a doctor, and in a Third World country no less! He would easily have all of this even without the sick religion. Quacky weird Puerto Rican puke.

The ganger monkeys hold up a chunk of wood and hatchet. They are giggling as if a circus magic act or somethin' were about to take place. They chop off the little girl's hands! Her handless arms are flailing about, as are the massive amounts of blood. Matrix firmly grasps the blood gushing arms, and offers them for several of his monkeys to lap and lick. The little girl's head is recoiling in whip-like spazzes of vacant disorder, much how one sees mindless retard children do when having a silent fit. The child is no longer in there, but she is. Tears are felt streamin' down my cheeks. (And we don't care, do we buddy? We don't care that Matrix and monkeys have taken notice of us cryin', and havin' great sport with it. No man, we do not.)

Much like the chilling squeal from a rabbit just before being killed in the night, the girl child, surprisingly, produces a shrill sound similar. Two chops, and she is beheaded. Her head, hanging from tangled mass of dark hair, is then held forth for horrific display.

With strength and speed startling even myself, I reach back seizing the Puerto Rican around the neck, and send him soaring across the room, bumping into the old man sleeping upon side wall counter top! In doing, Sparky quickly removes wretched mask for wiping away tears and blowing out globs of black snot to already filthy floor. Fueled by jeering laughter from windows above, the fuming Puerto Rican prick recovers for revenge, but before lunging, I shout, "No! Goddamn you. Touch me again and I'll break your fuckin' arm!" Seeing him hesitate, I add, "Then I will begin announcing to all, that you are one of them," nodding up toward Matrix and monkeys "and you are molesting me! The lady doctor already knows you are. I know I'm dead. I got nothin' to lose, fucker!"

The old rag of a man has stirred for awakening, and is now rasping out—between fits of coughing—calls, wanting attention. Matrix is enraged, spewing forth (despite his bouncing, laughing, cheering monkeys) a jumble of sharp hissing sadistic threats to both me and the rat-puke doctor. Young Doctor Puerto Rico, now all wide-eyed, and looking quite confused, decides it's best to just play it safe, and pay exaggerated attention to frail raggedy man.

Somethin' is tellin' me to put the flimsy carbon-tar smeared mask back on, so I do; leaving a good-sized crack in the seal for breathing in air along with foul freezin' gas. With teeth clanking and muscles spazzing from cold, Sparky listens, listens, and watches, watches the Puerto Rican and withered old frail man. And of course, corners of eyes are constantly darting up toward windows as well. Matrix can no longer be seen; however, it is guessed he's not too far away. A young voodoo bitch comments, as if genuinely perplexed, "Devon has no *problemo* fightin', yet he cries tears when we hurt and kill te *niñas* dat are nuttin' to 'im." A big, blood splattered male answers, as if she had asked a question, "Aw, it is how te Orc say: Devon tinks he be John Wayne." O yeah, "Devon" here is really feelin' like Ol' John Wayne. (Isn't that right buddy? He he! Hey buddy, can you picture John Wayne getting' a huge flashlight shoved up his ass? Or bein' forced to suck dick? Or bashing in the whole backside of some poor bastard's head, just because a room full of scary Central American cops tell him to? Or bein' cornered and bawlin' out, beggin' for life like some sissy, whimpering pansy? Or— Man, shut up! Must stay sharp, sharp and focused. We are seriously bein' drained here by this gas. Man, I'm not sure how long we can go on like this. Okay—okay, buddy, you're right. Hhmm, wonder where those cult bitches went with the babies?)

Listening now to punk Puerto Rican and old man, it is learnt that the raggedy man has been laying up there on the counter top for over three weeks, detoxing from cocaine. He and every male member of his family are, and have been for generations, *coca* farmers. Yepper, they grow the green *coca* leaves, and for payment, they receive a certain amount of processed cocaine, to do with as they please, which seems to be consuming. They are life long heavy cocaine addicts, farming the *coca* leaves, yet, living as the poorest of poor.

Two uniformed UN soldiers suddenly appear, stepping over the corpse of woman having gaping throat slash. They do this as normal people would for a large pile of dog shit, or the likes. Hospital staff are now behind them, working to raise the poor woman's gurney and roll her away. The UN soldiers enter, only within the room's threshold, and visually scan. Their eyes lock onto the windows above, then me. They both see the voodoo cannibal monkeys up there; still, their expressions remain indifferent (buddy, these guys don't give a fuck about us). The Puerto Rican yaps, "Yes? Yes? May I help you?" They both ignore him, giving no answer. "No? Perhaps you are lost then. As you can see there is nothing in this room that should concern soldiers." Without a word they turn and are gone. Nurse big mouth, fat ass, comes a-hoofin' it in for gettin' up close to the young rat doctor. Using quiet tone, they speak, but there is no problem in hearing them. While filling a syringe (buddy, sure hope that damn thing ain't for us), Doctor Rico asks Nurse Piggy why the UN soldiers are here? She answers, it is being said that there has been a serious auto collision involving Americans. The Americans have been brought in through the back. But no one has reported seeing them. "It is all very suspicious." Both dart a glance to Sparky, before turning and injecting the loaded syringe into trembling raggedy man.

Upon nurse's waddling exit from the room, in come Matrix and gray Nazi doctor. (Ught-O!). The Puerto Rican steps to greet them. With Matrix glaring dangerously. (Buddy, he is one mean lookin' son-a-bitch! Wow, let's just stare down at our toes. Man, stop trembling; he will notice. Fuck buddy, easier said than done. Sparky is freezin', and scared to death, 'cept we ain't dead.) They begin speaking in low voices. Matrix, of course, wants to take "Devon" out of here. The Nazi doctor, however, explains that it is impossible. And the reasons are obvious—too many witnesses, including, now, two UN soldiers. Matrix then demands "alone time with Devon for some fun." Again, Doctor Nazi won't allow, hissing, "This is not the time nor place. When you have finished your careless juvenile play with him, you will not be here to answer, only I will; and I do not have the time for such things. We will simply wait for his file to arrive in the morning. He will be dealt with then." Stomping his gleaming US army jump boots, Matrix growls, "I want the faggot hurting now!" (Oh shit, fuck!) The little Puerto Rican worm excitedly offers, "We can give Devon AIDS via injection!" (Oh-ho! That's just great. Are you hearin' this buddy? HIV—AIDS! Well, you just go right on ahead there, little Doctor Beaner Boy. Geez, it sure sounds better than what Matrix has in mind. Gosh, what a big, bad-ass, *satanico*, voodoo wimp!) Matrix, eyein' the young doctor, as if thinkin' the same as Sparky, answers, spitting, "No, I have plans for Devon. I do not want him having AIDS!' The gray Nazi Doctor, appearing annoyed, instructs, "With that much gas, Devon should be out soon. Have him laid on a gurney and put in the center of the floor." He turns and leaves, with Matrix following.

BANG! Bang, bang—BOOM! BANG—bang! (Holy crap! Hey man, man! It's just the firecrackers, the same we've been hearing all night, except now they are closer.) BOOM, bang-bang! (Man, stop with the jumping. The Puerto Rican and monkeys have taken notice and are laughing. We must stay strong. Okay buddy, you're right. Oh, buddy guess who's rejoined the monkeys. And buddy, look what he's got!) Matrix is at the windows holding an infant by the ankle, dangling it upside down. The infant baby is wailing its little heart out, struggling for bending up like a macaroni noodle to get at the clutching hand responsible for subjecting it to a hanging so frightful and degrading. Babies should not be handled like that. No they should not! But then again, babies should not be laid across a Goddamn chopping block and have their heads chopped off! They beheaded the baby. The head is, of course, held forth for "Devon" to see. The young voodoo bitches are excitedly reaching in the air around the infant's blood dripping head, claiming that angels have been released and are now all about. Yep, the psycho freaks are cooing and wavin' as if ol' God himself had come down and is personally touching a blessing to each and everyone of the murderin' monsters. (Aughg, fuck you God! Fuck you, and your whore of a mother! Hhmm, buddy, does God even have a mother, or am I thinkin' of Jesus? Buddy, wasn't the mother supposed to be a virgin, yet, still got knocked up keeping the precious hymie-hymen intact? Skippy Joe! Now that's a darn good trick, huh buddy? O shut up fool. Shut up and stay sharp. We can't afford mind wandering. Hey buddy, no *problemo*! Looky, Matrix has himself another dangling infant. Aw, buddy, they're gonna do it again; can't watch; gotta blow my nose, and wipe away these tears. Buddy they are seein—seein' us cry. We mustn't let 'em, huh buddy? But—but, can't help it, can't watch, not another one! Hey man, hey, calm down, nice and easy—breathe. Yes, the gas is freezing cold. Man, now you know what I've been dealing with. Breathe through the crack, in, out, okay? We are no longer going to watch this shit. Watching is just what Matrix and monkeys want us to do. It's to mess us up mentally. And it's working on you. So now bounce this chair around and deal with the Puerto Rican. Yeah, okay buddy.)

Matrix, seeing my actions for ignoring him, snarls hissing threats of how if I do not watch, he will hurt and behead one infant every fifteen minutes; and just for that little added attention getter, he begins to torture another dangling baby. But still, Sparky holds strong, and does not watch. No he does not! The grinnin' Puerto Rican, advancing with airs of bantering pretext, asks, "What is the problem Devon? You are not enjoying the show? You do not approve of our religion?" (Buddy? Matrix obviously can't touch us at this point in time. Like the gray Nazi doctor has instructed, they are to wait until morning. Yes, but don't count on this, and do try practicing restraint. Sure buddy, will do.) Removing the mask for sucking in long gulps for air, using tone dead serious, yet keepin' it low, too low for any but the Puerto Rican to hear: "Touch me, and I'll humiliate you in front of your friends again." This instantly stops him short of my reach! " Look, I truly don't give a fuck what you people kill or torture for your religion. If you were in the United States, that would be a different story. But here, in Guatemala? This is not my country. The people of Guatemala obviously do not object to these practices; if they did, it would be stopped. Here, as an American visitor only, it is not my place to interfere. Surely you, an educated scientist of medicine—much emphasis is placed on pronouncing the distinguished title—must be of the belief for free choice of religion, or so one would assume. Right? This is your religion after all, not mine. So why force me to watch or partake? Not very good for your religion's image, if you ask me.'

Snapping the flimsy mask back to its irritating spot on the face, there is a strange sense of words having actually touched the Puerto Rican idiot, perhaps reminding him that he is a human being. Uh, or maybe not; maybe he's just remembering that he is an educated doctor, and not some little murdering monkey dangling from strings of deranged psychopaths. Hell, I don't know, but do know his demeanor has changed. Without so much as a word for responding, Doc Beaner retreats, leans against the side counter, crosses arms and legs, looks now very tired, glances to wristwatch, then stares down to the floor. Matrix is hissing at us both for attention, but we ignore him, or try to anyways; such things are really impossible to ignore, you know.

A cell phone rings; it is Matrix's. He must leave, but shouts promise to return quickly. He is gonna bring back more *niñas* and, oh yeah, scorpions and black spiders too! Yeah, can't wait.

Coming down the stairs is a filthy, nappy headed, young, not quite white man of early twenties. Entering the room, he greets the Puerto Rican doctor, strolls right on past, and jumps to take up seat on counter top just below windows of horror. He is wearing a large blue nylon windbreaker type jacket. From beneath, in abdominal region, there is a protruding somethin'. (Hey buddy, do you see—do you see? Yes, yes I see. He's a yellow man, literally. Look at the whites of his eyes—solid yellow. Hepatitis much? Ugly chump isn't he? No buddy, not that! The bulge under his jacket! He's got somethin' hid there. Somethin' bad to hurt us with! I bet he's gonna... Man, shut up! Yes, of course, I see. Don't let him come to close. And if he does, throttle the yellow bastard! Hell be damned with the consequences. Buddy, are you sure? Yes. Buddy, we are in real bad shape, huh? I mean like seriously fallin' apart shape? Yes. Buddy, why have we lasted this long? Because I have held us together, that's why. Now shut up, and be ready for this yellow man.)

The Puerto Rican, using tone of bored weariness, asks the sordid yellow chump what it is he wants. As it turns out, the yellow man is wanting professional medical advice. Advice on why the "*Bebe's*" head that he is carrying is not doing so well. He is very concerned. It (the head) makes no movement on its own, nor does it ever speak; and the angels never come to visit. Evidently this is all very unusual, qualifying for concern. According to the yellow retard, all others that carry a "*Bebe's*" head have the benefits of the head giving prosperous direction to its carrier. Also, the angels are supposed to come visiting, thus making life euphoric. And so, after giving the matter some serious thoughts, the lunatic brilliantly concludes, "*Bebe's* head must be hungry!" (Buddy, are you hearing this? Yes; the whacked-out fuck is out of his mind. Just watch his hands, and don't let him come near.) Solution? Feed the "*Bebe's*" head. (Buddy, this guy is talkin' about an infant's head—no body, just the head—a real human baby's head!) And of course it must be fed breast milk, the yellow freak babbles on. He describes how he's been applying a pump to his own nipples for getting them to lactate. And he has succeeded in getting his nipples to grow and secrete milk, but still, the head won't feed.

Upon bein' asked if he himself carries a *Bebe's* head, the Puerto Rican doctor perks up as if this might be amusing, of course at my expense. Answering in tone of MD, God, know-it-all, "Yes, though I hardly have need of it. I am a doctor after all." Nappy, the half-breed banana boy, asks, patting the protrusion beneath the jacket, "You do? I see no bulge."

Clearing his throat, the upstanding, honorable doctor answers, "Well, I certainly cannot carry my infant's head here at work. No, I prefer carrying mine in the privacy of my own home. There, I can show it respect, and make comfortable the angels that come. I personally do not think it proper carrying an infant's head on one's self at all times. It is quite selfish, asking far too much of the angels; but, eh, to each his own" With brows raised and eyes rollin', I look toward him mocking. Doc Rat notices, yet pretends to ignore for continuing. He explains that the secretions being pumped from retard's nipples is not milk, but rather some sort of lymphatic discharge. Banana boy, lookin' confused, disappointed, and not quite believing, hurriedly raises his jacket up over dirty cloth wrapped protrusion of lower stomach for exposing the indeed swollen inflamed nipples. Squeezing one, he does succeed in gettin' a sticky yellow discharge to surface. After grimacing from the pain, the idiot proudly smiles as if possibly proving the doctor wrong. He receives an impatient wave, and is again told it is not *lactancia*—milk—and even if it were, the infant's *cabeza*—head—would have no need of it. They do not require feeding, nor do they move or speak to their carriers as a live human might. No, they speak in spiritual form only. (Buddy, are these sick assholes talkin' about heads that have been preserved via dehydration or somethin'? Oh—fuck me! Buddy look—look!) The yellow retard has undone his wrappings and is now holding forth a large jumbo plastic zipper bag containing the decaying little head! (Look away! Look away! Man, just don't even look at it, but do keep your eyes alert! You know what to do if the yellow bastard comes near. Yeah sure, but buddy, did you see that thing? Man, you've seen worse. Stay sharp!)

Despite the plastic baggy bein' covered with its carrier's sweat, and the inside all fogged up from the heat of decay, the contents are quite visible. The nappy freak is proudly showing it off to Doctor Rico, and in doin' asks, "Perhaps the American would like a better look? Eh, *Americano*, you should look and see; my *bebé* is very beautiful. Want to see it up closer? Yes? No?" Turning to the Puerto Rican. "What, the American does not speak?"

"Oh yes, our Devon here actually speaks quite eloquently when the mood strikes. However, he is also very unpredictable; we do not want to agitate him. I think we are finished here, yes?" Banana freak understands the dismissal, but before going, asks about the sore rash and festering spots all over his abdomen. The Puerto Rican waves him out, informing they are merely small mosquito and bug bites. And so, Nappy the weirdo leaves, taking with him his beloved decomposing *bebé* head, and my *watch*! It had been with my dirty red Converse high-tops and wet clothes piled in corner on floor. Now outside, from through windows of horror, the yellow retard is seen showing off his new watch to the ganger monkeys.

Fuming, and just about to begin bellowing for my watch, when damn! A gob of snotty tar goo lodges itself in throat as if it can't decide whether or not to come up, or go down. The gunk burns, and Sparky can't breathe—silently choking! During this, young Doctor Puerto Rico is speaking. (What the fuck is he goin' on about?) Turning, feeling very much like my eyes are gonna pop and explode, I see him looking down to the floor, explaining that the children they use, are bought or taken from homes and orphanages where they are not wanted. "Using them as we do, is actually very humane and an act of goodness. We take them from a life where they have no future, only to grow becoming like those outside—" his head nods to the windows "—social cancer; all of them. Whereas, the infants and children that die by our hand cross over to a world of love and enchantment. They are cared for by angels who teach them the way to becoming angels themselves. The pain and suffering inflicted upon them in this world is a small price, and only temporary. It is how the angels wish the cross over." His beady rat eyes dart up to meet mine. Mine are teared up, not from his psychotic ramblings defending the insanity, but rather, from the acid burning tar ball stuck halfway between lungs and throat! "These methods you do not understand and frown upon, but who are you to question or judge? You—you are a social cancer yourself. It is too late for you. Even after we have killed you, the angels will have nothing of you. You are an insult to their purity." (Aw shoot, darny! Buddy, do you hear? We insult the angel's purity. Yeah well, all you little cunt skank angels need to take this here tar ball and shove it up your asses! Ught, too late, it just went south, and stomach is protesting!)

With racking constriction, Sparky clears his throat. The pompous doctor gleams, as if excited for hearing my response to his babbling bullshit. He receives none. Shrugging his wimpy narrow shoulders, the beady eyes go back to staring down at filthy crawlin' floor, but not for long. A young, somewhat attractive couple come down the stairs, and enter the foul cubicle of a room. The young woman is quiet, leery, and acting nervous. It is obvious that she is not wanting to be here in this stinking room. The beau greets the Puerto Rican, handing him a fat baggy full of chunky crack rock, and explains the purpose for their visit. His girl has recently become pregnant, and now, she is concerned that smoking crack might affect the health of her unborn child. The beau is wanting to know if this is true or not?

Doctor Rico, putting away his new baggy of crack, yawns in exaggerated boredom, answering, "No, despite popular belief, it is not true. Crack, if used in moderation, does not harm the mother or fetus. Actually, it can be beneficial. The crack will stimulate the fetus's growth and development. Do not worry; I am quite certain you will have a strong healthy child." (Hey buddy, do you believe this crap?

Another Guatemalan crack baby in the making. Oh well, the poor thing will most likely end up goin' to the Goddamn angels anyway.) As if reading my thoughts, the Puerto Rican shoots a sharp glance warning against verbalizing opinion. (Uh, no *problemo* doc.) The young couple are smiling, very pleased with this tidbit of medical assurance. An invite is offered to the doctor, for briefly steppin' outside and sampling some of the new crack with them. "It is very fresh; bein' made on just this night." The Puerto Rican, nodding his head as if already aware of the fact, declines, with excuse of bein' tired and wanting only sleep. If he smokes any crack now, he will not be able to sleep when his shift is over. (Aw, is the poor doc now sleepy? Whew, the rat prick oughta be in our shoes, huh buddy? Buddy, how we doin'? Man, how do you think? This cold has our muscles spazzing tremors that are difficult to keep concealed. Also, we must stop jumping every time one of those blasting cap firecrackers go off. And the babies, constant wailings from the infant ward isn't helping either. Buddy? Yes? Matrix is gonna be back soon. Do you hear the monkeys at the windows? They won't stop with the taunting jests of what's to come. Looky at 'em buddy, crazed' baboons; jumpin' up and down, makin' stupid faces, screechin' their vicious laughter and mockery. Christ, more and more just keep appearin'. They're gatherin' for a show. Buddy maybe we should… Ught-oh, shit, Matrix is back. And with him is that old woman, the witch. Yepper, from her arms, dangles a bawlin' baby. *Fuck*! Man, do not watch this. No matter what, don't give them the satisfaction. Yeah okay buddy, but…)

Like a critter for the butcher's block, the infant is handed over by its feet, upside down, to the big blood splattered male, for first chopping off its little hands, and then head.

There's a moment where the old witch and I meet eyes. Again, Sparky reads her as not bein' all to approving of this business concerning me. It is almost like there is a bit of sympathy? But how can this be? The old bitch is handing over live babies for dismembering death, without even so much as battin' an eye. She turns, and begins shooing some monkeys away, fussing; they are attracting too much attention. Matrix is now snarling orders for Puerto Rican doctor to lay me out on top of the counter below the windows. He's got a special surprise for "Devon"! Fortunately the orders are ignored. After waving the young pregnant couple quickly from the room, the Puerto Rican feigns temporary deafness, appearing to be deep in thought, staring down at the floor. I follow suit, and do the same. The forced gas has become noticeably less acrid, and after some moments, it is only cold air, sputtering to a stop.

The tank is empty: Sparky has drained two whole tanks! Lookin' up, the Puerto Rican notices. Our eyes briefly meet. (Uh, what now Doc?) I can see the uncertainty as he tries to decide. Nervous, rat-like, his squinty eyes dart from me, to empty gas cylinder, to windows of horror, and back again. Still undecided, and remaining silent, he merely recrosses arms, and resumes the floor-staring stance.

From the grim ghastly circus above comes a man-freak bouncing down the stairs. He is a short grubby hunchback. His eyes are large, animated, and flitting. Its arms, seemingly way too long for his bent body, are cradling something. He does not enter our room; no, instead, using hunchbacked bounding strides, he dashes for one of the two now unoccupied gurneys in the center of the waiting room floor. Up 'til now, every gurney out there had been occupied with bodies of the ailing, broken, and dying or dead. However, there presently are two empty, and they just happen to be beside the stiff corpse of the woman having gaping throat cut. (Gosh, buddy, guess they don't believe in the practice of covering their dead in these parts, huh? Not even the gruesome mutilated ones.) Hunchback slides onto a gurney, one over from the hideous corpse. He, smilin' like a sly idiot, hurriedly unwraps the thing in crook of arm, wrapped with a sickly unclean, greatly stained sheet. (Buddy, what's he got there?) Using some quick adjustments, the hunchback gets himself laid down comfortable and is covered with his awful sheet.

The Puerto Rican, having also watched this, menacingly laughs quietly, goes to the doorless doorway, and calls for Nurse Piggy. After giving her some whispered instructions, which Sparky can't hear, he turns, is all grins, lookin' much like a rotten kid about to play a cruel joke. Informs me that in here, I am taking up much needed space, and therefore need to be moved out into the *centro* waiting room. Nurse Piggy is also smiling wickedly. Glancin' up, Matrix sure ain't smilin'; no he is not! Pushing aside one of the hatchet wielding monkeys, he roars, demanding to know what is going on. Nurse Piggy immediately drops her smile and becomes nervous. The Puerto Rican, ignoring Matrix, is barking orders for me to rise to my feet and follow the nurse. (Oh buddy, this oughta be fun, huh? Man, stop dickin' around. Get up, and walk. We must get out of this room now! Matrix is going to be down here any second! Okay—okay! And man, do not slip or fall. We must stand tall. Every asshole in this place is going to be watching us.)

Sparky removes irritating flimsy mask, plants feet firmly on floor, both hands grippin' arms of wheelchair—and umph! We are up and standin', yepper, despite knees bein' about to buckle, floor rollin', and walls wavin'. (Buddy? Man, this you can overcome, just like in the old days, when we were drinking, must stay standing. Whoa! Man, roll with it—just roll with it. It will pass. But do hurry! I think Matrix is on his way down!) Inhaling deeply, center of balance is somewhat found, and in doing, cautiously reach down for wet pile of clothing… The Puerto Rican, snaps, "You will not be needing those. Now go—get out!" There is urgency in his voice.

Hearing jump boots on the stairs and knowing who they are belonging to, Sparky does get outta there, damn near trippin' on the heels of Nurse Piggy. Exiting the room as Matrix rounds the corner, I sidestep him, bein' sure to keep way clear from his reach. He stops for glaring intimidating evil. And I'm feelin' just fucked up enough to look him in the eyes without wavering. Pure hatred versus pure hatred, in atomizing lock-up. (Yeah right! The psychopath knows no fear, and Sparky is literally electrified with it. Ain't we buddy? Buddy? Yoo hoo, buddy? Oh geez, let me guess, you're checkin' out, right? Right? Pussy! Chicken! Sissy bitch! Aw buddy, why now?) Grunting in disgust, Matrix breaks eye contact for harshly questioning the Puerto Rican.

Nurse Piggy resumes leading the way toward the only remaining unoccupied gurney. You know? The one in between waxy lookin' corpse of ghastly throat cut woman, and Hunchback the Village Idiot? And of course, everyone (that's able) is watchin' "Devon." This time though, nobody's makin' fun, or sport. No they are not. Instead, there is much murmuring of awe, and quick finger pointing. During this, Sparky is doin' his best for standin' tall.

Another young nurse, having short black hair and narrow hips, struts over, joining Nurse Piggy. No awe from these two bitches; nope, they stand there, side by side, with arms crossed, and glaring. Skippy Joe, how these two nurses are hatin' Sparky. Still, behind that hatred, fear is revealed. Ha ha! They are afraid of the long-haired, tattooed, American! However, this does little in stopping 'em from actin' tough, ordering me up on the gurney for laying down.

The gurney is layered with unwashed sheets of disgusting body fluids and semi-fluids: blood, pus, urine, feces, you name it. And I don't mean no little spots here and there either. No, these sheets are ripe, sticky, and damp, having one seeping into the other, interfusing a macabre, intricate with ugliness. Knowing the answer before even asking, I politely ask anyway for a clean sheet. After both nurses have their fun, mocking and pretending my request as bein' the most outrageous thing they've ever heard, I'm flatly told "No." Gosh, Sparky really don't want to get on this gurney and lay down. No he does not! Hhmm, maybe I could just step over here, and sit in a chair, or somethin'? Yes? No? Guess not. Nurse

Piggy throws her arms up in exaggerated reaction, as the other nurse barks like a yappy dog, ordering me to get up on the gurney, and lay down! And, of course, everybody is watchin', including the grinnin' Puerto Rican and scowling Matrix... both standin' in doorless doorway of small room. Jesus, maybe it is best to do as told. Ught, but first, let's just take a quick look-see under these layers of flesh decaying sheets. Don't want to lay down and find creepy-crawlies comin' out. Sparky sure wouldn't put it past these two nurses for planting just such things. No he would not! Especially the one that keeps a-glancin' toward Matrix, sendin' quick flirty smiles.

Thumbing through the layers, ignoring the nurses' loud, bitching protests, I find no sign of live creepy-crawlies, but damn, there is some real pretty shit in here! And lucky me, I get to lay on it. Wow, the smell... Hey, where the fuck did he come from? As if from nowhere, a UN soldier appears, taking up a standing guard position at the head of my designated gurney, yet a few feet away, against the wall in front of a doorway having closed door. His eyes are serious, alert, and darting; from his position. He can observe the room's activity, including directly beyond Sparky to where Matrix and Rico the Rat Doctor are presently standin'. Matrix is challengingly glarin' the UN trooper up and down. The soldier, however, is solid and unmoving. Matrix don't intimidate him; no he don't. And why would he? The troop has a grease gun (submachine gun) hangin' from around his neck with right hand grasping. Also, he's from a way bigger army than anything Matrix has. Hhmm, but why is the UN troop here? Is he here for guarding me, like sheep head Todd Boil has promised? Or is he here for guarding the Americans that were in a supposed car wreck? "Very suspicious," Nurse Piggy had said of that. I bet there ain't no Americans back there at all. If there were, Todd Boil and American Embassy people would be all over this place, not to mention reporters and journalists, who were here, but only for *moi*—yours truly. No, "Devon" is the only dumb ass American here. So then, why is this UN trooper here? Oh boy, sure wish he was a US marine. Yeah well, at least this UN trooper don't look to be Central American—Latin, or Carib. He is brown, but appears Asiatic, and is much larger framed than most of this region, save for the black Caribs. And why is this slightly comforting? Who knows.

Rolling up onto the gurney, my weight settles, sinking into layers of sheets so vile. Shaking from the cold, I use my little airport-style blanky for tucking myself in, but not too much; don't want the thing hindering if quick movement is called for. Well well, now ain't this just comfy. On my right is the poor murdered woman, and on my left is hunchback, the local village idiot. The retard has poked his head out from under his filthy sheet; eyes are huge with eerie sparkle, and he is grinnin' from ear to ear.

A commanding grumble from Matrix gets the nurses' attention. Both bitches hurry over to him. At the same time, "Phisst! Phisst!" The grinnin' idiot is wanting my attention. Ught, looky what he's got. The fucker's got himself an IV bag half full of pinkish liquid; and in this bloody fluid is, oh yeah, a squirmin' little blunt nosed snake. Yep, a for-real, live snake! In an IV bag that is for real needled into the retard's inner arm! There, on the tube, he's of course, got himself a mini-valve for regulating the flow of his blood entering the IV bag. Having my attention, the hunchback is proud as punch, tapping and tinkering with valve and tube, tryin' to get more blood down into the bag. (Buddy, are you gettin' this? Wow, wonder if this weird freak of nature ever works the IV feeding fluid contents back into himself? Geez, after what we've seen, in this hell hole of the world, it would hardly be surprising, huh? Buddy? Buddy! Crap.) The insane grinnin' retard is actin' like this is just our little secret. Uh, okey-dokey. Goddamn, even if by some miracle I did make it back home alive, nobody would ever, ever believe any of this. Hhmm, that little snake there is probably feelin' much the same regarding his own predicament. He ain't likin' this arrangement at all, no he is not! And who could blame him? The poor critter is zigzaggin', almost standin' on end of tail, tryin' to get out of there.

Hearing the nurses giggle; it can be assumed Matrix has given them some fun instructions concerning "Devon." They are all lookin' my way, having fiendish smiles. Matrix, using his index finger pointing, pretends to shoot me, before bounding up the stairs. Jump boots reverberating a stompin' echo, audible even above the constant hollow crying of infants no longer heard. Well, nobody seems to hear 'em 'cept for Sparky; and even as is—in this self preserving survival mode—I cannot allow for truly hearing. No, not the infants, not anymore; for if so, insanity would surely follow.

Doctor Puerto Rico disappears back into the doorless doorway of a room. The nurses, smirking, sending deviant sneaky glances, stroll over to the *centro*'s front desk, located on far right wall. There, the cunts gossip and goof around with two male nurses. Through the giggling bullshit, my name is heard mentioned often. Imagine that. Wonder what they are up to?

Warmth begins to slowly seep into my so-called bones, and with it, heavy eyelids. Drowsiness is flooding… (Buddy! Buddy? Man, you can not fall asleep, not even for a second. Come on, we've played this game before: fight the sleep, fight it using everything from within. Must keep mind busy, but do not think thoughts of wife, sons, or home. If you do, the body will drift, drift into sleep... Yeah okay, buddy. But whew—I am, so tired. And this horizontal position does not help.)

The village idiot continues to busy himself with the very, very bizarre, weird intravenous snake-in-a-bag. He's pulled the needle from his arm and is tryin' to blow air into it. Damn, the freak's inner arm is all messed up: one big bruise of oozing perforated sores. After watching him shove the needle back into the pulpy mass and fiddle with some filthy med tape, I glance over to see if the UN trooper is watching. He is, but without expression. Also, he avoids all eye contact with me. Still though, the troop is on alert, locked and loaded. Hhmm, what is the model of that grease gun he's got?

I have, of course, had some experience in the past with the American M3-A1, a cheaply made submachine gun in .45 caliber. Like most cheap grease guns, it is made up almost entirely of soft stamped steel, having little to no machining. There is also the British Sten Mark 2, which I have fired on a couple of occasions. The Sten Mark 2 is a weapon so simplified and stripped down that firing one is much like burping out 550 rounds per minute through a hot piece of galvanized pipe. And, as with all such weapons of this class, accuracy is nil; still, they did and do, serve their intended purpose. At close range, they get the job done; that is, of course, if they don't have jamming malfunctions during course of rapid fire, a risk which due to their cheap overall construction, is always high. Well, guess that's pretty much it, for Sparky havin' any hands-on experience with mass produced grease gun type sub-machine guns. Most were manufactured during the World War 2 era, a wee bit before my time, you know. For purpose of keeping brain on track, thus diverting persistent sleep, I openly stare at the trooper's grease gun, and try recalling everything known within concerning such weapons. It's a struggle, indeed. The thought process is weary, worn down, frazzled. Still, it's somethin' to do. Anything for stayin' awake and keepin' from thinking about all that has happened, and yet to happen. Like how in the morning, if ol' Toddy Boil don't show up in time, and that worm of a Puerto Rican tries carrying out the gray Nazi doctor's orders to give me the death shot injections. Fuck! Almost makes one think getting' a little shut-eye nap beforehand not such a bad idea. Ught! Can't afford even the slightest notion of this direction. The brain and body are so tired, tryin' to pull tricks for justifying sleep... Can not sleep MOTHER FUCKER!

Uhmm, let's see, the trooper's gun has a rectangular stock of tubular metal, which now is folded flush on the right side. It is fed ammo via long stick magazines of guessing 32 or 36 rounds of 9 mm. Strange thing is the manner this trooper has two long stick magazines taped together. As most know, taping magazines together is a common practice the world over. You just take two magazines, lay one on top of the other, bringing it down a bit, having ports (lips) facing opposite direction, and wrap 'em up tightly together, using sturdy tape. Obviously the purpose of this practice is speed loading. Empty mag number one—simply eject, rotate, and insert mag number two—lock and load! This is how it is most commonly done, and most practical. However, our UN soldier here must, for whatever reason, disagree. He's got his two long stick mags taped in such a way as to look like a big letter L. Mag number one descends from magazine housing, vertically, with mag number two taped to its bottom, riding horizontal, having feed lips aimed in same direction as muzzle of barrel, and it's almost just as long! Wonder what the advantage (if any) there is to this? (Hey buddy, why does this trooper have his mags taped like that? Buddy? Buu-ddy, yoo hoo, buddy? Hhmm, guess you've checked out again. Well, you go right on ahead, you dung eatin' puke! Uh, aw buddy, just kiddin' there. You go on and rest up a bit. Sparky here will keep look out. But if that Puerto Rican approaches with a syringe, it's gonna take us both to hurt him. Yepper, all holy hell is gonna break loose. It will be interesting to see what this UN trooper does then, huh?)

Gosh, why are those mags taped that way? Let's see; as I recall, much of the problems associated with these old, cheap, stamped out sub-machine guns, were the magazines. This, and them bein' very susceptible to dirt-fouling, ammo jams, and, oh yeah, can't forget the accounts of some literally breaking apart in the shooters' hands during heavy use, or simply from bein' dropped, etc. Primarily though, their stick magazines suffer the same weakness as the guns themselves, and even more so. First and foremost, there are the feed lips, which are easily bent and damaged, thus causing all sorts of hair-standing-on-end fun! Maybe the trooper's magazines are too weak for holding back the pressure of stacked rounds if upside down? No, that can't be. And why is the UN soldier armed with an outdated grease gun anyways? He must be from some poor-ass country to be issued a piece of junk weapon like the one he's got. What kind of gun is it? For the type, it's not a bad looking weapon. No cut-outs exposing any springs or internal parts. The frame is flat and well streamlined. No round tube appearance here; nor does it have that boxy look. The main body, including pistol grip, seems to be made of two side pieces somehow hinged for opening and closing to get at internal mechanism works. The cocking handle is a round knob, riding on top of receiver. The barrel is short, having no heat shield or flash guard. A magazine well (housing) does extend down a bit; and directly behind this, bein' very noticeable, is a good-sized protruding latch. This would be an overly large mag release, or possibly a safety? If it's a safety, both hands then would be required to start-fire the weapon—not a good feature for small sub-machine guns or machine pistols.

Hey I know that gun! It's a… Uh. It's a…, a… Aw darn, had it there, but then forgot. My head hurts, and I need to big time blow my nose. Can't hardly breathe. Eugh, maybe Sparky should forget about the gun for awhile, and give the neck muscles a break, stare at the ceiling or somethin'. But must not fall asleep. Though, perhaps, a little pretending wouldn't hurt.

For this, a game is played, one where I mentally mimic a kitty cat bein' stuck in the same backyard as a bunch of mean slobbering dogs staring with big bad teeth, waiting for a chance at breaking chains to rip poor kitty to shreds and eat kitty. Still, kitty cat, bein' kitty, does what all cats do when in such trying situations; after calming, they must reserve all energy and feign sleep so as not to re-arouse easily excitable toothy numbskulls. In doing, kitty can watch and listen without exposing true magnitude of alarming fear within. The watching is done through narrow slits of eyelash curtains that open ever so slightly and close ever so slowly, in rhythmic deliberation hardly noticed.

Listening, above the sounds of infants no longer heard (not), Matrix and his monkeys are heard in the far off distance calling out my name, laughing and thumpin' the chopping block. The village idiot, with his intravenous snake-in-a-bag, is muttering "Devon", while adding strange gurgled hissing sounds, wanting more of my attention. Many people sitting in waiting chairs are engaged in whispering conversations about you know who. "Devon, Devon, Devon"—God, how I do hate the way they pronounce my name. The front desk, hell, the whole sewer of a hospital is all in a buzz with my name, discussing me and what I have done, etc.

Nurse Piggy and Nurse Yappy decide it's time to have their fun: carrying out Matrix's instructions no doubt. They each take turns coming to my gurney under pretense for checking up, and tuck-snugging the already tucked in mini blanket. But what the wicked bitches are really doin', is discreetly slippin' in, with their tuckings, little black mesh bags, full of squirming live small shiny black scorpions and spiders. Sick cunts. Knowing them to be doin' this for creating a wanting hysterical reaction, I give them none. Now, since I'm obviously not asleep, and very much aware of all approaching my gurney, uh gee, when they're slippin' somethin' under my blanky, well Skippy you better believe that the somethin' gets swished to the floor quicker than you can say "What the fuck?" And is done so in calm form, attracting not much attention. Once the mesh bags hit the floor, all the little ugly creepy-crawlies begin to scurry up and out through cut opening in mesh to scramble every which way across grimy tiled floor. However, before they can get far, along comes Nurse Piggy, or Nurse Yappy, to sweep 'em away using a big push broom. Finally, after several attempts at pulling this lame stunt, and failing to get the desired reaction, and having to sweep away the nasty biting bugs each and every time, a male nurse (or whatever he is) emerges from a room having a large tinted black window near the front desk. He, softly laughing, confronts the two nurses, and in doing, using hushed humored tone, explains this must stop. Reason? They are appearing too suspicious on video camera. "Anyone who views the video will be asking, what is it these nurses are doing to the *Americano*? Why do they strangely touch him and push the broom so often?" The skanks giggle with acknowledgment. "It is simply too obvious. I do not care what Matrix instructs; we cannot get Devon to respond how he is demanding. We must, for now, leave Devon be. Look how the UN soldier and others are watching. See? It is too suspicious, and we will be the ones held responsible. We tried, but now it must stop." He then begins joking around with Nurse Yappy, asking her if she knows "Devon" is bisexual? And does it excite her? Has she ever seen two men fucking before? "No? Not even on porno videos?" Of course Nurse Yappy is all giggles, blushing, while acting appalled and such, blurting exclamation, while doin' the Catholic chest-crossing thing, "No—no! Never! All these homosexuals need to be tortured for their sins, and exterminated!" Seeing that the male nurse is a bit taken back by her extremism, she justifies that it is how God wishes. "It is written so in the Bible! Man must be with woman, and woman must be with man!" And with a ridiculously stupid laugh of conceit, the cunt waves off her listeners, and prances over to the standing UN trooper, for flauntingly flirting.

Wow, what is with these people and their thing concerning me and bisexuality? I haven't been with another man since like for ever, uh, unless you're sick enough to count havin' to blow Mr. Big Shot, or gettin' a huge flashlight shoved up the ass during my most welcomed stay in charming Trujillo. Hardly consensual gay activity. Hhmm, and now a video camera here in this cesspool of an emergency room videoing yours truly. Why? The only logical conclusion I can come up with, is that they are obviously tryin' to get documented proof of Sparky bein' loony as a two-headed pup with a live June bug up its butt! This would explain also, maybe, sorta the purpose, besides pure cruelty, for Matrix ordering the skank nurses to slip the little biting creepy-crawlies under my blanky. They themselves would be too small for the video camera to pick up from such distance, but of course, not "Devon" spazzin', flopping about, tryin' to brush unseen critters off myself. No, the camera would indeed pick that up, and thus, I would certainly appear to be suffering from hysterical detox of chronic long-term, drug/alcohol abuse or such. Personally, I never knew anyone to actually behave this way when high or detoxing; and, believe you me, Sparky has known his share of drug addicts and serious alcoholics. I have, of course, like everyone else, heard the stories and read the accounts of these kinds of symptoms occurring; but really though, they can't be all that common. Like I say; Sparky has known the real deal when it comes to substance abusers. Hell, there have been times in my life when I have lived with them—the chronic of the chronic: whether it was under a roof, or sharing a bush in some squatter camp; it had always been a running joke. Sure, they (we) would black out, do crazy things, go to jail, get the shakes, and always suffer from night sweats of ghastly dreams; yet nobody would ever wake up believin' snakes, spiders and/or various creepy-crawlies were on them. I guess, though, if such a thing could be documented, say via video camera, then pretty much anything that the poor chump (me) might speak of thereafter could be considered unsound—having no merit—for example, anything and everything regarding my own bizarre story here in Central America.

Boy-O-Boy, it's gonna be tough as a mother fuck, not only stayin' alive, but defending my extreme actions while exposing the crimes and sadistic atrocities witnessed and forced. Matrix knows this, and so does that sheep dip of an Ambassador Todd Boil. Christ, even he is playin' up this "All in my mind" game. That guy is so full of it. He knows; he knows the truths. I saw it in his eyes. Besides, these horrid acts go on so openly down here that there is no way he could not know about them. Also, Sparky heard him talkin' to Laura Simms; sure as shit I did. Laura and Todd both know of Matrix; just as they know of PRISA International Airlines forcing backpackers to mule. That son-a-bitch Todd Boil set me up tonight. Yes he did! But why? The big question— why? And where is that schmuck anyways?

Except for infants, the emergency room becomes eerie quiet. Matrix and his monkeys must have left. The nurses have stayed away from my gurney, and the village idiot with intravenous snake-in-a-bag has hid himself under his disgusting sheet. The UN soldier is still standing in position, but his eyes are similar to my own, in that they appear to be seeing through slitted eyelash curtain only. And me? Well, much like soft lazy waves of chocolate Mississippi River water rolling hot August lappings, licking smooth muddy sloping shoreline, I am drifting, drifting into semi-consciousness. The pull for drawing this homesick huckleberry out far is constant, inviting, and full of trickery. (Buddy, ol' friend, Sparky is seriously not sure how long he can keep this up. Damn, buddy, I sure wish we were on that ol' river right now. God, I can even smell the earthy, fertile redolence, so enticing. Can you smell it, buddy? Man, STOP! STOP! STOP! It's a trick you asshole! Wake up—wake the fuck up!)

And with that, all lights flip on and the whole emergency room becomes brighter. I hear sounds coming from more and more people arriving all around: visitors, patients, workers, nurses, doctors, etc. Suddenly there is a harrowing shriek heard from a woman outside; she has discovered the many severed baby heads, left over from Matrix's slaughter. The woman is now joined by others, all acting to be terribly appalled, but really though, from the rapid Spanish and English, Sparky knows their display of shocked anguish is merely sympathetic disgust. One would think they had come across bloody puppy heads, instead of human infants! This is confirmed when a woman is heard ordering another to go get so-and-so, for cleaning up the mess. There is no mention for calling the police, or anything.

The despicable village idiot, as if on cue, quickly rolls up his intravenous snake-in-a-bag, using filthy sheet, jumps from gurney and bolting, is outta here! A man, wearing sunglasses and outdated nerd clothes, strolls over to the UN soldier, and boldly asks him if he is guarding "Devon?" The trooper simply answers "No." When further questioned as to why he is here, the trooper answers with a silent shoulder shrug. The man then points to the UN soldier's weapon, and comments on its uniqueness. (Aaaw-haw! Sparky remembers! Yep, finally remembers; the gun is a Madsen! And I think the Danish made it. It was supposed to be an upgraded improved version of the Finnish Suomi M-31, if one can believe that. The Finnish Suomi M-31, once all her bugs were worked out, was, in its day, a very fine sub-machine gun, having been made from heavy machined-milled steel with a reputation for exceptional reliability. The cheap stamped out Madsen hardly compared.) The UN soldier, having eyes again very much open, glinting alert cautious watch, simply answers, "It is from Canada." The man, nodding, looking absurd in those sunglasses, pulls forth a pack of cigarettes and offers the troop one. With a look of agitation and wary head shake, the offer is silently declined. The man, getting the hint, shrugs his shoulders as if insulted, lights his cigarette, swaggers over to a chair and takes a seat, while keeping ridiculous sunglasses fixed on both Sparky and the trooper. (Uh, *policia secreto* much?).

Obviously, it is now early morning. I have once again made it miraculously through yet another night of hell. But now what? Three men dressed much like the watchful, chain smoking cop descend the stairs. One has in hand a manila paper folder. From across the room, they stop, point, gawk, and make jokes regarding "Devon" who is, of course, pretending to be asleep. In doing, I watch them through squinted eyelashes. Sparky can see their stupid sunglasses and smirking Latin pig grins. Listening, it is learnt that they are here with my documents supposedly sent from the United States. Mrs. Benny had said that important American officials would be hand delivering this paperwork themselves. Yeah well, they might have; but these guys sure aren't Americans. No they are not! And, it's morning. Why-why-why are no Americans here to at least check up on me, and issues pertaining? Lordy, it just don't make any sense. Where did these Latin pigs get my documents anyway? One would think FBI, right—right? Come on. It's not like small town police departments are gonna to be sending out their tidbits of meaningless info on Devin L. Murfin to Guatemala! So it would have to be the FBI. Hhmm, and if so, wouldn't they send it through the American Embassy first? If only for collaboration? Geez, I am an American—husband, and father—in some serious deep trouble here! (Right buddy? Buddy! Aw man, get real; and stop being a dumb ass! Obviously, nobody gives two shits. Besides, Todd Boil and Laura Simms already have a folder on us. That was evident during questioning back at the embassy, remember? And you know, it would have only taken them minutes to get all FBI records on us via high speed fax. Okay buddy, then what's goin' on? Man, the question of all questions. Just stay sharp!)

The three piggies are met at the doorless doorway room by Doctor Rat Puerto Rican himself. Inside the room they go, and, purposely bein' loud, they aren't hard to hear. Using voices for exaggerative boisterous humor, the three pigs read off a list containing my illegal offenses, most bein' from long ago. And to spice it up a bit, they, of course, add some arrests and offenses that I have never done. They then share stories rumoured of my Cuban exploits, like how "Devon' was a known gun runner, having made several trips to Cuba for selling arms and buying drugs. Also there, "Devon" and his mercenary friends would run wild, drinking tequila, smoking crack, raping and even killing! (Jesus buddy, are you hearing this? What fantastic storytelling! And drinkin' tequila? Who drinks tequila in Cuba? I thought rum was the island's drink of choice? Don't matter, 'cause Sparky can't stand either drink. Even back in the hard drinkin' days, that stuff played havoc on our stomach ulcers, huh buddy? Ught, looky who's a comin' to join 'em.) The grey Nazi Doctor enters the doorless room, bringing the noisy theatrics to an abrupt stop.

Two male nurses approach and remove the ghastly throat-cut corpse of neighboring peasant woman. They replace her with a moaning female burn victim, guessed to be a teenager, having head, face, chest, and hands heavily wrapped in unclean, stained gauze bandages, oozing ugly colors from mutilating hurt. Also the gurney that had bedded retard-intravenous snake-in-a-bag is now occupied by a man gasping with stab wounds to the stomach. He's bleeding like a stuck pig, but Christ if anyone seems to care. Whew, wonder what the Nazi doctor, three cop goons and Puerto Rican are deciding in that room? Death shot injection. Yes? No? Damn, where is Todd Boil? Come on Toddy, you son-a-bitch! Please come get me the hell outta here! (Calm down man; just calm the fuck down. Pretend to be asleep; watch and wait. Yeah, okay.)

Canada? Hhmm, the UN trooper had said his weapon was Canadian. Gosh, what would Canada be doin' with submachine guns like the Madsen? I mean, even if, say, during World War 2 or shortly thereafter, they (Canada) had purchased large quantities of mass produced, stamped out, budget grade sub-machine guns of grease gun class for stockpiling, which in all probability was the case, one would think it would be the British Sten, not the Danish Madsen; but who knows? I remember reading once, how an American Navy officer had carried and used the Owen Austin (perhaps one of the silliest grease guns ever designed) throughout his entire Vietnam tour with the brown water river patrol. Of all the personal weapons the naval officer could have chosen, he chose the cheap outdated Australian Owen Austin having top feed long stick magazine and poor offset sights. Why? Because he thought it looked cool! Stupid Navy, even the Australians hated the gun. Looked cool? You know, this most certainly would not be a consideration for me in choosing a battle weapon. Though, who am I, other than one screwed American that has somehow managed to seriously piss off everybody who is anybody in this bizarre, cruel, insane region of the world? So golly, if the UN trooper wants his weapon to be Canadian, then well hell, it's Canadian!

Laying here, drifting in wondrous thoughts of bein' armed with choice options for various combat weapons, a pile of ammo, and how Sparky would play it all out. Let's throw in a few fresh grenades and an RPG, shall we? Ught-oh, here comes Doc Puerto Rican. In his hands are my wet soiled clothes and sooty, red, high-top Converse tennis shoes; fortunately there is no syringe. Rico the Rat looks tired, yet there is a sense of him feeling relief. It's guessed his shift is over, and they've decided against givin' "Devon" the fatal injection. Reaching the gurney, he drops my clothes to filthy crawlin' floor; while sternly ordering, 'Okay, wake up! Time to go. We have done all we can for you. You have been discharged. Now leave." The three grinnin' cop goons are across the room waiting by the stairs. And the sitting chain-smoking *policia secreto* is half off his seat, as if ready to pounce. And the UN trooper? Well, he hasn't moved, but his eyes are alert. Whoa, fuck this! Sparky ain't goin' nowhere! No-sirree-bob! They are gonna have to attack, fight, and drag my ass outta here. Yes they are! Where is that squirrelly dick Todd Boil? Aughg! Using very best dazed and confused expression, I look to the Puerto Rican and pretend *no entendimiento*. Of course, he knows it to be an act, but so what. Shruggin' his shoulders, he turns, and is gone. Soon, however, the gray Nazi doctor approaches, and is much more persistent, knuckle jabbing my ribs with each barking command: "You!" (jab) "Get up!" (jab) "Leave!" (jab) "Now!" (jab) "You!" etc. (Buddy? Man, just stay cool. Everyone is watching. Do not lose it. He's the one looking the asshole. Must keep playing the passive, weak, injured patient. He's trying to provoke you into violence, thus justifying the cops becoming involved. Bite your lip and suck it up, he can't hurt us—not with everybody watching. Yeah, okay buddy.) Suddenly, the same nice lady doctor from last night is heard shouting, "Enough! That is enough—no more!" She hurriedly appears for intervening; and in doing, has an escort of several colleagues obviously loyal to her, hence consequently sympathetic to the tattooed, long-haired American.

Following some brief hostile arguing, consisting of both English and rapid Spanish, the nice lady doctor wins out, declaring the patient "Devon" anything but fit for discharge at this time. "Look at him! And after all the gas you have pumped into this patient. You are now wanting to release him without even allowing the required recovery time for the gas alone. Not to mention the carbon poisoning he is suffering as well. No! This patient will be permitted to stay, if only for resting off the gas you deemed so *necesario*."

The gray Nazi doctor, throwing his arms up, retorts, using words something on the order of this being an emergency room and not a hotel! He turns, stomps across *centro's* floor, is joined by the three waiting cop goons, whereupon they ascend the stairs and are gone. The chain-smoking *policia secreto*, however, remains seated; and UN trooper stays on guard, maintaining position (whatever it may be).

The nice lady doctor, leaning forward for examining, uses tone soft and soothing, quietly assuring that for the time being, I am safe, and should use this "safe time" for sleeping. Also, she is personally going to try reaching the American Embassy via phone. She then turns to her entourage, consisting of both young men and women, and instructs them, "Keep a close watch on this man. Do not let anyone come near him. Not even the *policia*. As long as he is here, in this building, under my care, they cannot legally take Devon away. I am to be immediately notified if they, or anyone else comes for him. Understood?" With eyes large, they all nod.

Oh Boy, this woman has just become my new best friend! Hhmm, and if the understanding is correct, as long as Sparky is in a hospital, under the care of a doctor, the cops, goons, and military can not legally drag me out. (Not that legal law means all that much down here; but still, it's a nice tidbit to know anyways.)

A slow long time passes. I do not see the nice lady doctor again, and it's a pretty sure bet the man having stab wounds, laying on neighboring gurney, has died. His blood is pooled all over the floor, even fingering its way into my piled wet clothes. He is no longer moaning and doesn't appear to be breathin'. The blood, though still seeping, ain't pumpin' gushes. The man's mouth is locked open agape, as are eyes, having eyeballs flat and dry. Yep, he's dead. Nobody seems to care though. To be honest, I think most of the hospital staff enjoy having patients and visitors seeing "Devon" laid out here in the middle of the floor between two fly-infested, ghastly dead and dying. It sorta adds a visual setting accompanying the sensational rumors buzzin'. I am seriously starting to pick up that these people down here really dig this sort of thing, much like the cheap, pulpy fright Comix publications so popular here, and all throughout Central America.

A young, clean-cut white man, recognized as belonging to the nice lady doctor's entourage, approaches. Bending down close, he whispers that they have reached the American Embassy and the Ambassador will be here shortly. This kind man, wearing long white doctor's smock, is guessed to be European and here for serving a medical internship or the likes. Very much unnecessarily he suggests, "It might be wise to be ready." (Uh, duh!)

On pins and needles Sparky waits, and waits, and waits! And still no

Todd Boil. Around noon, the chain-smoking *policia secreto* cop stands, snuffs out yet another cigarette, sends a grinning look having promise for return, walks across *centro*'s floor, ascends stairs, and out the building he goes.

His exit pulls my being from the adhering crusty vile sheets. I'm off that gurney, standin', calling forth sureness of balance. After gathering up wet belongings, while trying hard to ignore all the gawking murmurs from pointing people, it's double time across that floor for the doorless doorway room, where the white intern was last seeing entering. He is there, and with him is another. Educated white men they are, and obviously friends. Feeling their kind warmth and possible admiration, it is sensed these two are wanting to help, but aren't sure how. They do, though, openly praise my conduct, referring to last night as being an "act of *valore*." For many here, I am considered a "hero." (Oh yeah, that's Sparky all right—a fearless hero of gallantry! Lordy, I shat all over myself, having done things best not ever known.)

Warning is then given concerning the extreme unsanitary condition of these floors and how they should not be walked while barefoot. Yes sir, time for this cowboy to be gettin' his boots on, lickety-split, and Sparky has feet in damp, filthy red Converse high-tops with strings pulled tight and tied. The white interns, approving, are now discussing the obvious oddity as to why there is nobody here yet from the American Embassy. In doing, one suggests I go take up a nearby seat there on the bench, just outside the room, where they can keep watch, while the other again tries calling the American Embassy. (Uh, okey-dokey; sure; you bet.)

The bench is, of course, full of seated waiting people. But they've left a few inches open on the end. Move it on over, you yappy Beaners! 'Cause this gaunt, wild-eyed, ridiculously dressed, long-haired, tattooed American is gonna sit down. In doing, well, slap my balls if every Beaner on the bench don't rise for standing or finding other seating. One is noticed as being a very pretty teenage girl, enduring extreme pain, clutching a severely broken wrist having jagged bone protruding from bloody torn flesh. And still, with tearing brown eyes, she is staring in questioning bewilderment at you know who. Geez, what is it with these people?

A man walks over to the front desk, boisterously loud, asking a nurse, "Who is the American, and why is he here?" The nurse, looking at him, as if perhaps he had just arrived from another planet, exclaims, "Him? You don't know who he is? He is *famoso*, and in all the papers. He is Devon the *Americano* that burned down a hotel to fight off *satanicos*.

397

Personally, I think he is *loco*. Also, it is rumored, he is homosexual!" The man, hearing, throws his arms up for acting aghast at this last remark. Laughin' and shakin' their heads, they both send looks of disgust my way.

Just when it's thought that surely no more sitting around and waiting can be tolerated, ol' Todd Boil, his long lanky self, comes a-bouncin' down the stairs. He glances first across *centro's* floor toward the UN trooper still standing guard. Silent nods of acknowledgement are exchanged. And Sparky? Oh, Skippy Joe! He's smilin' like a beaming imbecile. Uh, that is until Todd spins and begins to loudly tear a new asshole, when old one is not yet itself healed. Todd's words are angered, vicious, and spitting. Clearly, the intention is for having the whole damn hospital hear; and hear they all do. Yep, Todd Boil is center stage with his dramatic, slandering accusations, calling me a psychotic firebug, delusional pyromaniac, etc. According to him, I am mentally unstable, and in dire need of immediate institutionalization. (Fuckin' what?)

He begins to rant and rave, repeating things I told him yesterday regarding snakes, spiders, snuff films, and people wanting to kill me! Todd keeps shouting how it is all in my mind! None of it is real! (Oh you back-stabbin' traitor! First you put me in that hotel, knowing full well, and now you have the nerve to pull this shit!)

With head spinnin' in disbelief, my first impulse is to spring jump him! But buddy screams, "NO," instantly reminding of the stupidity resulting. And in doing, it quickly becomes obvious that Todd is tryin' just a little bit too hard, and loud, at workin' his ass chewin' perform- ance. He must surely be doin' this for a reason, though for whose benefit, I've no idea. However, Sparky decides it's best just to play along: acting the role of scolded pup with tail between legs. Todd, seeing, plainly approves. He barks orders commanding the pitiful, long-haired, head-hanging American dog to follow. And of course, this mutt does, thinkin' we are gonna bound up those stairs for getting the fuck outta here, but nooo! Toddy ain't done with his degrading verbal hammerings. No he is not!

He leads the way through the doorless doorway room where the two white European interns still are. Here, in front of them, and for the whole hospital to hear, same as before, Todd lays into me some more. His behavior is shocking to the Europeans: finally one intervenes for attempts of questioning this insanity, "Why? Why do you shout at Devon in this manner? He is not well; look at him. We are surprised after all he has been through that he is even still able to stand. We hear that the man known as Matrix, with his death squad and street gang, were here last night tormenting Devon. And this is after he went down in the hotel fire!'

Todd Boil, the American Ambassador, spins on them both, speaking very rapid Spanish. The interns nod understanding of his words, but their quizzical expressions never leave. Todd then turns to me, and acting as though he is doing an undeserving favor, explains what it was he had just said to them. Basically, he told them that while in our presence, everything spoken or heard within this room is considered confidential. He trusts them to respect this and warns that if they should ever repeat anything, he will simply deny it all. Lowering his voice, and using English, Todd asks both men what they know of "Devin." Both interns look at each other as if tryin' to decide what best to say, or not to say. Finally, the tall one calmly answers, "As you must know there are many different stories going around concerning Devon." Shrugging his shoulders, he adds "So we know what we know only. For whatever reason, certain people, of politically-corrupt strong influence, are wanting Devon dead. The man Matrix, and his army surrounded Devon's hotel room last night and tried to pull him out." There is a pause before continuing, as if expecting an interruption from the Ambassador. None comes. "This sort of thing happens here in this country often. You, of all people, must surely know this." Another pause. Todd still holds his tongue, but is rolling his eyes and tapping foot, as if running out of patience. "Devon, rather than be taken alive, fights to the end, sets fire to his own room, and goes down with it, thus denying the man Matrix and his death squad their conquest. To us, where we come from, this makes Devon a hero."

Wow, I can't believe what is bein' heard. These two white interns are most definitely on my good guys list. Hhmm, wonder where they are from anyways? Their accents are certainly not UK British. No, more like eastern European. Todd Boil, however, is not so impressed; no, he is not! With astounded expression on stupid elongated face, he looks to both interns as if they have lost their minds. His look grows more incredulous, after having asked them from what source they are getting their incorrect information. For answer, both interns give silent shrug of shoulders only. Todd's face, now flushed with restrained frustration, having temples throbbing a rhythm same as blue vein in neck, he tries to calmly persuade the interns that what they think they know concerning "Devin" is all wrong, being nothing more than rumors; blah, blah, blah! Then he tells them that I am a known serious alcoholic, suffering from acute paranoid hallucinations and border-line schizophrenia. Yepper, ol' Toddy himself, just this morning, had spoken to my wife regarding this, and she strongly confirmed, informing, "Devin has been a chronic alcoholic since childhood!" (Oh God, fuck me! Damn, I can just picture my wife there, back home, hysterical, blabbering on and on, saying everything and anything that this sheep-head Todd Boil might want to hear. My wife and her family are a loud, easily persuaded bunch. Todd must have had himself a field day scrambling her brain.)

Fortunately the two interns have more backbone and ain't buyin'. Now pretending to busy themselves doin' nothing, they do keep glancin' toward Todd the way men do when it's known bullshit is bein' laid thick. Toddy continues on with his blatant, unnecessary spewing, until a stern defiant "No!" is hissed from one of the interns, adding, "Explain then, the severed heads of infants and children—fifteen in all— found this morning just outside this very window where Devon spent a good part of the night being force-pumped with a gas that should never have been used, not in his condition. We are amazed that it did not kill him. No. They were here—here for Devon! Alcoholic or no, it took some big balls to do what he did!"

"Big balls indeed," agrees the other intern.

Todd, knowing he's been defeated, retorts, "Well, believe what you like." Turning to Sparky, "Devin, your wife is anxiously awaiting to hear from you. Let's go to the embassy and give her a call, shall we?"

Upon exit, both interns firmly shake my hand while offering sincere farewell, good luck, etc. And with that, I am on Todd's heels bounding up those stairs and outta that wretched building, into the warm bright sunshine. Just beyond the door, now standing guard at the entrance platform, is the UN trooper having Madsen sub-machine gun. He and Todd again nod to each other, confirming somethin'.

There, in the parking lot, leaning against a car, are the three grinnin' cop goons that had been down in the emergency room earlier. Pointing them out to Todd, he hisses, assuring they won't do anything, as long as I am with him. Then suddenly, from outta the fuckin' blue, he spins, and begins to verbally tear me a whole new asshole, again. (Ouch!) Just like before, he is loud, possibly even louder, with disgusted voice having even more hostility! This is a show of course, performed for the cop goons, and whoever else might be listening, but still, Sparky can't hardly stand it no more.

Defiantly, and on the verge of breakdown, I retaliate, asking Todd, "Why? Why weren't you here at the hospital first thing like you promised last night in the ambulance?" The acting Ambassador, lookin' dumbfounded, pretends not to have a clue; nor does he with any of my other questions. In a fit of rage, Todd counters, yelling, how he was not ever at my side in the ambulance, and certainly did not have a journalist friend with him, and never, never would he have promised a marine body guard!

"Devin, I do not have the authority to post marines for such duty. Besides, if I were to assign a marine bodyguard to every American that came down here and got themselves into trouble, there would be no more marines left to guard the embassy! This is all in your mind: nothing you are saying makes any sense. From all your drug and alcohol abuse, you are hallucinating it all—snakes, scorpions, torture snuff films. I don't believe any of it. What I do believe Devin, is that you are a serious alcoholic. You came down here and started drinking again; and your wife says she is convinced you have been doing drugs excessively as well." (Geez, why can't—just for once—the bitch keep her mouth shut.) "Devin, my own father died an alcoholic; so I do know a thing or two concerning alcoholic behavior and symptoms. Also Devin, I know that you burned down poor Mr. Benny's hotel room, for no reason other than having delusional paranoia. You set fire, causing major damage to a very good, hard-working man's family home and business! This morning, eight o'clock rolled around; I had all the required paperwork ready for getting you out of here on the first flight to the United States, and still no Devin! I called Mr. Benny, asking, how's my boy Devin doing? And why isn't he here at the embassy?" (Buddy, is this guy full of crap, or what?) "Poor Mr. Benny, furious, informs me that you went crazy last night, burning his room down for no reason! He wants to press charges against you, and sue the American Embassy! Devin, this is my job we are talking about." (Uh, and Sparky's life.) "Because of you, I most likely will not have a job after this!" (Yeah, sure.) "Also Devin—" his voice rising to loudest pitch yet "—you should know: the police found a large amount of cocaine hidden in your room's burnt-out A/C unit. They are wanting to place you under arrest for arson and possession of narcotics with intent to sell. And Devin, there is a special task force that thinks you may have committed murder during your stay in Livingston, Guatemala and Trujillo, Honduras." (Oh shit!) "Murder, Devin! MURDER! You are being suspected of not just one, but several deaths of young men and women, murdered with a machete for reasons no other than drug-induced perversity!" (Oh shit-fuck, shit-fuck! This just keeps getting better and better. Buddy! Why didn't we just die in the Goddamn fire? This fuckin' endless nightmare would have been over, done, no more!)

"Devin, I honestly did not expect to find you still here at the hospital. No, I was seriously expecting to have to search police stations and jails for you. Believe me, no easy task in Guatemala. If they do not want the embassy to find an American, the police simply keep us buried in paperwork, while moving the individual from place to place. It can take up to a month just for me to pinpoint the location, which is almost always in a jail or prison outside of Guatemala City. I don't need this Devin! Contrary to popular belief, this is not part of my job. I don't need any of this! And I do not have to do it; but I tried to be nice—tried to help—despite your long hair, tattoos, filthy appearance and wild delusional story. I overlooked it all because I am a faithful practicing Christian. I tried to see the good in you, offering what help I could. And this is what I get in return?"

Todd is now yelling at the top of his lungs, making Sparky cringe from the onslaught. "A psychotic, drug dealing firebug, wanted for possible multiple murders! This is the thanks I get? Devin, I will tell you right now; if it were not for your wife half convincing me you are a good father and husband, who when at home, does not drink or do drugs, I would at this very moment, walk you over to those three detectives, and personally hand you over to them myself, having absolutely nothing further to do with you. Oh, and for your information, I am the only one from the American Embassy who *can* do anything for you. The only one, Devin! And to be honest, after what I've seen and heard, and your actions last night, I am not sure you are a man worthy of what little help I might be able to offer. Do you hear me, Devin!"

Indeed, Sparky does hear! Trembling uncontrollably with fright and exhaustion, a break-down ensues, having black tar snot runnin' out from nose and down face, while pathetically whimpering, "Todd please, enough already! Please, enough—enough! No more—please! The false charges and lies are to be expected, but I can't take anymore hostility, not from you. I've endured enough hostility to last ten lifetimes. Please stop, no more. And..., and, I am no murderer or drug smuggler. You know I wasn't carrying when we walked to Mr. Benny's. Also, if cocaine was found hidden in the A/C unit as claimed, it would have melted down to nothing from the heat of the fire. Uh, right? Right? So obviously it had to have been planted there after the fire. See? Everywhere I go down here, they are doin' this sorta thing to me. Todd, please. Please, for sake of my wife and sons, I am worthy. You're all I have in this country. I will do whatever you say—anything—just please don't give up on me; it will be my death sentence if you do."

Clenching my wadded up wet filthy shirt, OD wool socks, and camo French BDU pants, the body's trembling is hard and very evident, as must be the desperate look within the eyes. Standing nervous, wearing the large old button shirt and fecal stained swim shorts given by the nice lady doctor, combine this with sooty, red Converse high-tops, I know Sparky must look a sight. Todd Boil, staring down from his six foot somethin' height, sighs a pause, and, in doing, drops the harsh angered facial expression for that of possible benignant antipathy, while lowering voice to inform, "Devin, right now me, and the fact that they cannot positively prove that the cocaine found in what remains of your room was actually yours, is really all we have going for you. I tell you what; you do everything how I instruct, and I just might be able to help. As far as the arson goes? Well, you did do that. The murders? We will just have to wait and see. Oftentimes, here in Guatemala, if a person pays stiff hard cash for restitution to compensate for one crime, and does so without protest or attracting media attention, the other crimes (that may not be so easily proven, or considered controversial) will more often than not be simply overlooked and swept under the rug, so to speak. Understand? Devin, as you know, this is a very poor country. The name of the game is money, money acquired through discreet means best left out of the public eye." (Yeah right, damn, he must be referring to big shots and the likes, because Sparky sure ain't seen where discretion has meant jack shit down here. But then again, we're talkin' about murder charges! Oh, Jesus fuckin' Christ!) "Devin, no one will want high profile attention; not on this one. And with you being an American, this is just what it will become: international news, involving all sorts of reporters coming down to investigate. Devin, if it does come to this? Believe me, you will not benefit! And I can not protect you twenty-four seven, but I think I can put you some place that can, at least until we get most of this mess settled."

"God, Todd, please, not another hotel."

Half smirking, he answers, "No Devin, not another hotel. After last night, I wouldn't put you up in a hotel even if it were our very last option. Pal, your hotel days in Guatemala are over! No, I'm thinking more on the lines of a first rate private hospital. It's a little pricey, but hey, what's your life worth? And how bad do you want to get back to your wife and sons?" (Uh, shucks. Let's see, hmm.) "Trust me Devin; you will be safe at this place. I've put Americans there for protection many times. And after each and every case, they have all had nothing but good things to say about the place."

(And there's that trust word again. Buddy, why didn't the asshole put us there last night if it's so safe, and if he truly thought Sparky was unstable and suffering from delusional paranoia borderline schizophrenia, as ol' Todd is so fondly of accusing? Damn, the fucker set us up last night. Sure as shit he did! But what to do about it? He's all I got. Buddy? Buddy! Crap.)

"Devin, right now there are only three places in this entire country that are safe for you. One—at my side. Two—on American Embassy soil. Three—a hospital under the care of a doctor."

(Yeah, like the gray Nazi doctor that you promised was a real nice guy, and close personal friend? Oh right; that was last night while bein' in the ambulance you're now claiming to have never been in.)

Todd Boil, now rubbing his temples, commenting on having a headache, explains I am not the only American here in Guatemala that is needing help; far from it. "The police here, like in most of Central America, have strict laws that are clearly defined with harsh consequences. However, these laws are selectively enforced. For this very reason, the United States has declared Guatemala as being an unsafe travel destination for Americans, and advises against; hence there is warning for those that insist. They do so at their own risk, and are to expect little help from the very limited resources of the American Embassy and it's personnel." (Hhmm, the colorful travel books must have conveniently forgot to add this little tidbit of info.) "And still Americans keep right on coming down. Once here, many lose all common sense, or something, because they do things down here that they would never do back home, like buying cocaine openly on the streets, or taking ten-year-old prostitutes back to their rooms, etc. And, of course, often, these illegal activities are being watched, or even instigated, by those that work as informers. The police merely wait for the word, to make an arrest. Those that can pay fines, do. Those that cannot, go to prison."

Sparky interrupts, "Uh, or they are forced to mule, or worse! After which, they just disappear, never to be seen again—ever!"

Todd, ignoring, continues, "Of course this isn't the case with all. Some of the offenses are very minor, involving Americans that simply find themselves in the wrong place at the wrong time, and for whatever reasons, they refuse to play the game down here, which in most cases, requires only paying a fine—bribe—call it what you like." He now has his head bent down, using fingers of both hands for massaging temples. "Most Guatemalans consider all Americans to be rich with money; except, of course, the backpackers, who are frowned upon as being undesirables. Guatemalans can't understand why anyone having means to do otherwise, would choose to look and dress the way backpackers do, not to mention, travel in that mode. They seem to take a strange sort of personal insult to the whole backpacking thing, as do the police with

Americans that refuse to pay fines—or bribes, to give an example."

Todd's glossy black embassy car pulls up; behind the wheel is his personal driver, bein' a little elderly male Beaner wearing chauffeur cap and jacket looking too large. Gosh, no armed security here. Toddy and Sparky both slide into the back seat. The A/C is on, and cold. The car goes into drive, and in doing, so does Todd Boil's informing elusive edification.

"There is this one American couple I know—very nice Christian people—educated, clean-cut white collar types. They own a house in the suburbs, are both very active with the local church and community. They have three children, a dog, cat, and even some goldfish, I think. You know, just your all-round good American family. Anyway, the couple drive all the way down here to see if this is a region their church might be interested in contributing charity funds and donated gifts to— that sorta thing. Well, while driving, they are pulled over and stopped by the police, and during questioning, the husband—a real nice guy— admits to having given to his wife one of his prescription sleeping pills. This is, of course, no big deal, but, never the less, still illegal. The police inform him of the law, and in doing, expected the fine to be paid to them, in cash. Devin, the fine was nothing, twenty dollars US I think. But, the husband refuses to pay, accusing the police of imposing bribery. He decides to fight it in court. Devin, not a wise idea down here. Thank God the children were left back home in the States, because the man—a real nice guy—is immediately taken to jail. After spending a full month in jail, he is then put before a judge and is sentenced to five years' prison time. Five years, Devin, for giving his wife one sleeping pill! This poor man has been in a Guatemalan prison for over a year, and still, neither I, nor anyone else from the United States can get him out. I have been trying to get him released, making deal after deal, but still nothing."

Todd pauses, sending searching glance, as if trying to read my thoughts. Sparky remains silent, but inner gears are processing, espe- cially regarding the "deal after deal" part. Could it possibly be that ol' Toddy here—after seeing my desperate, thought to be despicable state, and discovering just how bad important people are wanting "Devon's" hide—was perhaps, going to throw me in on one of these "deals"? Is this why Todd set me up last night to be Matrix's lamb for torture and slaughter? A long-haired, tattooed, rumored drug addict alcoholic and murdering sex pervert, in trade for the nice, clean-cut Christian from the suburbs, tryin' to do church charity work? Oh boy, it sure would explain some of Todd's earlier actions. Actions to a plan that backfired on everyone, including even myself. I lived, survived the hellish night; and did so in such a manner as to attract huge sensational attention. "American backpacker deliberately sets fire to his hotel room for last stand against surrounding *satanicos!*" Geez, no matter what for better or worse, "Devon" still lives! And in doing? Well, hopefully ol' Toddy here, and the American Embassy, will start doin' their job a wee bit better. God playin' mother fuckers!

"Devin, the poor man is serving time here at the prison in Guatemala City; this is where most Americans sentenced are eventually sent. Approximately one hundred Americans are presently serving time here. I visit the prison weekly to bring our guys care packages, cigarettes, old magazines and newspapers, etc." He pats my knee, adding, "Don't worry Devin, if you work with me, I will do everything possible to keep you out of there."

"Todd, you know if I am sent there, Matrix will have me gang raped, tortured, and murdered. I won't survive a week."

Toddy, looking out the window, as if deep in thought, finally responds, "Devin. What I'm about to reveal really isn't a concern of yours, but if you should notice me having, say, certain mood swings, well, there's a reason: like I mentioned yesterday, I'm in the middle of going through a very ugly divorce. You see Devin, I brought my wife down here, and what does she do? She falls in love with another man! And in doing, of course, leaves me for him; and now I'm expected to give her a divorce. But hey, am I bitter? Nooo, not at all!"

Damn, there he goes again, babbling on about his supposed divorce. Wonder what's up with this deliberate attempt at divulging personal information regarding my only acting savior's domestic problem? Could it be some psychological strategy taught in spook school for attempt at gaining trust or camaraderie with those you are about to royally screw over? Fuck, wish my problems were merely a divorce. Uh, instead of arson, drug, and murder charges. And that's not mentioning Matrix and the many, many others that are wanting "Devon" tortured, mutilated, and dead. Lordy, how this Todd Boil is a flakey son-a-bitch.

Arriving at the embassy, the car drives around to the side, where a UN soldier, marine (whatever) opens a gate, letting us roll on down into the underground parking lot. Exiting the car, and entering the sparkling clean embassy, having A/C turned up blasting, I am again cold with a serious need to pee. Sharing this with Todd, he, after some brief hesitation, glances to his watch, then gives the "okay" adding, "Be quick! I'll have your wife on the phone." Uh, Roger-Dodger *mon Capitaine!*

Wow, had it only been yesterday that I was last here, doin' the very same thing? Fuckin' A, it seems like a year has passed rather than just one horrendous night. Whew-wee! Pissing my brains out. Oh Skippy, it is indeed a good thing nothing was drunk while in that wretched emergency room. Shakin' off the last drops, and in doing, noticing again the brown stained mesh lining of oversized swim shorts, I'm disgusted that the stains are not from my bowels. The shorts are lowered and stepped out of. But now what? Hhmm can't put on my French camo BDU pants: no, they are still sopping wet, foul dirty, stinking of soot and excrement from yours truly. Yepper, so guess the swim shorts are gonna have to go back on. First though, let's rip out the stained lining. Okey-dokey, with that completed, the shorts are free from any visual traces of fecal matter. My cock and balls sure seem to have shrunk, also, there's stubble growth of course, itchy pubic hair, same as that on face. Stepping back into the stupid large swim shorts and pulling tight the fortunate drawstring accompanying. A funny thought emerges, one that actually brings forth a true-blue chuckle. What if Sparky gets a sudden boner? The material to these shorts is so thin and baggy, my ol' wiener will surely stick straight out! He he! A boner! Yeah well, I don't think that will be happening anytime soon. Not after the ghastly horrors witnessed and endured, Sparky will probably never have a desire for an erection ever. Good God, so much for the very short-lived, feel-good chuckle.

In the back private office, behind the now very busy open counter, fronting room full of waiting people, of course, all bein' Latins-Ladinos (whatever), trying to get American visas for travel to the United States. Laura Simms and another American are there: an elderly man, having a distinct left leg limp. They are handling the long lines of hopefuls wanting passes for the United States. Todd Boil, cups the mini cell phone, warning again that this is not a secure line and anyone could be listening and most likely are.

(Uh, okay—then why the fuck don't we use a secure line? Christ, surely the American Embassy, even here in Guatemala, must have a secure line or two. Right?)

Quickly Todd adds, "Devin, your wife is understandably hysterical, full of rage and anger towards you. She is having a very difficult time comprehending the fact that you set fire to poor Mr. Benny's bed and breakfast. Devin, she is suffering from shock and depression, accompanying symptoms of anxiety and excitability. If I were you pal, I would seriously not provoke her in any way: keep your wife calm, and let her vent. Don't even try persuading her that what you think might have been going on around you last night, actually was. Devin, mention nothing of your Matrix phantom. It's all ridiculous and unbelievable. Don't even go there. I've already spoken to her about this, and she won't believe you anyway. She agrees with me that it's all in your mind, and you need professional help. I told her that I am personally taking you to a very reputable private hospital where you will get the treatment needed. She strongly supports this, and, I sense, is somewhat relieved. I have told her nothing of the murder and drug charges, and Devin, neither should you. Remember Devin, you promised earlier to do as advised; well, here's where I start holding you to your word." With a smile challenging, Todd hands over the mini cell phone.

In keeping my word, Sparky says very little to hyperventilating shrieking wife. And, even if I wanted, she wouldn't let me get a word in anyways. No, she is more preoccupied with hissing vicious accusations of drinking, drugging, going crazy, burning down hotels for no reason, jeopardizing our family and marriage, etc. Blah, blah, blah! The woman is venting! Todd is grinnin' ear to ear, givin' the thumbs up, while at the same time indicating a need to hurry! Hurry in winding down this one way, ass chewin' phone conversation.

"Uh, baby. Hey. Hey Nancy! Enough! The Ambassador is motioning that we gotta hang up. Look, just remember, I love you. Always have, and always will. Bye sweetheart."

"Devin? Devin! Just do what Todd Boil says! He knows best. Please just do as he says, and we will get you back home. Devin? Devin?"

The mini cell phone gets handed back to a grinnin', stupid Todd Boil. Fuckin' prick. I'm the puppet, and he's the puppet master. But be damned if Sparky knows what to do about it, 'cept play along and dangle.

Glancing again to his watch, Todd's stupid grin drops to an expression of all business. His eyes expose sincere concern for the time. It's time to go! Todd Boil is a lean tall man, having long strides resembling a double time march. Sparky, senses the urgency, and guesses we are workin' within a window of safety that is in motion for closing. I'm on Todd's heels like stink on shit! Via private exits, we are descending stairs, and again back down in underground parking lot. The car and driver, having motor idling, are waiting. Lickety-split, the little driver is skillfully maneuvering the glossy black embassy car speedily through chaotic midday Guatemala City traffic.

I try hard not to dwell on wife's hurtful lack of understanding and, of course, the very real, serious, heavy legal charges, thus, prison, torture, and death. It could have all been so easily avoided, if ol' Toddy here had not set my ass up to be Matrix's voodoo sacrifice. (Buddy? Buddy are you there? Yes, Buddy we could be on that big plane for the United States right this very moment, if only— Man, shut up; stop reflecting on what could have been. Must live in the present moment only. Stay alert, sharp, and do take directional bearings of the route to this private hospital from embassy. Jesus buddy, easier said then done.) Wow, helter-skelter the traffic is—having crowded streets, winding up-down-all-around. Besides, Todd, as if trying deliberately to add distraction, is babbling on and on again about his divorce and, oh yeah, his headache has come back. And—and—Todd's got himself a shrink, whom he sees once a week, sometimes more, depending on the need. Todd is hoping his shrink will make some time for him later tonight. Obviously, Toddy is a bit stressed. (Dick head oughta be in my shoes!)

Turning a sharp left on to a very narrow road, it's like going down a winding mountainside. After descending two miles or so, I notice the woodsy unsettled appearance and wild overgrowth of green foliage and tightly interwoven trees (conforming how they please as all rough bush timber does). However, here, a plateau comes to be, giving brief glimpse of up-scale development. On the left is a manicured pocket park having tennis court and small adjoining clubhouse only. Directly across the road is a large iron gate, with an armed guard standing post, serving as entrance to newly built sprawling houses in valley far below. We don't stop though, no; the road leads us curving its way down and down, again quickly becoming remote and secluded. Eventually, the driver brings the car to a stop before a guard house, having red and white painted wood plank barring—to be raised and lowered—allowing entrance and exit onto the private hospital parking lot and grounds. From the guard house emerge two armed guards for inquiring our names, and our business with the hospital. Both guards have runny snot noses and bulgin' shifty eyes—extremely red. They look to be majorly pumped up high! Plus, there is no mistaking the distinct aroma of crack smoke following. The guards are each wearing old Sam Brown holstered revolvers; in addition, one is slingin' a pump shotgun, the other, a Ruger Mini 14. These guys are your typical scrawny bad-ass actin' greaseballs, even sportin' the regulation issue thin Beaner mustaches. Their attitude is hostile to say the least, no less toward the American Ambassador. How very strange, what with this bein' a "first rate private hospital" and all.

Mr. Mini 14 steps into the guard house for clearing our arrival via phone. After some time he reappears, slurring something to Señor Shotgun They both, then, just stand there, bug-eyed, staring at us as if challenging. It is more than evident that our driver is nervous, and I don't mean just a little bit either. Turning around, he whispers to Todd, that he fears they are not going to let us pass. He thinks they have been instructed to contain us here until the *policia* can arrive. Todd, hearing, is furious! Using voice to show just how much so, he roars a bellowing threat to the two guards, while pulling forth his cell phone, that if they do not let us pass, this very instant, he will call the embassy, and have an entire army of UN marines down here. "It will be an international incident! Get out of our way, and let us pass—NOW!"

Both bug-eyed Beaners jump with weapons pointing! (Oh shit!) After Mr. Mini 14 spits a snot goober on to the front of the windshield, causing our driver to recoil and flinch; they back step a retreat and reluctantly, the balanced ballast is lowered and striped red and white wooden arm barring our way is raised.

With tires spinning, our driver floors it, speeding across the hospital's parking lot, stopping at double glass doors of front entrance! Damn, not a good sign—definitely not a good sign! Still, if this does turn out to be another set-up, I don't think it will be from Todd's doing. No, not this time anyways. In a flash, he and Sparky are outta that car and through those front glass doors! And just within, as if waiting for us, several important looking hospital personnel staff are there to greet us. Their smiles are big and severely fake. Todd speaks with them in speedy Spanish, which he does not bother translating.

The place appears immaculate, squeaky clean, modern, and newly built. I am surprised at the lack of patient/visitor activity—none are seen, or heard. Also, it comes to mind that the large parking lot, had been, except for a few cars only, empty. There is noise, construction work can be heard, hammering and sawing etc.... It seems to be comin' from the building's lower level. But really, where are the normal hospital sounds? You know, those of people, patients, employees: conversing, bitching, moaning, gossiping, barkin' orders, or goofin' off, jokin' around the way folks do at the work place? Besides the distant construction and Todd Boil hotly arguing *en Español rapido*, Sparky, with ears straining, can't even hear one television set, radio, intercom, or or—even a phone ringin'! All very unusual, and uncommon for a hospital, even the ones specializing in tending to the living dead elderly, or the nut houses that dope their patients to the point of bein' literally zombies. It's sorta creepy. Plus, there's no shakin' this inner voice. (Buddy is that you? Buddy? Buddy! No, it ain't buddy.) It's screamin'. (The cops are comin'—the cops are comin'!)

A thick-short man, having extremely broad shoulders, large animated sparkling eyes, and giant crooked smile to match, comes a-pushin' a wheelchair in which I'm instructed to sit. Todd Boil takes a break from his winding down torrential Spanish to inform, "All is well!" Todd has been explaining my very unique situation, and the administration staff, have "agreed to grant you, Devin, hospital admittance. This is great news!"

(Oh boy. The administration staff is lookin' anything but pleased with this decision. Wonder what sort of deal ol' Todd had to make for getting their consent?)

"Devin look, it's international law; as long as a person is admitted into a hospital with attending doctors that can give medical reason for refusing the individual a release, they are then protected for the duration of the stay. The doctors here have agreed not to release you without first getting my personal confirmed approval. Hey pal, we have bought some time, time for you to get strong and healthy again, and time for me to work with your wife, and all others involved, on how best we can get you back home. So cheer up! Okay? Okay, they are going to take you now; they need blood, urine, and stool samples. Then you will be put into your very own private room. Don't worry, I'll be here for a while, busy filling out the required paperwork, etc. I will come to check up on you and say goodbye before leaving."

Gimpy, the wheelchair pusher, having ever present goofy smile, pats my shoulder fondly. The hospital smock he is wearing happens to be ridiculously small for the man's thick broad shoulders and extending Neanderthal arms. Indeed it's a funny contrast to overly lengthy blue jeans. Even rolled up, bunching, they are still way too long for his short stout legs. Also odd are his shoes: instead of bein' the typical clean soft rubber soled shoes that are worn in hospitals everywhere, ol' Gimpy's are dirty leather work boots. This guy must be a maintenance man, nurses' aid (or somethin'). Yet, he's the one to roll me down the hall, into a little room where I am to piss in a cup; no privacy here. Well, none from Gimpy the Gimp anyways. His big weird eyes stare intently at my dick. (Come-on Gimpy, give us a break here.)

Now as a general rule, Sparky has never been what you would call pee shy. No, growing up in my neighborhoods, as children, we boys and girls, when outside, would pretty much relieve bladders unabashed and natural, like how our free-roaming pet dogs did, having same rules applying: no peeing on flowerbeds, or cars, etc. This lack of inhibition carried on well into the teenage years of hard core partying with those found being same caliber. Hell, it was nothing, while at large kegger parties and the likes, to step off into the bush for a much frequent pee. Boys with boys, girls with girls, boys with girls, girls with boys—whatever. It was simply no big deal. Pissin' was pissin, and no one thought anything of it. However, I will admit, there were those incidental casual occurrences where the practice did become a wee bit more. Chance company should be a real hot chick number, neither of us personally knowing the other, but both sensing a strong magnetic curious attraction. Sparky stands above with swollen dick stretched out full of booze, showin' itself off proud. And her, femme fatale, a few feet away, squats below, exposing sensual, tenacious, taut curve of bare bottom. And there we both would be, checkin' each other out—though pretending not to—as we pissed away all cares, worries, and responsibility. Also, admittedly, there have been unique times when the golden shower bit has been invited during sexual play.

But geez, if Gimpy's grinnin' idiotic face comes any closer, it won't be this here cup that gets the splash. No it will not! I can not urinate like this! A turn-around has my back to him, and finally the bladder yields and Gimpy is handed a cupful. His eyes are a-gleamin' in delight, while he, oh so careful, using both scarred and calloused hands, gently sets down the little cup on the counter. He then lubes a wooden tongue depressor with tad of Vaseline, and from an autoclave tray, pulls forth a small empty baby food jar having had label removed and looking to be sterile. Gimpy snaps on a pair of latex exam gloves and motions Sparky to drop 'em and spread 'em.

Uh, I don't fuckin' think so! Gimpy, already animated to the hilt, resulting from gene pools having nasty sense of humor, is now taking the refusal to comply as rejection, and thus, his sensitive feelings have been deeply hurt. The retard's look makes me laugh aloud! Still, he ain't goin' digging around the inside of my already torn rectum! Reluctantly, he hands over the greased stick, and I, squatting like a girl, clench teeth and surprise myself by actually bein' able to hand him back a tongue depressor having traces of fecal matter (and blood). Christ, just where the excrement came from, I've no idea. Sparky thought, surely, everything got shat out back at ol' friendly Mr. Benny's bed and breakfast.

Treating the shit on a stick as if it were something truly special, the again grinnin' fool Gimpy seals stool sample into baby food jar. It is now time for blood collecting and just like a pro, Gimpy draws blood from my arm: tiny tube after tiny tube, marked and labeled. After this, all samples—blood, urine, and stool—are quickly sent across the hall to another room (obviously a small lab or somethin'). Voices are heard, including Todd Boil's, coming from there. They are discussing the microscope and what will be found in my specimen samples.

Gimpy, smilin' proud as punch, opens a drawer and brings out a slim hinged box; and from this comes an already loaded syringe. Shaking it, he informs, "We must now feed the *pequenos*; they are very hungry. Yeses?"

Clearly, ol' Gimpy here is used for a bit more than just maintenance man and/or nurses' aid. With syringe between teeth, he smartly pulls tight a rubber hose around my upper arm. Using thick thumbs, he works my bulging veins, while eerily hissing quietly to himself, "Hungry *pequenos*, must feed. *Pequenos* hungry; yesss, yesss. We must feed hungry *pequenos*." (Buddy, why is this idiot referring to our veins as *pequenos*? Ain't that Spanish for small, or little? Hhmm, also, what's up with him thinkin' our veins are hungry? Oh duh! Apparently, despite there bein' no sign of previous needle track marks, the weirdo thinks Sparky is a junky. Buddy, the syringe looks to be full of dull water. Ught, the retard is gonna shoot us up with coke! Well, spank my ass and call me Judy! This oughta be fun! But why is it bein' done? Buddy? Uh, yoo hoo, buddy.)

A woman, across the hall, viewing my specimen samples through the microscope, is loudly announcing for all to hear her findings. Yep, they've found traces of coke, meth, heroin, Valium, and alcohol. (Oh bullshit! She's just callin' out, claimin' to find what ol' Todd Boil is telling her.) Before Gimpy the numbskull can insert his needle to feed my hungry *pequenos,* the microscope woman barks (in Spanish) a questioning confirmation from Gimpy (or whatever his real name). Upon receiving reply, she gives a change in orders. Again looking hurt and denied an act of pleasure, he reluctantly un-snaps rubber hose, and puts away the still loaded syringe. So doing, it is heard that others have indeed arrived in lab across the hall. They are detectives *policia secreto*. And they are here wanting you know who! But fortunately, after a long ensuing much heated argument, where the cop-goons are definitely reminded of the rules concerning "international law," it just ain't gonna happen. No, not today. They leave, furious, shouting a promise for returning.

Lookin' over to Gimpy, his big stupid face is again grinnin' ear to ear. Patting my knee, he stands, and begins to roll wheelchair-bound "Devon" somewhere. The somewhere is down the hall and onto an elevator lowering us to floors beneath. Since we are at the hospital's rear, and it having been built on a sloping terrain, each descending floor stays, more or less, at ground level. The one we do get off on is not near as nice as that of the front entrance. No it is not. Other than the unseen sawing and hammering, now loudly revealed as bein' very near, the halls are vacant, empty, void. Gimpy rolls the chair briskly until bringing us to x-rays. Inside is one man, and one man only. He is lookin' bored, doin' nothin'. His eyes meet mine coldly, conveying blatant disapproval for my being. He and Gimpy converse using Spanish only. While doing, Sparky is able to decipher Gimpy here asking the x-ray man if he has any *acido*? The man has none; so we are outta there, back in the elevator goin' down to another level. (*Acido*? Hhmm, buddy ain't *acido* Spanish for acid? Now why does Gimpy need acid? Buddy? Buddy? Buddy! Crap.) Oh what the hell, let's just ask the idiot. "Uh, *mi amigo, porque la razón por necesidad acido?*"

Gimpy laughs a chuckling wheeze at my poor Spanish, during which his eyes dart to and fro, as if double-checkin' nobody is near for hearing. "Devon, there are times I need it to be rid of undesirable things, and cleanup. Yesss—understand? Devon, it is best not to ask questions here. You must only sleep, eat and wait for your Todd Boil. Yesss."

Uh, okay, that's comforting. And there's the Todd Boil thing again. No one ever seems to refer to him as Ambassador Todd Boil. Wonder why? Not that this means anything, but, well, noted it is.

Exiting the elevator, this floor is even worse than the last. Also, it is the level for source of construction. We roll 'er on down the narrow ghost hall, having one whole side of corridor boarded with rough plywood only, The other side, our left, is guessed to be standard patient rooms. The doors are closed and, for some reason, the rooms are known to be vacant. Straight ahead, this corridor leads on to a small reception area having short front desk and possibly a nurses' station as well. However, before reaching it, Gimpy stops, opens a door, and voila! My very own private patient room—Ught-O. There's the bed—a hospital bed—positioned to be parallel (of fucking course) against a wall of Goddamn large windows. The drapes are drawn open, showing that also running parallel against the other side of windows is an outside walkway leading down for passing. Jesus, it will be nothin' to have people out there stopping to gawk down through windows—or worse.

The bed's wall-butting headboard has, within reach, a nightstand, tabling small desk lamp. Mid-length of mattress, bein' front and center, is a simple stainless steel tray holder on wheels, and at the bed's foot end, facing, is, up in a corner, a mounted elevated television. Along this same wall, mounted also, there's a petite vanity sink and mirror, adjacent to door enclosing private toilet and shower. The room is small, and so that's pretty much it. All appears to be clean enough, but in this country, who knows.

Gimpy leaves, informing he will be back. In a flash, he returns, carrying a half used, still slippery bar of soap, and a plastic bag. I'm given smiling instructions to undress and take a shower. Accepting the soggy soap bar, I do as told, leaving the door open I am surprised to find hot water, which feels absolutely wonderful, but fuck if Sparky is gonna linger for enjoying. No, after the speed shower and quick piss, this cowboy is outta there.

From the plastic bag, out comes a hospital gown; and in go my filthy clothes, all of 'em, including sooty red Converse high-tops. Gimpy, rolling up my bag of clothes, indicates that it is now bedtime. Yes Gimpy, but first, "Devon" here is gonna close the drapes and do a quick search through the bedding. Gimpy, watchin', is all idiotic smiles. Settling my exhausted butt into bed, I ask grinnin' Gimpy for a comb, razor, and a toothbrush. "Yesss, yesss," no problem, he will be right back. Turning, Gimpy leaves and in doing, takes all my clothes!

Time passes, and still no sign of Gimpy; yet, in waiting, a nurse and/or doctor, will occasionally open the door for a quick look-see. They do this without entering the room, and their eyes betray this is done for voyeurism reasons only. Exception is this one particular annoying nurse that does enter, but only for purpose of sending scowling glares while insistently pulling wide open the window drapes. Of course, as soon as she leaves, Sparky is up re-closing them, only to have her shortly come back for a repeat. The construction work is winding down, and my name is bein' heard mentioned often by laborers and hospital staff outside my room in the hall, and on the window walkway. Most are discussing "Devon" during brief passing, but some do stop for congregated gossip sharing. Really though, it is all bein' spoken in Spanish, and so, I'm not too bothered. But bubba-o-bubba, please no Carib English! Funny how bein' in this foreign country and all, my worst enemies are those that prefer speakin' English. Yepper, real funny!

Eventually Todd Boil shows up, and he's put on his happy face, commenting, "So, down here is where they've decided to put you!" Seeing my disgruntled look of concern, "Hey pal, this is good! The room is nice enough, huh? And they have you tucked away safe and sound. Devin, even if someone wanted to bother you, they wouldn't be able to find your room, ha ha ha!" It took me twenty minutes to find it; and that's after getting directions, ha ha!"

(Oh, you fuckin' dumb ass. Everybody and their mangy dog already knows where "Devon" is, what room he's in, and how to get to it.)

"Devin, you will have plenty of privacy down here, and considering your present condition, I seriously doubt the noise from the construction crews will be disturbing you. Besides, they only work during the day. I see you've had a shower; hey, bet that felt good, huh? Have they brought you anything to eat yet? No? Well, I'll see to it that some nice hot food is brought pronto!"

Glancing to the nightstand, "What, no phone? Hhmm, I'll have one brought in. Devin, here—this is the embassy's number. Below it is my personal cell phone number. And just in case you feel like talking to someone having a much more pleasant voice than my own, here is Laura Simms's number as well. Okay then. Let's see; we got you tucked away in a nice safe room. A phone will be brought in shortly. You have all the important numbers, just in case you start feeling afraid, threatened, or hey, whatever! Feel free to call anytime—day or night. Okay? Well pal, I have to go. I finally got through to my psychiatrist, and I'm late in meeting him. He's wanting to have another sit-down with my wife and I—together! Can you believe this? See Devin, it could be worse, pal, you could be in my shoes! Doggone, I'm really not looking forward to this one. I mean, I call the guy—to make an appointment because I need to talk to him alone. You know, to get some things off my chest? Things that have absolutely nothing to do with my soon to be ex-wife! But hey, he's the doctor; he knows best and is insisting. And am I bitter? No sir! Devin, pal, must be going. Will have that food and phone brought in right away. Also, I will swing by tomorrow to checkup on you—see how everything is going. Tell you what: I've a stack of old magazines that I collect, and at the end of each month, I take them over to the prison for our guys there. Most of the magazines are, you know, women's types: like Better Homes and Garden, or Glamour, Vogue. You know that sort, but hey, the guys eat 'em up! The magazines remind them of home. I will bring some with me tomorrow. You might get bored watching TV, or staring at the ceiling, okay? All right then. Is there anything else you need? Ha ha! Besides the airplane ride home!"

I tell him that they took my clothes. Todd, hearing, shrugs his shoulders, commenting, the clothes were taken more than likely to be washed. Sparky, nodding, then politely asks ('cause Gimpy sure as hell ain't been back) if Todd could have a comb, razor, and toothbrush brought in? "Also, I really would like my clothes back."

"Devin, why are you so concerned about your clothes? I certainly hope you are not planning on going anywhere. Not after I've gone through all the trouble of getting you into this nice private hospital."

"No Todd, it's just that I'd feel more comfortable with them, that's all."

Todd Boil ignores this last comment, but does promise to have a comb, razor and toothbrush brought. And with that, he is gone. Shortly following, in comes a woman doctor, having with her a small Indian (Maya) looking woman nurse. Both women appear to be in their late thirties; and their faces are sincerely gentle. They both approach without hesitation, and the doctor actually does a routine examination while asking the usual questions during such. She seems to genuinely care! As does (or so is sensed) the little Indian nurse. They hook "Devon" up to an IV drip, tapping the needle into my veiny inner arm, and hangin' the plastic IV bottle up on a steel hook-bar suspended from a rod attached to the bed. Upon completion, the doctor then speaks. (Spanish? Oh no, please don't be that strange Garifuna language.) She gives stern instructions to her nurse, who, looking up, silently nods obediently. The doctor, resting her feminine hand on my chest, spreads long narrow fingers out over area of heart, and with deliberation, presses all fingertips firmly three times. After this, she and the nurse exit the room. (Buddy, wonder why she did that finger pressin' thing? There didn't seem to be any malice behind it. No, more like the opposite. But there was definitely some sort of meaning there. Hhmm, buddy, whatcha think? Buddy?)

Soon, the doctor's nurse returns, and with her is another small Indian nurse—carrying a tray of food. It is put down on the simple stainless steel wheeled tray holder. The food is puréed beans, rice, some sort of stewed yellow fruit, corn tortilla, small cup of beef broth, warm tea, and very sweet juice. Not bein' hungry, but knowin' it to be needed for strength, sparky gulps down the liquids and eats only the rice and fruit.

Upon retrieving my food tray, the little nurse frowns, pointing to food not eaten. Smilin', trying to look polite, respectful, harmless, and in need of serious sympathy, I slowly shake my head saying, "*Gracias, lo siento.*"

Night falls and still no comb, razor, or toothbrush. Every thirty minutes or so (guessing since my watch got stolen and there is no clock in here), my room door will slowly open for whisking eyes to peek in, tryin' to be sneaky. Now gone are the sounds of construction and the likes, but what can be heard is small children whimpering and wanting to cry. Eerily, each time one starts to cry out loud, there is an adult there hushing it, but not in the kind gentle way. No, not quite. And to be assured, the whispers concerning "Devon" never stop. Also, loud firecrackers blast off in the distance, throughout the night. Sleep in no way comes, but deep depression does.

In the morning, there are brief congregations of arriving hospital staff, construction workers, and laborers. They are all comin' and goin'—forming small groups, stopping just outside my windows and on the other side of my room's door: speakin' speedy Spanish in hurried conversations, topic bein' "Devon." While doing, many do try gettin' in those quick glimpses for a personal look-see. Gosh, from the excitement and intrigue within the voices, I am, for better or for worse, *famoso*! One certainly does not need to speak the language to grasp that understanding. Aughg, Sparky just wants to be left alone, disappear, and go home. But nooo! Laying here, stuck, I succumb to the deep depression that has now seeped into my being. Like muddy waters of a river on a slow rise; wetting hard, parched earth that had compacted itself to keep from fearfully bein' blown away in swirls of dust by omnipotent winds. I feel as if I too had endured dry-dry drought, hot licking fire, and the ever persistent evil gripping tires of shiny, gloss black Chevy blazer, nullifying mind, body, and present situation. Maybe not; but, benumbed I do become. Yet, head must maintain clarity for sharp focus, red alert, action mode. (Buddy, is this even possible when depressed? Oh, shut up! You know it's not. Buddy! Hey buddy, you're back! Goddamn, where have you been? Aw, forget that. Hey buddy, there's somethin' not right with this place. Can you feel it? Buddy, it's just like everything else in this fucked-up country; there is a whole lotta wrong here! Yes, I know. Man, just get rid of that depression shit you've been entertaining. It serves no purpose except to distract, drain energy, and make you feel oh so sorry for yourself. Get it out of us—and keep it out! We cannot afford it—not now! Okay buddy, all right, whatever you say.)

The loud hammering and sawin' begins; and with it comes a new nurse with a breakfast tray. She says nothing, but does pull open those drapes before leaving. Also, she deliberately leaves the door to my room half open (bitch). Sliding back into bed, after re-closing the door and drapes, the tea again is only lukewarm. Wishing it were hot, I gulp it down and eat some stewed fruit only. Shortly, a teenage black boy arrives, carrying razor, comb, and toothbrush. (Yippee!) At the wall sink, he holds up my now empty IV bottle (the thing has been empty for, uh, all night) and watches curiously as I brush my teeth and shave, using dull disposable plastic razor and soggy bar of soap for shaving cream. After which, feelin' a bit better, it's back to bed for Sparky, where he works tediously at combing out long tangled mess of hair with cheap little black plastic pocket comb. In doing, the empty IV bottle gets replaced with a full one, and a phone is brought in, put on the night-stand, and extension plugged into wall-jack.

Snapping the six elastic bungees, down length of two-foot-long ponytail, buddy gives assurance to keep watch, while Sparky and body takes a little nap. Fuck knows we need it. Besides, it is daytime, and buddy is now here with us. Buddy makes good on his word, giving alert each time someone pokes their ugly head in, or even walks past our half open door. (Damned if I can keep the thing closed. There are those now out in the hall insistent on the door remaining half open, no matter how often my agitated backside slides from the bed for closing. So be it.) With buddy pullin' guard duty, a brief nap of yo-yoing in and out of somethin' resembling light sleep is accomplished, until the construction crews take a lunch break.

Lunch time for them. Call home time for Sparky (or at least—try). Not having my wallet anymore with phone numbers and AT&T phone card, and not knowing the number for calling out of the country, and not really wantin', or trustin', to ask the hospital staff, or even Todd Boil for that matter. I, of course, try for an international operator. Suspiciously, the line keeps going dead before an operator can pick up. Hhmm, let's try Laura Simms. Surprisingly, this call does go through. Laura is at home. Yep, she didn't feel well today, so she took the day off. Her voice, despite the obvious discomfort in receiving my unexpected call, is soft, gentle, and sweet. Still, she is very sorry, but will not give up the number for calling directly out of the country. Laura feels it's not a good idea, no, not without first talking to Todd. She wants to know why I didn't call him before her? Sparky answers honestly, "Uh, I didn't think Todd would approve and give the number."

Breaking the brief pause of ensuing silence, "Laura, what's really going on? You know. Why was I chosen for this nightmare?" Sparky is indeed reaching—reaching for hint of anything that might be unintentionally revealed.

Laura surprises by answering, "Devin, I honestly do not know why you were chosen. Ex-ex, excuse me Devin; "chosen" wasn't the word I meant to use." (Ught, she slipped! Yes, but little good it does.) "Devin, what I meant to say, is that I don't know why you've had to endure what you have. Believe me, I wish I could give you answers, but I really don't have any. However, I do know that Todd is doing everything humanly possible to help. Devin, you really need to trust him and do everything he instructs. Meanwhile, you might want to try writing down what you have experienced. It could help in dealing with the post-traumatic stress you certainly must be suffering. Devin, if nothing else, the writing will give you something to do."

No more is to be gained from Ms. Laura Simms; so with soft, polite goodbyes, we hang up. Hhmm, she might have something there with the writing business. It will help to keep brain clear, sharp, and on track of things. Yeah okay, 'cept for such, pen and paper are needed. Aw, what the hell, let's give ol' Todd Boil a call. Oh fuck me! Surprise, sur-fuckin'-prise! The phone is now completely dead. No dial tone, no nothin'! Damn, don't this just beat all. (Hey buddy, whatcha think? Think maybe our phone here is bein' monitored—much? Gee, guess they don't want us makin' any more phone calls. Wonder why? Buddy! Man, just be cool. It might mean something, or it might mean nothing. Either way, we must wait and see. Buddy, this sucks, and you know it.)

A real greaseball of a male doctor enters my room. His hair is oiled (or unwashed), combed straight back, and his teeth are a foul rotting mess. His English is deliberately broken (and deliberately hissing). Doctor Greaseball, having eyes gleamin' somethin' on order of complete contempt, has no desire to examine "Devon" but does want to hear my story, "the whole sss-story." Of course he gets the major left-out-parts version. Despite myself, and truly tryin' not too, tears surface while recalling (and hiding) some parts. During this, the greaseball doctor just stands there, wide-eyed, clipboard in hand, writing nothin'. Every so often he hisses through rotting teeth, as if encouraging, "Yesss, yesss Devon. Pleassse continue—yesss." (Oh goody, we must have Gimpy's cousin here; the one that did get to go to college. Wow, who gives these guys their degrees? Again, so much for your higher educations.)

With story time over and me wipin' my eyes and blowin' nose full of still black burning snot tar, Doctor Greaseball is now appearing angrily disappointed: he knows there's more to my story, and it's pissin' him off to no end that he ain't gettin' it. The veins in the man's neck and forehead are dramatically visible, knurled rhizomes of off-shoots increasing in size and number. Yep, once again, I'm before a doctor that would for-real rather see "Devon" dead than alive. It is frightening, to say the least! So much so, that now is thought to be a good time for reminding him (surely he's already gotta know) that Sparky has just talked to Laura Simms via phone (Skippy Joe, yeah, we're real tight, you know) and she advises I am to write my story down, from beginning to end.

With that said—under pretense of polite respect, Doctor Mouth-Full-O-Rot is kindly asked for pen and notepad. Upon hearing, the greaseball just stares a piercing scowl of pure hatred. Finally, without sayin' a word, he hands over a torn sheet of paper from his clipboard, adding short pencil stub. (One sheet!) Lookin' at him as if he were a complete idiot, I try getting the guy to give up some more Goddamn paper! The asshole glares, pretending not to understand. "Uh, *mas papel, por favor.*" (Fuckin' Beaner.) Nope, he ain't givin' up no more paper. But he does give hissing exhortation: I have sinned and instead of writing, I should be praying, and begging God for forgiveness! (Uh, what?) The greaseball does a heel spin and is gone, deliberately leaving my door half open.

Yeah well, you have a nice day too—dog face! The man went to college; got himself a doctor's degree, for diagnosing patients; and treats them with that God shit! Fuck you, fuck you, fuck you! Oh, and Skippy is feelin' a whole lot better now! Real calm and relaxed—you know! Hhmm, glad to be rid of the creep. Sparky quickly searches the night-stand for a Bible. What the hell. If the greaseball doctor is of such an opinion, then so must others. It can't hurt to be seen reading the Bible, maybe even learning a few passages for reciting; that might impress some of these monkeys. Except there ain't no Bible to be found; and it occurs—duh—even if there were, it would surely be in Spanish.

Toward the end of the day, Todd Boil comes. He's got on his happy-happy, I'm-in-a-big-hurry face. Setting the promised magazines down on top of the nightstand, he talks fast, saying he thinks my situation is improving. Todd can't give all the details right now, but things are "Looking up!" Oh, also, he talked to my wife today and she sends her love, etc. "Pal, you're getting some living color back into that brown tan of yours. See what a hot shower, healthy food, and a good night's sleep can do? And you're feeling much better too; aren't you? Well, except for being bored out of your mind, I bet. Have you had the TV on?" He reaches up to turn it on, but the TV don't work.

Todd, shrugging shoulders, says, "Devin, I have been working on your case all day. You wouldn't believe the phone calls I've made. Whew! Boy, pal, you sure left one long crazy trail behind you. So crazy, in fact, that I think it's going to work in our favor. Everybody seems to have a different story on you. No two stories are alike, and they just keep on getting wilder and wilder! It's now so scrambled up, that nobody seems to have a clue as to whose version to believe. The one sure crime that you have committed without any doubts, is the burning down of poor Mr. Benny's hotel room. I have talked to Mr. Benny; and Devin, he is upset, angry, that's for sure; but hey, who can blame the poor guy, right? However, he is a businessman. I think if we offer to pay for all damages, he just might be persuaded not to press charges. Oops! There I go again, saying more than I should. Devin, even if Mr. Benny doesn't press charges, we are still not out of the woods yet. I just want you to know that I'm on your side, doing everything possible to get you back home. And it's looking a lot better today than it was yesterday; that's for sure! You just hang in there. Stay put, and pal, please, do not cause any more trouble—eh? Just let me do all the work and worrying, okay? I know, yesterday, I told you this sorta thing wasn't my job; and really, it's not. But hey, you have a family waiting for you back home: so I'm now making it my job! Well, I got to go, pal. I will swing by tomorrow morning and check up on you. Laura might just come with me. Speaking of which, Devin, I talked to her earlier, and she told me you had called wanting to know if it was a good idea to phone home. Devin, I don't think it is, not at this point. Trust me pal, it is simply not good timing. Not when we are in the middle of trying to make deals for getting you back home, okay? Also pal, upstairs here, they like to listen in on the phone conversations. Hey, what can I say? Welcome to Guatemala! So, you just use that phone for calling Laura, myself, and the embassy only, okay? Got your word on that? Good—all right pal."

I tell Todd about the phone goin' dead right after my conversation with Laura. He steps over, picking up the phone. Yep, it's dead. Shrugging his shoulders, he comments, "This is nothing; the phones go down in the city all the time." My eyes roll for conveying serious doubts to this bein' the case. Todd is also told of the strange doctor that had come, wanting to hear my story, also afterwards advised me to beg forgiveness from God for my sins, etc. "Uh, Todd, do you have a Bible in English I can perhaps borrow?"

"Devin, I have many Bibles: I have Bibles printed in at least eight different languages. Plus, I have a personal collection of what I call my special Bibles. Devin, I read my Bible every night without fail; I am a very religious man. And guessing, Devin, I would have to say that you are not. Am I right? Yes, that's what I thought. You don't need a Bible, pal. Don't worry, I am not seeing God on your shoulder." (What the hell does that mean?) "Tell you what: I won't give you a Bible now, but if after you get back home, you still want a Bible, give me a call. I'll send you one from my personal special collection. How about that? Okay?" (Uh, no! If Sparky does make it back home alive he won't need a Goddamn Bible! Jesus fuckin' Christ! Whoever heard of a supposed religious Christian sitting on a pile of Bibles and not lending one out to someone that is down, hurting, and asking for one? And a fellow American to boot!) "Hey pal, gotta go. We will be seeing you in the morning!"

Todd Boil leaves; and shortly following, so do the Construction workers, laborers, and hospital staff—changing shifts. Night comes and my two small Mayan Indian nurses are back. Both have soft warm comforting smiles. Hhmm, wonder if the nice woman doctor is also here tonight. After the kind nurses take away my mostly untouched dinner tray, and change empty IV bottle for full one; they leave the room, quietly closing the door completely behind themselves. And in doing—I hear it! Garifuna English! My heart machine-guns a pounding for surging blood throughout entire core of body, mind, and soul. The Garifuna black Caribs are heard, having just arrived, surprising my two nurses, and (guessing) most of the hospital staff. How large are their numbers? Sparky does not know. But with them is definitely a very important family. An old man leads the way from down the hall, barking out orders and instructions. The Caribs are easily heard, as they approach and pass, asking the nurses if this is "Devon's room." The younger, teenage-sounding females in the bunch are bitching about having to stay here for the night, referring to the place as an "organ factory." They talk amongst themselves about how here is where they cut up people, keeping only the important organs to sell for big money to the United States and Europe. Also, the old ones are always wanting the flesh to eat—still believing in the old ways. The girls aren't real keen on this, as they too are expected to eat the human flesh. Plus, they don't like having to stay down here, in the building, on the lower level, to be bored, while the old man does the *coca* business, etc. An old woman, ushering some of the small children (or so it sounds), sharply scolds the fussing young bitches, instantly bringing them to silence.

(Oh fuuuck! Buddy—buddy! They're back! They are Goddamn BACK—BACK, BACK, BACK—BACK! Buddy are you there? Yes.

Buddy what are we gonna do? The sick mother fuckers are back! They are here! Damn, what are we gonna do? And that voice—the old woman's voice! We sure the fuck recognize her voice. God, how could we ever forget that voice. It's the old woman-witch! The same one from Hotel Hell Trujillo, the same with Matrix at Mr. Benny's! Buddy! Yes, you're right. The old hag certainly gets around. I wonder if this bunch is her personal family. Man, you notice how they aren't calling her witch? Also, thus far, hers is the only voice we do recognize. Buddy, that don't mean nothin'. Oh shit, what are we gonna do? Listen to 'em, buddy; do you hear? They are settling in all around us. The old man and some others are in the rooms on our left; others have taken rooms to the right; and the majority seem to be directly across the hall, beyond boarded plywood. The whole damn hospital sounds to be rushing around, catering to these people's every want and need. Do you hear buddy? Of course I hear. Man, just stay calm, and be cool. We've been through this before. Yeah right, but buddy, Sparky don't wanta play no more. No he does not! Aughg, why didn't we just die in that fuckin' fire?

Man, shut up, and stop being a pussy. Remember the objective. They can kill us, and most likely will; but under no circumstances can we be caught alive for them to torture! And preferably, we go-out fighting in such a way that they cannot take our body. Understand? UNDER- STAND? Nancy and the boys need our body sent home. So, wipe away those tears. I'm guessing since these people are like for-real cannibals, they must be of a crazed, bloody warrior descent. You remember? Those that Martin and friend had talked about back in Trujillo, concerning families heading the Mosquito Coast *coca* routes? Either way, we cannot let them see weakness! Yeah, but buddy, the witch, she saw; she saw in Trujillo how we bawled out, begging for help and mercy! Yes, true, but she also saw how you cut and hacked—how many people? Plus, you charged cops with only a machete when they had loaded guns pointed close range on you. These people think all your screaming and begging for help is just a tactical trick used to attract attention and distract. Anyway, it doesn't matter much, does it? Just put on your killer face and get ready for going into lean mean fighting machine mode. Show no fear! They know you have killed, even with bare hands. Eugh, buddy, no, please don't bring that up. We ll, you sure as hell did! Man, you pulverized that guy's head. Look at your knuckles, and remember: look at the bite on your finger and remember. Remember what they did to you! You and all those poor people, children and babies. You have killed, and you will kill again—so suck it up! March or die, right? RIGHT? Yeah buddy, damn straight! Mother fuckers! Let's kill 'em all. Kill 'em all! Yepper, hhmm, uh, buddy, how are we gonna kill 'em when they do come?

Well, that is the big question now, isn't it? Let's see, they think you are a family man that had once been a hardened combat vet: soldier, mercenary, and legionnaire. Yeah, but buddy, what about my file and documents sent from the United States? Wouldn't those show otherwise? Man, who knows. Since you are an American, and the files came from America, there is probably much doubt pertaining to the accuracy of info within, or purposely left out from those files and documents. However, these people do know what they know: they know you kill, and are not afraid to fight and die, even if it's suicidal. And there is no greater opponent more annoying or treacherous as those filling that degree of commitment and desperation. So, let's not let them down, shall we? Oooh, buddy, I'm scared—really scared. Wow, you'd think after all we've been through, that the mind and body would sorta just become numb to all fears, but that ain't happenin'. Hhmm, maybe it is. Man, look at you. Here we are once again surrounded by sadistic cannibal Garifuna black Caribs (whatevers), all having this bizarre personal vendetta for us, and really, you're sitting in bed, calculating the situation, for the most part cool as a cucumber; see? Yeah, sure buddy. If I appear that way, it's only because you are here with me. Yes, well man, when the shit hits the fan, we are gonna fly it together! Now let's get a battle plan in order, or at least, a major diversion for possibly getting us through the night. In the morning Todd Boil will be here: or so he said. Try the phone. Of course it's dead. See what we can take from the bed for a weapon. Too bad the IV bottle is plastic and not glass. Let's see, we have the obvious stuff for berserker time: lamp, phone, TV. All these can be thrown through the windows for acquiring sharp pieces of glass, and possible flight from room, though I doubt we would get far. No, best to hold the room, and bloody the walls! Hhmm, the steel bar suspending IV bottle comes off. Good, good, good!)

Suddenly, the door opens a bit. One of my small nurses pokes her head in, having eyes spooked big, full of fear. She hurriedly puts a finger to her lips, indicating the need for remaining silent. Sparky nods affirmative. Soundlessly, she withdraws her head, fully closing the door. More and more activity is now bein' heard all around. Laughin', giggles, orders, and instructions; preparations are in progress for somethin', seeming to have the old woman-witch in charge. She is very busy, perturbed, and not real happy. The teenagers of the clan are bothering her, reminding that it is time again for their *coca* injections. Several are complaining, and even pleading, that the amount given is not enough.

The witch has my nurses out there, helping with the administering of needy injections and other tasks. Soon, the whiny junkies, upon receiving their professed inadequate fixes, are none the less rejoicing with evident up-lifts. Oh what fine young cannibals they are now! The witch announces she has much serious work to do tonight. Shoos 'em all, warning them to stay out of her way.

The old man has sent word down the hall, that he has just spoken to Matrix via cell phone, and it has been agreed that tonight will be filmed on what the witch calls a "mirror memory machine" (obviously a video camera). She is now seeming quite flustered; the "mirror memory machine" needs a fresh battery, and also, they've just been informed, there is no gas for the torch. (Buddy, here we go again. Fuck, fuck, fuck!) Orders are given for fetching the needed supplies. Also, the witch wants the chosen patients to be brought down, and the "wood block" set up just so.

Meanwhile, the now coked-up young cannibals are runnin' all over the place—around and outside—lighting off those blasting cap firecrackers. It's sounding just like a barrage of incoming mortar rounds! Sparky is doin' his best to control hyper, jumpy reflexes, wantin' to take cover, run, hide, fight, whatever! The cannibal monkeys are now right outside my window, lighting the damn things. I can see the flashes and smell the black powder.

My drapes, even when closed, have gaps exposing large sections of glass window; especially up in the corners of open jalousies. And there baboons are, on other side, gathered, gawking in. (Buddy? Be cool, man, be cool). Finally, the witch orders the firecracker play to stop. The old man, or rather, Señor Santos (sounds to be pronounced Santos; but who knows, it's spoken so fast) is demanding a need for sleep, as are the *niños*. And so, the blasting outside my room stops. The tweakin' teenagers move on, only to be replaced by men. The men are hangin' out, lookin' in, smoking crack and cigarettes, while discussing "Devon" and what the "witch" (these guys do refer to her as "the witch"), is doing inside, etc. I still do not recognize any of the voices; well, except for those of the witch, my two nurses, and that teenage black boy, who had earlier brought the comb, razor, and toothbrush. He is now with the men outside, cranked up on coke and talkin' tough.

The witch is heard barking orders and giving instructions. Patients (victims) are to be gagged and bound. A cut is to go around the ankle—here—and sawed—there. After the foot comes off, the torch man must burn, cauterizing the artery.

There are sounds of serious struggling, then, the unnerving beep,

beep, beep from that wretched torch! (Yepper, they are indeed, cutting off people's feet!) The smell of burning human flesh floats in, wafting a nauseating horror cloud! Laying here, Sparky don't know what to do! There is, though, consolation in that Matrix and gang are not here; nor are they comin'. This is learnt from listening to those outside my window. Yes-sirree, Matrix is on official business, thus, can't be present tonight. Oh shoot, darny, bet he's pissed as all get-up! The men above, gawkin' down, are laughin', smokin', and jokin'; telling rumored stories of "Devon." Also, these guys are wanting my feet! Whoa, what's with the feet thing? Fortunately, none seem all too eager for storming the room to get 'em (my feet). No they are not! Yet, they are big on discussing. During this, buddy encourages Sparky to put on a little show. Plus, I really gotta pee.

My left hand grabs the steel hanging bar from the bed and has it a spinnin' menacingly overhead, while feet spring to floor's center. Even the plastic IV bottle (hoped to be considered glass) is held like a weapon in right hand. The floor is paced challengingly—as if bein' felt out, and squared off, for a battle arena—including the bathroom, where—out of view—fear is allowed to surface and full bladder is quickly drained. Whew! Exiting the bathroom, the show must go on!

Back in bed, leg lifts are performed for pointing feet, enticingly inviting. (Uh, buddy, maybe we are going too far with this show-off bit. I mean, the Beaners are surely crazy high on crack. Why are we tryin' to provoke 'em? Man, because at the moment, we do not have anything else to do; and we must demonstrate a presentation of having no fear! Understand? No fear, mother fuckers! Bring it on! Goddamn buddy, I sure hope you know what you're doin'. Man, just stay pumped! Pumped and ready! Uh, okay—shit.)

Buddy is right. The act has the men in confused awe, and a bit leery. However, one decides to just up and try shooting my foot off through the window, using his shotgun. (Buddy!) The man, bitching, trying to take aim, is told not to. No, they instead want to see if "the kid" (black boy) is man enough to go down there, enter the room and shoot "Devon." The teenager accepts the dare and the shotgun.

Sliding from the bed, Sparky gets ready for him. The door knob slowly begins to turn. My adrenaline is screamin'! Really, the only plan I have is to charge the little black punk when that door opens! If nothin' else, he will surely blast me head on—killing quickly—thus ending the sick nightmare. Ught, too late. Blacky, the teenage bad-ass wannabe, has been spotted by the witch, who sternly orders him to be gone, and away from her "business!"

Blacky returns to the men, now laughin' and teasing him. After which, they conclude that using shotguns for shooting "Devon" and the room up might not be the wisest of moves. Instead they opt to wait, wait until I'm asleep. Then they will attack, drag me out from here, cut off my feet, and (of course) fill Matrix's order—all before the video camera. These guys decide, brilliantly, that my lack of being should look like I just up and ran away, disappearing into the night, never to be seen again. Therefore, the room can't have any evidence of a struggle, or abduction. It is then mentioned by one amongst them, how "Devon" never sleeps— ever! Eh, no *problema*. The black boy is sent back down to tell the witch she must "dope Devon for deep sleep."

Blacky returns, relaying that the witch has agreed, and will start "druggin' Devon" upon completing her "foot work." The men waiting come up with another beaming idea: two of them are sent over to Mr. Benny's for my wallet. They are gonna steal some of my travelers checks; so-and-so will cash them. Yes, even at this hour!

All too soon, the witch and one of my sad-eyed nurses enter the room. They have no men or weapons with them and, surprisingly, the witch's eyes are not malicious; on the contrary, they appear to convey pitiful doubts toward everything having anything to do with this long-enduring, long-haired, tattooed American. I exhale, putting on my best poor-kicked-puppy face. The angle here, is sympathy big time! I'm handed a 10 mg Valium tablet, and plastic one-ounce cap containing some cough syrup type medicine, the kind having strong alcohol contents. Jesus, witch, this is supposed to knock me out? Oh woman, you sure don't know this cowboy. No you do not! You can feed him Valiums and cough syrup all night long!

Before leaving my room, both women glance up toward the gaps in the drapes as if disapproving. They close the door completely on their way out. The two men that had left for my wallet are back, and excited as all get-up! Yep, they've cashed a fifty, and guess what else they found in the wallet? (Ught-O.) They found the nude photo of my wife. This one has her on our bed, having jeans pulled down around black heeled boots; knees are up, exposing smooth pussy and ass. A full breast is in view, as is her gorgeous face with flowing long black hair. The retards go on and on about my wife: her beauty, big tits and (geez) the fact that she shaves her pussy, and would willingly pose in such a manner. They begin to brag themselves up (the macho way), each goin' into exaggerated detail describing the various sexual acts they would do to her, etc. The photo is serving to sexually stimulate; but also, it is feeding their lust for my blood and torment. The men are growing impatient. Three times they have sent Blacky down for telling the witch to administer more sleeping drugs, and three times the witch and nurse (wiping blood from themselves) enter my room, and give a 10 mg Valium with cough syrup chaser. Each time, the witch becomes noticeably more and more agitated. Her rile is not directed toward me per se, but rather the men up in the windows. She obviously does not appreciate them giving her orders. Also, from the sound of things, the witch is still very busy— cutting, sawing, burning, and tending to her victims. This business concerning "Devon," is clearly a distraction she does not need. The men, watching the witch doping, are baffled, thinking that surely I should be passed out cold by now.

Sparky hears a woman moaning the low haunting groans of one having just surfaced from shock shutdown. The poor woman seems to be floating in mental delirium, while gasping, "Oooh, te dam witch has cut me foot off. Aw-ooo!" One of my nurses is there, desperately tryin' to hush the woman. "Nooo! Dey cut me foot off, to be eatin' it! Te dam witch and her *satanicos* need to go back to hell, where dey come from!" More eerie moaning, with the nurse urgently pleading for quiet. But it's too late. The witch is now there, threatening: if the *"niños"* are awakened, she will cut the complaining woman "piece by piece."

Defiantly, the delirious footless woman does not care; she begins yelling gasping insults to the witch and her kind, bein' "demon cannibals from hell!" Muffled sounds of struggling ensue, and the poor maimed woman is silenced. Blacky is heard walking in on this, reporting instructions for "Devon" to be drugged more. The witch, exasperated, declares she has nothing more to give. She must see what the doctor has. (Oh buddy, this can't be good!)

The men at the window, are starting to get over the effects of my wife, and her posed erotic nudity. They turn to discussing again the mission at hand. A few now share doubts in their plan actually bein' credible. "Devon disappeared, running off into the night… Especially since the American Embassy is now working so closely with him… Devon talked today with that Laura woman; and Todd Boil came to visit, bringing all those magazines and informing him that deals are being made for his return home. Eh, I don't know; it does not feel right… Why would Devon leave the hospital?" A heated debate follows.

My door suddenly opens! In walks the witch and nurse, and with 'em is the nice woman doctor! Unlike the witch and little nurse, there are no visible traces of splattered blood on this woman doctor. No, but still… Our eyes meet, and hers, acknowledging the fearful alarm, discreetly soften while bending down close under pretense for examining my pupils. She whispers, "Devon, do not fear. I have something that will help you to stay awake and even fight if you must. The men above are cowards, and not very determined. I do not believe they are a threat to you."

Wanting so very much to believe, large tears surface as I nod, mouthing a silent "Thank you." From white smock, out comes a syringe, loaded with what looks to be clear, yet unclean water (same as Gimpy's had been). The woman doctor inserts the needle into the injection port (whatever it's called) of the IV valve, and turning the valve wide open, she depresses the syringe plunger, givin' one big shot of somethin'! Watchin' it all drain into my arm, the valve is shut off. Her hand again drops to my chest—doin' the three time fingertip press thing—and gone they are, with door closing behind.

CLICK! My breaker switch just got pulled, instantly shutting down all circuits, for what surely must have been a split micro second only! Then it's WHAM BAM THANK YA MA'AM! WHOA HOSS, WHOA! WOW-WEE-KAZAWEE! What the hell was that shit? Wide awake and rarin' to go is puttin' it mildly. SKIPPY! Light just turned green and I'm on a race horse, flyin' a hundred thousand million billion miles an hour! Bring it on Daddy-O! This cowboy is ready to kick ass and take names! Aw, screw the names; he can't pronounce 'em anyways. Sparky will just kill the mother fuckers—all of 'em! Yeah! Not bein' able to contain myself, it's off the bed, grabbin' steel bar and IV bottle for doin' some quick knee squats and room pacin'!

The men above obviously notice the difference in my jump-started, overly motivated nature. Catching bits of their questioning comments and wantin' to hear more, it's back to bed with a jump! The witch is now heard bein' outside confronting the men, barking for them to leave! "Devon will not be sleepin' on dis night." (Oh, she's got that right.) "Te injection te doctor give 'im had te opposite effect. No! Dis happens wit a rare few." (Yeah right; and if you believe that one… Damn, they seem to be actually buyin' it.) "No, dis not te fault of te doctor! How be she te know, eh? Devon, he is not like others. He be most uncommon; you know dis. Go now, leave 'im be! El Señor Santos will tend wit Devon. You have been here all night long. Tis almost mornin' time. Now go, lest anger Santos, you fools!"

Grumbling, the men decide she has a point. They do not want to anger Señor Santos (or whatever his name). Leaving, they are heard comforting themselves discussing a new plan. This one—if Señor Santos allows—consists of actually keeping "Devon" alive, alive long enough to have my wife bring down money for paying fines. Once she is here, they will do with me as they please, and force my wife into prostitution. "Yes—yes! She is *Americano,* class A pussy, same as *Baywatch* TV. We will make much money from her; plus, we can fuck her brains out, showing her what real men are like. She will love us so much; she will thank us, begging for more, just like it is done in the American porno videos." Blah, blah, blah. Their bullshit fades—following them away. Laying here, flyin' on the massive amount of quality coke injected into my arm, I am relieved at still bein' alive and havin' those assholes gone, but, now what? The witch had said that what's his name—Santos—would be tending to me. What the fuck does that mean? (Buddy, any ideas? Buddy? Buddy! Are you there? Yes, I'm here; and no, I don't have any ideas. Wow, this is some really good cocaine. Buddy! Forget the coke! What are we gonna do? It's all quiet now, no activity. The torch man has finally stopped his Goddamn torching—Ught! Buddy, did you hear that? A rooster crowin'—and now some children are cryin'. We need a plan, buddy. This Santos guy ain't gonna just let us be. No he is not! He will probably have us cut into stew meat! Uh-hhmm, yes, you're more than likely right. Okay okay, let's see: Señor Santos didn't kill us last night. Wonder why? Surely he wasn't leaving the task solely up to those goons; they weren't hardly motivated enough. But maybe he was allowing them to have their chance for purpose of perhaps appeasing Matrix, or whomever. In any case, we appear to be now in this Santos's lap. Man, all we can do, is wait, be ready, and hope like hell Todd Boil gets here early, as promised. Yeah okay. God buddy, how I do hate goin' through this shit. Still, buddy, you are right in this coke bein' out-fuckin'-standing!)

Light of morning comes, but no construction workers or laborers; no, not today. Also there are no gatherings of hurried hospital staff exchanging news or gossip before shift changes. From the next room or so, I can hear where old man Santos is now awake and about. It sounds very much as if his wife, or the likes, is the witch. Others too are with them in the room—all gathered (guessing) sitting around a table talking in comfortable tones of a clearly close family, sharing breakfast and discussing last night. The hospital intercom is now periodically announcing current, ever changing market prices for *coca* and marijuana. My small, sad-eyed nurse enters my room. Saying nothing, she sets down a breakfast tray and then leaves, closing the door completely behind.

The breakfast is lukewarm tea, juice, and a plate full of rice loaded with much meat having been diced into tiny cubes. Unusual breakfast food indeed. The meat looks to be like none Sparky's ever seen. Pinkish white, it's similar to pork, but not quite. After last night, I think I know what it might be. Hhmm, maybe it is, maybe it's not? (Hey buddy, shall we taste some? What the fuck, right? Yes, sure; what the fuck.) A sampling is chewed and swallowed. Mmm-mmm, tastes like chicken. He he he! Naw, Christ—who knows? It's not like we are gonna be eating it, or anything else, for that matter. No this coke high is way too good for putting food on. However, thirst is another matter.

Gulping down the tea, I strain ears for hearing what's bein' said from old man Santos's room. It's difficult to grasp everything, but Sparky can comprehend enough. A young man is in there; and somehow, he's now got the nude photo of my wife, and is showing it around. Old Santos is indeed impressed with the photo, though he is not with the police last night. No, and especially not after learning they had gotten into "Devon's" traveler's checks. "All this business concerning the American Devon is becoming too messy and complicated." Santos blames Matrix and Todd Boil for this.

The old man's English is surprisingly good, even for grumbling, "When I want someone dead I kill them! And they are no more. *No problemas*—*nada*—nothing. But Matrix, he must always make a grand show of it, playin' the big Orc, always adding the sex and torturing. I like his video movies, same as everybody, and they sell for good money—eh? Yes. But these days, he goes too far. Like with this Devon, the *Americano* that got away—and just keeps gettin' away! One difficult *problema* that just keeps runnin' about... What am I to do with him? I do not want him. Yes, yes, now Todd Boil wants to make another deal. Eh, everything about this Todd Boil is a deal. Now he is wanting to pay cash for this Devon's life. He is always thinkin' he runs the show. What? Eh, maybe you are right. Maybe it is time we teach Todd Boil a lesson. No, not yet. It is not like how it was in the old days. The time has come where they must first scratch our backs, before we scratch theirs. No more them tellin' us how it is to be. Yes, let's hear what he has to offer. If we do not like it, eh, then we teach him a very important lesson. Yes, I will have Devon taken away, up into the hills, shot dead, and buried. It is that simple. No more of this Devon business! Eh? No, I do not want him killed and buried here. He is *Americano*; too many know he is here. There will be investigations to contend with. Eh? Aw, possibly you are right. Then we will have Devon's body tossed along the roadside, where it can easily be found. This will then look as if he ran away from here, and *banditos* killed him. Yes, that way, there will be no investigations, or people snooping around, asking questions and possibly digging things up. Eh? Matrix? Aw, he had his chance. I do not care what he wants. All of that has now changed."

The knob of my door turns, but does not open. Todd Boil's voice is heard bein' just on the other side. The little nurse has stopped him from entering. Using excited whispering tone, she is quickly telling Todd about last night: the Santos family arriving, all night long cutting off patient's feet, and killing. Also, the family has brought prisoners; they have them tied up in the back shed. The *policia* and *gauchos* were here too. The nurse proudly describes how she, the witch, and the doctor had tricked them from taking "Devon" away. But now, she warns of her fear, believing the family is now making plans for my disappearance and death.

Upon hearing, Todd is furious! Thanking the nurse, he stomps down to the room where the chief and cannibal clan are havin' their mornin' chat. (Oh Todd, oh pal, you came! You actually came! But now don't blow it. Let's just get the hell outta here!) I am off the bed and doin' some serious floor pacing, fightin urge to run—run out that door—for Todd. But if Sparky does, Santos might just up and kill us both! (Come on Todd, do not blow this. Fuckin' Hannibal the Cannibal is just achin' to teach you a lesson. Uh, what's a *gaucho*? Oh forget that. Buddy? Buddy! What should we do? Man, just hold tight. Let's listen and hear what is gonna go down first. Yeah right, okay, but I hate this shit!)

Todd enters the room of cannibals, but sounds like he ain't showin' his anger. No, instead, he sounds to have put on his happy-happy face, and he's talkin' like they are all old friends. After some pretentious small talk, with which the cannibals are amusing themselves in playin' along, Todd cautiously inquires as to what their intentions are concerning "Devon." The old man laughs a wicked raspy chuckle, answering, that it depends on what Todd has to offer.

"Show us how much you want this Devon, and possibly we will consider. Remember Todd Boil, this is a very bad man. And a pervert! Look, Devon carries a picture of his wife naked! He has her showing off everything. Look, ha ha! You can see, his wife even shaves the hair there. She is looking to be wanting it, in both holes—ha ha! And you call this Devon a nice family man? Eh? He is nothing but trash. The *policia* are wanting him very much, as do others—eh?"

Todd asks to use their cell phone, claiming his own is low on batteries. He then excuses himself, stepping outside. Now he is right there, on the other side of my corner window! His silhouette is easily seen, leaning against the building, facing away, while speaking into a cell phone, "Yes, it's me. Devin had another long night last night... Yes, they are here. They had a little foot removing party. There are prisoners as well... tied in one of the sheds. Also, the police were here... Yes, last night. Yes, I know… No, Devin doesn't know that I am here yet. I'm standing right outside his window. The nurse told me he is fine, but they did coke him up pretty good to help him stay awake. How much can I offer them? And if they don't go for that?… Yes, I guess he will be then… If that does happen? I honestly don't know what his chances will be. Probably nil; but hey, who knows? He's gotten through worse… Okay, out." And with that Todd is gone, having taken no notice of my window tapping for his attention. (Hmm, he ignored it on purpose. Wonder why?)

Back inside the cannibal den, the old man sarcastically asks Todd if he's come up with a respectable offer? Before Todd can answer, the old cannibal hisses, "Remember Todd Boil, I said respectable. This sex pervert Devon knows nothing of respect. Just look and see the picture he carries of his own wife."

Todd, now sounding very annoyed, informs cannibal retard that it is a very common practice for American men to carry such photos of their wives, or girlfriends. It has nothing to do with disrespecting. Todd then asks, from where did they get the photo? Hannibal the cannibal snarls, "In his wallet. Devon had it hid amongst the nice proper pictures of his *familia*."

Todd replies, "Hey, well there you go. Devin had it hid because it is private. And here you all are; you have the man's wallet, without his permission. You have searched it, finding a private photo of his wife; and now, you are showing it around as if you've never seen a nude woman before. I don't see where Devin is the pervert here, or the one showing disrespect."

The old man growls warningly, "Watch your tongue Todd Boil. You are in my house now."

After some moments of silence, Todd speaks, "Okay, let's get this over with. We can spend all day going back and forth bickering price, but let's not. Instead, why don't you just tell me how much? How much is it going to take for getting Devin safely back home to his wife and sons?"

Grumbling, the old man, calm as can be, answers, "We want fifty thousand US and his—" Todd interrupts with a loud mocking laugh, adding, "No—no, I don't think so. It is ten thousand US and you will consider yourselves lucky to be even getting that much!"

"No! I do not think so, Todd Boil. If you are wanting this Devon to live, it will cost you fifty thousand US. Plus, his wife is to deliver the amount herself, and offer—let's say—special services for helping make amends to those her husband has caused to lose face. Ha ha! This should be no *problema* for such a woman that can so willingly flaunt her ass for the camera. Ha ha ha!"

Todd, enraged: "That's insane! Has all the cocaine made you people lose your minds? No way would we ever allow for that! We have tolerated enough from you people. No more! No more Mr. Nice Guy; no more deals, and no more asking! From here on out, it's going to be me telling you how it is! And I'm telling you, that there is no deal for Devin! No money! No nothing! And you will leave him alone! He is going back home to his wife and sons, and you get nothing! Is that understood?"

The old man has had enough. Todd is jumped! There is a strong struggle, with Todd shouting, demanding they remove their hands at once! But to no avail. Hannibal the cannibal orders his men to take Todd out to the shed. "The time has come for Todd Boil to be taught a lesson in respect." Todd is hollering in serious pain; they are for-real hurting him! And I am literally bouncing from foot to foot. (Oh Todd, you blew it! Now what are we gonna do?) Dashing for my door, but stop short of opening it on buddy's command. (Man, what are you doing? No plan, no nothing; and you are going to just run out into the hall, and do what? Try to help Todd Boil? Man, that is stupid! They will just up and shoot, or they will use us for torture as part of Todd's lesson.) "Devin! Awh! Devin!" It's Todd shouting my name, but he ain't yellin' what I'm to do!

From across the room, through the drapes, there they are! The silhouettes of 'em, a group of five or six men, half draggin', half carrying a kickin' screamin' Todd Boil! A couple of men have weapons slung over their shoulders, and one appears to have a hold of Todd's balls—squeezin' hard. One man hurries, putting a revolver against Todd's head; still, Todd ain't submitting, or givin' up. No, he's just simply overpowered and outnumbered. Down the steps they take him, and I see them no more, but they are heard. Yes they are!

The old man is barking orders. "Hold him tight—hold him tight! Put the clamp tool on his *huevos*. Ha ha! That will settle him down." Todd roars with pain! "Eh, gag him. Now turn his head. He is to watch, watch what it is that we do to those that think they tell us how it is."

Fuck, Sparky is guessin' they are now in the shed with the bound prisoners. The torch has fired up, and with it that unnerving beep, beep, beeping!

"Ha ha ha! Cut that one slowly, then burn him. I want our Todd Boil to see."

The poor man, whomever he may be, is wailing out the long muffled gasping moans how people do when helpless, bein' purposely maimed and mutilated. Sparky just stands here, listening, shocked, stupefied, and in dis-fucking-belief! Tears are swellin' and lips are trembling. I don't know what to do! (Buddy, we are in some deep, deep shit! Jesus Christ, they can do this to the American Ambassador? Hell, even if ol' Todd Boil there ain't the real Ambassador, he still works for the American Embassy, US government, whatever. And, and, these guys can just up and do this to him, like it is nothin'? Good God! Buddy? Buddy!) There! It's Todd. We hear him. His gag has been removed, and he's yellin' hateful threats toward the old man. (Damn, at least Todd ain't backin' down, or losing any of his arrogance. Good for him!) BANG! A gunshot—and another! No more sounds from Todd. There is though, much Garifuna/Carib laughter.

The old man barks orders for his men to start working on the others. He then wants the bodies cut up and put into barrels, same as the rest, also all blood traces should be torched, leaving no evidence. Suddenly another man begins loudly screamin' out my name, as they start in on him. This man's voice is a high-pitched howling: "Devon! Devon help! Oh God, Devon, please help me!" His desperate pleadings are quickly dropped to those of low haunting moans, begging for mercy between gut-wrenching spasms.

Covered with crawlin' goose bumps, it's pace the floor time, and try to figure a plan. Aughg, I think they just shot and killed Todd Boil! And the other guy callin' out "Devon," sure sounded sorta like Pio? My pacing stops abruptly to the blasting BANG of another gunshot! The poor man, maybe Pio, is now at least dead. The torch keeps goin', and approaching, passing my windows, is old Hannibal and his laughing cannibals. Stopping, one of the younger from the bunch suggests showing "Devon" their "trophies," but old Santos won't have it. When asked why? "Devon will soon be dead anyway." The answer is still "No!" And so back to their cannibal den they go.

Fuck me Judy! (Buddy, why, why, why didn't we make a run for it while they were outside, busy torturing? Buddy! Man, and what? Leave Todd Boil here, not knowing if he were dead or alive, or whatever? Oh right buddy, like we really ran out there to help him! You're the one that said not to leave the room! And so we didn't—nooo! We didn't do jack-shit! Yes, well let's not forget Rabbit Boy, there was no plan! None, *nada, pas de, rein*! Yeah well, uh, buddy, you were here with Sparky all the time; so Rabbit Boy yourself! Uh, and…, and, uh, it's your job to come up with the Goddamn plans! So, where is the plan? Buddy! Buddy? Uh, buddy? Yes. Buddy, they killed Todd Boil, didn't they? It would appear so. Jesus buddy, we really need a plan, and like quick!)

The door opens, and in walks Doctor Greaseball, mouthful o' rot, his grin ever wicked. He roughly removes the IV needle from my arm, while hissing, I have been released, discharged, and am no longer in their care. The nurse will be bringing in my clothes, at which time, I am to leave the hospital and grounds, at once. No, he knows nothing of either Todd Boil or Laura Simms. Also, all phones are still down, and no, he does not have a cell phone. His exit leaves the door wide open. Gimpy emerges; from his large knurly hand hangs a black plastic trash bag, dripping blood droplets, and conforming to shape of weighty contents within. It's guessed (due to having handled before, back during brief embalming days) that ol' Gimpy here, has himself several human hearts in that there trash bag. Well, ain't this the sight for beholdin': Smilin' Gimpy, the way too happy retard, standin' here with a bloody trash bag of human hearts, happily informing "Devon" that he is all healed and can now go home! (Uh yeah, sure Gimp, go home now.) Mimicking him, bein' all big idiotic smiles, having happy bouncing face, I explain the need for my clothes. "Can't go home wearin' this butt exposing hospital gown, can we? Ha ha!" (Fuckin' haw.) Snickering Gimpy agrees, promising to be quick in bringing the nurse having my clothes. (Yeah, you go do that Gimpy. Uh, and bring a grenade while you're at it.)

The hospital intercom announces Señor Don So-and-so's arrival for El Señor Santos (or whatever the name). This Don So-and-so, is another important honcho chief. Passing my room, he and his small entourage engage themselves with curious small talk about the ever popular "Devon." Listening, it sounds as if the two honcho chiefs are bein' left alone in the cannibal den to discuss *coca* business. Don So-and-so is here for purchasing a large amount from Santos. A price is quickly agreed upon. The coke is sampled by both men (snorting), and drinks are poured. Spirits become lifted, and voices grow louder. To further heighten the mood, they pop in a torture video.

As the video victim gasps out the mournful moaning of one begging for death, the two sickos laugh it up (as if watchin' a comedy), making comments on order of "Ha ha! You know that's gotta hurt! There are thousands of them on him! Look-see, how they cut the poor bastard to make them bite him all the more? Ha ha ha! I would not want to be in his shoes! Ha! Ha ha ha, ho, ho, ha! Now watch: *puta* is goin' to be cuttin' his cock off. Ha ha! Haw, ha ha! Haw! They will saw him up now, and see? He is still breathin'! Ha-haw! Ho ho, ha! Oh that gotta hurt!" etc., etc. (Buddy, we gotta get the hell out of here; and like now! Yes, agreed. Let's step into the hall and get a look around. We must get our bearings straight for the run. Ught! Don So-and-so is now leaving.

Wait until he is gone. Fuck buddy, I hate this shit!)

Hearing them leave, all is now silent. Sparky slips out into the eerie hallway. Taking a left, and on tiptoes, I sneak past the rooms guessed to house Hannibal the cannibal and immediate clan. From the plywood side of the corridor comes muffled sounds from unseen children in pain. (Buddy? Man, head on down toward this floor's front desk/nurses' station. Okay.) Oh crap, there, from behind the front desk, is another little Mayan nurse. She, quickly spotting, gives silent look of urgent alert, warning! Nodding acknowledgment, and following her gaze— aughg! Across from the front desk, to the right of a semicircle open floor entrance level, against a sidewall, is a short waiting bench. Sitting upon it, appearing very much to be that leaving no doubt, is a rough faced, cruel eyed bad man. He is wearing dirty blue jeans, cowboy boots, and long duster coat. (Damn, the only thing he's missin' is a cowboy hat and pair of six shooters.) Santos is standing above the seated man, giving him instructions, "Drive Devon into the hills, and shoot him, twice, in the head. Leave his body on the road, for all to see. It must look like the work of *banditos*. Use this gun. It is a very good gun and has killed many." Old Hannibal hands the cowboy hit man a pistol, bein' wrapped in cloth rag. Not caring who might be watchin', the cowboy opens the cloth, holds up a well used six-inch barrel .38 revolver, checks it to be loaded, spinning cylinder, and shoves the revolver down into belted waist of jeans, while asking, "And what if even at gunpoint, I can still not get Devon to come with me, or he runs?"

The old man, smiling, snarls, "Use, then, the *cuchillo*. Stick him like a pig once or twice; he will come. And if he runs? Eh, let him, a small distance from here, and shoot him where you think best, preferably not before many seeing, but you do what you must. I do not care, so long as you make him dead."

(Buddy? Yes, we've heard enough. Go back to the room, and let's see if we can get out unnoticed, through a window. Yeah, okey-dokey.) Slippin' back into room, and closing door behind—oh fuck! Gun totin' men can be seen just outside the windows! Sparky, turnin' back for the door— Whoa! In comes the sad-eyed little nurse, carrying a sack containing my still wet, ripe clothes.

Okay, it is get dressed time! Toss the hospital gown. Tucking in tail of thin cotton grey long sleeve crew neck tee, cinching belt fast, snap-tying French, camo, BDU leggings around pulled tight laces of sooty red Converse high-tops, over soggy wool OD socks. Wow! The cocaine is still felt surgin'. Also, now, just bein' back into my old clothes (despite foul state of their condition), has given some degree for positive charge.

Uh, and the ridiculous swim shorts and old button shirt? Eh, roll 'em in the sack and hang on to 'em. Why? Good question. Lookin' up from right hand clutching sack for purpose not quite understood, my eyes meet those of the little nurse's: hers are swelled with tears. Tears conveying that, already known. (Christ, buddy, any ideas? As usual, we need a distraction; gotta buy some time! That Beaner cowboy hit man is gonna be comin' for us at any moment. Buddy? Man, try the poor, pathetic, wanting to die with passive dignity, while having peaceful thoughts of loving wife and sons bit. The same asked of Pio and Partner. The difference being, we ask to be injected with a drug overdose, here in the hospital, and left to die in peace, alone in this room. Afterwards, of course, Santos can still have "Devon's" body dropped along the road, or whatever. No mess, no fuss, no *problemas*! Old Hannibal would be a fool not to go for it. Uh buddy, he just killed Todd Boil! Buddy, Santos ain't gonna play into this one. No fuckin' way! Man, he most likely will not. But it just might buy some time. Jesus buddy.)

Breaking the silence, Sparky asks the little nurse outright, "I am to die. Yes?"

Having tears streaming, she answers, barely audible, "Yes, yes—*si*."

Nodding my head, confirming understanding for fate willingly accepted, I, being of stance (seemingly) completely submissive and defeated, begin to tell the little nurse about my wife and two young sons; also, how it is known I have offended very important people and therefore must die. Blah, blah, blah. She is given the same heavy-hearted song and dance as what Pio and Partner got. The little nurse, intently listening, breaks into chest heaving sobs, and dashes out the door! (Uh buddy, was that good, or bad? Ught! Guess we are gonna find out.)

The little nurse is back, and with her is the other Mayan nurse, and old witch! Whereupon, I am instructed to repeat my request. (Hey man, it's for real—show time! You must convince the witch. So make it look good. Oh, you got that right buddy.) Surprisingly, the witch is very attentive, even nodding head for sharing understanding of the desire to die left alone, in peace, without torture or video camera, in order to leave this world thinking last thoughts of beloved wife and sons only. Both nurses are now literally blubbering weeping tears; and the witch is lookin' just a bit more than a little sympathetic herself. She turns to the nurses, reminding them they must first receive permission from El Señor (Hannibal the cannibal). She then holds my gaze with eyes piercing, as if searching; finally she breaks it, informing, "I twill see what con be arranged. Meanwhile, you must stay here as you are. Remain quiet and wait for our return. Yes? You give your word—no tricks? Okay."

Back in the cannibal den, the two nurses and witch are heard with Santos. The witch calmly explains my request in detail. The old man silently listens, as the witch concludes, "Devon twill still be dead. His body con still be dumped on te roadside to be easily found. Good ting, is dat dey will tink he run off to get te *coca,* and he do too much and die. Dis be proof dat all de long he is just te crazy junkie—*coca loco.*" Both nurses interrupt, acting like young school girls pleading, "Please! Please El Señor, we beg you. Let this Devon die as he wishes. We beg you—please, please, please! We will do anything you ask."

The old man, as if agitated, quiets them, informing, "I have already made arrangements for Devon. He is to be simply shot in the head. He will die quickly, feeling no pain. Aw, this Devon business, I do not understand. So many hate him, and yet there are so many that love him. Eh, no matter, his time is short; he must die. Eh, and what difference does it make how he dies? The video and cutting, I understand; no man wants to go like that; but why the *coca* and not the gun?"

The witch shrieks, "He desires to die in peace from te *coca* to help his mind for reachin' out to his *familia* as he passes over to de utter side! Dis twill take only a small time. Devon needs only te *coca,* and to be left in peace. Shortly, he twill be no more as we know 'im."

Old Santos has heard enough; grumbling, he will consider the request. The nurses, hearing, are shrieking with joy, and sound to be huggin' and kissin' him. One nurse rushes into my room, excitedly announcing, "Good news Devon! El Señor is considering!" Returning her big happy smile, and nodding grateful thanks, I turn, and offer her the magazines there on the nightstand. Oh boy! Thrilled is describing mildly. The little nurse appears to be about on verge for peeing herself! Grasping up the stack of old magazines, she exits the room, declaring she is needed for helping with preparations of my *coca* injection. (Damn, buddy, is this some fuckin' weird shit, or what? How they are actin', you'd think "Devon" was at the airport wavin' bye-bye! Geez, instead, it's soon to be a convulsing, vomit spewing death from cocaine overdose: and that's if we are lucky. Whatcha think? Do we stay, or run? Odds are, this is the only chance for goin' out in death so comfortably. But then again, buddy, what if it's a trick? You know, what if the witch don't inject a large enough dose, and they decide to do a little torture movie making? Hey buddy, help out here. Do we run, or stay? Ught, buddy, listen.)

From across the hall, behind the plywood partitions, the witch and nurses are heard bein' all chipper, while preparing the *coca* for injecting. Word must have spread, because now a couple of young cannibal bitches are there, whining for fixes themselves. The witch is scolding that it is still too early for their injections. However, the bitches are insistent, countering that if they receive their injections now, they will then be ready to cut on "Devon" for the video camera. One is even giggling how much fun it will be "cuttin' on his cock. He he he!"

The witch screams, "No! Der twill be no mirror memory machine, or cuttin' on Devon! He is to be left alone for dyin' in peace! You fools, get out de me way. I have work to do. Go now!" Both girls reluctantly obey, but not without some strange language cussing, and a mention of going to El Señor Santos for conveying personal complaint. (Oooh, buddy what does that mean? Man, who knows. Hhmm, maybe we should run; only, crap! Let's just give it a little more time and see. Jesus H. Christ, buddy, Sparky is literally climbin' the fuckin' walls here!)

Time passes—too much time. Someone should have come in here by now. Somethin' is most definitely not right. (Buddy? Sparky can't stand this waitin' no more. We gotta get outta this room—like now! Buddy, at least for a recon? Okay, confirmed, but man, do tread softly... Roger-Dodger that. God, buddy, I do hate this shit.) Out the door, down the eerie empty hall. Whoa! Old Hannibal the cannibal is heard speaking from the other side of the plywood. He is instructing the cowboy hit man, givin' him the green light: "Go get Devon. Remember to shoot him twice." (Uh buddy, guess we can forget about the overdosing idea, huh? Right, man, find one of the nurses. Maybe they can help you hide, call the embassy, or at least give best route out of this place. Move! Okay!)

Double-timing it, passing the now vacant front desk. (Hhmm, wonder where that nurse went?) Cross the open semicircle floor, ascend adjacent curved stairwell (cautiously avoiding the bored, stupid armed men, supposedly guarding the entrance doors from outside). Up the stairs. Ught-o! Down comes a young cannibal man, leading by the hand a small boy child that (guessin') is his son. From the young man's shoulder hangs a Ruger 10/22 rifle. (Not your typical combat weapon; that's for sure.) The young man and the child, upon spotting "Devon," instantly stop! Fear is in the little boy's eyes, and uncertainty is in the young man's. Letting go of the child's hand, he slowly reaches around for unshouldering the .22 rifle. In doing, the small boy clutches the young man's thigh, stepping behind. And me? Well, I'm about to haul some serious ass! Fortunately though, right at the very moment, a male, light-skinned doctor (of approximately early thirties) appears on the stairs. He comments with much disgust, "What's this? Guns now in the hospital? You people fear him—Devon—this much? Incredible!" Nodding his head side to side while mumbling somethin' on the order of having a real dislike for this country, he steps on past descending down the stairs, with Sparky bein' right on his heels! Glancing back—the silent young man cannibal has not moved, except to follow aim through sights on his 10/22. (Go ahead dick wad, pull that trigger!) However, upon the doctor having noticed, the .22 squirrel gun is reshouldered, and hurriedly back up the stairs young man and child go!

The doctor walks over to the front desk, now again having the same Mayan nurse standing behind. He instructs her to quickly call the American Embassy. The nurse's eyes are darting with fear; she whispers that the phone call cannot be made, "Not from here. Understand?" Nodding, the doctor quietly asks for the number. The number, on a small piece of paper, is discreetly slid to him. Having number in hand, he pulls forth, from his white smock, a cell phone, and walks away. I of course, try goin' with, but receive stern reprimand, almost bordering on hostile. (What the fuck?)

Looking to the little nurse, who has now become teary-eyed, while commenting, "May God forgive us. We are not a gentle country." (Oh, you got that right!) For the hell of it, Sparky asks her what she thinks I should do? Wiping away tears, she seems surprised with the question, but yet considers. Waiting for her reply, we both hear the cowboy's raspy voice, calling out for "Devon!" He is searching, and will soon be here! The little nurse, quickly points to the doors leading outside, motioning for me to run!

"Uh-uh, but the men guarding, they must surely still be just out beyond the doors!"

She urgently whispers, "No. They are with the *gaucho*! Go, go now; and may God be with you!' (Aw lady, why didn't you share this tidbit earlier! Hang on buddy, here we go!) Out those doors Sparky does fly, having hot sunshine hitting! The nurse had been right. The armed men are not present, but there is a tall chain-link fence topped with angled tight barbed wire. No problem; it's up with a kick—using the bounce from the fencing (both hands have gripped top strand of barbed wire) to flip in handspring fashion up and over, to land a jolting thump on the other side. The ground is overgrown, scrubby brush and twisted trees. The earth is hard and parched, thus enabling only the hardiest, most persistent foliage to exist. Mostly this is rugged, viney, intertwining underbrush country, sprouting sharp saw grasses, thorn bushes, and low knurly trees. A maze of well-worn earthen paths lead every which way, pocked with erratically placed (hopefully empty) man-sized foxholes.

They are sandbagged right up to US military spec. (Hey buddy, whatcha bet they have tripwires spread throughout? Yes, we die now—we die running! Do not stumble. If we injure a leg or ankle, it is torture city for us! So watch for wires, hidden holes, etc. Also, keep eyes open for anything that possibly can be used for a weapon. Now run! Uh, duh! But which way? Which way do we go buddy! ...Hhmm, the front entrance, parking lot, and guard house is back to our right. See the hills? Uh no! Well man, they are there. Therefore, we must run straight forward through this mess, far enough for swinging around entire flank of the compound, and get up that mountain road, using cover. Christ, here they come! *Run mother fucker, run!*)

The voices are angry, mean, hurried, and all conveying source bein' that of several groups. The sporting party hunt is on! God, please don't let 'em have dogs. Runnin' like a deer I am. Runnin' with heart racin' and eyes wide alert for anything and everything. Oh yeah, they got tripwires! However, they are thick, and stretched tight—therefore, easily detectable, in irregular terrain where nothin' natural is straight. Plus, these wires are obviously placed for tripping up and slowing down intruders or those—like myself—fleeing, rather than actually tripping off any explosives. Consequently, they are positioned at a height making proper camouflaging impossible. The run is all about speed, calling for agile, sharp, vigilant calculations. What can't be jumped, sidestepped, or climbed, is dived through. BANG! BANG-BANG, BANG! BANG! (Fuck! buddy, they are shootin' at us! Man, just *run*! Ught, buddy, do yah hear? *Dogs*! Dogs are barkin' like— Man, watch that wire! Buddy, dogs are barkin'. Oh shit! We are runnin' directly for 'em.) *Aughg-ooo-oomph*! Goddamn! (Man, hold on! Land on your ass! Not the feet! Tuck legs and ankles—must protect. Here comes another drop buddy. Oh-ho-ho, it's a high steep fuuuckerr! Man, roll—go with it—and *bounce*!)

Landing hard, the body struggles desperately for quickly getting' air back into deflated lungs now constrictin', while at the same time—on hands and knees, I'm crawlin' along narrow rough clay-dirt mountainside road, lookin' about for bearings. First, look up toward the jagged cliff, I had just ran-fell down, and bounced off of. (Jesus buddy, that was one hell of a fall. Man, get up. Must get up—check for injuries, and get moving! Yeah okay. Buddy, we've pulled a hamstring and are bruised like a mother fuck, still, no broken bones. He he! Hey buddy, look, after all that, we still got hold of clothes in rolled sack, and..., and, oh good, here's the piece of paper having phone numbers. Man, retard, there is no time. *Move*! Follow this ascending trail road. We must get up the mountain.)

Dogs are still heard, barkin' mad! A quick glance over edge of dangerous four-wheel drive only type winding cliff road, having no guard rails. Aw, there they are. The dogs barking aren't givin' chase, but rather are tied, or fenced, within the yards of many houses built in valley level below. And, uh, well, since I am up here, pretty much in plain view, what with bein' on this ridge road ledge. They, all below, can see. The dogs, most bein' of Rottweiler variety, do sound-off an excited frenzy! Several owners can be seen out in their yards angrily tryin' to silence the beasts. These dog owners (and there are quite a few) do keep glancin' up toward me, yet none give impression they are in any way surprised. (Oh that? No, that happens all the time. People are always runnin' from the hospital up there, to come bustin' through the bush, tumblin' over the side of the mountain, landing on that old road. Yes, all the time! Especially the *blondo gringos*. They do this all the time. It is nothing; though it does upset the dogs.)

Time to run; and for this, the body is screamin' pain and reluctance. My left buttock and entire leg are awkward and stiff, sending fears of buckling. Also, left ankle is getting in some crybaby whining, as are several ribs. Fuckin' sissy bitches! You will stop this shit, and run. Do you hear? Run! Oh fuck. I don't Goddamn believe this: my right shoelace has come untied. Sparky didn't double knot ties! (Somethin' all athletes, soldiers, *and escapees* know to do.)

Bending, quickly, retie, double knotting, both shoelaces. Glancing down, a dog owner from in the valley below is pointin' and motioning, givin' warning that he can see my pursuers above searching. With that, wavin' him thanks, I am runnin'!

At first, due to injuries, the run is hobbled, but then, mental stress of fear and physical charge demanded for the all uphill trek takes over, and in like no time, it's runnin' full throttle!

The ragged narrow dirt road comes out just above the armed guard house, fronting entrance to hospital parking lot. Here, a moment is taken for hunkering down in some scrubby brush for a quick look-see and listen. Lungs are heaving for air; however, they must be suppressed, least I hear nothin' 'cept them gaspin'. There is one coke head guard inside the little guard house, but where is the other? Ught, there he is, with his Mini 14, playin' soldier, patrolling the perimeter of parking lot. He's across, to the furthest end. Sounds are heard comin' from unseen men approaching, searching the surrounding grounds. Several armed men exit the hospital's front doors, escorting an older man (obviously another very important honcho) to his gleamin', expensive, *grandiose* car. None are lookin' my way. And I am guessin' the coked-up Beaner inside the guard house is most likely watchin' the doting entourage.

The time is now or never; go lickety-split! Crossing the open ground, diving behind backside of guard house. A quick peek around the corner is done for seeing if any had noticed: nope, so slip into dense thickets Sparky does with no lookin' back. Haulin' ass, all up hill, zigzaggin', doin' the whole deer in the woods thing. And I do mean woods! Thick as can be, havin' leafy trees canopying a density of plant life all doin' its best in mimicking a box full of corkscrews, seemingly endless. Still though, I was made for runnin' terrain like this. Despite limited visibility, direction is simple; just keep movin', ascending up, up, up!

With eyes full of blinding sweat, shoulder's bust like a plow through brush. What the fuck? Using sopping wet shirt sleeve for wiping eyes, vision clears, revealing two men playin' tennis. They have stopped their game; and are now lookin' at me quite how one would imagine. (Uh buddy, we are at the clubhouse tennis court thing, noticed on drive down to this hospital of cannibals. How do you want to work it? Man, run to them. Be non-threatening, and tell them your name; explain you are a tourist, and bad men are chasing you without proper reason. See if these guys will lend a cell phone, or, at the very least, give directions for the American Embassy. Now go—we must keep moving!)

The two middle-aged men playin' tennis are clearly upper class Guatemalans. And "No, no," they don't have their cell phones with them. (Dirty rotten liars! These Goddamn Guatemalans eat, sleep, and shit with their precious cell phones.) Also, the clubhouse phone is broken, and no, they do not know where the American Embassy is. (Yeah well, thanks for nothin'!) Across the street is the armed guard standing position at the gated entrance leading down to nice houses in valley below. The guard is wearin' an old Sam Brown rig, holstering a revolver. He, of course, has taken notice, and is watchin' closely; however, his stance betrays that of bein' more curious than anything else. There is no reaching for revolver or cell phone. Nor is he abandoning his post in approaching: not yet anyways.

From the small clubhouse emerges an old black Carib cleaning woman, havin' eyes darting. She is wavin' for my attention and motioning urgency. Hesitantly, goin' over to her, she quickly begins givin' directions for the American Embassy. In doing, the tennis players (pretending) resume their game. The cleaning woman's eyes meet those of the standing guard's across the street. Both she and him are nodding in silent communication of somethin'.

Thanking the kind woman for the directions, suddenly, she steps before me, pressing us both against clubhouse wall! She hisses a shush for quiet, while pointing. Fuck! It's the cowboy hit man. He's walkin' up the road, and has stopped before the standing gate guard, who just keeps slowly shaking his head, as if answering "No, no." The shielding cleaning woman whispers, "Do not fret, the guard twill not tell."

A burgundy Mercedes arrives, stopping; behind the wheel is the head honcho seen earlier. The gate guard is still shaking his head, when another car, containing four serious cannibal types, pulls up, stopping behind the Mercedes. Upon seeing, my new best friend—the cleaning lady—lets out a soft whistle, whispering, "I know of you Devon; as do most. You must get to te embassy. Dey, here, are huntin' you; en will kill you, evon out in te open like dis. See dat one? Wit te long coat? We call 'im a *gaucho*."

The cannibals back their car up, turn around, and drive slowly back down the winding road. The Mercedes drives quickly onwards, uphill; and *Gaucho* follows, on foot, having duster coat flappin', revealing the waistband-riding revolver. (Buddy, it is time we fly! Yes. Man, you understand the directions? Uh, well sorta. Hhmm, we are to follow this road up, all the way. At the top, it meets with a very busy city street, where we are to take a right—followin' for a very long distance—again it too bein' all uphill. Yes man, I remember that from the drive down here. Okay, uh, well then, at some park, or somethin' it's a left for a few blocks, then right for a couple more, then left, and uh, I guess we will see the embassy from there? Buddy, you know I suck at takin' directions. Yes man, however, remember—fake it 'til you make it. Let's go! Yepper!)

Sincerely thanking the nice woman, Sparky turns to leave, but her hand again clutches a hold, while asking, "Devon, what way you be goin'?"

"Uh, Ma'am, up through the woods. I will get to the top via cover of the woods."

She, hearing, sternly shakes her head no, explaining that the car and *Gaucho,* having not found me on the road, will guess I'm comin' up through the bush. "Dey twill be der waitin'. Devon, you must use te road. Devon, be still, and watch. If'n te car and *Gaucho* not soon come back down, din you understand I be correct." She turns out to be "correct." On her "Go now!" Sparky is a runnin'—haulin' ass!

According to her calculations, the *gaucho* and car should be now at top, waiting, where they are predicting my emergence from the "bush" will occur. She figured, since the road had already been searched, my best bet, therefore, is runnin' it. Whereupon, reachin' the top, there will at least be many people and much busy traffic. Perhaps, if I stay runnin' close near people witnessing, those that are pursuing may become hesitant with their shooting.

The road is a steep one. If memory serves, it's guessed bein' at the very least, a good two miles before reachin' the top from this spot. My pace is set at an all-out wide open run! Buddy, is, of course, screamin' for slowing the pace! He knows, as does Sparky, that we will never be able to maintain such a grueling speed. Hell, even on a flat run, the pace would be impossible. In our younger days we had been quite the runner: both as civilian and soldier. Yeah, how we could run! Just like in the movies, this abused body—despite size—could toss a full-grown man across shoulders and run! And I ain't talkin' no hobbled spit of a distance. No, Sparky is talkin' runnin'! So, buddy and I do know a thing about running. Like how if the pace is slowed, keepin' it fixed and steady, the destination will be reached quicker than flyin' now in overdrive, rapidly consuming limited steam.

Ignoring buddy and the obvious logic, the pace stays as it is. That carload of cannibals could be (and probably is) circling back. If bullets are gonna fly, then, fuck me, I'm runnin'! The Legion adamantly believes that most men will consider themselves fully spent after exhausting only seventy percent of their energy. The Legion demands one hundred percent from its troops; therefore, *La Legion Etrangère* is always pushin' for that extra hidden thirty percent, hence maximum endurance.

All too soon, my seventy percent is nearing depletion. Chest is heavin' with lungs painfully yelpin', gasping for air. What little they do get is seemingly worthless. Legs are jell-O, havin' no feeling, as are feet flappin' slappety-slap-slap, much like that of a doofus duck. One big gasping noodle I am! Bent forward, I'm damn near to point of draggin' swollen parched tongue along scorching pavement. Still, Gumby the rubber man keeps goin' onwards. Oh, and talk about acid reflux? Yepper, ol' Gumby has it, a very bad, bad case, spewing forth burning black tar, mucus, phlegm, whatever! (But we don't stop runnin'; do we buddy? No-sirree, it's march or die! Man, you dumb ass! This isn't running. We've slowed so much that a one-legged goose could pass us. Why didn't you listen to me, and pace yourself properly? Ught, Oh shit, here comes the Mercedes! Man, find that thirty percent; and *run!*)

Buddy is right! The burgundy Mercedes, in sighting, speeds past, goin' down the road, turning around and haulin' back again. Fortunately, it is the lone old head honcho only. Still though, even if he don't shoot, he's gonna fetch someone that will. Uh, the *gaucho*, and bunch! Honcho did have a cell phone to his ear. They will be comin'!

Hacking up a goober-glob tar ball, raspin' a loud, *"March or die, mother fucker!"* The thirty percent is called on, and away we go! Again runnin' hard, huffin' and puffin' like the Little Engine That Could, up that mountain, to rhythm of march or die, march or die, march or die. The Mercedes swishes past, not firing a shot; however, it takes no genius to figure out who he's goin' for. No it does not! Runnin' to beat all hell, having legs simulating imagined pistons in song, "Son you're gonna drive me to drinkin' if you don't stop drivin' that hot rod Lincoln!" Euphoria engulfs, lifting and carrying. Buddy and I, of course, know what this is, and are enlightened by the most welcomed euphoric embracing presence—riding her out for all she's worth. It is, though, short-lived, rapidly evaporating upon approach of the head-on intersecting busy city street. Wow, what a run! Ught-o! Can't slow now!

Amongst the heavy traffic, zippin' up and down this extremely steep street, here comes the burgundy Mercedes! *Gaucho* is now in the front seat with honcho, and they're floorin' it! From the curb, I spin lookin' to and fro with obvious intent for zigzaggin' my ass up and across this chaos of horn blarin', speeding traffic! (What the fuck? Buddy, look— look! Far down the street, on the sidewalk; it's white backpackers—for real, white backpackers! Two of 'em, bent forward with large packs, they are slowly humpin' their way uphill. Buddy, do you see? Yes, man, get to them—*now*!)

Kickin' in high gear, down that sidewalk, sooty red Converse high-tops do fly, with Mercedes hot in pursuit! Yet, despite the circumstances, or maybe because of, exhilaration takes hold. Goddamn, what a rush! To be runnin' down hill at such speed that feet don't hardly even touch concrete sidewalk. Yeah! Just like with sky divin', wind is blowin' through head as if it were hollow. Bullets could (at this moment) thump hotly, plowin' their damaging dance of a whole lotta hurt; and to be honest. Sparky wouldn't even mind (much).

The two backpackers, huffin' and a-puffin', bent, staring to hiking shoes, concentrating on steep trek before them, have no notice of barreling Sparky. (What's the plan? Buddy, they are gonna freak! Man, who cares. Maybe they are going to the embassy, or have just come from, or possibly have in possession a cell phone. Doesn't matter much; either way, they will know where the embassy is. And as long as their path leads them up this steep-ass street, we will try using the two for cover. Oh buddy, they are just gonna love this!)

In surprised unison, both heads jerk up as sooty, red Converse high-tops slam on brakes, dodging around backsides to come up parallel. Side by side the backpacking couple are between me and the street. They just have time for a quick startled glance over to yours truly, when the Mercedes locks 'er up, skidding, damn near popping the curb, forcing both backpackers to hurriedly sidestep, shocked in wondering, What the fuck? And I'm right there, sidesteppin' with 'em. *Gaucho* opens the passenger door partway, as if for getting out, the honcho is yellin' and shakin' his head, disapproving. Cars, now behind them, are loudly honking horns, blaring protests. Hence *Gaucho* stays seated, and Mercedes, with angry squealing tires, takes off drivin' on down the street. (Fuckin' A, buddy! This is indeed a good sign, proving that the bastards ain't all that keen blasting my brains out here before a street full of witnesses. Yes, except, this doesn't mean they won't—especially the cops. Oh shit, shit, shit! The cops! Buddy, you're right, the cops! Hey man, just stay sharp! Frosty sharp; and ready to haul. Also, hadn't we better introduce ourselves?)

With a big happy-happy face, "Hi! How y'all doin'? My name is Devin. I'm from the United States, and I have bad people chasing me. They want to torture and kill me. Uh, and you guys?" (Ha! Geez, these pink backpackin' yuppies are lookin' as if they have just stepped out from an L. L. Bean catalog of horrors! They themselves, bein' good Americans, seem intent on following newly revised standard procedures for all Americans traveling abroad when encountering a fellow American in need of help—don't! Do give pretense for deep concern followed with much sympathy, but do not, yourself, in any way, become involved, or attempt to help this troubled American. Instead, do get as far away from this fellow American as possible.)

The yuppie backpackers, of course, have no cell phone, though, oh boy, they sure know where the American Embassy is. Yep, they do. Uh, no; these two aren't goin' there themselves, but are more than eager in quickly givin' Sparky the directions, while double timin' now their own pace up this long steep stretch of ascending street that goes up and up, having no end in sight. The male, between gulps for air, kindly suggests, that it might be in my best interest, considering present situation, to be moving on and away from them, as they are burdened with such heavy packs. (Holdin' back a laugh.) Eyes catch glimpse of angry Mercedes, now slowing traffic for again cruising pass. The old honcho is on his cell phone, and *Gaucho*, seeing I'm watchin', pulls forth the revolver, and is openly pointing, taking aim, mouthing silent "bang, bang."

"Hhmm, you guys might be right; still, I'll just walk a spell with you two. You know, sorta keep y'all company, 'til at least we reach the top of this here hill."

The male yuppie, puttin' to use those expensive new style hiking shoes, snarls between deep rhythmic hard breathin', "Keep us company? Don't you really mean use us? Use us for your human shield?" The female yuppie looks a lot like the actress that played Shirley from the old Laverne and Shirley show—well, actually, right now, she is of facial appearance resembling how I'd imagine Shirley's to be during a rectal exam. Upon hearing this, bent, sweaty backpackin' Shirley moans, "Oh God, no! I hate this country. Why did we even come here?"

Her anguish is felt, and guilt is engulfing. (Buddy, what should we do? Sparky really don't wanta involve these folks. Yes, okay, just stay with them for a little while longer. The more people that see us with them, the better. Damn, here comes the Mercedes again. And Christ, from the hospital turn-off road, approaching fast, is the carload of cannibals! Buddy? Man, keep it cool. Get between the backpacking couple, turn, and give big grinning waves toward both cars. This just might temporarily confuse the inbred cannibals long enough for achieving brief hesitancy. Jesus buddy!)

Both cars slow down, yet, must keep movin' on past, due to heavy traffic. The number of bystanders has increased tenfold, and is clearly ever growing, seemingly appearing from nowhere, and everywhere! A drive-by shooting or abduction would be anything but discreet. However, for cops, such trivialities do not apply. (Buddy, cops are gonna be here any moment. Give the green light! Yes, *go*!)

"Okay folks, thanks for the chat. Remember my name is Devin! Devin Murfin from Illinois. I am outta here! And if I were you guys, I'd do the same. This country, and everybody in it, is fucking insane! *Adios!*"

With horns blarin, brake-skidding tires, and people shoutin', Sparky is haulin' ass, zigzaggin' across that street! Thus ensues another all-out run! (Of course, entirely uphill.) Traffic has slowed and people are hurriedly steppin' for clearing "Devon" a way. Many voices are heard callin' out my name. Some are on order of excited encouragement, while others… Shit! A cop car suddenly appears with lights a-flashin'! A young black man separates himself from his cheering group, and is quickly waving my attention, urgently pointing towards an alleyway veerin' left between towering squalid buildings of commerce. (Fuck me!) Kickin' hot, sooty, red Converse high-tops up on edge, sharp left turn is taken, and down that alley I do fly! In doin', the young black man is heard shouting for his friends to "block de way!" His voice becomes a distant echo, "Devon, follow dis passageway, keepin' to te right!"

The alley is narrow, ripe with litter, rot, debris, and disorder, much how one would expect. Crude intersections grid in typical Third World fashion. (Buddy? Man, run these grids, first left, then right, left, right, etc. But do keep directional objective. Instead of being a deer in the woods, you are now a rat in the sewer! Make the Beaners work for capture of "Devon." Yeah sure buddy, easier said than done. Oooh, by anyone's standards, this has been one hellacious run. Buddy, I'm seriously afraid of total collapse. Man, we do not have time for this. March or die, old friend. Surrender is not an option. So giddy-up and run, sissy boy! Oh blow me.)

Rounding a left corner unexpectedly, exit the alleyway's gridwork for flyin' across a busy open city street, just in time to see the ass end of a cop car go past. Sooty, red Converse high-tops are slappin' down the center for crossing one intersection for another. Vehicles are honking, swerving, and skidding on brakes. People are filling sidewalks, themselves runnin', so as not to miss the outcome.

Suddenly, Sparky is upon a park/courtyard type thing: it's a sorta manicured city block boulevard between streets. Oh fuck me runnin'! There, on far side of grass avenue, is now parked the Mercedes. *Gaucho* is standing, leaning against the car, actin' look-out. And here comin' straight on, haulin', is speeding carload of cannibals! Spinnin'—aughg! Cop cars havin' lights flashin' are closing in fast, from seemingly all directions! (Buddy! They're boxin' us in! And I've lost directional objective! What to do—what to do? Man, snap out of it! The embassy is that way! Now run! But, but, but… Man, work it out like an ambush. No retreat, no surrender, no hesitation! Run—*run*! Right through the damn thing, and hope for the best. Buddy, I hate this crap.)

Charging diagonally, with vision blurred and body pretty much just doin', boulevard breakout is (somehow) achieved. Sparky runs full blast down a street's center, fleeing fast-gaining pursuit from growlin', hot revving engines, flashing lights, and squealin' tires, closing in for prize.

Flags! Long low brick perimeter wall, and UN soldiers! My embassy has indeed come into view. It's so close, yet… Posted UN troops and standing people waiting in long, snaking lines have, of course, all noticed this oncoming arresting sight.

The horn blaring cannibals' car is working in unison with a racing cop car for sandwiching this desperate, rode hard fugitive. Almost succeed they do, but Sparky don't think so! Bringing left foot down hard, pushin' up, and back, both cars pass—instantly slammin' brakes—thus, colliding a front bumper crunch! I land to roll 'er over rear-end of cop car, just in time for glimpsin' another barreling down, head on for makin' me its new hood ornament! (Fuck this!) Two leapin' bounces, following some exceedingly impressive footwork, surpassing limits never thought personally possible, I am kickin' off that skiddin' cop car. Piston pumpin' legs to street curb, crossing sidewalk, and hurdlin' that low embassy perimeter wall, I use velocity of remaining momentum for bolting across grounds towards my embassy's revolving door entrance. In doin', UN troops are dashing forth, intent on intercepting. All to the loud ruckus from spectating, long lines of waiting people, who are now behaving much how one can imagine over-excited holler monkeys would.

Ignoring shouted commands, "Stop—*alto*—stop!" and dodging rushing troop attempts at enforcing, Sparky is able to reach waist high, independent standing nothing of L-shaped brick barrier wall; obviously built for bein' a barricade fire-wall, fronting revolving doors. The thing is easily jumped, damn near bowling over the old Sergeant standing his post before the enternace. Reclaiming his balance, holding on to my shoulders, his eyes are sparkling, and mouth is curved for gentle smile.

Acknowledging the old Sarge and his most welcomed present mien, Sparky glances left, and immediately takes notice. Yep, there, short distance up on the steps overlooking, is the same fearless, squinty-eyed, intimidating, tall, big, lean, black Carib, having dramatically slanted powder blue UN beret, and large veiny hand restin' on Glock pistol, holstered at hip. Despite him glarin' at me, conveying he would like nothing more than to blast my brains out, I am elated beyond belief! (Buddy, we made it! Actually made it out of that Santo hell of a hospital, to arrive here—alive—at the American Embassy! Lordy, who'd have ever thought?)

But whoa, tryin' to speak, there is no air! I can't catch breath! Bending forward, with hands on knees, heavin' sporadic gaspin' gulps, tryin' to get a flow steady and constant. There is very real fear of hyperventilation; also, stomach and lungs are seriously wanting to barf up carbon tar, and the likes. (Man, do not puke—not here!)

The old Sarge, seein' oxygen deprived wobbly state, sympathetically pats my sweat soaked back, while at the same time, askin' "Devon" for the rolled sack. (Ught, I still got hold of that thing? Jesus, held on to 'er for the entire run. Whew, wonder why?) Sarge, upon opening the sack, and finding only old swim shorts and shirt, turns toward surrounding troops, motions for 'em to lower weapons and go back to posted positions.

Sharp shooting pain from hurtin' ribs constricts a reminder, thus triggering lungs to open and bellow: "Sarge! Sarge! Somethin's bad has happened to Todd Boil! I must get inside! Must tell Laura. Ohh Sarge! Let me through!"

Sarge, gently nodding, is however, unwavering. "Procedures first." Aughg, okay-okay; following his instructions, I lean back against protective short barricade of brick L-shape fire-wall, and squat down on heels (ready to fly, if need be). Sarge kindly asks for my passport.

"Passport? Uh, that's a funny Sarge. I used to have one, plus lots of other things—but not anymore! Sarge, they took everything—everything! Well, except for the filthy clothes on my back, and this stupid sack!"

Old Sarge, half grinnin', silently motions for calm, while he himself speaks garbled words into his squelchin' walkie-talkie. Waiting patiently for the expected squawking reply to come, Sarge gazes out across the grounds toward the street. Sparky, seein' Sarge's eyes become fixed, jumps up to see. Fuck me! Cop cars are parked up and down the street with lights a-flashin', and there with 'em is the Mercedes and carload of cannibals. All are standing beside the vehicles, intermingling, talking into cell phones, and facing my known position! Shit, shit, shit! Sarge, with understanding firmness, pushes me back down to sit on my heels. Lookin' into his eyes, he whispers, "Do not worry Devon, they cannot come on to embassy grounds."

Yeah well, still, unnerving it is. Also, just like the time before last, the jabbering monkeys are again attempting to break lines—pushing, bunching up, for that better look-see of "Devon." Oh boy! Fortunately, the troops have anticipated, and are doin' a much better job in holding the lines (sorta).

The walkie-talkie crackles with Sarge confirming, "Out." He then relays, "Devon, you must remain as you are. Todd Boil will be down shortly."

"Sarge, Sarge! Todd Boil is here? He is okay? Not hurt!"

"Yes Devon, si—si, yes; he is fine; soon you will see. Now you must only remain calm, relax, rest. You are all *loco* from your long run. Eh? You are presently safe; so, simply do as instructed. Relax Devon."

(Buddy, the Sarge said "long run." He said it as if he knew where I had run from. Buddy? Buddy! What! Man, think about it. The Sergeant is door guard to the embassy. From all the scuttlebutt that must surely get siphoned to him, he probably hears more about what goes on concerning this place, and its dealings, than the important officials that work it themselves. Man, you know how this works; does it really surprise you? Uh—guess not. Buddy you're right. Damn, after learnin' that Todd Boil is here, okay, and alive; geez, nothin' surprises me anymore—and I do mean nothin'!)

"Hello Devon."

What the...? Sur-fuckin'-prise! I'll be Goddamned; go to hell! Standin' there, side by side, at head of monkey line—not even eight feet away—is the two grinnin' Bobsey twins! The Bobsey twins from lovely town of Livingston. Blinkity-blink, eyes are tryin' to register the reality. (Buddy, are we seein' things?) Why, how, what? Like brilliant vivid color slides flashin' at lightning speed, visions of Sparky in that stinkin' rotting building, violently bashing the poor drunk man's skull. Killing, murdering him for amusement of those sick cops and, of course, the Bobsey twins!

Shakin' my head for clearing brain—yep, it's them all right: very real, and very here! Smartly dressed they are; having big assured bemused smiles beaming down upon my confused surprise. Not able to think of anything better, "Uh, hi guys! Whatcha doin' here?"

With grins set, acting much how old acquaintances do when bumpin' into each other at unexpected odd places (boy oh boy, don't get much odder than this); they nonchalantly explain, that though both live and work in Livingston, their families are here, in the city. So, they come often for visiting... Oh the embassy? Well, both are here with hopes of obtaining traveling visas for the United States. (Gosh, that's great; uh-huh, yes sirree-bob. Just what the United States needs.) Wow, what are the odds of these two just happening to be here, in the city, at the embassy, standin' head of line, right at the very moment that I (just barely) made it to the embassy myself, after running guts out from cops, goons, and murdering cannibals? Huh—what are the odds! (Buddy? Man, if it is how they are saying, well then, the odds would be astronomical. Hhmm, wonder what these guys are really doing here? Uh, golly buddy, do ya think it might concern "Devon" much?)

The Bobsey twins, both smilin' slyly, ask, "And so Devon, why are you here? We thought you had a job in Livingston?"

"Yeah well, guys, that job didn't quite work out. The benefits, you know, weren't all that good; plus, the pay really sucked! Ha ha ha! My gear? What happened to all my stuff? Funny you guys should ask. See, every time my kit got searched it got lighter and lighter, 'til finally, there just wasn't anything left to search! Ha ha ha! Yepper, it just plum got searched away! Ha ha! Oh, it's for the best, really, considering the circumstances. Humpin' all that weight sorta became tiresome. Ha ha! Hey, you guys got a cigarette? No? Neither of you smoke! Hhmm, really? Oh that's right! You guys only smoke when helpin' yourselves to my cigarettes, yes? Huh, yes, right! Ha ha ha!" (You puke fucks!)

The accusatory jesting brings forth, from them both, dry laughter, containing evident traces of embarrassed awkwardness. They ain't so damn cocky no more. The one having brown hair, glances around, while sincerely offering, "If you want Devon, I can get you a cigarette from somebody here in the line."

Remembering what a comfort these two were on that grisly horrifying night, I drop the sarcasm, and politely decline. (Plus, do my poor lungs really need a cigarette right now? Hhmm, let's think on this one.) BOOM! POP-POP! Like a cat gettin' smacked in the ass with a sling shot, my strained, jumpy, over-alert reflexes *kick*, flyin' body straight *up*! Instant loud bursts of blurting laughter, and Sarge, rushin' over for urgent calming, help brain in registering that it had only been a car out on the street, backfiring belches of compressed exhaust. Sparky, recovering, acts the good sport. While attemptin' to hide ripplin' nerves and thumpin' heart lodged in throat, tries laughin' along with everyone else.

The Sarge's walkie-talkie crackles. Reaching, he escorts me over to the revolving doors. Both Bobsey twins call out goodbyes as I step on through.

Inside, to the left, a smiling Laura Simms is there, motioning for me to follow. Up the stairs we go, entering the American Embassy waiting room of old benches, assorted straight back chairs, and funny school desk units. The long customer service counter is now open, having (rolled/sliding) partition divider up. An older white American man and Todd Boil are working seemingly feverishly, dealing with the present lines of frustrated Guatemalans, all wanting visas for entering the United States. Some are almost pleading, while others are argumentative. All are loud! Todd glances up for a brief instant only; his eyes betray gleam of genuine delight in seeing me; and for the very first time, I see his true smile. Vanishing though it does, as he quickly recovers old façade and regains fake haughty smile, he calls out greetings, and informs, "See Devin, do you see what I am doing here? This is ninety percent of my job. It's all about passports and visas! Pretty exciting job, huh?"

Guatemalans, hearing my name, all turn to look, murmuring buzzes of "Devon" travel throughout the room like a giant confused bumble bee flyin' about, not knowin' which way to go, 'cept up, down, round and round.

Laura gently suggests, "Why don't you have a seat Devin. Todd will be with you as soon as possible." She then goes to take up his place behind the service counter. Todd steps away—disappearing.

Ignoring the gawkin' monkeys, Sparky does as told, settling into lone straight back chair. Despite throbbing pains resulting from injuries sustained from bouncing fall and hard run, I am in a euphoric state of exhilaration! (Buddy, we made it. Again we made it—here to the embassy—alive! Goddamn, buddy what are the odds? Also, looky, ha ha! Looks like most every single Beaner is bein' denied a visa for the States. Do ya see buddy? Yes, man, but more importantly, I see Todd Boil is still alive, and acting his usual self. Which means... Buddy, which means that the asshole left us there, in Santos's hospital, knowing full well our intended fate. Christ, buddy, he didn't even send no help. Wonder why? Especially after what they did to him. Man, you remember his phone conversation outside the window. Todd has a ranking superior that he must answer to. He's been following orders concerning us from day one.

Yeah, but still, buddy—orders or no orders—after what Santos had done to him, and those in the shed, fuck orders! Geez, buddy, elation just became deflation. Back on the clock for us, huh? Man, off the clock, we never were.)

Laura and the older American man, are makin' short work of the lines. Todd comes into view behind Laura, whispering somethin' into her ear. She, nodding, reaches up and pulls down her window partition, leaving those left still waiting in line to bark their screeching primate protests!

The door leading through opens a crack; Todd motions a silent command—come. I do, tryin' hard to conceal my new limp and, in doing, notice his.

Back in the office with Laura, Todd has put on his major prick act, demanding answers, "Okay Devin, what's going on now? Why are you here, and not at the hospital? Devin! This is becom—"

Tired of his games, I interrupt, hissing, "Uh, gee, I don't know Todd, why don't you tell me what's going on, and why I am here." You were there at the hospital! The deal didn't go as planned, did it? And they hurt you, didn't they? Todd, I saw it all. I notice you've got quite the limp there. They clamped your testicles didn't they? Todd, you are lucky they didn't kill you. I thought they did! Only they didn't. And you just left me! You left me there. You knew they were gonna kill me—or worse! And still you left, not caring enough even to send help! So Todd, you tell me what's goin' on and why I got the hell outta there!"

Cool as a cucumber Todd is, as he silently listens to my venting (Hhmm, man, you might want to shut up, now. Yeah okay, okay.) "Devin, are you finished? Good. First of all, I don't know what you are talking about." My eyes sharply meet his, conveying silent resentment. "Okay Devin, yes, last night I did promise to come visit you this morning, but hey, sorry pal, I just couldn't make it. As you see, things can get pretty busy around here; I could not get away. Devin, despite what you think—or want to think—the American Embassy does have duties and responsibilities that exceed simply helping you deal with your psychosis, which, by the way, in my opinion, you brought on yourself, by heavy, self-inflicted drug and alcohol abuse. So, you see pal, I was not at the hospital this morning, and have no idea what you are talking about clamping my testicles. That's just absurd! My limp, if you must know, is a result of a pulled groin muscle acquired early this morning during my routine daily jog. But hey, Devin, this really is none of your business. And you mention a deal not going as planned, and people arriving at the hospital, cutting off feet, and again wanting to torture and kill you. Is this correct? And let me guess—they had a video camera, I suppose, and were filming it all for one of your imaginary so-called torture/snuff films. Yes?" (Buddy, we never told him nothin' about the people showin' up, cuttin' off feet, did we? No, nothing of the sort was said. Hmm, also, he hasn't even asked who "they" are. Buddy, ol' Toddy here is a-slippin'.) "See Devin, from where I stand, at this very moment, I am more convinced than ever that you are suffering from acute paranoia. Your behavior is proof."

From out of the blue, Sparky barks, "Oh yeah? Todd, explain then how one of my fifty dollar traveler's checks got cashed last night? Huh? How? I sure the hell didn't crawl out of bed, stroll up that Goddamn mountain road, give ol' Mr. Benny and wife a visit, ask for my wallet, and then go around the city in search of someone to cash the damn thing, all in the middle of the night! And…, and, explain please, where is the photo of my wife! Todd, stop shaking your head. You know what photo; you saw it! My wife is very beautiful, isn't she? I want it back! Goddamn it! I want my photo back!" Todd actually flinches each time I use the so-called Lord's name in vain. Sparky had known wimp fucks like this while in the military, big bad-ass infantry grunts that would just about go into a fit of tears every time we'd sound off our favorite Goddamn son-o-bitch Jesus mother fuckin' Christ! "Todd, I want the photo back. You know what they have planned for her if she comes down here." Voice is cracking. "They want $50,000 US, plus my wife is to work for 'em as a prostitute! A prostitute— my wife!" Coughin' up a scorchin' tar ball, and re-swallowing, "Todd, you know this! You know this, and you know what they will end up doin' to her when they're finished."

Todd and Laura remain momentarily silent, watching as I sit here with face scrunched, squeezin' back tears wanting to cascade. Finally, Todd clears his throat, and calmly insists, "Sorry pal, but it's all in your mind; none of it is real."

Lookin' at him as if he were the world's biggest asshole, brain is racin' for answer as to why? It concludes the obvious. Todd must convince everyone, including myself, that I am a for-real nut-case. Thus, everything seen, heard, endured, and forced to commit would have then all been one big (never-ending) psychotic hallucination; hence, everyone, including Todd Boil, gets off the hook! Boy Skippy, let's hope this is what he's up to. And if by chance it is, well, sorta only makes sense to assume the game must first start with the persuasion of primary pawn—yours truly!

Letting out a long exhausted exhale, "Okay, Todd you are probably right. Cannibals, torturing/snuff films, beheaded babies, snakes, scorpions, giant toads! Todd, you're right—it's all insane! I must be suffering from some sort of psychotic mental breakdown, most likely resulting from drug abuse, and bein' so far away from home, my wife and sons. You know, I never did really get over the recent deaths of my father and grandfather." Tears (with some help) are now flowin' down cheeks like mad! "Todd, I am the last surviving adult male in my family. God, Todd, I gotta get home! Get home and receive long-term psychoanalysis. Please Todd, I gotta go home. Help me get back home. I will do whatever you say."

Todd, listening, is now all smiles, nodding his head as if he is hearing exactly what he wants to hear. Also, his eyes keep darting up strangely before responding, "Great! Hey, in that case Devin, let's get you back to the hospital; shall we? And I will continue working with your wife and others on the best means for getting you home."

"Wha-wha-what? No—no! Please Todd, Laura. Please, not there—not back there! Oooh, I know that none of this nightmare is real—honestly I do—but please understand, knowing isn't enough. I can't go back there—not to that hospital! The hallucinations will reappear there. I am for-real *terrified* of the place! Todd, please, just put me on a plane to anywhere, USA! Look, you can have me institutionalized into a psych ward, or…, or, uh, hell whatever you want; I don't care, so long as it's on American soil!"

"Hey Devin, pal, hey, understand, I'd like nothing better; however, unfortunately it's not that simple. You've heard the use of good news/bad news scenarios? Well, the good news here is that it's looking pretty positive that I can get you legally out of Guatemala on condition of terms agreed: you pay Mr. Benny full compensation for all damages."

"Yes! Todd, no problem there. Let's call my wife; I will have her transfer the money today! I don't know where she'll get it, but she will." (Actually, if it's the 50,000 that Hannibal the cannibal Santos had demanded, well, there is Nancy's rich brother in California, he might help out, under such circumstances. And if not, there is always my old friend Brent, also now living in California. We grew up together, both poor, and close like brothers we were; yet when he got wealthy with money, things just sorta changed between us. We haven't spoken in over two years; still, he would make good with the money, if it was to save my life.) "Todd, how much are we talkin' here? Fifty thousand, or ten thousand?"

After a moment of intense eyeing, Todd shrugs his shoulders, claiming the exact amount hasn't been determined, though he is guessin' it to be around the ten thousand figure. "Wonderful! Todd, let's call my wife!"

"Hey Devin, okay, we will, but after the bad news part, pal." (Oh shit.) "And that is, even after Mr. Benny gets paid, Devin, I still cannot put you on a plane, not by yourself."

Havin' a general idea where ol' Todd is goin' with this, Sparky bites down hard on tip of tongue to keep it from flappin' what it shouldn't. "Uh, Todd, and why is this?"

Rubbing his temples with eyes rollin' to throb from evident head-ache, he answers, "Because Devin, I am not going to be held responsible for boarding a known firebug onto a plane full of innocent people, not without an escort I won't. Devin, I can't; there's just no way! Besides my superiors won't allow for it; and neither will the airlines."

Wanting to shout protest in bein' declared a firebug, I don't, tasting the blood from tongue with jaw quivering. "Uh, okay Todd, I under-stand; but really, this shouldn't be a problem. Surely the embassy has people—uh, or, soldiers—that fly out of Guatemala City for the States every day; righ-right? No! Todd, you've got to be kidding; how can that be? I don't believe it. Okay, okay, how about this: just have 'em search me before boarding, and then handcuff my ass to a seat on the plane! Why not? How the hell can I possibly burn up a plane when handcuffed to a seat without any source of fire? No? Goddamn it! Okay Todd, what if Nancy hires a private investigator to come down here, and in handcuffs, he escorts me to anywhere you say, USA! No! Come on Todd, please! Why not? Hey Todd, you're not thinkin' what... Oh no, no way! Todd I'll die first! The dirty sick bastards can torture me to death in prison before I let my wife come down here! Todd, she cannot come down here! You know this! No way—no fuckin' way!"

"Devin! Hey pal, relax. Nobody is asking for Nancy here in Guate-mala. Hey, I'm on your side. Do you think I want your wife leaving those two sons of yours to travel down here? No Devin, I do not. Besides, I need her stateside to continue working things from her end. We are a team, right? All having the common goal of getting you home? Well pal, you're just going to have to trust me on this. In order to get you home, we need one—the money—and two—a very close family member of yours. No, not Nancy! We need someone other than her to fly down here and take care of the required business, you know, face to face? Signing forms, etc. And to act as guardian, shouldering responsi-bility on escorting you safely back home. Sorry pal, but it does have to be a family member, understand?" His eyes search mine for seeing if I'm getting the picture. "Don't worry pal, I'll be here to walk them through every step of the way."

Yes, Sparky is indeed seein' where ol' Todd is goin' with this. If it's a family member, the stage will be set for a much more viable exit, in closing confirmation of my unique mental situation. Hhmm, and uh, for such drama-effect, who, other than my wife, would be best suited? Aw geez, guess that would have to be my mother. Damn, who better, right? Everybody is sure gonna know you're a raving lunatic, when at age thirty-eight, you go a-travelin'—gettin' yourself into trouble—and your Mommy must come to fetch your butt back home. Jesus Christ, wait 'til they all see my mother: a small, beautiful, stylish woman, of middle age, lookin' easily twenty years her junior, having intellectual level exceeding life's cup. Thus there is, more often than not, a constant overflow of run-offs goin' every which way across flat surface before forming into erratic stream like channels for course of direction. And to add, she is a frustrated artist and hopeless romantic, always on the side of the world's little underdogs.

Aughg, they will literally eat her alive down here! Matrix and his cannibals will have a fuckin' field day with my mother. There is no way her safety can be guaranteed; not after knowin' what they did to Todd Boil, without even so much blinkin' an eye. They can do, and *do* do just as they please.

Looking to Todd, his eyes tell he's already spoken to Nancy (probably while I sat in my chair out in the waiting room, before bein' brought back here for this little chat) and they have both decided on my mother. Asking Todd, he confirms I'm right, while pullin' forth his cell phone for calling Nancy again.

"Whoa—wait! Todd, after we talk to my wife, then what?"

"Well, hey pal, that's up to you. I mean if it were me, I'd simply go back to my room at the hospital and wait for my mother to come. But, you claim you're not comfortable and don't feel safe there, uh okay. Personally, I don't understand why; it seems like a nice enough place, and all the people I've put there have been satisfied. Okay, so you're afraid there! Hey, no problem: there are other hospitals in the city. No Devin, we have been through this before; you cannot stay here at the embassy. Sorry pal, it's got to be a hospital, or hey, there's always prison! Oh come on now, cheer up; I'm not going to let you go to prison. Not after that record-breaking run you did in getting here, I'm not! Holy cow, think you ran that fast enough? Ha ha ha! And to think, it was all uphill. That's some serious determination! Uhmm, okay hey, don't worry; I know of a hospital I think will be perfect for you. Devin, I personally guarantee you will feel safe at this one. It's a good, old-fashioned Catholic hospital, you know, the kind having nuns for nurses that still wear the traditional winged bonnets and long flowing robes?

Devin, I will tell you, demons and cannibals will certainly think twice before entering this place; believe you me, they will. Ha ha!" (The prick is mockin' me.) Seeing I don't in no way share his humor, and almost as if a shooting pain from the groin reminds him of his stupidity, he drops the grin, suggesting we make that call.

Watching him punch the little lit up numbers on the cell phone, Sparky's gotta pee, but decides it can wait. With miniature phone to his ear, Todd again instructs that the conversation should be brief, mentioning as little as possible. Also, he is getting my attention on his eyes which are darting up toward a corner of the ceiling. (What? Cameras? Oh great, hidden cameras, but no safe room or secure phone line, right!) Laura has just been quietly sitting here, without much expression, occasionally jotting down a note or two in her ever-present clipboard file.

"Nancy? Hi! Yes, it's your old pal Todd Boil... Yes, I have him right here in front of me... He looks about how you would expect... No, Devin, claims he didn't feel safe in that one. But like I told you before, I can get him into another one, one that he feels safe in... Ho! That's for sure; he is a slippery one!" (Slippery? What the hell is she talkin' about? Wow, she ain't got a clue as to what's really goin' on down here. Slippery, fuck me!) "Yes Nancy, don't worry; I sure will be watching him closely. Laura and I will be visiting him every day... Hey, I personally know the doctor... Yes, he's a good one, and a real nice guy! Don't worry. Now about Devin's mother coming down. Oh, you did get a hold of her? Just got off the phone with her, and she's agreed to come down... She will be bringing Devin's little sister with her, she is twenty-one. Hey, that's great. When?" Todd's voice drops its performing up beat tone to that of solemn concern. "Excuse me Nancy, after the holidays? You mean after Christmas? Nancy, that's over a week away. No, no problem. Hey, it's your guy's money! Every day we keep Devin down here in a hospital, it's costing you money. Also, Nancy, remember this is Guatemala. Devin's situation can change daily. I just think it's best we get Devin out while the gettin' is good! That's all... No, now calm down; that's not what I meant. I know you are Jewish and Christmas doesn't mean anything to you. Hey, I don't blame you. What? You found a flight and now you want to come down instead? No, Nancy, I don't think that is wise. Like I said before, situations can change on a dime in these parts. Hey, we are talkin' Devin here! Ha ha! I might need you right where you are, to work things out from your end. Nancy! Nancy look, we will talk more on this tomorrow? Okay, but do work on trying to get Devin's mother down here, preferably before Christmas Soon as possible, okay? OK, look, here's your husband. We will talk tomorrow—

bye." Todd, now lookin' very concerned, hands over the little phone.

"Uh, hi, sweetheart."

"Devin? Devin, Oh God! Are you all right? Devin, why did you leave the hospital? It's all in your mind Devin! None of the shit you think is happening to you is real! God, what have you done to yourself? You must be so Goddamn fucked up! Do you even care that you have two sons here at home waiting for you? Every night they are asking where's Daddy—where's daddy? What? Devin, what? I don't know Devin; what is the deal with your mother? What do you mean why is she bringing your little sister? She's bringing her because your sister can speak Spanish, and your mother believes it will help convince the police and whoever else you have obviously pissed off, to see that you have family that seriously cares... Oh God Devin, I don't know. Trying to get a straight answer from her is like pulling teeth—she's your mother! How do I know? No! She wants to wait... Wait until after her precious Christmas! She says flights will be cheaper... I don't know... Yes, Devin I am aware, thanks to you, that every day you are there is costing us money! Your mother doesn't care! All she seems to care about is her pre-planned Christmas with her daughters. God, Devin, do you have any idea how much money all of this is going to cost us? Yes? Yes you do! Well, how are we going to pay for it? Are you fucking insane? I'm not calling my brother. Fuck no! My family doesn't know anything about this mess.... No, I am not telling them! I don't care... I don't want them knowing, that's why! What Brent? Brent! Devin, get real; I'm not calling him either. Look Devin, since you and Todd don't want me coming down there. I guess we have no other choice; you're just going to have to wait it out in this other hospital that Todd is going to be taking you to. Devin, please, just stay there; you will be safe. Todd has given me his word, and I believe him. But Devin, you must stay there—do not leave! Promise me; God, just promise me you will stay there—Devin please. Yes, I will keep working on your mother. Devin, remember, you brought all of this on yourself. I haven't slept since you started this nightmare! Devin... Devin! All right, bye. I love you too."

Well now, wasn't that a cheery conversation? Yep, so much for the euphoric state of exhilaration; geez, that puppy is long gone. Reaching for his cell phone, Todd instructs me to go wait in the front waiting room. I inform him of my need to pee. He impatiently points toward a door bein' a private bathroom. Todd, with urgency now in voice, snaps at me to be quick!

After a much needed bladder drain, followed by some serious nose blowin'—using up half a roll of toilet paper, and stuffing remainder down into side cargo pocket for future use—Laura is at the door for escorting to the front. My injuries have now stiffened so that it is impossible to hide the limping (though not from lack of tryin').

Entering the waiting room, I am surprised to see only one short line left. Laura relieves the older American man to deal with the last monkeys wanting visas for the States. And Sparky? Well, he takes a careful seat, while fighting inner floods of depression and cradling ribcage. (Whew, buddy, I think we fractured some ribs. We've had 'em fractured before, haven't we buddy? Buddy remember the time, years ago, we lost a fight with that great big fucker? Wow, he literally kicked the piss out of us! Buddy, remember? Buddy? Buddy! Aw, crap. I don't wanta talk to you either. Guess Sparky will just talk to himself then. Hhmm, wonder why Nancy is bein' the way she is? Oh, and now my mother! I surely don't want her anywhere near this stinkin' hell hole of a country, but Goddamn, if she's gotta be the one to come, then come! Lordy-Lordy, forget the fact that everybody and his mangy dog down here wants to torture, kill, and *eat me*! Just fuckin' forget all that shit. What I don't understand, is who the hell, other than my intellectually spaced out mother, could, or even would, think of Christmas, when their only son is stuck down in Guatemala, having got himself into a wee bit of trouble, so much so, that the supposed American Ambassador must hide his ass in wretched hospitals? We are talkin' Guatemalan hospitals here—central fuckin' America! Come on Ma! Forget your stupid Christmas and bring your boy home! Jesus bloody Christ! What's wrong with her? Oh man, stop! Stop the whining. You sound like a punk sissy bitch! And you're making me want to puke. Buddy! You're back! Gosh, I was afraid there that maybe you were gone for good. Yes, well man, I just might be, if you don't stop this crybaby, feeling sorry for yourself bit. Think about it. This is your mess—yours—and save for me, you are alone. This is what you deserve, think about it: what kind of man would be sitting here bellyaching over his Mommy not wanting to ruin her special Christmas plans, risking not only her own life, but now, also the life of her favorite daughter; and for what? Just to get your worthless butt out of Guatemala? Man, it's not like you've done anything with your weird life making it worth saving. Oh, and your wife? Hey, she can replace you on a dime! Man, you know damn good and well, she's cock riding her troubles away. Back home man, word is out; you are gone—left the country. Think Nancy is receiving visitors much? He he he! Yes sir, you know she is. Can't blame her for dealing with them how she chooses. Oh shut up buddy, I know what you are doin'. Aughg, does everything down here gotta be a Goddamn mind-fuck? Geez, okay buddy, Sparky is hearin' you. I am in no position to be bitchin' about no one from home. All right then; man, suck it up, and get tough! Because, old friend, this ride is still going around—and around! God Buddy, I am tired.)

The older American man is noticed having himself a wicked stiff leg. I could be wrong, but damn, this guy sure has that CIA look about him (whatever that may be). He limps over with big untrusting smile, asking, "You must be the Devin I've heard so much about? Yes, I thought as much. Well Devin, you look like a man that's seen some hard travels."

"Uh, yes sir. You could say that. Hard travels indeed."

We both eye each other, searching. It sorta becomes a bizarre contest. An eye contest that neither is willing to break. It continues to point of bein' beyond a little strange, even by Guatemala standards, where bizarre, strange weirdness is the norm. To survive, one must not only accept it but also expect it, while stayin' on top of the game not wasting lifetime asking why.

The waiting room door opens, with American English bein' spoken. Game over. We both turn to see. Ught, looky, it's my very favorite backpackin' couple! Ol' Shirley ain't lookin' so good. Obviously, she has not been enjoying her stay in the exciting splendors of Guatemala! Golly, how can this be?

My suspected CIA staring partner limps over to 'em for inquiring their needs. They see me, though pretend not to; they are wanting Todd Boil. Nodding, limpy marble eyes leaves for fetchin' him. Soon, Todd emerges, having one hand holding his abdomen and workin' hard at hiding his own limp (not so easy, with such long legs). Todd and the backpacking couple begin a whispering discussion. Shirley does shriek out somethin' on the order of wanting to go home! Todd, with his happy-happy phony facade, is trying to give positive assurance, even patting them both on the shoulders. Sparky, not bein' able to resist, yells out, "Hey guys! How ya-all doin'?"

The greeting is not returned, but Shirley does flinch, and Todd drops his smile long enough for sending a look—silently ordering yours truly to shut up! After this, he escorts the couple to the door, and sees them out. Todd then turns, and motions me to follow. We are now in a hurry; even passing the now arguing backpacking couple on the stairs. Shirley is in tears—sobbing.

For whatever reason, the embassy is closing early today; thus, they are not allowing any more people in. No more monkey lines. Hhmm, wonder what became of the Bobsey twins? Todd is having his car pick us up out on the street. Knowin' it pointless, the reason is not even questioned; still wow, Sparky does stay close on Todd's heels! Out on the street sidewalk, we stand, waiting side by side, almost like he is wanting as many people as possible to see us together. Gone now are the parked cop cars, cannibals, and burgundy Mercedes. However, cruising cop cars do keep circling the large compound for slowin' down, gawking, and givin' mean, intimidating, threatening glares while passing in the busy traffic. Todd ignores them for bein' nothin', but not me—I am jumpy as all get-up! Todd keeps glancin' to his watch and mumbling for his car. Then, abruptly, he starts ranting and raving, goin' on and on about his wife, divorce, and how because of me, again he is going to be late for yet another session with his psychiatrist! (Christ, what a moody fucker! And what does he have to do anyways? Meet with his shrink every damn night? Jeepers, and he calls Sparky psychotic; no wonder his wife is divorcing his weird ass. Oh, and he's a Bible collector at that!)

To stop his whining, get his goat, and somewhat poke him for bein' a general prick, I ask in tone using sarcasm, again, how he got his limp and evident groin pain. Todd sternly looks me up and down, having eyes of ice. Without giving answer, his expression softens for commenting, "Devin, you look like a runner yourself, yes? No? Hey, come on; are you sure? Well, you certainly have everyone in Guatemala fooled, including myself. Devin, did you ever compete in track? No? Ha ha! Yes, I know you smoke and have short legs. Still you do have the muscle definition and frame. I think you must have been trained somewhere along the line… No, besides the military. By the way, there seems to be some confusion even from our own intel concerning your military history. Doesn't matter. No, I'm talking about formal athletic training." (Buddy, what's he up to with this shit?) "Devin, it's not like just anybody could have made that run from the hospital the way you did. Not that distance. Not being all uphill, and definitely not at the speed you did it in. No, you have had some serious training, I think… Excuse me? Devin, what difference does that make now? I can't tell you anyway. Besides, by the time I could have got a car to you, you were already at the embassy. Ha ha ha! Also, Devin, we both know there wasn't anybody chasing you, right? It's all in your head, remember? So you see, it really doesn't matter now, does it? The hospital simply discharged you early, probably forgetting all about our agreement. Hey, it happens; this is Guatemala. Ha ha! You simply saw some armed security guards dressed in civilian clothes. Guatemala is crawling with them; they are everywhere. And you lost it—thinking bad men were out to kill you. Don't you agree? Okay then. No more questions about my limp. By the way, I notice you're limping yourself. Are you all right?"

"Yes, I am, Todd, thanks for asking. Uh, look who's comin'."

The little Indian nurse from the hospital that had given "Devon" the green light to run is walkin' up the sidewalk toward us. Her approach is steady, yet timid. Not meeting my eyes, she stands before Todd with head bowed subserviently. Todd, exposing a side I've never seen, changes mannerisms for greeting this pitiful petite woman. His mien becomes that of ultra gentle, sincere respect. They speak, using soft rapid Spanish. Tears are flowing down the woman's brown cheeks, while she explains and apologizes. Listening, Todd's own facial expression becomes that of contemplating concern, as he warmly thanks her for personally walking all this way to speak with him. (Yeah, like she really had a choice.)

Turning, Todd explains, "Devin, in a nutshell, she is saying, last night they gave you cough syrup for inducing required sleep for your condition. However, the cough syrup is the kind that contains a small amount of alcohol. After reviewing your file which clearly states you as being an alcoholic, they, at the hospital, think possibly you might have had a negative reaction, resulting in hallucinating certain activities during your stay, that never really occurred. The hallucinations, of course, were brought on by the alcohol in the cough syrup. Wóuldn't you agree Devin?" Todd ignores my rolling eyes for silent answer. "Devin, also, the hospital is demanding we return to settle your bill—pay it."

"The fuck you say!" (Oh shit, shit, shit!) "Todd, no way! We aren't really goin' back there. Uh, are we?"

Rubbing his forehead, looking right miserable, Todd answers in low haunting tone, "Yes Devin, I'm afraid we are." The little humble nurse is sobbing with eyes staring down toward oversized hospital shoes. Todd, too, has head bowed, with veins of temples a-bulgin', revealing his brain is flyin' a hundred miles an hour! Both he and the nurse are afraid! Yes they are—and so is Sparky!

Clearing my throat, "Uh, Todd, please. You know I can't go back there, and uh, neither should you! It's a set-up! A God damn set-up! They will be there just waiting for us. It's fuckin' crazy! Todd, look at her—she's terrified! Why? Duh! She knows!" Addressing her, "Uh, Mademois—uhm, huh—Señora. Señora, no! El Hospital muy perverso. Mucho hombres querer matar—matar! Aseinto, homocida! Tortura Huh, uhm—" (God, I suck at Spanish) "—huh, torturing cannibals por me en Ambassador Todd Boil! Uh, ellos espera Asesinato! Si? Si! El Hospital mucho malo! No vamos."

Todd irritably hisses, "Devin, will you please shut up! As usual, you aren't making any sense and, pal, your Spanish is a joke. She doesn't understand a word you are saying." (The hell she don't.) "Devin, I don't know why she is crying. Maybe, like myself, she's just having a bad day. Who knows—it does not matter."

Todd's car and driver suddenly appear. Todd gently offers the little nurse a ride back to the hospital. She, wiping tears, sheepishly declines; Todd, however, is insistent, holding the rear passenger door open for her, then sliding in himself, barking command for me to join. "Devin, get in this car now! No! You cannot wait here at the embassy, and no, we can't take you to the other hospital first! Devin, I need you with me to settle this bill! *Get in the car!*"

(Fuck me.) I slide in next to him, and close the door. Todd lowers voice for sarcastic "Thank you," then he casually informs the driver of destination. Via rear-view mirror, the driver and I are able to (momentarily) lock eyes. His eyes betray a surprised reluctance— hesitancy. (Well now, ain't this nice. Even the driver is objecting.) Todd loses patience, sternly scolding. And so, away we go! Depressing ride it is, and to top it, Sparky now has this damn Beaner driver constantly glarin' up through the rear-view mirror, as if this is all my fault (which it is—sorta). Todd busies himself with an open briefcase now in his lap, while occasionally makin' a call or two. The little nurse has stopped crying, and I'm wanting to start.

Descending the dreaded narrow, snaking road, before rounding the bend for the hospital's guard house, our timid nurse politely asks to be let out. No one must see that she has accepted this ride. Todd, in full understanding, has his driver pull over and stop. Exiting the vehicle, the small woman is sweet and very grateful. The driver, however, is not, whining excuses for also not goin' on any further. Blurtin' both English and Spanish, he shares his concerns. The driver fears the gate guards will not let him drive through, and if by chance they do, they most certainly will not allow him to drive back out.

Todd, closing his eyes and rubbing his temples, uses tone of deliberate forced calm for instructing the driver, "Just get us within several yards of the guard house. Park the car and wait. We will walk through."

The driver still complains (justly) that if need be, he will not have room for turning the car around—not down there, by the gated guard house, he won't. (Todd, why are you taking us back into this obvious ambush of a whole lotta horror?) Todd, chewing on bottom lip, takes a moment to think. In doin', both driver and Sparky are hopin' like no tomorrow that he will see the light, change his mind, and order this car back up and off this Goddamn road! But nooo. Toddy instead instructs the driver to turn the car around here, and back it down, in reverse, for the guard house. Upon hearing, the driver looks to me, I look to him, we both look to Todd. We look at him like he's outta his mind! Ignoring us, with cell phone in hand, Todd motions for the driver to do as told. Closing his briefcase, he makes one more call, while overseein' the driver's backing skills. (Of course, all calls are in hushed rapid Spanish, so there's no way Sparky has a fuckin' clue what's bein' said.)

Oh shit, there they are! The two armed gate guards are waiting, with weapons at ready. Both are standing side by side before the wooden red and white striped, ballast balanced plank for barring way. Several yards short of reaching, the driver curbs the car, throwin 'er in park. Receiving sharp jab to throbbin' ribs from Todd sends Sparky outta that car for following. We both, tryin' hard to hide limps, march with shoulders squared, straight for the grinnin', coked-up greaseball guards. Again, Todd is holding forth, in full view, his mini cell phone: the thing is held as one would threatening with detonator device.

The jumpy bug-eyed Beaners, reekin' of wafting crack smoke, let us pass without much trouble, save only some spitting and verbal insults.

The parking lot is void of all vehicles, and inside the hospital there is no one to meet us. Hell, we see not a soul. And eerie quiet? Oh Skippy, you better believe. Leading the way, Todd is rigid serious, and in a hurry! Sparky stays on his heels, up some stairs, down the hall, and right into a clerical/accounting type room. It is small and cramped, with short office desks, chairs, computers, etc., oh, and also, smartly dressed, fair skinned Guatemalan women sitting—doin' nothin'. Upon entering the room, their eyes silently land on us as if expecting. Not a one stands for greeting us, or to inquire our wants and needs. They just sit there, eyeing us up and down, having the demeanor of those with much haughty arrogance. Todd immediately goes into his all business motor mouth bit. The room suddenly bursts into loud argumentative hostile (Spanish and English) accusations with fingers bein' pointed at me! (Yepper, imagine that.) "Devon," the rich American, running out on his bill. here in a country so poor as Guatemala! (Or so they are barkin'.) Todd hotly retaliates his grievance of the hospital staff administering cough syrup having alcohol content to an alcoholic patient. He then faults the hospital for wrongful neglect (or somethin' on that order). Hearing this, the women all have themselves a good mocking laugh, belittling "Devon" for comparison to a "niños!" Abruptly, the teasing laughter stops, and again, payment of bill—cuenta—is demanded. Todd, acting just as arrogant, explains regret, that for reasons he cannot disclose, we are not able to pay the bill at this time; but, he gives the word of the American Embassy that the bill will be paid within a week or so. (Instant bitter laughter!)

Nope, no way! Not good enough: the bill/*cuenta* gets paid now, in full, or they are going to call the *policia*. (Oh shit, shit, shit! Todd, why, oh why did we come here? You fuckin' dumb ass! Just look at 'em. They're all grinnin' like a pack of dung eatin' hyenas! Oooh, they know full well the weight of this threat.)

Todd has become sincerely pissed off and is showin' it! He is vein-bulgin', beet red, and loudly charges them with insulting the integrity of the United States of America! How dare they! (Well, they do dare, and they do it laughin'.) Todd is furious; however, this does no good. The hospital is demanding payment now, or the *policia* will come. (Fuck me! Todd, what are you doin'? Just hand them your Goddamn credit card and let's get the hell outta here! You know Nancy will reimburse.) I tell him this, but does he do it? Fuck nooo! Instead he hisses, "Devin, shut up, and stay out of this!" Again more boisterous laughter from the baboon bitches. Whoa, these women are not only uppity as all get-up, they are hard to the core and mean to the bone! It is more than evident that they hate me, hate Todd, hate Americans! Yet, you can bet the farm, they'd do most anything to have their stuck-up wannabe asses over for living in anywhere United States. (Fuckin' hateful jealous cunts!)

Finally, Todd, rubbing his forehead—havin' had enough— thumbs his cell phone, calling Nancy for her credit card numbers and approval. (Christ almighty, why didn't he do this in the first place?) Over an hour later, we are outta there! Double timin' it across the big vacant parking lot, with Todd whinin' like a limpin', long-legged pussy about his throbbing headache. The fucked-up gate guards again attempt toying with us, but, quickly realizing Todd's mood, they step aside and are content with merely targeting our feet for spitting. The driver is still parked, with engine hummin'. Upon seeing us, his eyes betray huge relief. And away we go, for the nice, old-fashioned, Catholic hospital.

Damn, this is a big nice place. Todd had been right in it certainly bein' Catholic; inside the busy place, everywhere you look, there are statues and paintings of saints, priests, Jesus, Mary and that gang, to say nothin' of all the weird hangin' crosses and crucifixes. The nurses are indeed nuns, wearing funny winged hooded hats and long flowing gowns exposing only face and hands. Nursing nuns they are, though, warm and friendly they are not. The nuns keep glancin' at me as if they already know of "Devon," and in no way or form do they approve.

So it comes as no surprise, when after an hour's wait of havin' to listen to more of Todd's nonsense concerning his wife, divorce, shrink, and—oh yeah, check this out—he informs that along with his Bible collection, he also collects Disney videos. Yes sirree-bob! Ol' Todd's got himself a whole library of Disney flicks. Many are the same, yet in different languages. See, according to Todd, some are better when watched in certain languages, depending on video and language. He gives the example of one about a mouse—no, not Mickey. Uh, some other Disney mouse. Anyway, this particular Disney video isn't all that great in English; however, in German? Oh boy—watch out! (What a nut!) Yepper, Disney is about the only kind of movie he will watch. Again, according to Todd, "If it isn't Disney, it isn't worth watching!" Gee, why is his wife divorcing him? Oh yeah, right. She's leavin' (left) for his best friend! (Sucker.) Anyway, after an hour of listening to his ramblings, we are politely informed (lied to) that the hospital cannot at this time admit me as a patient; reason being, they presently have no rooms or beds available. Todd ain't buyin' it; and asks to speak to a Mr. So-and-so. "No, so sorry, he is not here today." Todd asks for another name. Again, the lying nun answers, "Not here." Todd turns red with silent anger. (Ha ha! Welcome to Guatemala, right?)

With me on his heels, we stomp outta there! Exiting the building, we see two plain clothes cops leaning against their car. Todd whispers not to worry. Yes, they are detectives. He personally knows them. "Most likely they are only following us."

(Only following us! Following us for what? To learn where I'm stayin' tonight, so that they may have their fun? FUCK!) Back in the car, Todd is in a piss-poor mood, barking out the name and location of our new destination. After calming himself with uninterrupted deep breathing exercises, he begins telling (somewhat) a little about this other hospital we are now goin' to. Actually, it's really not a hospital at all, but more like a "Well Devin, let's just say, it's a very professional facility for people much like yourself. What do I mean by this? Well pal, like I said, it's a facility created for individuals much like yourself, that have lost their, hmm, way? Whether it is resulting from drugs, alcohol, or other various mental struggles. You know, they have simply lost their, hmm, way." (Lost their way? What the hell is he talkin' about now?) "Devin, you have lost your way, haven't you? Devin? You have lost your way. Right? Suffering from mental fatigue." (Oh boy, it's mental fatigue now?) "Drug and alcohol abuse while still grieving the deaths of your father and grandfather. Yourself being so far away from the home and family. Devin, it has brought about some pretty bizarre hallucinations that have made you do things, uhm, like burning down poor Mr. Benny's bed and breakfast, just to name one incident, right? Devin, we won't speak of the others, right? All being incidents, uhm, or rather, should I say, actions, that you would not normally ever even think of doing. Right? Well, Devin, this place that I am now taking you to is a safe place that specializes in caring for and healing people suffering from similar problems such as yourself. Understand?" (Oh God.)

"Todd, no! You're takin' me to a fuckin' nuthouse! And a Goddamn Guatemalan nuthouse at that! Why—WHY?"

"Well, Devin, you can call it what you like. I admit, you will see that some, if not most of the patients have become full-time occupants, or uhm, residents. "Yes, most are long-term, and to be honest, they are incurable; living at the center full-time, having been admitted by family, the law, or by their own accord. Hey, Devin, I've really nowhere else to take you. Word is out on you pal! All of the hospitals—if not most, anyway—now consider you to be a high risk, one that they are not willing to take. I don't know about you pal, but this became more than apparent back at the Catholic hospital. Seriously pal, I think it's going to be pretty much that way wherever we go. Let's just hope they admit you here. Don't worry, I'm sure they will. I personally know the doctor; he's a real nice guy! Okay, yes. Yes, I know, I make this claim with every place. Really though, to an extent, it's true. However, in this case, things are a little different. What? Devin, it just is. Anyway, the doctor, besides being a real nice guy, has lived in the United States, and is a Harvard graduate. After earning his degrees, he decided to move back here to Guatemala City and open his own practice. What? Devin, I don't know why. Probably because Guatemala City is his home, and he feels he is more needed here by his own people. I don't know pal, it's not important. What is, I think, is that unlike the other places—gosh, now thinking about it, we should of just came here in the first place—here, they will be much more sympathetic to our unique situation. Not that there was anything wrong with the first hospital; it's just that I don't think, there, they fully understood." (The fuck they didn't.) "What? Yes Devin, I have brought other Americans here. What did they think of the place? Did they like it? Devin, what do you think? The place is what it is. I mean, who cares if they liked it or not. All that really counts is that they were safe, received professional care, and they got well enough to go home. Right? Hey pal, you had a room at one of the nicest hospitals in the city, but hey, you didn't like it there. Okay, okay, felt afraid there. Well, I very much doubt you will feel afraid here. What? What do you mean, I was also afraid? That's ridiculous! Devin, we surely aren't going through this again, are we? Good! Hey, your wife tells me that you and your youngest sister both have very high IQs. How high are they? You don't know?

Well, I don't know about your sister's, but do know yours. Ha ha! It's in your file. Hhmm, it's not bad. Now guess what mine is." (Damn, IQs? What the fuck do those things got to do with anything? Especially now, since he's takin' Sparky to a stinkin' Guatemalan nuthouse, that may or may not even allow admittance! Wow, I think my brain has dehydrated itself down to the size of a peanut. It's a-rattlin' around up there in hollow skull. Just what Sparky needs—more mind games. Todd, of course, brags his IQ level, and yes, it's off the chart. Eh, he's still a retard!) "My point Devin, is that I think you are smart enough to be by now seeing the picture, the whole picture. We must get you back home, preferably alive, and in one piece. Ha ha ha! Right? Right! So, in order to accomplish this, we all need your help. Now, this place I'm taking you to might not be the Ritz, and the occupants—uh, patients—will undoubtedly be far from normal. I mean, they are all here for a reason, right? Okay, so during your stay, you must be a sport, play the game. Don't let any witnessed behavior freak you out, and don't get spooked or afraid! Seriously, we cannot afford it, pal. Do you understand? Cooperate with the doctor and staff, and pal, you must stay put! Do not, under any circumstances, leave this *sanatorio*." (*Sanatorio*?) "Not until your wife and I can get your mother and sister down here. Devin, do you understand?"

"Yes, I do Todd. You are puttin' my ass into a Guatemalan nuthouse, because no reputable hospital will have anything to do with me. Why? Well uh, obviously they wisely aren't wantin' police, goons, *gauchos*, Matrix, Hannibal the cannibal, and clan landing on their doorstep— movin' in. It's bad for business, terrifying as all get-up, and really makes a bloody mess of things! I am to stay put, eat the time, and not let the crazies drive me crazy; all the while hoping like hell that the satanic powers that be chill long enough for Mommy and baby sis to come down here, wrap things up, and then fly the fuck outta here! This is, of course, if—*if* they are even allowed to legally do so. Oh, and that's also *if* they don't, in the process, get themselves raped, tortured, and killed first. Right?" Todd doesn't bother responding; pretending distraction by havin' to give the driver directions, followed by glancing at wristwatch, followed by more (very annoying) whining, resulting from a seemingly ceaseless headache, while adding comment about again needin' to see about upping the time for that there shrink appointment of his.

Arriving at the destination, dark clouds roll in for a drenching wet downpour greeting. This neighborhood, like most we have been driving through, has streets which are constricted, having slightly curbed narrow sidewalks laid for giving little space between actual street and continuous, greatly varied, assortment of gated tall stone walls; all are adjoining and fronting adjacent street side properties. Some are over-grown, having thick entangling vines and leafy foliage lookin' to be almost gothic or medieval old, while others are newer, built of concrete blocks. All have gates of iron, whether it be for walkway or driveway; of course, the gates are sharply topped with menacing spear-like spikes. The stout walls themselves are similarly spiked, or topped with an embedded layer of jagged broken glass, the purpose bein' obvious. There is no evidence of street names or numbers; yet Todd knows where to go.

Jumpin' from the street parked car, Todd and I dash through the pissin' rain to a solid iron gate door (solid, exceptin' for the hinged from inside view slot—now closed). On the right of this door, in the stone wall, is a push button intercom. After repeatedly pushin' the button and getting no response—nothin', it becomes obvious that the thing is broke (always a good sign for a nuthouse).

The wetness has Sparky teeth clankin' cold! Soaked, we both dodge our way back across the street for Todd's car. In the car, Todd immedi-ately begins makin' phone calls. He discovers that the *sanatorio* (sanitarium, nuthouse) has moved. Informing the driver of general whereabouts for new location, we are off.

Todd, rubbin' his forehead, explains that the *sanatorio* has needed a larger facility for quite some time. And though everyone is moved in, with this new place in operation, they are still very much in the process of getting adjusted and settled. Doctor So-and-So has advised Todd to relay that yes, the *sanatorio* will admit me, but only on condition that it is understood they are going through a major adjustment period; not just for the staff and faculty, but more importantly, the patients. The *sanatorio* normally operates with regimental routine. This routine is required for maintaining the delicate stability of fragile minds. While many patients are handling the move surprisingly well, others are understandably not. Thus, I will more than likely witness some of the more unsound patients behaving at their worst. (Oh, lucky lucky me.)

It has stopped raining and the day's last rays of sunshine stream through. The driver eventually finds the *sanatorio's* new location (an unmarked cop car is following). The only entrance to the compound is via a drive-through rod iron gate, surrounded (somewhat) by walls of stone, bein' a good eight feet tall and crowned with embedded jagged glass from broken bottles and such. Our arrival is expected, and so the large iron gate is open for Todd's car to enter onto the narrow, enclosed parking lot, bein' not much wider than your average driveway, adjacent to the building itself.

Jesus fucking Christ! Guess what the ol' *sanatorio*/sanitarium/ whatever new larger facility is? Come on, guess? Fuck me. It's a Goddamn old *hotel*! A fuckin' *hotel*! Why, oh why did it have to be a hotel? Of all things a hotel? Admittedly, at one time—long ago—the place was probably quite charming. Now? Now it's just another rundown shit hole!

The doctor himself is not presently here; though his wife, sons, and daughters are. They're all working seemingly feverishly together from one of the smaller front abutting rooms, sorting through many scattered boxes containing files, paperwork, and the likes. The entire compound is in a state of complete disarray. It is clearly evident that this once hotel has been derelict for a very, very long time. The wife is nice, greeting us warmly, and dialing' up her husband via telephone. He is back at the old location overseeing the move still in progress. Todd speaks to him first, deliberately using speedy Spanish, so I can't follow. Several minutes later, the phone is unexpectedly put to Sparky's ear; whereupon the doctor, using gentle, clean English, introduces himself and informs yes, he does know a little something about my unique situation, and is willing to help. The doctor apologizes for the timing in unfortunately having to endure this most inconvenient transitional period of facility relocation. However, the main concern is will I "feel safe" here at his *sanatorio*. Staring at a nearby small black blunt nosed snake, tryin' desperately to free itself from the jar it has been placed in, havin' just been caught by the doctor's youngest son. I lie, answering, "Yes sir, yes, here, I will feel safe and not afraid." Thus, with that tidbit of matter resolved, a male nurse appears for escorting. Todd, seizing the phone, waves his goodbyes, with promise of returning tomorrow for checking up, and keeping in touch. (Yeah, sure you will Toddy.)

Entering, directly across the main floor from once public access door, is what was the reception/front desk and cubicle post station; now it's a… um, I don't know. On our left is the lobby area, having a TV turned on in far corner. The lobby's furnishings are that bein' old second-hand couches, chairs, and the common sorts. From these, many strange lookin', bug-eyed people (patients—male and female) are cautiously rising for gawkin' at Sparky as if I were indeed the crazy-*loco*, tattooed, *blondo* long-haired American. Diagonally right, bein' only several feet away from the public access door, is a wide grand staircase leading up to circular second floor.

Following my male nurse, we cross to the reception desk, where, in broken English, he politely introduces "Devon" to another male nurse standin' behind the front desk counter. Here is where I am to come when in need of anything. Anything? Well, no, not anything. (Hhmm, cigarettes?) Using my retarded Spanish, I respectfully express the need, askin' for cigarettes. Nodding their heads, chuckling, the one from behind the front desk, asks, "What brand? No, no, no Camels. The only American cigarettes we have at this time are Marlboros." And quite proud he seems in having these. Well, Marlboro is Skippy by me. A hard pack is slid over the counter, with it bein' explained, while more and more bug-eyed zombies move in, gatherin' around, that the cost of the cigarettes will be added to my account. Smoking is only allowed outside, or in the back screened open air room at rear of lobby. I am not allowed matches or lighter. When needing a light, it must be acquired here, at the front desk.

My nurse, after shooing away curious patients surrounding, motions me to follow; up the grand staircase we go. The stairs, surprisingly, prove themselves incredibly difficult. Difficult due to sustained injuries from long run and bouncy ball fall (and Sparky ain't bein' no pussy here. The pain is shooting sharp!). However, the worst is my legs are almost jell-O-like; goin' up these stairs, they won't work right. With each step up, they are wanting to seriously buckle. Oh bubba, cannot expose this weakness, and with them all watchin', it will be exposed! Must lean forward, pushin' with hands on knees for gettin' self up these stairs.

My room, at the top, is first one on the right. It is a good-sized room, havin' six small institutional style beds. One has a frail old man laying with jacket over his head. Four other beds, though now empty, do have individual belongings and nightstands about. The bathroom and shower are through a door to the back. Walking over for seeing, I check out the large colonial style windows that open outwards on to a mini ledge/balcony. Of course, they have no locks or latches, and two won't even shut all the way. The bathroom—despite pooled water, exposed, rusty, leaking pipe, chipped, cracked, broken, missing tiles, and no toilet seat—is actually somewhat clean. In passing, I notice another doorway leading from the room into an overly large closet area, presently suffer-ing from a water damaged fall-out ceiling dropping itself with moldy debris, etc.

My nurse leaves. Quickly returning, he hands me a thin rag for a towel, half roll of toilet paper, used black plastic pocket comb, missin' several teeth, toothbrush appearin' new, a micro tube of toothpaste half used, plastic cup containing not near enough shampoo, and one unused disposable razor. Oh, also, an empty baby food jar. Yepper, a stool sample is needed. Fortunately Sparky can use finger, in privacy of bathroom, for excreting (way better than havin' weird Gimpy and his tongue depressor). After this, a shower is in order. There is no hot water. A speedy (cold, very cold) shower is managed, whereupon the nurse informs that I must now wear the old frayed button shirt and stupid swim shorts. He's gonna have my other clothes washed. Asked when? He answers, "Soon, soon!"

God, how I do hate gettin' back into these ridiculous swim shorts. Why the hell did Sparky even hang on to 'em? Fuck only knows—they just sorta tagged along. Strange. Hhmm, yeah, but these days, what ain't strange?

Gathering up my clothes—French camo BDU pants, long sleeved cotton t-shirt, etc.—the nurse explains the strictly enforced rule of mandatory morning shower, brush teeth, and shave. For those not able, or allowed, a nurse will dutifully assist. There are both male and female nurses. Men are never allowed in the female rooms and vice versa.

Hearing quite the commotion comin' from the bedroom, Sparky quickly double knot ties sooty, red Converse high-top tennis shoes. (Damn, at least they are letting me keep these puppies.) The nurse— holding my clothes—and I—holdin' baby food jar-o-shit, and used toiletries—exit the bathroom. We view the occupants of the four other beds; they are now present and very busy expeditiously packin' up their stuff for movin' out from this room, to another. Seeing "Devon," they accelerate, kickin' into gear, and rambling blurted excited Spanish, revealing fear! No way are they sleepin' in the same room with yours truly. And gone they are! Christ, can't say as I blame 'em, but a good sign, this is not! Handing over fecal jar, I am shown to my bed; it's right beside the door. (Gee, wonder why?)

Soon, the sleeping frail old man and myself are the only two left in the room. Closing the door all the way, it's a quick room search. From the mess of the closet area, Sparky finds an abandoned hefty four-foot-long steel clothes hanging rod. Doin' a couple of practice moves for feel and balance, I notice the old frail man, peekin' out from under his head-covered jacket. His eyes are sparkling in a smile, silently conveying he ain't gonna tell. Deciding the risk is worth taking, the steel rod gets tucked under my mattress. With the rod under the mattress and my tired body now (sitting upright) on top, the mind races with thoughts of what surely this night will bring. In doin', ears perk for hearing the ruckus below. Of course, "Devon" is the main topic, havin' many patients shrieking panicky screams, protesting my bein' here. Ught, the gate buzzer! Instant silence. A visitor? Yes, a very important visitor. (Hhmm, wonder who it is? Probably the cops, but what to do? Buddy, whatcha think? Buddy? Buddy! Aw crap, buddy, where are you?)

The room's door suddenly swings open! Reflexes bolt me up off the bed for defensive standing! My male nurse is so startled by the reaction that he himself jumps, nearly tripping, with only the door catching his fall! Recovering composure—though still lookin' very nervous and embarrassed—he informs that everybody is now being seated in *el comedor por la cena* (dinner). They would all greatly appreciate if "Devon" would join. (Oh fuck, hungry I am not; and really, really in no mood for forcin' myself to eat, especially amongst a room full of gawkin' Guatemalan nutcases. And, uh, oh goody, there's still that important big shot visitor—whoever—down there. It's not the doctor, because he hasn't the boomin', overly self assured voice that visiting man downstairs has.)

Lookin' into somewhat understanding eyes of my male nurse, they are silently communicating. Come on Devon, just get it over with; besides, you have no choice. (Aughg!) Nodding acknowledgment, I reluctantly (involuntarily wincing with every cautious step) follow him down the stairs. Inside the dining room, there is one rectangular table surrounded with many assorted chairs of people seated, waiting my emergence, which brings about complete hushed silence, accompanying expected intense center stage freak show spotlighting yours truly. Wow, the for-real shit is indeed deep, when the abortion-should-have-beens are bug-eyed, gawkin' at you as bein' the star blood clot. And accordingly, as if it were necessary, the nurse addresses the room by announcing my name. (Geez, from what was overheard upstairs, they all know my name; even here, these people have heard of "Devon" and his story. Of course, like everywhere, story versions vary greatly with exaggeration leaving little correct). The patients are all adults, ranging from young to middle aged, excepting for my old frail roommate, who is now bein' escorted to the table by another male nurse. Oddly, the old man is still wearin' his jacket draped over his head.

Seated at the head of the table—to the far end—I see him, the important big shot. He is also intently engrossed in lookin' me up and down, although he seems to be doin' so for deciding my fate! He must be in his early sixties: not an ugly man, but does carry the mien of bein' very capable (and experienced) in becoming extremely ugly, cruel, and mean. About him is much power and arrogant confidence. Sunglasses hang from the pocket of his olive green Fidel Castro jumpsuit, cinched at thick waist via standard web military pistol belt. Not knowin' what else to do, Sparky stands straight, tall, proud, and yet humble. I am softly instructed to sit. Complying, a grim-lookin' old woman immediately brings forth my plate of food containing over cooked chicken leg and thigh, lightly coated with thin BBQ sauce; beside this is some soggy, cold broccoli. And the drink is a plastic *vaso* of nauseatingly sweet Kool-Aid type stuff.

Slowly a bite is tasted, then a drink; however, nobody is joining. No, they are all too preoccupied watchin'. (Oh Jesus, buddy, we sure got us one of those pleasant dining experiences goin' now. Buddy, I don't know what to do. The food is wantin' to come back up, and this drink ain't helpin'.) Starin' down at my plate, feelin' all eyes upon me, it just happens; I don't know why, still, it does. Fuckin' tears surface to flow down constricting face; chest is heavin' with that damn black tar snot spewing. What a despicable display of weakness we are now exposing. (God, buddy, we are really fallin' apart here. Buddy? Buddy! Aw, you asshole fuckin' prick son-a-bitch! Whoa, I gotta snap out of this shit!)

Wiping away tears, using paper napkin for somewhat cleaning smeared black tar snot, lookin' around, Sparky is surprised in seein' that most eyes now have softened, with some even givin' encouraging nods of perhaps—understanding? A young guy, sittin' on direct right, hesitantly and quickly gives my shoulder two fast light speed pats. It was a forced effort, similar to how one pats a dog they aren't sure won't rip their hand off. Almost comical it is, and very appreciated. I give him a thankful smile, which he sincerely returns. Clearin' my throat, and tryin' my best Spanish, I apologize to those at the table. Unexpectedly, several, using English, offer short comments of there being no need. The young fellow on my right softly suggests, "Devon, you should eat. It will help for making you feel better." Glancin' down at the food, then back to him, while deliberately making funny face communicating that the food don't look so good, I offer it to him. He and others at the table immediately burst into laughter, with the young man explaining, "No, no, Devon, you must eat. It is not allowed, giving food to others. You must eat it all yourself. *Sanatorio* rule, understand?"

"Yes, yes I do. Thank you my friend."

A large beamin' smile, makes it evident the young man is delighted at now bein' considered my friend. (Yeah well, just wait until later tonight, or, whenever the cannibals, Matrix, and goons show up. And, uh, wonder what the deal is gonna be with this Mr. Big Shot, silently sitting at the end of the table, closely watchin', havin' no expression.)

Using Spanish, Sparky asks *"por, la Sal? Pimienta? Picante Salsa?"* No, no, no! Most everyone is now giggling.

My new friend explains, "Devon, what you asked for is not allowed here. You must eat the food as is."

Okey-dokey! Actin' the role of bein' the good nuthouse patient, I slowly begin forcin' the swallows down. Euw, it's not the food so much.

Fuck knows we've certainly ate stuff worse than this. There have been many times in my life when this meal would have been considered a feast! The problem now though, is the stomach simply ain't in the mood.

Meanwhile, Mr. Big Shot has turned his attentions toward his own plate, and in like two bites, has inhaled everything. Finished, he rises from the table, loudly boomin', "Compliments to the chef!" He thanks everyone for having him; however, regretfully he is a very busy man, and therefore must take leave. The table is now in a ruckus of loud, exaggerated delighted dramatics. The patients (most anyways) are expressing much disappointment at the departure of their most honored visitor, who had so surprisingly arrived, showing his personal presence before them, for first time ever, even sharing a sit-down meal! Oh what an honor, for he is the Commander! (Commander who? Though the name is very short, Sparky don't know. Most simply refer to him as "the Commander" only.) The Commander is now impatient, having seen what he had come to see. (Gee, golly, whatcha think that might be?) He ignores the few monkeys from the table gettin' a bit too carried away with the excitement from farewell moment. One ditzy bimbo is even offering herself sexually. She quickly receives scornful reprimand from a female nurse/aid. The Commander, giving the jumpin' table an irritable wave, stops before me, locking eyes as if searching or deciding. Breaking piercing gaze, the Commander spins, informing the nearest male nurse of his desire for speaking to the doctor now. The nurse, nodding, quickly leads the way, exiting the dining room.

Alone, back up in the dark empty bedroom, it's a quick check around the room, and then the bed itself. No creepy-crawlies, and steel rod is still in place under mattress. Sitting on the bed, slowly removing sooty red Converse high-tops, I place them carefully side by side, pulled open with laces positioned just so, for fast tyin'. Holding sore ribs, ignoring pained hips, bruised buttocks, and pullin' up now bum leg, reluctantly, I lean the ol' tired body to lay out on top of the bed. (Feelin' vulnerable much?) Hands are resting on chest, free from each other for that possible needed speed!

Listening, others are also goin', and/or bein' put to bed, with some screamin' out spine chilling shrieks of protests! Also, floating from the bottom of the stairs, I can hear now the doctor and Commander speaking near the front door. The Commander is confirming an evident previous agreement between him and the doctor, granting permission for "Devon" to stay here at the *sanatorio*. In doing, the Commander expresses concern, "This Devon is very fast, too fast! He must be slowed with medication. I do not want him capable of running about. Not that he will have need for running. Ha ha-ha!" The doctor agrees to do as asked; and so the Commander takes leave. Approximately fifteen minutes later, the front gate buzzer buzzes; the front door opens for greeting—guess who? Come on, guess. Guess mother fucker—guess! Shit, it's Matrix! The sound of his voice has Sparky upright, swinging in one fluid motion, with fingers a-flyin', lacin' sooty red Converse high-tops! And for the door I am listening with ears strainin'. The doctor and several male nurses are at the door, refusing Matrix admittance, giving warning that Commander So-and-so was just here, having personally seen "Devon" and declared him off limits. No one is to molest him, or take him. "Devon" must stay here until further decided by the Commander himself. Matrix is, of course, jump boot stompin' mad! But his fuming horrific threats are to no avail. (Aaa ha! They ain't gonna let him in! Nope, they sure aren't. Whoa! Let's just hope the psychotic maniac goes away without killin' and torturin'.)

Matrix snarls, hissing that he is goin' to meet with the Commander himself. In two days' time, with or without the Commander's permission, Matrix will be back, "for pulling that faggot Devon out of here. He will be taken to the hills, dealt with by my hand, cut into little pieces and buried throughout. This Devon will be no more! Two days' time. Devon will be mine!"

Out in the side driveway, Matrix snaps orders to two gang youths, placing them here and there. From my bedroom windows, I can see where they are. One is up on crowned broken glass embedded stone wall. He is usin' somethin' resembling a piece of carpet for protection against the glass. His position allows him easy access for watching the *sanatorio*'s back and side. The other punk is down toward the front gate, hunkered in shadows of overgrown foliage. Both are sternly instructed to stay in position, watch, and report. If anyone comes for "Devon," Matrix is to be immediately notified. The gangers remind him, asking "de Orc" for crack to smoke while on look-out watch. Matrix barks, and soon each has a baggy of crack, and aluminum foil for rolling into pipes, which, upon receiving, they begin doin'. Matrix, growling like a vicious lunatic, jumps into his glossy black Chevy blazer and is gone.

Hearing footsteps on the stairs, the room's door opens just as I've completed removing sooty red Converse high-tops. Two male nurses enter, escorting the frail old man. One turns and gives Sparky two pills with cup of water. After swallowing down the pills (guessed bein' sleepers), I'm told that wearing a shirt for sleeping is not allowed; mine must be removed. (Christ.) The night air is now cool, and I'm cold, wanting a blanket. But nooo, the *sanatorio* don't have blankets; only sheets. (Oh boy Skippy, can't hardly wait for that freezin' cold mandatory mornin' shower.) Meanwhile, the old man is puttin' up quite the fuss. He won't get into his bed. Nope, not until it has been stripped down for him to see that there is nothin' in there that shouldn't be. Both nurses, behaving as if this were routine for him, comply. Upon approval, before sliding into bed, the old man glances over, our eyes meet, and with ever-present jacket hangin' from head, his wrinkled face smiles a grin, conveying that his example might want to be followed.

Shortly thereafter, out in the hall, the doctor is heard softly whispering to my nurse, that if "Devon" at any time requests cocaine, he is to receive it. The doctor doesn't care how much, or my preference for intake, whether it be snorting, smoking, or injecting. He just wants the cocaine, discreet from others, available for "Devon" if the need is expressed.

Moments later, my nurse re-enters the room, quietly relaying the doctor's orders, and excitedly asking if there is a personal need or want for *coca* or crack? (Oh Bubba, you got that straight! Damn, snortin' some big fat lines of top grade A cocaine would indeed hit the spot, and be delicious beyond... Uh, wait a minute. What are they up to?) Wincing with anguished reluctance, the answer is a polite "No thank you."

The night is spent not sleeping; instead, it is endured, listening to whispered gossiping *sanatorio* staff, and night-long shrieking howls from the more neurotic patients. My elderly sleeping roommate, when not gasping sporadic gulps for air, snores, talks, and walks in his sleep. He likes to get up, stumble about the room, and prefers pissing on the floor in trashed-out ruins of the decrepit closet area. I do a lot of pissin' myself; however, mine is done in the dark bathroom. The walk across the room enables me to see and watch Matrix's two posted look-outs. They are doin' nothin' 'cept sitting, smokin' cigarettes and crack. Goddamn the doctor and the nurse for makin' offer of available coke. Uh, like already battling persistent depression, confusion, and all other jumbled bizarre crap (say nothin' about ingrained steadfast red alert mode), now Sparky gets to play the cocaine temptation game! Do I go to my nurse and ask for coke? Hhmm, really good coke at that and as much as I want? Or do I not? (Whew, buddy ain't no help. He's gone; and who knows when he will be back—if ever!)

Occasionally, my nurse will quietly open the door for a peek in. Each and every time, it makes me jump, which in turn, makes him jump!

Darkness of the night slowly gives way to glow of first morning light. Matrix's look-outs are gone; they don't come back. And despite Matrix's promising threats, neither does he. No glossy black Chevy blazer, no Matrix, no cops, no goons, *gauchos* or cannibals, and no trip to the hills!

Being a good *sanatorio* patient, it's a super fast shit, shower, and shave! The shower is like ice water, and I'm freezin' cold, with sinuses still draining the never-ending flow of stinging black tar. (God, how Sparky is tired of bein' cold in Guatemala. Aughg!) Shiverin' to beat holy hell, it's a hurried limp down those stairs. The male nightshift nurses are sprawled out on couches and chairs, asleep. They, awakin' quickly, jumping to their feet! My nurse, seeing me dripping and shiverin', rubbin' sleep from his eyes, kindly offers to fetch coffee. (Damn straight Skippy! Plus, I need a light.) He unlocks the door leading into the kitchen, and disappears. Meanwhile, another nurse lights my cigarette, gettin' a real kick from watchin' the filter-snap thing. Inhaling deeply— hoo, spank my ass silly, that is *good*! Smiling, the nurse motions for "Devon" to take the smoking out to the open air room. Seeing the direction of rising sun, I opt for walkin' on through the screened open air room to outside yard, and taking a seat in a cheap plastic chair, facing the somewhat warm escalating sunshine.

The *sanatorio* is—well it is what it is—a Guatemalan sanitarium. The days are long and boring. Yes, despite witnessing seemingly endless daily displays of sudden on-going shriek fits, flaring temper tantrums, arguments, brief physical fighting, and mood swing bursts, it's boring as all get-up and weird. The kind of boring weirdness that only such a place as this can be. The patients (most anyways) yell and cry a lot. They are all here for chronic drug and/or alcohol abuse, manic depression, and post-traumatic stress, caused from whatever. One guy is in here after bein' tied to a bed, gang raped, and covered with scorpions. (All while being filmed via video. Imagine that!) His entire backside is peppered with dark swollen pustules of seeping sores from the ugly stingin' bugs. Another guy is here after bein' a soldier and having to participate in the clearing of a peasant village—death squad style. Others are here because they are simply insane. All are hurting and sad. For most, the fear of "Devon" quickly wears off, and so I'm treated as something on the order of a peculiar celebrity. And it is soon learnt that Todd Boil had lied. (Again, imagine that!) He never brought anyone here before. Also, this place has never had an American for a, ahem, guest. Yepper, "Devon" is the lucky first!

A full week goes by before actually seeing the doctor. Mostly, he just wants to hear my version of my story. The stiff interview/chat takes up a whole thirty minutes, if that. Also, a week passes before seeing Todd Boil again. It too is brief, bein' just a show of face, and to give update on his divorce (okey-dokey), and share frustration concerning my mother's lack for urgency in getting down here. Seeming truly perplexed, Todd also adds he is in communication with my wife daily, and from her he is sensing an odd matter that he does not understand, regarding the amount of money bein' required for my safe return home. According to him, he is not receiving positive feedback from either my wife or mother. "Devin, I tell them, hey, let's get him out while the gettin' is good! Who cares what the costs are? After all, we are talking Devin's life here! How much is Devin's life worth to you people? Can you even put a dollar price value for his life? Well, there are those here in Guatemala that certainly have, and there is no more negotiating."

Todd's eyes go to mine, as if asking for an explanation—or two? Seeing I have none, he leaves, promising to be back tomorrow. (He isn't).

The days are mostly spent amusing those few patients that desire and make great effort in befriending. They sneak "Devon" lights, and offer cigarettes. I smoke a pack a day plus, which here, at the *sanatorio*, is considered a lot. The staff (doctor's orders) won't allow for the purchase of more than one pack per day. Mostly due to boredom, this is often not enough; so some of my new friends give me their smokes, and in return, I slip them my breakfast and lunches. These guys love practicing their English; and in turn, I try bettering my adolescent Spanish. Also, they are constantly wanting "Devon" to join them in playing board games. (Sparky hates board games, always has, but what the fuck—it's good PR.)

Group session is held every single day—two times a day. And for all that are able, mandatory it is. The damn boring things are a minimum two hours long, with every single one running overtime. Most of these people (patients) truly have a lot to say; and it's during these group sessions that they are able to be heard. For myself, this is just time spent observing and thinking. I've pretty much thought out all courses for plans of action, if and when the place gets attacked for my removal. Believe you me, I have many; also, besides the undiscovered steel rod kept under my mattress, there are many similar such unsuspected items for hand weapons stashed all about the grounds. I've various battle plans and weapons within quick reach for every section of the compound, including very much the outside yards. Escape isn't even really a consideration. No, best just fight it out here, dying, than on the streets, havin' nowhere to run.

So, Sparky spends much of his true mental energy thinking, scheming strategies, and rehatching everything, tryin' to make sense (where there is little) from all that has happened. And after Todd's visit, seeing his bewildered frustration concerning my wife and mother, I'm now spending far too much energy tryin' to figure them out as well. Wonder why they aren't rushin' down here for getting me the hell outta this Guatemalan sanitarium? Again, according to Todd, my mother absolutely will not come down here until after Christmas. Geez, Ma has always been squirrelly about this over-commercialized Christian holiday. Why? Who knows! The woman is not even religious, but still, she has always had in her mind that Christmas is some warm, loving wondrous family time of giving, sharing, and bonding. (Yeah well, hope she has herself a real good one this year.)

Here, at the *sanatorio*, Christmas day comes, and our big holiday meal is some strong, ripe canned tuna, having soggy cold broccoli on the side, and of course, the standard dry corn tortillas, which Sparky really hates! Since bein' here, even the smell of those things makes the stomach cringe. Afterwards, we all get to watch on TV *The Ten Commandments*, starring ol' Charlton Heston. Throughout the movie, every retard in the place asks "Devon" if he's a Christian. What? No, I'm not Catholic. I am a, a, a Baptist Protestant Presbyterian. Yepper, uh-huh, you bet.

With Christmas over, maybe Ma will come soon? Lordy, how pathetic, a grown man awaiting rescue from Mommy—who clearly is in no hurry for task required. What's worse though, is, yes, I surely do want her down here for attempts at gettin' my ass out of this sick fucked-up country, but whoa, I'm scared. Scared as all get-up for when she and little sis do come. I mean, the *sanatorio* hasn't been hit yet. Why not? Are Matrix, cops, goons, cannibals, waiting for Ma and sis? Damn, Matrix would just love getting his hands on them, if only for hurting me.

And so, the days are long, strange, and boring. Still, the nights are worse. Despite the administered intake of such pharmaceuticals as Alprazolam, Paufer, and Ziprexa, I don't sleep. Nope, nope, nope! Won't allow it; can't allow it; and so I don't. There is drifting though. A state of forced relaxation, floating along ethereal perimeter for what has long become feared strangeness of sleep, which torments me like some mystical deep dark forest, haunted with unknown wonders, or a river of whispers, heavy in unearthly fog, having never before seen the other side.

To pass the long sanitarium nights, this game of wavering will and endurance is played. Yep, like a young cautious girl virgin, rolling with a boy, whose closeness is lightly caressing, enticing the untrusted yearning urges, seducing the call to give in, surrendering an openness to come.

But does she? No-sirree-bob! No fuckin' way. And does this frustrate the boy? Oh-ho! You better believe! However, does he stop his persistence? Nooo, for he is determined. (God, I gotta get out of this place!)

Time slowly passes, and finally—my clothes! Gee, it only took the idiots two weeks to wash them. Enjoying the feel of bein' back in old clothes—French camo pants, long sleeve gray cotton t-shirt, OD wool socks cushioning feet inside sooty red Converse high-tops—sitting outside alone, smokin' a cig, and warmin' tired bones in the sun. "Hey Dev!"

Spinning out of chair—what the—? From the other side of the iron barred gate is my sparkling eyed, smiling, beautiful young adult baby sister! My sweet Lord, what a sight! Ma is here too; she and Todd are up in the front office, goin' through some required paperwork with the (rarely seen) doctor. Soon, Ma strolls from around the corner, wearin' her usual short linen dress and high heels, lookin' very much like an older hot chick on vacation, rather than a mother on a mission for rescuing burnt-out shell of a screw-up son. (Ught-o, is Ma's choice here of dressed appearance good or bad? Who knows. Sparky would ask buddy, but buddy has been silent these days. Guess he figures his voice ain't needed no more. Hhmm, yeah well, we will see; won't we? Buddy, ol' friend, please don't venture too far.)

"What?" After warm greetings, with hugs through the iron gate's bars, and well intended offered assurance that I am lookin' good, despite weight loss, etc., Ma, watching me light a smoke, asks about the gashed cut healing on my finger. (Uh, well, gee Ma, you see, there was this room full of whacked out Garifunas that really wanted my twenty-inch steel black MAGLITE flashlight for shovin' up my ass, while attempting to cut on me with creepy-crawlies all over, so's an American cameraman could get it on film, and well, uh well, I sorta wouldn't let go of my flashlight. That is, until this big toothed Garifuna started chompin' down on my finger. What? Yeah, it sure did get shoved up my ass, but don't worry, in the end… Ught, get it? In the end? Never mind. In the end, after some persuading, I got my steel twenty-inch MAGLITE flashlight back. Yepper, sure did.) Christ, can't be tellin' her any of that. No, instead, Sparky answers, "Aw Ma, it's nothin'. Just a cut from a crab that pinched hard."

Okay, so that sounded completely retarded; big deal. Only thing that matters now is that my mother and sister grasp full understanding of very real serious danger involved with bein' down here. But how to convey this without explaining truth of whole story, which they are both asking to hear, yet would never believe?

Sidesteppin' questions, warning attempts are put forth in expressing the magnitude of enemies made, and how while down here, Ma and sis must be at all time on red alert, trusting no one, believing no one, and never are they to go out at night—*ever*! Ma, listening, casually interrupts, "Not to worry, Todd Boil has assured us of our safety." (Oh has he? Gee, golly, then, Sparky ain't worried!)

Ma also shares that the process of getting my release legally final for leaving the country will take a couple of days; during which time she and little sis will be staying at Mr. Benny's bed and breakfast.

Upon hearin', my jaw drops in shocked disbelief, while at the same time, quivering to find words for objecting! "Wha-wha-wha."

"Devin? Devin look, Todd thinks this is the best. According to him, us staying at Mr. Benny's will act as confirmation for those watching, and involved, validating our stance of not being afraid, and that in no way or form do we support or believe your, quote, "crazy story". Whatever it may be. Devin, we must convince them, whoever "*them*" are, that we do not believe any part of it. Again, according to Todd, this cannot be stressed enough. What we do believe though? Again Devin, this is just Todd's game plan; it is that you are mentally unstable, and we are more than willing to pay for all damages caused, and debts acquired. And Devin, if for any reason this does not work, or problems do arise, Todd assures he can get us out of the country, back to the United States via some secret Cuba route. He claims it's no big deal; the embassy has had to do this often for people needing out of Guatemala."

Oh that full-of-shit mother-fucker! Holdin' back the urge for screamin': "Ma, Todd said that? And how does he do this? Right, he won't say. It's a last resort sorta thing." (Bullshit!) My mother's eyes are betraying a sparkle. Yes, sparkling with excitement for possible opportunity in going to her beloved Cuba. (Jesus, she's probably visualizing some fantastic adventure. Who knows. Ma is one of these Che Guevara groupies, and has always expressed a strong want for seein' Cuba.)

"Aw geez Ma, are you outta your mind? We can't get out via Cuba. Trust me, we can't. I don't care what Todd Boil says. I've been to Cuba, remember? And I can't go back! What? Why not? Because I just can't! And Todd knows this! Look, Cuba survives by being a huge drop-off point for major drug routes that snake through these regions. Literally tons of cocaine passes through Cuba before entering the United States. What? What does this mean? Ma, it means, those wanting me dead here want me dead there. The drug routes connect everything. One call from a cell phone is all it takes. Besides, how are we gonna get through customs of either country? Oh, okay, Todd's secret route avoids all customs. Yeah right, sure, it's a secret route. I don't know Ma, maybe Todd's talkin' about flyin' us out on a US military flight into Guantanamo Bay, and then into the United States." My mother's eyes have lost their sparkle. "Ma, if so, then Todd Boil could have got me out of this hell hole of a country anytime, yet he didn't, and it damn near cost me my life more than once! And now he's got you two down here, knowin' full well, your lives are at risk! Oh Goddamn it!" Tears are swellin', with chest constricting. "See? See how it is? You can't believe, or trust the guy for nothin', 'cept, he's all we got!"

Soon all three of us are havin' an emotional moment. We are wipin' wet eyes and tellin' each other that everything is gonna be all right, etc. when along comes jolly Todd Boil having on his happy-happy face. Ignoring our obvious teary-eyed state, he cheerfully informs that it is time for going back to the embassy, then on to Mr. Benny's bed and breakfast. From through the gate's bars, it's goodbye hugs and kisses, with promises of being careful, etc. Todd, hangin' back, shares his delight in how smoothly everything is coming along. Our eyes meet; he drops the happy-jolly act for sincerely askin' how I am holdin' up, and if there is anything I need?

"Todd, they are here; my mother and sister are finally here. I don't understand why they had to come, when—"

"Hey pal, if you want to get back home—back to your wife and sons—it had to go this way."

"Yeah well, I wish it didn't; I now regret havin' you send for them. Todd, this is the last place my mother and sister should be."

"No Devin, not if you want to get back home, it isn't."

"Todd, my life and gettin' back home ain't worth Ma and my sister comin' down here, puttin' themselves at risk; geez, what was I thinkin'?" After some silence, "Todd, you will give me your word —the one your God hears—that you will look after them, and do all that is within your power to keep them safe. And Todd, if things do start to get weird—you know what I mean—forget about me. Just get my mother and sister safely the hell outta here! Promise Todd, give me your *word*." He does, and for once, I believe him. But this is Guatemala, remember? So, who the fuck knows.

New Years Eve day; Todd, Ma and little sis, arrive at the *sanatorio* for taking me out of the country. Todd is wearing casual shirt and worn blue jeans. He is driving an old car, borrowed from a friend. My sister, has all that is left of my belongings from Mr. Benny's bed and breakfast. Her and Ma's stay, though safe, has been an exhaustingly educational one; one they are both eager to be done with. They have had their fill of dealing with scary grinnin' Guatemalan greaseball officials—and non-officials—where nothin' adds up (excepting, of course, money owed), and nothing much makes sense. Straight answers for questions (discouraged) are simply not to be had.

Todd's demeanor is indeed more tolerable, mostly, I think, because of his obvious attraction toward my mother. However, he does have my big zipper baggy containing codeine horse pills and Valium: he is wanting to donate them to the *sanatorio*. (My ass!). Against his protests, I snatch 'em, tucking the zipper baggy down deep into my old French pack (good havin' you back, ol' pack). Don't believe we will be voluntarily doin' no more donatin' of anything to this sanitarium. Yes, they have kept me alive thus far, and Sparky is grateful; but, at a charge of over one hundred dollars US per day, for this place? A Guatemalan nuthouse in the ruins of a decrepit hotel? Shit, the doc here made out pretty damn good off this *gringo*. I mean, even if Sparky is right, in thinkin' at least half of that price went out for pay-offs and such, by Guatemalan standards, it's still a ridiculous high price for such services. Aw, fuck it. The pills are mine, and I intend on tryin' to keep 'em.

Pulling Todd aside, I ask him about the American journalist murdered last night? (The *sanatorio* staff had been overheard discussing it this morning.) Todd, nodding his head, confirms the murder bein' true.

"Todd, was the journalist your friend? The same one that had been with you the night I burnt down Mr. Benny's motel room? Todd, you might wanta know, while in the emergency room that night, Matrix told me he was gonna kill that journalist."

Rubbing his forehead, appearing sincerely saddened, wavin' my words off as bein' more psychotic ramblings, "Devin, he was a close friend and a good man. What? How was he killed? They brutally stabbed him repeatedly, before cutting his throat. It was very bloody Devin. But I don't have to tell you how bloody a crime such as this is, do I, pal?"

Not answering that, lookin' down to sooty red Converse high-tops, "Todd, do you think they killed him because of me? Like maybe some sort of message, due to me possibly leaving the country—some sort of sick farewell?"

Our eyes meet. "Devin, I honestly don't know."

Todd has the timing calculated just so. While driving to the airport, he advises us on how to act, once there: we are simply ordinary tourists on our way home from vacation. Don't separate, don't attract any unnecessary attention, and don't act nervous! Tickets and reservations are all set; once at the airport, Todd is gonna follow us inside, but will inconspicuously stand back, keepin' look-out, so as to be available only if problems do arise. Todd warns if airport security does suspect he's with us, curiosity will become aroused, and we will more than likely be detained for questioning.

(Oooh, no fuckin' way are they gonna let "Devon" leave this country! The very best I'm hopin' for is that they pull me aside, letting Ma and little sis board for goin' safely back home! That first day, seein' them at the sanitarium, had convinced Sparky just how wrong it was in havin' any family come down here. But whoa, now, here at the airport! And after last night's murder of the American journalist, oh God, what have I done!)

However, for whatever reason, despite all doubts, everything at the airport goes smooth as can be! Oh, there's the nerve-racking weird moments of certain people speaking my name, and pointing: some even call out, waving mocking goodbyes. Ma and sis are now very much realizing the very real perplexing dilemma of our situation. Before, they had no way for really understanding just how notoriously recognized I am. Well, they are discovering now! Especially after (check this out) we three, shoulder to shoulder, holding our breaths with anticipation, knowin' inconspicuous we are not, waiting to board, when guess who should mosey on over, grinnin' slyly, patting my back for personally expressing goodbyes. Come on, guess! Guess! Why it's my ol' pals from Livingston—the Bobsey twins! What are the odds, huh? Can you believe? My mother and sister can't hardly, and they don't even know the story behind these guys (Goddamn).

Strolling past, the intimidating security, down tunnel walkway, onto plane and into seats; Ma and little sis, smiling, snap seatbelts, and let out long sighs of relief. Though not Sparky. Nope! I don't even ex-fuckin'-hale until landing on United States soil of Houston Texas airport; and even then—still, whoa, is this real? Can it possibly be? One simple plane ride, and I am safe—alive, intact, unharmed? Uh, uh, uh, shit, this don't seem quite right. And it's not. Oh, Matrix, voodoo psychopaths, cannibals, *gauchos*, drug runnin' bad men, street gangs, vicious cops, goons, soldiers, evil men of power, and torture snuff film makers have (so far, at least) all stayed away; yet, the horror has not, and probably never will. There is no safety from haunting horror. Ever!

Two weeks after arriving home, Todd Boil calls my mother to inquire how everyone is doin', and for stressing just how lucky we all were in getting me out of Guatemala. (According to him, under such circumstances, it doesn't happen very often. Hhmm, imagine that.) Also, Todd asks my mother if she would write a letter to his superior. The letter is for commending Todd, expressing her gratitude on what a fine job he is doing, and how very grateful we all are for his outstanding help, etc.

Now, Ma, like everybody else, has only received the major left-out-parts version of my story. (Hhmm, the reasons for this are numerous, and obvious. Mostly though, the majority of people presently surrounding, living in their safe secure protective white bread elements, simply would not allow themselves to realistically comprehend. I mean, for most Americans, these sort of horrendous mind fuck atrocities only happen in the movies. Right? Or, in the mind of a burnt-out, drug-induced paranoid schizoid). However, ol' Ma does have an appetite for history; and since bein' home (her home, in California), she has begun doin' some research on Central America—namely Honduras and Guatemala. Ma's simple search has brought forth a flood of mind-boggling data, all relating to the regions' true colors, revealing. Her son though—yes—did partake in what many, no doubt, would consider somewhat heavy drug use. Still, the parts of his story that he has shared are now very much holding water. So, when Todd Boil does call, Ma (understandably) has many questions. And, of course, he gives no answers. None that are solid anyways. Therefore it is doubted ol' Toddy got his letter of commendation. Not from my Ma anyways.

Stubbing out a Camel, I gotta pee. (Christ, I've been sitting here all night.) Shiftin' sweaty nudity in slippery cheap vinyl chair, the pregnant calico cat from out on the deck uses claws hooking mesh screening of sliding doors for stretchin' a big yawning self. Her one beautiful eye locks onto mine, ensuing a questioning "Meow," almost as if she is informing that it will be daylight soon, and askin' are we gonna raise lines. (She don't actually go out on the boat and fish; still she does faithfully wait for my return off the river, to excitedly check the day's catch). Lester, the Great Blue Heron, swooshes, a-landin' on his log for his own beginning day of fishin'. Always standin' tall and proud that bird is; but whew lookin' like he does now—with the sun cresting only a sliver of its brilliant orange, cutting through the river's blanket of dying night—he's fuckin' magnificent! The boat, too, rhythmically bumping its bow up against groaning wooden dock, yearns for the call to be a-goin'. The black Merc outboard glistens with sparkles from dew, reflecting streamin' orange light. The nightshift is over, converging with all that is to be the dayshift. Shortly the old beaver will come, paddling his way up river for worksite. Like a laborer needin' to punch a time clock, that beaver is. "Soon Puss, soon we will go raise lines. It will be a good catch today; lots of thick catfish belly meat for you and your unborn kits."

END

Made in the USA
Las Vegas, NV
22 November 2024

12403027R00288